The Last Secret
of the Temple

ALSO BY PAUL SUSSMAN
FROM CLIPPER LARGE PRINT

The Lost Army of Cambyses

The Last Secret
of the Temple

Paul Sussman

W F HOWES LTD

This large print edition published in 2007 by
W F Howes Ltd
Unit 4, Rearsby Business Park, Gaddesby Lane,
Rearsby, Leicester LE7 4YH

1 3 5 7 9 10 8 6 4 2

First published in the United Kingdom in 2005
by Bantam Press

A CIP catalogue record for this book is available
from the British Library

ISBN 978 1 84632 935 7

Typeset by Palimpsest Book Production Limited,
Grangemouth, Stirlingshire
Printed and bound in Great Britain
by Antony Rowe Ltd, Chippenham, Wilts.

For Alicky,
whose light shines brightest of all.
And for our beautiful,
beloved Layla Rose.

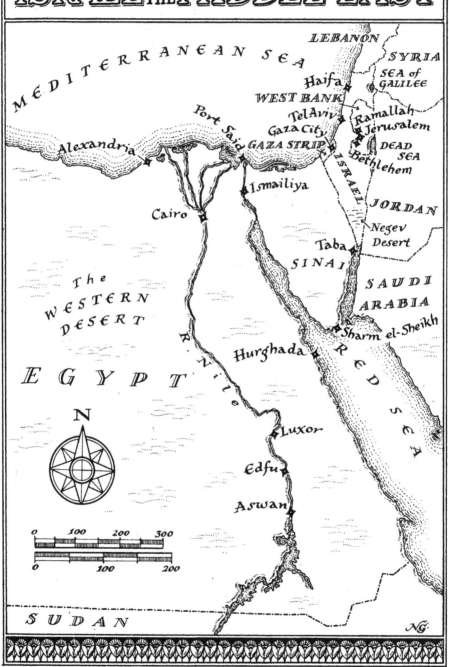

ISRAEL & THE MIDDLE EAST

MEDITERRANEAN SEA

LEBANON

SYRIA

SEA of GALILEE

Haifa

WEST BANK

Tel Aviv

Ramallah

Gaza City

Jerusalem

GAZA STRIP

DEAD SEA

Bethlehem

Alexandria

Port Said

ISRAEL

Ismailiya

JORDAN

Cairo

Negev Desert

Taba

SINAI

The

SAUDI

WESTERN

ARABIA

DESERT

Sharm el-Sheikh

EGYPT

Hurghada

RED SEA

R. Nile

N

Luxor

Edfu

Aswan

0   100   200   300

0   100   200

SUDAN

NG

The OLD CITY of JERUSALEM

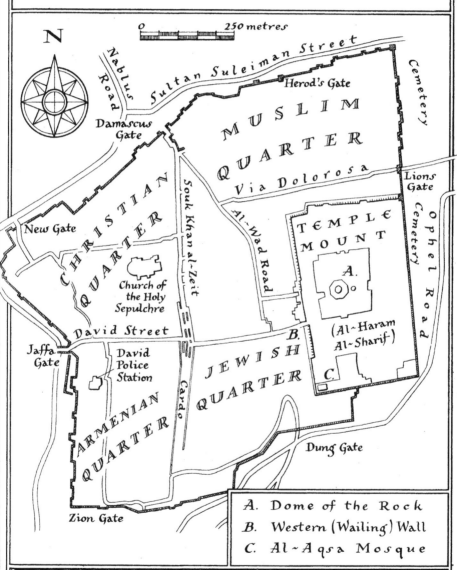

N

0 |—————| 250 metres

Nablus Road

Sultan Suleiman Street

Herod's Gate

Damascus Gate

MUSLIM QUARTER

Via Dolorosa

Cemetery

Lions Gate

CHRISTIAN QUARTER

Souk Khan al-Zeit

Al-Wad Road

Ophel Road

Cemetery

New Gate

TEMPLE MOUNT

A.

Church of the Holy Sepulchre

David Street

B.

(Al-Haram Al-Sharif)

Jaffa Gate

David Police Station

JEWISH QUARTER

C.

Cardo

ARMENIAN QUARTER

Dung Gate

Zion Gate

A. Dome of the Rock
B. Western (Wailing) Wall
C. Al-Aqsa Mosque

PROLOGUE

THE HOLY TEMPLE, JERUSALEM
AUGUST AD 70

The heads flew over the Temple wall with a hiss, dozens of them, like a flock of ungainly birds, eyes open, mouths agape, tendrils of flesh fluttering where they had been crudely severed at the neck. Some came down in the Court of Women, thudding onto the soot-blackened flagstones with an arhythmic, drum-like patter, causing old folk and children to scatter in horror. Others went further, passing right over the Nicanor Gate into the Court of Israel, where they rained down around the great Altar of Holocausts like giant hailstones. A few flew further still, slamming against the walls and roof of the Mishkan itself, the holy sanctuary at the very heart of the Temple complex, which seemed to groan and echo under the assault, as though in physical pain.

'Bastards,' choked the boy, tears of despair pricking his sapphire-blue eyes. 'Filthy Roman bastards!'

From his vantage point on the Temple ramparts he gazed down at the ant-like mass of legionaries moving around below him, their weapons and armour glinting in the angry firelight. Their cries filled the night, mingling with the whoosh of the mangonels, the pounding of drums, the screams of the dying and, enveloping all else, the metronomic, baritone thud of the battering rams, so that it seemed to the boy the entire world was slowly cleaving apart.

'Be gracious to me, oh Lord,' he whispered, quoting the Psalm. 'For I am in distress; my eye is wasted from grief, my soul and my body also.'

For six months the siege had tightened around the city like a garrotte, throttling the life out of it. From their initial positions on Mount Scopus and the Mount of Olives, the Roman legions, four of them swelled by thousands of auxiliaries, had moved inexorably inwards, breaching every line of defence, driving the Jews backwards, crushing them into the centre. Countless numbers had died, cut down as they tried to repel the attackers or crucified along the city walls and throughout the Kidron Valley, where the flocks of vultures were now so thick they blacked out the sun. The smell of death was everywhere, a corrosive, overpowering stench that tore into the nostrils like flame.

Nine days ago the Antonia fortress had fallen; six days after that the outer courts and colonnades of the Temple compound. Now all that was left was the fortified Inner Temple, where what remained of the city's once proud population was crammed like fish in a barrel, filthy, starving, reduced to eating rats and leather, and drinking their own urine, so pitiful was their thirst. Still they fought, frantically, hopelessly, raining rocks and flaming beams of wood down on the attackers below, occasionally sallying forth to drive the Romans back from the outer courts, only to be driven back themselves, with terrible losses. The boy's two elder brothers had died in the last such sortie, hacked down as they tried to topple a Roman siege engine. For all he knew, their mutilated heads were among those now being catapulted back over the walls into the Temple enclosure.

'*Vivat Titus! Vincet Roma! Vivat Titus!*'

The voices of the Romans swelled upwards in a roaring wave of sound, chanting the name of their general, Titus, son of the emperor Vespasian. Along the battlements the defenders tried to raise a counter-chant, calling out the names of their own leaders, John of Gischala and Simon Bar-Giora. The cry was frail, however, for their mouths were parched and their lungs weak, and anyway, it was hard to muster much enthusiasm for men who, it was rumoured, had already struck a deal with the Romans for their own lives. They kept it up for half a minute and then their voices slowly dropped away.

The boy removed a pebble from the pocket of his tunic and began sucking it, trying to forget how thirsty he was. David was his name, son of

Judah the winemaker. Before the great revolt his family had worked a vineyard on the terraced hills outside Bethlehem, its ruby-red grapes producing the lightest, sweetest wine you had ever tasted, like sunlight on spring mornings, like a soft breeze through shady groves of tamarind. In the summer the boy had helped with the harvest and the treading of the grapes, laughing at the feel of the mushy fruit beneath his feet, the way the juice stained his legs blood-red. Now the wine-presses were smashed, the vines burnt down, and his family dead, all of them. He was alone in the world. Twelve years old, and already he carried the grief of a man five times his age.

'Here they come again! Ready! Ready!'

Along the ramparts the cry rang out as a new wave of Roman auxiliaries poured towards the Temple walls, scaling-ladders held above their heads so that in the infernal shadowy firelight it looked as if dozens of giant centipedes were scuttling across the ground. A desperate hail of rocks showered down on them, causing the charge to falter for a moment before sweeping onwards again, reaching the walls and raising the ladders, each one anchored by two men on the ground while a dozen more used poles to heave it upwards and over against the battlements. Swarms of soldiers began scrambling onto them, streaming up the sides of the Temple like a rising tide of black ink.

The boy spat out his pebble, grabbed a rock from the pile at his feet, placed it in his leather sling and leant out over the ramparts, looking for a suitable target, oblivious to the blizzard of arrows hissing up from below. Beside him a woman, one of the many helping to defend the walls, stumbled backwards, her throat pierced by a harpoon-headed *pilum*, blood spraying through her hands. He ignored her and continued surveying the ranks of the enemy beneath, eventually spotting a Roman standard bearer holding aloft the insignia of Apollinaris, the Fifteenth Legion. He gritted his teeth and began swinging the sling above his head, eyes nailed to his target. One circle, two, three.

His arm was grabbed from behind. He wheeled round, punching with his free fist, kicking.

'David! It's me! Eleazar. Eleazar the Goldsmith!'

A huge bearded man was standing behind him, a heavy iron hammer slotted into his belt, his head wrapped round with a bloodied bandage. The boy stopped punching.

'Eleazar! I thought you were—'

'A Roman?' The man laughed mirthlessly, releasing his grip on the boy's arm. 'I don't smell that bad, do I?'

'I would have hit their standard bearer,' admonished the boy. 'It was an easy shot. I would have smashed the bastard's skull!'

Again the man laughed, with more warmth this time. 'I'm sure you would have. Everyone knows David Bar-Judah is the best sling-shot in the land. But there are more important things now.'

He glanced around, then lowered his voice.

'Matthias has summoned you.'

'Matthias!' The boy's eyes widened. 'The High—'

The man clamped his hand over the boy's mouth, again glancing around. 'Quietly!' he hissed. 'There are things here, secret things. Simon and John would not be happy if they knew this was done without their consent.'

The boy's eyes sparkled with confusion, uncertain what the man was talking about. The goldsmith made no effort to explain himself, simply looked down to make sure his words had hit home, then removed his hand and, taking the boy's arm, steered him along the top of the battlements and down a narrow stairwell into the Court of Women, the stonework beneath their feet trembling as the Roman battering rams punched into the Temple gates with renewed vigour.

'Quickly,' he urged. 'The walls won't hold for long.'

They hurried across the court, dodging the severed heads scattered on the flagstones, arrows clattering all around them. At the far end they climbed the fifteen steps to the Nicanor Gate and passed through into a second open space where crowds of *kohenim* were furiously sacrificing on the great Altar of Holocausts, their robes stained black with soot, their wailing voices all but drowning out the rage of battle.

Oh God, thou hast rejected us, broken our defences;
Thou hast been angry;

6

Oh restore us!
Thou hast made the land to quake, thou hast rent
  it open,
Repair its breaches, for it totters!

They crossed this court too and ascended the twelve steps to the porch of the Mishkan, its massive façade rearing over them like a cliff, a hundred cubits high and hung with a magnificent vine worked of pure gold. Here Eleazar stopped, turning to the boy and squatting so that their eyes were level.

'This is as far as I go. Only the *kohenim* and the High Priest may pass into the sanctuary itself.'

'And me?' The boy's voice was unsteady.

'For you it is allowed. At this time, in this extremity. Matthias has said so. The Lord will understand.' He laid his hands on the boy's shoulders, squeezing. 'Do not be afraid, David. Your heart is pure. You will come to no harm.'

He looked into the boy's eyes, then, standing, pushed him away towards the great doorway, with its twin silver pillars and embroidered curtain of red, blue and purple silk.

'Go now. May God be with you.'

The boy looked back at him, a huge figure silhouetted against the flaming sky, then turned and, pushing aside the curtain, passed into a long pillared hall with a floor of polished marble and a ceiling so high it was lost in shadow. It was cool in here, and silent, with sweet, intoxicating fragrance in the air. The battle seemed to recede and disappear, as though it was happening in another world.

'*Shema Yisrael, adonai elohenu, adonai ehud,*' he whispered. 'Hear, Oh Israel, the Lord is our God, the Lord is one.'

He paused a moment, overawed, then, slowly, started walking towards the far end of the hall, his feet falling soundlessly onto the white marble. Ahead of him stood the Temple's sacred objects – the table of the shewbread, the golden incense altar, the great seven-branched Menorah – and beyond them a shimmering, diaphanous veil of silk, the entrance to the *debir*, the Holy of Holies, which no man could enter save the High Priest alone, and he only once a year, on the Day of Atonement.

'Welcome, David,' said a voice. 'I have been waiting.'

Matthias, the High Priest, stepped from the shadows to the boy's left. He wore a sky-blue robe bound with a red and gold apron, a thin diadem about his head and, on his chest, the Ephod, the sacred breastplate, with its twelve precious stones, each representing one of the tribes of Israel. His face was deeply lined, his beard white.

'At last we meet, son of Judah,' he said softly, coming over to the boy and staring down at him, his movement accompanied by a soft tinkling sound from the dozens of tiny bells sewn around the hem of his robe. 'Eleazar the Goldsmith has told me much about you. Of all those defending the Holy places, he says, you are the most fearless. And the most worthy of trust. Like the David of old come again. This is what he says.'

He gazed at the boy, then, taking his hand, led him forward, right to the end of the hall, where they stopped in front of the golden Menorah, with its curving branches and intricately decorated stem, the whole beaten from a single block of pure gold to a design laid down by the Almighty himself. The boy stared up at its flickering lamps, eyes glinting like sun-dappled water, overwhelmed.

'Beautiful, isn't it?' said the old man, noting the wonder in the boy's face, laying a hand on his shoulder. 'No object on earth is more sacred to us, nothing more precious to our people, for the light of the Holy Menorah is the light of the Lord God himself. If ever it was to be lost to us . . .'

He sighed and raised a hand, touching it to the breastplate on his chest.

'Eleazar is a good man,' he added, as if as an afterthought. 'A second Bezalel.'

For a long moment they stood in silence contemplating the great candelabrum, its radiance surrounding and enveloping them. Then, with a nod, the High Priest turned so that he was facing the boy directly.

'Today the Lord has decreed that his Holy Temple will fall,' he said quietly, 'just as it did before, on this very day, Tish B'Av, more than six hundred years ago, when the House of Solomon was lost to the Babylonians. The sacred stones will be hammered to dust, the roof-beams torn asunder, our people led into exile and scattered to the four winds.'

He leant back a little, gazing deep into the boy's eyes.

'One hope we have, David, and one hope alone. A secret, a great secret, known only to a few of us. Now, in this final hour, you too shall know it.'

He bent towards the boy, lowering his voice and speaking rapidly, as if afraid they should be over-heard, even though they were quite alone. The boy's eyes widened as he listened, his gaze flicking from the floor to the Menorah and back to the floor again, his shoulders trembling. When the priest had finished he straightened and took a step backwards.

'See,' he said, a faint smile pulling at the edges of his pale lips, 'even in defeat there shall still be victory. Even in darkness there shall be light.'

The boy said nothing, his face tangled, caught between amazement and disbelief. The priest reached out and stroked his hair.

'Already it has gone from the city, out beyond the Roman palisade. Now it must leave this land altogether, for our ruin is nigh and its safety can no longer be guaranteed. All has been arranged. One thing alone remains, and that is to name a guardian, one who will convey the thing to its final destination, and there wait with it until better times shall come. To this task you have been appointed, David son of Judah. If you will accept it. Will you accept the task?'

The boy felt his gaze drawn upwards towards that of the priest, as if pulled by invisible cords. The old man's eyes were grey, but with a strange hypnotic translucence behind them, like clouds floating on a vast clear sky. He felt a heaviness inside him, and a weightlessness too, as if he was flying.

'What must I do?' he asked, his voice a croak.

The old man looked down at him, eyes running back and forth across his face, scanning the features as though they were words in a book. Then, with a nod, he reached into his robe and drew out a small roll of parchment, handing it to the boy.

'This will guide you,' he said. 'Do as it says and all will be well.'

He took the boy's face in his hands.

'You alone are now our hope, David son of Judah. With you alone the flame shall burn. Tell this secret to no-one. Guard it with your life. Pass it to your sons, and your sons' sons, and their sons after them, until the time shall come for it to be revealed.'

The boy stared up at him.

'But when, master?' he whispered. 'How will I know the time is right?'

The priest held his gaze a moment longer, then straightened and turned back to the Menorah, staring at the flickering lamps, his eyes gradually closing, as if he was slipping into a trance. The silence around them deepened and thickened; the gemstones on his breastplate seemed to burn with an inner light.

'Three signs to guide you,' he said softly, his voice suddenly distant, as if he was speaking from a great height. 'First, the youngest of the twelve shall come and in his hand a hawk; second, a son of Ishmael and a son of Isaac shall stand together as friends in the House of God; third, the lion and the shepherd shall be as one, and about their neck a lamp. When these things come to pass, then it will be time.'

Ahead of them the veil across the Holy of Holies seemed to billow slightly, and the boy felt a soft, cool breeze pass across his face. Strange voices seemed to echo in his ears, his skin tingled; there was a curious smell, rich and musty, like Time itself, if Time can be said to have a smell. It lasted only a moment and then suddenly, shockingly, there was a great boom and a crash from outside, and the cry of a thousand voices lifted in terror and despair. The priest's eyes snapped open.

'It is the end,' he said. 'Repeat the signs to me!'

The boy repeated them, stumbling over the words. The old man made him do it again, and again, until he had them perfect. The sounds of battle were now rushing into the sanctuary like a flood – screams of pain, the clang of weapons, the crash of falling masonry. Matthias hurried across the hall, looked through the entrance, then hurried back again.

'They have passed the Nicanor Gate!' he cried. 'You cannot go back that way. Come, help me!'

Stepping forward, the old man grasped the stem of the Menorah and started pulling, inching it across the floor. The boy joined him and together they moved it a metre to the left, revealing a square marble slab with two handholds sunk into it. These the priest grasped, heaving the slab away to reveal a dark cavity within which a narrow stone stairway spiralled downwards into blackness.

'The Temple has many secret ways,' he said, seizing the boy's arm and guiding him into the opening, 'and this the most secret of them all. Go down the stair and follow the tunnel. Do not deviate to left or right. It will take you far out of the city, south, well beyond the Roman palisade.'

'But what about—'

'There is no time! Go! You are now the hope of our people. I name you Shomer Ha-Or. Take this name. Keep it. Have pride in it. Pass it down. God will guard you. And judge you too.'

He leant forward, kissed the boy on each cheek and then, placing his hand on his head, pushed him downwards. He heaved the marble slab back into the hole and, grasping the Menorah, scraped it across the floor, grunting with the strain. He only just had time to get it back in position before there were cries from the far end of the hall, and the ring of clashing blades. Eleazar the Goldsmith staggered backwards through the entrance, one arm hanging limp at his side, a bloody stump where his hand had been, his other hand clutching his hammer with which he swung madly at a wall of legionaries coming after him. For a moment he managed to hold them at bay. Then, with a roar, they rushed forward and he was overpowered, stumbling backwards onto the floor where his limbs were hacked off and his body trampled.

'Yahweh!' he screamed. 'Yahweh!'

The High Priest watched, his face expressionless, then turned away, taking a handful of incense and casting it onto the coals of the golden altar. A cloud of perfumed steam spiralled upwards into the air. Behind him he could hear the Romans approaching, their iron-shod boots clinking on the floor, the rattle of their armour echoing around the walls.

'The Lord has become like an enemy,' he whispered, repeating the words of the Prophet Jeremiah. 'He has destroyed Israel; he has destroyed all its palaces, laid in ruins its strongholds.'

The Romans were at his back now. He closed his eyes. There was laughter, and the soft whoosh of a sword being raised high into the air. For a moment Time seemed to stand still; then the sword was driven downwards, drilling between the High Priest's shoulder blades and right the way through his body. He staggered forward and slumped to his knees.

'In Babylon let it rest!' he coughed, blood bubbling

from the corners of his mouth. 'In Babylon, in the house of Abner.'

And with that he crashed face down at the foot of the great Menorah, dead. The legionaries kicked away his corpse, hefted the Temple treasures onto their shoulders and carried them from the sanctuary.

'*Vicerunt Romani! Victi Iudaei! Vivat Titus!*' they cried. 'Rome has conquered! The Jews are defeated! Long live Titus!'

SOUTHERN GERMANY
DECEMBER 1944

Yitzhak Edelstein hugged his striped work fatigues around him and blew onto his hands, which had turned purple with the cold. Leaning forward, he tried to peer out of the back of the truck but could see little beneath the low canvas flap other than damp tarmac, tree-trunks and the bumper of the truck behind. He turned and pressed his face to a rip in the side of the canvas, briefly glimpsing steep, tree-covered slopes, white with snow, before a rifle butt banged into his ankle.

'Face forward. Sit still.'

He straightened and peered down at his feet, sockless, thrust into battered boots, scant protection against the freezing winter weather. Beside him the rabbi had started coughing again, his frail body trembling as though someone was shaking him. Yitzhak took the old man's hands between his own and rubbed them, trying to impart some warmth.

'Leave it,' snapped the guard.

'But he's—'

'Are you deaf? I said leave it.'

He levelled his gun at Yitzhak. The old man withdrew his hands.

'Don't you worry about me, my young friend. Us rabbis are a lot tougher than you think.'

He smiled weakly and they lapsed into silence, eyes fixed on the floor, shivering, swaying into one another as the truck turned this way and that.

There were six of them, excluding the two guards: four Jews, one homosexual, one communist. They had been herded from the camp and into the truck at dawn and had been driving ever since, east and south, Yitzhak thought, although he couldn't be sure. Initially the land had been flat and damp, the road straight. For the past hour, however, they had been winding steadily upwards, the pastures and forests gradually turning white with snow. There was another truck behind theirs, with a driver and one other man in the cab. No prisoners in the back, so far as Yitzhak could tell.

He ran his hand over his shaved head – even after four years he still couldn't get used to the feel – and, clasping his hands between his thighs and hunching his shoulders, tried to let his mind drift, fighting off the cold and hunger with thoughts of warmer and better times. Family dinners at their house in Dresden; Mishnah studies at the old *yeshiva*; the joy of the Holy days, especially Hanukkah, the festival of lights, his favourite of all the commemorative feasts. And of course Rivka, beautiful Rivka, his little sister.

'Yitzi, schmitzy, itzy bitzy!' she had used to chant, flicking at his *pe'ot*, tugging the tassles of his *tallit katan*. 'Yitzi, witzy, mitzy, ditzy!' How funny she had been with her tangle of coal-black hair and flaming eyes! How wilful and naughty! 'You pigs!' she had screamed when they had dragged their father out into the street and cut off his side curls. 'You filthy, dirty pigs!' For which they had ripped out hunks of her hair, pushed her against a wall and shot her.

Thirteen years old, and so beautiful. Poor Rivka. Poor little Rivka.

The truck hit a rut and jumped violently, jerking him back to the present. Glancing out of the back, he saw that they were passing through a large village. He craned his neck and through the rip in the canvas caught sight of a signpost beside the road: Berchtesgaden. The name sounded vaguely familiar, although he couldn't place it.

'Face forward,' growled the guard. 'I won't tell you again.'

They drove for another thirty minutes, the road climbing ever more steeply, the bends getting ever tighter, until eventually there was a sharp toot from the truck behind and they pulled over.

'Out!' ordered the guards, jabbing at them with their guns.

They struggled from the truck, billows of steam ballooning from their mouths. They were in the middle of a thick pine forest, parked in a lay-by beside an old stone building with empty windows and a caved-in roof. Far below, between snow-laden branches, patches of green pasture were visible, with houses here and there, small as toys, curls of smoke rising from their chimneys. Above, heavily wooded slopes ran steeply upwards, disappearing into a haze of mist and cloud within which a deeper darkness suggested high mountains. It was very quiet, and very, very cold. Yitzhak stamped his feet to stop them going numb.

The second truck had pulled in behind theirs. Leaning from the window, the man in the passenger seat, who wore a high-collared leather coat and seemed to be in overall charge, said something to one of the guards, motioning with his hand.

'Right,' shouted the guard, 'get over here.'

They were herded round to the back of the second truck. The canvas flap was thrown up, revealing a large wooden crate.

'Get it out! Come on! Hurry!'

Yitzhak and the communist, an emaciated middle-aged man with a red triangle sewn onto the leg of his trousers – Yitzhak wore overlapping yellow triangles to denote that he was a Jew – clambered into the truck and grasped the sides of the crate. It was heavy, and it took both of them just to shunt it across the metal floor and get it level with the tail-board. The others then took hold of it, and slowly they manhandled it onto the icy road.

'No, no, no!' shouted the man in the coat, leaning from the cab window. 'They carry it.

There.' He pointed past the ruined building to where a narrow avenue of virgin snow ran upwards into the trees above, presumably some sort of road or track. 'And make sure they're careful with it!'

The prisoners looked at one another, silently communicating their fear and exhaustion, then bent down and, slowly, heaved the crate up again, one on each corner, two in the middle, grunting with the strain.

'This is going to be bad,' mumbled the communist. 'This is going to be very bad.'

They started into the forest, feet sinking into the snow up to their calves. The guards and the man in the leather coat followed, although Yitzhak dared not look round for fear of losing his balance. In front of him the rabbi was coughing violently.

'Let me take a little of the weight,' Yitzhak whispered. 'I am strong. It is easy for me.'

'You're a liar, Yitzhak,' croaked the old man. 'And a bad one at that.'

'Shut up!' cried one of the guards behind them. 'No talking.'

They staggered onwards, grunting with exertion, skin burning with the cold. The track, which had initially followed a fold in the land, rising reasonably gently, now began to climb at a harsher gradient, coiling upwards through the trees, switching back on itself, the snow getting ever deeper. On one particularly steep section the homosexual lost his footing and stumbled, causing the crate to lurch forwards and smash against a tree-trunk, its top left-hand corner cracking and splintering.

'Idiot!' screamed the man in the leather coat. 'Get him up!'

The guards waded forward and hoisted the man to his feet, forcing him to heave the crate back onto his shoulders.

'My shoe,' he pleaded, indicating his left boot, which had somehow come off and was lying half-buried in the snow.

The guards laughed and, kicking the boot away, ordered them all to get moving again.

'God help him,' whispered the rabbi. 'God help the poor boy.'

Up and up they climbed, higher and higher, gasping and groaning, every step seeming to suck a little bit more life out of them, until eventually, at a point when Yitzhak felt that he must surely drop and die, the track suddenly came level and emerged from the trees into what looked like an abandoned quarry cut deep into the hillside. At the same moment the clouds above them drew back, revealing a huge mountain rearing overhead with, far away to the right, a small building perched on the edge of a cliff. The vision lasted only a few seconds and was then lost again behind a heavy curtain of mist, disappearing so quickly that Yitzhak wondered whether he had not just imagined it in his exhaustion and despair.

'Over there,' shouted the man in the leather coat. 'Into the mine!'

At the back of the quarry rose a vertical rock-face, in the centre of which gaped a doorway, wide and black, like a screaming mouth. They stumbled towards it, past heaps of snow-covered rock and slag, a broken winching device and an upturned cart with a single rusted wheel, picking their way carefully over the uneven ground. As they reached the opening Yitzhak noticed the words GLÜCK AUF crudely scratched into the rock above its lintel, and beneath it, in white paint, no bigger than the size of half a thumb, the legend sw16.

'Go on! Inside! Take it in!'

They did as they were told, bending their knees and backs so as not to smash the crate on the low ceiling. One of the guards produced a torch and shone it ahead into the blackness, revealing a long corridor running back into the hillside, supported at regular intervals by wooden props. Iron rails ran along the flat stone floor; the walls were rough and uneven, hewn out of the bare grey rock, with here and there thick veins of orangey-pink crystal exploding through the stone like forks of lightning across a dark sky. Abandoned tools lay scattered on the ground – a rusted oil lamp, a pick-axe head, an old tin bucket – giving the place an eerie, abandoned feel.

They were made to go about fifty metres, at which point the rails on the floor branched, one set continuing straight ahead, the other twisting off to the right into another tunnel that ran perpendicular to the main shaft, its walls lined with stacks of boxes and crates. There was a flat cart sitting near the entrance to this side-passage, and they were ordered to place their load on top of it.

'That's it,' came a voice from the darkness behind them. 'Out. Get them out!'

They turned and shuffled back the way they had come, breathing heavily, relieved that their ordeal seemed to be over, one of the other Jews supporting the homosexual, whose bare foot had turned black. There was a muttered exchange behind them, and then the guards came out as well. The man in the leather coat remained inside the mine.

'Over there,' said one of the guards when they emerged into the open air. 'There, by that heap of rock.'

They did as they were told, walking over to the pile of stones and turning. The guards had their guns levelled at them.

'*Oy vey*,' whispered Yitzhak, suddenly realizing what was about to happen. 'Oh God.'

The guards laughed, and the winter silence was shattered by a raucous bark of gunfire.

PART I

THE PRESENT

THE VALLEY OF THE KINGS, LUXOR, EGYPT

'Can we go home soon, Dad? It's *Alim al-Simsim* on TV.'

Inspector Yusuf Ezz el-Din Khalifa stubbed out his cigarette and sighed, gazing down at his son Ali, who was standing beside him picking his nose. A slim, wiry man with high cheekbones, neatly brushed hair and large, sparkling eyes, he exuded an air of quiet intensity edged with humour – a serious man who enjoyed laughing.

'It's not every day you get a private tour of the greatest archaeological site in Egypt, Ali,' he chided.

'But I've been here with school,' grumbled his son. 'Twice. Mrs Wadood showed us everything.'

'I bet she didn't show you the tomb of Ramesses II,' said Khalifa, 'which we've seen today. And Yuya and Tjuyu.'

'There was nothing in that one,' complained Ali. 'Just bats and a load of old bandages.'

'We were still lucky to be allowed inside it,' insisted his father. 'It hasn't been open to the public since it was found in 1905. And for your information, those old bandages were the original mummy wrappings, just as the tomb robbers left them in ancient times, after they'd ripped them from the bodies.'

The boy looked up, finger still wedged into his nostril, a flicker of interest in his eyes.

'Why did they do that?'

'Well,' explained Khalifa, 'when the priests wrapped the mummies they put jewels and precious amulets in among the bindings, and the robbers were trying to get at them.'

The boy's face lit up.

'Did they dig out their eyes too?'

'Not that I know of,' replied Khalifa with a smile. 'Although sometimes they snapped off the odd finger or hand. Which is exactly what I'm going to do to you if you don't stop picking your nose!'

He seized his son's wrist and tugged playfully at his fingers, as though trying to break them off. Ali squirmed and struggled, roaring with laughter.

'I'm stronger than you, Dad!' he cried.

'I don't think so,' said Khalifa, grasping the boy round the waist and turning him upside down. 'I don't think you're even half as strong.'

They were standing in the middle of the Valley of the Kings, close to the entrance to the tomb of Ramesses VI. It was late afternoon, and the crowds of tourists that had choked the valley for most of the day had now filtered away, leaving the place eerily empty. Nearby, a group of workmen were clearing debris from an excavation trench, singing tunelessly as they scraped chunks of shattered limestone into rubber buckets; further down the valley a tour party was filing into the tomb of Ramesses IX. Otherwise the place was deserted, save for a few tourist police, Ahmed the bin man and, on the slopes above the valley, squatting in whatever shade they could find, the odd postcard hawker and refreshment seller, gazing intently downwards in the hope of spotting some late business.

'I'll tell you what,' said Khalifa, setting his son down and ruffling his hair. 'We'll have a quick look in Amenhotep II, and then we'll call it a day, eh? It would be rude to leave now after Said's gone to all the trouble to find the key.'

As he spoke, there was a shout from the inspector's office fifty metres away, and a tall, gangly figure came loping towards them.

'Got it!' called the figure, brandishing a key. 'Someone had put it on the wrong hook.'

Said ibn-Bassat, popularly known as Ginger on account of his bright copper-coloured hair, was an old friend of Khalifa's. They had met years ago, at Cairo University, where they had both been studying ancient history. Money problems had forced Khalifa to abandon his studies and take a job with the police force. Said, on the other hand, had finished the course, graduating with distinction, and joined the Antiquities Service, where he had risen to the rank of assistant director of Valley of the Kings.

Although he never said as much it was the life Khalifa would have chosen for himself, had necessity not pushed him in another direction. He loved the ancient past and would have done anything to have been able to devote his time to working with its remains. Not that he bore his friend any grudges, of course. And Ginger didn't have a family like him, which was something he would never have given up, not for all the monuments in Egypt.

The three of them set off up the valley together, passing the tombs of Ramesses III and Horemheb before branching off to the right and following a path up to the doorway of Amenhotep II's tomb, which was at the bottom of a set of steps and secured with a heavy iron gate: Ginger began fiddling with the padlock.

'How long is it going to stay closed?' asked Khalifa.

'Only another month or so. The restoration's almost complete.'

Ali pushed between them, coming up on tiptoes and peering through a grille into the darkness beyond.

'Is there any treasure?'

'Afraid not,' said Ginger, lifting the boy out of the way and swinging open the gate. 'It was all robbed out in ancient times.'

He flicked a switch and lights came on, illuminating a long, steeply sloping corridor cut back into the rock, its walls and ceiling still bearing the telltale white ripples of ancient chisel marks. Ali started down it.

'Do you know what I'd have done if I was King of Egypt?' he called back to them, his voice echoing in the narrow confines of the tomb. 'I'd have had a secret hidden room with all my treasure in it, and then another room with just a bit of treasure in it to fool the robbers. Like that guy you told me about, Dad. Horrible Inkyman.'

'Hor-ankh-amun,' corrected Khalifa, smiling.

'Yes. And then I'd have booby traps so that if any robbers did get in they'd be caught. And then I'd put them in prison.'

'Then they'd have been lucky,' said Ginger, laughing. 'The usual punishment for tomb-robbing in ancient Egypt was to have your nose cut off and be sent to the salt mines of Libya. That or impalement on a spike.'

He winked at Khalifa and, chuckling, the two men set off down the corridor after Ali. They had only gone a few metres when there was a sound of hurried footsteps behind them. A man in a djellaba appeared in the tomb doorway, silhouetted against the bright rectangle of afternoon sky, breathing heavily.

'Is there an Inspector Khalifa here?' he called, panting.

The detective glanced at his friend, then took a step back up the shaft.

'That's me.'

'You're to come quickly, over the other side. They've found . . .'

The man paused, trying to catch his breath.

31

'What?' said Khalifa. 'What have they found?'

The man looked down at him, eyes wide. 'A body!'

From further down the shaft Ali's voice came floating up to them.

'Cool! Can I come too. Dad?'

The corpse had been discovered at Malqata, an archaeological site at the far southern end of the Theban massif, once the palace of the pharaoh Amenhotep III, now a desolate expanse of sand-blown ruins visited only by the most dedicated of Egyptophiles. A dusty Daewoo police car was waiting for Khalifa outside the valley office, and, leaving his son with Ginger, who promised to get him home safely, he climbed into the passenger seat and the car sped off, Ali's cries of protest echoing behind them.

'I don't want to go home, Dad! I want to see the dead body!'

It took them twenty minutes to reach the site. The police driver, a surly young man with freckled cheeks and bad teeth, kept his foot to the floor all the way, winding down through the hills to the Nile plain and then turning south along the edge of the massif. Khalifa stared out the window at the passing sugar cane and *molochia* fields, smoking a Cleopatra cigarette and half-listening to a news report on the car's battered stereo about the spiralling violence between Israelis and Palestinians – another suicide bomb, another Israeli retaliation, more death and misery.

'It's going to be war,' said the driver.

'It already is war,' sighed Khalifa, taking a final puff on his cigarette and flicking it out of the window. 'Has been for the last fifty years.'

The driver reached for a packet of gum on the dashboard, slipping two pieces into his mouth and chewing vigorously.

'You think there can ever be peace?'

'Not the way things are at the moment. Watch out for the cart.'

The driver swerved to avoid a donkey-drawn cart piled high with harvested sugar cane, pulling back in front of it just in time to avoid a head-on collision with a tourist coach.

'Allah protect me,' muttered the detective, gripping the dashboard. 'Allah have mercy.'

They passed Deir el-Bahri, the Ramesseum and the scattered remains of the mortuary temple of Merenptah before eventually reaching a point where the road branched, one arm turning east towards the Nile, the other west up to the ancient workers' village at Dier el-Medina and the Valley of the Queens. They went straight ahead, bumping off the smooth tarmac onto a dusty, rutted track which led them past the great temple at Medinet Habu and out onto an undulating expanse of rubbly desert, its surface covered with litter and tangled blooms of spiny camel thorn. They continued for a further kilometre, swerving and jolting, occasionally passing the slumped remains of ancient mud-brick walls, brown and shapeless like melted chocolate, before eventually coming upon four police cars and an ambulance drawn up beside a rusty telephone pylon, with beyond them a fifth car, a dusty blue Mercedes, set slightly apart. They skidded to a halt and Khalifa got out.

'I don't know why you can't just get a mobile,' grumbled Mohammed Sariya, Khalifa's deputy, detaching himself from a huddle of paramedics and walking over to greet them. 'It's taken us over an hour to find you.'

'During which time I have had the pleasure of visiting two of the most interesting tombs in the Wadi Biban el-Muluk,' replied Khalifa. 'About as good an advert as I can think of for not having one. Besides, mobile phones give you cancer.'

He pulled out his cigarettes and lit one.

'So, what have we got?'

Sariya gave an exasperated shake of the head.

'A body,' he said. 'Male. Caucasian. Name of Jansen. Piet Jansen.'

He fumbled in his jacket pocket and produced a plastic bag with a battered leather wallet inside, which he handed to Khalifa.

'Egyptian national,' he said, 'although you wouldn't think it from the name. Owned a hotel down in Gezira. The Menna-Ra.'

'Beside the lake? Yes, I know it.'

34

Khalifa took the wallet from the bag and flicked through its contents, noting the Egyptian identity card.

'Born 1925. You're sure he didn't just die of old age?'

'Not if the state of the body's anything to go by,' said Sariya.

The detective pulled out a Banque Misr credit card and a wad of Egyptian twenty-pound notes. In a side pocket he found a membership card for the Egyptian Horticultural Society, and behind it a crumpled black-and-white photo of a large, fierce-looking Alsatian dog. On the back was written, in faded pencil, 'Arminius, 1930'. He stared at it for a moment, sensing the name was somehow familiar but unable to pinpoint precisely why, then put it back, replaced the wallet in its bag and returned it to his deputy.

'You've informed the next of kin?'

'No living relatives,' said Sariya. 'We contacted the hotel.'

'And the Mercedes? His?'

Sariya nodded. 'We found the keys in his pocket.' He produced another bag, this one containing an improbably large set of keys. 'We checked it out. Nothing unusual inside.'

They walked over to the Mercedes and peered through the window. The interior – cracked leather upholstery, polished walnut dashboard, a fragrance holder dangling from the rear-view mirror – was empty save for a two-day-old *al-Ahram* on the passenger seat and, on the floor in the back, an expensive-looking Nikon camera.

'Who found him?' asked Khalifa.

'A French girl. She was out taking photographs among the ruins, came on the body by accident.' Sariya opened his notebook and squinted down at it. 'Claudia Champollion,' he read, struggling to get his mouth round the unfamiliar vowels. 'Twenty-nine. Archaeologist. She's staying over there.' He nodded towards a tree-filled compound further along the track, surrounded by a high mud-brick wall. The home of the French Archaeological Mission in Thebes.

'No relation to *the* Champollion, I take it?' asked Khalifa.

'Hmm?'

'Jean Francois Champollion.'

Sariya looked confused.

'The man who deciphered hieroglyphs,' sighed Khalifa in mock exasperation. 'God Almighty, Mohammed, don't you know anything about the history of this country?'

His deputy shrugged. 'She was quite good-looking, I know that much. Big . . . you know . . .' He motioned with his hands. 'Firm.'

Khalifa shook his head and took a drag on his cigarette. 'If policework was simply a matter of ogling women, Mohammed, you'd be chief commissioner by now. You get a statement?'

Sariya held out his notebook to indicate that he had.

'And?'

'Nothing. She didn't see anything, didn't hear anything. Just found the body, went back to the compound, called 122.'

Khalifa finished his Cleopatra and ground it out beneath the heel of his shoe.

'I guess we ought to take a look at him, then. You've notified Anwar?'

'He's got some paperwork to finish, then he'll be over. Said to make sure the body didn't go wandering off anywhere.'

The detective tutted wearily, used to Anwar the pathologist's tasteless sense of humour, and the two of them set off across the site, feet crunching on the fragments of pottery that littered the desert surface like discarded biscuits. Away to their right some children were sitting on top of a hummock of rubble, one of them clutching a football, watching as lines of policemen combed the desert for clues; ahead, the sun was slowly sinking behind the egg-shaped domes of the Deir el-Muharab monastery, its light thickening from a pale yellow to a rich honey-orange. Here and there shoulders of mud-brick wall heaved themselves from the sand, weathered and forlorn, like primordial creatures rising up from the desert deeps. Otherwise there was little to suggest that they were passing through what must once have been one of the most magnificent buildings in ancient Egypt.

'Hard to believe this used to be a palace, isn't it?' sighed Khalifa, slowing to pick up a piece of pottery with traces of pale blue paint on it. 'In his day, Amenhotep III ruled half the known world. And now . . .'

He turned over the potsherd between his fingers, rubbing at the pigment with his thumb. Sariya said nothing, just made a chopping motion with his hand indicating that they needed to angle to the right.

'Over there,' he said, 'just beyond that wall.'

They crossed a stretch of mud-brick pavement, cracked and broken, and passed through what must once have been a substantial doorway, now reduced to two heaps of rubble with a worn limestone step between them. On the other side a policeman was squatting in a sliver of shade at the foot of a wall. A few metres away lay a heavy canvas sheet with a corpse-shaped hummock beneath it. Sariya stepped forward, grasped the corner of the sheet and whipped it back.

'*Allah-u-akhbar!*' grimaced Khalifa. 'God Almighty!'

In front of him lay an old man, very old, his body frail and emaciated, his sallow skin wrinkled and peppered with liverspots. He was lying on his front, one arm beneath him, the other splayed out at his side. He wore a khaki safari suit and his head, bald save for a few wisps of whitish-yellow hair, was jerked back and twisted slightly, like a swimmer taking a gulp of air before plunging his face into the water again – an unnatural posture caused by the rusty iron peg spearing upwards

38

from the ground into his left eye socket. His cheeks, lips and chin were caked with a heavy crust of dried blood; a shallow gash angled across the side of his head, just above the right ear.

Khalifa stood staring down at the corpse, noting the dusty hands and clothes, a small rip in the knee of the trousers, the way the head-wound was choked with sand and grit, then squatted and gently poked at the bottom of the iron peg, where it emerged from the sand. It was firmly embedded in the ground.

'From a tent?' asked Sariya, uncertain.

Khalifa shook his head. 'Part of a surveying grid. Left over from an excavation. Been here for years by the look of it.'

He straightened, waving his hand at the flies that had already started buzzing around the body, and walked a few metres away, to a point where the sand was churned up and disturbed. He could make out at least three different sets of footprints, possibly belonging to the police who had been combing the area, possibly not. He squatted again and, removing his handkerchief, picked up a sharp lump of flint with spatters of blood on it.

'Looks like someone hit him on the head,' said Sariya. 'Then he fell forward onto the peg. Or was pushed.'

Khalifa turned over the stone in his hand, gazing at the red-black blood smudges.

'Strange the attacker should leave a wallet full

of money in his pocket,' he said. 'And the keys to his car.'

'Maybe he was disturbed,' suggested Sariya. 'Or perhaps robbery wasn't the motive.'

Before Khalifa could offer an opinion there was a shout from further out across the ruin field. Two hundred metres away a policeman was standing on top of a sandy hummock waving his arms.

'Looks like he's found something,' said Sariya.

Khalifa replaced the rock as he had found it and the two of them started towards the man. By the time they reached him he had descended from the hummock and was standing beside a length of crumbled wall along the lower part of which, on cracked mud plaster, was painted a line of blue lotus flowers, faded but still clearly visible. In the centre of the line was a gap where a chunk of plaster appeared to have been removed. On the ground nearby sat a canvas knapsack, a hammer and chisel, and a black walking cane with a silver pommel. Sariya squatted beside the knapsack and lifted back its flap.

'Well, well, well,' he said, removing a brick with painted plaster on it. 'Someone has been a naughty boy.'

He held the brick out towards Khalifa. The detective wasn't looking at him. Instead he had squatted down, lifted the cane, and was staring at its pommel, around which was incised a pattern of miniature rosettes interspersed with *ankh* signs.

'Sir?'

Khalifa didn't reply.

'Sir?' repeated Sariya, louder.

'Sorry, Mohammed.' The detective laid aside the cane and turned towards his deputy. 'What have you got?'

Sariya handed him the mud brick. Khalifa held it out in front of him, examining the decoration. As he did so his gaze kept flicking back down towards the cane, brow furrowed as if trying to remember something.

'What?' asked Sariya.

'Oh, nothing. Nothing. Just an odd coincidence.'

He shook his head dismissively and smiled. Even as he did so, however, there was a hint of unease in his eyes, a faint echo of some deeper disquiet.

Away to the right a large crow landed on a wall and stood staring at them, flapping its wings and cawing loudly.

TEL AVIV, ISRAEL

Having changed into the police uniform, the young man walked swiftly through Independence Park towards the vast concrete rectangle of the Hilton Hotel. Around him families and young couples were out strolling in the cool evening air, chatting and laughing, but he took no notice of them, keeping his eyes focused firmly on the building in front of him, his forehead glistening with sweat, his lips quivering as he mumbled inaudible prayers to himself.

He reached the hotel entrance and passed through into the foyer, a pair of security guards flicking him a cursory glance before noting his uniform and looking away again. He raised a trembling hand to wipe the dampness from his brow, then, in an extension of the same movement, reached beneath his jacket and tugged the first of the ripcords to arm the explosive. Terror, hatred, nausea, excitement – he felt them all. Beyond these, however, enveloping all else, like the outer shell of a Russian doll, was an ecstatic, trance-like euphoria, a searing bliss that hovered right at the very edge of his consciousness like a bright white flame. Revenge, glory, paradise and an eternity in the arms of the beautiful *houris*.

Thank you for choosing me, Allah. Thank you for allowing me to be the vehicle of your vengeance.

He crossed the foyer and passed through a set of double doors into a large, light-filled room where the wedding party was taking place. Music and laughter washed over him; a little girl ran up and asked if he wanted to dance. He shrugged her off and pushed his way through the guests, the world around him seeming to recede and evaporate like a coloured mist. Someone asked what he was doing there, if there was some problem, but he just continued forward, muttering to himself, thinking of his elderly grandfather, his little cousin killed by an Israeli bullet; his own life, empty, hopeless, choked with shame and impotent anger. And then he was beside the bride and groom. With a scream of mingled fury and joy, he reached down and yanked the second cord, unleashing a whirlwind of heat, light and metal ball-bearings that reduced himself, the newlyweds and everyone else within a radius of three metres to little more than a bloody vapour.

At almost precisely the same moment three faxes were received in swift succession, one by the Jerusalem Office of the World Jewish Congress, one by the news desk of *Ha'aretz*, one by the Tel Aviv police. All were sent via a mobile network, making their precise place of origin impossible to trace, and all conveyed the same message: the bomb was the work of al-Mulatham and the Palestinian Brotherhood; it was in response to the continued Zionist occupation of the Palestinian homeland; so long as that occupation lasted, all Israelis, of whatever age or sex, would be held accountable for the atrocities inflicted on the Palestinian people.

LUXOR

They remained at Malqata until almost seven p.m., by which point Anwar the pathologist still hadn't arrived. Rather than hang around any longer, Khalifa detailed a group of constables to guard the site and, accompanied by Sariya, set off to visit the dead man's hotel.

'Knowing Anwar, we could be here till midnight,' he grumbled. 'Might as well do something useful with the time.'

The Menna-Ra occupied a prominent position at the heart of Gezira village, a large, bustling settlement of shops and ramshackle houses on the west bank of the river Nile, opposite Luxor Temple. A whitewashed, two-storey building, it was accessed by a narrow dirt road and hemmed in on either side by a jumble of mud-brick dwellings that clung to its flanks like sprays of brown fungus. Khalifa and Sariya arrived early in the evening and were admitted by a slim, middle-aged English woman who, in fluent if heavily accented Arabic, introduced herself as Carla Shaw, the hotel manager. She called for tea and showed them onto a gravelled terrace at the rear of the building, where they sat down on wicker-work chairs beneath a canopy of fragrant red hibiscus blossom. A long, narrow lake ran left to right in front of them, black and murky, its surface rippled by shoals of sleek Nile perch, its palm-fringed shores clogged with pontoons of discarded Baraka water bottles. On the far side an adver-tisement for Hod-Hod Suliman Balloon Flights was just visible through the trees, painted onto the wall of a house. The air echoed with the barking of dogs, the toot of service taxis and, in the distance, the rhythmic putter of an irrigation pump.

'It wasn't really a shock,' said the woman, curling one jean-clad leg under the other and lighting a Merit cigarette. 'He hadn't been at all well. Cancer, I think, although he never talked about it.'

Khalifa lit a cigarette of his own and threw a glance across at Sariya.

'We'll know more when we get the autopsy,' he said, 'but it seems that Mr Jansen might have . . .'

He broke off, drawing on his cigarette, uncer-tain how to phrase what he wanted to say.

'There are certain irregularities about his death,' he said finally.

The woman looked over at him, eyes widening slightly. She wore heavy black eyeliner that seemed to accentuate her expression of surprise.

'How do you mean, irregularities? You're saying he was—'

'I'm not saying anything as yet,' said Khalifa gently. 'The body needs to be properly examined. There were unusual aspects to Mr Jansen's death, however, and we need to ask some questions. All perfectly routine.'

The woman took another deep puff on her cigarette, reaching up with her free hand to fiddle with a crescent-shaped earring in her left ear. Her hair was an unnatural jet black, as though it had been dyed. She was attractive, in a slightly faded sort of way.

'Ask away,' she said. 'Although I don't know if I can be any help. Piet kept himself pretty much to himself.'

Khalifa nodded at Sariya, who pulled out his notebook and pen.

'How long have you worked for Mr Jansen?' he asked.

'Almost three years.' She inclined her head slightly, tugging at the earring. 'It's a long story, but basically I was out here on holiday, made some local friends, they told me Piet was looking for someone to run the hotel – he was too old to cover the day-to-day business himself – and I thought, "Hell, why not?" I'd just got divorced, you see. There was nothing for me back in England.'

'He had no immediate family?'

'Not that I know of.'

'He was never married?'

The woman took another drag on her cigarette.

'My impression was that Piet wasn't particularly interested in women.'

Khalifa and Sariya exchanged a look.

'Men?' asked the detective.

The woman waved a hand noncommittally. 'I heard he liked to go to Banana Island. He never said anything about it, and I never asked. It was his business.'

There was a crunch of feet on gravel and a young man appeared carrying a tray with three glasses of tea and a small candle lamp on it. He set it down on a table beside them and disappeared again. Khalifa reached for a glass.

'It's not an Egyptian name, Jansen,' he said, sipping.

'I think he was from Holland originally. Came to Egypt fifty, sixty years ago. I'm not exactly sure when. A long time.'

'Did he always live in Luxor?'

'He bought the hotel back in the 1970s, so far as I know. After he retired. I think he was in Alexandria before that. He never really talked about his past.'

She took a last puff on her Merit and ground it out into a scarab-shaped brass ashtray beside her. Above them the first stars were appearing, fat and blue, like fireflies.

'He didn't live here, by the way,' she said, stretching back and clasping both hands behind her neck so that her breasts thrust outwards against the material of her shirt. 'In the hotel. He's got a house over on the east bank. Up near Karnak. He used to drive over each morning.'

Khalifa's brow furrowed slightly, then he motioned his deputy to take down the address.

'So when did you last see Mr Jansen alive?' asked Sariya once he'd finished scribbling, eyes focused on the point where the woman's shirt pulled open slightly, revealing a hint of pink bra.

'About nine this morning. He came over at seven as usual, did some paperwork in the office, then left a couple of hours later. Said he had some business to attend to.'

'Did he say what sort of business?'

This from Khalifa.

'Not in so many words, but I guessed he was going to look at the monuments. It's what he seemed to spend most of his time doing. He was always visiting them. Seemed to know more about them than most experts.'

A small grey cat came stalking along the edge of the terrace, pausing for a moment to size them up before leaping into the woman's lap. She ran her hand gently along its back, tracing the line of its spine, tickling its ears.

'We found certain items near his body,' said Khalifa. 'A walking cane, a canvas bag.'

'Yes, those were his. He always took them when he went exploring. The cane was for his leg. Some old injury. Car accident, I think.'

There was a splashing sound from the far side of the lake as a small boat moved out onto the water, one man rowing, another standing in the prow holding a net, their figures shadowy and indistinct in the thickening darkness. Khalifa sucked away the last of his cigarette and tamped it out in the ashtray.

'Did Mr Jansen have any enemies?' he asked. 'Anyone who would wish him any harm?'

The woman shrugged. 'Not that I know of. But then, like I told you, he kept himself to himself. Never gave much away.'

'Friends?' asked Khalifa. 'Anybody at all he was close to?'

Another shrug. 'Not in Luxor, so far as I'm aware. There was a couple he used to visit up in Cairo. He was there only last week. Anton, I think the husband was called. Anton, Anders, something like that. Swiss. Or German. Or maybe Dutch.' She threw up her hands apologetically. 'Sorry. I'm not really being much use.'

'Not at all,' said Khalifa. 'You're being extremely helpful.'

'The truth is, Piet was a bit of a loner. Kept his private life private. In three years I never once saw the inside of his house, you know. He was . . . secretive almost. I dealt with the hotel and that was it. We didn't have much to do with each other outside business.'

The young man who had brought their tea returned, leaning down and muttering something in the woman's ear.

'OK, Taib,' she said. 'I'll be along in a minute.' She turned to Khalifa.

'I'm sorry, inspector. We've got a private party tonight and I need to start organizing dinner.'

'Of course,' said Khalifa. 'I think we've covered everything we need to.'

The three of them stood and walked back into the hotel lobby, a large, whitewashed space with a reception desk at one end and a narrow stair-case in the corner leading to the upper storey. An elderly man in a dirty djellaba was mopping the tiled floor, humming to himself.

'There was a photo in Mr Jansen's wallet,' said Khalifa as they stopped to admire a row of Gaddis prints on the wall. 'Of a dog.'

'Arminius,' said the woman, smiling. 'A child-hood pet. Piet was always going on about him. Used to say he was the only real friend he'd ever had. The only person he'd ever really trusted. Talked about him like he was a human.' She paused, then added, 'He was a lonely man, I think. Unhappy. A lot of demons.'

They gazed up at the prints for a moment longer – two men operating a shaduf beside the Nile; a group of women selling vegetables inside the Bab Zuwela gateway of Cairo's Islamic quarter; a young boy in a tarboosh, staring at the camera and laughing – then crossed to the front door and stepped out onto the street. Two children scuttled past, wheeling a rubber tyre.

'There was one thing,' she said as they were about to walk away. 'It's probably not relevant, but Piet was extremely anti-semitic.'

She said this last word in English. Khalifa's eyes narrowed.

'What does this mean?'

'I don't know how you say it in Arabic. He was . . . *ma habbish el-yehudi-een.* He didn't like Jews.'

The detective's shoulders tensed slightly, imperceptibly, as though he had received a small electric shock, not enough to hurt him, just sufficient to make him feel uncomfortable.

'Go on.'

'There's not much to tell really. He never said anything in front of me. I overheard him a couple of times talking to other people, though – guests, local men. Awful stuff. How the only problem with the Holocaust was that they hadn't finished the job. How they ought to drop a nuclear bomb on Israel. I mean, I hate what's happening there as much as the next person, but this was sick stuff. Nasty.' She shrugged, fiddling with her earring. 'I guess I should have taken him to task about it, but then I figured he was old, and old people tend to have weird opinions. And anyway, I didn't want to get in a row and lose my job. Like I say, it's probably not relevant.'

Khalifa pulled out his cigarettes and lit one, inhaling deeply.

'Probably not,' he said. 'But thank you for mentioning it. If there's anything else we'll be in touch.'

He nodded a farewell and, turning, set off down

the street, hands thrust into his pockets, forehead furrowed in thought. Sariya came up beside him.

'Can't say I disagree,' he said as they walked. 'About the Jews.'

Khalifa shot him a glance.

'You think the Holocaust was a good thing?'

'I don't think it even happened,' snorted Sariya. 'Israeli propaganda. They had a piece about it this week in *al-Akhbar*.'

'You believe that?'

Sariya shrugged. 'The sooner Israel is wiped off the map the better,' he said, sidestepping the question. 'What they're doing to the Palestinians . . . it's unforgivable. Butchering women and children.'

For a moment it seemed Khalifa was going to take issue with him. He decided against it, however, and, turning a corner at the end of the street, the two of them continued down towards the Nile in silence, the amplified wail of a muezzin ringing out behind them, summoning the faithful to evening prayer.

ISRAEL – THE DEAD SEA DESERT, OUTSIDE JERICHO

The man paced up and down beside the helicopter, puffing on a stubby cigar, his eyes flicking from the empty dirt road in front of him down to his watch and back again. It was dark, the only light coming from a rising three-quarter moon that bathed the desert in a buttery yellow glow, and silent too, so that the man's footsteps sounded unnaturally loud, grinding deep holes in the still night air. The shadows were too heavy to make out his appearance clearly, save that he was of medium height and very thin, with a hooked nose, a white *yarmulke* on his head and a livid, sickle-shaped scar slicing down his right check.

'Any idea how long?' came a voice from the cockpit of the helicopter.

'Soon,' replied the man. 'He'll be here soon.'

He continued pacing, drumming his palm nervously against his thigh, stopping every now and then to cock his head and listen. Five minutes passed, ten, then the faint sound of an engine insinuated itself into the night, accompanied a moment later by the crunch of tyres on gravel. The man moved out into the centre of the road, watching as a car gradually detached itself from the shapeless generality of shadows and bumped its way towards them, moving slowly, headlamps off.

It pulled up ten metres away and the driver got out. The man joined him, and together they went round to the rear of the vehicle, where the driver opened the boot. There was a groan and a rustle, and a figure clambered out into the night, clutching the driver's arm for support. Again it was too dark to make out much about him, other than the fact that he was younger than the cigar-smoker, with an unruly mop of dark hair and a checked *keffiyeh* wrapped around his neck.

'You're late,' said the older man. 'I was worried.'

The newcomer was taking deep gulps of air, raising his arms above his head to stretch out the stiffness.

'I have to be careful. If some of my people find out about this . . .'

He drew a finger across his throat, the movement accompanied by a sharp hissing sound, as of a knife slicing through meat. The cigar-smoker nodded and, laying an arm across the newcomer's shoulders, steered him towards the helicopter.

'I know,' he said quietly. 'We're walking a tightrope here.'

'I hope we can reach the other side.'

'We have to reach the other side. For all our sakes. Otherwise . . .'

He waved his cigar helplessly and the two of them disappeared into the helicopter, the desert echoing to the rising whine of its engines as the blades started to turn, slashing at the darkness.

LUXOR

The two policemen crossed the Nile on the local ferry, a hulking, rusty affair that ploughed through the water in a haze of diesel fumes and with much tooting of its horn. Sariya nibbled a packet of yellow *termous* beans; Khalifa sat gazing at the floodlit shell of Luxor Temple, lost in his own thoughts, his fake leather jacket zipped up to his chin against the evening chill. On the eastern shore they climbed a set of steps up onto the Corniche, where Khalifa asked his deputy for the keys to the dead man's house.

'You're going down there tonight?' asked Sariya, surprised.

'Thought I'd just have a quick look around. See if there's anything . . . unusual.'

Sariya's eyes narrowed. 'How do you mean?'

'Just . . . unusual. Come on, give me the keys.'

Shrugging, Sariya reached into his pocket and handed over the plastic bag with Jansen's keys in it. He then took out his notebook, tore off the page on which he had scribbled Jansen's address and handed that over too.

'You want me to come with you?'

'No, you get off home,' replied Khalifa, glancing down at the address before folding it and putting it in his pocket. 'I won't be long. Just need to check a few things. I'll see you at the station tomorrow.'

He clapped his deputy on the shoulder and, pushing him away along the Corniche, turned and flagged down a passing taxi. It swung into the kerb where the driver, a plump man with an *imma* wrapped around his head and a cigarette dangling from the corner of his mouth, reached behind him and opened the back door.

'Where to, inspector?' he asked. Like most Luxor cabbies he knew Khalifa personally, having been arrested by him at least once for driving without the proper documentation.

'Karnak,' said Khalifa. 'Just go straight down the Corniche. I'll tell you where to stop.'

They set off, heading north past the Mercure Hotel, Luxor Museum, the old hospital and Chicago House, weaving in and out of the traffic, the town's buildings gradually fragmenting into a scatter of ramshackle houses surrounded by swathes of scrub parkland. Five hundred metres past the town's northern fringes Khalifa signalled the driver to pull over, opposite a broad avenue of laurel and eucalyptus trees that led off to the right, towards the floodlit first pylon of Karnak Temple.

'You want me to wait?' asked the driver as Khalifa got out.

'Don't worry, I'll walk back.'

He reached into his pocket for money, but the driver waved him away.

'Forget it, inspector. I owe you.'

'How do you work that one out, Mahmoud? Last time we met I arrested you for being out of date with your insurance.'

'True,' acknowledged the driver. 'But then I hadn't paid my road tax either, so I figure I got off lightly.'

He grinned, revealing two rows of uneven brown teeth, and, with a cheeky toot, swung the car around and disappeared back the way he had come.

Khalifa stood for a moment staring at the Nile, its surface glinting in the moonlight like a sheet of rippling grey silk, then turned and set off towards the temple entrance.

It took him ten minutes to reach the dead man's house, which sat in a secluded enclosure two hundred metres from the north-west corner of the temple complex, at the end of a rutted dirt track. A low, single-storey villa, surrounded by a tall, barred fence and half-hidden behind a screen of palm and mimosa trees, it harked back to the days before Luxor became a major tourist centre, when the only visitors were archaeologists or wealthy Europeans come to winter in the balmy climes of upper Egypt. A scraggy mist had risen from a nearby irrigation canal and wrapped itself around the base of the house, giving the place an eerie, haunted feel, as if it was floating just above the ground.

Khalifa gazed through the fence at the neatly tended flower beds, the heavily shuttered windows, the KHAAS! MAMNU' EL-DUKHUUL! PRIVATE! NO ENTRY! signs posted at regular intervals around the fence's circumference, then stepped up to the front gate and turned the handle. Locked. He pulled the dead man's keys from his pocket and, in the pale moonlight, tried them one by one until he found the right fit, swinging the gate open and crunching along a gravel path. As he climbed onto the building's front porch an animal of some sort, a cat or a fox, shot out of the shadows to his right, knocking over a rake and disappearing into a clump of bushes around the side of the house.

'Dammit!' he hissed, startled.

He lit a cigarette and fiddled with the keys, undoing the door's three heavy locks and stepping into the dark interior. He located a switch on the wall and turned on the lights.

He was in a large living room, wood-floored and scrupulously tidy; with four armchairs arranged around a circular brass coffee table in the centre, a sideboard with a television and telephone on it, and a bulky chaise-longue arranged against the right-hand wall. Opposite, a dark corridor led away towards the back of the house.

He gazed around for a while, familiarizing himself with his surroundings, then wandered over to the left-hand wall where a large oil painting of a craggy, snow-covered mountain hung above a rack of newspapers and magazines. He stared up at the painting, admiring it – he had never seen snow before, not real snow – then bent down and flicked through the contents of the rack. There were two *al-Ahrams*, an Egyptian Horticultural Society magazine and a bulletin from the Egyptian Museum in Berlin. At the back was a copy of *Time*, its cover bearing photos of two men, one squat, heavy-set and bearded, the other thin and hawk-faced, with a livid scar arcing down his right cheek almost to the line of his chin. Khalifa pulled it out and read the headline: HAR-ZION AND MILAN: WHICH WAY FOR ISRAEL? by Layla al-Madani. He recognized the writer's name. Opening the magazine, he flipped through it to the relevant article, which was topped with a photo by-line of a young woman, beautiful, with short dark hair and large green eyes. He gazed at it for a moment, curiously compelled, then, with a shake of the head, closed the magazine, replaced it in the rack and set off to explore the rest of the house.

There were five further rooms: two bedrooms, a bathroom, a study and, at the rear of the building, a large kitchen. All were immaculately tidy, unnaturally so, as though no-one actually lived there, and in addition to thick shutters there were heavy brass security locks on all the windows. Khalifa went through them one by one, poking and prying, not really looking for anything in particular, just trying to get a feel for the place, for the man who had lived there.

He took the study first, a large room with a pair of metal filing cabinets in one corner, floor-to-ceiling bookcases along two of the walls and a large desk pushed up beneath the window. The filing cabinets were both locked, but he found the keys on the dead man's key-ring and opened them one after another. The first contained plastic envelopes full of business and legal documents. The second was a mini-library of photographic slides, hundreds upon hundreds of them, all neatly labelled and arranged in plastic sleeves, depicting, so far as he could make out, almost every major historical site in Egypt, from Tel el-Fara'in in the Delta right the way down to Wadi Halfa in northern Sudan.

He picked out a couple of the images at random and held them up to the light, squinting, recognizing the Temple of Seti I at Abydos, the rock tombs at Beni Hassan, the Precinct of Khonsu at Karnak. He stared at this last slide for over a minute, moving it towards and away from the light to get the focus sharp, a troubled furrow creasing his brow, before returning it to its sleeve, closing and relocking the cabinets and wandering across to one of the bookcases.

Its volumes were arranged alphabetically by author name and, with the exception of a couple of dictionaries and a small section on plants and gardening, were almost exclusively historical works, some popular history, most academic. A cursory skim across their spines revealed titles in Latin, French, English, German, Arabic and – surprisingly, given what the Shaw woman had said about Jansen's attitude towards Jews – Hebrew. Whatever else Jansen was, he was clearly extremely well read and educated.

'How did someone like you end up running a cheap hotel in Luxor?' Khalifa murmured to himself. 'What's your story, eh, Mr Jansen? And why all the security? What were you afraid of? What were you trying to hide?'

He remained in the study for a while, examining books and rifling through the desk drawers, then moved on to the bathroom, and then the two bedrooms, in the first of which, in a small cabinet beside the bed, he unearthed a pair of magazines – German, pornographic, with young boys on the front posing nude for the camera. He gazed at them, fascinated and repelled, then threw them back in the cabinet and slammed it shut.

He came to the kitchen last. Two further doors opened off this. One, secured with two mortise locks and a heavy steel bolt, led out on to a wooden veranda at the rear of the villa. The second door, which also had to be opened with a key from the dead man's ring, revealed a steep set of stairs descending into darkness. He started cautiously down them, the wooden steps creaking beneath his feet, the blackness slowly enveloping and disorientating him so that he was forced to keep his right hand against the cool stone wall to maintain his balance. At the bottom his fingertips brushed a chunky switch, which he flicked on.

It took him a second to register what he was looking at, then he gasped in astonishment.

'My God!'

Antiquities. Everywhere antiquities. On trestle tables arranged down the centre of the room, on shelves around the walls, in boxes and chests stacked in the corners. Hundreds upon hundreds of objects, each sealed in its own plastic bag, each accompanied by a neat, handwritten tag detailing what it was, where and when it had been found, and its estimated date.

'It's like a museum,' Khalifa whispered incredulously. 'His own private museum.'

For a moment he stood rooted to the spot, then stepped forward to the nearest of the tables, picking up a bag with a tiny wooden figure inside it. 'Shabti, KV39, East corridor fill,' read the accompanying card. 'Wood. No text or decoration. 18th Dynasty, probably Amenhotep I (c.1525–1504 BC). Found March 3, 1982.' KV39 was a large, rubble-filled tomb in a fold of the hills above the Valley of the Kings, considered by many to be the final resting place of the Eighteenth Dynasty pharaoh Amenhotep I. It had never been properly excavated. Jansen had clearly been in there doing a bit of private digging of his own.

Khalifa replaced the figure and picked up another object. 'Fragment glazed floor tile,

Amarna (Akhetaten), Northern palace. Papyrus reed design in green, yellow and blue. 18th Dynasty, reign of Akhenaten (*c*.1353–1335 BC). Found 12th November 1963.' It was a beautiful piece, if broken, the colours rich and vibrant, the painted papyrus reeds leaning slightly as if blowing in a gentle wind. Again, it seemed to have been dug up by Jansen himself. Khalifa turned it over in his hand, shaking his head, then laid it down and wandered off around the rest of the cellar.

It was an extraordinary collection, mind-boggling, the result, judging from the accompanying tags, of over five decades' surreptitious – and illegal – scavenging. Some of the objects – a small faience hippopotamus; a beautifully decorated ostracon bearing the Theban triad of Amun, Mut and Khonsu – were extremely valuable. The majority, however, were either damaged or else so common as to be worth virtually nothing. The guiding principle seemed to be not so much the desire to amass rare or beautiful objects, but rather a simple joy in digging things up, recovering and labelling tiny shards of the past. It was, Khalifa thought to himself, the sort of collection he himself would have loved to own. A history lover's collection. An archaeologist's.

In the far corner he found a small iron safe, squat and chunky, with a dial and lever on the front. He tried turning the latter, but the door remained resolutely closed and after a minute or so he gave up and wandered off again.

Eventually he looked down at his watch.
'Dammit!'

He had promised his wife Zenab he would be home by nine p.m. so he could read the children a story, and it was now past ten. Tutting at himself, he took a final look around, then moved back to the stairs and raised his hand to switch off the light. As he did so he noticed that the door above, which opened inwards, had swung half closed again so that he could see the back of it. There, on a hook, hung a broad-brimmed green felt hat with a spray of long feathers protruding from its side. He paused, then climbed the stairs, slowly, as if reluctant to do so, and lifted it from the hook, holding it out in front of him.

'Like he had a bird on his head,' he mumbled, voice hoarse suddenly, as though something had been pushed deep down into his throat. 'A funny little bird.'

He gazed at the hat, then suddenly, angrily, smashed his hand against the back of the door, causing it to slam shut.

'Dammit!' he hissed. 'It has to be a coincidence! It has to be!'

JERUSALEM

The Old City of Jerusalem, that bewildering labyrinth of streets and squares, shrines and holy places, spice markets and souvenir shops, is by night as silent and empty as a ghost town. The bustling crowds that during the day throng its thoroughfares and passages – especially those of the Muslim quarter, where you can hardly move for shoppers and fruit sellers and scuttling children – swiftly drain away with the setting of the sun, leaving forlorn vistas of shuttered shop-fronts, shadowy and echoing, like stone veins from which all the lifeblood has been drained. The few people who remain seem ill at ease, glancing around nervously, walking faster and more purposefully than they would by day, as if menaced by the dream-like emptiness of the place, and the corrosive orange glow of its street lamps.

It was almost three in the morning when Baruch Har-Zion and his two companions came through Jaffa Gate and made their way down into this dim twilight world, the most deserted hour of the night, when even the stray cats have gone to ground and the sharp quarterly clangs of the city's church bells seem blunted by the enshrouding silence. A short, thick-set man, almost as broad as he was tall, he had greying hair, a bearded, square-jawed face, and carried an Uzi submachine gun in one gloved hand and a leather holdall in the other. His companions were also armed with Uzis, one of them slight and milky-pale, the tassles of a *tallit katan* dangling from beneath his jacket; the other tall and tanned, his hair crew-cut almost down to the scalp, his arms and neck thick with knotted muscle. All three wore black *yarmulkes* on their heads.

'What about the cameras?' asked the pale man as they walked, nodding at the security monitors bolted at regular intervals along the street.

'Forget them,' said Har-Zion, waving a hand dismissively, a certain stiffness to the movement as though his roll-neck sweater, which came up almost to the level of his jawline, was a little too tight for him. 'I've got friends in the David control centre. They'll turn a blind eye.'

'But what if—'

'Forget them,' repeated Har-Zion, firmer this time. 'Everything's been taken care of.'

He threw the man a glance, his granite-grey eyes narrowed slightly as if to say 'I don't want you here if you're afraid', then looked to the front again.

The three of them strode onwards, following the stepped slope of David Street down towards the

Jewish quarter before swinging left into one of the souks that thrust deep into the heart of the Muslim part of the city. Walls of shuttered shop-fronts stretched away to either side of them, grey and uniform, their metal plates scrawled with Arabic graffiti, interspersed here and there with the odd word or phrase in English: FATAH, HAMAS, FUCK OFF JEWS. They passed a Coptic priest hurrying up to prayers in the Holy Sepulchre, and a pair of tourists, male, drunk, struggling to locate their hostel in the maze of narrow streets. Otherwise they were alone.

A bell clanked the hour, the sound echoing dully across the rooftops.

'I hope we *are* fucking seen,' growled the crew-cut man as they went, patting his Uzi. 'It's our city. Screw the Arabs.'

Har-Zion smiled faintly but said nothing, just pointed them down a narrow alley flanked by high stone walls. They passed a courtyard full of rubbish, a wooden door behind which they could hear the faint babble of a television, and the gateway of a small mosque before emerging into an empty cobbled street that ran perpendicular to the one they had just descended. To the right it disappeared beneath a series of low stone arches, running down towards the Western Wall; to the left it inclined upwards in the direction of the Via Dolorosa and the Damascus Gate. A sign in front of them read AL-WAD ROAD.

Har-Zion checked both ways, then dropped to

his haunches – again with that tightness of movement, as if something was somehow constricting
him – and unzipped his holdall, producing two
crowbars, which he handed to his companions,
and a canister of spray paint, which he kept for
himself.

'Let's get started.'

He led them over to a tall, shabby-looking
building – a typical old-city house with chunky
stone façade, wooden doorway and arched
windows, grilled and shuttered.

'You're sure it's empty?' asked the pale man
nervously.

Again Har-Zion gave him that piercing, grey-
eyed stare. 'This is no place for a *nebbish*,
Schmuely.'

The smaller man blinked and lowered his head,
ashamed.

'Let's get to work,' said Har-Zion.

He shook the canister, the clack of ball-bearings
echoing down the street, and began to spray,
drawing a crude seven-branched menorah onto
the walls to either side of the doorway, the paint
dripping in places so that in the uncertain light it
looked as if a huge claw was scratching into the
stone, causing it to bleed. His companions began
working their crowbars into the gap between the
door and its jamb, easing them in about two
inches, levering them back to widen the crack and
forcing them in further until the door-bolt gave
with a sharp splintering sound. They looked up

and down the street, then stepped into the dark interior. Har-Zion finished spraying the second menorah, picked up the leather holdall and followed them in, pushing the door to behind him.

They had heard about the house from a friend in the Jerusalem police. Its Arab owners were away on 'umra and had left the place empty, a perfect target for occupation. Har-Zion would have preferred something even closer to the Temple Mount, something more confrontational, more hurtful and insulting to the Muslims, but for the moment this was good enough.

He rummaged in the holdall and pulled out a heavy metal flashlight, switching it on and playing the beam around them. They were in a large room, sparsely furnished, with a stone staircase in the far corner and a tang of polish and tobacco smoke in the air. A poster on the wall above one of the sofas carried nine lines of swirling Arabic script, white against a green background, verses from the Koran. Har-Zion held it in the torch-beam, then stepped forward and ripped it down.

'Avi, you check the back. I'll do the upper levels. Schmuely, you come with me.'

He handed a second torch to the crew-cut man, then started up the staircase, taking the holdall with him, glancing into various rooms as he went, the pale-skinned man trailing in his wake. At the top he unbolted a metal door and stepped out onto the building's flat roof, a tangled thicket of washing lines, TV aerials, satellite dishes and solar panels fanning out all around him. Ahead rose the domes of the Holy Sepulchre and the rearing steeple of the Church of St Saviour. Behind stretched the vast paved expanse of the Temple Mount, at its centre, floodlit, the bulbous golden crown of the Dome of the Rock.

'For you will spread abroad to the right and to the left,' murmured Har-Zion, 'and your descendants will possess the nations, and will people the desolate cities.'

How often he had imagined this moment: during the dark days of persecution back in his native Ukraine; in the army hospital, where the burns had been so agonizing he'd felt his very soul was being ripped out of him. They'd taken land elsewhere these last few years – outside Nazareth, down near Hebron, along the Gaza seafront – but it meant nothing if Jerusalem itself could not be theirs. That Mount Moria, the Even Shetiyah, where Abraham had come to sacrifice his only son Isaac; where Jacob had dreamt of a ladder rising all the way to heaven; where Solomon had raised the first Holy Temple . . . that this, of all places, should be in the hands of the Muslims was something that pained him physically, like an open wound.

And now, at last, they were taking it back. Reclaiming what was rightfully theirs. Yerushalyim the Golden, capital of Eretz Israel Ha-Shlema, homeland of the Jewish people. That was all they were asking. That they should have a homeland.

But the Arabs and Jew-haters would deny them even that. Scum. All of them. Cockroaches. It was them who should be put in gas chambers.

He turned slowly round, taking in the scene, then he delved into the holdall and removed a large roll of cloth with two pieces of rope attached to it.

'Do it,' he said, handing the roll to his companion.

The man moved forwards to the front edge of the roof where he knelt and began tying the rope-ends to a couple of steel rods protruding from the concrete floor. Har-Zion pulled a mobile phone from his pocket and jabbed a number into the keypad.

'We're in,' he said when it was answered. 'Start sending the others down.'

He rang off and slipped the phone back into his pocket. As he did so his companion finished securing the ropes and dropped the bundle off the side of the building. It unfurled with a muffled whoosh, leaving a long white and blue flag draped down the front of the stonework like a waterfall, a bold Star of David at its centre.

'Praise be to God,' he smiled.

'Hallelujah,' said Har-Zion.

KALANDIA REFUGEE CAMP, BETWEEN JERUSALEM AND RAMALLAH

Layla al-Madani ran a hand through her close-cropped black hair and stared at the young man sitting opposite, in his neatly pressed trousers and Dome of the Rock T-shirt.

'The idea of killing women and children doesn't concern you?'

The young man met her gaze.

'Does it concern the Israelis when our women and children are killed? Deir Yassin? Sabra and Chatila? Rafah? This is a war, Miss Madani, and in war bad things happen.'

'So if al-Mulatham approached you—'

'I would consider it an honour. To become a *shaheed*, to martyr myself for my people, my God. I would consider myself lucky.'

He was a handsome man, with large brown eyes and the hands of a piano player, long-fingered and delicate. She was interviewing him for an article about antiquities plunderers – young Palestinians who, because of the Israeli economic stranglehold on the Palestinian territories, had been reduced to stealing and selling ancient arte-facts in order to make ends meet. The conversation had, as it always did with these sort of interviews, moved on to a wider discussion of Israeli military oppression, and thence to the subject of suicide bombing.

'Look at me,' he said, shaking his head. 'Look at this.'

He circled his hand, indicating the cheap, three-room cinder-block house, with its couches that doubled as beds and small primus stove in the corner.

'Our family used to own a vineyard down near Bethlehem, two hundred *dunum*. Then the Zionists came and drove us out and all we are left with is this. I have a degree in engineering but cannot find employment because the Israelis have revoked my work permit, so I sell stolen antiquities so we can eat. Do you think this makes me feel good about myself? Do you think I have high hopes for the future? Believe me, if the chance to martyr myself came along I would jump at it. The more of them I kill the better. Women, children, it makes no difference. They are all guilty. I hate them. All of them.'

He smiled, a thin, bitter expression that cracked the lower part of his face, revealing an immensity of fury and despair within. There was a silence, broken by the sound of children playing in the alleyway outside, then Layla closed her notebook and slipped it back into her bag.

'Thank you, Yunis.'

The man shrugged, but said no more.

She joined her driver Kamel outside and together they bumped their way out of the camp, the car slaloming down a potholed road and onto the main Ramallah-Jerusalem highway where they joined a queue of traffic stacked up behind the Kalandia checkpoint. To their left the drab camp buildings spread away across a hillside, grey and ramshackle, like a bed of decaying coral; to their right the runway of Atarot airport lay flat and lifeless, as if someone had slashed a line of dirty yellow paint across the landscape. Ahead, four lanes of stationary traffic stretched off up the road like dusty ribbons, tapering to a single lane at the Israeli roadblock two hundred metres further on, where documents were being checked and vehicles searched. It was a pointless exercise – anybody who didn't have the requisite papers could simply skirt the checkpoint on foot and pick up a lift on the far side – but the Israelis insisted on doing it, less for security reasons than to humiliate the Palestinians, show them who was boss. No-one fucks with us, that was the message. We're in control.

'*Kosominumhum kul il-Israelieen*,' muttered Layla, dropping her head back and staring up at the car ceiling. 'Fucking Israelis.'

Twenty minutes passed, the queue remaining exactly as it was, and eventually, throwing open the car door, she got out. She walked up and down, stretching her legs, then reached back into the car and pulled out her camera, a Nikkon D1X digital, removing it from its case and switching it on, fiddling with the lens.

'Watch it,' said Kamel, his head leant forward on the steering wheel in anticipation of the long wait to come. 'You know what happened the last time you took photos at a checkpoint.'

How could she forget? The Israelis had confiscated her camera, spent an hour taking apart Kamel's car and, just for good measure, given her a strip-search as well.

'I'll be careful,' she said. 'Trust me.'

A large brown eye swivelled towards her.

'Miss Madani, you are the least trustworthy person I know. With your face you say one thing, but—'

'Yes, yes, always there is something different in my eyes.'

She threw him an annoyed glance and, draping the camera around her neck, turned and wandered off between the rows of vehicles towards the checkpoint.

They'd left Jerusalem early the previous afternoon, driving out to Ramallah to cover a story about a Palestinian collaborator whose mutilated body had been found floating in the fountain at the centre of town, the perfect hook for a wider feature on collaborators she was doing for the *Guardian*. It had only taken a couple of hours to research. While they'd been there, however, there'd been another al-Mulatham suicide bombing, at a wedding in Tel Aviv, and the Israelis had closed off the entire West Bank, leaving her no choice but to bed down with an old university friend while American-built Apache AH-64 helicopter gunships hovered overhead, blowing the shit out of various Palestinian Authority buildings that were still half-ruined from the last time they'd had the shit blown out of them.

It hadn't been a completely wasted stay. She'd picked up the antiquities plundering story, and had managed to wangle an interview with Sa'eb Marsoudi, one of the leaders of the First Intifada and a rising star of Palestinian politics. He was a charismatic man – young, passionate, handsome, with a mop of jet-black hair and a checked *keffiyeh* slung around his neck – and, as always, had given her some good quotes. Now, however, she was anxious to get back to Jerusalem. Chayalei David, the Warriors of David, had apparently seized a building in the Old City, which sounded like a good feature; and she was already a week overdue with an *al-Ahram* piece she was doing about malnutrition among Palestinian children. More than anything she just wanted to get back to her flat and take a shower – the IDF had cut the Ramallah water supply and she hadn't washed properly since the previous morning. A faintly sour smell wafted from her shirt and cords.

She came to within twenty metres of the checkpoint and stopped. A pick-up truck piled high with watermelons was being ordered to turn round, the driver shouting and gesticulating at one of the soldiers who just stared at him through mirror shades, uninterested, occasionally mouthing the word '*Ijmia*' – go back. Vehicles were queuing from the opposite direction as well, coming out of Jerusalem, although not as many as on this side. To her left, a Red Crescent ambulance sat grid-locked, its red light rotating helplessly.

She'd been writing about scenes like this for over a decade now, publishing in both Arabic and English, writing for everything from the *Guardian* to *al-Ahram*, the *Palestinian Times* to the *New Internationalist*. After what had happened to her father it hadn't been easy establishing herself, especially in the early days after her return from England when she'd had to put up with all manner of shit. She'd worked hard to gain people's trust, however, to prove herself, to show she was a true Palestinian, and although there would always be those such as Kamel who would never be entirely convinced, the majority had, in the end, accepted her, won over by her outspokenness in the name of the Palestinian cause. 'Assadiqa' they now called her – the truth teller. The Israelis were somewhat less enthusiastic. 'Liar', 'Jew-hater', 'Terrorist' and 'Interfering Bitch' were just a few of the titles she had amassed over the years. And those were the nice ones.

She pulled a tab of chewing gum from her pocket and popped it into her mouth, wondering if she should go forward to the checkpoint and flash her press ID, try to speed things up a bit. She'd just be wasting her time, though – press card or no press card, it didn't change the fact she was a Palestinian. She gazed at the scene a while longer, then turned away and started back the way she had come, shaking her head wearily, the ground beneath her feet trembling as a pair of Merkava tanks rumbled past on the opposite side of the road, blue and white Israeli flags fluttering from their turrets.

'*Kosominumhum kul il-Israelieen*,' she muttered.

LUXOR

Dr Ibrahim Anwar, chief pathologist at Luxor Hospital, had many annoying habits, not the least of which was his refusal ever to let work get in the way of a good game of dominoes. Anwar's passion for what he referred to as 'the board game of the gods' had delayed many an investigation over the years, and it did so again with the Jansen case. He had carried out an initial examination of the body at Malqata and then sent it back over the river to the morgue at Luxor General. Rather than performing an autopsy that same evening, however, as Khalifa had hoped he would, the pathologist had instead postponed it so he could participate in an inter-departmental dominoes competition. The upshot was that it was almost noon the next day before he finally called the police station to inform Khalifa that the post-mortem results were ready.

'About time,' snapped the detective, angrily stubbing out his fifteenth cigarette of the day into an already overflowing ashtray. 'I was hoping I'd get them last night.'

'All good things to those who wait,' said Anwar

81

with a cheerful chuckle. 'Interesting case, by the way. Very . . . thought-provoking. Anyway, my secretary's just finishing typing up the report. I can send it over to you, or you can come down here and pick it up yourself. Your choice.'

'I'll come down,' said Khalifa, knowing that if it was left to Anwar he might wait days for the report. 'Just tell me if it was an accident or foul play.'

'Oh, definitely foul play,' replied the pathologist. 'Extremely foul, although not perhaps in the way you imagine.'

'What the hell does that mean?'

'Let's just say it's a complicated story, and one with a bit of a sting in the tail. Come on over and all will be revealed. I think you'll find I've excelled myself on this one, Khalifa. Really excelled myself.'

The detective let out an exasperated sigh and, telling Anwar he'd be at the hospital in twenty minutes, hung up.

Mohammed Sariya walked into the office.

'That damned pathologist,' grumbled Khalifa. 'He's a disgrace.'

'He's finished the autopsy?'

'Only just. The man couldn't move slower if he was a bloody tortoise. I'm going over to get the report now. Any progress?'

While Khalifa had stayed in the office waiting for Anwar's call, Sariya had spent the morning following up the leads his boss had found in the dead man's house the previous night.

'Not much,' he replied, crossing to his desk and sitting down. 'Banque Misr are faxing over copies of his statements for the last four quarters and I've been on to the phone company for a breakdown of his calls over the same period. I also managed to track down his housekeeper.'

'Anything?'

'About the best way to cook *molochia*, more than you could ever want to know. About Jansen, almost nothing. She came in for a few hours twice a week, cleaned, did his shopping. He cooked for himself. She never went in the cellar, apparently. Wasn't allowed.'

'His will?' asked Khalifa. 'Did you speak to his solicitor?'

Sariya nodded. 'He definitely made one because the solicitor witnessed it. He hasn't got a copy, though. Said Jansen kept one for himself and gave another to some friend down in Cairo.'

Khalifa sighed and, standing, removed his jacket from the back of his chair.

'OK, start looking into Jansen's background, will you? How long he's lived in Egypt, where he was from originally, what he was doing when he lived in Alexandria. Anything you can dig up. There's something wrong about this guy. Or at least something not right. I can feel it.'

He pulled on the jacket and started across the room. When he reached the door he turned.

'By the way, you didn't happen to find out where the name Arminius comes from, did you?'

'I did actually,' said Sariya, looking pleased with himself. 'I did an internet search.'

'And?'

'Apparently it was some ancient German guy. Bit of a national hero, apparently.'

Khalifa clicked his fingers in recognition.

'I knew I'd heard the name before. Good work, Mohammed. Very good work.'

He stepped through the door and set off down the corridor, hands thrust into his pockets, wondering why on earth someone from Holland would want to name his dog after a German national hero.

True to form, Anwar wasn't in his office when Khalifa arrived fifteen minutes later. While a green-uniformed nurse went looking for him the detective stood at his window gazing down into the hospital grounds below, where a group of workmen were digging a trench across a stretch of lawn, the rhythmic thwack of their *tourias* echoing dully up to him. His lungs ached for a cigarette, but he resisted the temptation. Anwar was fiercely anti-smoking, and aching lungs, however uncomfortable, were infinitely preferable to one of the pathologist's 'If-you-want-to-poison-yourself-go-right-ahead-just-don't -do-it-anywhere-near-me' lectures. He nibbled his nails instead and, heaving open the window, leant out with his elbows on the sill, staring down at a child chasing a butterfly around the hospital car park.

There was something wrong here. He'd tried to tell himself he was just imagining things, reading too much into the situation, but it made no difference. Each little element, each fragment of the picture – the dead man's cane, his hatred of Jews, the house beside Karnak Temple, the strange feathered hat – all had added to his growing sense of unease, so that what had started as a faint pulse of uncertainty had now expanded into a corrosive panicky ache deep in the pit of his stomach.

True, he always experienced an adrenalin rush at the start of a case, a furious overworking of the mind as he struggled to master all the elements of the problem and arrange them into recognizable patterns. This, however, was different, for what was troubling him now was not so much the current investigation, but rather a previous one, years ago, right at the start of his police career. A murder, the first one he had ever worked on, horrible affair, brutal. Schlegel. That had been her name. Hannah Schlegel. Israeli. Jewish. Dreadful case. And now, suddenly, from nowhere . . . echoes. Nothing concrete. Nothing he could clutch on to with certainty. Just coincidences, momentary flashes in the blackness of the past. Cane, Jew-hater, Karnak, feathers – the words kept ringing in his ears like a mantra, boring into his skull.

'This is crazy,' he muttered to himself, nibbling on his thumbnail. 'It was fifteen years ago, for God's sake. It's finished!'

Even as he said it, however, he sensed that it wasn't finished at all. On the contrary, he had the uncomfortable feeling that something was only just beginning.

'Damn you, Jansen,' he growled. 'Damn you for dying like this.'

'My sentiments exactly,' came a voice behind him. 'Although of course if he hadn't died I wouldn't have had the satisfaction of solving the case for you.'

Khalifa turned, annoyed that his thoughts had been disturbed. Anwar was standing in the doorway holding a steaming glass.

'I didn't hear you.'

'I'm not surprised,' said the pathologist. 'You were miles away.'

He sipped his drink and raised the glass, staring at the pale yellow liquid inside.

'*Yansoon*,' he said with a smile. 'The best in Luxor. One of the matrons brews it for me. Marvellous stuff. Very calming. You should try some.'

He winked at Khalifa, then crossed to his desk and sat down, balancing the glass on one corner while he burrowed his way into the snowdrift of paperwork that was heaped up in front of him.

'Now, where the hell did I put it. I had it only . . . ah, here we are!'

He sat back, brandishing a thin typewritten document.

'Report of autopsy findings for Mr Piet Jansen,'

he said, reading out the title at the top of the document. 'Another Anwar triumph!'

He looked up at Khalifa, smirking. The detective reached towards his pocket for his cigarettes, an involuntary motion he aborted halfway through, laying his hand on the windowsill instead.

'Go on then,' he said. 'Talk me through it.'

'With pleasure,' said Anwar, settling back in his chair. 'To start with, I can tell you that our man was murdered.'

Khalifa leant forward slightly.

'I can also tell you that I'm pretty certain I know the identity of the guilty party. They were, I suspect, acting in self-defence, although that in no way reduces the enormity of the crime, nor the fact that Jansen would have died an extremely unpleasant and painful death.'

He paused for dramatic effect. He's been rehearsing this, Khalifa thought to himself.

'Before I reveal the murderer's name, however, I think it might be instructive to remind ourselves of the precise circumstances in which Jansen's body was found.'

Khalifa opened his mouth to say that he remembered the circumstances perfectly well, but then shut it again, accepting from long experience that Anwar was going to do this at his own pace and no amount of complaining on Khalifa's part was going to change that.

'In your own time,' he muttered, waving his hand in weary resignation.

'Thank you. I don't think you'll be disappointed.'

The pathologist took another long, slow sip of his drink and set the glass down again.

'So,' he resumed, 'the scene. Our man's body, you will remember, is found lying face down in the dirt with a rather unsightly iron spike jammed through his left eye socket. As well as massive trauma to zygomatic, sphenoid and lachrymal bones, and to the entire left side of the brain – his cerebrum, frankly, looked like a bowl of mashed aubergine – he had also suffered a size-able laceration to the right side of the skull, just above the level of the ear, clearly caused by an agent other than the spike. In addition there were minor lacerations to his left palm' – the pathologist held up his hand to illustrate the point – 'and left knee, as well as an area of discoloura-tion and swelling around the base of the right thumb, just below the first synovial joint. You probably didn't notice this because that particular hand was positioned beneath the body. There were also traces of dried mud beneath the fingernails of the same hand.'

He drained the last of the *yansoon* and, with a slight burp, set the glass aside.

'Three metres from the corpse,' he continued, 'there were signs of disturbance to the desert surface, as though it had been the scene of a struggle of some sort, and also a lump of rock with traces of blood on one edge. Two hundred metres beyond that the deceased's bag and walking cane were discovered beside a section of painted mud-brick wall that he was evidently in the process of dismantling. To achieve this it would appear that he loosened the bricks with hammer and chisel, then prised them out with his hand, hence the mud-traces beneath his nails.'

He brought his elbows up onto the table and clasped his hands in front of him.

'So much for the scene-setting. The question is, how do all these different parts of the picture actually relate to one another?'

Again Khalifa's hand, as if independent of the rest of his body, reached for his cigarettes. Again he diverted it at the last minute, thrusting it into the pocket of his trousers.

'Do tell me.'

'I most certainly will,' replied Anwar. 'Let's look at each piece of the jigsaw separately, shall we? First, the metal spike. The injuries it inflicted were, of course, fatal. It was not, however, the cause of death. Or rather, Jansen would have died anyway, irrespective of whether or not he had fallen on it.'

Khalifa's eyes narrowed. Despite himself, he was interested.

'Go on.'

'The laceration on the side of the head is likewise a red herring. It was certainly caused by the bloodstained rock. It was in no way life-threatening, however, even to a man as old and frail as Jansen. There was no damage to the skull beneath, and no significant deep bruising. It was a nasty flesh wound, no more.'

'So if he didn't die from a blow to the head, and he didn't die from having his brain pulped by the spike, how the hell did he die?'

Anwar slapped a hand against his chest.

'Myocardial infarction.'

'What?'

'Heart attack. The man suffered a massive coronary thrombosis and subsequent cardiac arrest. Chances are he was dead before he even hit the spike.'

Khalifa came forward a step.

'So what are you saying? Someone sliced him across the head with a rock and his heart gave out?'

The pathologist grinned, enjoying the game.

'No-one sliced him over the head with the rock. The laceration was an accident.'

'But you said he was murdered!'

'And so he was.'

'Then how?'

'He was poisoned.'

Khalifa slammed his hand against the wall in frustration.

'Dammit, Anwar, what the hell are you talking about?'

'Exactly what I say. Piet Jansen's murderer poisoned him, and that poison, either directly or indirectly, precipitated a heart attack which subsequently killed the poor man. I really can't put it any clearer than that. What exactly is it you don't understand?'

Khalifa gritted his teeth, determined not to be provoked by the pathologist's patronizing tone.

'And who precisely is this mysterious poisoner?' he asked, trying to keep his voice steady. 'You said you knew who he was.'

'Oh, I do.' Anwar chuckled. 'I most certainly do.'

Again he allowed a pause for dramatic effect, then, leaning forward, he held out his hand palmside upwards. He bunched it into a fist, extended the first finger and, with a sharp jerking motion, curled the finger back in on itself.

'The villain's name,' he announced portentously, 'is Mr Akarab.'

He repeated the strange jerking motion, jabbing the index finger in towards his palm.

'Akarab,' repeated Khalifa, bemused. 'You mean . . .'

The pathologist smiled. 'Exactly. Our friend Jansen was stung by an *akarab*. A scorpion.'

He curled the finger one more time, mimicking the action of a scorpion tail, then collapsed backwards into his chair, guffawing.

'I told you it was a story with a sting in the tail!' he roared. 'Just wait till I tell the boys about this one. The Tale of the Malqata Poisoner! Or should that be the *Tail* of the Malqata poisoner? Ha, ha, ha!'

'Very funny,' grunted Khalifa, smiling despite

himself. 'I presume the swelling beneath his thumb was—'

'Where he got stung,' Anwar spluttered, trying to catch his breath. 'Exactly. Judging by the colour and extent it was a pretty severe sting, too. An adult scorpion rather than a nipper. Unbelievably painful.'

He got to his feet and, still chuckling to himself, crossed to a washbasin in the corner of the room, turned on the cold tap and poured himself a cup of water.

'My guess is that things happened roughly like this. Jansen goes out to Malqata to pilfer some decorated mud bricks. He loosens one with his hammer and chisel, puts his hand into the cavity to pull it free and bang! Gets walloped by Mr Scorpion. In too much pain to bother about his bag and cane he staggers off towards his car, presumably intending to drive for help. After a couple of hundred yards the shock provokes a monumental heart attack and he keels over, in the process grazing his hand and knee and cutting his head on the rock, although it's conceivable he suffered the coronary after falling over. Either way he scrabbles around on the ground for a bit, somehow manages to get up, staggers another few metres and again keels over, this time skewering his eyeball on the peg. Bye-bye Mr Jansen.'

Khalifa mulled the sequence of events over in his head. He felt annoyed at the ease with which Anwar appeared to have solved the case. Relieved as well, though. No murder meant no criminal investigation, and although the antiquities in Jansen's cellar obviously required looking into, there no longer seemed any necessity to delve too deeply into the man's past. Which was good news, because if he was honest with himself Khalifa had been terrified of what he might find in that past.

'Oh well,' he said, letting out a deep sigh, 'at least that clears that up.'

'It certainly does,' said Anwar, draining his cup of water and crossing back to his desk, where he picked up the autopsy report and passed it across. 'It's all there, along with a few other observations that might be of interest.'

Khalifa flicked through the pages.

'What sort of observations?'

'Oh, just general medical stuff. He had pretty advanced prostate cancer, for one thing. Would probably only have survived a few more months anyway. And there was a lot of old scar tissue around his left knee, which probably accounts for the walking cane. He also lied about his age. Or at least he did on his ID card.'

Khalifa looked up questioningly.

'Admittedly I'm not an expert in these things,' said Anwar, 'but according to the card he was born in 1925, which would have made him about eighty years old. If the state of his teeth and gums was anything to go by, however, I'd have put money on him being at least ten years older than that. Doesn't really change anything, but I thought I'd point it out anyway.'

Khalifa considered this for a moment, then, with a nod, slipped the report into his jacket pocket and started towards the door.

'Good work, Anwar,' he said over his shoulder. 'I hate to say it, but I'm impressed.'

He reached the door, and was about to walk into the hallway when Anwar called after him.

'One funny thing.'

Khalifa turned.

'I didn't bother to mention it in the notes, didn't seem relevant to anything, but our man suffered from syndactylism of the feet.'

The detective came back a step, his face registering confusion.

'What does that mean?'

'Basically, it's a congenital fusing of the phalanges, the toes. Very rare. In layman's terms, the man had webbed feet. He was like—'

'A frog.'

The colour had drained from Khalifa's face.

'Are you all right?' asked Anwar. 'You look like you've seen a ghost.'

'I have,' whispered the detective. 'Her name's Hannah Schlegel, and I've done something terrible. Truly terrible.'

JERUSALEM

It was mid-afternoon before Layla finally made it back to Jerusalem. Kamel dropped her at the bottom end of the Nablus Road and, with a desultory nod of his head, drove off again, disappearing round the corner into Sultan Suleiman Street. It had started to drizzle, a cool, soft spray that drifted down from above like a billowing veil, dampening her hair and jacket, settling soundlessly onto the rooftops and pavements. Patches of blue sky were visible above Mount Scopus away to the east, but overhead the sky was grey and heavy, pressing down on the city like a vast steel dustbin lid.

She bought herself half a dozen freshly baked pitta breads from a roadside stall and started up the hill, past the entrance to the Garden Tomb, the Jerusalem Hotel and a line of weary-looking Palestinians queuing to renew their residency permits outside the grey metal turnstile of the Israeli Interior Ministry office, eventually turning into a narrow doorway slashed between a bakery and a grocer's shop, opposite the high-walled enclosure of the Ecole Biblique. An old man in a shabby grey suit and *keffiyeh* was sitting just inside, leaning on his walking stick, staring out at the rain.

'*Salaam alekum*, Fathi,' she said.

The old man looked up, squinting, then raised an arthritic hand in greeting.

'We've been worried about you.' He coughed. 'We thought maybe you had been arrested.'

Layla laughed. 'The Israelis wouldn't dare. How's Ataf?'

The old man shrugged, his wrinkled fingers tapping the handle of the stick.

'So-so. Her back is bad today so she stays in bed. You want some tea?'

Layla shook her head.

'I need a shower, and then I've got work to do. Maybe later. Tell Ataf to let me know if she needs any shopping.'

She stepped past the man and, crossing the entrance hall, climbed two flights of stone stairs up to her flat, which occupied the upper floor of the house. It was a simple space, high-ceilinged and cool, with two bedrooms, one of which doubled as her study, a large living room and, at the back, a kitchenette and bathroom, a narrow concrete stairway leading up from the latter to the flat roof above, with views down to the Damascus Gate and the jumbled checkerboard of the Old City. She had lived there for almost five years, renting it from a local businessman whose parents, Fathi and Ataf, lived on the ground floor and acted as the building's caretakers. With the amount she earned from freelancing she could easily have afforded something more up-market – in the Sheikh Jarrah district for example, with its plush apartment blocks and high-walled houses. She had taken a conscious decision to remain down here in the heart of East Jerusalem, however, among the bustle and noise and rubbish. It sent out a message: I am not one of those journalists who gets what they want from you and then retires to the security of the Hilton or American Colony. I am one of you. A Palestinian. It was a small gesture, but a necessary one. Always she had to keep proving herself, maintain the façade.

She dumped her things on the sofa – which with a small dining table, a television and a couple of shabby armchairs made up all the furniture in the living room, and, grabbing a bottle of Evian from the fridge, went through into the study. The message light was flashing on her answerphone and, taking a gulp of water, she crossed the room and sat down at her desk, glancing up, as she always did, at the large framed photograph of her father on the wall above, in his white doctor's coat and stethoscope. It was her favourite picture of him, the only one she had kept after his death, and she felt a momentary tightening in her throat before looking down again and jabbing the play button.

There were eleven messages. One was from the *Guardian* chasing up her piece on Palestinian collaborators; one from Tom Roberts, a guy at the British Consulate who had been trying, and failing, to chat her up for the last six months; one from her friend Nuha asking if she wanted to meet later for a drink at the Jerusalem Hotel; and one from Sam Rogerson, a Reuters contact, alerting her to the Warriors of David occupation in the Old City, which she had already heard about in Ramallah. The rest were either insults or death threats. 'You disgust me, you filthy, lying, cocksucking whore.' 'Enjoy today, Layla, because it's going to be your last.' 'We're watching you, and one day we're going to come up and put a bullet through your head. After we've raped you, of course.' 'We're going to stick a knife up your stinking Arab-loving cunt and slice you open, you dirty, lying bitch!' 'Death to Arabs! Israel! Israel!'

Judging by the accents, most of the calls were, as usual, from either Israelis or Americans. She changed her phone number regularly, but they always seemed to find out the new one within a day or so of it being assigned, and the calls continued unabated. Years ago, when she was first starting out, they had upset her. She was by now so used to them that they no longer had any effect; she got more stressed by editors hassling for copy. Only at night, silent, alone, did the cracks appear, did the horror of what she was involved in filter through, like poison into her blood-stream. The nights could be terrible. Truly terrible.

She sat through the messages, then wiped the

tape clean, plugged her mobile into its recharge unit and made a couple of quick calls, one to Nuha to arrange a drink for later that evening, another to get details of the Jewish house occupation in the Old City. She'd written several pieces over the last few years on Chayalei David, and had recently been commissioned by the *New York Review* to produce an in-depth profile of the group's leader, the militant, Soviet-born settler Baruch Har-Zion. The current occupation would provide a good hook for it, and she wondered if she shouldn't go down to the Old City immediately. She decided a couple of hours wouldn't make any difference, and, finishing the water, went through into the bedroom and stripped off her clothes.

She took a long, hot shower, vigorously soaping her slim body, leaning her head back and allowing the water to dash against her face and scalp, groaning with pleasure as the warm jets scoured the dirt and sweat from her skin. For the last thirty seconds she turned the dial to cold, then, slipping into a towelling robe, went back into the study where she sat at her desk and switched on her Apple laptop.

She worked for the next two hours, finishing a piece she had already begun on malnutrition among Palestinian children, and making a start on the *Guardian* collaborators article, occasionally referring to her scribbled shorthand notes but mostly composing from memory, her fingers dancing across the keypad, the images and sounds in her head translating effortlessly into words on the screen.

Curiously, given how easily it came to her, journalism had not been her first or even second choice of career. As a teenager, before her father's murder, she had envisaged herself becoming a doctor like him, working in the refugee camps of Gaza and the West Bank. Then later, at Beir Zeit University, where she had read contemporary Arab history, she had toyed with the idea of going into politics. In the end, however, she had decided it was journalism that would give her the best opportunity to carry out what she had come to see as her life's mission.

After graduating she had got herself a job on the Palestinian daily *al-Ayyam*, where the then editor, a hunch-backed chain-smoker named Nizar Suleiman, had taken her under his wing, drawing a lot of flak in the process, for her family history was well known. Her first feature, a piece on Palestinian indoctrination camps where kids as young as six were taught anti-Israeli songs and the art of Molotov cocktail making (plenty of Vaseline round the rim, that was the key, so the flaming petrol would adhere to the target), had gone through sixteen rewrites before Suleiman grudgingly consented to publish it. She had been so despondent she had thought of giving up her career there and then. He had refused to let her – 'If you give up now I'll damn well sack you!' –

and her second feature, on Israel's displacement of native Bedouin tribes in the Negev, had only gone through five rewrites. Her third feature, on Palestinians who, out of economic necessity, were forced to take jobs helping to build Israeli settlements, had been syndicated to three different newspapers and won her her first journalism award.

Thereafter her fame had steadily grown. Her hybrid background – English mother, Palestinian father – and intimate knowledge of the Palestinian world, not to mention fluency in Arabic, Hebrew, English and French, gave her a head-start on many other correspondents, and she received offers of staff posts on both the *Guardian* and the *New York Times* (she turned them down). She worked with *al-Ayyam* for four years then went freelance, writing on everything from the use of torture by the Israeli security services to spinach-growing projects in Lower Galilee, gaining a reputation – depending on which way you looked at it – for either passionate campaigning journalism or blinkered anti-Israeli bias.

The bias charge was one her critics – and there were plenty of them – were constantly levelling at her: that she only ever told one side of the story; gave voice to Palestinian suffering but ignored that of Israeli civilians; reported the horror of the refugee camps but never that of the innocent people reduced to mincemeat by car bombs and suicide bombers. It wasn't entirely fair. She had, over the years, done plenty of articles on Israeli civilian casualties, not to mention the rife corruption and human rights abuses within the Palestinian Authority. The reality, however, was that this was not a conflict you could report objectively. However hard you strived for balance, in the end you couldn't help but be partisan. And anyway, given her background, she couldn't afford to be seen pandering to Israeli sensibilities.

She banged out about a thousand words on the collaborator piece, then emailed the malnutrition article to the *al-Ahram* offices in Cairo and shut down her laptop. She hadn't got much sleep over the last few days and her eyelids felt heavy. Years of reporting, with its unpredictable hours and tight deadlines, had inured her to tiredness, however, and anyway, she wanted to get down to the Old City to check out the occupation. Throwing some clothes on, therefore, and swiftly munching an apple, she grabbed her notebook and camera, crossed the flat and opened the front door.

Fathi the caretaker was just coming to the top of the stairs, wheezing heavily, one hand clutching his walking stick, the other holding an envelope.

'This came for you this morning,' he said. 'I forgot to tell you earlier. Sorry.'

He handed over the envelope. It bore no postmark or address, just her name written in blood-red ink, the lettering forceful and regimented, like a row of soldiers standing to attention.

'Who delivered it?' she asked.

'Some kid,' replied the old man, turning and starting back down the stairs again. 'Never seen him before. He just came up, asked if you lived here, handed it to me and ran away again.'

'Palestinian?'

'Of course Palestinian. Since when did Jewish kids come round this part of town?'

He waved his hand as if to say 'what a ridiculous question' and disappeared round the corner.

Layla turned the envelope over in her hand, examining it, feeling for wires or other potentially threatening contents. Satisfied it was safe, she took it back into the flat and, laying it on her desk, carefully opened it, pulling out two pieces of paper stapled together, the top one a covering letter in the same curling gothic script as that in which the envelope had been addressed, the other an A4 photocopy of what looked like an old document of some kind. She glanced briefly at the latter, then turned her attention to the accompanying note, which was written in English.

Miss al-Madani,
I have long been an admirer of your journalism, and would like to put to you a proposition. Some while ago you interviewed the leader known as al-Mulatham. I am in possession of information that could prove invaluable to this man in his struggle against the Zionist oppressor, and should very much like to contact him. I believe

you can help me do so. In return I can offer what would, I believe, be the biggest scoop of your already illustrious career.

Given the delicacy of the situation, you will appreciate my desire to proceed with caution in this matter. I shall reveal no more at this stage. Please consider the proposition and, if possible, convey it to our mutual friend. I shall be in contact in the near future. PS. A small clue, just to whet your appetite. The information of which I speak is intimately connected with the enclosed document. If you are half the journalist I believe you to be, it should not take you too long to discover the significance of my offer.

There was no signature.

Zbxnufgmhiuynzupnzmimindoygzikdmong
uukxpgpnzpogouzhdzqohidpcpdngbuuhmzdzi
konugdmonumnhodgpdnohmuumyhhuhpnxou
ndnzyoxdmzkzmziaomhpguinufzggunzznhdz
qohguzhpxlgupdgqhhzuonzznhondhdnimofdv
uminzufzomvguuxxzgufdpfdguhdqnnhzloupu
goygzodioophdoxopmunzzocoxdpuzooghuuonz
nopoofododozuapoodnuopzhzxnnmuidzkdmp
oumdnloipbyumzquyhggpnzznhoguzmznonh
udolpnddnugxuikzoohnddnugxumbounddnu
ghuzodazhughhddmznpfugzrzvdximppupofuu
zanumzoomppn

GR

She read and re-read the note, then looked again at the photocopied sheet. It seemed to be of a letter, old to judge by the style of the script, very old. It used the Roman alphabet, but beyond that she could make neither head nor tail of it, for rather than individual words and sentences it seemed to consist of a single unbroken sequence of letters which, however hard she looked, failed to resolve itself into any language she could recognize.

At the bottom, set slightly apart and in larger writing, were the initials GR, which meant no more to her than the confused sequence above them.

She gazed at it for a while, eyes narrowed, confused, then she returned to the covering letter. The interview it referred to was one she had published over a year ago. It had attracted considerable interest at the time for it was the only occasion on which its subject, the Palestinian terrorist al-Mulatham, had parted the obsessive veil of secrecy in which he shrouded himself and consented to speak publicly. The Israeli security services had shown particular interest, impounding her notepad and laptop and bringing her in for extensive questioning. She had been able to reveal little of any use – as she had explained in the article, the interview had taken place in a secret location and she had been blindfolded throughout – and her suspicion now was that the curious letter and photocopy were a not very good Shin Bet ruse to find out whether she knew more about the terrorist leader's whereabouts than she had been letting on. It certainly wouldn't be the first time they had tried to trap or discredit her. A few years back she had been approached by a man purporting to be a Palestinian activist and asked if she could use her press status to help run guns through the Erez checkpoint into Gaza – a case of agent-provocateuring so transparent she had burst out laughing and replied in Hebrew that she would be delighted provided Ami Ayalon took her out for dinner afterwards.

Yes, she thought, the letter was definitely some security service stunt. That or an elaborate prank. Either way it wasn't worth wasting any time over. Taking one last look at the photocopied document, she consigned it and the accompanying letter to her wastepaper basket and left the flat.

LUXOR

'You're a dreamer, Khalifa! Always have been, always will be! A bloody dreamer!' Chief Inspector Abdul ibn-Hassani slammed a meaty fist onto his desk, stood and clumped over to his office window, staring angrily out at the first pylon of Luxor Temple, where a crowd of tourists were gathered around the obelisk of Ramesses II, listening to their guide.

A broad-shouldered, overweight man with heavy eyebrows and a flattened boxer's nose, he was renowned both for his bad temper and his vanity, the former manifesting itself, as it was doing now, in a raised voice, red face and a small pulsating vein beneath his right eye; the latter in all manner of little indulgences, the latest being an exquisitely coiffured wig that sat atop his balding head like a clump of tangled Nile weed. The desk-banging had dislodged it slightly, and, pretending to scratch his forehead, he nudged it carefully back into place, leaning slightly to his left to check his reflection in a mirror hanging on the wall.

'Bloody ridiculous!' he growled. 'I mean, for God's sake, man, it was twenty years ago.'

'Fifteen.'

'Fifteen, twenty – what does it matter? Too long to be worrying about it, that's the point. You spend too much time with your head stuck in the past. You should come up for air once in a while.'

He turned to Khalifa, glowering, an expression that, topped as it was with the toupee, didn't quite come off, like someone trying to be serious with a flattened rodent sitting on his head. In any other situation Khalifa would have struggled to contain his laughter. Today, he barely noticed the wig, so focused was he on what he was trying to say.

'But sir—'

'The present!' Hassani shouted, striding forward and positioning himself, arms crossed, beneath a framed photograph of President Hosni Mubarak, a stance he always adopted when he was about to deliver a homily. 'That's where our work is, Khalifa. The here and now. There are crimes being committed every day, every hour of every day, and those are what we should be concentrating on, not something that happened a decade or more ago. Something that was solved at the time, I should add!'

His brow knitted momentarily, as if he wasn't quite convinced this last sentence made sense. It passed almost immediately and, puffing out his chest, he jabbed a finger at Khalifa, who was sitting on a low chair in front of his desk.

'It's always been your problem. If I've said it

once I've said it a hundred times – a complete inability to focus on the present. Too much time poking around in museums, that's what does it. Tutankhamun this, Antenaben that—'

'Akhenaten,' corrected Khalifa.

'There you go again! Who cares what his fucking name was! The past is over and done with, finished, irrelevant. Today, that's what's important.'

Khalifa's fascination with the ancient past had always been a bone of contention between the two men; that and the fact that he was one of the few policemen in the station who refused to be intimidated by Hassani. Why the chief should have such a disregard for history, an aversion even, Khalifa had never discovered, although he suspected it was because he knew nothing about it and was therefore at a disadvantage whenever the conversation turned that way. Whatever the case, it was always the thing Hassani brought up whenever he wanted to browbeat Khalifa, as if detective work and an interest in his country's heritage were somehow incompatible.

'Wouldn't they just love it!' Hassani was shouting, working himself up into a lather. 'The pimps and the thieves and the fraudsters. Wouldn't they just be so happy if we spent all our time pissing around with cases that were finished fifteen years ago while they were left in peace to get on with their pimping and thieving and . . .' He paused for an instant, searching for the right word. 'Fraudering!' he cried eventually. 'Oh yes, wouldn't they just love it! We'd be a fucking laughing stock!'

The vein beside his eye was pulsing more furiously than ever, a plump green worm wriggling about beneath his skin. Khalifa pulled out his cigarettes and, bending forward, lit one, staring down at the floor.

'It's possible there might have been a grave miscarriage of justice,' he said quietly, drawing on his cigarette, craving the nicotine, the focus and clarity it gave him. 'Not definite; but certainly possible. And whether it was fifteen years ago or thirty years ago I think we have a duty to investigate it.'

'But what evidence have you got?' cried Hassani. 'What evidence, man? I know you've never been one to let facts stand in the way of a good conspiracy theory, but I'll need more than just a "possibly maybe".'

'Like I said, there's nothing definite—'

'Nothing at all, you mean!'

'There are similarities.'

'There are similarities between my wife and fucking water buffalo, but that doesn't mean she sits in a pool of her own shit eating palm leaves all day!'

'Too many similarities for it to be mere coincidence,' continued Khalifa, speaking over his boss, refusing to be beaten down. 'Piet Jansen was involved in the murder of Hannah Schlegel. I know it. I know it!'

He could feel his own voice rising and, clenching his knee with one hand, took a deep pull on the cigarette to steady himself.

'Look,' he said, trying to keep his tone slow and measured. 'Hannah Schlegel was murdered at Karnak. Jansen lived beside Karnak.'

'So do a thousand other people,' snorted Hassani. 'And five thousand people visit the place every day. What are you saying? They're all involved?'

Khalifa ignored the question and pressed on.

'The *ankh* and rosette decoration on the pommel of Jansen's cane match the impact-marks that were found on Schlegel's face and skull. Those marks were never properly accounted for.'

Hassani waved his hand dismissively.

'There are thousands of objects with that sort of design on them. Tens of thousands. It's too tenuous, Khalifa. Too tenuous by far.'

Again, the detective ignored his boss and pressed on.

'Schlegel was an Israeli Jew. Jansen hated Jews.'

'For God's sake, Khalifa! After what they've done to the Palestinians everyone in Egypt hates fucking Jews. What are we going to do? Bring the entire population in for questioning?'

Still Khalifa refused to be deflected.

'The guard at Karnak said he saw someone hurrying away from the scene with something strange on his head. "Like a funny little bird" – that's how he described it. When I was in Jansen's house I found a hat that matched that description hanging on the back of his cellar door. A hat with feathers sticking out of it.'

Hassani exploded into a gale of derisive laughter.

'This is getting more ridiculous by the minute. That guard, if I remember right, was half fucking blind. He could barely see his hand in front of his face, let alone someone fifty metres away. You're clutching at straws, Khalifa! Or feathers, more like. A funny little bird? You're losing the plot, man!'

Khalifa took a last puff on his cigarette and, leaning forward, tamped it out into an ashtray on the edge of the desk.

'There was one other thing.'

'Oh, please tell me,' cried Hassani, clapping his hands together. 'I haven't had a laugh like this in ages.'

Khalifa sat back again.

'Before she died, Schlegel managed to say two words: Thoth, which is the name of the Egyptian god of writing and wisdom—'

'Yes, yes, I know!' huffed Hassani.

'And *tzfardeah*, which is apparently the Hebrew word for frog.'

Hassani's eyes narrowed.

'So?'

'Jansen had a genetic condition that gave him webbed feet. Like a frog.'

He spoke quickly, trying to get the words out before the expected hoot of ridicule. To his surprise Hassani said nothing, merely crossed back to the window and stood looking out, his back to Khalifa, hands clenched at his sides as if he was holding a pair of invisible suitcases.

'I know that individually none of these things means very much,' Khalifa continued, trying to press home his advantage, 'but when you take them all together you have to stop and think. It's too much of a coincidence. And even if it is all circumstantial there's still the matter of the antiquities in the man's basement. Jansen was dodgy. I know it. I can feel it. He needs to be investigated.'

Hassani's fists were clenched so tight his knuckles had turned white. There was a long pause, then he turned towards Khalifa.

'We are not going to waste any more time on this,' he said slowly, deliberately, the controlled fury of his voice more threatening than any amount of shouting. 'Do you understand? The man is dead, and whatever he was involved in, whatever he's done, it's over. There's nothing we can do about it.'

Khalifa looked at him incredulously.

'And Mohammed Gemal? An innocent man might have been wrongly convicted.'

'Gemal's dead too. There's nothing we can do.'

'His family's still alive. We owe it—'

'Gemal was found guilty in a court of law, for fuck's sake. He openly admitted he'd robbed the old woman.'

'But not that he'd killed her. He always denied that.'

'He committed suicide, for God's sake. What more of a fucking admission do you want?'

Hassani came forward another step.

'The man was guilty, Khalifa! Guilty as sin! He knew it and we knew it. We all knew it. All of us!'

His eyes were wide with fury. There was something else there as well, however. An edge of desperation, fear even. It was not something Khalifa had seen before. He lit another cigarette.

'I didn't.'

'What? What did you say?'

'I didn't think Gemal was guilty. I had doubts then, I've had doubts ever since, and now they're stronger than ever. He might have robbed her, but Mohammed Gemal did not murder Hannah Schlegel. I knew it at the time but to my lasting shame didn't have the guts to say so. I think deep down we all knew it – you, me, Chief Mahfouz—'

Hassani stepped forward and slammed his fist on the edge of the desk, sending a sheaf of papers tumbling to the floor.

'That's enough, Khalifa! Enough, do you hear?' His entire body was trembling. Flecks of froth had gathered at the corners of his mouth. 'Your psychological problems are your own business, but I've got a police station to run and I'm not going to re-open a fifteen-year-old case just because some spineless idiot is having a crisis of conscience. You've got no evidence, nothing whatsoever to suggest that Mohammed Gemal did not murder Hannah Schlegel, except in your own mind, which from what you've just been saying about feathers and frogs would appear to be in a far from stable condition. I always knew you weren't made of the right stuff, Khalifa, and this just confirms it. If you can't stand the heat, get out of the kitchen. Piss off and become an archaeologist or whatever it is you always wanted to do and leave me to get on with the job of catching criminals. Real criminals, not imaginary ones.'

Forgetting he was wearing a wig, he reached up and vigorously scratched the top of his scalp, dislodging the hairpiece, which slipped halfway down his forehead. With a furious growl he ripped it off altogether and threw it across the room, stomping back to his desk and sitting down, breathing heavily.

'Just drop it, Khalifa,' he said, his voice weary suddenly, subdued. 'Do you understand me? For everybody's sake. Mohammed Gemal murdered Hannah Schlegel, Jansen died accidentally, and there's no link between the two. I am not re-opening the case.'

His eyes flicked up and then down again, refusing to hold Khalifa's stare.

'Now, there's some *hawagaya* at the Winter Palace who thinks her jewellery's been stolen and I want you to go and look into it. Forget Jansen and do some proper police work for once in your life.'

He shuffled a pile of papers in front of him,

jaw clenched. Khalifa realized it was pointless continuing the argument. He stood and moved towards the door.

'The keys,' growled Hassani. 'I'm not having you nosing around Jansen's house behind my back.'

Khalifa turned, removed Jansen's keys from his pocket and threw them across the room to Hassani, who caught them one-handed.

'Don't cross me on this one, Khalifa. Do you understand? Not on this one.'

The detective paused, then opened the door and strode out into the corridor.

JERUSALEM

Layla could never pass through the Old City's Damascus Gate, with its imposing, twin-towered arch, grime-blackened flagstones and crush of beggars and fruit sellers, without recalling the first time she had come here with her parents, when she was five.

'Look, Layla,' her father had said proudly, squatting beside her and stroking her waist-length black hair. 'Al-Quds! The most beautiful city in the world. Our city. See how bright the stone looks in the morning sunshine; smell the *za'atar* and the newly baked bread, listen to the call of the muezzin and the cry of the *tamar hindi* sellers. Remember these things, Layla, keep them inside you. Because if the Israelis have their way we will all be driven out and al-Quds will become no more than a place we read about in history books.'

Layla had thrown an arm protectively around his neck.

'I won't let them, Daddy!' she had cried. 'I'll fight them. I'm not scared.'

Her father had laughed and, sweeping her up

into his arms, pulled her tightly to his breast, which was flat and hard, like marble.

'My little warrior! Layla the Invincible! Oh what a daughter I have been given!'

The three of them had walked right the way around the outside of the city, following the line of the walls, which at the time had struck her as immeasurably huge and threatening, a great tidal wave of stone rearing overhead, and had then passed through the Damascus Gate into the bustling labyrinth of streets beyond. They had drunk Coca-cola at a small roadside café, her father puffing on a *shisha* pipe and talking animatedly with a group of old men, before wandering down al-Wad Road towards the Haram al-Sharif, stopping every now and then so he could point out a bakery where he had eaten cakes as a child, a square where he had played football, an old fig tree growing out of a wall whose fruit he had used to pick.

'Not to eat,' he had explained. 'It was way too hard and bitter. We used to throw them at each other. I got hit right on the nose once. You should have heard the crack! There was blood every-where!'

He had burst out laughing at the memory, and Layla had laughed too, told him how funny she thought it was, even though the story had horrified her, the thought of her father being hurt. She had loved him so much, so wanted to please him, show that she was not weak or afraid, but strong like him – brave, a true Palestinian.

From the fig tree they had weaved up into a maze of narrow side streets, eventually coming to a spot where the buildings on either side arched right the way over their heads, forming a tunnel. A group of Israeli soldiers had been standing just inside the entrance and had stared at them suspiciously as they walked past.

'See how they look at us,' her father had sighed. 'They make us feel like thieves in our own house.'

He had taken her hand and steered her towards a low wooden doorway surmounted by a lintel carved with an intricate design of grapes and vine stems. A brass plaque declared that it was the Alder Cohen Memorial Yeshiva; a *mezuzah* was screwed onto the stone jamb to its right.

'Our house,' he had said sadly, reaching out and touching the door. 'Our beautiful house.'

His family – her family – had fled during the fighting of June 1967, leaving the city with just a few treasured possessions and taking refuge in the Aqabat Jabr camp outside Jericho, forty kilometres away. It was only supposed to have been a temporary measure, and they had returned as soon as the fighting had stopped. By then, however, the house had been taken over by the Israelis and no amount of complaining to the city's new masters could get it back again. They had lived as refugees ever since.

'I was born here,' her father had said, running his hand lovingly over the door's gnarled wooden panels, touching the carved lintel. 'So was my father. And his father too, and his father before him. Fourteen generations. Three hundred years. All gone, just like that.'

He snapped his fingers into the air. Looking up, she had seen tears welling in his huge brown eyes.

'It's OK, Daddy,' she had said, hugging him, trying to squeeze all her strength and love into his thin, hard body. 'You'll get it back one day. We'll all live here together. Everything will be OK.'

He had leant down and run his face back and forth through her long black hair.

'If only that was true, my darling Layla,' he had whispered. 'But not all stories have happy endings. Especially for our people. This you will learn as you grow older.'

These and other memories scudded across her mind now as she passed through the gate's gloomy dog-leg and out onto the paved slope of al-Wad Road.

Normally this part of the city would be bustling, with multi-coloured stalls selling flowers and fruit and spices, throngs of shoppers jostling back and forth, boys whizzing past on wooden barrows piled high with meat or refuse. Today, everything was unnaturally quiet – a result, no doubt, of the Warriors of David stand-off further into the city. A couple of old men were sitting beneath the corrugated tin awning of a deserted café; to her left a peasant woman was squatting in a shuttered doorway, a forlorn pyramid of limes piled in front of her, her face buried in her wrinkled brown hands. Otherwise the only people present were Israeli military and police personnel: a trio of young Giv'ati brigade conscripts hunkered down behind a sandbag emplacement; a unit of border police in green berets lounging around on the steps in front of the café; a gaggle of regular police patrolling just inside the gateway, their blue flak-jackets melding into the shadows so that their heads, arms and legs seemed to disappear into an empty hole where their torsos should be.

Layla flashed her press card at one of them, a pretty girl who could have passed as a model had she not been a policewoman, and asked if she could get through to the occupied house.

'The road's blocked further down,' said the girl, eyeing the card disapprovingly. 'Ask there.'

Layla nodded and continued down into the city, passing the Austrian Hospice, the Via Dolorosa, the alley containing the fig tree her father had pointed out all those years ago – it seemed hardly to have grown in all that time. As she went she heard shouting up ahead and the police and military presence steadily became heavier. She started to pass straggling groups of *shebab*, Palestinian youths, some wearing black and white Fatah head-bands, others carrying the red, green, black and white Palestinian flag, the groups coalescing into a crowd and the crowd into a crush, the narrow street echoing to the sound of their chanting, a forest of clenched fists punching the air. Israeli troops were massed in every side street, preventing the protest fanning outwards across the city, the soldiers' expressionless faces contrasting with those of the protesters, which were twisted in fury and defiance. Smudges of ash and charred cardboard stained the cobbles where makeshift fires had been lit; Israeli surveillance cameras dangled from their wall-brackets like the carcasses of dead animals, their lenses smashed.

Layla pushed her way through the throng, the crush growing tighter with every step, and it was starting to look like she might not get through at all until she was recognized by a young man she'd interviewed a couple of months earlier for an article she had been doing on the Fatah Youth Movement. He greeted her and, appointing himself her chaperone, forced a way through the mass of bodies until they reached the crash barriers the Israelis had erected across the street. There was a small group of Israeli Peace Now protesters gathered here among the Palestinians, and one, an elderly woman in a knitted hat, called out to her.

'I hope you're going to write about these bastards, Layla! They're going to start a war!'

'That's exactly what they want to do,' shouted a man beside her. 'They're going to kill us all! Settlers out! We want peace! Peace now!'

He leant forward and waved his fist at the row of heavily armed border police lined up on the far side of the barrier. Beyond them a scrum of journalists and TV crews, many wearing helmets and bulletproof jackets, was gathered outside the occupied house. Further down the street a second roadblock had been erected, this one holding back a crowd of Haredi Jews and Israeli right-wingers, there to show solidarity with the settlers. One was holding a placard reading KAHANE WAS RIGHT!, another a banner proclaiming ARAB MURDERERS OFF JEWISH LAND.

Layla showed her press card to one of the soldiers at the barrier and, after some consultation with his superior, she was allowed through, pushing her way into the pack of journalists where she ended up beside a paunchy, bearded man wearing wire-rimmed spectacles and a plastic protective helmet.

'The great Layla al-Madani finally graces us with her presence,' he snorted, his voice all but drowned out by the shouting of the crowd. 'I was wondering when you'd turn up.'

Onz Schenker was a political correspondent for the *Jerusalem Post*. The first time they'd met she'd thrown a glass of water at him for making a disparaging remark about Palestinian women, and that had just about set the tone of their relationship ever since. They maintained a frosty cordiality, but there was little love lost on either side.

'Dig the hat, Schenker,' she grunted.

'You'll wish you had one when your Arab mates start throwing rocks and bottles,' he retorted.

As if to emphasize his point a bottle came arcing over from among the Palestinian protesters, smashing onto the paving slabs a few metres to his right.

'Told you,' he shouted. 'But then I guess they'd never throw anything at you, would they, Assad-fucking-iqa. It's the proper journalists they want to hurt!'

Layla half opened her mouth to bat the insult back, but couldn't be bothered and instead just gave him the finger and moved away, working her way forward right to the front of the press pack. Jerold Kessel from CNN was struggling to deliver a piece to camera amid the mayhem; to her left the Israeli border police had lifted the crash barriers and were forcing the Palestinian protesters back, driving them further up the street. The shouting grew even louder. A tear-gas canister was fired. More bottles were thrown.

For a moment Layla stood motionless, taking in the scene, then swung her camera from her shoulder and started snapping, getting shots of the spray-painted menorahs to either side of the front door – the traditional Warriors of David calling card – the Israeli flag draped down the front of the building, the troops stationed on the roofs to either side, presumably to prevent locals storming the house from above. She had just turned to her right to photograph the pro-settlement protesters when she suddenly felt the pack around her tighten and surge forwards.

The door of the occupied house had opened. There was a pause, then the squat, cuboid figure of Baruch Har-Zion stepped out onto the street, accompanied by his crew-cut bodyguard, Avi Steiner. The pro-settlement protesters cheered and broke into a rendition of the 'Hatikva', the Israeli national anthem. The Palestinians and peace protesters, who had by now been driven almost a hundred metres up the street and couldn't see properly what was happening, rattled the crash barriers and raised their own song, 'My Homeland, My Homeland'. Steiner pushed angrily at the semi-circle of journalists, trying to keep them back. Cameras flashed like strobe lights.

For a brief instant Har-Zion's eye caught Layla's, then slid away again. Questions flew at him like gunfire, but he ignored them, turning his head this way and that, a faint smile creasing the edges of his mouth, before slowly raising his right hand, indicating that he wished for silence. The questions died away and the pack pressed forward a few more inches, a bristling hedge of tape-recorders held out towards him. Layla swung her camera back over her shoulder and pulled out her notebook.

'There is an old Hebrew saying,' Har-Zion intoned, speaking in heavily accented English, his voice gruff and low, like tumbling rocks. *'Hamechadesh betuvo bechol yom tamid ma'aseh bereishit.* God makes the world new every single day. Yesterday this land was in the hands of our enemies. Today it has been returned to its rightful owners, the Jewish people. This is a great day. A historic day. A day that will never be forgotten. And believe me, ladies and gentlemen, there are many more such days to come.'

LUXOR

Even at a distance of fifteen years, Khalifa remembered the Schlegel case as though it had happened only yesterday.

Her body had been found by a local man, Mohammed Ibrahim Gemal, in the Precinct of Khonsu, a dark, shadowy, rarely visited building in the south-western corner of the Karnak Temple complex. Sixty years old, Israeli, Jewish, single, she had, according to the autopsy report, suffered a series of violent blows to the head and face inflicted by a blunt instrument of indeterminate type. As well as shattering her jawbone and fracturing her skull in three separate places, the murder weapon had left a curious pattern of marks on her skin – *ankh* signs interspersed with miniature rosettes, presumably from some sort of decorative design on the weapon's surface.

Despite her massive injuries, Gemal had been adamant Schlegel was still alive when he had found her. Blood-covered and incoherent, she had, he insisted, whispered two words, Thoth and *tzfardeah*, repeating both several times before slipping into a coma from which she had not emerged.

There were no other witnesses to corroborate his statement, and no witnesses at all to the murder itself, save for an old temple guard who claimed to have heard muffled screams from the interior of the temple and had glimpsed someone hurrying away from the scene of the crime, limping heavily and with 'something on his head, like a funny little bird'. Since the man was old and half-blind, and had a reputation for drinking on the job, no-one had taken his evidence especially seriously.

The then head of Luxor Police, Chief Inspector Ehab Ali Mahfouz, had assumed control of the case personally, assisted by his deputy, Inspector Abdul ibn-Hassani. Khalifa, who had only just been posted to Luxor from his native Giza, was also appointed to the investigating team. He was twenty-four at the time, on his first murder case.

From the outset the investigation had focused on two possible motives for the killing. The obvious one, favoured by Mahfouz, was robbery, since the woman's wallet and watch were both missing. The second, less likely option, although one that couldn't be ruled out, was that it had been a fundamentalist attack. Only a month previously nine Israelis had been shot dead on a tour bus on the highway between Cairo and Ismailiya.

Khalifa, the least experienced and most junior member of the team, had from the first had doubts about both these scenarios. If robbery had been the motive, why had the attacker not taken the gold Star of David hanging on a chain around the

woman's neck? And if it had been fundamentalists, why had they not claimed credit for their
actions, as they invariably did after an attack of
this sort?

There were further puzzling aspects to the case.
Schlegel had arrived in Egypt the previous day
from Tel Aviv, travelling alone, and had flown
straight down to Luxor where she had booked
into the Mina Palace, a budget hotel on the
Corniche el-Nil. According to the hotel concierge,
she had remained in her room from the moment
she had checked in until 3.30 p.m. on the afternoon of her death, when, at her request, he had
arranged a taxi to take her down to Karnak. She
only had a small overnight bag with her and her
return ticket to Israel had been for that same night.
Whatever her reason for being in Luxor she clearly
wasn't there for a holiday.

She had, apparently, made at least one call from
her bedroom phone, on the evening of her arrival
– the hotel housekeeper had overheard her when
she had brought up towels and soap. And a large
kitchen knife had been found in the handbag
beside her body, newly sharpened, as if she had
been expecting to do violence to someone, or else
to defend herself in the face of violence from
someone else.

The more Khalifa had thought about the case,
the more convinced he had become that it had
nothing to do with theft or extremism. The key,
he felt sure, was the phone call. Who had Schlegel

been speaking to? What had been said? He had requested a print-out from the hotel's telephone meter, but as luck would have it the meter had chosen that evening to go on the blink, and before he had had time to chase up Egypt Telecom for a call breakdown for the entire building the investigation had taken an unexpected turn: Schlegel's watch had been found in the house of Mohammed Gemal.

Gemal was well known to the Luxor Police. An inveterate petty criminal, he had a string of convictions as long as your arm, from assault and battery – for which he had done three years in al-Wadi al-Gadid – to car theft and supply of cannabis (six months in Abu Zaabal). At the time of the murder he was working as an unlicensed tourist guide, and claimed to have been clean for several years, a claim Chief Mahfouz had roundly dismissed. 'Once a criminal, always a criminal,' he had said. 'A leopard doesn't change its spots, and a shit like Gemal doesn't turn angel overnight.'

Khalifa had sat in on Gemal's interrogation. It had been an unpleasant affair, brutal, both Mahfouz and Hassani giving the suspect a real working over. At first he had denied all knowledge of the watch. After twenty minutes of slapping and punching he had broken down and admitted that, yes, he had taken it, on the spur of the moment. He had debts, you see, his family were about to be evicted from their home, his daughter was sick. He vehemently denied that he had murdered Schlegel or taken her wallet, however, and continued to do so throughout two days of increasingly violent treatment. By the time the interrogation ended he was urinating blood and his eyes were so swollen he could barely see out of them. Still he continued to protest his innocence.

Khalifa had sat through all of this, disgusted to the core of his being yet too afraid to speak out, fearful that to do so might in some way jeopardize his fledgling police career. What made it worse was that from the first he had been certain Gemal was telling the truth. There was something in the desperate fury with which he screamed he hadn't killed the woman, in his refusal to buckle even under the hammer blows of Hassani's fists, that had convinced Khalifa he had, as he said, found Schlegel after she had been attacked. The man might have been a thief, but he certainly wasn't a murderer.

Mahfouz, however, had been unmoved. And Khalifa had said nothing. Not during the interrogation, nor when Gemal had been sent for trial, nor when he was sentenced to twenty-five years' hard labour in the Tura quarries, nor even when, four months after his conviction, he had taken his own life by hanging himself from the bars of his cell with a length of washing line.

In the intervening years he had tried to justify this silence to himself, arguing that Gemal was a nasty piece of work, an inveterate lawbreaker, and that his conviction, whether fair or not, was probably no less than he deserved. The truth was, however, that his cowardice had allowed an innocent man to be convicted of a crime he hadn't committed, and a woman to die without her murderer being brought to justice. And now that cowardice had come back to haunt him. As deep down he had always known it would.

JERUSALEM

To his supporters – and there was a growing band of them – Baruch Har-Zion was the new David, the Lord's chosen warrior battling against overwhelming odds to deliver his people to their Promised Land. Tough, fearless, battle-scarred, devout, he was the epitome of the *schtarker* – the Jewish tough-guy hero who looks out for himself, his people and his God, and suffers no qualms whatsoever about the means he uses to do it.

Born Boris Zegowsky in a small village in the southern Ukraine, he had come to Israel in 1970, at the age of sixteen, after he and his younger brother had smuggled themselves out of the Soviet Union, crossed half of Europe on foot and presented themselves at the Israeli Embassy in Vienna claiming their right as Jews to make *aliyah*. The journey had, for Har-Zion, been as much a pilgrimage as an escape, a voyage to a mythical land that offered not merely sanctuary from the corrosive anti-semitism of his native country, but also a physical manifestation of God's covenant with his chosen people.

He had devoted the rest of his life to defending and expanding that land, first as a soldier with the IDF, where he had served with distinction in the elite Sayeret Matkal regiment; subsequently, after incurring horrific burns when his Humvee ran over a landmine in southern Lebanon, with Military Intelligence, heading a unit devoted to the recruitment and running of Palestinian informers. An absolute and unwavering devotion to the Israeli cause was what defined and consumed him, a devotion that manifested itself both in acts of extreme heroism – he had twice been awarded the Medal of Valour, Israel's equivalent of the Victoria Cross – and also of extreme brutality. In 1982 he had received an official reprimand for covering a young Lebanese girl in petrol and ordering his men to set her alight unless she divulged the whereabouts of a Hizbollah weapons cache (she did). During his time with Military Intelligence he had been sent for court-martial following allegations that he had authorized the threat of gang rape as a means of coercing Palestinian women into turning collaborator (all charges had been dropped after the main prosecution witness had died in a mysterious car accident).

And that was just the tip of the iceberg. Tales of violence, brutality and intimidation followed him everywhere – something that, far from causing him concern, appeared to be a greater source of pride than all his awards for gallantry. 'It is nice to be admired,' he was once quoted as saying, 'but far better to be feared.'

A fierce opponent of the Oslo peace accords – of any peace accord that involved surrendering an inch of the biblical land of Israel – he left Military Intelligence in the mid-1990s and went into politics, allying himself first with the militant settlers organization Gush Emunim before breaking away to found the even more militant Chayalei David. The latter's campaign of seizure and resettlement of Arab land was initially dismissed as the work of a lunatic fringe. With the appearance of al-Mulatham and the Palestinian Brotherhood, however, his hard-line message – that there could be no safety from the suicide bombers until the whole land of Eretz Israel had been settled by Jews and every Palestinian driven across the border into Jordan – gained increasing popularity. His rallies attracted ever larger crowds, his fundraising dinners ever more prominent guests. In the 2000 election he had won a seat in the Knesset, and in some quarters he was now being seriously talked of as a future Israeli leader. 'If Baruch Har-Zion ever became Prime Minister it would be the end of this country,' moderate Israeli politician Yehuda Milan once commented. 'If Baruch Har-Zion ever became Prime Minister it would be the end of *yutzim* like Yehuda Milan,' had been Har-Zion's response.

This résumé scrolled through Layla's mind as she stood staring at the man in front of her, with his gloved hands, greying hair and square-jawed face, pale and bearded, like a moss-covered cube of granite. Around her the press pack was once again screaming questions, Dictaphones waving.

'Mr Har-Zion, do you accept that you are breaking the law by occupying this house?'

'Do you believe any sort of accommodation is possible between Israelis and Palestinians?'

'Can you comment on claims that your actions are tacitly supported by Prime Minister Sharon?'

'Is it true you wish to demolish the Dome of the Rock and rebuild the ancient Temple in its place?'

Har-Zion fielded the questions one by one, arms held stiffly at his sides, iterating and reiterating in his low, gruff voice that this was neither an occupation nor a settlement but rather a liberation, the recovery of land that belonged to the Jewish people by divine right, continuing thus for twenty minutes before signalling that he had no more to say and turning to go back inside. As he did so, Layla stepped forward and shouted after him.

'Over the last three years members of Chayalei David have poisoned Palestinian wells, destroyed Palestinian irrigation equipment, cut down Palestinian orchards. Three separate members of your organization have been jailed for the murder of Palestinian civilians, including one case in which an eleven-year-old boy was beaten to death with a pick-axe handle. You yourself have spoken with approval of the actions of

Baruch Goldstein and Yigal Amir. Are you really not just an Israeli al-Mulatham, Mr Har-Zion?'

Har-Zion froze, then turned slowly back towards the press-pack, searching for Layla's face, finding her eyes, holding them. His stare was hard, angry, although there was something flickering behind it, amusement almost, as if the two of them were playing some private game to which only they were privy.

'Explain to me, Miss al-Madani' – he spat her name, as if it tasted bitter in his mouth – 'why is it that when an Arab kills twenty civilians he is called a victim, but when a Jew defends himself and his family he is condemned as a murderer?'

Layla held his stare, refusing to be intimidated.

'So you support the unprovoked murder of Palestinian civilians?'

'I support the right of my people to live in peace and security on the land that was given to them by God.'

'Even if that involves systematic acts of terrorism?'

Har-Zion's face crumpled into a scowl. The rest of the pack were staring at them, silent suddenly, absorbed in the private duel.

'There is only one group of terrorists in this region,' he said, 'and it is not the Jews. Although you would not guess that from your reporting.'

'You don't call the murder of a child terrorism?'

'I call it a tragedy of war, Miss al-Madani. But it was not us who started the war.'

He paused a moment, eyes boring into her.

'Although it will certainly be us who finish it.'

He held her gaze, then turned on his heel and stepped back into the house.

'Bitch,' hissed one of his followers as he came in. 'She needs a bullet through her head.'

Har-Zion smiled. 'Maybe. But not just yet. Even she has her uses.'

LUXOR

Khalifa loved the ruins of Karnak Temple, especially at the end of the day, when the crowds had thinned and the setting sun suffused the entire complex with a hazy golden radiance. *Iput-Isut* the ancients used to call it, 'the most esteemed of places', and he could understand why, for there was indeed something magical about it, a ruined city suspended midway between earth and the heavens. Being there invariably took him out of himself, soothed and calmed him, as if he had been transported to some different dimension of time and space, leaving all his troubles behind.

Not today, though. Today, the monumental statues and hieroglyph-covered walls left him cold. Indeed he barely noticed them, so lost was he in his own thoughts, striding through the first and second pylons and into the column-forest of the great Hypostyle Hall with barely a glance at his surroundings.

It was almost five p.m. He had, on Chief Hassani's orders, wasted most of the afternoon at the Winter Palace dealing with an elderly English

139

tourist who had reported her jewellery stolen. He and Sariya had spent three hours interviewing the entire house-keeping staff before the woman had finally remembered she hadn't brought the jewellery with her in the first place. 'My daughter told me to leave it at home,' she'd explained, 'in case it got stolen. You know, in Arab countries . . .'

Having sorted that out he had returned to the station where he had sat alone at his desk, chain-smoking, doodling on his pad, thinking about Piet Jansen and Hannah Schlegel and the meeting with Chief Hassani, going over and over the whole thing in his head. After an hour he had got up and gone down into the records room in the basement to pull out the notes on the Schlegel case, knowing he should just leave it, but unable to stop himself. Here, however, another mystery had greeted him, for the notes were nowhere to be found. Miss Zafouli, the elderly spinster who, for as long as Khalifa could remember – as long as anyone could remember – had been the guardian of the station's past cases, had searched high and low for them, but without success. The file had disappeared.

'I can't explain it,' she had muttered. 'I just can't explain it.'

He had left the basement more uneasy than ever and, without really thinking about it, hopped a service taxi down to Karnak, not so much to clear his mind as because it was the place where Hannah Schlegel had been murdered and therefore, somehow, the focal point of all his doubts and worries.

He passed now through the great Hypostyle Hall, its papyrus-shaped columns towering above him like sequoia trunks, and exited through a doorway in the southern wall. It was near closing time, and the tourist police were starting to herd visitors back towards the main entrance. One approached Khalifa, wagging his finger, but the detective flashed his ID and was allowed to continue.

Why had Hassani been so adamant he shouldn't go back into the Schlegel case? That was the question he couldn't get out of his mind. Why had the chief seemed so nervous? There was something wrong here. Badly wrong. And trying to find out what was going to bring him trouble. A lot of trouble. But still he couldn't drop it.

'Dammit,' he muttered, grinding one Cleopatra out beneath the sole of his shoe and immediately lighting another one. 'Bloody dammit.'

He angled towards the south-east corner of the temple enclosure, following a path between rows of hieroglyph-covered sandstone blocks, like the pieces of an enormous jigsaw puzzle, before eventually coming to a long, rectangular building set slightly apart from the rest of the complex. The Precinct of Khonsu. He slowed momentarily, taking in the monumental walls of weathered sandstone, then, his heart pounding suddenly, slipped through a side door into the interior.

It was cool and shady inside, very silent, very still, with a solitary shaft of sunlight spearing across the paved floor from a doorway opposite, like a stream of molten gold. To his left a pillared forecourt opened out; to his right was another open court, and beyond it a low doorway leading into the temple's main shrine. He himself was standing in a narrow hypostyle hall spanning the centre of the building, with eight papyrus-shaped columns marching away in front of him, four on either side. It was beneath the third column on the left that Hannah Schlegel's body had been found.

He allowed his eyes to adjust to the gloom, then moved forward. Although he had visited Karnak numerous times in the intervening years, he had always studiously avoided this particular part of it, and as he crossed the hall now he half expected to find spatters of sticky red blood still marking the paving slabs, a body-shaped chalk outline. There was nothing to suggest that violence had once been done here, however; no bloodstains, no chalk, no memory whatsoever, unless it was in the stones themselves, which seemed to possess a sort of elemental awareness, a knowing impassivity. 'We have witnessed many things,' they seemed to say, 'both good and bad. But of them we will not speak.'

He reached the relevant column and squatted, recalling the moment he had first seen the dead woman's corpse. For some reason the overall state of the body had affected him less than the extraneous details: the victim's green underpants, visible where her skirt had rucked up above her waist; a line of ants marching across her shoeless right foot; a jagged scar meandering across her abdomen like a pencil-line scrawled by a drunk; above all, the strange tattoo on her left forearm, a triangle followed by five numbers, in faded blue-black ink, like veins seeping their way through cheese. A Jewish thing, Chief Mahfouz had explained. Some religious sign or something. Like the marks you get on meat to show where it's come from. The analogy had shocked Khalifa, as though the victim was just some anonymous carcass lying on a butcher's slab. Like the marks you get on meat. Horrible.

He scuffed his hand across the floor, his palm making a dry hissing sound on the dusty sandstone, then stood again, raising his eyes to the wall behind the column, on which was inscribed an ancient relief depicting the pharaoh Ramesses XI being purified by the gods Horus and Thoth, the latter depicted with a human body surmounted by the head of an ibis.

Thoth and *tzfardeah*, that's what Schlegel had said just before she died. *Tzfardeah*, he felt certain, was a reference to Jansen's deformed feet. But what about Thoth? Had she simply, in her dying delirium, been stating what she could see above her? Thoth the Ibis, the last image upon which her eyes had focused. Or had there been some deeper meaning, some more revealing resonance?

He took a drag on his cigarette and rubbed his temples, digging into his mind, pulling out everything he could remember about the god. Wisdom, writing, counting and medicine – these were Thoth's particular preserves. Magic also, for it was he, according to Egyptian mythology, who had provided the spells that enabled the goddess Isis to bring her murdered husband/brother Osiris back to life. What else? He was the gods' scribe and messenger, the creator of hieroglyphs, the author of Egypt's sacred laws, the recorder of the eternal verdict on a deceased person's heart. He was closely associated with the moon – he was often depicted with a lunar disc over his head – and had his chief cult centre at Hermopolis in Middle Egypt, where he was known, among other things, as 'The Heart of Ra', 'The Measurer of Time' and 'Master of the Words of God'. His silver barque transported the souls of the dead across the night sky. He was married to Seshat, the 'Lady of Books', the gods' librarian.

There were plenty of possible connections in all of this, plenty of ways for Khalifa to bend Schlegel's mention of Thoth into a coded accusation against Piet Jansen. Jansen was intelligent and well read, after all; he spoke many languages, he had a large library of books. If the ancient Egyptians had had any interest in archaeology, Thoth would almost certainly have been its patron deity.

Yet despite these similarities, Khalifa still had the sense that he was missing something; that he had still not got to the heart of what Schlegel had been trying to convey. She had meant something specific, and he wasn't getting it. He just wasn't getting it.

He finished his Cleopatra and stamped the butt out beneath his shoe. Maybe Hassani's right, he thought to himself. Maybe I *am* just imagining things, trying to hammer a square peg into a round hole. And even if I'm not, what can I do about it? Carry on an investigation behind the chief's back, risk my entire career? And for what? When all was said and done, after all, Schlegel was only an old—

A sound of footsteps echoed at the far end of the temple. At first he thought it must be a guard. As the steps came closer, he realized they were too soft for a man. Five seconds passed, ten, then a woman in a *djellaba suda* entered the hall from its southern end, a bunch of wild flowers clutched in her hand, a black shawl draped over her head so that her face was all but hidden. The sun was gone now, and in the thickening twilight she didn't notice Khalifa, who had backed away into the shadows behind a pillar. She came up to the spot where Hannah Schlegel had died and, throwing off the shawl, squatted and laid the flowers on the floor. Khalifa stepped forward.

'Hello, Nur.'

She spun round, startled.

'Please, don't be afraid,' he said, holding up a hand to indicate that he meant her no harm. 'I didn't mean to scare you.'

She came to her feet, backing away, gazing at him suspiciously. A grimace of recognition slowly puckered her mouth.

'Khalifa,' she whispered. There was a brief pause, then: 'The man who killed my husband. One of the men.'

She had changed since he had last seen her, in the courtroom on the day of Mohammed Gemal's conviction. Then she had been young and pretty. Now she was a different person, worn, tired-looking, her face weathered like ancient wood.

'Why were you watching me?' she asked.

'I wasn't watching you. I was just . . .'

He broke off, unable to explain exactly why he had come to the temple. She stared at him, then, lowering her eyes, returned to the flowers, squatting and arranging them around the base of the column. A white egret appeared outside in the forecourt, pecking at the dust.

'I come here every now and then,' she said after a while, talking more to herself than to Khalifa, tweaking at the flower stems with her wrinkled fingers. 'Mohammed doesn't have a proper grave. They just dumped him in a pit outside the prison. It's too far for me to go all the way up to Cairo. So I come here. I don't know why. I suppose it's . . . well, the place where he died, in a way.'

Her tone was matter-of-fact, not overtly

accusing, which somehow made it even worse for Khalifa. He shifted uncomfortably, fiddling with a coin in his pocket.

'I leave them for the old woman as well,' she continued. 'It wasn't her fault, was it? She didn't accuse Mohammed.'

She got the flowers laid out to her satisfaction and stood again, ready to leave. Khalifa took another step towards her.

'The children?' he asked, anxious, suddenly, that the conversation shouldn't end.

She shrugged. 'Mansour's got a job as a mechanic. Abdul's just finishing school. Fatma's married, with a kid on the way. She lives up in Armant now. Her husband works in the cane factory.'

'And you. Have you—'

'Remarried?' She looked up at him through dull eyes. 'Mohammed's my husband. He might not have been a good man, but he's still my husband.'

The white egret had pecked its way up to the doorway and now came stalking into the hall, its head jerking this way and that, its knitting-needle legs rising and falling with the controlled, rhythmic delicacy of a ballet dancer. It came to within a metre of the woman, then moved off again.

'He didn't do it, you know,' she said quietly. 'He took the watch, which was bad. Very bad. But he didn't kill the old woman. And he didn't take the wallet. Not the wallet.'

Khalifa was staring at the floor.

'I know,' he mumbled. 'I'm . . . sorry.'

She followed the egret with her eyes, tracking it as it weaved its way through the pillars.

'You were the only good one,' she whispered. 'The only one I thought might help him. But then you . . .'

She sighed and turned to leave, moving a couple of steps before turning back again.

'The money's helped. It can't bring him back, but it's helped. So thank you for that.'

Khalifa looked up, confused.

'I don't . . . what money?'

'The money you've been sending. I know it's you. You were the only good one.'

'I haven't . . . what money? I don't know what you're talking about.'

She was gazing over his shoulder into the webs of shadow thickening at the back of the hall, her eyes dry and empty – the eyes of someone from whom all hope has been drained.

'Every year. Just before Eid el-Adha. It comes in the post. No note, no name, nothing. Just three thousand Egyptian pounds, in hundred notes. Always in hundred notes. It started a week after Mohammed killed himself, and has carried on ever since. Every year. It's how I got the kids through school, how I managed to survive. I know it's you. You are a good man, despite it all.'

She looked across at him, then turned and hurried out of the temple.

JERUSALEM

On the way home from the Old City Layla stopped into the Jerusalem Hotel for a drink and a bite to eat with her friend Nuha.

A handsome, Ottoman-style building near the lower end of the Nablus Road, Palestinian-owned and run, with a cool, stone-floored interior and vine-covered front terrace, the hotel had been a part of her life for as long as she could remember. It was here that she had met Nizar Suleiman, the editor of *al-Ayyam*, who had given her her first writing job; here that she had picked up some of her best story leads; here that she had lost her virginity (aged nineteen, to a chain-smoking French journalist, an uneasy, fumbled affair that had left her feeling soiled and confused). And, of course, it was at the Jerusalem Hotel that her parents had first met, and, if her mother was to be believed, Layla herself had been conceived.

'There was a terrible storm that night,' her mother had later told her. 'Thunder, lightning, rain like you've never seen. The whole world seemed to be tearing itself apart. I sometimes think that's why you're like you are.'

'Like what, Mum?'

Her mother had smiled, but said no more.

They had been an unlikely couple, her parents, the fun-loving English girl from a resolutely middle-class Cambridgeshire family and the intense, introverted doctor ten years her senior whose every waking hour was dedicated to the care and well-being of his fellow Palestinians.

They had met in 1972, at a gathering to celebrate the marriage of a mutual friend. Alexandra Bale, as Layla's mother was then known, had just left university and was working as a volunteer teacher in an East Jerusalem girls' school, uncertain about what she wanted to do with her life. Mohammed Faisal al-Madani lived in the Gaza Strip where he ran a medical clinic in the Jabaliya refugee camp, working fourteen-hour days, seven days a week, ministering to the camp's population.

'It was his eyes that hooked me,' Layla's mother later recalled. 'They were so dark, so sad. Like looking into a well of black water.'

Despite, or possibly because of, their wildly differing backgrounds, they had clicked instantly, Layla's father swept away by the young woman's beauty and wit, her mother hypnotized by the elder man's intensity, his quiet, brooding strength. They had started going out almost immediately and, much to the horror of Alexandra's parents, married six months later, enjoying a one-night honeymoon in the Jerusalem Hotel before setting up home in the cramped rabbit warren of Gaza City. Layla was born on 6 October 1973, the day the Ramadan war broke out.

'One day this child will do great things,' her father had predicted, proudly cradling the newborn daughter he himself had just delivered. 'Her future and that of our people will be inextricably bound. One day every Palestinian will know the name Layla Hanan al-Madani.'

From the first she had loved her father. Loved him with a devotion that was almost painful in its intensity. While other memories of her earliest youth were fragmented and confused, blurred flashes of people and places and sounds, her feelings for her father retained a brilliant and undiminished clarity. She had loved her mother too, of course – her mass of unruly red hair, her laughing eyes, the way she would suddenly burst into song or dance, reducing the young Layla to fits of giggles. In her mother's case, however, it had been a gentle love, warm, simple, like spring sunshine, like a subtle caress. With her father, it had been something altogether fiercer and more elemental, a white-hot flame of affection, consuming and overwhelming her, the defining emotion of her existence beside which all other emotions paled into insignificance.

He had been such a good man, so handsome and patient and clever and strong. Always he would be there for her, always he would make her feel calm and secure. When Israeli tanks rumbled

151

through the streets at night she would run to him and he would hold her, stroking the silken waves of her hair, humming an old Arab lullaby in his deep, slightly out-of-tune voice. When other children teased her because of her pale skin and green eyes, calling her mongrel and half-caste, he would take her on his knee and, wiping away her tears, explain that her classmates were only jealous because she was so pretty, so intelligent.

'You are the most beautiful girl in the world, my Layla. Never forget that. And I am the happiest man in the world, because you are my daughter.'

As she had grown, her feelings for him had only intensified. In her earliest years she had loved him simply because he was her father, an omnipresent figure who sang songs to her, read her stories and fashioned wonderful toys out of pieces of cloth and scrap wood. As time had passed, however, and her focus widened, she had come to appreciate him in a broader context, not just as a parent, but as a human being: a selfless, driven, courageous man who had devoted his life to helping others. She would visit him at his clinic – a single room with whitewashed walls and a bare concrete floor – sitting in the courtyard outside as one by one patients trooped in to see 'el-doktor', thinking to herself how special he was, how clever and magical to be able to make all these people well again. 'He's the best man in the world,' she had written in the personal diary she kept at that time, 'because he always helps other people, and he's never afraid, and he's good at making things. Also, he gave old Mrs Falouji medsins for free because she hasn't got any money, which was good.'

If her love had grown and deepened with age, each day seeming to bring some new aspect of her father to admire and respect, so too had her protectiveness towards him. With the intuitive emotional radar of childhood, she had sensed early on that despite his broad, white-toothed smile and the way he laughed and joked with her, he was an unhappy man, weighed down not merely with the pressures of his work, which left him drained, exhausted and prematurely greying, but with the hopelessness of occupation, the shaming impotence of watching his homeland being taken bit by bit from beneath his feet and being powerless to do anything about it.

'Your father is a proud man,' her mother once told her. 'It hurts him very deeply to see his people suffering like this. It makes him so sad.'

From the moment she had become aware of this pain she had made it her mission to help her father. As a child she had put on plays for him, done drawings, written stories in which handsome doctors saved beautiful princesses from wicked Israeli soldiers with M16 rifles (such was the nature of Palestinian childhood that she'd known what guns the Israelis carried before she could even place their country on a map). Later, as she entered her teens, she had begun helping him in his surgery, making tea, ushering patients in and out, running errands, even doing basic medical work.

'Why did you become a doctor?' she had asked him one day, as she and her parents were eating lunch together.

He had thought for a long moment.

'Because it was the best way I could see to serve my people,' he had replied eventually.

'But did you never want to fight the Israelis? To kill them?'

He had taken her hand.

'If the Israelis ever threatened those I love, then yes, I would fight. I would fight with every ounce of strength in my body and to the very last drop of my blood. But I do not believe violence is the way, Layla, however much I hate what the Israelis have done. I wish to save lives, not take them.'

It was the afternoon of her fifteenth birthday. Later that same night she had watched as the person she loved most in the world, the finest human being she had ever known, was dragged from his car and beaten to death with a baseball bat.

The lunch had, of course, been held at the Jerusalem Hotel.

Her friend Nuha was already there when Layla arrived, sitting at a table on the front terrace, her face buried in a copy of the *Herald Tribune*. A plump woman with heavily lacquered hair, slightly older than Layla, she wore a pair of wire-rimmed spectacles and an overly tight T-shirt bearing the logo PALESTINIAN RIGHT OF RETURN: NO RETURN, NO PEACE. Layla came up behind her and, bending, kissed her on the cheek. Nuha looked round, squeezed Layla's arm and, waving her into a chair, handed her the paper.

'Have you seen this shit?'

She pointed to a story headlined US CONDEMNS PALESTINIAN WEAPONS SHIPMENT. Opposite was another story: CONGRESS APPROVES $1 BILLION ARMS SALES TO ISRAEL.

'The hypocrisy of these fucking people! It's like a bad joke. Beer?'

Layla nodded, and Nuha waved a hand at Sami the barman.

'So, how's it looking down there?' she asked, nodding towards the Old City.

Layla shrugged. 'Tense, like you'd expect. Har-Zion gave a press conference, all the usual crap about God and Abraham and how anyone who criticizes Israel is a Jew-hating anti-semite. He talks a good talk, you've got to hand it to him.'

'So did Hitler,' snorted Nuha, lighting a Marlboro. 'Are they going to evict them?'

'Sure,' grunted Layla. 'And Sharon's going to dance male lead with the Bolshoi. Of course they're not going to bloody evict them.'

There was a burst of laughter from another table where a group of Scandinavian-looking men and women – NGO workers, probably, or minor diplomats – were eating. Outside there was the rumble of an engine as an Israeli Izuzu trooper jeep motored slowly past, like some giant armour-plated reptile. Sami arrived with two glasses of Taybeh and a plate of olives.

'You hear about the bomb?' he asked, setting down the glasses and plate and lighting a candle in the middle of the table.

'Oh God,' sighed Nuha. 'Not another one. Where?'

'Haifa. It was just on the news.'

'Al-Mulatham?'

'Looks like it. Two killed.'

Layla shook her head. 'Between him and Har-Zion they're going to start World War Three.'

Nuha swept up her beer and took a long gulp.

'You know what I think,' she said, laying the glass down again and taking a puff on her cigarette. 'I think they're working together. Look at it: the more people al-Mulatham kills, the more support Har-Zion gets. The more support Har-Zion gets, the more excuse al-Mulatham has for killing. They help each other.'

'You know, you might just have something there,' said Layla with a laugh. 'Maybe I'll do an article.'

'Well, just remember where you heard it first, girl. I know what you journalists are like. The biggest scoop of your career and you'll claim all the credit yourself.'

Again Layla laughed. While the amusement registered in her lower face, however, her eyes seemed suddenly to have drifted elsewhere, into some other circle of thought. 'The biggest scoop of your career.' Where had she heard that phrase recently? It took her a couple of moments before she remembered it was in the letter she had received earlier that afternoon. How had it gone? *I've got information that could help al-Mulatham in his struggle against the Zionist oppressor, and should like to contact him. I believe you can help me. In return I would give you the biggest scoop of your career.* Something like that. She'd dismissed it as a prank or a Shin Bet stunt, and it still struck her that this was the most likely explanation. Yet, now that a couple of hours had gone by . . .

'Do the initials GR mean anything to you?' Layla asked suddenly.

'Sorry?'

'GR. Do the initials mean anything to you?'

Her friend thought for a moment.

'Greg Rickman? The guy from Save the Children, the one who fancies you?'

Layla shook her head. 'He doesn't fancy me. And this is someone old, someone in the past.'

Nuha looked confused.

'Forget it,' said Layla after a moment, lifting her beer and taking a sip. 'It's nothing important. How's your day been?'

Her friend worked for an organization that monitored Israeli land confiscations around Jerusalem, and she needed no further prompting to launch into a long story about an elderly farmer whose olive grove had just been bulldozed by the

IDF. Layla tried to listen, but her mind was else-where. The letter, al-Mulatham, her father, that last lunch they had had here at the Jerusalem Hotel. It had been such a happy afternoon, just her and her parents, all laughing together, talking, telling stories. And just a few hours later he was dead.

'Oh God, my daddy!' she had screamed, her hair slopping in his blood. 'Oh God, my poor daddy!'

And from that everything else had sprung.

JERUSALEM

They had a rabbi with them in the house, a thin, intense young man, American-born and raised, like so many militant settlers, with wisps of beard clinging to his chin and thick glasses that magnified his eyes so that they seemed to fill half his face. As night fell he gathered them all in the house's downstairs living room and began to preach to them, choosing as his *parasha*, or portion of text, Genesis chapter 17, verse 8: 'And I will give to you, and your descendants after you, the land of your sojournings, all the land of Canaan, for an everlasting possession, and I will be your God.'

Har-Zion sat listening with the others, nodding and smiling as the rabbi assured them this was the Lord's true work they were engaged in here, a holy crusade that future generations would look back on with the same sense of pride and gratitude they themselves felt towards the great Jewish heroes of old. He loved to hear the Torah discussed like this, to feel himself a part of that rich tapestry that was the history of the Jewish people. As a boy, after his mother had died and his father

159

descended into madness, he and his brother Benjamin had spent hours together at the government orphanage reliving all the old tales, dreaming that one day they too would visit the land of the Patriarchs, defend it against Israel's enemies, like Joshua and David and the great Judah Maccabee. The stories had, for them, been as immediate as their own surroundings, a separate reality within which they would immerse themselves to escape the cold and the hunger and the Jew-bashing that were their daily lot.

'The Torah and the Mishnah and the Talmud, these are what is real,' their father had once told them. 'Everything else is just an illusion.'

He had been a devout man, their *abba*. Too devout, in a sense, disappearing into his books of law when he should have been providing for his family. It had been left to their mother to keep things together, sewing through the night to bring in enough money to feed and clothe them all and put wood on the fire. But then his mother had died and, rather than rising to his responsibilities, their father had simply withdrawn even further into his studies, sitting for days on end reading and muttering to himself, occasionally breaking into wild, ecstatic cries of joy, telling them that he had seen a great menorah in the sky and that the day of redemption was near, until eventually they had taken him away and he and his brother had been consigned to a government home where the least mention of their Judaism would result in the most brutal thrashings.

Yes, thought Har-Zion, you could be too devout. He did not begrudge those who devoted their lives to the *halakhah*, the rabbis and the *matmidim* and the *talmid hakhamim*. In a way he envied them, their ability to withdraw from the physical world and exist solely in a landscape of faith and spirit. It was not for him, however. *Frumm* as he was, he was a man of action. That's why he and his brother had run away from the orphanage and come to Israel; that's why he had joined the army and fought the Arabs; that's why he was sitting here now. Because if his early experiences had taught him anything, it was that faith on its own was not enough. You had to *do* too; stand up and defend yourself in the real world. Cling to the Torah by all means. But always make sure that in the other hand you are holding an Uzi.

The rabbi finished his sermon and the group dispersed, the women into the kitchen to start preparing food, the men to guard the house, or to engage in private Talmud study. Har-Zion went up onto the roof where he took a couple of calls on his mobile, one from a donor in America to congratulate him on the occupation, another from a cabinet contact to tell him he was a fucking nuisance but that, provided there was no overt violence, the government would make no move to evict them.

'At times like this we need to stick together, Baruch,' the man told him. 'Although there's going to be a lot of international pressure, particularly from Europe and the UN.'

'Fuck them,' Har-Zion replied. 'They won't do anything. They never do. They're worms.'

He rang off and stood for a while gazing east towards Mount Scopus and the Hebrew University, watching as an Arab bus heaved itself slowly up the steep slope of Ben Adaya Road, smoke belching from its exhaust, then ducked back into the house, descended the stairs and went into one of the rooms on the second floor, switching on the light and closing the door behind him.

He and Avi would leave later that night, he decided, once things outside had calmed down a bit and they could slip out without too much trouble. That's how it worked with these actions: he'd be there at the start to organize things and secure maximum publicity; then, once the occupation was secure, he'd hand over to someone else, leaving them to direct the actual business of settlement, the stripping out of every hint of the building's former owners and its replacement with a new Jewish identity. There was other, more pressing business to attend to – interviews, meetings, his Knesset work, al-Mulatham.

He turned the key in the lock, crossed the room to check the window shutters were properly closed, then slowly, stiffly, started removing his clothes. There was a mirror on the wall opposite, cracked and murky, and, once he was naked, he took a couple of steps towards it, staring at his reflection. From the neck down the skin was a swirling patchwork of reds, browns and pinks, glassy-smooth and hairless, more like plastic than real skin. He ran his eyes up and down, a faint look of surprise on his face, as if even after thirteen years and a hundred skin grafts he still couldn't believe he looked like this.

Landmine, southern Lebanon. That's what had done it. A crude thing, makeshift. Half the time they didn't even go off. Their Humvee had run over it and erupted, swathing everyone inside in a searing cloak of flame. He would have died there and then had Avi, who was in a vehicle behind, not sprinted forward and dragged him from the flames.

'No chance,' the army doctors had said when they'd brought him in. 'He's dead.' But he hadn't died. He had survived, clinging to life with a ferocious determination, like a man dangling by his fingertips from the edge of a precipice. The pain had been unbelievable, weeks of it, months, a pain measured against which all other pain was exquisite pleasure, tearing him apart cell by cell, atom by atom, until there was nothing left of him but pain; he became pain, a creature formed from the purest and most intense primordial agony. Yet he'd held on, sustained by an adamantine conviction that God needed him to survive. And, also, by fury. Not for what had happened to him, although that was bad enough, but for his younger brother, his beloved Benjamin, who had been in the Humvee with him and had been incinerated by the blast. Dear, brave Benjamin.

He gazed into the mirror, at once repulsed and fascinated by the difference in texture between his head and face, which had by some miracle escaped the ravages of the fire, and the livid, glassy kaleidoscope of everything beneath. Then, with a grunt, he picked up a bottle of balm sitting on the table beside him, squeezed some into the palm of his hand and began rubbing it into the patchwork flesh of his arms and torso.

Five times a day he had to go through this ritual. The skin needs to be kept supple, the doctors had told him. Moist, pliant. Otherwise it would tighten around him like a straitjacket, ripping open with any sudden or expansive movement. That's why he had had to give up active service and take a desk job with Military Intelligence. Because there could be no break in this ritual; even to miss one session would cause him to literally tear apart at the seams.

He worked the almond-white liquid into his shoulders, chest and stomach, moving down towards his penis and testicles, a tight, bunched fruit dangling from the shelf of shiny scar tissue that was his groin. 'Do you have children?' the doctors had asked him. When he had said no they had shaken their heads sadly. No chance now. Everything inside had been ruined. He was empty. Incapable of bringing forth life. It wasn't just his

164

brother they'd killed, but his children too. His future. The future he and his wife Miriam had so often dreamt of.

Benjamin, his children, his flesh, and three years ago Miriam too, from cancer – all had been taken from him, stripped away like bark from a tree, leaving nothing but his faith, his fury and his country, Israel. That was his family now. And, also, his revenge. His cry of defiance against the Arabs and the goyim and the Jew-haters everywhere. And he would do whatever he had to do to ensure its survival.

He finished massaging himself and, laying aside the balm bottle, stared into the mirror. You might be scarred, he thought, but still you are strong. *We* might be scarred, but still we are strong. *Va'avarecha me'-varakhecha umekalelecha.* I will bless those who bless you, and he who curses you I will curse.

He nodded and, turning away, started dressing again.

JERUSALEM

There were so many 'if onlys' that might have saved her father's life: if only they hadn't driven up to Jerusalem for her fifteenth birthday; if only they had come back earlier; if only they hadn't diverted into the camp; if only the Israeli soldier had been dumped somewhere else. Above all, if only her father hadn't been such a good man. That, ultimately, is what had killed him, as surely as the blows of the baseball bat – that he cared for other people, that he was a human being who couldn't help but help. A lesser person would have turned away and lived. But her father was not a lesser person, and for that he'd been butchered.

They had found the soldier on a roadside on the outskirts of Jabaliya refugee camp, late at night. They were on their way back from her birthday lunch at the Jerusalem Hotel, and had diverted off the main Erez Checkpoint-Gaza City road in order to collect something from her father's surgery in the centre of the camp. Their headlights had picked up a shape in the darkness and, slowing, they discovered it was a young man, half-naked and unconscious, his face so badly beaten it was barely recognizable as something human. Her father stopped, got out and went over to him.

'Is he alive?' her mother had asked.

Her father had nodded.

'Israeli?'

Another nod.

'Christ.'

The First Intifada was then at its height, and anti-Israeli feeling was intense, especially in the pressure cooker of the Gaza Strip, where the revolt had first erupted the previous December. How and when the soldier had ended up on the road-side was uncertain. What was clear was that to help him at this time, in this place, would be extremely dangerous. Palestinians who aided Israelis were hated as much as the Israelis them-selves. More, even.

'Leave him,' Layla had said. 'The Jews don't care about us. Why should we do anything for them?'

Her father shook his head. 'I am a doctor, Layla. I can't leave someone to die in the dust like a dog. Whoever they might be.'

And so they lifted the soldier into their car and drove him to the surgery, where her father had done his best to clean the man's wounds and bandage him. He regained consciousness as he was being treated and started to buck and weep.

'Please hold his hand, Layla,' her father ordered her. 'Try to reassure him.'

She did as she was instructed. It was the first time she had ever touched an Israeli.

Afterwards, when they'd patched him up as best they could, they wrapped the soldier in a blanket, got him back into the car and drove out of the camp, intending to drop him off at one of the Israeli checkpoints that bottlenecked the main highway. They had barely gone a hundred metres when, sickeningly, two cars appeared out of nowhere and came up alongside them, forcing them over to the edge of the road.

'Oh God,' Layla's mother whispered. 'Oh God, help us.'

Who the men were, what faction they belonged to, how they had found out about her father's good deed, and so quickly, Layla never discovered. All she remembered was a sudden mass of people around the car, their faces hidden behind checked *keffiyehs*, the crack of a pistol as they shot the Israeli at pointblank range through the open window, and then her father being dragged out onto the street to screams of *'Radar! A'mee!'* – 'Traitor! Collaborator!' Her mother had tried to follow, but they had slammed the car door against her head, knocking her unconscious. They had beaten her father, viciously, unremittingly, a crowd of onlookers gathering to watch, many of them patients of his, not one of them trying to help, not one of them offering even the faintest whimper of protest, then handcuffed his hands behind his back and dragged him out onto the sandy wasteground that surrounded the camp. She had gone after them, weeping and screaming and pleading for her father's life, but to no avail. They pushed him down into a hollow, a baseball bat appeared out of nowhere and, with a sickening crack, was smashed into the back of her father's head, pitching him face forwards onto the ground. Three further blows rained down, opening his skull like a watermelon, before, as suddenly as they had come, the men were gone again, leaving her to crawl across and cradle her father's broken body in her arms, her long black tresses slopping in his blood, the howls of wild dogs echoing in the distance.

'Oh God, my daddy! Oh God, my poor daddy!'

Of the events of that night Layla had never spoken to anyone, not even her mother. The following day, after her father's funeral, she had taken a pair of scissors and hacked off her hair, unable to bear the feel of her father's blood that still seemed to linger however many times she washed it. Two days after that she and her mother had packed up and left Palestine for good, returning to England where they set up home with Layla's grandparents, who owned a large cottage in a village on the outskirts of Cambridge. She remained there for four years before, to her mother's horror, she announced she was going back.

'But why?' her mother had cried. 'For God's sake, Layla! After what's happened? After what they did? How can you?'

She had been unable to explain, beyond saying that she needed to put things right, wipe the slate clean. Which was, in a sense, what she had been doing ever since.

LUXOR

It was only when he arrived back home that evening that Khalifa remembered they were having people round for dinner.

'They'll be here in a minute!' huffed his wife Zenab as he came through the front door, bustling past him with a tray of *torshi* and *babaghanoush* and disappearing into the living room of their small, cramped apartment. 'Where have you been all this time?'

'Down at Karnak,' replied Khalifa, lighting a cigarette. 'Business.'

There was a clatter of plates and Zenab reappeared, plucking the cigarette from his mouth, kissing him swiftly on the lips and popping the cigarette back in again. She was wearing an embroidered cotton caftan, the top three buttons open to reveal a hint of swelling breast, and had plaited her ebony-black hair into a long tress that hung down her back almost to the level of her waist.

'You look beautiful,' he said.

'And you,' she countered with a smile, flicking his earlobe playfully, 'look terrible. Why don't you go and have a shave while I finish up with Batah? And try not to wake the baby. I've only just got him down.'

She kissed him again, on the cheek this time, and disappeared back into the kitchen.

'Where's Ali?' he called after her.

'Staying with a friend. And put on a clean shirt, will you? Your collar's all grimy!'

He wandered through into the bathroom, unbuttoning his shirt and standing in front of the mirror above the sink, staring at his reflection. Zenab was right – he did look terrible. His eyes were dull and puffy, his cheekbones jutted out like the ribs of an undernourished donkey and his skin was an unhealthy grey colour, like the surface of a stagnant canal. He flicked his cigarette out of the window, turned on the cold tap and, bending down, splashed his face with water, coming up again and looking himself in the eye.

'What are you going to do, eh?' he asked his reflection. 'What are you going to do?'

He stared at his mirror image for a while longer, shaking his head as if he saw something there that he didn't like, then quickly shaved and went through into the bedroom where he splashed some cologne on his face and changed his shirt. He was just doing up the last of the buttons, bending down as he did so to kiss baby Yusuf, who was asleep in his cot, when the doorbell rang.

'We're here!'

The voice of his brother-in-law Hosni barged in from outside the front door. Khalifa sighed.

'Whatever you do in life,' he whispered to the baby, rubbing his nose back and forth across its smooth, soft forehead, 'promise me you won't end up like your uncle.'

'Come on, you two!' boomed the voice. 'What're you doing in there? Or shouldn't I ask!'

There was a raucous snort as Hosni's wife Sama, Zenab's elder sister, laughed at her husband's joke, which Hosni seemed to crack every time a doorbell wasn't answered within a nanosecond of him ringing it.

'God help us,' muttered Khalifa, going through into the entrance hall to welcome the guests.

There were six of them in total: Khalifa, Zenab, Sama, Hosni, and two of Zenab's friends from Cairo – Nawal, a small, intense woman who taught classical Arabic at Cairo University; and Tawfiq, a *mashrabiya* dealer whom everyone referred to as 'Goggle-eyes' on account of his unnaturally large, saucer-shaped eyes. They ate around a small table in the living room, with Batah, Khalifa's daughter, serving the food, which she liked to do because it made her seem grown up. Like her mother she wore an embroidered caftan and had her long dark hair done in a plait down her back.

'I must say, Batah, you look more beautiful every time I see you,' said Sama as the girl passed round bowls of chicken broth. 'And I simply love that caftan. I bought one just like it for Ama. Three hundred pounds, would you believe!'

Unlike Batah, Sama and Hosni's daughter was short, plump and extremely slothful, a difference her mother did her best to disguise by ensuring the girl always wore more expensive clothes than her cousin.

'She looks just like you did at that age,' said Nawal, smiling at Zenab. 'I bet you've got all the boys running after you, eh, Batah?'

'If I was a bit younger I'd be running after you,' said Tawfiq, laughing. 'Or sprinting more like!'

Batah giggled shyly and left the room.

'It's time you started thinking about a husband for her,' grunted Hosni, slurping his soup.

'For God's sake!' cried Zenab. 'She's only fourteen!'

'It's never too early to think about these things. Forward planning – that's the key. Always look to the future. Take edible oils.' Hosni worked in the edible oils business, and never missed an opportunity to nudge the conversation in that direction. 'When we relaunched our sunflower range last year it was on the back of eighteen months' careful preparation. And the result? An eight per cent increase in sales and a Best Domestic Oil award. You don't achieve that sort of success without thinking ahead.'

He took another slurp of his soup.

'We got a commendation for our nut oil as well. It's simply flying out of the shops!'

Everyone tried to look suitably impressed, finishing their soup and moving on to the main course: lamb *torly* served with peas, okra, rice and potatoes. The conversation switched to mutual friends, then the recent Cairo football derby between Zamelak and al-Ahli, then politics, Hosni and Nawal getting into a heated debate about America's ongoing war against terrorism.

'So what are you saying?' cried Hosni. 'They should have done nothing after September eleven? Just let them get away with it?'

'I'm saying that before they start bombing other countries they should sort their own house out. I mean, why is it that when any other country in the world supports terrorism they get invaded, but when America does it it's justified as "foreign policy"?'

Khalifa sat silently through all this, prodding at his food, occasionally interjecting the odd comment but for the most part lost in his own thoughts. The corpse at Malqata, Jansen's antiquities collection, the meeting with Hassani, the curious encounter at Karnak – all bounced around his brain like reflections in a hall of mirrors. And behind everything, like the backdrop to a stage play, always the same even when the scenes before it changed, that curious tattoo on the dead woman's forearm, a triangle and five numbers. Like the marks you get on meat to show where it's come from.

'More lamb?'

Zenab's voice echoed in his ear. She was holding out the bowl of *torly*.

'What? Oh, no, thank you.'

'So what do you think of him, Yusuf?'

Tawfiq was looking at him expectantly.

'Sorry?' said Khalifa.

'He was miles away,' Nawal observed with a laugh. 'Probably thinking about tombs and hiero-glyphs.'

'Or women's bums!' Hosni chuckled, receiving a sharp slap on the wrist from his wife.

'Al-Mulatham,' said Tawfiq. 'What do you think about the suicide bombings?'

Khalifa took a sip of Coca-cola – as a devout Muslim he did not drink alcohol – and, pushing his chair back, lit a cigarette.

'I think that anybody who kills innocent civil-ians in cold blood is disgusting.'

'The Israelis kill Palestinians in cold blood and no-one seems to complain about that,' said Nawal. 'Look what happened the other day. Two children killed by an Israeli helicopter.'

'That still doesn't justify it,' replied Khalifa. 'What's the point seeking revenge by killing more children?'

'But what other way do they have of standing up for themselves?' countered Tawfiq. 'They're facing the most powerful army in the Middle East, the fourth most powerful army in the world. How the hell else are they supposed to make their point? I agree that it's horrible, but that's what people do when they've been systematically brutalized for fifty years.'

'Like the Palestinian Authority's got such a great human rights record,' grunted Zenab. 'Like *we've* got such a great record.'

'That's not the point,' said Tawfiq. 'The point is that people don't strap explosives to their waists and blow themselves up just for the hell of it. They do it because they're desperate.'

'I'm not defending the Israelis,' said Khalifa, holding out a match to light Nawal's cigarette. 'I just think . . . well, like Zenab says, it doesn't help the situation.'

'You're telling me you don't feel a hint of pleasure when you hear another bomb's gone off?' asked Tawfiq. 'That a part of you doesn't feel, "Serves them bloody right."'

Khalifa stared down at the table, a spiral of smoke drifting upwards from the end of his cigarette. Before he could answer, Sama butted in.

'I'll tell you what I feel like,' she said, 'and that's some pudding! Is that *umm ali* I can smell, Zenab? Why don't I help Batah serve? This really is a wonderful dinner party!'

It was past midnight before they finally got to bed. Zenab fell asleep almost immediately. Khalifa tossed and turned, listening to baby Yusuf breathing in the cot beside him, watching as parallelograms of light slipped across the ceiling from the passing cars below, feeling the beating of his own heart.

After twenty minutes he got up again and padded out into the front hall where he flicked a switch on the wall. A miniature fountain in the centre of the floor bubbled into life. He flicked another switch, illuminating a string of multi-coloured fairy lights arranged around the plastic pool into which the fountain trickled, and sat down on the floor with his back to the wall, rubbing his eyes. He had built the fountain himself, to add a bit of colour to their otherwise drab apartment. It wasn't the greatest piece of work in the world – the water didn't pump properly, and the tiles surrounding the pool were slightly misaligned – but he still found it soothing to gaze at it, to hear the rhythmic plop of the water and watch the refracted glint of the lights.

For a long while he sat in silence, then leant to his right and punched the play button of a small tape recorder sitting on a wooden stool. The rich, ululating voice of Umm Kulthoum wrapped itself around him, singing a song about love and loss:

Your eyes take me back to days that are gone,
They teach me to regret the pain of the past,
All that I saw before my eyes saw you
Was just a wasted life. How could it not be,
When you are my life, your light my dawn?
Before you my heart never knew happiness,
It felt nothing but the taste of suffering and pain.

There was a movement behind him and Zenab came out into the hall, eyes bleary, her long, slim legs protruding from beneath the hem of one of his shirts which she wore in bed. She leant down and kissed his forehead, the shirt riding up around her thighs so that he could see the vague shadow of her pubic hair, then she settled herself down on the floor beside him with her head on his shoulder, her long hair spilling across his chest like a dark waterfall.

'You didn't enjoy tonight, did you?' she said sleepily.

'Yes I did,' he protested. 'It was . . .'

'Boring,' she said. 'I could see it in your eyes. I know you too well, Yusuf.'

He stroked her hair.

'I'm sorry,' he said. 'I've got things on my mind.'

'Work?'

He nodded, enjoying the feel of her breast against his arm.

'Do you want to talk?'

He shrugged, but said nothing. The silken ribbon of Umm Kulthoum's voice curled around them.

> *You are worth more to me than my days,*
> *You are worth more to me than my dreams.*
> *Take me to your goodness,*
> *Far away from this world,*
> *Far away, far away, just me and you*
> *Far away, far away, just us alone.*

'You know what this reminds me of?' Zenab said, stroking his hand, running her finger back and forth along a small scar on his wrist where he had been bitten by a dog as a child. 'That day we went to Gebel el-Silsilla. When you caught that catfish for our lunch, and we went swimming in the Nile. Do you remember?'

Khalifa smiled. 'How could I forget? You snagged your foot on a piece of weed and thought you were being attacked by a crocodile.'

'And you slipped over in the mud and spoilt your new trousers. I've never heard such swearing!'

He laughed and kissed her on the cheek. She pushed herself closer to him, wrapping her arms around his waist.

'What's wrong, Yusuf? You were so distant tonight. And last night too. What's troubling you?'

He sighed and stroked her hair.

'It's nothing. Just office stuff.'

'Tell me,' she said. 'Maybe I can help.'

He was silent for a long moment, staring at the glittering droplets of the fountain, then laid his head back against the wall, eyes moving back and forth along a crack in the ceiling above.

'I've done something terrible, Zenab,' he said quietly. 'And I don't know how to put it right. Or at least I do, but I'm afraid.'

'Nothing you do is bad, Yusuf,' she whispered, unwrapping her arms and lifting a hand to stroke his face. 'You are a good man. I know this, our children know this, God knows this.'

'I'm not, Zenab. I am weak and scared and have let you down. Have let myself down.'

He reached up his hands and rubbed his temples. There was another long silence, broken by the sound of the tape and the soft bubble of water from the fountain, and then he started to talk, slowly at first, then faster, spilling out the whole story: Piet Jansen, Hannah Schlegel, Mohammed Gemal, the meeting at Karnak, everything. Zenab sat and listened, saying nothing, her hands stroking his face and neck, her soft breath caressing his shoulder.

'I was too afraid to say anything at the time, you see,' he said when he had finished. 'I was young, I was new at the station, I didn't want to rock the boat. I allowed them to convict an innocent man because I didn't have the guts to speak out. And now . . . I'm still afraid. Afraid of what will happen if I start digging, if I go back into the case. There are bad things here, Zenab. I can feel it. And I don't know if it's worth risking my job for a . . .'

He broke off, shaking his head.

'For a what? A man like Mohammed Gemal?'

'That, yes, and . . . well, like Chief Hassani says, Jansen is dead. It won't make any practical difference what we find out.'

She looked into his eyes, holding them with hers.

'There's something else,' she said. 'I can see it inside you. I can feel it. What are you thinking, Yusuf?'

'Nothing, Zenab. Nothing. It's just . . .'

He brought his legs up to his chest and leant forward, resting his forehead on his knees.

'She was an Israeli,' he whispered. 'A Jew. Look what they're doing, Zenab. Is it worth it, I ask myself? Is it worth all the trouble for someone like that?'

The words just spilled out of him, without him really thinking about them. Yet once he had said them it struck him that deep down this was what had really been bothering him all along; not just now, but fifteen years ago too, as he had sat watching Mohammed Gemal being taken apart by Hassani and Chief Mahfouz. That to speak out would mean not simply putting his career on the line for a low-life criminal, but also – and it was this that had given him more pause for thought, both then and now – for someone from a country and a faith he had been brought up to despise. It shamed him, this bigotry, shamed him deeply, for he tried in all things to be a tolerant man, judging each person for themselves rather than their background or nationality or creed. Yet it was hard. From his earliest years he had been taught that Israel was evil, that the Jews were trying to take over the world, that they were a cruel, arrogant, greedy people who had committed unspeakable atrocities against his Muslim brothers.

'They are wicked,' his father used to tell him when he was a child, 'all of them. They drive people off their land and steal it from them. They kill women and children. They wish to destroy the Ummah. Be careful of them, Yusuf. Always be careful of the Jews.'

As he had grown and his circle of experience widened he had come to see that things were not, of course, as black and white as he had been told. Not all Jews supported the oppression of the Palestinians; being Israeli did not automatically make you a monster; the Jews themselves had suffered terribly as a people. Yet despite this mellowing of his outlook he could not completely scour away the things that had been ingrained in him from his earliest years.

In discussions with friends and colleagues, whenever the subject turned that way he would try to take the moderate line, as he had done that evening. Deep down, however, in the places that only he knew about, the old bigotry still remained, a dark stain that however hard he tried he could not completely scrub away. It was not something he was proud of. He knew that it diminished him as a person, yet he could no more get rid of it than he could his own marrow. It had dictated his actions fifteen years ago, and it seemed to be doing the same now.

'When Tawfiq asked me tonight if I feel pleasure when a bomb goes off in Israel,' he said quietly, 'if a part of me doesn't think "serves you right"? – well, the truth is that I do, Zenab. I wouldn't have said so, but I do. I can't help myself.'

He shook his head, ashamed to be telling her such things, to be revealing so much of his secret self.

'With this case, I feel like I'm two people. One

knows there's been a terrible miscarriage of justice, that a woman was murdered and the wrong man convicted for it, that it's my duty to try and find out the truth. But then there's this other person who just thinks to hell with it. Who cares that an old Jew was battered to death? Why put myself to all the trouble? I hate myself for it, but it's there nonetheless.'

Zenab leant back slightly, staring at him, her almond eyes narrowed, her face wrapped in shadows, as if covered with a thin veil.

'We all have bad thoughts,' she said quietly. 'It is our actions that are important.'

'But that's just the point, Zenab. I don't know if I can act. My thoughts are . . . it's like they're holding me back. It's easier for you. You come from a clever, well-read family. Your parents had travelled, seen something of the world. You didn't grow up with these prejudices. But when you're told from the word go that Jews and Israelis are evil, that it's our duty as Muslims to hate them, that if we don't kill them then they'd kill us – it's hard to move away from that. Up here' – he reached up and tapped his head – 'I know that these things are wrong. And here too.' Now he touched his heart. 'But here' – he moved his hand down to his stomach – 'deep down, I can't help hating them. It's like I can't control my own emotions. It frightens me.'

Zenab reached out and stroked his hair, running her hand down across the back of his neck. He could feel her thigh warm against his. There was a long silence.

'Do you remember my grandmother?' she said eventually, massaging the muscles of his neck and shoulders. 'Grandma Jamila.'

Khalifa smiled. There had been a wide social gap between Zenab's family, well-to-do business people from the posh part of Cairo, and his own, peasant labourers from the poor Giza backstreets. Grandma Jamila had been the only one to take the trouble to make him feel welcome, always sitting him beside her when they went round to the family home and asking him all manner of questions about his interest in Egypt's history, a subject on which she was formidably well read. When she had died a few years ago he had felt as much sadness as when he had lost his own mother.

'Of course I remember her.'

'There was something she once said to me, years and years ago, when I was a child. I can't even remember the context, but her words stuck with me. "Always go towards what you fear, Zenab. And always seek out what you don't understand. Because that is how you grow and become a better person." I've never told you what to do in your work, Yusuf, but that is what I think you must do here.'

'But how?' He sighed. 'I can't just carry on an investigation behind Chief Hassani's back.'

She took his hand, brought it to her lips and kissed it.

'I don't know how, Yusuf. All I know is that this case has somehow been sent to test you, and you mustn't back away from it.'

'But it could cause so many problems.'

'We'll get through it together. As we always do.'

He looked across at her. She was so beautiful, so strong.

'No man could want a better wife,' he said.

'And no woman could want a better husband. I love you, Yusuf.'

They gazed at each other and then, bending forward, kissed, gently at first, then more passionately, her breasts pushing against him, her leg curling around his.

'Do you remember what we did that day at Gebel el-Silsilla,' she whispered into his ear, 'after you fell in the mud and had to take off your trousers to wash them?'

He didn't answer, simply got to his feet and, lifting her into his arms, carried his wife back into the bedroom, leaving Umm Kulthoum to play herself out.

JERUSALEM

There are two of them, or at least two that I am aware of. They come at me from behind and take my arms, one of them holding my head so that I cannot look round at their faces. They do not hurt me, they are calm and well spoken. It is clear as they push me into the car, however, and throw a blanket over my head, that they will not tolerate resistance.

We drive for two hours, maybe more – after only a few minutes I have lost track of both time and direction. Early on we climb steeply up, and then down again, which suggests to me we are heading south-east out of Jerusalem towards Jericho and the Dead Sea plain, although it is possible – probable – that they are simply driving around to disorientate me and ensure that we are not being followed.

Half an hour into the journey we pull up and a third person climbs into the front passenger seat. There is a smell of cigarette smoke. Farid, I think, although I can't be sure.

Strangely, I am not frightened. During a lifetime in the region I have been in many situations where my instincts tell me I am going to be harmed, but this is not one of them. Whatever the purpose of my abduction it is not violence. So long as I do as I am told.

For the last twenty minutes we are on a bumpy track, and then in some sort of village or settlement – a refugee camp? – for I can hear voices, and occasional music, and the car swerves back and forth as though negotiating a series of narrow alleys.

Eventually we stop and, the blanket still over my head, I am hurried into a building. I am taken up a set of stairs and into a room where I am made to sit on a wooden chair. From beneath the blanket I glimpse a blue and white tiled floor before what feels like a pair of diving goggles are slipped over my head, the lenses blacked out with tape so that I am to all intents and purposes blind. I can feel someone behind me, a woman to judge by the sound of her breathing, and can hear voices somewhere else within the house, very faint and muffled. I think I catch a couple of words in Egyptian Arabic, which is slightly different from the Palestinian dialect, although I am so disorientated I can't be sure.

I do not hear him enter or sit down. All that alerts me to his arrival is a sudden faint waft of aftershave – Manio (I had a friend who used to wear it). Although I cannot see him I have the sense of a tall, slim man, very self-contained. The woman behind me steps forward and places a pad and pen in my hands. There is a long silence during which I can hear his soft breathing, feel his eyes on me.

'You may commence the interview,' he says eventually, his voice slow and measured, educated, a voice that gives no hint of his age or origin. 'You have thirty minutes.'

'And who exactly am I supposed to be interviewing?'

'My real name I prefer to keep to myself. It would mean nothing to you anyway. My nom de guerre is more appropriate.'

'And that is?'

There is a faint, amused exhalation of breath, as though the man in front of me is smiling.

'You may call me al-Mulatham. You now have twenty-nine and a half minutes.'

Layla yawned and, laying aside the magazine, stood and padded through into her small kitchenette. It was 2.30 a.m. and, aside from the faint rumble of Fathi the caretaker's snores drifting up from deep within the bowels of the building below, the world was wholly silent. She boiled the kettle, made herself some strong black coffee and returned to the living room, slurping at her cup.

She had arrived home half an hour earlier, drunk, having demolished two bottles of wine and several brandies with Nuha. She had taken a cold shower to clear her head, gulped several glasses of water, then gone through into the study and recovered the mysterious letter from the bin, the one she had received earlier in the day, with its heavy script in blood-red ink and attached photocopy.

> *Miss al-Madani,*
> *I have long been an admirer of your journalism, and would like to put to you a proposition. Some while ago you interviewed the leader known as al-Mulatham . . .*

She had looked again at the photocopy, then crossed to her filing cabinet and searched through her cuttings for the interview to which the letter referred. It had appeared in the *Observer Magazine* under the headline THE HIDDEN ONE REVEALED – AN EXCLUSIVE INTERVIEW WITH THE MOST FEARED MAN IN THE MIDDLE EAST. She had pulled it out, taken it through into the living room and started reading.

> He has been described as the new Saladin, the Devil incarnate, the man who makes Hamas and Islamic Jihad look like Israel's

best friends. Since Al-khwan al-Filistinioun – the Palestinian Brotherhood – launched its first suicide attack three years ago, killing five people at a hotel in Netanya, he has been responsible for over 400 deaths, the majority of them civilians. While other Palestinian extremist groups have at least shown some willingness to enter into ceasefires and negotiations, al-Mulatham – the name means 'the veiled' or 'the hidden one' – has continued his campaign unabated.

It is a campaign that is polarizing the politics of an already polarized region, scuppering any lingering hopes of a meaningful peace process and driving Israelis and Palestinians inexorably towards all-out war.

Polls show that with each attack Israeli public opinion, already hardened by the activities of other Palestinian extremist groups, is pushed even further to the right, with support for right-wing politicians such as Baruch Har-Zion rising by the day. At the same time the increasing severity and arbitrariness of Israeli retaliatory action has in turn seen an upsurge in support for militant organizations such as the Palestinian Brotherhood. In the words of moderate Palestinian politician Sa'eb Marsoudi, a man whose lifelong involvement in Palestinian activism – not to mention five years in prison for helping smuggle arms into Gaza – lends particular weight to his criticism of al-Mulatham: 'It is a vicious circle. The extremists feed off and encourage each other. When al-Mulatham kills five Israelis, the Israelis kill ten Palestinians, so al-Mulatham kills fifteen Israelis, and so on and so on. We are diving headlong into a lake of blood.'

What has set the Brotherhood apart is not simply the regularity and ferocity of its attacks, but the fact that despite extensive efforts by the security services of Israel and a dozen other countries, including the Palestinian Authority itself, virtually nothing is known about either the organisation itself or the man who leads it. Where it is based, who belongs to it, how its 'martyrs' are recruited and its operations funded – all remain a complete mystery. No reliable informers have ever come forward, no member of the group has ever been arrested. It is a level of organization and secrecy unprecedented in the history of Palestinian activism, and one that has led many experts to speculate that an established state security operation must ultimately be behind the attacks. Iran, Libya and Syria have all been mooted as possible background sponsors, as has the al-Qaeda network of Osama bin Laden.

'The Palestinians simply aren't that good,' one Israeli security expert has commented. 'There are always informers, you can always

find an in. The way the Brotherhood operates is way too sophisticated for a renegade
Palestinian cell. The impetus has to be
external.'

Despite such speculation, no-one has come
any closer to discovering the truth about al-
Mulatham. And now I am sitting in front of
him. The new Saladin. The Devil incarnate.
The most dangerous man in the Middle East.
He asks if I would like some tea and a biscuit.

From outside there came the clatter of a bin lid.
Layla rubbed her eyes, stood up and went over to
the window, looking out at the street below. Two
men were loading freshly baked bread into the
back of a van; further down the hill a small group
of people had already started queuing outside the
Israeli Interior Ministry office in the forlorn hope
of getting their city residency permits renewed. A
little beyond them, on the other side of the road,
a battered white BMW was parked in front of the
entrance to the Garden Tomb, with yellow Israeli
number plates and, just visible inside, a shadowy
figure sitting motionless in the driving seat. She
had seen the same car parked there a number of
times before, and although the rational explanation for its presence was that it was a Shin Bet
vehicle keeping tabs on the Palestinians queuing
opposite, she couldn't shake a carping suspicion
that its driver was in fact staring directly up at the
windows of her flat. She looked down at it now,

more intrigued than discomforted, then, with a shake of the head, went back to the sofa and picked up the article again.

She skimmed the rest of it – basically an extended series of quotes in which al-Mulatham justified his campaign of violence and vowed to continue it 'until the soil of Palestine runs red with the blood of Jewish children' – before slowing again for the final few paragraphs, which always sent a slight shiver down her spine.

And then suddenly, as abruptly as it started, the interview is at an end. One minute we are talking, the next I am heaved to my feet and led downstairs again, the blacked-out goggles still over my head. As I reach the ground floor I hear his voice from above.

'There are many who will question whether this interview actually took place, Miss al-Madani. To silence any doubters, please inform the Israeli security services that at precisely 9.05 p.m. tonight one of our operatives will martyr himself in the name of a free Palestine. I wish you a safe journey.'

Two hours later I am abandoned on a roadside just south of Bethlehem. I inform the Israeli authorities what has happened. That same night, at the time specified, a bomb goes off in Hagar Square in West Jerusalem, killing eight people and injuring ninety-three. It says more than any interview could about the

194

nihilism of the man known as al-Mulatham that those killed and maimed were attending a Gush Shalom peace rally.

'He has done almost as much damage to my people as the creation of the State of Israel,' Sa'eb Marsoudi has said. 'More, perhaps, for where once we were seen as victims, now, thanks to him, we are regarded as murderers.'

I suspect al-Mulatham would regard this as a compliment.

She laid the article aside and picked up the curious letter again, reading through it one final time, brow furrowed. There was definitely something about it, something . . . compelling. She was too tired to do anything more about it now, however, and, leaving both the article and the letter on her study desk, she went to bed, falling asleep almost as soon as her head hit the pillow, the initials GR echoing at the edge of her mind like distant rumbles of thunder on a dark winter's night.

EGYPT, THE SINAI PENINSULA, CLOSE TO THE BORDER WITH ISRAEL

It was a mystery. That was all the old man could say about it. Like so many things in the desert. Lights where there shouldn't be lights, shadowy figures that came and went with the darkness, a neatly furnished room in the middle of the wilderness. In seventy years he had never seen anything like it. A very great mystery.

It had started a year ago, as he searched for one of his goats amid the shallow, twisting wadis that wound along the border with Israel. Night had fallen, and he had been about to abandon his hunt when, coming to the top of a gravelly ridge, he had noticed a faint light glowing below inside an abandoned army border post. There had been no soldiers in this part of the desert for decades, no people at all aside from occasional Bedouin such as himself, and then only passing through, for it was a barren, lonely place, inhospitable even to those used to the harshness of the desert. Yet now there was a light where there hadn't been light before, and people too, just visible inside the low stone building.

196

He had crept downwards, his goat forgotten, approaching the building and coming up on tiptoe to peer through the window. Inside, illuminated by the oily glow of a kerosene lamp, were two men, one with a cigar wedged into the corner of his mouth, a long scar running down his right cheek and a white skullcap on his head, such as was worn by the *yehudi-een*; the other younger, handsome, with thick black hair and a checked *keffiyeh* slung across his shoulders. They were hunched over a collapsible camp table staring at a map, talking together in a language he didn't understand, their fingers tracing patterns across the crumpled paper. To their right, two comfortable armchairs were set side by side against the wall; on another table sat a thermos flask and a half-eaten plate of sandwiches.

He had watched for a few minutes, then, fearful of being spotted, moved away, wrapping his *schal* around him against the cold and crouching down behind a rock, waiting to see what would happen. At one point he heard angry shouting; a little later the younger man came out and urinated against the wall.

All night he had stayed there, watching, listening, until in the chill hour before dawn the light had gone out and the two men emerged into the night, moving off around the side of the building. He counted to fifty and followed, weaving among the scattered boulders, keeping his distance, eventually coming round a high shoulder of rock just in time to see a large helicopter hoisting itself into the air, its down-draft enveloping him in a choking cloud of dust. It had hovered overhead for a moment, then swung off into the greying eastern sky.

After that he had seen the two mysterious figures many times. Sometimes they would appear once or even twice a week; sometimes as much as two months would elapse between visits. Always, however, they came in the dead of night, and always they left with the first hint of day, as if afraid of the sun's revealing light. He mentioned it to some of his fellow Bedouin, but they laughed and said his brain had been softened by the sun, and after that he did not speak of it again, which was fine by him, for he rather liked the idea of being privy to a secret no-one else knew about.

'One day you will be involved in great events,' his grandmother had once told him, when he had been a child, before the *yehudi-een* had come and there had been war. 'Events that will change the world.'

Squatting there behind his rock, gazing at the ghostly flickering light and listening to the men's voices, he felt sure that this is what she had meant. And he was happy for that, because somehow, deep down, he had always known that his life would amount to more than simply tending a flock of scrawny desert goats.

PART II

A WEEK LATER

JERUSALEM

They walk close to the front of the procession, arm in arm, singing with the others, each holding a flaming taper so that the evening is freckled with a thousand points of flickering light. She has long brown hair gathered into an untidy bun on top of her head, and wears a thin spring dress of yellow cotton, the contours of her young, slim body echoing through the flimsy material, a rumour of veiled shapeliness. He is taller than her, and broader, a bear beside a gazelle, his face huge and craggy, like something crudely hewn out of wood, ugly and handsome at the same time. He keeps looking down at her, shaking his head as if unable to believe he is with someone so beautiful, so fragile and so gentle. She reads his thoughts and laughs. 'It's me who's the lucky one, Ari-yari,' she says. 'I'm going to be the happiest wife in the whole wide world.'

They come to an open space and the procession breaks and spreads, rearranging itself in front of a makeshift stage where speeches are made beneath a banner bearing the word PEACE. They hold hands and listen, applauding, cheering, glancing at each other constantly, eyes bright with love and hope.

After a while he leaves her, saying that he wants to get something to drink. Instead, chuckling to himself, he slips into a late-night florist's and buys her a flower, a single white lily, her favourite. He is on his way back, smiling at the thought of her delight as he sweeps the bloom out from behind his back, when he hears the explosion. At first he is uncertain from which direction the sound comes. Then he sees the plume of smoke and breaks into a jog, then a sprint, stomach tight with foreboding.

In the square there are bodies everywhere, and parts of bodies, and people screaming. He stumbles around yelling her name, feet slopping in blood, the trill of unanswered mobile phones echoing in his ears, eventually finding her beneath a shattered cypress tree, her dress blown away so that she is almost naked. Her legs have been torn off and are lying nearby.

'Oh my darling.' He chokes on his words, cradling her in his arms, her warm blood pumping over his shirt and jeans. 'Oh my beautiful darling Galia.'

Somehow she manages to raise her arm and, clasping a blistered hand round the back of his head, pulls his face down towards her own. She kisses him, her mouth broken and bloody, like a crushed crayon, and whispers into his ear, faintly, words that only he can hear, words that will stay with him for ever. And then her head flops back and she is dead.

Bewildered, empty, lonely beyond any loneliness he has ever known, he gazes down at her torn body, the lily still clutched in his hand, its petals red now. All around him the night fills with the wailing of sirens, as if the air itself is screaming in despair.

'Arieh!'

Sirens everywhere.

'Arieh!'

Lights, shouting, people running.

'Ben-Roi, you stupid cunt, what the fuck are you doing?'

Arieh Ben-Roi jerked awake, banging his head on the car window. His silver hip-flask had slipped from his hand, spilling what was left of the vodka into his lap, soaking his jeans. Sirens were blaring. His earpiece was going berserk.

'Go, man! For fuck's sake go!'

For a moment he sat there flummoxed, suspended between past and present; then, realizing what was going on, he flipped open the glove compartment, snatched his Jericho pistol and stumbled out of the taxi. In front of him a steep tarmaced road ran up towards the Lions Gate, where a black Mercedes was frantically trying to reverse, its tyres screeching. Behind, a phalanx of police cars had come skidding to a halt, blocking any escape from the Old City, their flashing lights throwing psychedelic patterns across the old

Muslim cemeteries ranged across the slopes to either side. He broke into a loping run, ripping the *keffiyeh* from his head and casting it aside.

They'd been planning the bust for over a month. An informer had tipped them off about a big dope delivery to the Old City dealers. No definite date, just a time and place: midnight, the Lions Gate. They'd been staking it out ever since, working undercover as vagrants, refuse collectors, tourists, lovers. For the past three nights Ben-Roi had been parked on the hill leading up to the gate disguised as an Arab taxi driver, waiting, watching, swigging from his hip-flask. And now, finally, the balloon had gone up. And he'd been asleep.

'Fuck it,' he muttered, blundering on up the hill, the car in front of him roaring and skidding like a cornered animal. 'Bloody fuck it!'

To his right, marksmen were stalking forward through the undergrowth of the Yusefiya cemetery; ahead, inside the Lions Gate, three men were spread-eagled, face down on the cobbles, surrounded by police.

'Take out the tyres!' screeched his earpiece. 'Shoot low!'

Ben-Roi dropped to his knees and raised his pistol. His hand was trembling with the vodka, and before he had time to steady it three cracks echoed around him, two from the cemetery, one from the wall above the gate. The Mercedes' front tyres exploded in unison, slewing the car into a wall. There was a pause, then the doors opened and three Palestinian men emerged, arms raised above their heads.

'*Udrubu aal ard! Sakro ayunuk!*' came an amplified voice. 'Hit the ground and close your eyes!'

The men obeyed, going down on their knees and then their bellies. A swarm of police flew from the shadows and descended on them, yanking their arms behind their backs, slapping handcuffs on their wrists, searching them.

'OK, guys, we've got them,' echoed the earpiece. 'Good work, everyone.'

Ben-Roi remained on his knees, breathing heavily; then, with a sigh, he flicked on the Jericho's safety catch, got to his feet and plodded up the hill towards the stricken Mercedes, fingers playing with a miniature silver menorah hanging on a chain around his neck.

'Kind of you to join us,' said a wiry man who was squatting beside one of the prisoners, hand clasped tightly around the back of the man's neck.

'Bloody radio,' muttered Ben-Roi, tapping his earpiece. 'Couldn't hear a thing.'

'Yeah, right.'

The man threw him a sceptical glance, hoisted the prisoner to his feet and marched him away towards a nearby police van. Ben-Roi considered going after him, arguing his case, but couldn't be bothered. What was the point? What was the point of anything these days? It was all a waste of time. Let Feldman think what he wanted. He didn't give a shit.

He stood watching as forensics officers in plastic gloves and white body-suits gathered around the Mercedes, then turned and, removing his earpiece, started back towards his car, alone, useless, unable to share in the general sense of satisfaction at a job well done. He remembered the time when, as a kid, he'd been sent out of class for wetting his shorts and felt the same sense of isolation now, of awkwardness and embarrassment and shame. Always he felt ashamed. That he should be like this. That he'd let himself go so badly. That he'd gone to buy the lily. That he'd lived.

Reaching the car, he threw a forlorn glance over his shoulder, then got in, started the engine and idled downhill, swinging out onto the Ophel Road. To his left, the shadowy, tree-filled well of the Kidron Valley dropped away below him; to his right, a three-metre walled embankment ran alongside the road, with above it the overgrown slope of the Muslim cemetery sweeping upwards towards the floodlit line of the Old City walls. He pushed down on the accelerator and changed up to third, covering a hundred metres before slowing again and, keeping one hand on the wheel, leaning down to retrieve his hip-flask. Most of its contents had spilled away, but there was still a trace of liquid in the bottom and, slowing the car still further, he put the flask to his lips, arched his head back and drained what was left, grimacing at the fiery taste in his throat and the sharpness of his self-loathing.

'You disgust me,' he mumbled. 'You're pathetic. Pathetic.'

He held the flask until the last few drops had splashed down into his mouth, then threw it over his shoulder into the back seat and depressed the accelerator again, jerking the steering wheel round to straighten the car, which had started to drift into the opposite carriageway, attracting a furious honking from an oncoming lorry.

'Fuck you!' he shouted, hammering his own horn. 'Fuck all of you!'

The lorry flashed past to his left. At the same moment something seemed to drop from the embankment to his right. It happened in a flash and, fuzzed as he was with vodka and weariness, his first, incoherent thought was that a large animal had leapt from the cemetery above. He slowed and glanced in his rear-view mirror, travelling a further fifty metres up the road before it registered that what he'd actually seen was a man jumping down from the embankment onto the pavement below, where he was now squatting, clutching his knee, which he seemed to have injured. Again, Ben-Roi's mind struggled to deal coherently with the information, and another fifty metres rolled by before it occurred to him that the man must be one of the dope pushers who'd somehow slipped through the police net. He swung into the kerb and grabbed his walkie-talkie.

'There's still one out here!' he shouted into the mouthpiece. 'Do you read? There's still one out here! Ophel Road, top of the Kidron path. I need back-up. Repeat. Need back-up.'

There was a cough of static, and a crackly voice acknowledged his request. He jammed the walkie-talkie into his pocket, grabbed his pistol and clambered out of the car. The Palestinian, aware that he had been spotted, had by now hobbled over the road and onto a broad stepped path leading down into the Kidron Valley. Ben-Roi broke into a lumbering sprint, dodging a truck full of aubergines coming from one direction and a pair of taxis from the other as he too crossed the road. A year ago the adrenalin would have been pumping through him. Now he was overweight and out of shape, and all he could think of was why the hell was he bothering to do this.

'Come on!' he urged himself, his lungs already starting to burn. 'Come on, you fat cunt!'

He reached the top of the path and saw his quarry limping along below him. He raised his Jericho, but the man was now too far away to be sure of the shot so he resumed running, down and down, a vicious stitch cutting into his side, his breath coming in short, painful rasps. The Palestinian was clearly in distress with his knee, and had he been fitter Ben-Roi would have swiftly narrowed the gap between them. As it was, he gained on the man only slowly and was still a good forty metres behind by the time they reached the valley floor, where the path started to level out, running alongside a row of ancient rock tombs cut back into the lower slopes of the Mount of Olives.

A line of blue flashing lights appeared ahead, cutting off his quarry's escape in that direction, forcing the man to clamber over a low retaining wall beside the path and double back on himself along the valley bottom. He was now below Ben-Roi and to his right, and, heaving himself over the wall, the detective bounded down a steep, grassy slope towards him. The man veered left, scrabbling up a rocky incline alongside the pyramid-roofed Tomb of Zechariah. Ben-Roi followed, feet scrabbling on the loose, sandy soil, hands tearing frantically at rocks and brambles and tufts of coarse grass, coughing and panting. He was by now almost at the end of his physical reserves, and halfway up the incline they gave out altogether, like a car suddenly running out of petrol, leaving him stranded, watching helplessly as the Palestinian continued upwards and disappeared above him.

'Fuck,' he groaned. 'Fuck, fuck, fucking fuck.'

He remained where he was for a moment, furiously sucking air deep down into his crumpled lungs, then, feebly, started upwards again, clambering over the top of the slope on all fours and collapsing in a heap at the foot of a twisted acacia tree. There was a burst of laughter.

'Dear oh dear, Ben-Roi, my grandmother could run faster than that!'

Feldman, the wiry detective with whom he had

spoken earlier, was standing above him accompanied by four uniformed policeman, two of them holding the Palestinian in an arm lock. He reached out a hand, which Ben-Roi slapped away.

'*Lech zayen et ima shelcha.* Go fuck your mother, Feldman.'

He struggled to his feet and took a step forward so that he was in front of the Palestinian. The man was younger than he'd expected. His left eye was starting to swell and blacken, his lip was cut. Feldman nodded at the policemen holding him, who tightened their grip.

'Go on,' he said, winking at Ben-Roi. 'You know you want to. We didn't see anything.'

Ben-Roi glanced at Feldman, then back at the Palestinian. God, he'd love to do it. Smash the little bastard's face in. Show him what he thought of him. Of all his kind. He came forward another half step, fist clenching. As he did so a soft voice echoed in his ear, near yet at the same time immeasurably distant, accompanied by a fleeting vision of a woman's face, grey-eyed, beautiful. It lasted only a fraction of a second and then was gone, along with the voice. He gazed at the Palestinian, breathing heavily, then, touching his hand to the menorah around his neck, turned away and started back down the slope again.

Behind him, Feldman shook his head. 'Poor Arieh,' he muttered. 'Poor stupid fucking Arieh.'

EGYPT – BETWEEN LUXOR AND EDFU

Khalifa swung out from behind the lorry, pulled past it and swung back in again, pumping the car horn throughout the manoeuvre. Away to his left a distant range of yellow hills undulated and swelled like a line of crumbling sandcastles; to his right, nearer, beyond a patchwork swathe of cane and banana fields, the Nile meandered its way slowly northwards, its surface black and smooth, like a band of polished metal. He lit a cigarette, pushed the accelerator to the floor and turned on the radio. Shaaban Abdel-Rehim blasted out, singing his hit song 'Ana Bakrah Israel' – 'I Hate Israel'. Khalifa listened for a moment, then changed to another station. A sign flashed past indicating it was sixty kilometres to Edfu.

It was over a week since the body had been found at Malqata, and in that time he had managed to dig up almost no new information about the mysterious Piet Jansen. Admittedly he'd had to conduct his investigations surreptitiously behind Chief Hassani's back, coming into the office early, staying late, making a few snatched calls at lunchtime, fitting it in wherever he could around other police work. Even without these constraints, however, he doubted he would have uncovered a great deal more about his subject. Everything about Jansen's life, from the obsessive security at his villa to the complete lack of information about his past, seemed geared towards keeping that life private. More than private. Secret. Walled in. Inaccessible.

He had applied for and been granted Egyptian citizenship in October 1945. That much at least Khalifa had found out from an old contact at the Interior Ministry. Thereafter he'd lived in Alexandria, running a moderately successful bookbinding business from a house on Sharia Amin Fikhry, before moving down to Luxor in March 1972, buying first his villa and then, seven months later, the hotel (changing its name to Menna-Ra from the more prosaic Hotel Good Welcome). His bank statements revealed that he was, if not well off, at least financially comfortable, while according to medical reports he suffered from piles, arthritis, bunions and angina, as well as advanced prostate cancer, which had been diagnosed in January 2005. His limp was the legacy of a car accident in 1982 that had shattered his right knee.

There were a few other random pieces of information – Jansen was a regular user of the Egyptological library at Chicago House, a keen gardener, had no police record – but that was about it. When he had first come to Egypt, why and where from, and what, if any, his connection with Hannah Schlegel was – all remained lost in a fog of obscurity. Plenty of people knew him, it seemed, but, when pushed, nobody actually seemed to know anything about him. It was as if he didn't have a past, as if there was nothing below the surface. Even Carla Shaw's suggestion that he was originally from Holland had proved a dead end, the Dutch Embassy informing him that Piet Jansen was one of their country's most common names and that without a birth date or location it would be impossible to trace him.

There had been just one potentially interesting lead, and that had come from the dead man's phone bill. Jansen hadn't made many calls, and most of those had been to the Menna-Ra. Only one other number, in Cairo, had figured with any degree of frequency on the bill – nine times in the last three months. Khalifa had checked it out with Egypt Telecom, thinking that it might be one of the friends Carla Shaw had mentioned when they'd interviewed her a week ago. Ultimately, however, this too had proved to be a red herring, the number belonging not to a private address but to a public payphone, in the El-Maadi district of the city.

He had, in short, hardly moved forward at all. Which is why he was in the car now.

He sped on, passing through small, ramshackle

villages, the hills and river to either side sometimes pressing right up close to the road,
sometimes veering away into the far distance as
though startled by the speeding traffic. The sun
was lifting to his left, floating up into the sky like
an egg-yolk rising through boiling water, its
growing heat causing the moist, alluvial earth of
the cultivation to shimmer and steam like a
baking cake.

He hit Edfu thirty minutes later, crossing the Nile
on the town's four-lane bridge and negotiating his
way through its dusty, gridlocked streets before
continuing south again, on the west bank of the
river this time. Six kilometres on he pulled up beside
a roadside stall to ask for directions. Two kilometres
beyond that he turned left off the main highway
onto a sandy track that wound its way through
fields of onions and cabbages, occasionally plunging
into dense groves of *falak* trees, before eventually
petering out in front of an ornate, whitewashed
house perched beside the river. The home of Ehab
Ali Mahfouz, Khalifa's former boss, the man who
had led the Schlegel investigation. He pulled up
and switched off the engine.

Coming here was a major gamble for Khalifa.
Although he had retired from the force three years
earlier, Mahfouz still wielded considerable influence. If he took offence at the visit he would only
have to say the word for Khalifa to be busted
straight down to constable and posted to some
godforsaken station out in the middle of the

214

Western Desert. That or be kicked out of the force altogether. If he wanted to get the case officially reopened, however – and he'd reached a point in his investigations where he could go no further working unofficially – it was a gamble Khalifa had no choice but to take. Chief Hassani wasn't going to help him. If he went over Hassani's head – to the district commissioner, say – it would snag him in a bureaucratic tangle that could take months to resolve. Mahfouz had the power to get things moving immediately. The question was, would he be prepared to wield that power? Khalifa didn't remember him as a man who liked to admit to mistakes.

He drummed his fingers nervously on the steering wheel, then grabbed a typewritten report of his findings so far, got out and, crossing to the front door, rang the bell. There was a pause, then a sound of approaching footsteps. The door opened, revealing a dark-skinned, middle-aged woman dressed in black robes and *tarha*. The housekeeper, Khalifa guessed.

'*Sabah el-khayr*,' he said. 'I've come to see the chief inspector.'

'Commander Mahfouz isn't seeing anyone at the moment,' said the woman, emphasizing the word 'commander', the rank with which Mahfouz had retired from the force.

'If I could just have a few minutes. I've come all the way from Luxor. It's important.'

'Do you have an appointment?'

Khalifa admitted he didn't.

'Then he won't see you.'

She started to close the door, but Khalifa stepped into the narrowing gap.

'Please tell him that Inspector Yusuf Khalifa is here,' he said firmly. 'Tell him it's urgent.'

She glared at him angrily, then, ordering him to stay where he was, disappeared into the house.

Khalifa leant against the doorframe and lit a cigarette, inhaling deeply. Despite his habitual run-ins with Hassani he wasn't an innately confrontational person, and situations like this didn't come easily to him. He found himself thinking of the time at university when he had contradicted a teacher in front of the whole class, told him he'd got some fact wrong, and the stomach-churning fear he had felt at holding up his hand and speaking out. It was the same fear he felt now – that of the poor man who has clawed his way up the ladder and is terrified of doing anything that might pitch him back down to where he has come from.

He took another drag and, turning, stared out across the fields through which he'd just driven, watching as a distant, half-naked figure hacked at the earth with a *touria*, his body rising and falling with the slow, rhythmic precision of a clockwork toy.

'What am I doing?' he thought to himself. 'What the hell am I doing?'

The woman returned a couple of minutes later. He was half-expecting her to say Mahfouz did not wish to see him. As it was, she told him to extinguish his cigarette and, throwing him a look that said 'this is against my better judgement', ushered him into the cool interior of the house.

'The commander's not well,' she explained tersely as they passed through a series of rooms towards the rear of the building. 'He only came out of hospital a fortnight ago. The doctor said he wasn't to be disturbed.'

They came into a large, sunlit lounge with a tiled floor and an ornate chandelier hanging from the ceiling. On the far side a set of glass doors gave on to a flower-filled garden.

'He's through there,' she said. 'I'll bring some tea. And no smoking.'

She eyeballed Khalifa to make sure he had got the message, then turned and disappeared.

For a moment he stood gazing up at a large framed photograph of Mahfouz shaking hands with President Mubarak, then stepped through the doors into the garden. Ahead, across an immaculately manicured lawn bordered by beds of pink and yellow roses, a small wooden platform jutted out into the river. On it, its back to him, sat a sun lounger shaded by a green and white striped parasol. He muttered a swift prayer and started forwards across the grass, reaching the jetty and ducking beneath the umbrella.

'I was wondering when you'd come,' said a croaking voice. 'I've been expecting you for over a week now.'

Mahfouz was lying propped up on pillows, one hand flopped across the lounger's arm rest, the other clutching a plastic oxygen mask from which a thick, intestine-like tube led down to a metal cylinder on the decking beneath him. Khalifa was shocked by the change in his appearance. The last time he had seen him, over five years ago, he had been a huge, broad-shouldered man, muscular and physically imposing, like a heavyweight wrestler (the Edfu Ox, they used to call him). Now he was barely recognizable, his body shrivelled and shrunken into something resembling a strip of worn leather, with a hollow, skull-like face and spindly, fleshless limbs. Most of his hair and teeth had gone, and his brown eyes, which Khalifa remembered as having been bright and fierce, had dulled to the colour of stagnant water. Beneath his white djellaba swelled the tell-tale bulge of a urostomy bag.

'Not much of me left.' He chuckled mirthlessly, noting the expression on Khalifa's face. 'Bladder, bowel, one lung – all gone. I feel like an empty suitcase.'

He started coughing and, raising the oxygen mask to his face, pressed a button on the front of it and sucked.

'I'm sorry,' mumbled Khalifa. 'I didn't know.'

Mahfouz shrugged weakly, drawing in oxygen, gazing at a tangled raft of *ward-i-Nil* drifting slowly by on the river. It was almost a minute before his breathing stabilized and he was able to lower the mask again, nodding Khalifa into a chair beside him.

'I've got about a month,' he rasped. 'Two at the outside. With the morphine it's just about bearable.'

Khalifa didn't know what to say.

'I'm sorry,' he repeated.

Mahfouz smiled humourlessly.

'Punishment,' he wheezed. 'What goes around comes around.'

Before Khalifa could ask what he meant, the housekeeper appeared carrying a tray with two glasses of tea on it. She laid it down on a low wooden table, plumped up her employer's pillows and, with a surly glance at Khalifa, departed again.

'Omm Mohammed,' grunted Mahfouz. 'Miserable bitch, eh? Don't take it personally. She's the same with everyone.'

He leant to one side and stretched out a trembling hand towards his tea. He couldn't reach it, and Khalifa had to pick up the glass and pass it across.

'Mrs Mahfouz?' he asked, trying to make conversation.

'Died. Last year.'

Khalifa hung his head. He hadn't expected any of this. Mahfouz sipped his tea, peering at Khalifa over the top of the glass.

'You're thinking you shouldn't have come, aren't you?' he wheezed, reading the detective's thoughts.

'That the old man's suffering enough. Why add to his problems?'

Khalifa shrugged, staring down through the slats of the platform at the muddy water sliding past beneath.

'You said you were expecting me,' he muttered after a brief silence.

Mahfouz shrugged.

'Hassani called. Told me what was going on. That you were nosing around the Schlegel case. If you were the Khalifa I remembered, I knew you'd come eventually.'

He smiled to himself, the expression more pained than mirthful, and broke into a renewed fit of coughing, his glass shaking in his hand, droplets of tea splashing onto his djellaba. He motioned Khalifa to take the glass from him and, raising his mask, took another long, slow gulp of oxygen. The detective turned away and gazed out across the river. It was a glorious view – the blue-black water, the whispering reed beds, a lone felucca gliding past close to the opposite shore, its billowing sail pushing at the sky like a cheek on a pillow. Mahfouz noticed the direction of his gaze and dragged the mask aside.

'My one consolation,' he croaked. 'At least I'll die with a nice view.'

He replaced the mask and slumped back, gulping oxygen like a fish stranded on a mudbank. Khalifa took a sip of his own tea and started to reach for his cigarettes, then remembered what the housekeeper had told him about not smoking and clasped his hands in his lap instead. Back across the garden a bee-eater was fluttering over one of the rose-beds, peering down at the flowers beneath.

Eventually, Mahfouz recovered sufficiently to remove the mask again. Khalifa leant forward and handed him the typewritten report.

'I thought you ought to see this, sir.'

Mahfouz took the report and, wincing as he adjusted his position, read slowly through it, turning the pages with trembling hands. When he came to the end he laid it aside and dropped his shrivelled head back onto his pillows.

'I always suspected.'

His voice was so quiet Khalifa thought he'd misheard him.

'Sir?'

'That it was Jansen who killed the old woman. I always suspected.'

Khalifa sat staring at him, shocked.

'Not what you were expecting, eh?' said Mahfouz with a weak chuckle.

He turned his head slightly, looking across towards the far shore of the river where a herd of water buffalo had lumbered down to the water to drink, their bony hindquarters swaying pendulously from side to side. Khalifa reached up and rubbed his temples, trying to gather his thoughts. He felt as if a heavy wave had swept over him, choking and disorientating him.

'You knew?' he managed to mumble.

'Not for sure,' said Mahfouz. 'But the evidence certainly seemed to point that way. The hat, the walking stick, the house near Karnak. The feet-thing was interesting. I didn't know about that.'

A small bulb of spittle had formed at the corner of his mouth and he wiped at it with the sleeve of his djellaba.

'I knew him, you see. Jansen. Not well, but well enough. We both loved gardens. Belonged to the Horticultural Society. Used to go to the same meetings. Nasty man. Cold. Good with roses, though.' He was still trying to wipe away the glob of spit. 'When I saw the marks on Schlegel's body, heard the guard's story about a bird or whatever it was, it seemed a strange coincidence. Especially with Jansen's attitude towards the Jews, and his living so near to the murder scene. It was circum-stantial, admittedly, but if we'd followed it up I'm sure we'd have got him.'

He lowered his arm again, breathing heavily. There was a loud splash as a pair of geese came down in the middle of the river, legs splayed in front of them, wings spread. Khalifa found that his hands were trembling.

'But why?' he asked, voice hoarse, bewildered. 'If you thought Jansen was guilty, why convict Gemal?'

Mahfouz was staring at the geese.

'Because I was told to.' After a brief pause, he added, 'By al-Hakim.'

Again Khalifa had that feeling of being hit by a heavy wave, rolled over and over, everything around him out of control, all his points of reference swept away. Until his death the previous year Farouk al-Hakim had been the head of the Jihaz Amn al Daoula, Egypt's state security service.

'I always knew it would catch up with me,' wheezed Mahfouz. 'These things invariably do. In a sense it's a relief. It's been with me too long. Better to get it out in the open. Face up to it.'

There was a loud horn blast away to their right, around a bend in the river, and a giant Nile barge hove slowly into view, laden down with a cargo of quarried sandstone, its prow scoring a deep furrow through the flat surface of the water, like a chisel being hammered across a length of smooth, dark wood. It had reached and passed them before Mahfouz spoke again.

'I knew from the start it was going to be a difficult case,' he sighed, his voice barely louder than a whisper. 'They always are when politics gets involved. Schlegel was killed less than a month after the Ismailiya massacre. You remember that? Nine Israeli tourists butchered on a bus. And now another dead Israeli. Didn't look good. Especially with the Americans. They were about to sign off on some big loan programme. Millions of dollars at stake. You know what they're like about Israel. The Schlegel thing could have fucked it all up. Believe me, there were a lot of worried people up in Cairo. Al-Hakim took charge personally. There was massive pressure for a quick conviction.'

He paused, trying to catch his breath. Khalifa was drumming his fingers on his knees, trying to get a grip on what he was hearing. From the outset he had assumed he was simply dealing with an accidental miscarriage of justice. Now it appeared he was involved in something far more complex and insidious.

'But if you knew it was Jansen, why did al-Hakim tell you to convict someone else?'

Mahfouz waved a hand helplessly.

'No idea. Didn't know then, don't know now. I told al-Hakim about Jansen, but he said he was off limits. Said dragging him into it would only make matters worse. Piss the Jews off even more. Those were his words. If we investigated Jansen it would just piss the Jews off even more. He told me to find someone else to take the rap. So we fingered Gemal instead.'

His wheezing was becoming progressively worse and, raising the oxygen mask, he took another series of gulps, his frail chest jerking up and down like a set of punctured bellows, his hands trembling uncontrollably. With a faint shiver of disgust, Khalifa noticed the bag beneath his djellaba slowly swelling as urine flowed into it through the valve in his abdomen. There was another horn blast as the Nile barge disappeared northwards round another bend in the river.

'Set me up for life, that case,' choked Mahfouz,

lowering the mask again. 'Got a promotion, my name in the papers, a telegram from Mubarak. It meant fuck all compared to the guilt, though. Not about Gemal. The man was a piece of shit. Deserved everything he got. But his wife and kids . . .'

He broke off, raising a stick-like arm and running it over his eyes. The strange meeting with Gemal's wife flashed into Khalifa's mind. *It comes in the post. No note, no name, nothing. Just three thousand Egyptian pounds, in hundred notes.*

'It's you that's been sending them money,' he said quietly.

Mahfouz looked up, surprised, then dropped his head again.

'It was the least I could do. Help them survive. Get the kids through school. A pretty empty gesture, considering.'

Khalifa shook his head, stood up and walked to the edge of the jetty, gazing down at a shoal of Nile perch drifting in the shallows beaneath.

'Did Hassani know?'

Mahfouz shook his head. 'Not at the time. I told him later, after Gemal hanged himself. He was just trying to protect me. Don't judge him too harshly.'

'And the case file? It's missing from the records room.'

'Hassani burnt it. We thought it would be best. Just forget the whole thing. Consign it to the past.' He chuckled bitterly. 'But then that's the problem with the past, isn't it? It's never really past. It's always there. Clinging on. Like a leech. Sucking out the blood. Whatever you do, whatever you say, you can never really get away from it. I've tried. Believe me. Like a fucking leech. Draining you.'

He motioned weakly towards his tea, indicating that his throat was dry, that he needed liquid. Khalifa stepped forward and passed him the glass. He couldn't keep it steady on his own, and in the end Khalifa had to hold it for him as he leant forward and slurped. When he had finished he slumped backwards again, as floppy and helpless as a rag doll.

'I was a good policeman,' he whispered. 'Whatever you might think. Forty years I gave to the service. Lost count of the number of cases I solved. The Aswan Express Robbery. The Gezira Murders. Girgis Wahdi. You remember him? Girgis al-Gazzar, the Butcher of Butneya. So many cases. But it's this one that lives with me. I let a murderer get away with it.'

He was tiring rapidly now, his breathing coming in short, sharp gasps, his limbs trembling. He grasped the oxygen mask and took several breaths, grimacing as though in pain.

'Reopen the case,' he murmured, laying the mask aside. 'That's what you want, isn't it? I'll speak to Hassani and whoever else needs to be spoken to. It won't have any practical effect. Al-Hakim's dead. Jansen's dead. Gemal's dead. But at least you can find out the truth. It's about time.'

There was a sound of footsteps as the house-keeper approached across the lawn, carrying a small surgical tray.

'You?' asked Khalifa.

Mahfouz coughed.

'What about me? I'll be dead in a few weeks. At least I'll go knowing I did the right thing in the end.'

He raised the oxygen mask, took another gulp, then, with what strength he had left, fumbled out a hand and grasped Khalifa's arm.

'Find out the truth,' he whispered. 'For me, for Gemal's wife, for Allah if you want. But be careful. He was a dangerous man, Jansen. Had friends in high places. Nasty secrets. I'll try to protect you. But be careful.'

A cloudy eye swivelled wearily towards Khalifa, then slumped shut. The detective gazed down at him for a moment, then, slipping his arm free, he set off past the housekeeper and back across the lawn. Half an hour ago he'd been praying for Mahfouz to allow the case to be reopened. After what he'd just heard, he now rather wished he hadn't.

JERUSALEM

Layla couldn't remember when she had first become a member of the American Colony Breakfast Club, but its Friday-morning meetings had for several years been a regular fixture in her weekly diary. It wasn't a proper club as such, more an informal gathering at the American Colony Hotel in East Jerusalem where, over coffee and croissants, a group of journalists, aid workers and minor diplomats – whoever happened to be in town at the time – would discuss the major issues of the moment. Breakfast would generally segue into lunch, lunch into tea and, a few times a year, tea into an alcohol-fuelled dinner, where arguments would rage. On one memorable occasion the *Washington Post* bureau chief had broken a bottle of wine over the head of the Danish cultural attaché.

Layla arrived a little after ten, and after slowing to drop a letter into the hotel's post box, continued through the cool, stone-floored foyer and out into the sunny central courtyard behind, with its bubbling fountain, pots of flowering plants and metal tables shaded beneath cream-coloured parasols. Several 'club' regulars were already there – her friend Nuha, Onz Schenker of the *Jerusalem Post*, Sam Rogerson from Reuters, Tom Roberts, the guy from the British Consulate who was forever trying to chat her up – as well as a couple of new faces she didn't recognize, all sitting beneath a gnarled orange tree. They were already deep in discussion.

Pulling up a chair, she poured herself a cup of black coffee from a pot on the table beside them. Roberts glanced across at her, smiled nervously, then looked away again.

'The whole thing's a joke,' Rogerson was saying, running a hand over his balding head. 'It's a road map to fucking nowhere. Until Israel gets to grips with the central issue, which is that they've shat on the Palestinians and need to make significant concessions to redress that, the blood's just going to flow and flow.'

'I'll tell you what the central fucking issue is,' growled Schenker, puffing on a Noblesse and scowling. 'It's that in the final analysis the Arabs aren't interested in talking peace. There's fuck all point in offering concessions when all they really want to do is to wipe Israel off the map.'

'That's bullshit,' said Nuha.

'Really? You're telling me al-Mulatham suddenly wants to negotiate? That Hamas are about to acknowledge Israel's right to exist?'

'Come on, Onz, they're not representative of the Palestinian people,' said a small, heavily made-up woman named Deborah Zelon, a stringer for Associated Press.

'So who is representative? Abbas? Qurei? Guys most of the population don't even bloody trust? Arafat, the man who tortured his own people, embezzled their aid money, was offered peace on a plate at Camp David—'

'Not that again!' cried Nuha.

'Barak offered him ninety-seven per cent of the West Bank!' shouted Schenker, jabbing his cigarette at her. 'His own bloody state. And he turned it down!'

'What he was offered, as you well know,' said Nuha, glaring, 'were a collection of cantons surrounded by illegal Israeli settlements and with no international borders. That and a shitty bit of desert that you lot have used as a toxic dumping ground for the last twenty years. There was no way he could have accepted it. He would have been lynched.'

Schenker snorted, grinding his cigarette out in an ashtray. A waiter came out with more coffee and a large plate of croissants, followed a moment later by an elderly man in a tweed jacket and half-moon spectacles, who pulled up a chair and joined the group. Nuha introduced him as Professor Faisal Bekal of Al-Quds University. He raised an arthritic hand in greeting.

'Loath as I am to say it,' said Rogerson, picking up the conversation where it had left off, 'but I agree with Schenker on that last point. Arafat screwed up. Abbas and Qurei mean well, but they just don't command enough respect to cut a realistic deal and bring all their people with them. The Palestinians need a new figurehead.'

'The Israelis don't?' snorted Nuha.

'Of course they do,' said Rogerson, taking an apple from a bowl in the centre of the table and starting to peel it with his penknife. 'Sharon's a fucking disaster. But that doesn't change the fact that the guys you've got at the moment aren't going to sort this thing out. Not permanently.'

'So who is?' put in Deborah Zelon. 'Dahlan and Rajoub haven't got the power base. Erekat's a non-starter. Barghouti's in prison. There's no-one else.'

Professor Bekal reached slowly for a croissant, breaking it in two and laying one half on the edge of the table while nibbling on the other.

'There's Sa'eb Marsoudi,' he said quietly, wiping crumbs from his lips, his voice thin and slightly tremulous.

'You think?' asked Rogerson.

The old man tilted his head to one side.

'Why not? He's young, he's intelligent, the people love him. And he's got the credentials. Son of an activist, grandson of an activist, leader of the First Intifada, yet enough of a pragmatist to know there's never going to be a free Palestine without negotiation and compromise.'

'He's also got Jewish blood on his hands,' snarled Schenker.

'In this part of the world everyone's got someone's

blood on their hands, Mr Schenker,' sighed Bekal. 'The point is what they do now, not what they have done in the past. Yes, Marsoudi smuggled arms into Gaza. And yes, those same arms were no doubt used to kill Israelis. Perhaps the same Israelis who evicted his family from their land, imprisoned his father, blew up his brother. He served his time. Now he's one of the few Palestinians with the courage to openly reject violent resistance. I think he could do some good things.'

'If he lives long enough,' grunted Nuha. 'Hamas want to cut his throat.'

'There you go, Onz,' said Rogerson, who had managed to remove his apple peel in a single, unbroken spiral. 'On that basis he should be your best mate.'

Schenker gulped at his coffee and lit another Noblesse.

'They're all as bad as each other,' he grunted. 'You can't trust any of the bastards.'

'Hark the voice of reason and hope!' laughed Deborah Zelon.

The discussion moved on to other topics, opinions flying back and forth like ping-pong balls, the babble of voices rising and falling, its rhythm broken every now and then by a sudden burst of laughter or explosion of shouting, the latter usually from Onz Schenker, whose conversational spectrum appeared to contain only two postures – angry, and very angry. Other people drifted into the courtyard and joined the gathering, the numbers gradually swelling until there were more than twenty of them and what had been a single debate gradually fragmented into a series of subsidiary discussions between smaller groups.

Tom Roberts came over and sat down beside Layla.

'Hello, Layla,' he said, his tongue lingering slightly on the first 'L' of her name – a hangover from his childhood, he had once explained, when he had had a bad stutter. 'How are you doing?'

'Good,' she said. 'I'm sorry I didn't return your call. I've been a bit . . .'

He waved his hand to show it didn't matter. He was older than her, mid-forties, tall and thin, bookish, with round glasses and a shy, self-deprecating manner. Not unattractive, but not particularly attractive either. Bland. For some reason he reminded her of a giraffe.

'You're very quiet today,' he went on, his mouth again catching slightly, this time on the 'v' of very. 'Normally you give Schenker a good run for his money.'

She smiled. 'Thought I'd give him a day off.'

'Things on your mind?'

'You could say that.'

It had been a busy week for her. The day after the meal with Nuha she had written two and a half articles, good-going even by her standards, including a two-thousand-word profile of Baruch Har-Zion for the *New York Review* (it was out that very day). After that she'd gone down to Gaza to do a colour piece on domestic violence – an increasing and rarely acknowledged problem in Palestinian society – barely having time to write that up before the *Guardian* had sent her over to Limassol to cover a conference on Palestinian aid programmes. She had arrived back late the previous evening and had spent half the night transcribing tapes, only finally falling into bed at four a.m. for a few hours' restless sleep.

It was not tiredness that was troubling her now, however, but that damned letter. She couldn't seem to get the thing off her mind. All week it had been there, lurking at the back of her thoughts, intriguing her, goading her. *I am in possession of information that could prove invaluable to this man in his struggle against the Zionist oppressor... In return I can offer what would, I believe, be the biggest scoop of your already illustrious career... The information of which I speak is intimately connected with the enclosed document.* The more she had thought about it the more convinced she had become that her initial assessment had been wrong; that the letter was neither a prank nor an attempt to entrap her, but rather the genuine article. She had no concrete evidence for this, just a gut feeling, an instinct, the same instinct that told her a story lead was worth following, an interviewee trustworthy.

In what little time had been left to her between writing articles and travelling she had made some tentative enquiries as to the identity of the boy who had delivered the letter, but had drawn a blank. The curious construction of the introductory 'would like to put to you a proposition' suggested to her that the letter's author was not a native English speaker, but beyond that there were no clues as to his identity (somehow she felt sure it was a man). Whoever it was had said they would be in contact again in the near future, but so far she had heard nothing.

Which left the curious photocopied document. She had run it past a contact at the Hebrew University, who had suggested it might be some sort of code, although he had had no idea how to decipher it. A search for GR on the internet had, as expected, thrown up an enormous number of matches – more than a million of them, for God's sake – and after scrolling through the first thirty or so she had given it up as a waste of time. She had hit a dead end.

'Anything I can help with?'

Tom Roberts was looking at her expectantly.

'You said you had things on your mind,' he added, noting the confused look on her face. 'I was wondering if I could help.'

'I doubt it,' she said, finishing her coffee. 'Unless you're any good at cracking codes.'

'Actually, I'm not bad. Sort of an amateur hobby. What's the context?'

She raised her eyebrows questioningly.

'Is it a letter, an official document?'

'A letter, I think,' replied Layla. 'Old. Medieval

maybe. Or ancient. I can't make head or tail of it. It's just a long sequence of letters with some sort of signature at the bottom. GR.'

He pursed his lips, thinking, then shook his head to indicate that the initials meant nothing to him.

'It's my day off,' he said after a short pause. 'I could take a look if you like.'

She hesitated, knowing that he was attracted to her and not wanting to complicate things.

Before she could refuse the offer, he added, 'No strings attached. Scout's honour. I think after six months I've just about got the message.'

She looked at him for a moment, then smiled and laid her hand on his.

'I'm sorry, Tom. You must think I'm a real bitch.'

'Part of the attraction, to be honest,' he said, grinning wistfully.

She squeezed his hand.

'It would be great if you could take a look. One condition, though. You let me make you lunch.'

'If only you had a code to crack every day,' he said, smiling. 'When's good for you?'

'No time like the present,' said Layla, pushing back her chair and coming to her feet. 'I think I've had my Schenker fix for the week.'

Roberts grabbed his jacket and they made their farewells, Nuha throwing Layla a questioning glance which she returned with a slight shake of her head, as if to say, 'It's not what you think.' As they crossed the courtyard into the hotel foyer, Onz Schenker's voice exploded behind them.

'Yehuda Milan is the last fucking person that can save this country! War hero or no war hero, the man's a fucking liability.'

'Why's that, Onz?' came Sam Rogerson's voice, shouting. 'Because he might actually cut a realistic deal with the Palestinians? It's people like you who are the liability!'

'You're an anti-semite, Rogerson!'

'My wife's a fucking Jew! How can I be an anti-semite?'

'Fuck you, Rogerson!'

'No, fuck you, Schenker! Fuck you right up your fat stinking fascist fucking arse!'

There was a scraping of chairs, the sound of a plate smashing, and a cacophony of shouts telling the two men to sit down and stop being stupid. By that point Layla and Tom Roberts had passed through the hotel foyer and out beneath its arched, bougainvillea-covered front entrance, the voices of their Breakfast Club colleagues fading behind them.

TEL AVIV, THE SHERATON HOTEL

'When people ask me why I oppose the so-called peace process, why I believe in a strong Israel governed by Jews, for Jews, with no Arab presence in our midst, I like to tell them the story of my grandmother.'

Har-Zion leant away from the microphone and took a short sip of water, gazing out at the lunch guests seated in front of him. It was a good crowd, business people mostly, plenty of Americans. A hundred guests, two hundred dollars a head – that was a lot of money for Chayalei David. And that was before the promises of private donations, which would at least double the total. Fifty thousand dollars, say. A lot of money.

Despite that, he wasn't enjoying himself. He never did at these sort of occasions. The suits, the polite conversation, the glad-handing – it wasn't for him. Give him a battlefield any day, or a crowd of screaming Arabs protesting at another Warriors of David occupation. Give him action.

Involuntarily he glanced down at the seat to his right, where his wife Miriam had always used to sit, before the cancer had taken her. Instead of her small, neatly dressed frame he was confronted by an elderly rabbi in a large, fur-trimmed *shtreimel*. He stared at him for a moment as if confused by his presence, then, with a shake of his head, leant back to the microphone and continued speaking.

'My grandmother, my mother's mother, died when I was only ten, so I never got to know her properly. Even in the few years I did know her, however, I realized she was a remarkable woman. She made food like you never tasted – borscht, *gefilte* fish, *kneidls*. The perfect Jewish grandmother!'

A ripple of laughter echoed around the room.

'She did more than cook, however. She knew the Torah better than any rabbi I ever met – no offence.'

He turned to the rabbi beside him, who smiled magnanimously. Another ripple of laughter.

'And sung like no *hazzan* you have ever heard. Even today, if I close my eyes, I can hear her chanting the *kerovah*, so sweet, like a nightingale. If she was here now she would enchant you. More than I am doing, certainly!'

A third echo of laughter, accompanied by a few muffled shouts of 'Not true!' Har-Zion raised his glass and took another sip of water.

'She was a strong woman too. Brave. She had to be to survive two years in Gross-Rosen.'

This time there were no shouts or laughter. All eyes were focused on him.

'I loved my grandmother very dearly,' he continued, putting down his glass. 'She taught me so much, told such wonderful stories, invented such great games to play. There was only one thing about her that made me sad: in the time I knew her she never once took me to her breast and hugged me, as grandmothers are meant to. Especially Jewish grandmothers.'

The audience was quiet now, wondering where the story was leading. Beneath his suit Har-Zion's skin felt tight and itchy, as though he had been bound into a pepper-filled straitjacket. He ran his finger around the inside of his collar, trying to loosen it a bit.

'At first I did not take much notice of this. As I grew older, however, it began to affect me. Maybe my *bubeh* does not love me, I thought. Maybe I have done something wrong. I wanted to ask her why she would never take me in her arms, but I sensed it was not something she wished to speak about, so nothing was ever said. It made me sad and confused.'

Behind him, his bodyguard Avi coughed. It sounded unnaturally loud in the rapt silence that had enveloped the room.

'Only after she died did my mother explain to me the solution to this strange mystery. As a young woman my grandmother had lived in a *shtetl* in southern Russia. Every Saturday night, after they had been drinking, the Cossacks would come. The Jews would lock themselves in their houses, but the Cossacks would kick down the doors and drag people out onto the street, where they would beat and even kill them. It was fun for them, sport. They were only dirty Jews, after all.'

A hundred pairs of eyes bored into Har-Zion. Beside him, the rabbi was staring at his lap, his head shaking sadly from side to side.

'On one of these occasion the Cossacks seized my grandmother. She was fifteen at the time, a beautiful girl, with long hair and bright eyes. I don't think I need to tell you what they did to her. Five of them. Drunk. In the street, where everyone could see. Afterwards, when they had finished, they wanted a souvenir of their night out. Do you know what souvenir they chose?'

He let the question hang a moment.

'One of my grandmother's breasts. They sliced it off with a knife and carried it away with them, a trophy to hang on their wall.'

There were murmurs of horror. At a table near the front a woman held her napkin to her mouth. The rabbi whispered, 'Dear God.'

'This is why my grandmother would never hug me,' said Har-Zion quietly. 'Because she knew I would notice something wrong, and she was ashamed. She did not want me to know about her pain. She did not want me to be sad for her.'

He stopped, letting his words sink in. There were other stories he could have told, in the same vein. So many other stories. About his own experiences – the teasing, the beatings, the time at the orphanage when they had forced a broom-handle deep into his rectum to cries of 'Fuck the Jew-boy! Fuck the Jew-boy!' Every day of his childhood seemed to have been shadowed with fear and humiliation. But he preferred not to speak about it. Had never spoken about it. Not even to Miriam, his own wife. It was too raw, too painful, worse even than the burns that had scoured his body and left him looking like a melted waxwork. So he told the story of his grandmother instead, which was close, but not so close as to make him crack, to open up the floodgates. There was so much pain inside. So much horror. Sometimes he felt as if he was drowning in blackness.

He took a third sip of water and, coughing to clear his throat, drove on to the end of the speech, vowing that what had happened to his grandmother would never happen to any Jew again, that he would do whatever he had to do to defend his people, to keep Israel strong.

When he had finished, the audience came to its feet as one, cheering and applauding. He acknowledged the ovation, skin itching uncontrollably beneath his suit, then sat down, Avi stepping forward and helping him ease his chair into the table. The rabbi patted him on the arm.

'You are a good man, Baruch.'

Har-Zion smiled, but made no reply. Am I, he wondered? Good and bad, right and wrong – they no longer seemed to have any meaning. All there was was belief in God and the struggle for survival. It's what he'd been doing his whole life. What his people had been doing for their whole life. He turned slightly, stiffly, gazing at the seven-branched menorah stencilled onto a panel behind his table, thinking about Layla al-Madani and al-Mulatham and all the rest of it, before turning back to the front again and smiling as a photographer came up to take his picture.

JERUSALEM

It was early afternoon when Arieh Ben-Roi drove his battered white BMW through the Jaffa Gate into the Old City, pulling up at the electronic iron barrier in front of the David Police Station, an imposing two-storeyed building in yellow-white Jerusalem stone, with the flags of Israel and the Israeli police fluttering outside and a tall radio mast on the roof, like a tree stripped of all its foliage. The duty guard recognized him and, activating the barrier, waved him through the arched tunnel that cut through the centre of the building and into the walled compound at the rear, where he parked up beside a white Kawasaki Mule police truck. Behind him, a couple of bomb disposal guys were fiddling with one of their robots, adjusting its retractable arm; to his right a horse was being exercised inside a fenced enclosure surrounded by blooming oleander bushes.

He felt like shit, as he did most days, and told himself he ought to cut down on the drinking. As he did most days. He knew he wouldn't, though. It was the only thing that eased the pain, that helped him forget. Without the drink things would be . . . unbearable.

He sat where he was for a moment, wishing he was back in his flat, hidden from the world, alone with his thoughts, then got out of the car and walked slowly back towards the tunnel, turning into a low doorway just inside it and climbing a set of stone stairs to the first floor. His office was halfway down a whitewashed corridor, a small, cramped room with plywood furniture, a computer on a trolley in the corner and, above his desk, a framed photo of a younger, fitter-looking Ben-Roi being awarded the Valiant Conduct Order. He'd got it three years ago for saving a young Palestinian girl from a house fire down near the Mauristan, risking his life kicking in the front door, fighting his way upstairs through the flames and carrying her to safety across the rooftops. At the time he'd been proud of himself; now he thought what a bloody stupid thing to do. He should have left her to burn. Shame there hadn't been more of them in there.

The office was empty when he arrived and, shutting the door behind him, he sat down at his desk, pulled out his hip-flask and took a long, slow swig. The liquid drilled down his throat, sending warmth radiating outwards through his chest and stomach. He took another swig and his mind started to clear, his mood improve. A third swig and he felt just about ready for the day ahead.

The door flew open.

'Don't you ever fucking knock, Feldman?' he snapped, ducking the flask down below the desk and struggling to screw the lid back on.

Feldman noted what he was doing and shook his head.

'For fuck's sake, it's not even lunchtime.'

Ben-Roi ignored him, slipping the flask into the pocket of his jeans.

'What do you want?'

'We're starting prelim interviews of the guys we brought in last night. Thought you might want to do the one you caught.'

Feldman smirked slightly on the phrase 'one you caught', reminding Ben-Roi of his failed chase through the Kidron Valley. Wanker.

'Where is he?'

'Interview Three. You think you can handle him on your own?'

Ben-Roi ignored the sarcasm, got to his feet, snatched a folder off the desk and crossed the office. As he pushed past Feldman he felt a hand on his arm.

'Sort yourself out, man. You can't go on like this.'

There was a momentary pause, then Feldman withdrew his hand.

'Look, Arieh, I know what you've—'

'You know fuck all, Feldman. You understand me? Fuck all.'

Ben-Roi glared down at his colleague, then strode out of the office and down the corridor, fighting back the urge to take another long glug of vodka. Pity and rebuke, that's all he seemed to get these days. Pity for what had happened, and rebuke for how he'd dealt with it. The latter he could handle. But not the pity. Not that. It unmanned him. God, he wished he'd stayed with her in the square that night.

He descended the staircase back into the tunnel. The interview rooms were through a doorway in the opposite wall, but instead of going directly there he turned left, back into the compound, and then right into a modern, glass-fronted annexe tacked onto the rear of the station, passing through a cool, softly lit foyer and into a large control room with a double bank of colour television screens on its far wall. Each screen carried a different image of the Old City – the Western Wall, the Damascus Gate, the Haram al-Sharif, the Cardo – relayed by one of the three hundred security cameras bolted at every street corner. The images changed frequently as the system switched from camera to camera, while every now and then one of the screens would turn orange and a CAMERA DOWN legend would appear.

Two semi-circular control desks, one inside the other like a pair of inverted commas, sat in front of the screens, manned by uniformed officers. Ben-Roi crossed to the first of these and tapped a large, blonde-haired girl on the shoulder.

'I need some footage from last night,' he said. 'Interior Lions Gate. From about eleven forty-five.'

The girl nodded and, after calling to one of her colleagues that she was leaving her post for a few minutes, ushered Ben-Roi into a side room where she sat him down in front of a computer and, leaning over his shoulder, clicked various icons with a mouse until she had located the footage he wanted, of the previous night's drugs bust.

He sat and watched as the operation played itself out, occasionally asking the girl to rewind, zoom in on something or click to a different camera, tracking the young Palestinian man he had chased from the moment he arrived at the gate with his three colleagues, through the appearance of the dope-laden Mercedes, to the point where the police swooped and, unnoticed in the confusion, the man scrambled over a gate into the Haram al-Sharif and then over the Old City walls into the Muslim cemetery below, flitting from tombstone to tombstone down towards the Ophel Road.

'OK, that's enough,' he said eventually. 'Can I get a copy?'

The blonde girl disappeared, returning a couple of minutes later with a CD. He slipped it into the folder he was carrying and left the control centre, heading back into the main building.

Interview Room 3 was in the basement, a bare, whitewashed room with a stone floor and single strip light in the ceiling. The Palestinian man was sitting behind a rickety plywood table, his wrists handcuffed, his left eye swollen and puffy. Ben-Roi pulled up a chair and sat down opposite him.

'I want a lawyer,' mumbled the man, staring at the table.

'You're going to fucking need one,' grunted the detective, opening his file, laying the CD to one side and removing a typewritten sheet – the arrest report he'd filled out the previous night.

'Hani al-Hajjar Hani-Jamal,' he said, reading the personal details at the top of the report. 'That's a fucking stupid name.'

He put the sheet down.

'Look at me.'

The young man looked up, biting his lip, eyes bright with fear. He looked tiny beside Ben-Roi, a child in front of a teacher.

'You're going to tell me the truth, aren't you, Hani? Every question I ask you. The truth.'

There was an imperceptible nod. The young man's thighs were clenched tightly together as if he was expecting some assault from beneath the table. Ben-Roi stared at him, enjoying his fear, gratified by it. Then, without taking his eyes away, he reached out with his left hand and slid the CD across the desktop.

'This is for you.'

The man stared down at it, confused, frightened.

'It's all there,' said Ben-Roi. 'Everything that happened last night. All recorded, all admissible in a court of law. So no fucking lies, you understand? No bullshit about how you just happened to be walking past, how you've never dealt drugs in your life. Because if you do bullshit me I'll damage you. I'll really fucking damage you.'

He reached out and grasped the man's wrist, squeezing, fingers biting into the flesh, then released his grip and sat back.

'Now start talking, you pathetic piece of shit.'

LUXOR

By the time Khalifa got back from Edfu, Mahfouz had spoken to Chief Hassani and filled him in on the situation.

He took it surprisingly well. Better, certainly, than Khalifa had been expecting. There were a few muttered expletives when he first came into his office, and the usual Hassani glare, but the anticipated yelling and hammering of fists on desk, for which Khalifa had been preparing himself throughout the journey back, singularly failed to materialize. On the contrary, the chief was uncharacteristically subdued about the whole thing, accepting the reopening of the case with barely a murmur of dissent, as if he no longer had either the energy or the will to resist it. Khalifa even thought he caught the vaguest flicker of relief in his eyes, like a man who is finally able to lay down a burden he had never wanted to pick up in the first place.

'Let's get one thing clear,' said Hassani, staring out of the window of his office, his toupee clinging to his head like a clump of brown candyfloss. 'You're on your own on this. I'm short

251

on manpower as it is. I can't spare anyone else. Understood?'

'Yes, sir.'

'I'm moving Sariya on to another case. Until you've got this thing sorted he'll work out of a different office.'

'Yes, sir.'

'And I don't want you mouthing off around the station. You keep it to yourself. If anyone asks, just say some new evidence has come to light and you're looking into it. Don't go into details.'

'Yes, sir.'

There was a loud clip-clopping as a horse-drawn *caleche* clattered past along the street below, its driver whistling at tourists, importuning them to take a ride. Hassani stared down at it for a moment, then turned and came back to his desk.

'So, what are you going to do?' he asked.

Khalifa shrugged, taking a swift puff on the Cleopatra he had clasped between his fingers.

'Try and find out more about Jansen's background, I guess. See if I can turn up anything to link him with Schlegel. Some motive for killing her. Everything we've got at the moment is circumstantial.'

Hassani nodded, opened his desk drawer, removed Jansen's keys and threw them over.

'You'll be needing these.'

Khalifa caught the keys and put them in his jacket pocket.

'I'll have to contact the Israelis at some point,'

he said. 'See if they've got anything on the woman.'

Hassani grimaced but said nothing. He held Khalifa's gaze for a long moment, then, slowly, pushed himself away from the desk, got to his feet again, crossed to a filing cabinet in the corner, squatted and unlocked the bottom drawer, removing a slim red file. He came back to the desk and handed the file to Khalifa. On the front was written '2345/1 – Schlegel, Hannah. March 10, 1990'.

'I expect the leads are all cold by now, but you never know.'

Khalifa stared down at the file.

'Mahfouz said you'd burnt it.'

Hassani grunted. 'You're not the only one round here with a fucking conscience, you know.'

Again he held Khalifa's eyes, then, with a wave of the hand, dismissed him.

'And I want regular updates!' he shouted to his back. 'Which means *regular* updates.'

JERUSALEM

After the fund-raising lunch was finished and he had seen Har-Zion back to his office at the Knesset building on Derekh Ruppin, Avi Steiner took a bus up to Romema to check the mail box, his eyes roving suspiciously over his fellow passengers, less for potential suicide bombers – God, what an irony that would be, to end up on a bus with one of al-Mulatham's people! – than on the off-chance he was being followed. It *was* an off-chance, minuscule – the whole thing was such a closely guarded secret most of those involved didn't even know they *were* involved – but you could never be too careful. That's why Har-Zion trusted him, had nicknamed him Ha-Nesher, the Eagle – because he was so careful, saw everything. Ha-Nesher, and also Ha-Ne-eman – the Loyal. He would have done anything for Har-Zion. Anything. He was like a father to him.

He got off the bus at the top end of Jaffa Street and, again glancing suspiciously around him, walked up the hill into the heart of Romema, a drab residential suburb of yellow-stone apartment blocks interspersed with clumps of pine and cypress trees, taking the odd sudden turning, doubling back on himself, confirming and recon-firming he wasn't being tailed before eventually ducking into a shop with a sign over the door announcing GROCERIES, STATIONERY, PRIVATE MAIL BOXES.

He didn't check the box on a regular basis – regularity meant routine, and routine aroused suspicion. Sometimes he would come only a couple of days after his last visit; sometimes he would leave it a week, a fortnight, even a month. You could never be too careful.

The boxes were along a wall at the back, out of the eyeline of the shop owner, an elderly Sephardee woman who in the three years he had been coming here never once seemed to have moved from her armchair behind the low plywood counter. He took one final look around, then, producing a key, went over and opened box number 13, removing a single envelope which he slipped into the pocket of his jacket before locking the box again and exiting. He had been inside for less than a minute.

Back on the street he zig-zagged around for a while, then opened the envelope. Inside was a single sheet of paper on which was written, in uniform capital letters so that the hand could not be traced, a name and an address. He memo-rized them, then tore the sheet into small pieces, mixing them in his hand and depositing them in four separate bins before returning to Jaffa

Street and catching a bus back across town, content in the knowledge that what he was doing was ultimately for the greater good of his people and his country.

JERUSALEM

Come five p.m., Tom Roberts was still hunched over the desk in Layla's study, surrounded by pieces of scrap paper, seemingly no nearer to deciphering the cryptic document than he had been six hours earlier when he had first started looking at it.

The two of them had walked back from the American Colony Hotel together and, having made him a cup of coffee, Layla had handed over the photocopied sheet, which she had detached from its covering letter (like most journalists she made a rule of never giving out more information than she had to).

'And you've no idea where it's from?' he had asked, staring down at the document, fiddling distractedly with his tie.

'None at all. Someone sent it to me in the post. You know as much as I do.'

He had turned the sheet over, glanced at its blank reverse side, then turned it back again, eyes squinting behind his glasses. With his spare hand he had scratched at a small blotch of eczema at the back of his neck, just above the line of his shirt collar.

'Well, it's hard to be certain without looking at the original, but my guess is it's medieval – early medieval if the palaeography is anything to go by.'

He caught the sceptical look on Layla's face.

'I studied the period for my Ph.D.,' he explained. 'You get a feel for these things.'

She smiled. 'I never knew you were Doctor Roberts.'

'It's not something I make a point of advertising. Early medieval Latin jurisprudence tends to be a bit of a conversation killer.'

She had laughed, and for a moment their eyes had caught before he looked away again, embarrassed.

'Anyway,' he went on, 'assuming it *is* early medieval, it shouldn't be too hard to work out what it means. Encryption was pretty rudimentary in those days. No Enigma machines or anything. Let's see how we go.'

Layla had installed him at the desk in her study where he had removed his jacket, loosened his tie and got to work, starting by transcribing the sequence of letters onto a separate sheet of paper so that he could read them clearly.

'We don't know what language has been encrypted,' he had said, 'although if it's medieval it's a fair guess it'll be Latin, or possibly Greek. For the moment we'll leave that to one side and concentrate on the algorithm.'

She raised her eyebrows questioningly. 'That being?'

'Basically, the method that's been used to encode the message. Like I said, early medieval encryption was a pretty unsophisticated science. Or at least it was in Europe. The Arabs were streaks ahead, like they were in most things in those days. Anyway, chances are we've got a fairly simple algorithm here, either a substitution cipher, or possibly transposition.'

Again Layla had raised her eyebrows. 'Speak to me in English, Tom.'

'Sorry.' He smiled. 'One of my many faults – always assuming people are interested in the same things as me. Basically, a substitution cipher is when you generate a new alphabet by substituting the letters of the existing alphabet either for other letters or symbols.'

He wrote out an alphabet on a piece of paper, and then beneath it a second alphabet in which all the letters had been shifted one space to the right, so that A was twinned with Z, B with A, C with B, etc.

'You then rewrite your original message, or plain-text, replacing each letter with its equivalent letter in the new alphabet. So, "cat" comes out as BZS, for instance. Or Layla as KZXKZ. Transposition, on the other hand, is when you simply rearrange the existing letters of the plain-text according to some prearranged system, effectively generating a giant anagram. Any clearer?'

'A bit.' Layla had laughed. 'Although not much.'

'A bit's good enough for the moment,' he had

said, arranging the transposed message in front of him and staring down at it, tapping at his spectacles with the end of his pencil. 'So what we need to do is pin down the algorithm, and then try and work out the key, or the precise formula that's being used to generate the cipher text. It might simply be a matter of a basic Caesar shift, or it could be something more opaque, in which case we're going to have to get into frequency analysis.'

This time she hadn't bothered asking what he was talking about. Instead, with an amused shake of the head, she had patted him on the shoulder and left him to it, heading into the kitchen to prepare a simple lunch of stuffed peppers, cheese and salad. They had eaten an hour later, by which point he still hadn't made any progress.

'I'm pretty sure it's a regular monoalphabetic substitution cipher rather than transposition,' he had said, removing his glasses and rubbing his eyes. 'Unfortunately I'm no nearer to finding the key. It's looking more complex than I thought.'

They had talked about his work at the consulate, her journalism, the current situation in the Middle East – nothing too heavy, just chatting. At one point he had asked about the framed photograph of her father hanging above her desk, but she had closed off the conversation quickly, moving on to another topic, not wanting to get drawn into a personal discussion, to reveal anything of herself. Within forty minutes he had been back at the desk wrestling once again with the mysterious code.

And now it was four hours later, and the Old City clocks had just chimed five, and still he hadn't cracked it. He let out a deep sigh and sat back in his chair, hands locked behind his neck, the desk in front of him half hidden beneath a snowdrift of scribble-covered sheets of paper.

'For God's sake!' he muttered, shaking his head.

Layla, who had spent most of the afternoon curled up on the sofa working on an article about the Palestinian aid conference she had attended in Limassol, came through and stood beside him.

'Leave it, Tom,' she said. 'It doesn't matter.'

'I just can't understand it,' he complained, removing his glasses and polishing the lenses with the end of his tie. 'Ciphers from this period are always child's play.'

'Maybe it's not monoalphabetic substitution after all,' she joked, not really understanding the term, simply trying to lighten his mood.

He said nothing, just finished polishing his glasses. Then he picked up the sheet with the transcribed code on it and held it away from him, staring at it, his left knee bouncing up and down beneath the table.

'It's going to be something simple,' he muttered to himself. 'I know it's going to be something simple. I just can't see it. I just can't bloody see it.'

He threw the sheet back on the table and, leaning over, picked up a handful of other sheets, flicking through them, tapping his rubber-tipped pencil on the chair-arm. One sheet in particular occupied his attention for almost a minute, his eyes scanning back and forth along the rows of seemingly random letters scrawled thereon, before he laid it aside again, only to return to it a moment later, staring at it even more intently than he had done before. His pencil tapping gradually slowed and stopped, as did the jogging of his knee. He held the sheet away from him, teeth biting at his lower lip, then placed it flat on the table and, taking a blank sheet from a pile on the floor, began writing on it, slowly at first, then faster, eyes darting to the sheet he had been looking at and back to the one on which he was scribbling. After thirty seconds he started to chuckle.

'What?' she asked.

'Layla al-Madani, you're a bloody genius!'

She leant over his shoulder, trying to read what he was writing.

'You've worked it out?'

'No, Layla, *you've* worked it out. You were right. It wasn't a substitution cipher. Or rather it wasn't *only* a substitution cipher. Whoever encrypted this used transposition *and* substitution. On its own each system would be simple to decipher. Taken together, they make the whole thing that bit more confusing. Especially when the original message is in medieval Latin, as I suspected.'

He had continued scribbling as he spoke. Now he sat back and showed her what he had written.

G. esclarmondae suae sorori sd
temporis tam paucum est ut mea inventio huius magnae rei post maris transitum sit narranda. nunc satis est dicere per fortunam solam eam esse inventam; nec umquam inventa esset nisi nostri labores latebram caecam illuminavissent. quam ad te mitto ut in C. tuta restet. hic autem tanta est stultitia et fatuitas ut necessario peritura sit; quod grave damnum esset, nam res est antiquissima ac potentissima ac gratissima. ante finem anni ierusalem exibo. cura ut ualeas. Frater tuus.
GR

'What they did,' he explained, 'was firstly to encrypt the message using a simple Caesar shift cipher.'

He grabbed another blank sheet of paper and wrote out the alphabet, as he had done earlier, missing out the letters J and W (they didn't use them in the early medieval alphabet, he explained). Beneath that he wrote a second alphabet with all the letters moved five spaces to the right.

'That gave him – I'm presuming it was a him – his primary level of encryption. The first couple of words thus change from G. esclarmondae to b znxfumgihyuz.'

He sounded excited, pleased with himself, like a scientist explaining a new discovery.

'What he then did, however, and what threw me off the scent, was to transpose the first and second letters of the coded message, and the third and fourth, and the fifth and sixth, and so on and so on right the way through the text. So *b* swaps with *z*, *n* with *x*, *f* with *u*, etc. It's transposition in its most simple form, but if you're working on the basis that they've only used substitution, it can make things somewhat confusing. It was only when you said that maybe they weren't using substitution that I got to thinking maybe I'd missed a trick.'

He looked up at her, smiling. His excitement was infectious and, leaning down, she kissed him on the cheek.

'Oh, the joys of decryption!' He chuckled.

'So what does it mean?' she asked, picking up the sheet with the deciphered text on it. 'Or was translation not part of the deal?'

His brow furrowed in mock contemplation.

'Well, normally I'd charge extra for that sort of service. But seeing as it's you . . .'

She laughed and handed the sheet back to him.

'Go on then, Dr Roberts. Do your stuff.'

He took the sheet from her.

'I should say that my medieval Latin is a bit rusty. It's been a while since I last used it.'

'I can assure you it's a lot better than mine,' she said. 'Go on.'

264

He sat back, adjusted his glasses and started to translate, slowly, stopping every now and then to consider an unfamiliar word, interjecting frequent comments along the lines of 'I think that's what it means', or 'I'm paraphrasing slightly here', or 'I could be wrong'. Layla took a blank sheet of paper and, leaning over the desk beside him, wrote down what he said.

'G., to his sister Esclarmonde, greetings,' he began. 'S.D. stands for salutem dicit – "says hello". Time is short, so the tale of how this great thing came to me must await my return from across the sea. Suffice to say that it was found quite by chance, and might never have been found at all had our work not happened to reveal its secret hiding place. I send it to you now in the knowledge it will rest safe at C. Here there is such ignorance and foolishness it must surely be destroyed, which would be a grievous loss, for it is an ancient thing, and one of great power and beauty. I shall leave Jerusalem before the year's end. I trust and pray you are in good health. Your brother, GR.'

Layla finished copying down the translation and, sitting on the edge of the desk, read through it. Whatever she'd been expecting from the document, it wasn't this. It sounded like some sort of riddle.

'Any idea what it means?' she asked.

Roberts took the sheet from her and skimmed through it. There was a long silence.

'It's certainly unusual,' he said eventually.

'Judging by the references to "Jerusalem" and "across the sea" I'd say it was written during the crusader period, although that's just an educated guess so don't go quoting me.'

'And this was when exactly?' she asked. 'Crusader history not being my strong point.'

'Mine neither,' he replied, scratching at the eczema-blotch on his neck. 'Let's see. The First Crusade captured Jerusalem from the Saracens in 1099. After that there was a crusader state in the Holy Land for, what, the next two hundred years, until the end of the thirteenth century, although Jerusalem itself was recaptured by Saladin in' – he paused for a moment, thinking – '1187, I think. Yes, 1187. After the Horns of Hattin. So this must have been written before that. Some time between 1099 and 1187, that's my guess. Although like I say, I could be talking complete rubbish.'

He put the translation down and, removing his glasses, started polishing them again.

'The crusader kingdom was known as Outremer, incidentally,' he added, 'which means "across the sea".'

Layla stared down at the cryptic message.

'So you think whoever wrote this was a crusader?'

'Well, not one of the rank-and-file crusaders, certainly. Most of them were illiterate. The fact that this GR knew Latin and was educated enough to encrypt it would suggest he was either a nobleman, a scribe, or a member of the clergy.'

He held his glasses in front of him, examined them, then put them back on.

'Esclarmonde is a medieval French name, so far as I'm aware only used in the Languedoc region, so it's probably a fair bet GR was from that part of the country too. Who exactly he was, however, and what this ancient thing is he found I have no idea. It's certainly intriguing. Very intriguing.'

'"C"?' quieried Layla, pointing at the letter in the text.

'Presumably an abbreviation of a place name, but . . .' He shrugged as if to say 'who knows?'

'And it's genuine?' she asked. 'Not a fake?'

Again, that noncommittal shrug of the shoulders.

'I simply can't tell you, Layla. Not without the original. Even then, it's not at all my subject. You need to go and talk to an expert. A palaeographer or something.'

He smiled apologetically.

'I think my usefulness is rapidly starting to run out.'

'Not at all,' she said, reaching over and squeezing his shoulder. 'You've been fantastic.'

They cleared up all the sheets of scrap paper and dumped them in the bin, then headed back through into the living room. Layla thought of offering him a drink, but decided against it. He seemed to sense her reticence, because he said it was time he was leaving.

'I can't thank you enough, Tom,' she said,

opening the front door for him. 'You've been so helpful.'

'I've enjoyed it.' He smiled. 'Really. It's been a challenge. And lunch was excellent.'

He stepped out onto the landing.

'Look, Layla, I know I said no strings attached, and I meant it when I said no strings attached, but I was wondering . . . I don't want to hassle you, but would you . . .'

He seemed nervous, tripping over his words. She came forward a step and kissed him on the cheek.

'I'd love to go for dinner,' she said, smiling. 'Can I call you?'

He beamed. 'Of course. Wonderful. I'll wait to hear from you, then.'

He set off down the stairs with a spring in his step and she closed the door behind her, leaning her back against it. She'd been lying, of course. She had no intention of calling him. Not for a while, anyway. All she wanted to do now was to find out more about the mysterious letter.

'Who are you, GR?' she muttered to herself, gazing down at the translation in her hand, Tom Roberts already forgotten. 'Who the hell are you? What did you find? And who sent you to me?'

JERUSALEM

At the end of the day Ben-Roi drove home to his grubby, lonely, one-bedroom flat in Romema, where he showered, dabbed on some cologne and then set off on foot to his sister Chava's apartment for Shabbat dinner.

It was a cool, clear evening, with a translucent blue sky and a slight breeze drifting in from the north, unnaturally quiet and still, the streets having all but emptied for the Sabbath observance. He passed a group of Haredi Jews hurrying home from synagogue, their side-curls bobbing up and down like coiled springs, and a line of young female soldiers sitting in a shelter above the main Egged bus station, laughing and smoking, their M16s balanced on their slim, khaki-clad legs. Otherwise the city seemed deserted. He liked it like that – clean, empty, silent. There was something pure about it, unsullied, as if everything that had gone before had been swept away, leaving a new city, a new beginning. He wished it could be like that all the time.

Chava's flat was back towards the Old City, on Ha-Ma'alot, a plush, tree-lined avenue in the heart of West Jerusalem. Arriving in front of the yellow-stone building he took a swig of vodka from his flask and pressed the intercom beside the glass door. There was a pause, then his nephew Chaim's voice echoed from the panel.

'Uncle Arieh?'

'No,' he replied, putting on an American accent, 'it's Spiderman.'

There was a pause as the boy considered this, then a guffaw of laughter.

'It's not Spiderman,' he cried. 'It's Uncle Arieh! Come quickly!'

There was a loud buzzing and the door clicked open. Ben-Roi went through into the foyer, smiling to himself, and took a lift to the fourth floor, removing a mint from his pocket and popping it in his mouth to mask the smell of alcohol.

He enjoyed Shabbat evenings at his sister's. It was one of the few social occasions he was able to deal with these days – just himself, Chava, her husband Shimon and their two kids, Chaim and Ezer. The religious element didn't mean much to him now. Since Galia's death his faith, once such a central part of his existence, seemed to have crumbled away, to the extent that it was now almost a year since he had last set foot inside a *shul*, missing even the High Holy days of Passover, Rosh Hashanah and Yom Kippur, the first time in his life he had ever done so.

No, it wasn't the religion that made Friday nights

so special to him, nor even so much the fact of being with his family, his own blood, although that was of course important. Rather, it was a simple pleasure in being with people who were happy, who could laugh, who saw the world as something full of light and hope rather than the maelstrom of pain and confusion that it was for him. They were such a contented family, so warm, so close. To be with them helped him, if not to forget, at least to remember a little less.

The lift door opened and he stepped out onto the landing. Four-year-old Chaim and his elder brother Ezer charged from their front door and leapt at him.

'Did you catch any killers today, Uncle Arieh?'

'Have you got your gun with you?'

'Will you take us swimming next week?'

'To the zoo! To the zoo!'

He swept the two boys up into his arms and carried them into the flat, kicking the door closed behind him. His brother-in-law Shimon, a short, plump man with curly afro hair – hard to believe he was a decorated paratrooper – came out of the kitchen, an apron tied round his waist, a smell of roasting chicken drifting after him.

'You OK, brother?' he said, clapping Ben-Roi on the shoulder.

Ben-Roi nodded and deposited the children on the floor. They scuttled away into their bedroom, laughing and making shooting noises.

'Drink?' asked Shimon.

'Is the Chief Rabbi *frumm*?' grunted Ben-Roi. 'Where's Chava?'

'Doing the candles. With Sarah.'

The detective frowned. He hadn't expected anyone else to be there.

'A friend of hers,' explained Shimon. 'She was at a loose end tonight so we invited her round.'

He glanced down the corridor, then dropped his voice.

'Seriously good-looking. And single!'

He winked and disappeared into the kitchen to get their drinks. Ben-Roi wandered down the corridor towards the lounge, glancing through into the dining room as he passed. His sister, a tall, broad-hipped woman with bobbed hair, was leaning over the table blessing the Shabbat candles. Beside her stood another woman, smaller, slimmer, with auburn hair almost down to her waist, dressed in chinos, sandals and a white shirt. She glanced up, caught sight of him and smiled. Ben-Roi held her eyes a second, then, without reciprocating the gesture, continued into the living room. The sound of his sister's voice echoed behind him, reciting the traditional Shabbat blessing.

'Baruch ata Adonai, eloheinu melech ha'olam, asher kid'shanu b'mitz'votav v'tzivanu l'hadlich ner shel Shabbat.'

He was joined a moment later by Shimon, who handed him a large whisky. The two women came in shortly after that, Chava coming over and hugging him.

'I just love that aftershave,' she said, kissing him on the cheek. 'This is Sarah.'

She pulled away and indicated her friend, who smiled and held out her hand.

'Chava's told me a lot about you,' she said.

Ben-Roi took the hand and muttered a greeting, making little effort to be polite. He found the woman's presence unsettling. He liked it when it was just the five of them, family, no outsiders. That way he could be himself, didn't have to make an effort. Now, with a stranger here, the intimacy of the evening was somehow polluted, spoilt before it had even begun. He was starting to wish he hadn't come.

'Don't mind him,' his sister joked, jerking her head in Ben-Roi's direction. 'He's the super *sabra*. Give him till dessert and he'll be the life and soul.'

The young woman smiled, but said nothing. Ben-Roi downed his whisky in two long gulps.

They exchanged pleasantries for a few minutes, then Chava excused herself and went off to the kitchen to check dinner. Ben-Roi followed her on the pretext of refilling his glass.

'So what do you think?' she asked when they were alone.

'What do you mean, what do I think?'

'Of Sarah, stupid. She's beautiful, isn't she?'

Ben-Roi shrugged, pouring himself another slug of whisky from a bottle on the sideboard.

'Hadn't noticed.'

'Right,' said his sister with a laugh, opening the

oven and checking a large chicken that was roasting inside.

Ben-Roi came forward and, lifting a lid, sniffed the contents of a pot that was simmering on the stove. Chicken *kneidlach* soup. His favourite.

'She's a good person,' said Chava, basting the chicken. 'Fun. Intelligent. Kind. And single.'

'So Shimon tells me,' said Ben-Roi, dipping a spoon into the pot and slurping a mouthful of soup.

Chava slapped his hand and replaced the lid.

'I know what you're thinking, Arieh. I'm not trying to fix you up—'

'You could have fucking fooled me.'

'*Zedakah* box! You know we don't have swearing in this house.'

Ben-Roi grumbled an apology, fiddled in his pocket and produced a five-shekel coin which he dropped into the charity box on the windowsill.

'I'm not trying to fix you up,' repeated Chava. 'I just think—'

'What? That it's time I started screwing someone else?'

He bit his lip, produced another coin, ten shekels this time, and dropped it in the box.

'Sorry.'

Chava smiled and, stepping forward, wrapped her arms around her brother's neck.

'Come on, Ari. Please. Lighten up a bit. I can't bear to see you like this. None of us can. So unhappy. So . . . tormented. Galia wouldn't have wanted it. I know that. She'd want you to start living again. Being happy.'

Ben-Roi let her hold him for a moment, then pushed her away, taking a long gulp of his whisky.

'Just let me deal with it in my own way, sis. I need time, that's all.'

'You can't mourn her for ever, Arieh. You have to move on. You know it, deep down.'

He drained the rest of the whisky, something hardening inside him.

'I'll mourn her for as long as I fucking want, Chava. It's no-one's business but my own.'

This time he neither apologized for the expletive nor put a coin in the box. He filled his glass again and made for the kitchen door. His sister grabbed his arm.

'At least try and be polite, Arieh. Please. At least try and be nice.'

He looked down at her, her eyes moist, imploring, then nodded and walked out into the corridor.

Twenty minutes later they gathered in the dining room. The men and boys donned *yarmulkes* and Shimon recited the *kiddush* over a cup of wine, everyone taking a sip before they all sat down to eat, Ezer and Chaim insisting on sitting to either side of Ben-Roi.

'You're under arrest, Uncle Arieh,' explained Ezer. 'And we're your guards.'

With a couple more drinks inside him Ben-Roi's mood had lightened slightly.

'OK,' he said. 'But remember, if you're proper guards you have to watch me all the time. *All* the time. Which means you can't have any dinner because it will distract you.'

The boys took up the challenge and, swivelling in their seats, stared at him. They managed to hold it until the soup was served, at which point they lost interest. Shimon nodded at Ben-Roi, who stood up and crossed to the sideboard, where he opened a bottle of wine.

'Some guards you turned out to be,' said Sarah, smiling. 'Look – your uncle's just escaped. And you didn't even notice.'

'He didn't escape,' countered Ezer, slurping at his soup. 'There are other guards, but they're invisible.'

Everyone laughed. Ben-Roi's eyes caught Sarah's for a fraction of a second, then flicked away again. He returned to the table with the opened bottle.

'So, what do you do?' he asked, pouring the wine.

'She's a teacher,' said Chava.

'Since when was she mute?' snorted Shimon. 'Let her answer for herself.'

'Sorry,' said Chava. 'Go on, Sarah, tell him what you do.'

The young woman shrugged.

'I'm a teacher.'

Despite himself, Ben-Roi smiled.

'Where?'

'Down in Silwan.'

'Silwan?'

'It's a special project. Experimental.'

Ben-Roi raised his eyebrows questioningly.

'We teach Israeli and Palestinian kids together, in the same school,' she explained. 'Try and integrate them. Break down the barriers.'

Ben-Roi stared at her for a moment, then lowered his eyes, his smile fading. Shimon took a piece of *hallah* and swiped it round his empty soup bowl.

'Did you get that funding you applied for?' he asked.

Sarah shook her head. 'They manage to find money for the bloody settlers, but for teaching . . . the way things are at the moment we can't even afford to buy colouring books and pens.'

Ben-Roi was poking a *kneidl* around his bowl.

'I don't see the point,' he muttered.

'Of colouring books?'

'Of trying to integrate Arab and Israeli kids.'

She looked at him, eyes sparkling.

'You don't think it's worth a try?'

Ben-Roi waved his spoon dismissively.

'Different worlds, different values. It's pointless thinking they can get on together. Naive.'

'Actually, we've had a lot of success,' she countered. 'The kids play together, share experiences, form friendships. It's amazing how open-minded they can be.'

'In a couple of years they'll be cutting each

277

other's throats,' said Ben-Roi. 'It's the way things are. There's no point trying to pretend any different.'

For a brief moment it seemed she was going to argue with him. As it was, she simply smiled and gave a slight shrug of her shoulders.

'We'll give it a go anyway. You never know, it might do some good. More good than encouraging them to grow up hating each other, that's for sure.'

There was a momentary silence, uneasy, broken by Chaim, who started into a story about how they'd found a rat in the toilets at their local swimming pool and the lifeguard had killed it with a broom.

'Good for him,' said Ben-Roi, finishing his soup and throwing a glance across the table at Sarah. 'That's the only way to deal with vermin. Crush the bastards.'

He didn't say much for the rest of the meal, eating in near silence while the others chatted among themselves, mainly, inevitably, about *ha-matzav*, the current political situation. Once they had finished eating they sang a couple of *zemirot*, Ben-Roi mumbling along tunelessly, then retired to the living room for coffee. At ten o'clock he said he ought to be going.

'Me too,' said Sarah, standing. 'It's been a lovely evening, Chava. Thank you so much.'

The two of them made their farewells, Ben-Roi annoyed that he couldn't get away alone, and descended in the lift together in embarrassed silence. When they came out onto the street he asked Sarah which way she was going.

'Right,' she said. 'You?'

He also needed to turn right.

'Left,' he muttered.

There was an awkward pause.

'Oh well,' she muttered eventually. 'It was nice meeting you.'

She smiled and held out her hand. He looked down at it, nodded, then turned and started walking away. After he'd gone a few metres she called after him.

'I'm sorry about what happened, Arieh. Chava told me. I'm so very sorry. It must be terrible for you.'

He slowed. 'You're not fucking sorry,' he wanted to yell at her. 'You're a dirty fucking Arab-lover. They murdered the only woman I ever loved and now you're playing games with their children. You're a stupid ignorant fucking *zonah*. Whore.'

He said nothing, just half-raised a hand in farewell and, picking up his pace, continued to the end of the street, disappearing round the corner onto Ha-Melekh George.

Later, much later, having spent three hours drinking alone in Champs Pub on Jaffa Street, Ben-Roi stumbled back to his flat, banged on a Schlomo Artzi CD and collapsed onto his sofa, head swimming.

There'd been a hooker in the bar, young, blonde, Russian, with mascara-stained eyes and the transparent, punctured arms of a regular smack user. He'd thought of bringing her back with him, fucking away a bit of his anger and loneliness, but decided against it. He was too pissed, wouldn't be able to get a hard-on, would end up despising himself even more than he already did, if such a thing were possible. The woman had made a play for him, but he'd told her to fuck off and carried on drinking alone, staring at his reflection in the mirrors behind the bar, his huge, craggy face bisected by the vertical join between two glass panels so that it looked as if his skull had been neatly split in half and the two halves eased apart, leaving a heavy black strip running right the way through his centre.

He lay back on the sofa and closed his eyes, but was overcome by a wave of nausea and opened them again almost immediately, his gaze veering around the room, trying to find something to focus on. He stared at his CD-player, a crack in the ceiling, a Batya Gur whodunnit, before eventually his eyes swooped down on a row of framed photographs sitting on a shelf opposite. Taking deep breaths, he worked his way along the line, using the images to steady himself, as though his eyes were hands and the photos a solid iron rail keeping him upright: him and his sister hanging upside down from the branch of an apricot tree on the family farm; his great-grandfather, old Ezekiel

Ben-Roi, a stern, heavily bearded Russian who had emigrated to Ottoman-ruled Palestine in 1882, making the Ben-Rois one of the longest-settled Jewish families in the region; him on his graduation from police school; him and Al Pacino, whose film *Serpico* was what had inspired him to become a policeman in the first place. And of course last of all, right at the end of the row, the largest photo of all, him and Galia, laughing into the camera, the rippled silken sheet of the Sea of Galilee behind them, at Ginosar, on the night of his thirtieth birthday, when she had given him his silver hip-flask and the menorah-shaped pendant he still wore on a chain around his neck.

He stared at the photo, the fingers of his left hand tweaking helplessly at the pendant, then, heaving himself up onto his feet, he staggered through into the bedroom. Sellotaped to the wall beside his bed was a photocopied newspaper article, the print enlarged to three times its original size, nooses of thick red ink circling certain words and phrases – *Jericho and the Dead Sea Plain; Manio; a tall, slim man; way too sophisticated for a renegade Palestinian cell; the impetus has to be external.* He leant against the wall with one hand to either side of the article and scanned the text, reading right the way through it, as he had done a thousand times this last year, before eventually slumping backwards onto the bed, where he lay staring at a bottle of aftershave on the bedside cabinet.

'Bellyache,' he mumbled drunkenly. 'You give me a fucking bellyache.'

And then his eyes folded shut and he was asleep, snoring heavily, his right hand bunched into a half-fist as though he was clutching the handle of a parachute ripcord.

JERUSALEM

It was the same dream she always had, every night, without fail. She was in an underground cell, very small and cramped, pitch dark, with a damp, slime-covered floor and sweaty concrete walls. There was something in there with her; she couldn't tell what – a snake, maybe, or a rat, or a large scorpion. Something dangerous, malevolent. She was naked, pressing her frail body into one corner of the cell, trying to keep out of the thing's way, terrified of any contact with it, of being bitten or stung. As she did so, there was a distant rumble of machinery, like huge iron wheels slowly revolving, and the walls began to inch together, driving her and the creature towards each other. She started screaming, calling for her daddy, insisting she wasn't a traitor, she was a good Palestinian. The walls kept coming, somehow pushing her legs up and open so that her private parts were exposed. She could feel the creature moving around down there between her thighs, crawling across her skin, exploring, moving steadily upwards. She tried to stay still, not to breathe, but it felt so disgusting she couldn't help but jerk, whereupon it tore into her crotch, biting and slashing and stinging, ripping her open, pushing right up inside her.

'No!' she screamed, snapping awake, arms and legs flailing. 'Please, God, no!'

She continued to convulse for several seconds, then collapsed back onto the bed, trembling, a distant ringing sound in her ears. Gradually her breathing calmed and her body relaxed, but the ringing continued, and as her mind cleared she suddenly realized the phone was going. She glanced across at the luminous dial of her clock – 1.30 a.m. – then swung her legs off the bed and, rubbing her eyes, went through into the study where she picked up the receiver.

'Layla?'

It was Tom Roberts.

'It's one-thirty,' she said, her voice groggy, annoyed.

'What? Oh sod, Layla! I'm so sorry. I had no idea it was so late. I just wanted to tell you . . . Forget it, forget it. I'll call back tomorrow.'

He sounded excited. Worked up.

'Wanted to tell me what?'

'It doesn't matter. I'll call you tomorrow.'

'I'm awake now, Tom. What do you want?'

She was still on edge from the nightmare and her tone was sharp, suspicious. She had a nasty feeling he was going to come out with something embarrassing, tell her he was in love with her or something.

'It's just that I've been turning things over in my mind since I left this afternoon . . .'

Oh God, she thought.

'And I think I might have an idea what GR stands for.'

It took a moment for the words to sink in, and then, suddenly, she was wide awake. She leant forward and switched on a lamp, fumbling for a pen and paper.

'Go on.'

'I don't know why it didn't occur to me at the time,' he said, 'what with the reference to Jerusalem and secret hiding places. It's certainly an amazing coincidence. Anyway, I think it might be someone called William de Relincourt.'

She frowned, her pen poised above the sheet of paper.

'The initials are *GR*, Tom, not WR.'

'I know,' he said. 'That's probably why it didn't leap out at me immediately. The thing is, in medieval Latin the name William was rendered Guillelmus, with a "G".'

She scribbled down the name, underlining it.

'Who is he?'

'Well, this is what's so fascinating,' said Roberts. 'So far as I remember – and like I said this afternoon, I'm not great on this period – he was the guy who built the Church of the Holy Sepulchre. Or rather rebuilt it. The original church was Byzantine, I think. Or was it Roman? I can't remember. Anyway, it doesn't matter. The point is that during the crusader era the church was completely rebuilt, and while they were digging the foundations this William de Relincourt was supposed to have unearthed some amazing treasure.'

Layla felt goose-bumps prickling her arms.

'What treasure?'

'I don't know. I don't think anybody knows. The story appears in one of the crusader chronicles. William of Tyre, I think, although I could be wrong. It just seems an extraordinary coincidence. Two people with the same initials, in Jerusalem at roughly the same time, finding some mysterious hidden object. Extraordinary.'

Layla scribbled a couple of notes to herself, then picked up the translation they had done earlier that afternoon and read through it.

'Layla?'

'Yes, I'm still here. I'm just going through the letter again.'

She finished reading and laid the sheet back down, running a hand through her close-cropped hair.

'I'm out of my depth here, Tom. If it's politics I've got an address book full of contacts, but medieval history . . . I just don't know anything about it. It's never interested me.'

There was a momentary pause.

'If you like we could—'

She knew what he was going to say and cut him off immediately.

'I prefer to research on my own, Tom. I'm sorry, it's just the way I work. Nothing personal.'

She sounded tough, cold. Under other circumstances she would have apologized – he'd done her a huge favour, after all – but tonight she wasn't in the mood.

'Of course, of course,' he mumbled, taken aback by her abruptness. 'I quite understand. I'm the same actually.'

'I just need a steer, Tom. A lead. Someone who knows about this stuff. Can you help me?'

She could hear him breathing at the other end of the line.

'Please?' she added.

There was another pause.

'There's a guy down in the Holy Sepulchre,' he said eventually, an edge of hurt in his voice. 'One of the Greek Orthodox priests. Father Sergius, I think his name is. Big fat man. Knows everything there is to know about the history of the church. He's written books on it. He might be a good starting point.'

She wrote down the name.

'Thank you, Tom,' she said. 'I owe you.'

She sensed that he needed more than that from her. That he was waiting for some kind word, some reassurance. She wasn't in the mood. William de Relincourt – that's all she could think about.

'Thank you,' she said again. 'I'll call you.'

She put down the phone, sat for a moment staring at the name in front of her, then plugged her laptop into the phone-line, logged on to Google and started searching.

LUXOR

The banana fields were still blanketed in early-morning mist when Khalifa arrived at Jansen's Karnak villa, unlocking its front gate and crunching along the gravel path towards the low, single-storey building ahead, with its wooden porch and shuttered windows.

He had spent the previous afternoon and evening working his way through the Schlegel file, scribbling notes, re-familiarizing himself with the case. As Hassani had suspected, it hadn't proved much help. It had furnished him with a few forgotten details – photographs of Schlegel's corpse, statements from witnesses who had seen her before her death, copies of correspondence with the Israeli Embassy arranging for the trans-port of the body back to Israel – but nothing that could realistically be considered new information. He had tried to re-establish contact with the two key witnesses – the housekeeper who had heard Schlegel talking on the phone in her hotel room and the Karnak guard who had seen someone hurrying from the scene of her murder – but after a bit of digging had discovered the guard was dead and the maid had married and moved away from the area, leaving no forwarding address. He was, effectively, having to start from scratch.

He reached the villa's front door, and, after some fiddling with keys, got it open and stepped into the cool, shadowy interior, flicking on a light-switch. Everything was exactly as it had been on his last visit – the armchairs, the rack of papers, the large oil painting of a craggy mountain summit, that same air of sterile neatness, of obsessive security. Half a dozen letters were lying scattered on the floor at his feet, and he bent over, picked them up and flicked through them. The first five were bills or circulars; the sixth had a handwritten envelope and a Luxor postmark. He ripped it open and pulled out a cheap, photo-copied flyer advertising a talk the following day: 'The Iniquities of the Jews'. The speaker was one Shaykh Omar Abd-el Karim, a local cleric renowned for his seditious, anti-Western preaching. Khalifa studied the flyer, puzzled that such a thing should be sent to someone like Jansen, then slipped it into his jacket pocket and, kicking the front door closed behind him, set off around the house.

An opening. That's what he was looking for. Some sort of window on to Jansen's secret world. Something, anything, that would tell him more about the villa's mysterious owner. Something to help him breach the impermeable façade the man seemed to have built up around himself.

He started in the living room, certain there were clues here to Jansen's story, but uncertain how to read them. The large oil painting, for instance. It was clearly telling him something about its owner, about his inner life. But what? That he simply liked mountains? Or was its message more specific? That this was the landscape of his native country, perhaps (but wasn't Holland supposed to be flat)? He felt as though all the information he needed to get to the heart of his quarry was here in front of him, but it was in code, and he didn't have the crib to decipher it.

He spent half an hour going over the room, then went through to the bedrooms, then the study, where he spent a long while going through Jansen's bookshelves, pulling out volumes at random, flicking through their pages: *Die Südlichen Raume des Tempels von Luxor* by H. Brunner; *The Complete Works of Josephus*, translated by William Whiston; *Cathares et Templiers* by Raimonde Reznikov; *From Solon to Socrates* by Victor Ehrnberg; *The Basilica of the Holy Sepulchre* by G.S.P. Freeman-Grenville. As on his first visit he was struck by the diversity of Jansen's reading matter, by the man's obvious intelligence and erudition. There were works on everything from Pre-dynastic Egypt to the Spanish Inquisition, the Crusades to Aztec burial customs, Byzantine Jerusalem to the art of rose growing. It was a rich, eclectic, scholarly collection, and Khalifa again got the feeling it was at odds with the outward life of the man who owned it.

'Who were you, Piet Jansen?' he muttered to himself. 'Who were you, and why were you here?'

From the bookcase he turned his attention to the desk, then the two filing cabinets. The first, containing plastic folders full of business, banking, insurance and legal documents, proved no more revealing than it had when he'd flicked through on his first visit to the house. The second, with its sleeves of photographic slides, was more interesting, if only because the slides were of places Khalifa either knew and loved or had always yearned to visit. Giza, Saqqara, Luxor, Abu Simbel – all the major monuments were there, expertly photographed and neatly labelled, as were numerous smaller sites few tourists would ever bother to go to: the great mudbrick walls at el-Kab; the boundary stela of Akhenaten at Tuna el-Gebel; the tomb of Djehutihotep at Deir el-Bersha. Some of the sites – Gebel Dosha, Kor, Qasr Dush – were so obscure Khalifa hadn't even heard of them.

One slide in particular held his attention, for it was the only one that appeared to feature Jansen himself. He was slightly younger here, with neatly brushed hair and an erect, straight-backed stance, standing in what looked like the tomb of Seti I in the Valley of the Kings, in front of an image of the king with the gods Horus and Osiris. There was something faintly menacing about the image, the way its subject stared straight through the camera lens, his gaze hard and knowing, arrogant, his expression hovering midway between a smile and a sneer.

'You were bad,' Khalifa whispered to himself. 'It's in your face, in your eyes. You did bad things, cruel things.'

He gazed at the image for a long while, then put it back and worked his way swiftly through the rest of the collection, not bothering to look at every slide, simply holding each sleeve up to the light and flicking his eyes back and forth across it, focusing on perhaps six or seven pictures before moving on to the next sleeve.

He would most likely have missed the tomb entrance had it been in a normal plastic frame like all the other slides, for by the time he came to it he was almost at the end of the collection and was giving each sleeve little more than a cursory glance. As it was, the picture stuck out from those around it because of its old-fashioned brown cardboard mounting. His interest piqued, Khalifa removed it and took a closer look.

It was in among a series of pictures of Middle and New Kingdom tomb doorways at Deir el-Bahri, on the eastern edge of the Theban necropolis. Although it was in black and white, unlike the richly coloured hues of its neighbours, and slightly out of focus to boot, his initial assumption was that its subject matter must be the same. Only when he held it up to the light did he start to have doubts, not simply because he didn't actually recognize the doorway – in his fifteen years in Luxor he had explored just about every tomb there was to explore in the vicinity – but because the dark, forbidding wall of perfectly flat rock at whose base the doorway opened was unlike any geological formation he had ever seen in the Luxor region.

He turned it over, intrigued, hoping it might have an explanatory label like every other picture in the collection. It didn't, which was frustrating, because for no reason he could explain he sensed the image was somehow significant. He gazed at it for a moment longer – 'What are you trying to tell me?' he murmured. 'Whose tomb are you?' – then slipped it into his inside pocket alongside the flyer and resumed his examination of the house.

He came to the basement last, as he had done on his first visit, descending the dark, creaking stairs, flicking the light switch at the bottom and gazing at the tables and shelves covered in plundered antiquities. He had, by this point, been in the house for over three hours and now spent a further ninety minutes sifting through the basement's contents, marvelling again at the sheer size and diversity of the collection, finding plenty to interest him but nothing whatsoever that shed any light on the man who had put the whole thing together.

He finished up beside the cuboid iron safe in the far corner of the room, with its numbered dial and chunky brass handle. Squatting down in front of it he idly turned the dial back and forth, the internal mechanism clicking softly as it rotated. There was no way he could force the door, and although he had, in his long association with the criminal classes, learnt how to pick a simple lock, this was way beyond his elementary breaking-and-entering skills. He either needed the combination, which had most likely gone to the grave with the safe's owner, or else . . .

He remained where he was for a moment, then, snorting as if to say 'What the hell?', went back up to the living room, lifted the phone and dialled. The line rang six times, and then a gruff voice answered.

'Aziz? It's Inspector Khalifa. No, no, it's nothing to do with that. I just need a favour.'

'If this is some sort of trick . . .'

'It's—'

'Because I'm straight now. You understand? Completely above board. All that stuff . . . it's in the past. I was a different person then.'

Aziz Ibrahim Abd-el Shakir, popularly known as 'The Ghost' because of his ability to pass through even the most heavily secured of doors, opened his tool-bag, removed a small foam pad, laid it on the floor in front of the safe and knelt down on it, edging his knees back and forth until he was comfortable. A small, plump man with a bulbous, turnip-like nose and permanently sweat-stained armpits, he took several deep, slow breaths as if about to start meditating, then reached out a hand

and ran it gently over the top and sides of the safe, as if stroking a nervous animal, calming it, winning its confidence.

'This is just between us,' Khalifa assured him. 'No-one will ever know.'

'They'd better not,' Aziz muttered, leaning forward and pressing his ear against the safe door, tweaking the dial back and forth, listening.

'You have my—'

'Ssshhh!'

He continued to manipulate the dial for almost a minute, face puckered in concentration, the sweat-blooms beneath his armpits seeming to grow and spread, then came upright again.

'Can you open it?' asked Khalifa.

Aziz ignored him, fiddling in his bag.

'Chubb casing, Mauser dial system,' he muttered, pulling out a stethoscope, pencil-torch and mini-hammer of the sort geologists use to break rocks. 'Frangible tumblers, three, maybe four; double levers. Oh, you're a sweet little lady!'

'Can you—'

'Of course I can open it!' snapped Aziz. 'I can open anything. Except my wife's legs.'

He smiled sourly at his joke and began tapping around the dial with his hammer, eyes closed in concentration.

Aziz Abd-el Shakir was generally regarded, by everyone including himself, as the finest safe-breaker in Upper Egypt. The man who had twice broken into the main vault at the National Bank of Egypt offices in Luxor, and cracked the supposedly uncrackable American Express safe in Aswan, he was a legend among both his fellow criminals and those whose job it was to bring him to justice. Khalifa had first encountered him back in 1992 after he had cleaned out the strongbox at the Luxor Sheraton, and their paths had crossed several times since, most recently two years ago when the detective had nailed him for a local jeweller's-shop robbery. On that particular occasion Khalifa had written to the trial judge recommending a lenient sentence on compassionate grounds, Aziz's youngest son having just been diagnosed with leukaemia. Aziz had heard about the letter and, with that curious code of morality that allows a man to make his living from stealing yet at the same time always to honour his debts, had contacted Khalifa and told him should he ever need a favour, he only had to ask. Which is why he was there now.

He laid aside the hammer and donned his stethoscope, holding its disc flat against the safe door with one hand while gently tweaking the dial back and forth with the other, his torch held in his mouth, his eyes closed as he listened intently to the movements of the tumblers inside. Khalifa knew full well that he was lying when he said he'd gone straight, that he was as active a criminal as he'd ever been. At this particular moment, however, he needed his expertise and wasn't about to argue the point.

'There's a good girl.' Aziz was whispering to himself, a faint smile etched across his face. 'Don't be difficult now. Oh, you're a sweet little lady. A real sweet lady.'

In the end it took him fewer than twenty minutes to work out the combination, a source of evident satisfaction for, as the last tumbler clicked into place, he broke into a broad, brown-toothed smile and, bending forward, planted a kiss on the top of the safe, his lips leaving a damp mark on the green-grey metal. 'The Ghost strikes again!' he said with a chuckle, opening the door a couple of inches and gathering up his equipment.

They went upstairs and Khalifa saw him out.

'Keep your nose clean,' he said as Aziz started down the front steps.

The safe-breaker grunted and set off along the gravel path to the front gate. When he reached it he turned.

'You're OK, Khalifa,' he called back. He paused, then added, 'For a pig, that is.'

He winked and disappeared through the screen of palm and mimosa trees.

Khalifa watched him go, then returned to the basement where he squatted in front of the safe and pulled open the door. There were only three things inside: an official-looking brown manila envelope which on closer inspection turned out to contain the dead man's will; a pistol of a type Khalifa had never seen before, with a thin barrel protruding from a chunky, L-shaped body;

and, right at the back of the safe, a rectangular object wrapped in a length of black cloth. The latter proved unexpectedly heavy, and after undoing the cloth Khalifa found himself gazing at a large gold bar. On its glistening upper surface was stamped an eagle with wings spread, clutching in its talons the interlocking arms of a Nazi swastika. Khalifa let out a low whistle.

'What the hell were you up to, Mr Jansen? Just what the bloody hell were you up to?'

KALANDIA REFUGEE CAMP

The summons to martyrdom, when it came, was not at all what Yunis Abu Jish had imagined it would be.

For months now he'd been praying that he would be approached and asked to give himself for his God and his people, picturing in his mind an intensive selection procedure through the course of which his courage and faith would be repeatedly tested and triumphantly proved. As it was, he received a single, brief phone call informing him that he had been chosen by al-Mulatham as a potential *shaheed*, and instructing him to consider carefully whether he felt himself ready for this honour. If he did not, he was to do nothing; he would not be contacted again. If he did, he was to don his Dome of the Rock T-shirt – how on earth did they know he had a T-shirt with a picture of the Qubbat al-Sakhra on the front? – and go at noon the following day to the Kalandia checkpoint on the Jerusalem-Ramallah road where he was to remain for exactly thirty minutes beneath the hoarding with the advertisement for Master Satellite Dishes. Thereafter he was to start preparing himself with prayer and study of the Holy Koran, informing no-one of his situation, not even close family. More detailed instructions would follow.

And that was it. No explanation of how or why or by whom he had been chosen; no indication of what his eventual mission might be. The cold precision of the call, the businesslike manner of the man at the other end, had frightened him, and after the line had gone dead he sat for a long while trembling, his face pale, the receiver still pressed against his ear. Can I do this, he wondered to himself. Am I strong enough? Am I worthy? To imagine, after all, is one thing, to do quite another. Fear and doubt almost overwhelmed him.

Gradually, however, his misgivings eased, giving way first to acceptance, then determination, and finally a swelling sense of euphoria and pride. He had been chosen! He, Yunis Abu Jish Sabah, hero of his people, instrument of God's vengeance. He imagined the honour his family would feel, the joy of every Palestinian. The glory.

With a yelp of delight he slammed down the phone and charged outside to where his mother was sitting peeling potatoes, kneeling in front of her and wrapping his arms around her waist.

'It's all going to be OK,' he said, laughing. 'Everything is going to be OK. God is with us. *Allah-u-akhbar.*'

JERUSALEM

It was almost midday before Ben-Roi finally surfaced from his drunken slumber and staggered out of bed, coughing and cursing. He took a cold shower, downed a Goldstar to drive off his hangover, then dressed, dabbed on some after-shave and took a bus over to the Jewish cemetery on the Mount of Olives, stopping en route to buy a single white lily.

He visited her at least once a day. More sometimes, if the loneliness became particularly acute. As a kid he remembered thinking it was something only old people did, going to cemeteries. A way of passing the time when you had nothing better to do with your life, when all the joy and hope was behind you. Yet here he was now, not even thirty-four, and the visit was the focal point of his day. Of his entire existence.

He alighted from the bus on the Jericho Road and entered the cemetery through a gate at its bottom left-hand corner, weaving his way upwards through the rows of flat, rectangular tombstones that covered the terraced hillside like a vast fragmented stairway. Away to his left the seven golden cupolas of the Church of St Mary Magdalen gleamed in the afternoon sun; ahead and above, the ugly arched façade of the Intercontinental Hotel loomed on the hill's summit, like a row of hoops graffiti'd onto the clean blue sky. Behind, across the Kidron Valley, sat the Dome of the Rock, the buildings of the Old City stacked up behind it like a jumble of children's play bricks.

Her grave was about halfway up, at the cemetery's southern edge, a simple flat stone bearing her name and dates – born 21 December 1976; died 12 March 2004 – and at the bottom a quotation from the Song of Solomon: 'I am a rose of Sharon, a lily of the valleys.'

He stood staring down at it, catching his breath after the steep climb, then squatted and laid the flower on top of the quotation, with beside it a small rock he had picked up on his way through the cemetery, as per Jewish custom. He bent and kissed the grave, running his hand over its warm yellow surface, allowing his lips to linger for a moment on the deep chiselled grooves of her name. Then, with a sigh, he straightened again.

Strangely, he'd never been able to cry for her. However intense the pain, however overwhelming, the tears just wouldn't come. He wept at lesser things – crap TV programmes, cheap song lyrics, schmaltzy novels – but for her there was nothing, just emptiness, the tears damming up inside him so that sometimes he struggled even to draw breath, like a drowning man only just able to keep his mouth above the waterline.

He clasped his hands together, part of him feeling he ought to recite a *kiddush*, or at least say a prayer of some sort. He dismissed the idea. What the fuck was the point of praying to a God who allowed things like that to happen? Who sat up in His heaven and gazed down dispassionately on so much horror and misery? No, he thought to himself, there's no comfort in belief; it's a hollow thing, empty, tuneless, like a cracked bell. He thrust his hands into his pockets and turned away from the grave, gazing across at the Old City, humming an old Jewish folk song his grandfather had taught him about a poor boy who falls in love with a rich rabbi's daughter.

He'd arrested her. That's how they'd met. Corny beyond belief, like something out of a cheap romance novel, but that's the way it had happened. She'd been part of a group protesting against Israeli settlement building on the outskirts of the city; he'd been in the police cordon thrown up to hold the protesters back. There was a mêlée, she kicked him in the shin, he slapped a pair of handcuffs on her and threw her in the back of a police van. It all happened so quickly he didn't have time to notice how beautiful she was. Only later, in the holding cell back at the station, while taking down her details as she held forth on the iniquities of Israel's occupation of the West Bank, did he find his gaze lingering on her unruly tangle of brown hair, her slim, sunbrowned arms, her sparkling grey eyes, angry and passionate yet gentle too, full of wit and laughter, so that somehow he knew she was a good person, a kind person, and that her raised voice and belligerent manner were just a front.

He could have charged her – should have charged her – but in the end he let her off with a caution. The fact that she showed no gratitude for this favour – on the contrary, seemed rather put out by it, as if his leniency somehow diminished the impact of her protest – for some reason attracted him to her even more than her physical appearance.

He had never been especially confident around women, uneasy within his bear-like frame and craggy, big-nosed face, and it took him three days to pluck up the courage to call her. When he finally did she mistook him for a friend playing a joke; then, realizing he was who he said he was, told him to fuck off and slammed down the phone. He called again the next day, and the day after that, and again the day after that, his interest (and humiliation) increasing in direct proportion to the number of rejections he received, until eventually, exasperated, she agreed to have a drink in a local bar 'just to get you off my bloody back'.

Even then it is doubtful anything would have happened between them had it not been for the spaghetti. Up to that point in the meeting they had struggled to make any sort of connection, their conversation stilted and uncomfortable, punctuated with embarrassed silences and occasional raised voices as she harangued him about their government's treatment of the Palestinians while he retorted that the Palestinians deserved everything they fucking got. They were actually in the process of leaving the bar, acknowledging that they had nothing in common, that the evening was going nowhere, when a waiter walked straight into him, depositing a plate of sauce-covered pasta down the front of his white shirt. She burst out laughing; he snapped at her, but then started chuckling too, appreciating the ludicrousness of the situation; and in that moment of shared amusement something finally sparked between them, like a match striking in the darkness, driving back the shadows. The waiter lent him a T-shirt, which lightened their mood further for it was way too tight for him and bore the embarrassingly inappropriate logo GAY AND PROUD. Accepting an offer of compensatory drinks, they returned to their table and started the conversation anew, this time steering away from politics and talking about themselves instead, their backgrounds and interests and families, exploring.

She worked as an editor for a small co-operative publishing house specializing in poetry and children's books, devoting three evenings a week to volunteer work with B'Tselem, the Israeli human rights organization. The daughter of one of the country's most decorated war heroes, now a

Labour Knesset member, she had grown up on a kibbutz on the northern edge of Galilee, the youngest of three sisters. Her two elder siblings were both married with children.

'Perfect Jewish mothers,' she said. 'I'm the black sheep.'

'Me too,' admitted Ben-Roi. 'All the men in my family are farmers. Dad was horrified when I said I wanted to be a policeman. Although not as horrified as he'd be if he could see me now.'

He glanced down at his T-shirt. She laughed.

'So what made you want to become a tool of the fascist regime?' she asked.

'Al Pacino, believe it or not.'

'Al Pacino?'

'Well, a film he made.'

She held up a hand. 'Let me guess.' There was a pause, then, '*Serpico.*'

His eyes widened. 'How did you know that?'

'It's one of my favourite movies.'

'You're the only person I've met who's ever seen it! I love that film. I remember when I first watched it, on TV, when I was fourteen. I thought, "That's what I want to be." Just like Al Pacino. Doing good things. Making a difference. I met him once, you know. After I graduated from police college. We had our photo taken together. He's tiny.'

He took a slug of wine and their eyes met, only momentarily but enough for each to know something was moving within them. Later he would recall that first meeting of gazes, that fleeting, uncertain acknowledgement of shared feeling, as one of the most perfect moments of his life.

They remained in the bar for almost three hours, talking and talking, delving ever deeper into each other, gently stripping back the layers, before, at her suggestion, moving on to a small restaurant she knew in the Armenian Quarter of the Old City where they ate *soujuk* and *khaghoghi derev* and drank a bottle of fragrant, slightly bitter red wine. Afterwards, half-drunk, they wandered through the deserted streets, exchanging the odd embarrassed glance but saying little, passing down into the Jewish Quarter and then doubling back on themselves through the Mauristan and eventually up to the New Gate, where they drank a final coffee at a late-night café and he presented her with a white lily he had plucked from a vase on the café counter.

'Thank you,' she said, clutching the flower to her chest. 'It's beautiful.'

They went outside and made their farewells, a huge moon bobbing above them like an orange in a pool of deep black water. He had an overwhelming urge to lean down and kiss her, but held back, not wanting to spoil the moment. She had no such qualms, and, brushing aside the hand he had proffered, seized his shoulders, got up on tiptoes and kissed him passionately on the lips.

'I'm sorry,' she said, drawing away, eyes sparkling. 'I couldn't resist. I think it must be that aftershave you're wearing.'

'I didn't think it was for my good looks.'

She kissed him again, gentler this time, slower, pressing herself against him.

'You look great to me.'

'Then maybe it's time for an eye-test.'

She smiled and, reaching up a hand, touched his huge chin, his nose, his cheek. They remained like that for a long moment, staring at each other. Then, with a final hug, they parted, agreeing to meet up again in a couple of nights' time. As he walked away she called after him.

'Open your eyes, Arieh. Look at what's going on in this country. I need you to do that. Because it's poisoning us all. And unless we do something to change it there's no future. Not for Israel, not for us, not for anyone. Open your eyes. Please.'

Over the ensuing weeks and months, as their relationship had grown and deepened, as love for her had filled his soul, he had done as she asked, seeing things he had never wanted to see, asking questions he had never wanted to ask. It had caused him great pain, this awakening, great confusion and uncertainty. Yet he had followed her lead nonetheless, because he loved her, and trusted her, and knew deep down she was helping him to grow, to become a better person.

And then, after all that, despite all that, they had killed her. The very people she had fought so hard to defend, whose cause she had so passionately advocated. Blown away her legs, shattered her face; her beautiful, gentle, laughing face. So that now, standing alone in the cemetery gazing down at her gravestone, it seemed to Ben-Roi that the future of which they had both dreamed, a future of peace and understanding and hope and light, was no more than an empty mirage. And like the thirsty desert traveller who endures the agony of watching a longed-for oasis evaporate before his eyes, no more than a trick of the light, he wished he had simply kept his eyes closed and never fallen for the illusion in the first place.

He finished mumbling his song, fingers fiddling with the silver menorah that hung against his chest, a tiny piece of her that he kept with him always, and then, after bending and kissing the grave one more time, he started back down through the cemetery.

Near the bottom he came upon a solitary figure in a *yarmulke* and *tallit* standing beside a pair of graves set slightly apart from the rest, on their own little plot of land. The man's back was to him, and it was only as he passed that he realized it was Baruch Har-Zion. He turned his head slightly and for a brief instant their eyes met, each nodding fractionally in acknowledgement of the other, before Ben-Roi turned away again and continued downwards to the gate at the bottom of the cemetery, where he found Har-Zion's bodyguard Avi Steiner leaning against a wall. Again, there was the briefest meeting of eyes, the faintest nod of acknowledgement, and then Ben-Roi was out on the road and walking back towards the Old City, wondering where he could get a drink before heading into the station for the start of his shift.

JERUSALEM

Layla crossed the paved courtyard in front of the Church of the Holy Sepulchre, pausing briefly to take in the double-arched entrance with its slim marble flanking pillars, straight and sinuous as saplings, before passing through into the gloomy, cavernous interior. A trio of elderly women were kneeling in front of the Stone of Unction, crossing themselves and bending forward to kiss the stone's grainy pink surface; to her right, a flight of stone steps led upwards into a gilded, softly lit chapel, the traditional site of Christ's crucifixion. From deep within the bowels of the building came the echo of chanting, the latter clashing and merging with a hymn being sung elsewhere in the church so that the entire interior seemed to throb with a low cacophony of sound. A group of Armenian oblates bustled past, led by a priest in a long cloak and pointed hood.

For a moment she hovered just inside the entrance, eyes adjusting to the murky half-light, nostrils absorbing the pervasive musky odour of incense, then turned to the left and walked into

311

the vast domed Rotunda that dominated the western end of the church. A young Greek Orthodox priest was sweeping the floor. Layla approached him and asked where she might find Father Sergius, the contact Tom Roberts had given her the previous night.

'He food,' said the priest in pidgin English, making an eating motion with his hand. 'Coming ten hour.'

'Tonight?'

The priest furrowed his brow, confused, then suddenly smiled.

'No ten hour. Ten . . .'

'Minutes?'

'Yes, yes. Minute. Ten minute.'

Layla thanked him and, leaving him to his sweeping, wandered across to one of the massive granite columns that bore the Rotunda's dome, sitting down on a bench beside it. In front of her rose the Aedicule, the gaudy, icon-filled shrine that marked the place of Christ's burial. Behind it the Katholicon, the Greek Orthodox choir that dominated the central portion of the building, stretched away eastwards, hemmed in on either side by a gloomy honeycomb of corridors and galleries and doorways and shrines, their masonry blackened and smoothed by centuries of candle-smoke and devotional touching.

She gazed around for a while, taking in the ponderous, jumbled architecture, the crowds of tourists and pilgrims, then opened her bag and removed her notepad, flicking through it until she came to the notes she had scribbled down the previous night.

Her search of the internet had thrown up several thousand web-page matches for the name William de Relincourt, most of which had nothing to do with the man she was interested in. A trawl through some of the hundred or so that did had revealed that, while he was the subject of a great deal of imaginative speculation, hard facts about de Relincourt were few and far between. What little *was* known – all that was known, indeed – appeared to come from two brief passages in medieval chronicles, both translated and reproduced on a number of the websites.

The shorter of these, from William of Tyre's *Historia Rerum in Partibus Transmarinis Gestarum* (*The History of Deeds Done Beyond the Sea*), written some time around 1170, recorded how 'After they had conquered the city the Crusaders found the church (of the Holy Sepulchre) too small, and they added to it a sturdy, high building. At the start William de Relincourt had this work, until he fell into dispute with King Baldwin and suffered a grievous fate. A bell tower was also built.' The second passage, longer and more detailed than the first, appeared in a work called *Massaoth Schel Rabbi Benjamin* (*The Itinerary of Rabbi Benjamin*), the author a Jew from the Spanish city of Tudela who had visited the Holy

Land in 1169 as part of a ten-year journey around the Mediterranean and the Near East:

A story is also told about the Frenchman Gillom of Relincar, who built that church known to the Christians as Holy Sepulchre. In the course of that great work, it is said, at a time when trenches were being dug for the laying-in of stones, as is common practice in such things, this Gillom found a secret place in which was concealed a treasure of very great power and beauty, unlike any treasure that was known before. Being of a wise disposition, and by no means approving of the treatment of the Jews, he spoke nothing of this thing, but rather hid it away, for such was its nature it would have aroused much greed and envy among the Christians. News of it came nonetheless to King Badouin who ordered that it should be given over. And when this Gillom refused his eyes were put out and he was cast into a deep well, where he died only after four days, for he was a man strong both of body and spirit. Few know of this thing, which was told to me by Simon the Jew, who had it from his grandfather.

Around these two passages a whole thicket of theory and supposition had sprung up, some of it relatively innocuous, most downright absurd. One website, for instance, which opened to a fanfare of Gregorian chants, claimed that William had discovered the mummified body of Christ, thereby undermining the entire Christian doctrine of the Resurrection. Another, decorated with mysterious-looking astrological symbols and entitled Sacred Guardians of the Cosmic Portal, had argued in all seriousness that de Relincourt had stumbled across some sort of intergalactic doorway that allowed him to access higher dimensions of space and time, thereby joining an exclusive club of time-travelling initiates that included Moses, Tutankhamun, Confucius and King Arthur. There had been plenty more in the same vein, linking de Relincourt with everything from Freemasons to the Holy Grail, the Knights Templar to the Bermuda Triangle. So far as Layla could make out, however, no realistic explanation had ever been put forward as to precisely what the two passages meant, nor had any independent evidence ever come to light either to corroborate the authenticity of the story they were telling or to confirm that someone named William de Relincourt had ever actually existed.

The whole thing seemed flimsy in the extreme. Yet despite this paucity of hard evidence, despite the niggling doubts in the back of her mind that she was being led on some elaborate wild-goose chase, the more she had read the more hooked she had found herself becoming. Even with her limited knowledge of things medieval she realized that if the photocopy she had been sent was of a genuine letter – and it remained a big 'if' – then the original must be an extremely important and valuable historical document, proving not only that de Relincourt was a real person, but that he *had* found some unnamed treasure beneath the church.

What had really whetted her journalistic appetite, however, and continued to whet it, was not so much the prospect of shedding light on some nine-hundred-year-old mystery, intriguing as that was, but rather the connection between that mystery and current events. *I am in possession of information that could prove invaluable to this man in his struggle against the Zionist oppressor . . . The information of which I speak is intimately connected with the enclosed document.* How could the story of William de Relincourt help a man like al-Mulatham? Why should a medieval legend be of any relevance to contemporary Palestine? What was the link between past and present? These were the questions that were occupying her mind now, spinning round and round inside her head like the sparks from a Catherine wheel. It was something important. She could feel it. Something big. But she needed more information. More facts. More pieces of the jigsaw.

'He here now.'

She looked up. The young Greek Orthodox priest was standing over her, still holding his broom.

'Father Sergius,' he said. 'He come.'

He pointed over her shoulder into the Katholicon, where an enormously fat man in black robes, his grey hair tied into a pony tail behind his head, was arranging a ladder in the angle between a wall and a pillar. Layla thanked the priest and, standing, set off across the choir towards the man, passing beneath a cartwheel-sized brass chandelier and coming up to him just as he clambered onto the first rung of the ladder.

'Father Sergius?'

He looked down at her.

'My name's Layla al-Madani. I'm a journalist. A friend of mine suggested you might be able to help me with a story I'm researching.'

The priest gazed at her for a moment, eyes bright, then stepped back down onto the paved floor. He had a jovial, pumpkin-like face, heavily creased and half-covered with a bushy grey beard. Beneath his robes, she noticed, he was wearing socks, sandals and baggy purple trousers.

'Apparently you know everything there is to know about the history of this church,' she added.

He smiled. 'Your friend gives me more credit than I deserve. No-one knows everything there is to know about the Church of the Holy Sepulchre. I've been here for thirty years and I haven't even scratched the surface. It can be an extremely . . . challenging place.'

317

His voice was deep and resonant, his English fluent. He smelt faintly sweet, either from after-shave or the scent of incense on his robes.

'What is it you wish to know?' he asked.

'I'm trying to find out about someone called William de Relincourt.'

His smile broadened and, reaching up, he stroked his beard thoughtfully, running his fingers through the wiry grey fronds of hair.

'William de Relincourt, eh? And why would you want to know about him, I wonder?'

Layla shrugged. 'It's just a story I'm researching. Mysteries of Jerusalem. A colour piece.'

'Not your usual sort of article.'

He noticed the puzzled look on her face and started chuckling.

'Oh, I know who you are, Ms al-Madani. We're not that cut off from the world here. I've read a lot of your articles over the years. Very . . . forth-right. You don't let the Israelis get away with anything. I can't recall you ever showing much interest in medieval history, though.'

'It's just a one-off,' she said, not wanting to give away too much information, trying to keep things vague. 'I'll get back to Israel-bashing as soon as it's done.'

The priest's chuckling redoubled, his eyes bright with knowing amusement, as if he was well aware that she wasn't giving him the full story but wasn't overly perturbed by the fact.

'In that case,' he said, lowering his hand from

his beard and resting it on his protuberant belly, 'we must help you get your article finished as soon as possible. We can't have the Israelis getting complacent, can we? Mind you, I shall require something from you in return.'

'That being?'

'To hold my ladder for me while I try and get rid of these damned birds.'

He nodded upwards to where a pair of white pigeons were fluttering around, banging themselves repeatedly against the windows set high in the walls of the church.

'I need to get one open,' he explained. 'Let them out. Otherwise they shit all over the tourists.'

As if to confirm his words, a large, paint-like glob descended from on high, spattering onto the brass chandelier. Father Sergius tutted and, turning, clambered back onto his ladder.

'Make sure you hold it steady,' he said. 'It sometimes slips.'

She stepped forward and anchored the ladder with her foot while he started climbing, moving with surprising agility for a man his size and weight. Four rungs up he leant over and grasped a long wooden pole that was leaning against the wall, clutching it in one hand while using the other to steady himself as he continued upwards, his billowing robes affording Layla a clear view of his pantaloon-clad legs and backside. A group of tourists wandered in, forming a circle around the *omphalos*, the ornately carved marble basin in the middle of the floor that according to Greek tradition marked the centre-point of the world.

'He attracts all sorts of unlikely people, you know,' called Father Sergius as he reached the top of the ladder. 'William de Relincourt. Last year we had some Italian scientist who wanted to go over the entire church with a . . . what are those things called for measuring radiation?'

'Geiger counter?'

'Exactly. He was convinced William had uncovered the remains of an alien spaceship and that it was still buried underneath the floor somewhere. Complete madman.'

He started raising the pole, grasping a ledge with his left hand while straining upwards towards the nearest window three metres above him.

'And then there's some American group who think he found a doorway into another world.'

'The Sacred Guardians of the Cosmic Portal,' Layla said with a smile.

'You've heard of them?'

'I saw their website.'

'Crazy. Absolutely crazy. We've even got an old Jewish guy who comes in every day because he thinks de Relincourt found the Ten Commandments or something. Only Jew I've ever seen in here. Stands outside the Aedicule praying like it's the Wailing Wall, poor old fool. Every day.'

He was almost at full stretch now, wobbling precariously on the second-from-top rung, prodding at the catch of the window with the pole, trying to get it open. Three times the pole slipped before he finally managed to wedge it directly beneath the catch, forcing the window outwards and open, in the process leaning so far back that Layla had the uncomfortable feeling he was going to fall directly on top of her. He somehow managed to steady himself and, clutching the ledge, waited until the pigeons had located the window and flown out. As soon as they had gone he raised the pole again and, using a hook attached to its end, pulled the window shut and clambered back down to earth, breathing heavily.

'We need to get a bigger ladder,' he puffed, laying his pole on the floor and brushing down his robes. 'I keep telling them. But then the Catholics say we don't need one and the Syrians say we can't afford it and the Armenians and Copts can't agree on whether it should be a wooden ladder or a metal one, so nothing ever gets done. Believe me, compared to some of the people in this place the de Relincourt lot are models of reason and good sense. Tea?'

She declined his offer and, leaving the pole and ladder, the two of them wandered back into the Rotunda. Two women, one elderly, the other young, both dressed in black, were kneeling inside the cramped interior of the Aedicule, holding candles and praying. The young Greek priest had disappeared.

'So,' said Father Sergius, motioning her to the bench she had sat on earlier and lowering himself down beside her, 'that's your side of the bargain. Now you'll be wanting to know about William de Relincourt. I'm not sure there's much I can tell you, but ask away. I'll be as much help as I can.'

Layla pulled out her notebook and pen and, crossing her legs, rested the book on her knee, biro poised above a blank page.

'The first thing I wanted to ask was about sources,' she said. 'I've been looking on the internet and as far as I can make out de Relincourt is only mentioned by two medieval writers: William of Tyre and . . .'

She leafed back through her notes, trying to find the name of the Jewish traveller.

'Benjamin of Tudela,' said Father Sergius.

'That's the one. You know the passages?'

'Not off by heart, but yes, I've read them. A while ago, mind you.'

Layla bent down and pulled a crumpled sheet of paper from her bag.

'I printed them off last night.'

She handed him the sheet. Holding it slightly away from him to catch the light, he read through it. When he'd finished he passed it back to her.

'So far as I can make out,' she said, 'Baldwin, or Badoiun as Benjamin calls him, was king of Jerusalem from 1100 to 1118.'

Father Sergius nodded.

'Which means that both Benjamin and William of Tyre were writing, what, sixty, seventy years after the events they were describing.'

He thought for a moment, then nodded again. 'Correct.'

'So is there anything else?' she asked. 'Any other chronicle that mentions de Relincourt, gives more information? Anything to corroborate the story?'

The priest clasped his hands on his belly where they sat like large pink crabs sunning themselves on a rock.

'Not that I've ever heard of. Certainly none of the early crusader chroniclers mention him. Ekkehard of Aura, Albert of Aachen, and . . . oh, what's the other one's name? . . . Fulcher of Chartres, that's it – all completely silent. William of Tyre and Benjamin of Tudela seem to be all we've got.'

'And only Benjamin says anything about a hidden treasure,' said Layla. 'William of Tyre just mentions that de Relincourt and King Baldwin had some sort of dispute.'

'I expect they probably heard different versions of the story,' he said. 'You often get that with medieval chroniclers. Especially when they're writing years after a particular event, describing it at second or third hand. They have different sources, pick up different details. It's simply a matter of emphasis.'

'So which version's more reliable in this case?'

He raised his eyebrows. 'Difficult to be sure, although on balance I'd say probably Benjamin of Tudela. Admittedly he was only passing through the Holy Land, unlike William of Tyre, who actually lived here. But the extra detail suggests he probably heard a fuller version of the story. William's account sounds like he's just repeating an old rumour.'

Layla scribbled a note in her book.

'And you think the story's true?'

Father Sergius shrugged. 'Who knows? There's no physical evidence to support it, but then that's no reason to discount it. Benjamin was an extremely scrupulous chronicler. Didn't go in for legends or old wives' tales or any of that sort of thing. Always checked his sources. I believe him.'

There was a sudden burst of flashing as a group of Japanese tourists trooped into the Rotunda, snapping pictures of the dome and Aedicule. Layla curled one leg underneath the other, resting her notebook on her knee.

'Which begs the obvious question,' she said. 'If Benjamin's story *is* true, what did William actually find? What was this . . .' She glanced down at the printed sheet. 'This "treasure of very great power and beauty, unlike any treasure that was known before"?'

Father Sergius smiled and, reaching behind his head, started fiddling with the band of his pony tail.

'As you say, the obvious question. And the one I can't answer, I'm afraid. Although I think you'll find it wasn't a spaceship.'

He chuckled to himself, fingers tweaking at the band, trying to arrange his hair more neatly. In front of them the two women came out of the Aedicule, their prayers finished, and the Japanese tourists started filing inside, the shrine's cramped interior only large enough to admit four of them at a go. The singing and chanting that Layla had heard when she first entered the building had died away, leaving just the echo of chattering voices, as though the church's stones were whispering to one another.

'No,' repeated Father Sergius, having adjusted the band to his satisfaction and laying his hands back down on his belly, 'I have no more idea what William de Relincourt found than the thousands of other people who have speculated on the subject over the last nine hundred years. Maybe some ancient relic, maybe the bones of an early saint, maybe a treasure from the original Byzantine basilica – you name it. We simply don't know.'

Layla was tapping her pen on her thigh.

'And you say there's no physical evidence. Nothing in the church itself?'

He shook his head. 'If William de Relincourt was ever here he left no traces.'

She raised the pen and scratched at her eyebrow.

'What's underneath us?' she asked. 'What would have been there when de. Relincourt was working?'

He stared up at the domed ceiling for a moment, fingers drumming on his belly, then heaved himself up and, indicating that Layla should follow, waddled across to the entrance to the

Rotunda where they had a clear view of both the Aedicule and the church's main doorway.

'A quick tour,' he said. 'Just to give you the background.'

He spread his arms, taking in the building around them.

'At the time of the crucifixion, so far as we know, this entire area used to lie outside the walls of the city, which were a hundred metres or so to the south.' He nodded to indicate the direction.

'According to the Bible and early Christian writers, Golgotha, the hill where the crucifixion took place, stood over there.' He pointed towards the elevated chapel Layla had passed on her way in. 'While over there' – he pointed back towards the Aedicule – 'lay an abandoned quarry in which various wealthy Jews had cut tombs for themselves. It was in one of these tombs, that of Joseph of Arimathea, that our Lord's body was laid to rest.'

The last of the Japanese tourists emerged from the Aedicule and trooped off into the Katholicon, cameras still flashing.

'For a hundred years after the crucifixion all this area was a place of pilgrimage and prayer for early Christians,' he continued. 'In AD 135, however, the emperor Hadrian levelled it and built a temple to the gods Juno, Jupiter and Minerva. That stood here for a further two hundred years until Constantine the Great, the first Christian emperor, tore Hadrian's temple down and built a magnificent church in its place incorporating all the holy sites.'

Again he pointed towards the elevated chapel and the Aedicule.

'Constantine's church was in its turn destroyed in the Persian invasion of 614. It was rebuilt two years later, knocked down by an earthquake, rebuilt, knocked down by the Fatimid Caliph Al-Hakim, rebuilt and knocked down several times more before finally the crusaders arrived and erected the structure we see today, which was completed in 1149. Even this has had extensive alterations in the intervening years. The dome of the Rotunda, for instance, and the Aedicule both date mainly from the nineteenth century.'

Layla was furiously scribbling in her book, trying to keep up with him.

'The point I'm making,' he said, stamping his foot on the floor, 'is that beneath us lie the remains of over a thousand years of building and rebuilding, right the way down to the original bedrock. Who knows what de Relincourt found when he started digging? Jews, Romans, early Christians, Byzantines, Persians, Muslims – any one of them could have buried something here which William subsequently unearthed. And of course before that there were Canaanites, Jebusites, Egyptians, Assyrians, Babylonians and Greeks. They've all been in Jerusalem at one point or another. The fact is we simply don't know what was down there, or who left it there. And to be honest I doubt we ever will. Which is, of course, part of the story's appeal.'

He fell silent, fiddling with a button on his robes. A pair of Coptic monks hurried past wearing their distinctive black skullcaps and carved wooden crosses. Layla finished scribbling and stared down at her notes, intrigued and frustrated in equal measure.

'It's like trying to put together a jigsaw where half the pieces are missing and you don't even know what the overall picture is supposed to be,' she muttered. 'And doing it blindfold.'

Father Sergius smiled. 'Such is history. A giant jigsaw puzzle.'

From somewhere behind them came the faint clack of a walking stick on stone, the sound growing louder until eventually an elderly man hobbled past them into the Rotunda and made his way across to the Aedicule. His back was bent, the skin of his face slack and covered with liverspots. He stopped in front of the shrine, produced a *yarmulke* and a small black book, and started to pray, bending stiffly back and forth, mumbling to himself, leaning heavily on his stick.

'That's the one I was telling you about,' said Father Sergius quietly. 'Every day he comes in, regular as clockwork. Convinced de Relincourt found the Ten Commandments, or the Ark of the Covenant, or King David's sword – I forget which. Some ancient Jewish thing. That's what these sort of stories do, ultimately – fulfil some inner need, some hope that can't be resolved in the real world.'

They stood watching the man for a while, then Layla looked back down at her notebook, flicking through the pages.

'Benjamin of Tudela says that de Relincourt was "by no means approving of the treatment of the Jews",' she said. 'What does that mean?'

Father Sergius smiled sadly, gazing up at the dome above.

'The crusaders treated the Jews appallingly,' he said with a sigh. 'Slaughtered thousands of them as they made their way across Europe. Tens of thousands. When they captured Jerusalem they herded the city's entire Jewish population into the main synagogue and burnt them all to death. Men, women, children. Every one of them.' He shook his head. 'Did the same to the Muslims. The mosques were ankle-deep in blood, it was said. You would have thought something like that, such shared horror, would draw the two religions together. But then you look at what's happening today . . .' He raised a hand and rubbed his temples. 'God's Holy Land, and so much pain. Always so much pain.'

He continued rubbing his temples for a moment, then lowered his hand and turned to Layla.

'It's time I started preparing for the midday service.'

'Of course,' said Layla. 'Thank you for your time.'

'I'm not sure I've been any help.'

'You have,' she said. 'A lot.'

She returned her notebook to her bag and swung the bag over her shoulder.

'Keep up with the writing,' he said. 'It will make a difference.'

She smiled and, raising a hand in farewell, turned to go.

'One interesting fact for your article,' he called out after her. 'Hitler was obsessed with him, apparently. William de Relincourt. Had a team of academics researching the story, trying to find out what de Relincourt found and what happened to it. Was convinced it was some sort of secret weapon he could use against the Jews. Or so the stories claim. Like I said, de Relincourt attracts all sorts of strange people. I wish you all the best, Ms al-Madani.'

He nodded at her and, clasping his hands behind his back, wandered off into the Katholicon.

LUXOR

'Hello? Hello? Yes, my name is Inspector Yusuf Khalifa of the Egyptian Police Force. I think I spoke to you . . . Khalifa. No, Khalifa. Khal-ee-far. Exactly. I am trying to find someone who can help me with a case I am working on involving an Israeli national. What? No, a case I am working . . . Do you speak English? What? . . . Yes, OK, I will hold, thank you, thank you.'

Khalifa cradled the telephone receiver between his head and shoulder and, reaching out, pulled a cigarette from the packet in front of him, clicking his tongue in frustration. He had spent the best part of an hour vainly trying to track down someone in the Israeli Police Force who could help him with background details on Hannah Schlegel, being shunted from department to department, office to office and person to person before eventually ending up back where he'd started, at the National Police Headquarters in Jerusalem, with a woman who hardly seemed to speak any English, let alone Arabic. He had the distinct feeling that because he was Egyptian they were not taking him as seriously as they would if he had been, say, American or European. He lit his cigarette, drew on it and exhaled an annoyed billow of smoke, listening to the silence at the other end of the line.

'Hello?' he called, thinking maybe he had been cut off. 'Hello?'

The line clicked back into life.

'I ask you to hold,' came the woman's voice, sharp, as though she was talking to a naughty child. 'Please do this.'

The line went dead again.

'Dammit,' muttered Khalifa, chewing on the filter of his cigarette, jaw tight with annoyance. 'I'm trying to *help* you, for God's sake. I'm trying to help you, woman!'

He took another drag and slumped back into his chair, looking up at a faded poster of the Step Pyramid of Djoser on the wall opposite, and then down at his desk, where the items he had brought back from Jansen's house were arranged in a neat line in front of him – the photographic slide, the flyer, the will and the pistol. The only thing that was missing was the gold bar, which he had entrusted to a certain Mr Mohammed Hasoon, bullion expert at Banque Misr, who had promised to try and find out more about the eagle and swastika legend stamped into its surface.

Of the remaining objects, Jansen's will had proved the most immediately informative. It set out detailed instructions for the sale of the dead man's property and possessions and, from the proceeds thereof, the granting of bequests to various individuals and organizations, including the staff of the Menna-Ra, the dead man's housekeeper, the Egyptian Horticultural Society, Luxor Museum and, somewhat incongruously, the Brooke Animal Hospital for Horses and Donkeys.

By far the largest bequest – comprising, so far as Khalifa could make out, the bulk of the dead man's estate – was to an Anton and Inga Gratz 'for the support of those causes that we all hold so dear'. Carla Shaw, the manager of the Menna-Ra, had mentioned friends of Jansen's, one of whom was called Anton, and Khalifa presumed these must be the same people. More interesting, 16 Orabi Street, the address given for the Gratzes in the will, was in the El-Maadi district of Cairo. The payphone whose number had figured so frequently on Jansen's telephone bill was also in that district, and after checking its precise location with Egypt Telecom Khalifa had found it was located literally just across the street from the apartment block in which Mr and Mrs Gratz resided, suggesting that they were the people Jansen had been speaking to on such a regular basis. Some further checking had revealed that the Gratzes had no private telephone number – presumably why they used the payphone – so Khalifa had contacted the neighbours to either side of them in the block, asking them to put a note under the Gratzes' door requesting them to contact Luxor Police immediately. He had, to date, heard nothing back.

Of the other items, the pistol had been identified by Mr Salah, the station ballistics expert, as a 9mm Walther P38 semi-automatic – a make rarely seen these days, apparently, although they were, according to Salah, much in demand among firearms collectors, the Walther P38 having been the official sidearm of the German military during World War Two. The gun had been kept clean and oiled and was in perfect working order, its eight-bullet magazine full. As with so many other aspects of Jansen's world, the information had raised more questions than it answered.

There had been no time to find out anything about the final two objects, the flyer and the slide, and, leaning forward now, Khalifa picked up the latter and held it to the light, puffing on his cigarette, the phone still clutched in his left hand. The image of the dark, narrow tomb doorway at the foot of a vertical wall of rock meant nothing to him, and after staring at it for a moment, wondering whether it had any relevance, he laid it back on the desk and took up the flyer instead, reading slowly through it, struck, as he had been the first time he'd looked at it, by the incongruity of someone of Jansen's evident breeding mixing with a fundamentalist firebrand like Shaykh Omar Abd-el Karim. He was just scribbling a note to himself to look in on the meeting the flyer was advertising when the line finally clicked back into life.

'Have you speak to Israeli Embassy in Cairo?'

'It was the Israeli Embassy in Cairo who gave me your number,' replied Khalifa, banging his cigarette out into the ashtray, trying not to lose his temper.

She put him on hold again, only for fifteen seconds this time, then came back and asked if he knew the victim's last known address, or rather her 'place of living before death', which he took to mean the same thing. He reached across the desk for Schlegel's murder file and leafed through it.

'Forty-six O-hor Har Chime Street,' he read, struggling with the unfamiliar words. 'Flat four.' He had to repeat it twice before the woman recognized it.

'Ohr Ha-Chaim,' she said. 'This is Old City. You must speak David Police Station.'

She gave him a phone number.

'Do you have a contact name?'

'You speak investigation department. They help you.'

'If possible I'd like a name,' pushed Khalifa, aware that without one he was liable to end up being fobbed off by some secretary. 'Someone I can speak to directly. Anyone. Please.'

The woman let out an annoyed sigh, making no effort to disguise the fact that she thought he was being a nuisance, and put him on hold for a third time, eventually coming back and reading out a name, which Khalifa wrote down on the pad in front of him.

'And this is a detective?' he asked.

'This detective,' she said curtly, and rang off.

He downed the receiver and lit another cigarette, grumbling to himself, all his worst suspicions about the Israelis confirmed. He took a couple of deep puffs, then picked up the phone again and dialled the number the woman had given him. The line rang seven times before someone answered.

'Good afternoon,' he said. 'My name is Inspector Yusuf Khalifa of the Egyptian Police Force. Can I please speak to . . .'

He squinted down at the pad in front of him.

'Detective Ar-ee-ay Ben-Ro-eye.'

JERUSALEM

The phone was ringing when Ben-Roi walked into his office, which he could have done without, fuzzed as he was by the two beers he'd drunk on the way up to the station, not to mention the unbearable sense of melancholy he always experienced after visiting Galia's grave. He snatched up the receiver, cursing whoever it was at the other end of the line.

'*Ken.*'

'Detective Ben-Ro-eye?'

'Ben-Roi,' corrected the Israeli, scowling. Who was this *maniak*?

'Forgive me. My name is Inspector Yusuf Khalifa of the Egyptian Police Force. Your name was given to me by Central Police Headquarters.'

Ben-Roi said nothing.

'Hello?'

'*Ken.*'

'Do you speak English, Mr Ben-Roi?'

'*Ata medaber Ivrit?*'

'Sorry?'

'Do you speak Hebrew?'

'I'm afraid I do not.'

'Then it looks like I'll *have* to speak English. What do you want?'

Khalifa puffed on his cigarette. He'd been speaking to the man for less than fifteen seconds and already he disliked him.

'I am currently investigating a case involving an Israeli national,' he said, struggling to keep his tone civil. 'A murder case.'

Ben-Roi transferred the receiver to his left hand and, with his right one, eased the hip-flask from his pocket.

'So?'

'The victim was a woman named Hannah Schlegel. She was killed in 1990.'

Ben-Roi snorted. 'And you're just investigating it now?'

'No, no, you misunderstand. We investigated it at the time. A man was convicted. But now new evidence has come to light and we are re-examining the case.'

Ben-Roi got the lid off the flask and took a swig.

'You convicted the wrong person?'

It was more an accusation than a question. An imputation of professional incompetence. Khalifa gritted his teeth.

'This is what I am now trying to find out.'

Ben-Roi took another swig.

'So what do you want from me?'

'I am trying to get . . . how do you say? . . . a little background information on the victim. Job,

338

family, friends, interests. Anything that might help us establish a motive for the killing.'

'And?'

'Sorry?'

'Why are you phoning me?'

'Oh, I see. Well, the victim used to live at' – Khalifa glanced down again at the file in front of him – 'Ohr Ha-Chaim Street. Number forty-six, flat four. I was told this address comes within the . . . how do you say? . . . care of your station.'

Ben-Roi sat back and, reaching up his free hand, began rubbing his temples. For fuck's sake! This was the last thing he needed, getting roped into a joint investigation with some bloody rag-head. Amateurs, the lot of them. Fucking amateurs. He should never have picked up the phone.

'I'm busy at the moment,' he said gruffly. 'Can you call back?'

'Later today?'

'Next week.'

'I'm afraid it can't wait that long,' said Khalifa, sensing the fob-off and refusing to accept it. 'Perhaps one of your colleagues can help me.' Someone a bit more professional, he felt like saying. Who takes a bit of pride in his work. 'Or perhaps I should speak to your superior,' he added.

Ben-Roi's scowl tightened into a snarl. Cheeky Arab cunt! He held the phone away from him and glowered at it, tempted simply to slam it back down into its cradle, to cut the man off. He got the feeling he wasn't going to get rid of him that easily, however. Why the hell hadn't he just left the phone to ring?

'Inspector Ben-Roi?' Khalifa's voice echoed down the line.

'Yes, yes,' growled Ben-Roi, taking a final swig from the flask and screwing the cap back on. 'OK, give me the name and address again.'

He grabbed a pen and started scribbling as Khalifa repeated Schlegel's details.

'And she was killed when?'

'March the tenth 1990. I can send you the case notes, if that would help.'

'Forget it,' said Ben-Roi, aware that the more information he had, the more work he'd be obliged to do. A couple of calls, maybe a quick visit to the woman's former address – that's as far as he was prepared to go. And if that wasn't enough, well, that was the Arab's problem. It was him who'd fucked up, after all.

'One thing you should know,' Khalifa continued. 'Our main suspect in this case is someone named Piet Jansen. Any connection you can find between this man and Hannah Schlegel would be very useful. That's—'

'Yeah, yeah, I've got it,' said Ben-Roi. 'Piet Hansen.'

'*Jansen*,' said Khalifa, no longer bothering to mask the annoyance in his voice. 'J . . . A . . . -N . . . S . . . E . . . N. Have you got that?'

Ben-Roi's hand bunched into a fist. 'Got it,' he growled.

Khalifa took an angry drag on his cigarette, taking it right down to the butt before grinding it out in the ashtray in front of him.

'You'll need my contact details.'

'I guess I will,' responded Ben-Roi, bristling.

Khalifa gave them to him.

'Yours?' he asked.

Ben-Roi gave him his email.

'Mobile?'

'Don't have one,' said the Israeli, gazing down at his Nokia.

Khalifa knew full well he was lying, but couldn't see any point pushing the issue so he simply said he would appreciate it if Ben-Roi could treat the matter with as much urgency as possible.

'Sure,' grumbled the Israeli.

There was a silence, the line between them seeming to crackle with mutual antipathy, and then Ben-Roi said that if that was all he had work to be getting on with. Khalifa thanked him, stiffly, and both men started to lower their phones.

'One question!'

Khalifa's voice echoed back down the line. For fuck's sake, thought Ben-Roi.

'What?'

Khalifa was flicking swiftly through the file in front of him.

'Something I do not understand. On the victim's arm. There was a . . . how do you say . . . tatter?'

'Tattoo?'

'Exactly.'

Khalifa came to a black and white photograph of the dead woman's forearm and pulled it out, holding it up in front of him.

'A number. Four-six-nine-six-six. With a triangle in front of it. This is some Jewish ritual?'

Ben-Roi sat back in his chair, shaking his head. Fucking ignorant, anti-semitic Arab.

'It's a concentration camp number. The Nazis tattooed them on the arms of Jewish prisoners during the Holocaust. Although seeing as you lot don't believe the Holocaust ever happened that probably won't help you much. Anything else?'

Khalifa was staring at the photo in front of him.

'Anything else?' repeated Ben-Roi, louder.

'No,' said Khalifa. 'Nothing else.'

'Then I'll be in touch.'

The line went dead. Khalifa continued gazing at the photo for a long moment, eyes dwelling on the five digits crawling across the dead woman's skin like a procession of insects emerging from the triangular mound of an ant-hill, then laid it aside and picked up Jansen's pistol. This too he stared at for some while, brow furrowed, before putting it down again, picking up his pen and, on the pad beside the phone, writing 'Nazi' and 'Holocaust', underscoring each with a double black line.

JERUSALEM

'The war between Israelis and Palestinians – and make no mistake, it is a war – is being fought on many different levels, and with many different weapons. Most obvious, of course, is the physical confrontation: rocks against Galil rifles, Molotov cocktails against Merkava tanks, car bombs and suicide attacks against Apache helicopters and F-16 jets.

'There are other elements to the conflict, however, which, if less overt, are no less significant. Diplomacy, religion, propaganda, the economy, intelligence, culture – all are arenas in which the ongoing struggle between my people and our Israeli oppressors is played out on a daily basis. In this article I shall concentrate on one of the less likely theatres of attrition, and yet in many ways the most crucial of all, one that sits at the very heart of this corrosive conflict: archaeology.'

Layla paused, fingers hovering over the keypad of her laptop, scanning what she had just written, reading the words out loud to check that they flowed smoothly, made sense. She added another sentence – 'For the Israelis, archaeology, specifically the unearthing of evidence to support the existence of a biblical State of Israel on the lands they now occupy, has from the outset been a key component of their war against the Palestinians' – then, with a sigh, pushed herself away from her desk, stood up and went through into the kitchen to make herself some coffee.

The article, for the *Palestine-Israel Journal*, was one she'd been turning over in her mind for the past week, since her meeting with the young man Yunis Abu Jish in Kalandia refugee camp. It was a good subject, and, given her usual speed of writing and the fact she'd already planned the whole thing out in her head, one she should have wrapped up in a couple of hours or less.

As it was she'd been working on it for twice that length of time, since returning from the meeting with Father Sergius, and although it was now early evening she'd still only produced a fraction of the two thousand words she intended to write. If it had been any other subject she might have concentrated better. The references to archaeology and history, however, were a constant reminder of the whole William de Relincourt thing; she would write a few words only for her mind to start drifting almost immediately, pulling her away from the job at hand and back to de Relincourt and the mysterious treasure he had supposedly found buried beneath the Holy Sepulchre. What was it, she kept asking herself? How did it tie in with al-Mulatham? Who was the mysterious correspondent who had alerted her to the story in the first place? What? How? Who? The questions echoed around her head like a constantly ringing bell, shattering her concentration.

She brewed her coffee, making it Palestinian-style, boiling water in a metal flask and adding coffee and sugar, then went up onto the roof and gazed eastwards at the darkening sky, trying to clear her head. On top of Mount Scopus the lights of the Hebrew University had come on, sharp and cold, as though the hilltop was covered in a glittering sheet of ice; to the right, on the Mount of Olives, the Church of the Ascension was just visible, enveloped in a warmer corona of illumination, like a halo. She smiled faintly to herself, recalling the time she and her father had raced all the way down the hill from the church to the Gethsemane Basilica below, her father betting her a dollar she couldn't beat him to the bottom. She had, just, and although she'd known he'd let her win, had held back deliberately, the knowledge had in no way diminished her sense of triumph as she crossed the agreed finishing line, raising her skinny arms and whooping in delight before breathlessly demanding her prize money.

It was, like so many of her memories of him, an ambivalent image, one replete with happiness, yet also a melancholy symbolism. In a way, after all, she was still running that race. Had been ever since his death, her father always at her shoulder, haunting her, pushing her, never receding, however hard she ran. The difference being that whereas once there had been a finite distance to cover, a clear end in sight, a reward for her exertions, now there was . . . what? Nothing. No expectation of triumph or delight, no enjoyment. Just the ceaseless running, the hopeless headlong sprint from emptiness into emptiness. And always her father's memory behind her, his skull shattered, his hands cuffed behind his back like an animal tethered in an abattoir. Always there. Always present. Always driving her.

She dragged her arm across her eyes, wiping away the moisture that had gathered there, and gazed out at the last faint band of twilight as it slowly dissolved into night. A breeze got up, pushing against her face, and she closed her eyes, enjoying the calming freshness of the night air. She remained like that for a long while, wishing she could just spring up above the rooftops and fly away, escape from the whole vicious thing, leave it all behind; then, with a sigh, she downed her coffee and descended once again into the study, sitting back in front of her laptop and reading through what she'd written. She added another couple of sentences, half-heartedly, then, realizing it was a waste of time, that she was too preoccupied, shut down the file she was working in, put away her notes and logged on to the internet, calling up Google and typing 'William de Relincourt' into the subject field.

She spent the next five hours going back over

every relevant de Relincourt entry listed, searching for some new lead, something she might have missed on her initial trawl through the listings the previous night. William de Relincourt and the Holy Grail, William de Relincourt and the Rosicrucians, William de Relincourt and the lost scrolls of Atlantis, William de Relincourt and the Vatican conspiracy to take over the world – she waded through them all, each match seemingly that bit more bizarre than the one preceding it. Had she been researching an article on New Age oddballs, or History as the New Mysticism, she would have had a field day. As it was, she found nothing whatsoever to add to the facts she already knew.

When she'd exhausted all the William de Relincourt matches, she began typing in variations, widening the net: Guillelmus de Relincourt; Gillom of Relincar; Esclarmonde de Relincourt; De Relincourt Jews; De Relincourt France; De Relincourt Languedoc; De Relincourt C. Still nothing. Sometimes there'd be no matches at all, sometimes dozens of them but all irrelevant, sometimes matches she'd already brought up and gone through under another heading.

Only one combination proved, if not necessarily helpful, at least interesting, and that was 'Guillelmus Relincourt Hitler', which she typed in on the basis of Father Sergius's parting shot that morning. Here again she was confronted by more than a few crazy theories, including one suggesting de Relincourt had unearthed some sort of secret magical weapon capable of vaporizing the world's entire Jewish population, a weapon that, for obvious reasons, Hitler had been anxious to lay his hands on (and the author too, to judge by the anti-semitic tone of the article). Among the dross, however, were a number of more plausible-sounding pieces in which de Relincourt was name-checked as an example of the Führer's well-documented obsession with archaeology and the occult. Most of the references were brief and lacking corroborating detail, but one, in an article by a Frenchman named Jean-Michel Dupont, carried an intriguing footnote quoting from the diary of one Dietrich Eckart, a Nazi ideologue and the man to whom Hitler had, apparently, dedicated *Mein Kampf*:

> November 13, 1938
> Thule Soc. Dinner, Wewelsburg. Spirits high after events of 9–10, with WvS making joke about the 'shattering of Jewish hopes'. DH said they'd be more than shattered if the Relincourt thing came off, after which long discussion on Cathars etc. Pheasant, champagne, cognac. Apologies from FK and WJ.

Some swift cross-referencing revealed that Wewelsburg was a castle in north-west Germany, the headquarters of Himmler's SS; the Thule Society a quasi-esoteric order devoted to the promotion of Aryan mythology; the 'events of 9–10' the mass destruction of Jewish property subsequently referred to as 'Kristallnacht'; and the Cathars, a name she had already come across in several other articles, some sort of heretical Christian sect that had flourished in the twelfth and thirteenth centuries (interestingly, they had been especially active in the Languedoc region of France). The initials WvS, FK and WJ, so far as she could make out, belonged to Wolfram von Sievers, Friedrich Krohn and Walter Jankuhn, Nazi academics and regular Thule Society members.

All of which was perfectly interesting. Unfortunately, the one part of the extract she really needed to source, namely the owner of the initials DH and the meaning of 'if the Relincourt thing came off', was the one she could find nothing about. There was no contact number or address for Jean-Michel Dupont, and after a futile half-hour zig-zagging around the net trying to clarify the issue she eventually decided the whole thing was just another red herring and gave up on it.

'For fuck's sake!' she hissed angrily, slamming her foot against the leg of the desk. 'What the fuck am I supposed to be looking for? Fuck it!'

It was by now almost midnight. She gazed at the screen, eyes swimming with weariness, then, reaching out, made to switch off the laptop, accepting that she wasn't going to get any further that night. As she did so, more for the exhausted, bloody-minded hell of it than because she thought it was going to do any good, she banged a final random combination of words into the subject field, the first that came into her head, not even thinking about it, just tapping the keyboard automatically as if it was her fingertips rather than her mind that had taken the initiative: 'Relincourt France treasure Nazis secret Jews'. She paused a fraction of a moment, staring at what she'd written, then, again more as a reflex than from any obvious rationale, replaced 'Relincourt' with 'William' and clicked on the search icon.

It was the first match listed.

> St John's College History Society . . . Professor Magnus Topping, with the show-stopping title 'Little William and the Secret of Castelombres: A tale of Nazis, treasure . . .
> www.joh.cam.ac.uk/historysoc/lent.html

The site, as its title suggested, belonged to the history society of St John's College, Cambridge, and consisted primarily of a long, rather flowery report of the previous term's events and activities, most of which, to judge by the accompanying j-pegs of inebriated undergraduates in togas and orange wigs, had little or nothing to do with the study of history. The report's penultimate paragraph read:

> The final talk in this bumper term of talks – nay, cornucopia of talks! – was given by

our very own Professor Magnus Topping, with the show-stopping title 'Little William and the Secret of Castelombres: A tale of Nazis, treasure, Cathars, and the Inquisition'. In this illuminating and typically colourful disquisition Professor Topping explained how his research into 13th Century inquisition records had revealed an unexpected link between the fabled treasure of the Cathars and the so-called 'Secret of Castelombres', the latter a castle in the Languedoc region of France where, according to medieval legend, some priceless if unspecified treasure was housed. From this starting point we were taken on a fascinating excursion into the world of Judaic mystery cults, Nazi archaeologists and the visoeral horrors of the Catholic Inquisition (Little William was a particularly brutal interrogator), the overall effect being not of your usual history seminar but rather a full-on, edge-of-the-seat historical who-dunnit. A truly memorable evening made doubly so by our honoured speaker's awesome demolition of an entire bottle of Lagavulin! Oh weep all ye who failed to attend!

Layla's immediate reaction, on reading through this, was one of mild amusement at the jejune pomposity of style, coupled with disappointment at the fact that, contrary to what she'd initially hoped, the William mentioned clearly had nothing to do with the one in whom she was interested. It was a sign of how exhausted and dull-headed she was, not to mention sceptical after an evening floundering around in a mire of historical hokum, that it was only on a second reading that the connections between the report and her own research started to hit home. And it was only as she went through it a third time that, like a bird springing noisily from a thicket, the word 'Castelombres' suddenly leapt out of the screen at her.

Castelombres. Languedoc. C.

For a moment she sat where she was, staring at the name, taking it in, then, with a giddy rush of adrenalin, started madly scrambling through the notes scattered across her desk, pulling out the translation of the coded letter and holding it under the lamp, eyes sprinting across the text. *I send it to you now in the knowledge it will rest safe at C.*

'Oh my God,' she whispered.

She went through the report one more time, carefully, scribbling notes to herself, then saved the website to her favourites folder and clicked back to Google, where she typed 'Castelombres' into the search box. Six matches came up. She clicked on the first, 'A Geneaology of the Comptes de Castelombres'. For a long moment the screen was blank, then, like a fog clearing before a strong gust of wind, a threadbare family tree slowly materialized, actually more of a family bush, for there were fewer than a dozen names suspended from its branches like tattered foliage. The one that caught her eye was right in the centre.

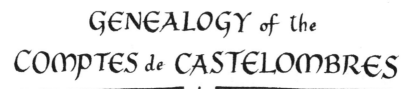

GENEALOGY of the
COMPTES de CASTELOMBRES

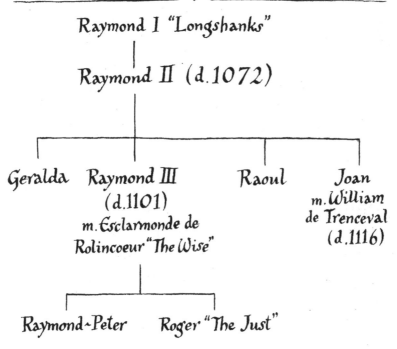

Raymond I "Longshanks"

Raymond II (d.1072)

Geralda Raymond III (d.1101) m. Esclarmonde de Rolincoeur "The Wise" Raoul Joan m. William de Trenceval (d.1116)

Raymond-Peter Roger "The Just"

She stared at it for a moment, checking and re-checking, then, with a sharp yelp, as much of relief as pleasure, slammed her fist on the desk.

'Gotcha!' she cried.

353

QUEYERAM VILLAGE, BETWEEN LUXOR AND QUS

'The Palestinians are our brothers in Allah. Remember this always. Their suffering is not distant or abstract. It is our suffering. When their houses are bulldozed it is our houses that are bulldozed. When their women are violated it is our women who are violated. When their children are slaughtered it is our own dear children that die.'

The voice of Shaykh Omar Abd-el Karim, shrill and impassioned, echoed around the village mosque, a simple, one-room affair with white-washed walls and a domed ceiling into which a circle of coloured glass bricks had been set, filtering and softening the harsh morning sun so that the room below was filled with a dim, sub-aquatic light, all blues and greens and misty greys. Several dozen men, young mostly, *fellaheen*, dressed in djellabas and *immam*, knelt on the mat-covered floor gazing up at the speaker in his pulpit, their hands clasped in their laps, their eyes bright with anger and indignation. Khalifa hovered in the doorway at the back of the room, neither inside nor out, fingers fiddling with a biro in his jacket pocket.

'It is our duty as Muslims to oppose the *yehudieen* to the utmost of our strength,' the Shaykh continued, his voice teetering on the edge of a falsetto, his bony finger jabbing at the air. 'For they are an ignorant race; a greedy, lying, murdering race, the enemies of Islam. Was it not the Jews who rejected the Holy Prophet Mohammed when he came to Yathrib? Does the Holy Koran not curse them for their wickedness and infidelity? Do the Protocols of Zion not lay bare their desire to dominate the world, to turn us all into slaves?'

He was an elderly man, stooped and heavily bearded, dressed in a dark *quftan* and simple knitted skullcap, with cheap plastic spectacles pressed tight into the bridge of his nose. He had long been banned from preaching in Luxor itself – less for his anti-semitism, Khalifa suspected, than for his outspoken attacks on government corruption – and so confined his activities to the outlying hamlets, travelling from village to village peddling his own particular brand of fundamentalist Islam.

'There can be no accord with the Zionists,' he was crying, banging an arthritic fist on the edge of the lectern. 'Do you talk to the spitting cobra? Do you make friends with the charging bull? Rather they must be cursed, driven out, wiped from the face of the earth like the pestilence that they are. This is our duty as Muslims. As it says in the Holy Koran, "We have prepared for the unbelievers an ignominious punishment"; "We have appointed hell to be the prison of the unbelievers."'

There were murmurs of assent from the listeners in front of him. One, a boy with a downy moss of hair smudged across his chin and upper lip – fourteen or fifteen, no older – punched a fist into the air and cried, 'Al-Maoot li yehudi-een! Death to the Jews!', his call taken up by the rest of the congregation until the entire room trembled with the chant: 'Death! Death! Death!' Khalifa stood gazing at them, mouth tight, then, shaking his head, he turned away into the mosque's covered porch and slipped his feet back into his shoes, which he had left there with those of the rest of the congregation, arranged in neat rows like cars in a dusty traffic queue. He lingered a moment longer, listening as behind him the Shaykh called for a Jihad, a Holy War against the Israelis and all those who supported them, then stepped outside into the fierce morning sun.

He was disgusted by what he had just heard. How could he not be? To use the teaching of the Holy Prophet to incite violence and hatred, to quote the Koran as a justification for bigotry and prejudice and intolerance – these were things he rejected with every cell and sinew in his body.

And yet . . . and yet . . .

Was there not a part of him that agreed with it?

356

A part of him that, when he heard news of another Palestinian killed by the Israelis, another family made homeless, another orchard bulldozed, also wanted to punch the air, cry for revenge and destruction, chant 'Death, death, death!' with his Muslim brothers?

He sighed and lit a cigarette, squatting down in a thin sliver of shade beside the mosque entrance. Never before had he experienced such confusion, about where he belonged, what he believed in, what he *ought* to believe in. Even in his most desperate moments – the crushing poverty of his youth, the deaths of his parents and elder brother, the enforced abandonment of his studies at Cairo University – there had always been some core of inner certainty, a kernel of solidity and assurance. But now, every turn of this investigation, every path down which it led him – Jews, Israelis, fundamentalists – seemed to open up ever wider cracks in his sense of self. *Go towards what you fear.* That's what Zenab had told him. *Seek out what you don't understand. Because that is how you grow and become a better person.* But he didn't feel like he was growing. On the contrary, his overriding impression was that everything inside him was crumbling, fragmenting like a shattered mirror into a series of jagged and contradictory constituent parts that, even when the case was finally closed, he doubted he'd ever be able to put back together again into a recognizable whole.

He pulled on his cigarette and looked up and

down the dusty street in front of the mosque. The village was only twenty kilometres north of Luxor, but might as well have been a different world, a ramshackle settlement of shabby mud-brick dwellings and brushwood animal pens, the building behind him the only structure with any sense of solidity or permanence. With his town clothes and lower Egyptian features – pale skin, straight hair – he stuck out like a sore thumb against the darker-skinned, traditionally dressed Saidee inhabitants, a fact that only added to his sense of alienation and unease.

'Dammit,' he muttered despondently. 'Bloody God dammit.'

Another twenty minutes passed before the sermon finally drew to a close. The congregation recited the *shahada*, chanted '*Al-salamu alekum wa rahmat Allah*,' and began filtering out onto the front porch, pushing and jostling as they struggled to retrieve their shoes. Khalifa stood and, removing his own shoes again, dropped them just inside the porch and started easing his way through the crowd into the interior of the mosque, ignoring the suspicious glances lancing into him from all around.

The Shaykh had now come down from his pulpit and was standing at the far end of the room, leaning on a walking stick, talking animatedly with a small group of followers. Khalifa knew full well the hazards of confronting him like this: a few years ago his supporters had badly beaten a pair of undercover policemen who'd tried to infiltrate one of his meetings up near Qift. The alternative was to pitch up with a truck full of uniforms and physically take the old man into custody, a provocative act that, given the Shaykh's popularity and the fiercely independent nature of these sort of out-of-the-way villages, could well have sparked a full-on riot. Khalifa preferred to take the less inflammatory option, even if it did carry an element of personal risk.

He lingered in the doorway for a moment, then started forward across the room, feet falling soundlessly onto the matted floor. He was almost beside the group before anyone noticed his presence. The men fell silent and turned towards him.

'Shaykh Omar?'

The old man looked up, squinting through his glasses.

'My name is Inspector Yusuf Khalifa. Of the Luxor Police.'

The group of followers shifted slightly, imperceptibly, tightening around their leader, suspicion radiating from them like heat from a burning coal. The Shaykh stared at him, his body tilted at a slight angle, like a weathered tree.

'You are here to arrest me?' he asked, sounding more amused than concerned.

'I'm here to talk to you,' said Khalifa. 'About a man named Piet Jansen.'

There was a sharp hiss from one of the group, a large, bullish figure with close-set eyes and freckles spattered across his upper cheeks.

'*Ya kalb!*' he spat. 'You dog! This is a holy man! How dare you insult him like this!'

The man came forward half a step, shoulders spread, squaring up. While Khalifa knew better than to rise to the challenge he was also aware that to back off would be an admission of weakness from which he'd struggle to reassert himself. He stood his ground, therefore, while simultaneously raising his hands, palms outwards, to show that he didn't want any trouble. There was a brief, tense silence; then, slowly, he reached into his pocket, produced the envelope with the flyer inside it and, as if offering a bone to a snarling dog, held it out towards the Shaykh.

'You sent Mr Jansen this,' he said.

There was another uneasy pause, then, with a faint nod, the Shaykh motioned the freckled man to take the envelope and pass it to him. He turned it over in his hand, squinting at the address on the front.

'This is not my writing,' he said, looking up.

He was playing cat-and-mouse, daring Khalifa to chase him.

'I'm not interested in who addressed the envelope,' said the detective. 'I'm interested in why it was sent.'

Another of the group, a small, plump man with a white *schal* draped over his head, took the envelope from the Shaykh and thrust it back at Khalifa.

360

'Are you not listening? It is not his writing! How can he know why it was sent?'

'Because a flyer for one of his meetings wouldn't be sent to a *kufr* like Jansen without his approval,' said Khalifa, taking the envelope and returning it to his pocket. 'As he well knows.'

His tone was sharper than he'd intended, more confrontational, and the followers didn't like it. Again they murmured disapprovingly, the murmur this time, like a flame catching on dry brushwood, swelling into a shout, the men closing in on Khalifa, yelling at him, jostling, their anger seeming to feed off and encourage itself. The Shaykh rapped his stick firmly against the side of the lectern, the crack of wood on wood echoing around the room like a gunshot.

'*Halas!*' he snapped. 'Enough!'

As suddenly as it had started, the commotion died away, the men shuffling backwards and to the side, leaving Khalifa and the Shaykh facing each other. There was a long silence, broken only by the sound of a donkey trumpeting outside, then the Shaykh waved at his followers.

'Leave us.'

The freckled man started to protest, but the Shaykh repeated his command and, grumbling, the men padded out of the mosque, muttering among themselves. Once they were gone, the old man removed his Koran from the pulpit and hobbled over to the far wall where he lowered himself onto a cushion on the floor.

'You are either very stupid or very brave to come like this,' he said, laying the book and walking stick on the mat beside him and tugging his spindly limbs into a cross-legged position. 'A bit of both, perhaps. Although more stupid than brave, I think. And arrogant. Like all policemen.'

He picked up the Koran again and started leafing through the pages. Khalifa came over and squatted down in front of him, flicking at a fly that had swung in over his head and was now weaving figure-of-eights in the air above. The donkey was still trumpeting outside.

'You disapproved of my sermon?' asked the old man, still turning the Koran's pages.

Khalifa shrugged noncommittally.

'Please, answer the question.'

'Yes,' said the detective, his voice sounding less firm than he would have liked. 'I thought it was . . . *ghir Islami*. Un-Islamic.'

The Shaykh smiled. 'You like the Jews?'

'I didn't come here to—'

The Shaykh held up a hand, cutting him off. Khalifa had the uncomfortable feeling that, although his eyes were fixed on the book in his lap, the old man was at the same time somehow staring straight at him, seeing not so much his physical form as everything within, his thoughts, his feelings. He shifted his position slightly.

'You are a Muslim?'

Khalifa muttered an impatient yes.

'And yet you like the Jews.'

'I did not think the two things were incompatible.'

'So you *do* like the Jews?'

'I don't . . . that's not . . .'

The detective flailed at the fly, confused, annoyed at himself for having been pulled into the conversation despite his determination not to be. The Shaykh continued turning pages, the yellowed paper making a dry, whispering sound beneath his fingertips. He eventually reached the *sura* for which he seemed to have been looking. He placed a finger on the swirling text and, turning the book, held it out to Khalifa.

'Read for me, please.'

'This is not what I—'

'It is only one *aya*. Please, read.'

Reluctantly, Khalifa took the book, aware that if he wanted any information from the old man he had no choice but to play by his rules. The passage was about midway down the page, from the fifth *sura* – Al-Ma'ida, 'The Table'. The detective looked down at it, biting his lip.

'Oh true believers,' he read, speaking fast and tonelessly, as if trying to get through the passage as swiftly as possible, to distance himself from what it was saying, 'take not the Jews and Christians for your friends; they are friends the one to the other; but whoso among you taketh them for his friends, he is surely one of them.'

The Shaykh nodded approvingly. 'You hear this? These are the words of the Holy Prophet

Mohammed. They are clear and unambiguous. To be friends with the Jews, with those of any other faith, to sympathize with them, to feel anything for them whatsoever other than hatred and disgust and loathing – this is to go against the will of Almighty Allah, blessed be his name.'

He reached out a trembling hand and took the book back. The detective wanted to argue, to tell him that this was not the Islam he knew and loved, to quote other passages that spoke well of the *ahl el-kitab*, praised them. But somehow his mind had gone blank and he could not find the words he needed. Or perhaps didn't want to find them. The Shaykh noted the troubled look on his face and smiled, not entirely kindly.

'To be a Muslim is to submit to the will of the Almighty,' he said, closing the Koran and running a hand gently over its cover. 'This is the meaning of Islam. If you do not submit you cannot be a Muslim. It is one thing or the other. Black or white, light or darkness. There is no middle way.'

He touched the book to his lips and laid it in his lap.

'Now, you said you wished to talk about *sais* Jansen.'

Khalifa dragged a sleeve across his sweat-stained forehead, struggling to gather his thoughts. After what had just been said the investigation seemed curiously distant, part of a separate reality.

'Mr Jansen died two weeks ago,' he mumbled,

the fly still circling above him, its buzzing unbearably loud, filling his head. 'We are investigating certain . . . irregularities in his lifestyle. I found your flyer in his house. It seemed an unusual thing for a man like that to be sent. A *kufr*. Not your average follower.'

The Shaykh said nothing, just leant forward and began massaging his ankle, gazing up at the dome overhead with its inset circle of coloured glass bricks.

'So?' pushed Khalifa. 'Why did you send it to him?'

The old man continued to knead his bony limb, fingers digging into the cracked, powdery skin.

'Courtesy.'

'Courtesy?'

'*Sais* Jansen had been extremely . . . generous. It seemed polite to let him know we were thinking of him.'

Khalifa's mind was starting to clear now; the case was coming back into view. As if put off by this sharpening of his focus the fly swung away and started banging itself against a small window at the far end of the room.

'Generous how?'

'He had given a donation. To one of our projects.'

'What project?'

The Shaykh released his ankle and folded his hands in his lap, his eyes revolving downwards until they were staring directly at Khalifa.

'To help those of our people who are suffering

under the oppression of Zionists,' he said, a faintly accusatory tone to his voice, as if by failing to admit to an unqualified hatred of Jews Khalifa had in some way allied himself with the enemies of Islam.

'Help in what way?'

The Shaykh was still staring at him.

'We collect money. Send it to Palestine. For food, clothes, school books. Charitable causes. Nothing illegal.'

'And Jansen was a contributor?'

'He contacted us. Six weeks ago, two months. Gave a one-off donation.'

'Out of the blue?'

The Shaykh shrugged. 'We too were surprised. For a *kufr* to come to us like that. He approached one of my men in Luxor, said he would like to help us. Asked if he could talk with me. Normally I would not mix with such people. In this case, however, he was offering a very substantial sum of money. Fifty thousand Egyptian pounds.'

Khalifa let out a low whistle. What the hell was Jansen doing giving that sort of money to a man like the Shaykh?

'You met him?' he asked.

The old man nodded, reaching up a wrinkled hand and scratching at his beard.

'And?'

'And nothing. We spoke. He said he had heard of our work with the Palestinians, admired it,

366

would like to help us. Handed over the money there and then. In cash. Who was I to refuse?'

Khalifa's legs were starting to ache after squatting for so long. He levered himself into an upright position, stretching.

'But why come to you? There are dozens of organizations that raise money for the Palestinians. Established charities. Legitimate charities. Why approach—'

The Shaykh smiled. 'A man with my reputation?'

'Exactly. Jansen must have known the risks involved, that to be seen with you could have got him in a lot of trouble. And yet he pops out of the blue, gives you all this money, doesn't want anything in return.'

Khalifa continued stretching for a moment longer, rubbing his knees, then, struck by a sudden thought, stopped.

'Did he want something in return?'

The Shaykh said nothing, just gazed up at him, a faint smile still lingering around the corners of his mouth, like the ripples left on sand by a receding wave. Khalifa squatted down in front of him again.

'Did he want something?' he repeated.

Again, no reply. The detective's pulse began imperceptibly to quicken.

'He did want something, didn't he? What? What did he want?'

The Shaykh tilted his head first to one side, then the other, the vertebrae of his neck clicking like a key in a lock, his gaze never leaving Khalifa's face.

'My help in contacting al-Mulatham.'

Khalifa's eyes widened in astonishment.

'You're serious?'

'Why should I lie? This is what he asked me.'

Khalifa sat back on his heels, head shaking. Every time he felt himself inching closer to Jansen some new piece of information seemed to emerge that left him further away from the man than ever, like a hunter who, after careful stalking, gets to within striking distance of his prey only for it to suddenly bolt out of range again.

'Why?' he asked. 'Why did he want to contact him?'

The Shaykh shrugged. 'He said he had something that could help him. A weapon he could use against the Jews. Something that would cause them great hurt.'

Outside there was a sharp clanging as someone began hammering a piece of metal. Khalifa barely registered the sound.

'What sort of weapon?'

The Shaykh raised his hands. 'This he wouldn't say. He told me he was a dying man, he didn't have long left to live, wanted this thing to go to someone who would use it well. Use it to hurt the Jews. That's what he said. Someone who would use it to hurt the Jews.'

The clanging stopped for a moment, then started again, even louder, the sound echoing around the interior of the mosque.

'And did you help him?'

The Shaykh snorted. 'What, you think I have al-Mulatham's address? His phone number? That I can just call him up? I admire the man, inspector; I rejoice every time he takes an Israeli life; if we met I would embrace him and call him my brother. But who he is and where he is, I have no more idea than you.'

He removed his glasses and began polishing them on the hem of his *quftan*, circling the material gently around the glass of the lenses. Outside, the hammering stopped again, flooding the mosque with a dull, watery silence.

'I gave him the names of some people I know in Gaza,' said the old man eventually, having finished his polishing and replaced his spectacles. 'It was the least I could do after the donation he had made.'

'And? Did he contact them?'

'I have no idea. Nor do I wish to know. I had no dealings with him after that first meeting. And in case you ask, I will not betray the trust of my Palestinian friends by giving you their names.'

He stared at Khalifa, then, uncrossing his legs, took his walking stick in one hand, his Koran in the other and began struggling to his feet. He got about halfway and stopped, clearly in pain. Standing himself, Khalifa took the old man's elbow and helped him the rest of the way, respect for his elders getting the better of his distaste for the old man's opinions. Once upright, the Shaykh brushed down his *quftan* and started hobbling across the room. At the doorway he turned.

'Remember, inspector: there is light and there is dark, Islam and the void. No middle way. No compromise. It is time you made your choice.'

He held Khalifa's eyes, then left the mosque. The interview, it seemed, was at an end.

KALANDIA CHECKPOINT, BETWEEN JERUSALEM AND RAMALLAH

As he had been instructed, Yunis Abu Jish went to the Kalandia checkpoint at midday wearing his Dome of the Rock T-shirt, taking up position beneath a giant dusty hoarding advertising Master Satellite Dishes.

For the past twenty-four hours, since receiving the phone call from al-Mulatham's representative, his mood had veered wildly between abject terror and giddy euphoria. One moment he would be trembling all over as if freezing, stunned by the enormity of what he was being invited to do; the next he would be swept away in an intoxicating surge of joy, like the time he had visited the seaside as a child and been rolled over and over in the warm, frothy waves, sputtering and laughing and thinking that this was the best feeling in the whole wide world.

Now, as he stood gazing at the lines of stationary traffic snailing their way towards the Israeli roadblock further along, he felt neither fear nor ecstasy, nor, indeed, anything very much at all – just a blank, emotionless conviction; a steely acceptance that this is what he had to do; that this was the destiny prescribed for him. What else was there, after all? A lifetime of subjugation and bitterness; of watching helpless from the sidelines as day by day the Israelis clawed away more of his people's lands, scraped away another layer of their self-respect? The ceaseless cycle of humiliation, shame and regret?

No, he could not bear that. Had been unable to bear it for a long time now. This was the way. The only way. The one path that conferred strength and dignity, permitted him to influence events rather than forever being ground down by them. And if it led to death . . . well, what was his life anyway but a sort of living entombment?

He remained beneath the hoarding for precisely thirty minutes, as he had been told to do, checking and rechecking his watch to make sure he got the timing just right. Then, with a nod of his head as if to say, 'You have your answer,' turned and set off back towards the refugee camp where he lived, its buildings eating their way across the landscape like an ugly grey fungus.

LUXOR

When Khalifa got back from his meeting with Shaykh Omar it was to find Mr Mohammed Hasoon, the Banque Misr official to whom he had entrusted Jansen's gold bullion bar, sitting in his office waiting for him. A plump, immaculately dressed man with oiled hair, wire-rimmed spectacles and startlingly shiny black shoes, he let out a muffled cry as the detective threw open the office door, clutching a silver Samsonite briefcase protectively to his chest, as though expecting someone to try and snatch it from him. He relaxed when he realized he wasn't about to be assaulted, although a nagging twitch in his left eye suggested he still wasn't entirely at ease.

'You gave me a fright,' he admonished, eye jerking open and shut like a car indicator. 'I've brought the . . . you know . . .'

He drummed his fingers on the case.

Khalifa apologized for startling him. 'Although I don't think anyone's going to mug you in the middle of a police station,' he added.

The banker fixed him with a disapproving stare.

'I have been mugged in many unlikely places and by many unlikely people, inspector, including once, I'm sad to say, by my own father-in-law. Where gold is concerned, you can never be too careful. Never.'

He held Khalifa's eye for a moment to emphasize the gravity of his message, then rose from his chair, crossed to Khalifa's desk and laid the case on top of it.

'Anyway, I've had a look at it for you. Interesting. Very interesting. Do you have time?'

'Of course.'

'Then if you wouldn't mind . . .'

He nodded towards the door. Khalifa turned and closed it.

'And the, uh . . .' The banker coughed nervously, winking at the lock. 'Just to be on the safe side.'

Khalifa turned again, this time twisting the key to lock the door.

'Would you like me to close the shutters as well?'

It was meant as a joke. Hasoon took him at face value and said that yes, in the circumstances it would probably be a very good idea. With an exasperated shake of his head Khalifa crossed to the window and creaked closed its iron shutters, plunging the room into semi-darkness.

'OK?'

'Much better,' said Hasoon. 'You really never can be too careful.'

He leant forward and switched on the desk lamp, casting a suspicious glance around the room as if, despite the evidence of his own eyes, he was still not entirely convinced that they were alone. He then unlocked the case, raised the lid and, reaching in, removed the ingot, still wrapped in the length of black cloth in which Khalifa had found it, placing it on the table under the light. Khalifa came up beside him and lit a cigarette, exhaling a dense cloud of blue-grey smoke.

'So, what did you find out?'

'Quite a lot actually,' said the banker, pulling aside the cloth, the lenses of his spectacles glowing yellow in the light reflected from the bar's glassy surface. 'Yes, yes, it's been something of an education. Even after thirty years in the business gold still retains the capacity to surprise. Extraordinary stuff. Truly extraordinary.'

He reached out and touched the bar reverentially, then straightened and, reaching into the case again, removed a typewritten report from a sleeve inside the lid.

'The basic details are all fairly obvious,' he began. 'Standard trapezoid ingot, twenty-six centimetres by nine by five, twelve and a quarter kilograms, nine-nine-five parts gold to the thousand, which is about twenty-four carats, maybe a little over.'

'Value?'

'Well obviously that fluctuates depending on the market, but at current prices I'd say about five hundred and twenty thousand Egyptian pounds. A hundred and forty thousand dollars.'

Khalifa coughed, the mist of cigarette smoke swirling in front of him like a torn curtain flapping in the wind.

'*Abadan!* No way!'

Hasoon shrugged. 'It's gold. Gold's valuable. Especially when it's of this quality.'

He reached out his hand again and gave the ingot a satisfied pat, as though congratulating a pet that has performed a particularly impressive trick. Khalifa leant forward and stared down at the bar, hands grasping the edge of the desk.

'And the stamp?' He nodded down at the eagle and swastika hammered into the surface of the ingot. 'Did you find out anything about that?'

'I most certainly did,' said Hasoon. 'And it's here that things start to get interesting.'

He stretched out his hands, clasped them together and cracked the knuckles, like a concert pianist about to begin a recital.

'I'd never come across that particular refining stamp before,' he said. 'So I had to do a bit of digging. I won't bore you with all the details.'

He said this rather wistfully, as though boring Khalifa with all the details was something that would have given him a great deal of pleasure. The detective sensed this and said nothing, anxious to get to the point.

'Anyway,' continued the banker after a momentary pause, realizing he wasn't going to get the hoped-for invitation to expound, 'it seems the eagle and swastika was the refining mark of the Prussian

State Mint, which was, until the end of the Second World War, Germany's national mint. Based in Berlin.'

Khalifa stared at the ingot, lianas of cigarette smoke winding upwards from the corners of his mouth.

'That in itself wasn't too hard to discover. Just a quick flick through some standard reference books, a couple of phone calls. Where the story gets more complex' – he grasped the ingot in both hands and, with an effort, turned it over – 'is with these.'

He pointed to a row of tiny numerals, barely visible, incised into the metal at the top left-hand corner of the bar's underside. Khalifa let out a grunt of surprise. He had completely missed the numbers on his initial, admittedly cursory examination of the ingot.

'Serial number?' he asked uncertainly.

'Exactly. Some bars have them, some don't. When they do, it basically allows you to trace the bar's history – when it was smelted, where, that sort of thing.'

'And this one?'

'Oh, this one has been very informative. Yes, yes, very informative. But it's not been easy. The numbers aren't part of a universal system or anything. They simply refer to a paper record at whatever institution happened to mint the bar. I spent half of yesterday and most of this morning on the phone to Germany trying to trace it. The

Prussian State Mint archives were either destroyed or scattered after 1945. The Bundesbank don't have any records. To be honest I'd just about given up, until someone in the Bundesbank museum suggested I try contacting . . .' He paused a moment, flicking through his report. 'The Degussa Corporation. In Dusseldorf. They used to be one of Germany's main smelting companies. Did a lot of work for the Nazis, by all accounts. Perfectly above board now, of course. Various diverse interests—'

'Yes, yes,' cut in Khalifa impatiently. 'But what did you find?'

'Well, the archivist at Degussa – nice fellow, very polite' – he put a slight emphasis on this last word, implying that the archivist at Degussa would never dream of interrupting anyone mid-sentence, as Khalifa had just done – 'had a trawl through their records, and amazingly he managed to come up with a serial number match. So efficient, the Germans.'

'And?' Khalifa's face was hovering directly above the ingot, a long cylinder of ash pivoting precariously at the end of his cigarette.

'Well, it seems that the ingot was one of a batch of fifty cast by Degussa in 1944. May 1944, to be precise. They were handed over to the State Mint on the seventeenth of that month and from there passed on to the Reichsbank, the forerunner of the Bundesbank.'

'And after that?'

'It seems that most of them got melted down and recast at the end of the war.'

'Most of them?'

'Well, this one obviously survived. And according to the Degussa man, so did at least two others.'

He paused for effect, drawing himself up like an actor about to deliver a soliloquy.

'They were found in Buenos Aires. In 1966. By Israeli secret agents. In the house of a man called . . .' He consulted his report again. 'Julius Schechtmann. A former Nazi army officer who had escaped to Argentina at the end of the war and lived there ever since, under an assumed name. The Israelis tracked him down and brought him and the bars back to Israel. They're now held at the Central Bank of Jerusalem.'

'And Schechtmann?'

Again that pause for dramatic effect, that drawing up of the shoulders.

'The Israelis hanged him.'

There was a sharp clanging sound as outside a gas vendor passed beneath the window in his donkey-drawn cart, banging the stacked metal cylinders with a spanner to alert potential customers to his presence. Khalifa's cigarette had burnt itself out and, flicking the butt into the waste-basket, he lit himself another, rubbing his eyes with his thumb and first finger. Everything about this case, every new piece of information – it just seemed to get more and more twisted and bewildering. He felt as if he was underwater, frantically trying to fight his way to the surface only somehow to drive himself deeper with every desperate sweep of his arms.

There was a long silence.

'Anything else?' he asked eventually, a weariness to his voice, as if he was wondering how many more turns the investigation could possibly take.

Hasoon shrugged. 'Not really. There are a few technical details about the actual composition of the gold, but they're probably not of much relevance.'

He ran his hand over the bar again, wiping away the flecks of cigarette ash that had settled themselves on its shiny surface, then wrapped it back up in the length of black cloth.

'You want to keep it here?'

Khalifa pulled on his cigarette.

'Can you hold it at the bank for me?'

'Our pleasure.'

Hasoon locked the ingot back in the case, then crossed to the windows and heaved open the shutters, blinking in the sharp afternoon sunlight. From below came a discordant babble of voices and the receding clank of the gas-vendor's cart.

'Actually, there *was* one thing,' Hasoon said, his voice suddenly subdued, thoughtful. 'Odd. Upsetting, really. Rather spoilt the lustre.' He curled his right foot behind his left leg and rubbed the face of his shoe up and down the calf. 'As I said, the serial number allows you to trace the date and place of the ingot's casting. In some cases extra information is recorded: the name of the foreman in charge of the smelting, the person at the mint who commissioned it, that sort of thing. Minor details.' He changed legs, rubbing his left shoe against his right calf. 'The Degussa files didn't have any of that. What they did have was a record of where the smelted gold came from in the first place.'

He finished polishing and turned towards Khalifa, slowly, hand fiddling nervously with the windowsill. The detective raised his eyebrows questioningly.

'Apparently it came from Auschwitz. It seems, inspector, your ingot is made from gold extracted from the teeth of dead Jews.'

After the banker had left, Khalifa sat staring up at the office ceiling, legs crossed on the corner of his desk, wreaths of cigarette smoke winding themselves around his head like a turban. There were things he should be getting on with: Hassani was hassling him for a report on his progress so far; Jansen's friend in Cairo still hadn't got in touch and needed to be chased up; and it probably wouldn't hurt if he put in a phone call to that damned Israeli either, checked that he'd got off his fat backside and started making the requested enquiries into Schlegel's past. So much to do. So much ground to cover. And all he could do was sit staring up at the ceiling, thinking about gold fillings, and shattered teeth, and the procession of mould-coloured numbers tattooed on Hannah Schlegel's forearm.

He knew about the Holocaust, of course, about Auschwitz. General things, rumours, not precise details – it was never something he'd felt the need to look into. He certainly accepted it had happened, the Israeli detective had been wrong when he'd accused him of not believing in it. At the same time it seemed so distant, so abstract, not something that had any relevance to him or his world. Until now. Now it seemed to have become very relevant.

He dropped his head back and blew a succession of lazy smoke-rings, the doughnut-shaped hoops of vapour chasing one another upwards to the ceiling where they broke and disintegrated into a dim, lingering haze. Five minutes passed, ten, the clock on the wall clacking out the seconds like the beat of a mechanical heart. Then, as if coming to a decision, he swung his feet to the floor, grabbed his jacket and left the station.

On the street he turned right, then left, working his way through the bustling afternoon crowd into the heart of the town's souk, past cafés, souvenir emporia and spice stalls piled high with heaps of hibiscus petals and powdery red saffron, before finally ducking into a brightly lit internet café with half a dozen computers ranged along the back wall. He nodded a greeting at the owner, a boy with gelled hair and a belt-buckle fashioned in the shape of a motorcycle, who pointed him to the furthest computer on the left, next to a European girl with badly sunburned shoulders. He went over, sat down and, after a moment's hesitation, logged on to Yahoo! and typed 'Holocaust' into the subject field, wincing slightly as he did so, like a child flicking its hand into a fire – afraid, yet at the same time anxious to know what the flames will feel like.

JERUSALEM – THE OLD CITY

'What have we ever done to them that they should come here and tell us how to run our country? Are we not even permitted to defend ourselves now? *Meshugina!* All of them! *Meshugina!*'

The old man rattled his *Yediot Ahronot* angrily, his saggy, thin-lipped mouth puckering up into a rictus of indignant fury, like a slug that has had salt poured on it.

Ben-Roi took a swig of his beer and stared at the object of the man's ire – a front-page story about a group of European peace activists who had come to Israel to protest at the three-hundred-kilometre security wall the government was erecting between Israel and the West Bank. The accompanying photograph showed an English comedian Ben-Roi had never heard of linking arms with a group of Palestinians in front of an IDF bulldozer, under the caption CELEBRITIES CONDEMN 'APARTHEID' BARRIER.

'Nazis!' cried the old man, crumpling the newspaper as if he was trying to strangle it. 'This is what they call us. See here? My brother died in

Buchenwald and they call me a Nazi! Shame on them! Shame on the dirty *goyim*!'

He cast the newspaper aside and slumped back in his chair, shaking his head. For a brief instant Ben-Roi thought of saying something, telling the man how he too despised these foreign do-gooders, the way they came over here to moan and condemn before scuttling back to their nice secure homes in their nice secure countries, congratulating themselves on being such wonderful, caring human beings while behind them women and children were being blown to offal by the poor old oppressed fucking Palestinians.

He said nothing, however, worried that if he started into the subject the fury would swiftly take over, filling him with a blinding, sludgy blackness so that before he knew what was happening he would be shouting and raging and banging his fists on the table, making a spectacle of himself. No, he thought, it was better just to hold his own counsel. Safer.

He reached up and grasped the menorah hanging around his neck, squeezing it, as though to try and force something back inside him, then, downing the remainder of his beer, he stood, slapped a twenty-shekel note onto the table and set off up the road to see what he could dig up about the murdered woman for that damned Egyptian.

Shabbier and less exclusive than the surrounding blocks, Ohr Ha-Chaim was a gloomy, claustrophobic street right at the top end of the Jewish Quarter, up near the Armenian sector, with a sloping paved floor worn shiny by the ceaseless slap of feet, and high houses pressing in on either side like the walls of a vice. Number forty-six was about halfway along, a dour stone building whose upper section was divided into apartments – empty washing lines drooped in slack parabolas from many of the windows – and whose basement was occupied by a cramped *yeshiva* with its own separate entrance. On arrival, Ben-Roi consulted the crumpled sheet of notepaper on which he had scribbled the details the Egyptian had given him the previous afternoon, then went up to the main door and pressed the intercom buzzer for flat four.

He could have got down here sooner – it wasn't as if he'd had a lot to do over the last twenty-four hours – but he hadn't liked the Egyptian's tone and didn't feel inclined to do him any favours. He'd actually been thinking of leaving it even longer, especially after yesterday evening when, despite the fact that Ben-Roi had specifically told him he didn't want them, the little prick had faxed over a whole spew of case notes, in the process jamming his fax machine which had beeped and squealed at him like a whining child until, in a fury of frustration, he'd ended up ripping it from its socket and throwing it across the room.

No, he didn't feel the remotest urge to be helpful. In the end, however, he'd decided he might as well get it over and done with, before Khediva or whatever the hell his name was started phoning up and badgering him, as he almost certainly would do, the pestering little cunt. So here he was.

He pressed the buzzer again, glancing down through the basement window at the rows of young Haredi men hunched over their Talmuds, their *pe'ot* dangling like spaniels' tails, their faces pale and sickly-looking behind their glasses (Jerusalem, he'd once heard, had the highest concentration of opticians of any city in the world). A slight scowl twisted his mouth – 'penguins' Galia used to call them – and, looking up again, he pressed the buzzer a third time, this one finally drawing a response.

'Shalom?'

A young woman was leaning out of a window above, her plump face framed by the traditional *sheitel* wig worn by Orthodox Jewish wives. He explained who he was and why he was there.

'We've only just moved in,' said the woman. 'And the people before us were only here for a couple of years.'

'Before them?'

The woman shrugged, turning to shout something at someone behind her.

'You want to talk to Mrs Weinberg,' she said, looking down again. 'At number two. She's been here for thirty years. Knows everyone. And everything.'

From her tone it was clear she thought Mrs

Weinberg was an interfering old busybody. Ben-Roi thanked her and, flicking his eyes across the intercom panel, jabbed the buzzer for flat two. He had barely withdrawn his finger when the front door creaked open to reveal a tiny wizened old lady, little taller than a child, wearing a crimplene housecoat and cheap slippers, her hands bunched and twisted with arthritis.

'Mrs Weinberg?' He pulled out his ID. 'My name is Inspector Ben-Roi of the—'

She let out a little gasp, bringing a hand up to her throat. 'Oh God! What's happened? It's Samuel, isn't it? Tell me what's happened to him!'

He assured her that nothing had happened to Samuel, whoever he was; he simply wished to ask her some questions. About a woman who used to live in the flat above. For a moment she didn't seem to believe him, her chest heaving, her eyes moist with frightened tears. Gradually she calmed down and, with a motion of her hand, beckoned him into her flat, which was on the building's ground floor, to the right of the entrance hall.

'Samuel's my grandson,' she explained as they went. 'The best boy in the world. They've got him down in Gaza, God help us, on his national service. Every time I turn on the news, whenever the phone rings . . . I can't sleep for worry. He's just a *boychik*, a child. They're all just children.'

She directed him into a small living room, cramped and gloomy, with a large wooden dresser at one end and two armchairs arranged in front of an old black and white television set, on top of which sat a cage with a yellow budgerigar inside. There were photographs everywhere, and a lingering smell of something sweet and rather unpleasant – exactly what, Ben-Roi couldn't work out. Bird-shit, maybe, or cooking fat. He tried not to dwell on it. From somewhere else in the flat he could hear the babble of Israel Army Radio.

The old woman prodded him into one of the armchairs and disappeared for a moment, turning off the radio before returning with a glass of orange juice, which she handed to him. He hadn't asked for it but accepted it anyway, taking a polite sip and laying it on a small table beside his chair. She settled herself in the other chair, picked up a tangled spaghetti of blue and white wool from the floor and started to knit, the needles held almost directly in front of her face, her hands moving with surprising dexterity for one so bent and arthritic. She seemed to be making a *yarmulke*, part of its circumference already realized at the end of the twin strands of wool, and Ben-Roi smiled faintly to himself, recalling an old family story about his grandmother, his father's mother, who during the 1967 war had knitted matching red skullcaps for every man in her son's artillery company, over fifty of them, the company as a result gaining the nickname the Blazing Yarmulkes, a title which, so far as he knew, they still bore to this day.

'So, what are these questions?'

'Hmm?'

'You said you wanted to ask me some questions. About flat four.'

'Yes, of course.'

He glanced down at the sheet of notepaper he was still holding in his hand, trying to gather his thoughts.

'Is it about that Goldstein woman? Because if I said it once, I said it a hundred times – she's going to come to a bad end. Three years she was here, and when she left the whole block applauded. I remember once, it was a Friday, Shabbat for God's sake—'

'It's about someone called Hannah Schlegel,' said Ben-Roi, butting in.

The clack of the needles slowed and stopped.

'Oh.'

'The woman above said you might have known her.'

She stared at her knitting for a moment, then laid it in her lap and sat back.

'A terrible thing,' she sighed. 'Terrible thing. Murdered, you know. By Arabs. In the pyramids. In cold blood. Terrible.'

She clasped her hands together, the swollen protuberant knuckles giving them the look of some barky deformity on the side of a tree.

'Quiet lady. Kept herself to herself. Always said good morning, though. She had a . . .' She unlocked her hands and made a tapping motion on the inside of her left forearm. 'You know . . . the numbers. Auschwitz.'

The budgerigar broke into a sudden brief chorus of song, then fell silent and started pecking at its claws, head bobbing up and down like an angler's float on choppy water. Ben-Roi took another sip of his orange juice.

'The Egyptian police are reinvestigating the case,' he explained. 'They want us to get a few personal details about Mrs Schlegel. Job, family, that sort of thing. Just the basics.'

The old woman raised her thin, pale eyebrows and resumed her knitting, the needles working slower than before, the woollen circle of the *yarmulke* imperceptibly spreading beneath her fingertips like some strange blooming algae.

'I didn't know her well,' she said. 'It wasn't like we were friends. Just said hello occasionally. She liked to keep herself to herself. Most of the time you'd hardly have known she was there. Not like that Mrs Goldstein. You always knew *she* was there. The noises you used to hear! *Oy vey!*'

She wrinkled her face in disgust. Ben-Roi patted his pockets, trying to find a pen, realizing after a moment that he'd forgotten to bring one. There was a biro sitting in a glass vase on the dresser, but he didn't like to ask for it, worried it might make him look unprofessional. Fuck it, he thought, I'll just scribble some notes when I get back to the station.

'She was already here when we arrived,' the old

woman was saying. 'That was 1969. We came up from Tel Aviv, me and Teddy. August 1969. He'd always wanted to live here. Me, I wasn't so sure. When I first saw the place I thought *klog iz mir!* What are we doing in a dump like this? Rubble everywhere from the Arabs, half the buildings fallen down. Now, of course, I wouldn't live anywhere else. That's him, over there.' She raised her needles, indicating a photo on the middle shelf of the dresser – a short, plump man wearing a trilby and a *tallit*, standing in front of the Western Wall. 'Forty years we were married. Not like today's kids. Forty years. How I miss him!'

She raised a wrist and dabbed at her eyes. Ben-Roi stared at the floor, embarrassed.

'Anyway, she was already here then. When we arrived. Moved in right after the liberation, apparently.'

Ben-Roi shifted in his chair.

'Before that?'

The old woman shrugged, squinting down at her knitting. 'I seem to remember her mentioning she lived up by Mea Sharim, but I can't be sure. She was from France originally. Before the war. She used to use French words, you know, talking to herself, when she came down the stairs.'

'And you say she was in Auschwitz.'

'Well, that's what old Dr Tauber told me. You know, Dr Tauber, from number sixteen.'

Ben-Roi didn't know at all, but said nothing.

'I saw her tattoo a couple of times, so I knew

she'd been in the camps. She never mentioned it herself. Very private. But then one day I was talking to Dr Tauber – lovely man, passed away, what, four, five years ago, God rest his soul – and he said "You know that lady who lives above you, Mrs Schlegel," and I said "Yes", and he said, "Guess what?" – he was like that, you know, good at telling a story, building it up – "Guess what?" he said. "We came over together on the same boat. In 1946. From Europe." The British tried to turn them back at Haifa, apparently, but they jumped into the sea and swam ashore. Over a mile it was. At night. And then twenty years later they end up living in the same street! What a coincidence!'

There was an echo of thudding feet from the flat above, as if someone was running around. The old woman looked up at the ceiling.

'And this Dr Tauber told you she was in Auschwitz?'

'Hmm?'

'Hannah Schlegel.'

For a moment she looked confused, then realized what he was talking about.

'Oh, yes, yes. He said they got talking on the boat. I told you they came over on the same boat, didn't I? Two weeks they were on it. Six hundred of them. Squashed in like sardines. Can you imagine? To survive the camps and then have to go through that! She was pretty, he said. Very young and very pretty. Tough. Hardened. The brother didn't say a word for the whole journey, apparently. Just sat there staring at the sea. Traumatized.'

Ben-Roi didn't recall the Egyptian detective mentioning any brother. He chewed his lip for a moment, then, pushing his pride to one side, stood up, crossed to the dresser and took the pen from the vase, raising his eyebrows at Mrs Weinberg as if to say 'Do you mind?' She was lost in her own thoughts and didn't even seem to notice that he'd moved from his chair.

'Poor things,' she was saying. 'Couldn't have been much more than fifteen or sixteen. To have been put through something like that. What is this world, I ask you? What is this world that things like that should happen to a child? To anyone?'

Ben-Roi crossed back to his chair and sat down again, scribbling the biro on his palm to get the ink moving.

'Is he still alive?' he asked. 'The brother?'

The old woman shrugged. 'According to Dr Tauber he was . . . you know . . .' She lifted a hand and tapped the side of her head, the gesture conveying disturbance, madness. 'And what do you expect? Cut open like that, injected, like some sort of animal.'

Ben-Roi looked up, his palm covered with a scrawled cross-hatch of biro-lines.

'How do you mean?'

'Well, they were twins, weren't they? Didn't I tell you? I'm sure I did. Mrs Schlegel and her brother. And you know what they did to twins in the camps. The experiments. You must have heard.'

Ben-Roi's throat tightened. He had indeed heard: how Nazi doctors had used twins as human guinea pigs, subjected them to the most vile and excruciating genetic experiments, cutting them up, sterilizing them, stripping pieces out of them. Butchery.

'Dear God,' he managed to mumble.

'Is it any wonder the poor boy was a bit . . .' Again she tapped the side of her head. 'Not the girl though. She was tough. Strong. That's what Dr Tauber said. Thin as a matchstick, but strong as iron inside. Looked after her brother. Cared for him. Wouldn't let him out of her sight.'

She looked across at Ben-Roi.

'Do you know what she said? When they were all on the boat. "I'm going to find them." That's what Dr Tauber told me. She didn't cry, didn't complain. Just said, "If it takes me the rest of my life I'm going to find the people who did this to us. And when I find them I'm going to kill them." Sixteen years old, for God's sake. No child should have to feel those things. Isaac. That was the brother's name. Isaac Schlegel.'

She ceased her knitting and, with a sigh, laid the needles and wool aside, came to her feet and hobbled over to the bird cage, tapping at its bars with the nail of her finger. The budgerigar hopped along its perch towards her, levering its wings up and down, twittering.

'Who's a pretty, then?' she cooed. 'Who's a pretty boy?'

Ben-Roi had spread the page of notepaper taut over his thigh and was scribbling notes on whatever blank space was available.

'Do you know if this brother is still alive?' he asked, repeating his question of a couple of minutes earlier.

'I couldn't tell you,' she said, running her finger along the bars of the cage, the movement making a rhythmic tang-tang-tang sound. 'I never even met him.'

'Did he live with her?'

'Oh no. He was much too ill. Last I heard he was over at Kfar Shaul. That's what Dr Tauber told me.'

Kfar Shaul was a psychiatric clinic out on the north-western periphery of the city. Ben-Roi scribbled a note to himself.

'She used to visit him every day, apparently. Never spoke about him, though. Not to me at least. I've no idea if he's still alive. None of us are getting younger, are we?'

The budgerigar had hopped up onto a swing in the corner of the cage, rocking itself back and forth. She whistled at it tunelessly.

'And you say they were from France originally.'

'Well, that's what she told me. It was the only time we ever had a proper chat. In twenty years. Can you believe it? She came in with a load of shopping – it must have been Pesah time because she had a bag full of *matzah* boxes – and we just got talking. Right out there in the hallway. Can't remember how we got on to the subject, but she definitely said she was born in France. And there was something about a farm and a ruined castle. Or am I imagining that? I really can't remember the details. I can still see those *matzah* boxes, though, clear as if they were here in front of me now. Funny what you remember, isn't it?'

She whistled at the budgerigar again, slipping one hand into the pocket of her housecoat.

'Did she have any other family that you know of?' asked Ben-Roi. 'Husband, children, parents?'

'Not that I ever saw.' She was fiddling in the pocket, searching for something. 'Lived all on her own, poor woman. No family, no friends. Completely alone. At least I had my Teddy, God rest his soul. Forty-four years we were together, and never once a cross word. I still wake up thinking he'll be there.'

She craned her neck to one side, peering down at the pocket, hand still groping.

'What about work?' asked Ben-Roi. 'Did Mrs Schlegel have a job?'

'I think she did something up at Yad Vashem. Filing, or something like that. She used to go out early in the morning and come back late in the afternoon with arms full of papers and files and God knows what else. She dropped some once, in the hall, and I helped her pick them up. Something about Dachau, it was, with a Yad

Vashem stamp on it. God knows why she'd want to bring something like that into her house after all she'd been through. Ah!'

She withdrew her hand, some sort of seed or small nut clasped within the gnarled pincer of her thumb and index finger. She waved it about in front of the cage as if to say, 'Look what I've got!' Then, clasping her wrist with her other hand to steady her arm, she pushed the seed through the bars. The budgerigar let out an excited trill and hopped down from its swing.

Ben-Roi stared at his notes, wondering if there was anything else he should cover. He noticed the name the Egyptian detective had given him.

'Does the name Piet Jansen mean anything to you?' he asked.

The old woman thought for a moment.

'I knew a Renee Jansen once,' she said. 'Lived on the next street but one to us in Tel Aviv. Had a hip replacement, and a son in the navy.'

'This is Piet Jansen.'

'Him I didn't know.'

Ben-Roi nodded and glanced down at his watch. He asked a few more questions – Did Mrs Schlegel have any enemies that she knew of? Any unusual interests? Did any of the other neighbours know her at all? – but the woman wasn't able to provide any more information and eventually, feeling he'd done as much as could reasonably be expected, he folded his sheet of notepaper, returned the biro to its vase on the dresser and said he wouldn't need to trouble her any further. She made him finish his orange juice – 'If you don't drink you get dehydrated!' – and led him back through the flat and out into the building's entrance hall.

'You know, I can't even think where they buried her,' she said as she opened the front door. 'Twenty-one years we were neighbours and I don't even know where her grave is. If you find out, will you let me know? I'd like to say a *kiddush* for her on her *yahrzeit*. Poor woman.'

Ben-Roi muttered something noncommittal and, thanking her, stepped out into the street. He took a couple of paces, then turned again.

'One final thing. You don't know what happened to Mrs Schlegel's possessions, do you?'

The old woman looked up at him, her eyebrows lifting slightly as if she was surprised by the question.

'They were burnt, of course.'

'Burnt?'

'In the fire. You must have heard about the fire.'

Ben-Roi stared down at her.

'The day after she died. Or was it two days? Some Arab kids climbed up the drainpipe at the back, covered everything in petrol and set it on fire. Destroyed the lot. If old Mr Stern hadn't raised the alarm the whole block would have gone up.' She shook her head. 'Poor woman. To have survived the camps, and then for her life to end like that, murdered, her home destroyed. What is this world we live in, I ask you? People killed, children sent into the army. What is this world?'

She sighed deeply and, raising a hand in farewell, heaved the door shut, leaving Ben-Roi standing on the street, his craggy brow cut with deep, uncertain furrows, like plough-marks grooved across a rocky hillside.

JERUSALEM

Bloody Castelombres. The night before Layla had been euphoric about the new lead, convinced it was the breakthrough she needed to solve the William de Relincourt conundrum. After a day of scratching and digging, however, she now felt almost as confused as she had before she'd even heard of the bloody place.

She'd called Cambridge first thing, hoping to speak to Professor Magnus Topping, only to be informed by a blandly officious college porter that the professor possessed neither a phone ('The ringing disturbs him, madam') nor an email address ('Prefers his typewriter, madam').

'So how the hell do I get in touch with him?' she had asked, picturing some crusty, pipe-smoking academic closeted away in a book-filled study, wholly oblivious to the outside world.

'Well, madam,' the porter had replied – he seemed to insinuate a polite-but-patronizing 'madam' into every sentence – 'you could write to him, although between you and me he's never been very good at answering his letters. Or you could simply turn up and knock on his door, which is generally the best way of getting hold of him.'

'I'm calling from Jerusalem.'

'Ah. Well, then, that's going to be a problem, isn't it? Madam.'

With the Topping option closed to her, she had gone back to the internet. Unlike William de Relincourt, Castelombres had barely figured on the web, half a day of careful searching and cross-referencing failing to add to the six brief matches she had turned up the previous night (of which the sixth had turned out to be for a Castelombres Sanitary Porcelain company in Antwerp). Of the other five, one was the truncated genealogy that had given her the Esclarmonde de Rolincoeur connection; one a rather bad translation of a French academic article on the troubadour tradition of twelfth-century Languedoc; one a site devoted to the history of the cabbala and Jewish mysticism; one a footnote to an article about a medieval Jewish scholar called Rashi; and one a passing reference in the 'Haunted Ruins' section of a site titled 'Hidden France'.

From these she had picked up various scattered shards of information, random glimmers of some wider mystery. Not, however, the revelation for which she had been hoping. On the contrary, far from helping to clarify the whole William de Relincourt thing, the Castelombres lead had only seemed to cloud the waters further, adding new and confusing angles to a picture that already resembled some obscure and muddled Braque composition – a jumble of disparate elements all hinting at something significant without ever fully resolving themselves into a form she could recognize.

She hunched forward and stared at the notepad in front of her, wondering what to make of the whole thing, where on earth it was leading her.

Castelombres

'The Castle of Shadows'. Seat of Comptes de Castelombres. Castle destroyed Cathar Crusade 1243 – only few ruins left (ghosts!) Arriege Dept. Castelombres village 3 km away.

Esclarmonde de Rolincoeur (Relincourt). 'Esclarmonde the Wise' 'White Lady of Castelombres'. Married Raymond III of Castelombres c.1097. No extant biog. details.

Renowned for intelligence, beauty, charity etc.

Popular figure in troubadour tradition.

Bona domna Esclarmonda,
Comtessa Castelombres,
Era bella e entendia
Esclarmonda la blanca

(Good lady Esclarmonde/Countess of Castelombres/She was beautiful and she was wise/Esclarmonde the White). Jaufre Rudel (1125–48) Occitane language.

C. important centre of learning. Renowned for religious tolerance. Many Jewish scholars. Cabbala. 'Lo Privat de Castelombres' – The Secret of Castelombres. References in troubadours. Esclarmonde the 'protector'. No-one certain what secret actually was.

The thing that made it so frustrating was that she knew she had made a significant leap forward. The links were too tight, the similarities too sharp, for it to be mere coincidence. In her mind there was no doubt that this Esclarmonde the White was the same Esclarmonde to whom William de Relincourt had addressed his coded letter, nor that 'C.' and the castle of Castelombres were one and the same. And if those pieces fitted it was a pretty fair guess that William's 'ancient thing . . . of great power and beauty' was in some way bound up with this mysterious 'Secret of Castelombres'.

Beyond that, however, she didn't seem able to progress. She had contacted a couple of experts at the Hebrew University, including the Gershom Scholem Professor of Cabbala, who added a few extra brushstrokes to the overall picture: Castelombres had not merely attracted Jewish scholars, he had informed her, but, from the mid-twelfth century, seemed to have been a specific site of Jewish pilgrimage. Why, however, and what, if anything, that had to do with William de Relincourt or the so-called 'treasure of the Cathars' remained wholly unclear. It was as though she had leapt across a chasm only to slam straight into a rock wall.

She read through her notes again and again, then picked up the print-out she had made the previous night of the St John's College History Society web page and re-read that. *In this illuminating and typically colourful disquisition Professor Topping explained how his research into 13th Century inquisition records had revealed an unexpected link between the fabled treasure of the Cathars and the so-called 'Secret of Castelombres'.* The more she thought about it the more convinced she became that Topping was the key; that she could surf the net ad infinitum, call every expert going, but without talking to him directly she was never going to move forward with this thing. And from what the college porter had said the only way she was going to be able to talk to Topping was to get on a plane and fly all the way over to England.

'No way,' she muttered. 'Absolutely no fucking way.'

Even as she said it, however, she was laying aside the print-out and starting to leaf through her address book, looking for the number of her travel-agent friend Salim.

JERUSALEM

Back in his office, Ben-Roi took a swig from his hip-flask and stared at the three-quarter-page report on the computer screen in front of him. He had, he told himself, done everything that could reasonably be expected of him. He'd interviewed the old woman on Ohr Ha-Chaim; called Kfar Shaul to enquire about Schlegel's twin brother (still alive, apparently, although in a 'very disturbed' state); even contacted Yad Vashem to confirm that Schlegel had actually been an employee there (she had, part-time, in the archives department). OK, there were other avenues he could have pursued; he hadn't exactly driven himself into the ground. But then why should he? 'A little background information', that's what Khediva had asked for. And that's what he'd given him. He'd type a couple of extra lines, push the report up over a page and leave it at that. Email it across and wash his hands of the whole damned thing.

Except . . . except . . .

That bloody house fire. He couldn't get it out of his mind. The last thing the Weinberg woman had told him, about all Hannah Schlegel's possessions being destroyed in an arson attack. He just couldn't get it out of his mind. Why, he kept thinking to himself – this despite his best efforts *not* to keep thinking to himself – would a group of Arab kids risk going into the Jewish Quarter and shinning all the way up a drainpipe for the sole purpose of covering an elderly woman's flat in petrol and setting it alight? It simply didn't make sense. He'd dealt with Arab burglars before, and Arab vandals, but this didn't fit into either category.

The bellyaches. That's what his mentor, old Commander Levi, used to call them. 'The bellyaches, Arieh, are what make the difference between a good detective and a great detective. The good detective will look at the evidence and use logic to work out there's something wrong. But the great detective will *feel* there's something wrong even before he's seen the evidence. It's a gut instinct. A bellyache.'

He used to get them all the time, those bellyaches – an uncertain tremor in the pit of his stomach, a sixth sense that things weren't quite what they seemed. He'd got them on the Rehevot fraud case, when everyone had told him he was shooting at shadows until the computer expert had recovered those dumped files and proved his suspicions right after all. And he'd got them on the Shapiro settler murder, when all the evidence had pointed at the Arab kid, every bit of it, yet

407

he'd still been convinced the kid was innocent, that there was some other angle. He'd taken a lot of flak over that case, but he'd kept digging, and of course eventually they'd found the cleaver in the rabbi's cellar and the truth had come out. 'I'm proud of you, Arieh,' Commander Levi had told him as he presented a citation for outstanding police work. 'You are a great detective. And you'll become even greater, so long as you keep listening to those bellyaches.'

But of course he'd stopped listening this last year. Stopped even having the bellyaches, aside from the whole al-Mulatham thing. He went through the motions, did what he had to, but the old fire, the passion for getting to the bottom of things, the desire to be like Al Pacino in the film – that had faded and died. He just didn't care any more. Right, wrong, truth, lies, justice, injustice – it no longer mattered. He didn't fucking care.

Until now. Because now he had one of the strongest bellyaches he'd ever experienced and it just wouldn't go away. He didn't want to have it, he was angry that he did have it, but it was there all the same, gnawing away at his insides. Kids, arson, murdered woman, Jewish Quarter. It was wrong. It was all bloody wrong.

'Damn you, Khediva,' he muttered. 'Bloody fucking damn you.'

He procrastinated a few minutes longer, desperate just to wash his hands of the whole thing, not get sucked in any further. Then, unable to stop himself, he snatched up the phone and tapped a number into the keypad.

'Feldman?' he said when it was answered. 'I need to find the file on an arson case from fifteen years ago . . . None of your fucking business. Just tell me where to look.'

It took almost two hours to track down the file, which had for some inexplicable reason ended up in the archive at Moriah, one of the city's other regional police stations. He'd had it sent over by bike, and now sat with his feet propped on the edge of his desk reading through it, taking occasional deep swigs from his hip-flask.

The thing that immediately leapt out at him, and only served to deepen his misgivings, was the date and time of the fire. Mrs Weinberg had told him it had happened a day or two after Hannah Schlegel's death; according to the notes, it had actually occurred on the very same day as her murder, just a matter of hours later, an extraordinary coincidence and one that even the most obtuse of investigators would have been pushed not to find suspicious.

Unfortunately, frustratingly, there was nothing in the rest of the file to explain this troubling synchronicity. There were statements from Schlegel's neighbours, including Mrs Weinberg; photographs of the gutted flat; and arrest forms for the three Arab kids who'd been brought in for the crime, two of whom had pleaded guilty and got eighteen months' youth detention each, while the third, the youngest, identified on his arrest sheet only as 'Ani', had been released without charge on account of his age – seven at the time – and a lack of evidence against him.

Why they had chosen that particular flat to torch on that particular day at that particular time, and what, if anything, the attack had to do with Hannah Schlegel's murder – all were questions that remained unanswered. 'We did it for a dare,' was all the boys had said, and the police interrogator, evidently satisfied with having wangled an admission of guilt out of them, seemed to have made no effort to delve any deeper into the matter.

Ben-Roi went through the notes twice, then leant his head back and drained the remaining vodka from his flask. It was all wrong. Massively, belly-achingly wrong. The question was, what could he do about it? The fire had been a decade and a half ago, the leads were all dead, the perpetrators had most likely moved or changed names, or probably both. He could spend months trying to get to the bottom of it. And for what? Some pushy, Jew-hating raghead.

'*Zoobi!*' he muttered. 'Fuck it. What's the point? Bellyaches or no bellyaches.'

He closed the file, threw it on the desk and, picking up the phone, punched in the number of the Moriah archives, intending to tell them he'd finished with the notes. As he did so something caught his eye, a line scribbled on the back of the file, in faded pencil. He hadn't noticed it before. Reaching out, he pulled the folder towards him. It was barely legible, and he had to squint to read it: 'Ani – Hani al-Hajjar Hani-Jamal. Born 11/2/83. Al-Amari camp.'

He stared down at the note, eyes narrowed, then, leaning to his left – slowly, as if reluctant to do so – he fumbled through a pile of papers, pulling out the case file for the Palestinian he had chased after the Old City drugs bust. He opened it and stared down at the man's arrest form.

Name: Hani al-Hajjar Hani-Jamal
Age: 22
D.O.B. 11 February 1983
Address: 14, Ginna Lane, Al-Amari camp, Ramallah

'Shalom, archive.'

The receiver echoed in his ear. His eyes were flicking from the scribbled note to the arrest form and back again.

'Archive,' repeated the voice.

'Yes,' he said. 'It's Ben-Roi. At David.'

'Hi. You finished with that file?'

'Ben-Roi bit his lip, torn.

'No,' he said after a pause. 'I think I'm going to be needing it a while longer.'

LUXOR

It was dark when Khalifa eventually emerged from the internet café, eyes bleary, mouth thick from cigarette smoke. He wandered back through the souk – bright lights, blaring music, jostling crowds – and down to the Corniche el-Nil, stopping en route to buy himself a can of Sprite before descending a set of worn stone steps onto the Nile quayside, the dark water slopping and glugging at his feet.

Strangely, after everything he had seen and read, all the images and statistics and testimonies and descriptions, the only thing he could think of was his family. Zenab, Batah, Ali, little Yusuf – the four cardinal points of his world, his light, his life. How would I feel if it was them, he wondered: Zenab standing skeletal and hollow-eyed, staring into the camera like some deranged ghost; Batah and Ali heaped in a pit with a thousand other corpses, anonymous as stacks of rotting lumber? What would that do to me? How could I ever live with the torment of something like that? He had lost loved ones before, of course – his father, his mother, his elder brother Ali, in whose memory he had named his own son. But to lose someone to senseless, hateful butchery; to see them starved and beaten and broken and slaughtered – this he had never experienced. Could not even imagine experiencing. It was too terrible, too painful, like the sound of fingernails being scraped down a blackboard.

He sighed and drained off the last of the Sprite, his mind drifting back over all the happy times they'd had together, those gentle, joyous family moments. The day they had sailed upriver on a felucca for Batah's thirteenth birthday, stopping to picnic on a small deserted island before skimming back to Luxor with the sunset, Batah standing on the prow with her dark hair stretched out behind her in the wind. The time they had visited the Bil'esh Camel Market in Cairo, before baby Yusuf was even born, when Batah had cried because the camels all looked so sad, and Ali had had a joke bid for one of the animals accepted by the auctioneer, causing all sorts of arguments and mayhem. His own birthday just gone, his thirty-ninth, when his wife and kids had arranged a surprise party for him, dressing up as ancient Egyptians and cheering and whooping as he came in through the front door.

He laughed out loud at the memory – little Yusuf burbling in a tissue-paper *nemes* head-dress; Zenab as Queen Nefertiti – the sound echoing through the masts of the feluccas lashed to the quayside before abruptly catching into a sort of choking half-sob, his eyes blurring as though he had opened them underwater. These people are so precious, he thought to himself, yet I spend so little time with them, provide so badly for them with my crappy police salary that hasn't gone up for the last five years and is less than what Hosni earns in a single month. And if they were to be suddenly taken away from me – how could I ever cope with that? With the thought that there is so much more I could have done for them, so much more of myself I could have given.

I'll try harder, he whispered to himself. Spend more time at home, not work so hard. Be a better husband and father.

Only when this case is over, however, came another voice. Only when I know the truth about Piet Jansen and Hannah Schlegel. Only when I have all the answers.

He gazed out across the river, the water slurping at his feet, the green lights on the minarets of a pair of neighbouring mosques peering at him out of the dark like snake eyes. Then, crunching his empty can into a ball and drop-kicking it into the river, he turned and climbed back up onto the Corniche.

JERUSALEM

Hani al-Hajjar Hani-Jamal had been transferred the previous day to a holding cell
up at Zion, the largest of Jerusalem's
regional police stations, and it was there that Ben-
Roi had to go to interview him, phoning ahead to
get the necessary authorizations.

A dour, forbidding complex of buildings on the
edge of what had once been the city's Russian
Compound, the station had grimy barred
windows, a patchy eczema of ivy crusted across
its face and walls topped with tangled tubes of
razor-wire. As well as ordinary criminals it had
long served as the main interrogation centre for
those suspected of Palestinian militancy, in the
process gaining an unwholesome reputation for
brutality and ill treatment of prisoners. Al-
Moscobiyyeh the Palestinians called it, after the
Arab word for Moscow, speaking its name with a
mixture of dread and foreboding.

Ben-Roi had always had a bad feeling about the
place – a couple of years back he'd turned down
a promotion because it would have meant trans-
ferring there – and as he entered now through a

door at the rear of the station, past a gaggle of distraught Arab women clamouring for news of some loved one who was being held there, he felt his stomach involuntarily tightening, like a frightened animal curling itself into a protective ball.

He announced himself to one of the duty sergeants, signed a couple of forms and was escorted through a maze of grim, harshly lit corridors and down into the basement, where he was shown into a small interview room with a table, two chairs and, incongruously, a poster of a bright purple tulip taped to the rear wall. Muffled sounds seeped into the room from elsewhere in the station – a ringing telephone, someone shouting, a barely audible staccato wail that could have been laughter or sobbing – leaving him with the uncomfortable feeling that he was listening not to external noises but to the ghostly echoes of every person who had ever had the misfortune to find themselves in this particular space. He waited until the sergeant had left, then sat down, pulled out his flask and took a long, comforting swig.

Five minutes passed, then the door of the room opened again and another policemen came in, leading the man Ben-Roi had arrested a few nights ago. For some reason he was wearing just a T-shirt and oversized boxer-shorts, no trousers. The policeman brought him over to the table and sat him down, handcuffing his left wrist to one of the chair legs, an unnatural position that left the prisoner bent forwards and to his left.

416

'Call when you're finished,' he said. 'I'll be down the corridor, third room on the right.'

He walked out and slammed the door behind him, leaving Ben-Roi and the Palestinian alone.

As well as the black eye he had received on the night of his arrest, the man now sported an ugly rosette of bruising on his upper left cheek. He was unshaven, and exuded a sour, sweaty, faintly faecal odour that slowly permeated the room. He looked up at Ben-Roi, then down at the floor, shifting back and forth in his seat, clearly uncomfortable in the position the hand-cuff had forced him into. Ben-Roi pulled a tab of chewing gum from his pocket and slipped it into his mouth.

'What happened to your trousers?'

The Palestinian shrugged, but said nothing.

'Someone steal them?'

Still the Palestinian didn't reply. Ben-Roi repeated the question.

'No-one fucking steal them,' snapped the man, his bloodshot eyes flicking upwards and then down again.

'So what happened to them?'

The man twisted his wrist in the handcuff.

'I ill,' he mumbled after a brief pause, face reddening. 'I need shit. I tell guard but he no let me out, so I shit my trousers. Other men in cell, they give me these, but no-one have new trousers. OK? Happy?'

He looked up again, eyes full of humiliation and

hatred. Ben-Roi stared at him, taking in the purpled cheek, the shorts and the handcuffed wrist, the squadge of his chewing gum echoing around the room like the sound of feet traipsing through a muddy bog. Thirty seconds passed, then, with an annoyed grunt, he got to his feet and, warning the man that if he tried anything funny he'd give him another black eye, except worse, left the room. He returned a moment later with a set of keys and, bending, undid the cuffs. The Palestinian straightened, rubbing at his wrist. Ben-Roi sat down again and opened the arson file he had brought with him.

'I've got some questions,' he growled, staring down at the notes. 'Same rules as before: you bull-shit me, I hurt you. Clear?'

The Palestinian was still massaging his wrist. Ben-Roi looked up.

'Clear?'

The Palestinian nodded.

'OK. On March the tenth 1990 you and two other guys went down to the Jewish Quarter and set light to an apartment there. You remember?'

Hani-Jamal mumbled a grudging affirmative. Ben-Roi leant forward.

'Why?'

In the end he didn't get much out of him. The Palestinian was nervous and evasive, convinced Ben-Roi was trying to trap him into some sort of admission of guilt. It wasn't this that was the

418

problem, however, but the fact that he simply didn't seem to know very much. His cousin Majdi, one of the two boys who had actually been convicted of the arson attack, had roped him into the whole enterprise, promising him twenty dollars if he came along and acted as lookout. He himself had not climbed up to the flat, just waited in the alleyway below while the others went up and set light to the old woman's property. Why they had done so and what, if anything, they had against the old woman he had no idea. Ben-Roi pushed and cajoled and probed, but to no avail, and eventually he realized he was not going to get anything more from the man and brought the interrogation to an end.

'This Majdi . . .' He flicked through the file in front of him. 'He still lives in Al-Amari camp? Number two, Al-Din Street?'

The Palestinian stared at his feet, silent.

'Come on, no pissing around.'

The man scowled. 'I no informer.'

'I'm not asking you to inform, you fucking idiot. I've got the address here in front of me. I just need you to confirm it.'

The Palestinian looked up, eyes full of mistrust and uncertainty, then gave a feeble nod. Ben-Roi scribbled a note to himself, closed the file, and, standing, went to the door and called down the corridor to say he was finished. When he turned back into the room again the Palestinian had swivelled in his seat and was staring at him.

'Why you take them off?'

The man indicated the open handcuffs lying on the desk. Ben-Roi didn't answer, just moved back to the table and picked up his file.

'Why you do this?' Hani-Jamal insisted.

Outside, the sound of approaching feet echoed down the corridor.

'You feel sorry me?'

'No I don't fucking feel sorry for you,' grunted Ben-Roi, annoyed by the question.

'Then why you do this?'

Ben-Roi stared down at him, the file clutched in his hand, fingers digging into the cardboard. Why had he removed the handcuffs? He couldn't really explain. A voice somewhere in his head – hers, and yet his as well, an earlier Arieh, a forgotten him. An Arieh he had thought was lost for ever.

'Because if you need to crap yourself again I don't want you doing it in front of me,' he answered gruffly. 'I didn't come down here to sit sniffing your dirty Arab shit.'

He crossed to the door and, with a curt nod at the policeman who had just arrived, set off down the corridor, the Palestinian's questions troubling him more than the fact that the interview had proved a waste of time.

EGYPT, THE SINAI PENINSULA, CLOSE TO THE BORDER WITH ISRAEL

The man gazed up at the stars, twirling a tassel of his *keffiyeh* around one of his fingers.

'You know what my father used to tell me? That the Holy Land is a mirror of the entire world. When this land is in pain, so is the world. And when it is at peace, then, and only then, will there be hope for everywhere else.'

Beside him a second figure, older, was also gazing upwards, a cigar clenched between his teeth, the glow of its tip alternating between a dull pastelly red and a fierce orange as he slowly puffed on it.

'He's still alive, your father?'

The younger man shook his head. 'Died in eighty-four. In Ketziot. Yours?'

The cigar smoker also gave a shake of the head. 'Sixty-seven. Golan Heights. Bullet in the gut.'

They fell silent, each sinking into his own private thoughts, the desert around them shadowy and still, a rusted shutter hinge creaking behind them like the chirruping of some giant nocturnal insect. A shooting star flashed overhead, streaking the sky for a fraction of an instant before disappearing again; strange twisted rock formations loomed in the shadows, like claws stretching from a deep, dark pool. Somewhere far off a startled bird rose suddenly into the air, cawing loudly.

'You really think it's going to work?' asked the younger man eventually, raising a hand and rubbing his eyes. 'You really think we can persuade them?'

His companion shrugged, but said nothing.

'Sometimes I worry we're too late. Ten years ago, five even – then, maybe, it would have been possible. But now, after all that's happened . . .'

He sighed, his head dropping despondently onto his chest. The man with the cigar looked at him for a moment, then came forward a step and laid his hand on his shoulder.

'Selling it was always going to be the hard part. This' – he nodded towards the building behind them – 'was never more than a first step. But now we've taken that step we have to keep going. We have to. For your father. For my daughter. For both our peoples.'

The young man looked up. For a moment his face was blank, heavy; then, suddenly and un-expectedly, he smiled.

'Who would have thought it, eh? You and me, meeting out here like lovers!'

The cigar smoker smiled too.

'If we can do it, anybody can. What say we go over Jerusalem one more time, just to be sure?'

The young man nodded and, turning, the two of them stepped back into the building, arms around each other's shoulders.

JERUSALEM

'You want me to take you where?'

The taxi driver stared up at Ben-Roi suspiciously.

'Al-Amari camp. Al-Din Street.'

The driver shook his head, fingers drumming nervously on the Peugeot's steering wheel.

'This across the line. You Israeli. Dangerous.'

'I want a car, not a fucking lecture,' growled Ben-Roi, in no mood for discussion. 'Either you take me or I find someone else. Your choice. Quick.'

The driver bit his lip, torn between desire for the fare and unease at carrying an Israeli in his taxi. In the end economics won the day, and with a grudging nod he leant across and opened the passenger door.

'You want to go Al-Amari I take you Al-Amari,' he muttered. 'It's your funeral.'

Ben-Roi climbed in and they set off, driving in silence, following Derekh Ha-Shalom up onto the main Jerusalem–Ramallah highway and then speeding north out of the city, the new Jewish suburb of Pisgat Ze'ev fanning out to their right, ranks of uniform yellow-stone houses marching across the landscape like the vanguard of some huge army. Ben-Roi stared at them through the open window, hair ruffling in the breeze, his blank, impassive face belying the unease he felt deep in the pit of his stomach.

The driver was right. It *was* dangerous for someone like him to cross the line. An Israeli policeman, alone, in an area under PA control, in the current political climate – fucking dangerous. The alternative was either to get the Palestinian authorities involved, or else call in a full military operation with armoured cars and God knows what else, both of which could delay him for days. And the bellyaches were too strong for that. He wanted to know what was going on with that arson attack. Needed to know. With a bit of luck he could be in and out without anyone noticing him. And if not . . . He reached up a hand and touched his jacket, feeling the reassuring metallic knot of his Jericho pistol beneath the material.

They came to the Kalandia checkpoint and pulled in at the back of the waiting queue of traffic, idling for twenty minutes before eventually being waved through and picking up speed again, the road on this, the Palestinian side, pitted and uneven, the buildings shabby and cheap and run-down, as if they hadn't just crossed a barrier between two areas of the same country but rather a border into a wholly different, more impoverished land. Three kilometres on they passed through a second checkpoint, Palestinian this time – just a couple of oil drums arranged haphazardly across the road, manned by a single, bored-looking police guard in a red beret – before eventually turning left off the main highway onto a sloping side road that ran down towards a bleak, grey mass of concrete and cinder-block buildings, all piled up on top of one another like a mound of sun-bleached bones.

The driver slowed and stopped.

'Welcome Al-Amari,' he grunted.

They lingered a moment, taking in the scene, then continued downwards, stopping briefly to ask directions from a dusty-haired boy before moving on into the camp proper, its crumbling grey buildings closing in around them, its inhabitants – old men in checked *keffiyehs*, groups of *shebab* hanging around on street corners – throwing suspicious glances at them as they motored past, the car bucking and juddering on the pot-holed road. Festoons of electricity cables sagged overhead; multi-coloured spaghettis of Arabic graffiti covered every available inch of wall space – Hamas, al-Mulatham, Death to Israel, Victory to the Intifada – with here and there rows of posters bearing the images of local suicide martyrs.

'What the fuck am I doing in this shithole?' Ben-Roi thought to himself, fighting the urge to tell the driver to turn round and get them the hell out of there. 'I must be fucking mad.'

Further and further they went, deeper and

deeper, the streets becoming ever narrower and harder to negotiate, Ben-Roi feeling ever more uneasy, until eventually, after what seemed like an age but was actually no more than a couple of minutes, they rounded a tight corner and pulled up in front of an alleyway choked with rubbish and discarded building materials.

'Al-Din,' said the driver. 'What number you want?'

'Two.'

The man leant out of the window and stared up the alley. 'That.' He pointed to a heavy steel door, the first on the left, above which was whitewashed a large Arabic numeral. 'You want me wait?'

'Fucking right I do,' muttered Ben-Roi, getting out of the car.

He glanced around, nervous, imagining eyes staring, voices whispering. Then, giving the Jericho another reassuring pat and checking his mobile was switched on, he started up the alleyway, weaving through heaps of discarded paint cans and sacks of refuse. The door the driver had indicated was slightly ajar, the sound of a television echoing from within. He went up to it and knocked.

'*Aiwa, idchol, al-bab maftouh.*'

A woman's voice echoed from inside, elderly by the sound of it. He hesitated, not understanding what was being said.

'*Idchol!*'

Still he hesitated, suspecting he was being told

to come in, but not sure. There was a pause, then another voice spoke, male this time, younger.

'*La, la, istanee hinnaak, ya omi. Ana rai'h.*'

There was a faint squeaking hiss, as of a bicycle being ridden across a concrete floor, and the door swung open. A young man – late twenties or early thirties, stick-thin, in jeans and a red Manchester United T-shirt – was sitting in front of him, his lower body strapped into a wheelchair. Over his shoulder Ben-Roi could see a large, bare room with a tiled floor, a couple of framed pictures on the wall – photographs, quotes from the Koran – and, through a doorway at the back, a cramped kitchen area. The old woman was out of sight somewhere to the right.

'*Mi-in hinaak?*' she called.

'*Yehudi,*' replied the young man, staring up at Ben-Roi.

'*Yehudi! Shoo bidoo?*'

'*Ma-ba'rif,*' he replied. Then, to Ben-Roi, 'What do you want?'

The detective removed his ID and held it out.

'Jerusalem Police. I'm looking for someone called Majdi.'

The man's eyes narrowed suspiciously.

'I'm Majdi.'

'Majdi al-Sufi, cousin of Hani Hani-Jamal?'

'*Shoo bidoo?*' came the old woman's voice again, concerned, insistent. The young man waved a hand impatiently, signalling her to be quiet.

'Yes, that's me.'

Ben-Roi was staring at the wheelchair.

'How long . . . ?'

The young man's eyes flared. 'Two years. Ever since I got my back broken by a rubber bullet. An Israeli rubber bullet. Now, what do you want here?'

Ben-Roi shifted uneasily.

'I need to ask you some questions.'

The young man snorted. 'This is a Palestinian area. You have no authority here.'

'Then I'll get the army in and drag you back to Jerusalem. That what you want?' He looked down at the man. 'I just thought it would be easier this way. For both of us. Keep it informal. You tell me what I need to know, I go away, you never hear from me again. Your choice.'

The young man held his gaze, face full of antipathy and mistrust, then, with a resigned grunt, he wheeled himself backwards into the room. Ben-Roi followed, pushing the door closed behind him, relieved to be off the street.

'*Shoo bidoo, Majdi? Shoo aam bi-mil?*'

The old woman was sitting on a couch to his right, dressed in a *mendil* and intricately embroidered *thobe*, her hands clasping and unclasping in her lap. Majdi wheeled himself over to her and touched her arm, speaking rapidly in Arabic, explaining what was going on, reassuring her.

'She's had bad experiences with Israelis,' he said, swivelling his chair so that he was facing Ben-Roi. 'We've all had bad experiences with Israelis.'

The three of them stared at one another, the

only sound the chatter of voices from the television. Then, grudgingly, the young man nodded towards a cot-bed pushed up against the wall beside the door, indicating that Ben-Roi should sit. He did so, glancing first at the old woman, then, finding the intensity of her gaze uncomfortable, at the wall above her head, where a pair of old Arabic legal documents were hanging in a frame. Property deeds, he guessed. He'd seen them before, in other Palestinian homes – a pathetic, defiant reminder of lands they'd once owned and still vainly hoped to recover.

'This about Hani?' asked the young man, removing a packet of Marlboro cigarettes from a pouch hanging beside his chair and dragging one out with his teeth. 'About the drug charges?'

Ben-Roi shook his head.

'What then?'

'It's about something you did back in 1990. A flat you burnt out. In the Old City.'

The young man let out a surprised snort. 'That was fifteen years ago! I served my time.'

'I know you did.'

'So?'

'I want you to tell me why you did it,' said Ben-Roi. 'Why you torched the flat.'

The young man let out another snort and, lighting his cigarette, propelled himself across the room and picked up an ashtray from the top of the television, balancing it on his knee and wheeling himself back to the old woman's side.

'You've had a wasted trip, man. I told them all this at the time.'

'So tell me again.'

'I was a kid. It was a bit of fun. No big deal.'

'If you wanted to fire an Israeli property there are easier targets than one right in the middle of the Jewish Quarter.'

Majdi waved a hand dismissively. 'It was a dare. That was the whole point. You're wasting your time, man.'

'Why that particular flat?'

No reply.

'Why that particular flat?' repeated Ben-Roi, pushing.

'I don't fucking know! It was the one we chose. There was no reason. I told them all this.'

'You know the woman who owned the flat was murdered the same day.'

The man muttered something.

'What?'

'We found out later. At the station. We didn't know at the time.'

He looked over at the television, then, as if struck by a sudden thought, jerked his head back towards Ben-Roi again.

'Hey! If you're trying to accuse—'

'I'm not accusing you of anything.'

'Because I know you fucking people—'

'I'm not accusing you of anything! The woman was murdered in Egypt. There's no way you could have been involved.'

The young man grumbled something and pulled angrily on his cigarette, tapping it into the ashtray on his knee.

'You're lying to me about the fire, though,' added Ben-Roi after a brief pause. 'I know it, you know it. A woman's murdered and two hours later someone burns out her flat. It's too much of a coincidence, Majdi. There's something else. Some other reason. Now, I want to know why you did it.'

The old woman jabbered something, asking what was going on. The young man muttered a reply, then looked up at the detective.

'It's like I told them at the time, and it's like I'm telling you now: we did it for a dare. You understand? That's all. There's nothing else. If you don't believe me, take me in and fucking charge me.'

He stared at the detective, defiant, then switched his gaze back to the television screen, where two men were fighting, rolling over and over in what looked like a large pool of black oil. Ben-Roi stared down at his notes, then at the old woman, then up at the dog-eared land-deeds above her head. He knew he was being bullshitted, could see it in the tightness of the man's shoulders, the short, nervous drags he was taking on his cigarette. He'd called the detective's bluff, though, knew full well he was shooting in the dark and had no proof he was lying. He could take him into custody, interrogate him properly, interrogate him till the fucking cows came home; it wouldn't do any good. He'd stuck to his story back in 1990, and he was sticking to it now. He wasn't going to get anything else out of him. Unless . . .

Ben-Roi got slowly to his feet, crossed to the television and switched it off, not feeling proud of what he was about to do but unable to see any other way forward.

'I could make things difficult for your cousin,' he said.

The young man's breath seemed to catch.

'He's already looking at two years, just for association. If the charge was upped to supplying, he could go down for five, six. Maybe more. You think he could handle that?'

'You fucking shit.'

Ben-Roi gritted his teeth. He wasn't comfortable playing these sort of mind games, had never been comfortable, even after Galia's death, when hurting Palestinians seemed to have become the prime imperative of his existence. Now he'd started the thing, however, he needed to see it through.

'Six years in Ashkelon,' he continued, laying it on. 'Six years with the rapists and murderers and arse-fuckers. And they're the good guys compared to the guards. That's hard time, Majdi. I'm not sure Hani would make it. So, do you want to tell me why you fired that flat?'

The old woman could see the tormented look on her son's face and gabbled at him, anxious, wanting to know what was being said. The young man replied to her, his eyes never leaving Ben-Roi, his body seeming to strain against the belt that held him in the chair.

'You fucking dirty Israeli shit,' he repeated.

The detective said nothing.

'You fucking shit.'

His cigarette had burnt down to the stub and, hand trembling, he ground it out into the ashtray, driving it down hard, crushing it, the muscles of his lower arm knotting and swelling. He looked down at the crumpled filter, shaking his head bitterly, as if he was somehow staring at a reflection of his own self; then, grasping the wheels of his chair, he spun himself across the room, laid the ashtray back on top of the television and returned to the old woman's side. There was a long silence.

'Off the record?' he mumbled eventually.

Ben-Roi nodded.

'And Hani? You'll leave him alone? You won't hurt him?'

'You have my word.'

The young man snorted derisively. He glanced up at Ben-Roi, then down at the floor.

'I was paid,' he muttered, voice barely audible.

Ben-Roi came forward half a step.

'By who?'

'My uncle. He had some business with a man in Cairo. Fruit exports – oranges, lemons, that sort of thing. One day this man calls, says he needs a favour. Wants this flat burnt out. Says he'll pay good money. Five hundred dollars. But it has to be done quickly. No questions. So my uncle calls me.'

'You know who this man was?'

Majdi shook his head. 'I never speak to him. My uncle arranges everything.' He brought up his hands and began rubbing his eyes. 'Gad, Getz, something like that. Not an Egyptian name.'

Ben-Roi scribbled it down in his notebook.

'And your uncle? Where's he?'

'Dead. Four years ago.'

Outside, there was a metallic clatter as if someone had just kicked a paint can. Ben-Roi was too immersed in the interview to notice it.

'So, this Gad, Getz, he phones from Cairo, offers five hundred dollars to torch this old woman's flat—'

'We didn't know whose flat it was. He just gave the address.'

'And he didn't say why? No explanation?'

The young man shook his head.

'You didn't think that was strange?'

'Of course we thought it was strange. What were we supposed to do? Turn it down? We needed the money.'

Ben-Roi stared at him, then went back to the cot-bed and sat down again.

'OK, so he tells you to burn the flat. Then what?'

The young man shrugged. 'Like I told them at the time, we went up to the Jewish Quarter.

There's an alley behind the building; Hani stayed down there to keep watch, we climbed up to the flat, broke in through the back window, covered everything in petrol, set it alight. Someone spotted us climbing down, they chased us, we got caught. That was it. Just like I told them at the time.'

'What was in there?'

'What do you mean?'

'In the flat. What was in the flat?'

'How the fuck am I supposed to remember that? It was fifteen years ago!'

'You must remember something.'

'I don't know! Furniture, a table, a TV . . . normal stuff. What everyone has.'

He pulled out another Marlboro, jamming it between his lips and lighting it. There was another clatter outside, and what sounded like muffled whispering.

'There was a lot of paper.'

'Paper?'

'That's why the place went up so quickly. There was paper everywhere.'

'Newspaper?'

'No, no. Files and stuff. Photocopies. Everywhere, stacks of them. Like some sort of . . .'

He paused, trying to find the right word. Ben-Roi recalled what the Weinberg woman had said, about Schlegel coming home with armfuls of papers from Yad Vashem.

'Archive?' he suggested.

'Yes, like some sort of archive. You could hardly

move for papers. And on one of the walls, in the living room, there was this huge photograph, blown up, this big . . .' He gestured with his hands. 'A man. In some sort of uniform. Black and white. You know, like it was taken a long time ago. It was the only picture in the place.'

There were more voices outside, the thud of feet. Quite a crowd seemed to be passing through the alley.

'And you didn't recognize the man in the photo?' asked Ben-Roi, oblivious to the sounds.

'Never seen him before. Like I said, it was old. Black and white. Not family, I don't think.'

The detective flicked his eyes up questioningly. 'How do you know that?'

'I don't. I just . . . it didn't feel like family. Blown up like that, taped to the wall. It was more like' – he took another pull on his cigarette – 'like the pictures you get in police stations. You know, of wanted people. That's what it was like. A police wanted picture. It was weird.'

He clamped the cigarette in his mouth and, wheeling himself back across to the television, picked up the ashtray, sat it on his knee and continued into the kitchen area. There was a groan of pipes, and then the splash of a running tap. He reappeared a moment later, a glass of water wedged between his thighs.

'That's everything I know,' he said. 'There's nothing else.'

He returned to the old woman's side and

437

cranked the chair around. Ben-Roi fired off a few more questions, but it was clear the young man was telling the truth, and after a couple of minutes, accepting he'd got all he was going to get, he closed his notebook and got to his feet.

'OK,' he muttered. 'That's it.'

There didn't seem much point in saying goodbye – it hadn't exactly been a social visit – so, slipping the notebook back into his pocket, he simply gave a curt nod and started towards the door. As he did so the old woman gabbled something at his back.

'*Ehna mish kilab.*'

He turned.

'What was that?'

Majdi looked up, dragging on his cigarette.

'What did she say?' repeated Ben-Roi.

The young man exhaled a curlicue of smoke.

'She says that we are not dogs.'

The old woman was staring up at the detective, her expression neither fearful nor defiant, just weary, infinitely sad. He half-opened his mouth to make some sort of response, tell her about Galia, the way they'd butchered her, blown away her legs, the same people whose faces were now plastered on posters all over the camp like fucking heroes. But he couldn't think of anything to say, any words to express adequately the enormity of his loneliness and hatred, so he simply shook his head, turned away, walked over to the door and threw it open.

'Al-Maoot li yehudi! Al-Maoot li yehudi!'

An explosion of noise blasted into his face. The alleyway, previously empty, was now crowded with young men, teeth bared, fists clenched, eyes alight with the jubilant, ecstatic blood-lust of hunters who know they have cornered their prey. There was a momentary pause, just a fraction of a second, like a wave teetering at its highest point before crashing down onto a beach, and then the mob surged towards him, screaming.

'I ktelo! Iktelo! Uktul il-yehudi!'

Ben-Roi didn't even have time to react. One instant he was standing in the doorway, the next a dozen pairs of hands had seized his coat, his shirt, his hair, and he was being dragged out into the alley. Someone pulled the pistol out of his shoulder holster and fired it off into the air right beside his ear, deafening him; near the back of the crowd he caught a glimpse of the young Palestinian boy his driver had earlier asked for directions, laughing, clapping his hands above his head. A noose was thrown around his neck and tightened; something slammed into his stomach – a baseball bat, a beam of wood – doubling him up, winding him.

'I'm dead,' he thought to himself, choking with horror and yet at the same time curiously detached, as though he was watching a video of the assault rather than actually being a part of it. 'Sweet Lord God, I'm dead.'

He tried to get his arms around his head, to protect himself from the barrage of punches that were raining down, but they were yanked away again and brought up behind his back. Spit showered at him from all directions, hot, viscous, sliming down his cheeks and chin like slug trails. He felt himself being propelled down the alley as if caught up in some roaring mudslide.

And then, as suddenly as it had started, the assault abruptly ceased. One moment he was being punched and dragged, the next, inexplicably, the crowd had split and withdrawn against the walls of the alley, leaving him bent double, a high, shrill sound echoing in his ears. At first he thought it was a result of the punching; then, as his senses started to clear, he realized it was a woman's voice yelling. He remained as he was, coughing, terrified that to move even a fraction of an inch would somehow trigger a renewed frenzy of violence. Then, slowly, he straightened, the rope still dangling from his neck like some sort of joke tie.

Majdi was sitting in the doorway of his house, face white, hands clenched around the wheels of his chair. His mother, stooped, frail, was standing just outside, waving her hands, jabbering at the crowd, admonishing them. Although she was by far the smallest person in the alley, the men seemed cowed by her presence, unable to meet her fiery gaze. She continued yelling for almost a minute, gesticulating, voice hoarse, then came forward a step towards Ben-Roi.

'*Keefak?*'

He looked wildly around, blood pounding in his temples, his whole body trembling, not knowing what she was saying.

'Are you hurt?' called Majdi.

Amazingly, given the ferocity of the attack, he wasn't. A few bruises, a cut lip, a nasty rope burn around his neck – superficial injuries, nothing serious. He tried to speak, but the words seemed to jam in the funnel of his throat, and in the end all he could do was give a sort of broken half nod, like a wooden doll with a snapped neck. The old woman stooped to retrieve his pistol, which had been dropped in the confusion, and, hobbling slowly forward, handed it to him, lifting her frail arm and drawing the sleeve of her dress roughly across his chin, which was spattered with blood.

'*Ehna mish kilah,*' she said quietly. '*Mish kilab.*'

He held her eyes for a moment, then turned and stumbled away down the alley, pulling the noose off his neck and slotting the pistol back into its holster, the whispering of the crowd following like an angry gust of wind.

At the bottom, the taxi driver was standing by his car, trembling.

'I tell you it dangerous come here,' he spat. 'I said you—'

'I don't fucking care what you said!' hissed

Ben-Roi, heaving open the passenger door, throwing himself into the car and yanking the hip-flask from his pocket. 'Just get me out of this fucking shithole. Get me out of here now.'

ISRAEL – BEN-GURION AIRPORT

Layla's travel-agent friend Salim had booked her on to BA's midday flight to London Heathrow. There was an earlier El-Al service to the same destination, but it was more expensive, and anyway, she made a point of never using Israel's national carrier so she had opted for the later, cheaper flight instead. Kamel, her driver, dropped her off at Ben-Gurion at 8.30 a.m., letting her out in the airport's main car park, in front of its giant Salvador Dalí menorah sculpture. He was in an even surlier mood than usual, and having ensured that Layla and her bag were out of the car he leant over, slammed the passenger door and sped off without even saying goodbye.

'Well fuck you too,' she muttered as he disappeared round a corner.

She checked her passport and tickets, and, as she seemed to do every time she came to the airport, stood for a moment gazing up at the surrealist menorah, its arms all lopsided, its dull brass surface swirling and chunky so that it looked as if the whole thing was slowly melting. As the emblem of Har-Zion's Warriors of David,

443

paraded every time they seized another pocket of Arab land, it was a symbol that carried distinctly malevolent connotations for her. At the same time, almost despite herself, she found something curiously hypnotic about it – its curving symmetry, the way its arms reached outwards and up, as though stretching to embrace the sky. Only last year she had researched an article on its iconic importance to the Jewish people, how in ancient times, before it was carried away by the Romans in AD 70, the Menorah had been the most revered of all the sacred objects in the Temple. Looking at the Dalí sculpture now, with its dedication to 'Thou people of Israel, chosen people', she felt both distaste and an indefinable sense of connection. Like her attitude towards Har-Zion himself, she had often thought. She gazed up at it for a while longer, then, grasping her bag, turned and set off towards the departures terminal.

Getting out of Israel was always a complicated business. She'd lost count of the number of times she'd only just made her flight – and in a couple of instances actually missed it – because Israeli security staff insisted on going through her baggage with the very finest of fine-tooth combs, subjecting her to an interminable series of questions about where she was going, why she was going there, who she would be meeting, when she would be returning – her entire itinerary, basically, with a raft of additional enquiries thrown in for good measure about her family, friends, colleagues and private and professional life. 'You've got enough here to write my fucking biography,' she had once snapped at her interrogator, an outburst that, far from speeding things up, had only served to intensify the questioning.

It was the same for every Palestinian who used the airport – the suspicion, the bullying, the obstructiveness. She suspected she copped it worse than most, however, because of her reputation as a journalist. 'They've got your details on file,' Nuha had once told her, only half-joking, 'and when you check in a flashing sign comes up on screen saying "Urgent: fuck this person over big time."'

She did what she could to make things easier, always arriving half an hour before the earliest check-in time and keeping her luggage down to a bare minimum – no address book, no anti-Israeli literature and definitely no electrical items (the one unavoidable exception being her mobile phone). It never seemed to make any difference, and it certainly didn't today. She was the first person to arrive for her flight and the last person to board, her phone, as always, having been laboriously examined by an in-house explosives expert who had accidentally-on-purpose succeeded in wiping out all her stored numbers. ('What the fuck's the point?' she had wanted to scream. 'The only people who plant bombs in mobile phones are the fucking Israelis!')

As she finally settled back in her seat – she had

requested a window or an aisle but had, inevitably, got one in the middle – and leafed through the book she had bought the previous day on the history of the Cathars, she drew scant comfort from the fact that she'd made it through. If leaving Israel was difficult, it was a piece of cake compared to the hassle of getting back into the bloody place.

LUXOR

Khalifa stubbed out his umpteenth cigarette of the day, drained his glass of tea
and slumped back in his chair, exhausted.
He'd been in the office since five that morning,
and it was now almost two o'clock. Nine hours
of banging his head against a brick wall.

First thing, he'd faxed pictures of Jansen over
to Interpol and the Dutch police in the vain hope
their files might throw up some sort of match –
they hadn't – and had then hoofed around Luxor
for a couple of hours doorstepping some of the
town's more renowned antiquities dealers,
trying, and failing, to establish some link between
Jansen and the trade in stolen artefacts. Whatever
else he was doing with all the objects in his basement, the dead man clearly hadn't been trying
to sell them. After that he'd returned to his office
and spent the rest of the morning sitting at his
desk going back over everything he'd discovered
these last two weeks, scribbling down what
seemed to him all the key elements of the case
onto blank filing cards – Thoth, al-Mulatham,
Nazis, Farouk al-Hakim, everything – and then,

like an epigrapher piecing together the fragments of some shattered inscription, trying to arrange the cards into some sort of recognizable pattern. Try as he might, though, he just couldn't make sense of it, couldn't work out where it was all leading him.

He lit another cigarette and, with a despondent groan, left his office and went downstairs, walking out of the station onto El-Matouf Street to get some fresh air. There was a small drinks stall on the corner with Sharia Karnak Temple. Wandering over to it, he bought himself a glass of *karkaday* and squatted down against the station wall, sipping at the cool ruby liquid. A baker's boy cycled past balancing a giant tray of *aish baladi* on his head.

The truth was he was fast running out of options. Farouk al-Hakim was dead so he couldn't talk to him, and although there remained a few minor leads to chase up, as he saw it the investigation had now come to hinge on two key factors: speaking to Jansen's friends up in Cairo, and getting some useful feedback from that dreadful Israeli detective. The Gratzes were still refusing to get in touch. They were definitely at home, both of their neighbours having independently reported hearing their voices inside their apartment. For reasons best known to themselves, however, the two of them were playing hard to get, and short of going all the way up to Cairo and hammering on their door personally, Khalifa didn't see much immediate hope of pinning them down.

Which left Ben-Roi. Rude, incompetent, lazy Ben-Roi. Khalifa had already called his office four times that morning, on each occasion getting an answerphone, and on each occasion leaving an increasingly curt message asking what, if anything, the Israeli had managed to dig up about Hannah Schlegel. He still hadn't replied, however, fuelling Khalifa's suspicions that he was simply giving him the runaround, not taking him seriously.

He let out a frustrated sigh and drained off his *karkaday*, closing his eyes and allowing the afternoon sun to play across his face. It was warm and relaxing, not yet possessed of the furious scorching heat that would come with summer.

'Bloody damn you, Ben-Roi,' he muttered, dragging on his cigarette. 'Bloody sodding damn you.'

'All going well, then!'

His eyes flicked open again. His deputy. Mohammed Sariya, was standing over him.

'You know, I think that's the first time I've ever heard you swear,' said Sariya, impressed.

'It's the first time I've ever had to deal with the sodding Israelis,' grunted Khalifa, flicking his cigarette into the gutter and coming to his feet. He handed his glass back to the street vendor and, slipping his arm through Sariya's, the two of them wandered back into the police station together.

'I hear you're working with Ibrahim Fathi now,' said Khalifa.

Fathi was another of the station's detectives, popularly known as *el-homaar* – the donkey – on account of his plodding, unimaginative approach to police work. Not surprisingly he was one of Chief Hassani's favourites.

'Anything interesting?'

'A pair of banana merchants who've been fiddling their weights up in el-Bayadiya,' replied Sariya, 'and an intriguing case of serial chicken theft over in Bayarram. Things were never this exciting when I was working with you.'

Khalifa smiled. He wouldn't have admitted as much, but a part of him had been worried Sariya might actually enjoy working with *el-homaar*, doing things by the book for a change. The fact that he clearly didn't was somehow a relief, made him feel a little less isolated. He had missed his deputy these last few days.

They passed between the twin guard emplacements set on either side of the station entrance and started up the main stairway.

'But seriously, how *is* it going?' asked Sariya as they climbed. 'Not so good, I take it.'

Khalifa shrugged, but said nothing.

'Anything I can do? Calls I can make, you know.'

Khalifa smiled and patted his deputy on the arm. 'Thanks, Mohammed, but it's probably best if I just get on with it on my own. I'm not overworked. Just confused. As usual.'

They reached the top of the stairs. *El-homaar*'s office, where Sariya was working, was down a corridor to the right; Khalifa's was to the left.

'Make sure you let me know what happens with

those banana merchants,' he said, releasing Sariya's arm, winking at him and turning away. He went a couple of paces, then turned back again.

'Hey, Mohammed! There is one thing.'

Sariya joined him and together they went down the hall to Khalifa's office. The phone was ringing as they came through the door.

'You want to get that?' asked Sariya.

Khalifa waved a hand dismissively. 'It'll just be Hassani phoning to check up on me. Let him wait.'

He crossed to his desk and, ignoring the phone, started rooting through the piles of paper heaped all over its surface, eventually pulling out the photographic slide he had taken from Jansen's house.

'It's probably nothing, but I was wondering if you could find out where this tomb is. To be honest, it's more personal interest than business, so don't bother wasting too much time on it – just whenever you get a moment.'

Sariya took the slide from him and held it up to the light. The ringing continued, shrill, insistent, filling the room.

'And probably best not mention anything to Fathi,' added Khalifa, throwing an annoyed look at the phone. 'I don't think he'd be too happy about you moonlighting.'

JERUSALEM

'Come on, you stupid Arab schmuck, where the fuck are you?'

Ben-Roi sat at his desk, scowling and drumming his fingers impatiently on its surface, the telephone receiver jammed to his ear. He was already in a foul mood after what had happened in the camp, and was in an even worse one now having listened to the four messages the Egyptian had left on his office answerphone. 'Inspector Ben-Roi, could you kindly give me a call.' 'Inspector Ben-Roi, I was hoping to have heard back from you by now.' 'Inspector Ben-Roi, can you please let me know how your investigations are going.' 'Inspector Ben-Roi, have you even started looking into the matter we discussed?'

He'd just risked his fucking life for the man and all he got by way of thanks were messages like that! He shouldn't even have bothered to ring him back; should have just let him stew for a few days. Teach him some manners. In fact, now he thought about it, that's exactly what he was going to do. Hang up and let the little tosser wait.

The line clicked into life.

'*Sabah el-khir.*'

'Khediva?'

A fractional pause.

'Khalifa. Kal-ee-far. I take it that's you, Inspector Ben-Roi.'

'Yes, it's me,' said the Israeli, resisting the urge to add 'you pushy little Muslim cunt' and instead taking a swift nip from his hip-flask.

At the other end of the line Khalifa lit a cigarette and bit hard onto the filter, disliking the man even more than he had the first time they'd spoken, not least because, by catching him unawares like this, he had made him feel disorganized and incompetent.

'I was hoping to have heard from you sooner,' he said, trying to reassert himself.

'Well, you're hearing from me now,' growled Ben-Roi. 'Which is as soon as I could manage.'

They lapsed into silence, each somehow sensing that to make the next move would be a sign of weakness. I mustn't sound like I need him, thought Khalifa, puffing on his cigarette. I mustn't seem too interested, thought Ben-Roi, taking another swig of vodka.

It was the Egyptian who cracked first.

'So?' he asked, his attempt at nonchalance not quite coming off. 'Have you found anything?'

Ben-Roi gave a satisfied nod, sensing that he had somehow gained the upper hand. Yes, he replied, he had found something. Several things. He let the statement hang a moment, lifting his legs and crossing them on the corner of the desk, enjoying the thought of Khalifa clenching his fists impatiently at the other end of the line, then launched in.

He started with all the personal stuff about Hannah Schlegel: France, Auschwitz, the filing job at Yad Vashem, the twin brother, everything the Weinberg woman had told him the previous day. The receiver echoed to the soft rasp of pen on paper as Khalifa scribbled notes at the other end of the line. He butted in with constant questions – Where in France? Filing what? Have you spoken to this brother? – which brought increasingly curt, mono-syllabic responses from Ben-Roi, partly because he didn't like being interrupted, mainly because, deep down, he knew he hadn't covered the ground as well as he should have, and by failing to provide adequate answers was being made to look sloppy.

'Look, I don't fucking know!' he snapped at one point after yet again being forced to admit he hadn't followed something up. 'I've only had two fucking days.'

At the other end of the line Khalifa smirked, perversely glad at having something to criticize, each unanswered question seeming to shift the balance of power a little further his way.

'I quite understand,' he said in the most sympathetic-yet-patronizing tone he could muster. 'Two days is really not very long at all. Especially if you have other things to do.'

'Bollocks,' thought Ben-Roi, holding the receiver away from his ear and giving it the finger.

He stumbled to the end of the background stuff, then moved on to the house fire, and here he was on firmer ground because, although he said it himself, he'd actually done a pretty good job. He took it slowly, starting with what Mrs Weinberg had told him and then going through it step by step – Hani Hani-Jamal, the trip to Al-Amari, Majdi's admission that he'd been paid to burn the apartment, the description of the flat's interior – building the story up piece by piece. Again Khalifa interrupted with numerous questions, but this time Ben-Roi had the answers and, despite himself, the Egyptian was forced to acknowledge it was a pretty good piece of detective work, one with which he himself would have been happy.

'Maybe he's not as stupid as I thought,' he conceded to himself. 'Rude, crass, objectionable. But not stupid.'

The Israeli ordered his narrative in such a way that the crowning piece of information, the revelation of who had actually commissioned the arson attack, came right at the end of the story. By this point Khalifa had become so absorbed in what was being said that he wasn't even bothering to ask questions any more; he was just listening and taking notes. When the Israeli finally mentioned the name the young Palestinian man had given him – Gad, Getzhe let out a low whistle.

'You know him?' asked Ben-Roi, trying, and failing, to mask his own interest.

'Maybe, maybe not,' replied Khalifa. 'Piet Jansen had a close friend named Anton Gratz, who also lives in Cairo. It's certainly a strange coincidence.'

He pondered a moment, wondering why on earth Gratz should have wanted to destroy Hannah Schlegel's flat, then, with a shake of the head, he sat back and stared down at the pad in front of him, scanning the notes he had just taken.

'I am interested in this incident on the boat,' he said after a long pause. 'When Mrs Schlegel first came to Israel. When she said . . .' He ran his pen down his notes, searching for the relevant quote.

'"I'm going to find them,"' put in Ben-Roi, helping him out. '"If it takes me the rest of my life I'm going to find the people who did this to us. And when I find them I'm going to kill them."'

'Exactly. Who is she talking about?'

'The ones who did whatever they did to her in Auschwitz, I guess,' grunted the Israeli. 'The doctors, the scientists. From what the Weinberg woman said, she had a pretty fucking bad time there.'

Khalifa pulled deeply on his cigarette. Before his search on the internet the previous afternoon he'd known almost nothing about Auschwitz save the name. Even now he found it hard to believe such a place could have existed. Gas chambers, ovens, medical experiments . . . He took another deep drag, thinking about the scar he'd seen on Hannah

456

Schlegel's abdomen, thick, zig-zagging, like some squirming reptile. Was that a legacy of the camp, he wondered? Had they cut her open, poked around inside her, torn bits out? An image flashed momentarily through his mind of a young girl strapped to a hospital gurney, naked, shaved, weeping, terrified, calling for her mother. He grimaced and shook his head, trying to dislodge the vision.

'You think Jansen could maybe have been one of these doctors?' he asked. 'That he could have been involved in these experiments in some way?'

He knew it was a long-shot, explaining as it did some pieces of evidence but leaving most dangling unresolved. Ben-Roi dismissed it immediately.

'All the Auschwitz doctors were either executed or imprisoned at the end of the war. Mengele escaped to South America, but he died thirty years ago. Whatever else your Mr Jansen was involved in, I don't think it was Nazi medical experiments.'

Khalifa nodded, disappointed but not particularly surprised, and sat back in his chair, exhaling a long, undulating ribbon of smoke and flicking through his notes one more time. There was some good stuff here. No blinding revelations, admittedly, but some important new pieces to add to the jigsaw. Schlegel's wartime experiences, the 'archive' in her flat, her twin brother, the arson attack – taken with what he himself had already dug up these were significant new leads. For the first time since the start of the investigation he felt the vaguest flicker of optimism, a rumbling sense that, despite the fog of uncertainty in which everything still seemed to be shrouded, he was at least starting to move forward, to get closer to the heart of the thing.

There was still a long way to go, however, and to cover that extra distance he needed more – more facts, more background, more information, more angles. Some, to be sure, he could ferret out himself; he'd already decided his next move would be to travel north to Cairo to confront the mysterious Mr Anton Gratz. But there were other leads that he couldn't chase up on his own, or at least not easily. Whether he liked it or not he still needed Ben-Roi. Which was frustrating, because if he was grudgingly impressed with some of the work the Israeli had done, that didn't mean he found him any more amenable as a person.

Ben-Roi, for his part, was grappling with much the same problem, albeit from the opposite direction: how to admit that he wanted to stay involved in the case without coming across as overly eager. OK, maybe the Egyptian wasn't quite as incompetent as he'd at first thought; some of the questions he'd asked and the comments he'd made had actually been pretty astute. He was still an irksome, pushy little towel-head, though, and he was fucked if he was going to go crawling to him asking for favours.

There was once more a long, charged silence, neither man wanting to make the move, to say what was on his mind, for fear of giving the other some invisible advantage. This time it was Ben-Roi who caved in first.

'I'll see what else I can turn up,' he said, gruffly, swiftly, as though downing a drink he didn't like.

'Right,' said Khalifa, relieved and slightly surprised. He sat down behind his desk again and screwed his cigarette out into an ashtray. 'I'll fax you a picture of Jansen. And a report of what I've found so far.'

'Do that. And you'd better take my mobile number.'

Khalifa distinctly recalled the Israeli saying he didn't have a mobile. Given that he was being so unexpectedly helpful, he didn't want to risk provoking him, so he just grabbed a pen and made a note of the number. Once he'd got it down there was another silence, neither man quite knowing how to end the conversation.

'I'll be in touch then,' said Ben-Roi eventually.

'Right,' said Khalifa. 'I will wait to hear from you.'

He quarter-lowered the receiver, then lifted it again.

'Ben-Roi?'

'What?'

'One thing . . . it may or may not be significant.'

'Yes?'

Khalifa paused.

'Piet Jansen . . . it seems he was trying to make contact with al-Mulatham. He said he had something that would be useful to him in his fight against Israel. I thought you ought to know.'

After he had put down the phone Ben-Roi sat for several minutes doing nothing, just staring into space, fingers playing with the menorah around his neck. Then he got to his feet and crossed to a metal cabinet in the corner of the office. Pulling a set of keys from his pocket, he unlocked it and, squatting, removed a chunky cardboard file crammed with papers. He kicked the cabinet door shut, went back to his desk, sat down and opened the file. Right at the top was a photo of a young woman with short-cropped black hair. Scrawled on a fix-it note stuck to the bottom of the photo was the name Layla al-Madani.

CAMBRIDGE, ENGLAND

It was past five o'clock when Layla eventually arrived in Cambridge, an unseasonably warm, hazy evening with a high, powdery sky and wafts of cherry blossom and mown grass in the air. She had come up from London by train, and under other circumstances would probably have walked the mile and a half from the station into the centre of town – it was years since she had last been in this part of the world and it would have been nice to take in some of the old sights again, from the days she had lived here with her grandparents, after she and her mother had fled from Palestine. As it was, time was pressing, and she was anxious to track down the elusive Professor Topping.

Emerging from the station building, therefore, she hailed a taxi and ten minutes later was walking through the arched gateway of St John's. A porter in the lodge informed her that Professor Topping's study was on I-Staircase Second Court and, thanking him, she set off through the college, crossing one large, silent court – neatly clipped lawns, red-brick Tudor buildings, an ornate, arch-windowed chapel – and passing into a second.

461

I-Staircase was in the far left-hand corner, with an in-out board screwed to the wall just inside its entrance bearing the names of all those with rooms above. The shutter beside Professor Topping's name was pushed firmly to the 'out' setting, causing her a moment of panic – Christ, she thought, have I come all this way for nothing? – before a burly student in a red-and-white hooped rugby shirt came clumping down the stairs and, in response to her query as to the professor's whereabouts, assured her that he was definitely in his rooms.

'I heard him shouting,' he explained. 'Don't take any notice of the board. I've lived below him for two years and he's never once had his name on "in".'

Relieved, although not exactly reassured – the professor didn't sound at all like the sort of person who would welcome unexpected callers – she started up the stairway, the wooden boards creaking and groaning beneath her feet, continuing right to the top of the building where she found a door with PROFESSOR M. TOPPING painted onto the wall beside it.

She hesitated, picturing, as she had done the previous afternoon, a crusty old academic with half-moon spectacles, tweed jacket and whiskers sprouting from his ears, then stepped forward and knocked. No response. She knocked again.

'Not now!'

'Professor Topping?'

'Not now!'

His tone was angry, harassed. She wondered if perhaps she should go away and get a cup of coffee, come back later when he was in a better mood. But she hadn't come all this way to pussy-foot around so, gritting her teeth, she raised her hand and knocked a third time, knuckles rapping insistently on the wooden door.

'I would appreciate a moment of your time, Professor Topping,' she called.

There was a brief, threatening pause – the calm before the storm – then the sound of rapidly approaching feet. An inner door was yanked open, then the outer one on which she had knocked.

'Don't you bloody understand English? I said not now! What the hell's wrong with you?'

For a moment Layla was too taken aback to speak, for rather than the fusty old scholar she had been expecting she found herself confronted by a tall, handsome, dark-haired man, early to mid-forties, in Bermuda shorts and a denim shirt, a fuzz of black chest-hair exploding from the shirt's open neck. Her surprise lasted only an instant, then, riled, she launched into him.

'Fuck you, you pompous arsehole! I've come all the way from Jerusalem because you haven't got a fucking telephone like any normal human being, so you just show me a bit of fucking respect.'

She fully expected the door to be slammed in her face. As it was, the professor merely stared at her, a mildly impressed look in his eyes, then, with

463

an arching of his eyebrows, turned and padded back into his room. She remained in the doorway, uncertain what to do.

'Well, come on,' he called over his shoulder. 'I might be a pompous arsehole, but at least I know when to back down gracefully. And close the door behind you. Both doors. I don't want this setting a precedent.'

Too surprised to debate the matter she did as she was told, pulling the outer and then inner door shut, and following him into the study.

The place was a shambles, every available inch of space – floor, mantelpiece, windowsill, desk – subsumed beneath teetering drifts of papers and books, as if the room had been hit by a particularly violent tornado. Such was the all-enveloping chaos it was a moment before she realized that two chair-shaped mounds over by the window were in fact exactly that – a pair of armchairs encased in a barrow of discarded clothes and heavily thumbed volumes of the *Cambridge Medieval History*. Topping picked his way over to them and started clearing a space for her to sit down.

'I don't think I caught your name.'

'Layla,' she replied. 'Layla al-Madani.'

'And you're a . . . ?'

'Journalist.'

'Didn't think you were an academic,' he said, stepping back and indicating the chair, now stripped of its camouflage of books and dirty laundry. 'Far too good-looking.'

His tone was so ingenuously matter-of-fact he managed to carry this off without it sounding like a bad chat-up line. She came over and sat down while he got to work clearing himself a space on the other chair.

'Coffee?' he asked, nodding to a small doorway in the corner of the room through which Layla glimpsed a cramped galley kitchen. She declined the offer.

'Drink?'

'It's a bit early for me.'

He seemed faintly surprised by this response, as if the idea of a connection between drink and the time of day had never occurred to him. He didn't push the point, just finished clearing his own armchair, then went through into the kitchen and fetched himself a bottle of Budwar from the fridge, banging the bottle's cap off on the edge of the sideboard.

'And you've really come all the way from Jerusalem?' he called. 'Or were you just trying to make me feel bad?'

She assured him she had been telling the truth.

'I suppose I ought to feel flattered,' he said, coming back in and sitting down opposite her. 'Half my students can't even make it here from the other side of college.'

He took a swig of his beer and stretched out his legs, staring at her.

'So?'

Their eyes held a moment – he really was very

good-looking – then she leant down and started rummaging in her bag.

'I wanted to ask you about a talk you gave a few weeks ago,' she said. '"Little William and the Secret of Castelombres".' She straightened, clutching her notepad, pen and the print-out she'd made of the St John's College History Society web page. 'I've been trying to look into this whole Castelombres thing for an article I'm doing, but I don't seem to be getting anywhere. I've managed to pick up a few vague pieces of information from the internet, but . . . well, from the description of your talk it sounded like you might be able to give me something a bit more detailed.'

He raised his eyebrows, surprised. 'And you've come all this way for that?'

'Well, it obviously would have been easier if you'd been on phone or email . . .'

He gave a half-smile, acknowledging her point, and, hunching forward, took another swig of beer.

'I should say straight out that the talk was more by way of light relief than serious academia,' he said. 'Cultural identity in medieval Languedoc, that's my area of interest, with a specialism in thirteenth-century Inquisition registers, so all this stuff about secrets and buried treasure and mysterious goings-on with Nazi archaeologists – I take it all with a slight pinch of salt.' He stared down at his bottle. 'Although it *was* interesting. Very interesting. Important, maybe.'

There was a brief pause, the professor momentarily seeming to sink into his own thoughts. Then, with a shake of his head, he held out a hand.

'What have you got so far?'

She pulled out the page of notes she'd taken the previous day and passed it over. He ran his eyes over it.

'To be honest, I'm not sure there's really an awful lot I can add to this. As I told you, it's not my specialist field. And even if it was . . .' He shrugged, handing the page back to her. He must have noticed the disappointed look on her face, however, because he added almost immediately, 'Still, I dare say I can fill in a bit of the background. Give you the context and all that. It's the least I can do given that you've come all this way. Whether it's any use or not . . . well, you'll have to be the judge of that.'

He heaved himself up and picked his way over to his desk where he began burrowing into a huge mound of papers.

'Have you ever been there?' he asked as he worked his way through the papers. 'To Castelombres?'

She admitted that she hadn't.

'It's worth a visit. Not much to see, admittedly. A stone window, a few tumbled walls. All completely overgrown. Atmospheric, though. Has a curiously melancholy feel to it. The Castle of Shadows. That's what the name means. Appropriate. Aha!'

He yanked a sheaf of papers out of the pile.

'The notes for my talk,' he explained.

He flicked through them, perching himself on

the edge of the desk, the movement causing the paper pile behind him, already rendered unstable by his rooting, to slump and cascade to the floor. He ignored it.

'OK,' he said, 'let's start at the beginning. So far as we can tell from the contemporary sources, and those are sparse to non-existent – just a couple of incomplete genealogies, a few extant land charters, wills, that sort of thing – there was, at least until the end of the eleventh century, nothing remotely out of the ordinary about Castelombres. It was just a typical minor Languedoc estate. Its lords owned land and property, intermarried with other local gentry, made bequests to religious institutions, owed allegiance to the Counts of Foix. Consummately normal. Then, some time around 1100, things suddenly seem to change. Quite dramatically.'

Layla came forward onto the edge of her seat, a ripple of excitement echoing down her spine. If her research was correct, and she had no reason to think it wasn't, some time around 1100 would have been exactly when William de Relincourt discovered his mysterious treasure beneath the Church of the Holy Sepulchre and sent it away to his sister at Castelombres.

'Again, the sources are scanty in the extreme,' continued Topping. 'Just a few troubadour poems, a couple of fleeting references in contemporary chronicles, and, most importantly, two fragments of letters written by the contemporary Jewish scholar Rashi. They all seem to agree, though, that from the early twelfth century onwards Castelombres starts to attract an increasing amount of attention. And the reason for this is that rumours start flying around that it's the repository of some extraordinary treasure of unparalleled power and beauty.'

Another, stronger, ripple reverberated through Layla's body. 'Power and beauty' were exactly the words de Relincourt used in his letter.

'Do we know what it was?' she asked, trying to keep her voice steady.

Topping shook his head. 'No idea. Even the sources don't seem to be entirely sure. Some refer to it as "Lo Tresor" – the treasure – others simply call it a secret or a mystery, which implies some sort of allegorical or symbolic meaning. It just isn't made clear.'

He downed the last of his beer and launched the bottle into a bin five feet away, where it landed with a loud clatter.

'If we don't know precise details, however, two things at least do seem to be certain. Firstly, whatever this mysterious object or secret was, it was intimately associated with Esclarmonde of Castelombres, wife of Count Raymond III, who from the outset seems to be regarded as some sort of guardian or protector figure. Secondly, it appears to have had some profound significance for the Jewish faith. As early as 1104, according to Rashi, we have the leaders of Languedoc's main Jewish communities in Toulouse, Beziers, Narbonne and Carcassonne – visiting the castle. By 1120 you've got Jews coming from as far afield as Cordoba and Sicily. And by 1150 the place seems to be well established as a centre of Jewish pilgrimage and cabbala study. Again, I have to stress how meagre the sources are. Even bearing that in mind, however, it's clear that something very unusual was going on at Castelombres during this period.'

Layla was sitting right forward on the edge of her chair.

'Go on.'

Topping shook his head. 'Unfortunately, from the mid-twelfth century the sources go completely silent. The next thing we hear of Castelombres, the last thing we hear, is in something called the Chronicle of Guillaume Pelhisson which records how in 1243, during the Cathar Crusade, the castle was razed to the ground by the forces of the Catholic Church, its lands redistributed and the House of Castelombres wiped out. Of the mysterious treasure or secret or whatever the hell it was, nothing is ever heard again.'

He paused a moment, then looked up at her over the top of his notes.

'Or at least it wasn't until I found a rather curious reference to it a few months ago in an Inquisition register I was studying at the Bibliothèque Nationale in Paris. Which is how this whole thing got started in the first place.'

There was a dull clank as, outside, a bell chimed the half-hour.

'Do you know about the Cathars?' he asked.

She had skim-read a book on the subject during the journey over which, along with the stuff she had already picked up from the internet, had given her the basic background.

'A bit,' she said. 'I know they were a heretical Christian sect that flourished in Languedoc in the twelfth and thirteenth centuries. That they believed' – she glanced down at the brief notes she had scribbled on the plane – 'the universe was ruled by a God of Light and a God of Darkness, and that everything in the material world was the work of the evil God. That the Catholic Church launched a crusade against them, the Cathar Crusade. That they made their last stand at the Castle of Montségur and that just before the castle fell they were supposed to have smuggled some fabulous treasure out past the besieging army.' She looked up at him. 'That's about it, I'm afraid.'

He gave her an impressed nod. 'It's a lot more than most people know, I can assure you.'

There was a momentary silence, the two of them staring at each other, then, with a cock of his head, Topping went through into the kitchen again and fetched himself another beer.

'You're sure you don't want one?' he called.

'Go on then.'

He opened two bottles and, after coming back in, handed one to her and sat down opposite, stretching out his legs – long, pale, honed – so that his bare feet were within an inch or so of her chair.

'The treasure of the Cathars has long been the subject of speculation,' he said, picking up the thread of his narrative, 'some of it academic, most just wild fantasy. All sorts of ideas have been floated as to what exactly it was, everything from sacks of gold to Cathar religious texts to the Holy Grail. The fact is, as with the whole Secret of Castelombres thing, the sources just aren't clear.'

He took a swig of his beer.

'We know about the treasure from a series of depositions given to the Inquisition by survivors of the siege of Montségur. When the castle fell to the Catholic crusaders in March 1244, about two hundred of the defenders refused to renounce their beliefs and were burnt to death. The rest were allowed to go free on condition they provided a full confession to the Inquisition interrogators. Twenty-two of these confession depositions have survived – over four hundred pages' worth – of which four mention the story of the mysterious smuggled treasure.'

Layla half raised her bottle to take a sip, but then lowered it again and instead scribbled a note of what Topping had just said.

'Then, last December, I turned up what seems to be part of a twenty-third Montségur survivor deposition. One that also mentions the treasure of the Cathars, but with some rather interesting extra details.'

He seemed outwardly relaxed as he said this, slumped in his chair with his beer bottle dangling from his hand. Despite this, Layla could tell from the brightness of his eyes and the slight speeding up in his delivery that he was as excited by the story as she was.

'The deposition had been bound, presumably by accident, into a register of much later documents,' he continued. 'It recorded the interrogation of a Montségur survivor named Berenger d'Ussat by an inquisitor called Guillaume Lepetit – William the Small, or Little Willy as I prefer to call him. In it, this Berenger describes how, some time around Christmas 1243, three months before Montségur fell to the Catholic besiegers, four Cathar leaders' – he referred to his notes – 'Amiel Aicart, Petari Laurent, Pierre Sabatier and a man named Hugon, managed to escape from the castle under cover of night carrying away some sort of important treasure. In itself that isn't particularly earth-shattering – the other four "treasure" depositions all say exactly the same thing. What comes next, however, *is* fascinating, because when William, the interrogator, pushes Berenger for more information about this mysterious treasure, he says' – he glanced down at his notes again – '"Credo id Castelombrium unde venerit relatum esse et ibi sepultum esse ne quis invenire posset." Which in translation means: "I believe it was returned to Castelombres, from where it came, and was buried there so no-one could find it."'

Layla's jaw dropped. 'They were the same thing! The Montségur treasure and the Secret of Castelombres!'

Topping sat up in his chair and took a swig of his beer, 'Well, admittedly it's just one piece of testimony,' he said, 'wholly uncorroborated. It's more than possible that Berenger was just trying to confuse his inquisitors, give them false leads. All the same, it's an intriguing notion. And not perhaps entirely unsurprising. Castelombres, after all, is fewer than ten kilometres as the crow flies from Montségur, so it's fair to assume there was some sort of interaction between the two castles. Also, the Cathars were renowned for their friendship with the Jews, so again it's probably fair to assume that in the face of a violently anti-semitic Catholic invading force the defenders of Montségur would have offered sanctuary to whatever secret or treasure was lodged at Castelombres. Whether the Lords of Castelombres themselves actually adopted the Cathar creed . . .' He shrugged. 'I doubt we'll ever know, although given their involvement with the Jews and the fact that their castle was destroyed by the crusaders it's a fair bet that they did. To be honest, it's neither here nor there. The important thing is that there do seem to be reasonably solid grounds for speculating that what have until now appeared to be two wholly separate mysteries are in fact one and the same.'

Layla still hadn't drunk any of her beer. She

raised the bottle now and took a swift gulp, struggling to process everything she'd just heard, to tie it into what she already knew: William de Relincourt finds some object beneath the Church of the Holy Sepulchre; he sends it to his sister Esclarmonde at Castelombres; Castelombres becomes the focus of some Jewish mystery cult; the object is transferred to Montségur for safekeeping during the upheavals of the Cathar Crusade; when Montségur falls it is returned to Castelombres and buried. It all seemed to fit together. Yet, fascinating as it was, it ultimately didn't move her any further forward. There was still so much she didn't know, so many questions to answer. What was this mysterious thing? Why was it so important to the Jews? What was its relevance to al-Mulatham? And what had happened to it?

'The report of your talk said something about Nazi archaeologists,' she said, taking another sip, bringing up her left foot and tucking it under her right knee. 'How do they come into it?'

Topping smiled. 'I was wondering when you'd get round to that. In many ways it's the most curious part of the whole story.'

He got to his feet and wandered over to the window, gazing down into the court below. Aside from the muffled thud of music from an adjoining room, everything was completely silent.

'Inquisition transcripts are a pretty obscure topic of study,' he said after a brief pause. 'Not many people are interested in them. Some of the registers in the Bibliothèque Nationale haven't been looked at for years, decades even. I once came across one that hadn't been opened since the middle of the nineteenth century.'

She tapped her pen on her knee, wondering where he was going with this.

'According to the Bibliothèque records,' he continued, turning back to her, 'the last time anyone looked at the register in which I found the Berenger d'Ussat transcript was at the beginning of September 1943, during the German occupation of Paris, when it was examined by a Nazi scholar named Dieter Hoth.'

The name seemed to spark a faint connection somewhere deep in Layla's mind. She was so overloaded with information that she couldn't immediately think why.

'Go on.'

'Well, initially I thought this Hoth – who incidentally I'd never heard of, which was strange given how narrow the field is – must have missed the Berenger transcript altogether because there's no record of him ever publishing anything about it. Anyway, just for the hell of it I checked him with a contact of mine down in Toulouse, a Nazi specialist, and guess what? Less than a week after looking at the register this same Dieter Hoth turns up down in the depths of Languedoc, staying in the modern village of Castelombres, this time accompanied by a unit of SS stormtroopers. And what do you think they were all doing down there?'

Layla shook her head. Topping took a swig of his beer and leant back against the windowsill, smiling wryly.

'Excavating.'

She gawped. 'You're serious?'

'That's what I was told.'

'And? Did they find anything?'

Again he gave a wry smile. 'Apparently so, although exactly what I can't tell you. Like I said, Nazi archaeologists aren't really my area of expertise.'

He stared down at her, then, pushing himself away from the windowsill, went through into the kitchen and began rummaging in a cupboard. Layla sat back and sipped her beer, her mind whirring. There was so much to follow up here, so many avenues to explore.

'Who's this friend of yours?' she asked after a moment. 'The one in Toulouse.'

'I wouldn't call him a friend as such,' replied Topping, 'more a passing acquaintance. I met him a couple of years ago, when I was on sabbatical at Toulouse University. Runs an antiques shop near the St Sernin. Odd man. Eccentric. Knows everything there is to know about the Nazis, though. Name of Jean-Michel Dupont.'

As with Dieter Hoth, this seemed to ring a vague bell somewhere deep inside Layla's head. She closed her eyes, trying to pin it down. Dieter Hoth,

Jean-Michel Dupont; Dieter Hoth, Jean-Michel Dupont. How did she know these people?

And then, suddenly, it came to her. Of course! From the web the other night. The article about Nazi archaeologists, with the footnote containing the unidentified initials DH. Her eyes snapped open and, after scrabbling through her notes, she pulled out the print-out she had made at the time:

> November 13, 1938
> Thule Soc. Dinner, Wewelsburg. Spirits high after events of 9–10, with WvS making joke about the 'shattering of Jewish hopes'. DH said they'd be more than shattered if the Relincourt thing came off, after which long discussion on Cathars etc. Pheasant, champagne, cognac. Apologies from FK and WJ.

'My God,' Layla whispered. 'He knew. De Relincourt, Castelombres, Montségur. He made the connection.'

'What was that?' said Topping.

She ignored the question.

'This Dieter Hoth. What happened to him?'

Topping came back into the room, munching on an apple.

'Died at the end of the war, apparently. Got his head blown off by a Russian artillery shell. No more than he deserved, by all accounts.'

He took another bite of his apple and leant against the door of the kitchen.

'Don't fancy something to eat, do you? I know a very nice little Greek taverna down on Trumpington Street.'

She looked up, distracted.

'Are you hitting on me, Professor Topping?'

He smiled.

'Absolutely.'

JERUSALEM

Har-Zion wound the leather straps of the *tefillah* anti-clockwise around the bicep of his left arm and down around his gloved fingers, ensuring that the box with the holy passages in it was positioned exactly adjacent to his heart. By rights, the bicep and hand should have been bare – that is what the Torah prescribed. With his ravaged flesh, however, he did not feel comfortable exposing himself, and had managed to gain a rabbinic dispensation permitting him to keep the relevant portions of his body covered.

He finished winding the seven loops and attached the second *tefillah* to his forehead, centring the scripture box midway between his eyes; then, with a nod at Avi as if to say 'wait for me', he heaved a prayer shawl over his shoulders and started forward across the floodlit esplanade towards the HaKotel Ha-Ma'aravi, the Western Wall, last vestige of the ancient Temple, holiest site in the Jewish world.

It had been a while since he was last down here, over a week. He would have liked to come more often, every day if possible, but what with all his various commitments there simply wasn't the time. Tonight, however, he had made the time. There were some things it wasn't safe to delegate.

He approached the Wall and positioned himself at its far left-hand end, gazing up at the twenty-metre-high patchwork of giant stone blocks rearing overhead, like some intricate gaming board, every nook and cranny of its lower courses jammed with a dandruff of folded paper notes on which were scribbled the prayers and supplications of previous visitors. By day this area would be crowded, with tourists in makeshift cardboard *yarmulkes*, Haredi Jews in their black coats and hats, boys performing their bar mitzvah ceremonies. Now, aside from himself and a lone Hasidic worshipper away to his right bowing back and forth in prayer like a pecking raven, the Wall was completely deserted. He cast a quick glance around, then placed a palm against the pockmarked stone, lowered his head and began to recite the *shema*.

'Like a story come to life.' That's how his brother Benjamin had described the Wall when the two of them had first come here all those years ago. 'Like something out of a book or a song.' The image had stayed with Har-Zion, elaborating and embellishing itself over time so that now, as he stood beneath the towering matrix of cream-yellow stone, he felt himself in the presence not of something dead and inanimate, an ossified relic of some long-forgotten world, but rather of something vibrant and alive and relevant. A voice. That's how he thought of it. A deep, sonorous voice singing to him from out of the void: of things that had once been – kings and prophets, the Ark and the Menorah, Moses and David and Solomon and Ezra – but also, more importantly, of things that were yet to come: God's people gathered together once again, the Temple rebuilt, the Holy Lamp recast and filled with light. The Wailing Wall some called it, those who came here to weep, pull their hair and fixate upon the centuries of exile and loss. Not Har-Zion. For him it was a Singing Wall, a place not of pain and remembrance but of hope and joy and expectation; a tangible, touchable reminder that God was with them, that they were not abandoned, that they were His chosen people, precious above all others. That they would endure, just as the Wall had endured, whatever man and nature might throw at them.

He continued reciting, the words of the prayer swooping and swirling within the soft musical hum of his voice, before eventually coming to the end and falling silent. At the same moment a figure, tall, broad-shouldered, came up beside him, positioning himself in a deep pool of shadow at the Wall's far-left extremity so that his face was lost in darkness. The solitary Hasid had by now departed, so the two of them were completely alone.

'You're late,' said Har-Zion, his voice so low as to be barely audible.

The man edged himself deeper into the shadows, mumbling an apology.

Har-Zion delved into his pocket and produced a small, folded sheet of paper which he slipped into the gap between two masonry blocks.

'All the details are there. The boy's name, contact address. Just follow the instructions. It will be—'

There was a sound of approaching footsteps and a young soldier came up to the Wall, stopping a few metres to their right. Har-Zion flicked his finger at his companion to indicate that their conversation, such as it had been, was at an end. He leant forward and kissed the wall, turned and, without a backward glance, walked back across the esplanade towards his bodyguard Avi.

Five minutes later, when the young soldier had finished his prayers and moved away, the man crept a hand up the wall, pulled the folded sheet of paper from the crack and slipped it into his trouser pocket.

CAMBRIDGE

Layla rose at five a.m. and, leaving Topping asleep, quietly gathered her things, tiptoed from the bedroom and left the house.

She wasn't sure why she'd slept with him. He'd been good company – witty, charming, attentive – and the sex had been great, among the best she'd ever had. Despite that, at no point had she felt fully engaged in the experience, allowed herself simply to let go and disappear into the whirlwind of his lovemaking. Even as she had ridden on top of him, hips grinding into his, beads of passionate sweat jerking down her small, tight breasts, still a part of her, most of her, had stayed detached, locked away in her own thoughts, turning over what she'd heard earlier, what was happening back in the Middle East, as if her body was simply some inanimate vehicle that had been programmed on to autodrive while she, the pilot, sat back inside and focused on something completely separate.

She clicked the front door closed and stepped out onto the empty street, rows of neat Victorian houses running off to either side, the world around her grey and still, no longer dark but not yet light either, the dim no-man's land between night and dawn.

She had called Jean-Michel Dupont, Topping's contact in Toulouse, the previous evening, explaining that she was interested in Dieter Hoth and his excavations at Castelombres. They had agreed to meet at his antique shop at 1.30 p.m., and she was now booked on to BA's ten a.m. flight from Heathrow. Briefly the thought struck her that with so much time to kill she could walk out to Grantchester, have a look at the old house where she had gone to live after her father's death. Although both her grandparents had long since passed away, her mother, so far as she was aware, still lived there, with her second husband. A barrister. Or was it a banker? Layla couldn't be sure. She hadn't spoken to her since she had remarried six years ago, unable to forgive what she regarded as a grotesque betrayal of her father's memory.

Yes, she thought, it would be nice to see the old place again, with its moss-covered roof and garden full of plum and apple trees, about as far away from the dust and horror of Palestine as you could possibly get. She even started to cross the street, aiming for the public footpath that, if memory served her right, led out through the water meadows that lapped against the town's eastern fringes. After only a few metres, however, she stopped and, with a shake of the head as if to say 'What's the fucking point?', turned and set off in the opposite direction, towards the station, tears pricking her eyes at the thought of how utterly and irrevocably alone she was in the world.

EGYPT – BETWEEN LUXOR
AND CAIRO

Khalifa sipped at the plastic beaker of tepid in-flight coffee, nibbled on the corner of his biscuit and glanced out of the aeroplane window at the miniature world beneath. It was a spectacular view – the Nile, the cultivation, the crumpled yellow sheet of the Western Desert – and under other circumstances he would have spent the entire journey staring down at it in wide-eyed wonder. It was, after all, only the second time in his life he had ever been in an aeroplane, and there was surely no better way of appreciating the natural miracle that was Egypt, the extraordinary juxtaposition of life and barrenness – Kemet and Deshret as the ancients had known it, the Black Land and the Red Land – than to view it from above in this way, stretched out from horizon to horizon like some vast unfolded map.

This morning, however, his mind was preoccupied with other things, and after gazing out of the window for only a moment he looked away again, draining the remainder of his coffee and refocusing on the business in hand.

He had wanted to travel down to Cairo the previous afternoon, immediately after his conversation with Ben-Roi. Unfortunately, force etiquette dictated that he couldn't just turn up on another station's patch without some sort of official notification, and by the time he had jumped through all the necessary bureaucratic hoops he had missed the last flight up to the capital. Which, as it turned out, had proved to be a blessing in disguise, because the delay had afforded him the time to do a bit of background checking into the mysterious Mr and Mrs Anton Gratz, with some extremely interesting results.

For a start, it turned out that Anton Gratz used to run a medium-scale fruit and vegetable import business. According to Ben-Roi, the 'Gad' or 'Getz' who had ordered the destruction of Hannah Schlegel's Jerusalem flat had also been involved in the fruit business. Khalifa had already assumed, of course, that 'Getz' and 'Gratz' were one and the same, but this new snippet of information seemed to provide absolute confirmation of the fact.

Equally if not more intriguing had been the similarities between the Gratzes' background and that of their friend Piet Jansen. Like Jansen, both were foreigners. Like Jansen, both had applied for and been granted Egyptian citizenship in October 1945. And like Jansen, neither seemed to have any discernible history prior to that date. Where they came from originally, when and why, whether

Gratz was even their real name – all were questions to which Khalifa had been unable to find answers. The more he had dug the more he had got the feeling that, like Jansen, the Gratzes had something to hide. And the more he had dug the more he had got the feeling that all three were trying to hide the same thing.

By far the most significant piece of information he had come up with, however – a real revelation – concerned Mr and Mrs Gratz's original citizenship applications. The contemporary paperwork for these had, inevitably, been lost or destroyed. What remained, according to a contact of Khalifa's in the Interior Ministry, was a basic administrative record of the receipt and subsequent approval of said applications. And who was the security official responsible for that approval? None other than Farouk al-Hakim, the man who, four and a half decades later, would step in to stop Jansen being investigated for the Schlegel murder. Some further digging had revealed that al-Hakim had also dealt with Jansen's citizenship application, thereby establishing for the first time a clear link between the two men. More importantly, it implied that whatever Jansen and the Gratzes had been up to prior to October 1945, whatever it was they were all so desperate to keep hidden, al-Hakim had most likely known about it. It still didn't explain why he should have been so intent on protecting Jansen back in 1990, but it did reinforce Khalifa's conviction that the key to the Schlegel murder and subsequent cover-up, the key to everything that had been troubling him this last fortnight, lay in those crucial years prior to Jansen's arrival in Egypt.

And the only people who, it seemed, could now shed any light on those years were the ones he was currently on his way to see.

As the plane banked and dipped, beginning its descent into Cairo Domestic, the ruins of Saqqara drifting slowly by as though viewed through deep, clear water, Khalifa closed his eyes and prayed that the trip wouldn't be a wasted one; that when he returned to Luxor later that evening it would, finally, be with some clear idea about what the hell this whole thing was all about.

El-Maadi, the Cairo suburb where the Gratzes lived, lay on the southern fringes of the city. A quiet, leafy district favoured by diplomats, ex-pats and wealthy businessmen, its expensive villas and long avenues shaded by flame and eucalyptus trees were a world away from the poverty and mayhem that defined most of the rest of Egypt's capital.

Khalifa arrived just after midday, having taken the Metro down from the city centre. He got directions to Orabi Street from a peanut-seller near the station, and ten minutes later was standing outside the Gratzes' apartment block, a large pink building with whirring air-conditioning units bolted to the outer walls, an underground car park, and, opposite, the public payphone whose number had figured so prominently on Piet Jansen's telephone bill.

He lingered for a moment on the front steps, struck by the depressing thought that however hard he worked, and for however long, he would never be able to afford to live in a place like this. Then, flicking away his half-smoked Cleopatra, he passed through into the glass-fronted foyer and took the lift up to the third floor. The Gratzes' flat was halfway down a brightly lit corridor, with a varnished wooden door from the centre of which, like a large, curled tusk, protruded a brass knocker, a matching brass letterbox beneath it.

The detective paused a moment, sensing that what followed was either going to make or break the investigation, then, with a deep breath, he reached out towards the knocker. Before his fingers had reached it, he seemed to have second thoughts, lowering his hand again and instead dropping to his haunches and gently pushing back the letterbox flap. Through the rectangular opening he could make out a dim carpeted hallway stretching off in front of him, very neat and tidy, with rooms opening off to either side. From one of these – the kitchen, to judge by the rack of plates and the corner of a fridge just visible through the doorway – came a faint hum of music, a radio or cassette, and, even fainter, the sound of someone moving around. He brought his ear right up to the letterbox to make sure he wasn't imagining things, then, assured that he had indeed heard movement, straightened up, grasped the knocker and gave three loud bangs.

He counted ten beats, then, when there was no response, he repeated the action, four knocks this time. Still no answer. He squatted and eased open the letterbox again, thinking perhaps whoever was in the kitchen was elderly or infirm and thus simply taking a long time to reach the front door. The hall was empty.

'Hello!' he called. 'Is there anyone there? Hello!'

Nothing.

'Mr Gratz! My name is Inspector Yusuf Khalifa of the Luxor Police. I have been trying to contact you for the last three days. I know you're in there. Please open the door.'

He waited a few seconds, then added, 'If you don't I will have no choice but to assume you are deliberately obstructing a police inquiry and to place you under arrest.'

He was bluffing, but it seemed to have the desired effect. There was a faint choking sob from the direction of the kitchen, and then slowly, hesitantly, a short, plump, elderly woman, Mrs Gratz presumably, shuffled a few steps out into the hallway, supporting herself on a metal walking stick, staring in terror at the letterbox.

'What do you want with us?' she said, her voice weak and unsteady. 'What have we done?'

She was clearly not well: both her calves were heavily bandaged and the skin of her face was cracked and grey, like dried putty. Khalifa felt a pang of guilt for having so obviously upset her.

'There's no need to be afraid,' he said, speaking as gently and reassuringly as the situation permitted. 'I'm not going to hurt you. I just need to ask you and your husband some questions.'

She shook her head, a tress of white hair dislodging from the bun in which it had been clipped and swinging down across her face, giving her a faintly deranged look.

'My husband's not here. He's . . . gone out.'

'Then if I could talk to you, Mrs Gratz. About your friend Piet—'

'No!' She cowered back, half raising her walking stick as though to ward off an attack. 'We haven't done anything, I tell you! We obey the law. We pay our taxes. What do you want with us?'

'Like I said, Mrs Gratz, I need to ask you some questions. About Piet Jansen, Farouk al-Hakim—'

At the mention of this last name her fear seemed to redouble, her entire body trembling as though a pair of invisible hands had grasped her frail shoulders and were vigorously shaking them.

'We don't know anyone called al-Hakim!' she wailed. 'We never had anything to do with him. Why can't you leave us alone? Why are you doing this to us?'

'If you could just—'

'No! I won't let you in without my husband here. I won't! I won't!'

She started to back away down the hall, one

hand clutching her stick, the other supporting herself against the wall.

'Please, Mrs Gratz,' said Khalifa, coming down onto both knees, fully aware of the ridiculousness of trying to conduct a conversation in this manner but unable to see any other way of proceeding. 'I have no wish to frighten or harm you. I believe, however, that you and your husband are in possession of important information concerning the murder of an Israeli woman named Hannah Schlegel.'

If the mention of al-Hakim's name had provoked a strong reaction, it was nothing compared to the look of abject terror that now swept across her face. She staggered backwards against the wall, one hand pawing at her throat as though she was struggling to draw breath, the other clasping and unclasping around the handle of her walking stick.

'We don't know anything,' she choked. 'Please, we don't know anything.'

'Mrs Gratz—'

'I won't talk to you! Not without my husband here. You can't make me! You can't!'

She began to sob, fierce spasms jerking her body, mucusy tears bubbling from her eyes. Khalifa remained as he was for a moment, then, with a sigh, he lowered the letterbox flap and stood up, shaking the stiffness from his legs.

There was no point pushing her any further. She was too distraught. Whatever she knew about Hannah Schlegel – and she certainly did know something – she wasn't going to tell him in her current state. Some of his colleagues would have simply kicked down the door and dragged her off into custody, but that wasn't the way Khalifa did things. He lit a cigarette, took a couple of drags, then dropped to his haunches again and pushed back the flap. The old woman was just as he'd left her.

'What time is your husband home, Mrs Gratz?'

She didn't answer.

'Mrs Gratz?'

She mumbled something inaudible.

'I'm sorry?'

'Five o'clock.'

He glanced down at his watch. Four and a half hours.

'He'll definitely be here then?'

She gave a weak nod.

'OK,' he said after a brief pause. 'I'll come back. Please tell your husband to expect me.'

He thought of adding 'and no tricks', but couldn't imagine what tricks they'd play so left it at that, lowering the flap, standing and setting off back down the corridor towards the lift. About halfway along he heard her voice calling after him, frail, desperate.

'Why are you hunting us like this? They're your enemies too, you know. Why are you helping them? Why? Why?'

He slowed, thinking of going back to ask what she meant, but then decided against it and, continuing to the lift, pressed the button for the ground floor. Things hadn't turned out quite as he'd hoped.

After he had gone the old woman remained as she was for a long moment, then she slowly hobbled down the hallway into the living room at the far end of the apartment. A small, erect man with a pencil moustache and a pinched, puckered face, like a piece of dried fruit, was waiting just behind the door, his hands held stiffly at his sides as though he was standing to attention on a parade ground. She shuffled across to him and, opening his arms, he wrapped them tenderly around her.

'There, there, my dear,' he said gently, speaking in German. 'You did the best you could. There, there.'

She pressed her cheek against his chest, shivering like a frightened child.

'They know,' she whimpered. 'They know it all.'

'Yes,' he said. 'It seems they do.'

He held her tight, stroking her neck and back, trying to calm her; then, easing her away, he took the tress of hair dangling across her face and tucked it back into the bun on top of her head.

'We always knew it might come to this,' he said softly. 'It was foolish to think it could last for ever. We had a good run. That's the main thing. Didn't we have a good run?'

She nodded weakly.

'That's my girl. That's my beautiful Inga.'

He reached into his pocket, removed a hand-kerchief and dabbed at her eyes and upper cheeks, wiping away the tears.

'Now, why don't you go and put on your dress while I sort things out here? No point hanging around, eh? We should be ready for them when they come back.'

TOULOUSE, FRANCE

Jean-Michel Dupont's antique shop was located in a quiet, winding street right in the centre of Toulouse, just a couple of hundred metres from the spectacular red-brick eruption of the Basilique St Sernin, the tip of whose belltower was just visible above the tiled rooftops, like a lighthouse rising above a sea of choppy orange waves.

As agreed, Layla arrived at 1.30 p.m. After pausing for a moment to take in the front of the shop, with its object-filled windows and faded sign announcing LA PETITE MAISON DES CURIOSITÉS, she opened the glass door and stepped inside, a bell clanging loudly above her head.

The interior smelt of polish and cigar smoke, and was crammed with a confused jumble of bric-a-brac, everything from furniture to books, paintings to glassware, china to brass ornaments, although the bulk of the collection appeared to be of a military nature. There were tailors' mannequins dressed in brocade-covered uniforms; shelves lined with caps and helmets; and, against one wall, flanked on either side by a stuffed bear and a panel from a stained-glass window, a long cabinet filled with an array of bayonets and pistols.

'Vous désirez quelque chose?'

A bulky, overweight man had appeared at the back of the shop, dressed in corduroys and a traditional Breton peasant's smock, his shoulder-length hair and goatee beard shot through with peppery streaks of grey. A pair of half-moon spectacles dangled from his neck by a gold chain; a half-smoked cigarillo was clutched between the nicotine-stained fingers of his right hand. With his heavy jowls and lugubrious expression, he looked like a large bloodhound.

'Monsieur Dupont?'

'Oui.'

Layla introduced herself, speaking in French. He nodded in recognition and, lodging the cigarillo in the corner of his mouth, came forward and shook her hand, beckoning her round the counter and up a narrow, creaking set of stairs to the first floor. He paused there for a moment, putting his head through a bead curtain and holding a brief muttered conversation with someone in the room beyond – 'My mother,' he explained, 'she'll watch the shop while we talk' – then continued upwards to the second floor, where he opened a heavy wooden door and led her through into a large office-cum-study that occupied the entire upper level of the building. Bookshelves lined two of the walls, a long work counter the third, the latter covered with a clutter of computer equipment – hard-drives, screens, keypads, piles of disks and CDs. Set against the fourth wall, the one furthest from her, was a large glass-fronted display cabinet similar to the one she had seen in the shop downstairs.

He asked if she would like coffee, and when she replied in the affirmative he crossed to one end of the work counter and began busying himself with an electric kettle. Layla hovered by the door; then, curious, she started wandering around the room, perusing first one of the bookshelves – a mixture of antique dealers' manuals and histories of the Third Reich – then the cabinet against the far wall. At first glance this seemed to contain a generalized collection of militaria such as had been displayed downstairs, and it was only after a moment that she realized, with a slight shudder, that it in fact housed a collection of specifically Nazi militaria – medals, bayonets, photographs, items of uniform. On one shelf was arrayed a row of iron crosses with red, white and black ribbons; on another a line of daggers, each with the twin lightning-bolt insignia of the SS inlaid into its handle and the legend MEIN EHRE HEISST TREUE inscribed on its blade.

'SS honour daggers,' explained Dupont, coming up behind her and handing her a steaming cup. 'My honour is loyalty.'

'You sell this stuff?' she asked, taking the cup.

'No, no. To do so in France is illegal. It's merely a private hobby. You disapprove?'

She shrugged. 'It's not the sort of thing I'd want in my house. Given the moral connotations.'

He smiled. 'My interest, I can assure you, is purely aesthetic. I no more sympathize with the activities of the Third Reich than a collector of, say, Roman artefacts sympathizes with that civilization's predilection for slavery and crucifixion. It is the craftsmanship that attracts me, not the ideology. That and the historical context. They are, after all, important artefacts. If you knew more of their background you too would be drawn.'

She gave another shrug, unconvinced.

'You do not believe me? Come, let me show you something.'

He led her to the far end of the cabinet where a safe was set into the wall. Spinning the dial, he opened it and removed a small square case bound in black leather, lifting its lid and holding it out towards her. Inside, lying on a bed of velvet, was a black metal cross surmounted by a magnificently worked silver clasp in the shape of oak leaves and crossed swords, the latter encrusted with what looked like tiny diamonds.

'The Knight's Cross with Oak Leaves, Swords and Diamonds,' he explained. 'Nazi Germany's highest military honour. One of only twenty-seven ever awarded, and the only one conferred for a non-combat role. It is worth more than the rest of my collection put together. More than everything in this building put together. Probably more than the building itself.' He paused a beat, then added, 'Its recipient, I believe, is the reason you have come here today.'

She looked up, eyes widening. 'Not . . . Dieter Hoth?'

He nodded.

'How the hell did you get it?' she asked, coming forward a step and staring at the medal.

'A long and boring story,' he replied, waving his cigarillo. 'And one that I won't waste your time by telling. I merely wanted to make the point that, now you know the context, you too are drawn, despite yourself. The fact that Hoth himself was an extremely unpleasant man, this is neither here nor there. You are interested in his story, and are thus inevitably attracted to the material remains of that story. Moral considerations do not enter the equation.'

He held out the box a moment longer, then returned it to the safe and ushered her into a creaking leather armchair, himself crossing to one of the bookshelves and running a finger along the spines of the volumes lined up along it.

'So, what exactly is it you wish to know about our friend Dr Hoth?' he asked, head tilted to one side, examining book titles.

'Anything you can tell me about what he was doing at Castelombres, basically,' replied Layla, putting down her coffee cup and rummaging in her bag. 'According to Magnus Topping you've done a lot of research into the subject.'

She pulled out her notebook and pen and sat back.

'I also wanted to ask about a footnote in an article you wrote for the web linking Hoth with a man named William de Relincourt.'

Dupont nodded, continuing to trace his finger along the book spines before eventually pulling out a volume and blowing dust off its cover. He flicked through its pages, then came over and handed it to Layla, open about midway through.

'Dieter Hoth,' he said, indicating a grainy black and white photograph. 'One of the very few pictures that exist of him.'

A tall, handsome man stared up at her, with sunken cheeks, coal-coloured eyes and a long, aquiline nose. He was dressed in a Nazi officer's uniform, with twin lightning-bolt flashes on the collars.

'Hoth was in the SS?' she asked, surprised.

'The Ahnenerbe,' replied Dupont. 'What you might call the cerebral branch of the SS. He was an archaeologist by profession. A very brilliant one, by all accounts. Headed the Ahnenerbe's Egyptian department.'

Layla's look of surprise intensified. 'He was an Egyptologist?'

'An Egyptian archaeologist is probably a more accurate description. But, yes, Egypt was his specialist field.'

'So what the hell was he doing excavating in the south of France?'

Dupont chuckled, a deep, throaty sound, like a car engine starting.

'An interesting question. And one to which, so far as I am aware, no-one has yet provided a satisfactory answer.'

He took a final puff on his cigarillo and, crossing to the workbench, tamped the butt out into an ashtray and heaved himself up onto a rickety swivel stool. From somewhere above them came the cooing of pigeons and the scratch of talons on tiles. There was a long pause.

'To understand Hoth's career you have to appreciate the extent to which the Nazis were obsessed with history,' said the Frenchman eventually. 'For Hitler et al it wasn't sufficient that the Third Reich should be militarily powerful. Like all despotic regimes they wished to justify and validate their power by wrapping it in an aura of historical legitimacy.'

He pulled a small flat tin from the pocket of his smock, removed another cigarillo and lit it.

'From the outset archaeology, and archaeologists, played a crucial role in that process. Himmler in particular realized their significance. In 1935 he set up Das Ahnenerbe, the Ancestral Heritage Society, a special department within the SS charged with finding material to bolster the ideal of German historical supremacy. Expeditions were sent all over the world – to Iran, Greece, Egypt, even Tibet.'

'To dig?'

'In part, yes. Himmler was determined to uncover evidence that Aryan Germanic culture

504

wasn't just confined to northern Europe but was in fact the prime moving force behind the whole of modern civilization. The Ahnenerbe also stole, however. Looted on an unprecedented scale. Shipped thousands, tens of thousands of artefacts back to Berlin for the greater glory of the Third Reich. If they were obsessed with the past, the Nazis were doubly so when it came to the remains of the past. Because of course if you control its remains, then in a sense you control history itself.'

'And Hoth?' she asked. 'How does he fit into all of this?'

'Well, as I told you, he was a brilliant archaeologist. He was also a devoted and enthusiastic supporter of the Nazi Party; his father, the industrialist Ludwig Hoth, was a close friend of Goebbels. So it was only a matter of time before Hoth junior was asked – or volunteered, we're not sure which – to deploy his skills for the benefit of the Nazi machine. He was only twenty-three when the Ahnenerbe was formed, but Himmler personally appointed him head of its Egyptian unit, with a special brief to dig up and loot as many ancient Egyptian artefacts as he possibly could.'

Dupont dragged on his cigarillo, wafting a hand back and forth in front of his face to dispel the sheets of blue-grey tobacco smoke.

'For the next three years Hoth travelled all over Egypt, ostensibly carrying out legitimate excavations under the guise of the Deutsche Orient-Gesellschaft, but in fact stealing anything he could lay his hands on and smuggling it back to Germany. We're talking thousands of objects here. A letter exists from Himmler to Hans Reinerth, another Nazi archaeologist, in which he jokingly complains that thanks to Hoth the Castle of Wewelsburg – the headquarters of the SS – was starting to look like something out of a Boris Karloff mummy film.'

'But how does all this lead to Castelombres?' asked Layla, butting in. 'I don't see the connection.'

'That's the whole point,' said Dupont. 'There doesn't seem to be a connection. Which is what makes the story so intriguing. Until 1938, Hoth's career is focused exclusively on ancient Egyptian archaeology. He displays no interest whatsoever in any other branch of history, least of all the sort of credulous, quasi-mystical hokum that appealed to people like Himmler – the Holy Grail, Atlantis, that sort of rubbish. He might have been a thief and a looter, but unlike many Nazi archaeologists, Hoth was never a fantasist.

'Yet in November 1938 this man for whom the Land of the Pharaohs has been everything, who is widely regarded as the finest Egyptian excavator of his generation, who has shown no previous interest in any other subject, suddenly abandons Egypt altogether and instead devotes himself to investigating what can best be described as a series of half-baked medieval legends about buried treasure. It's extraordinary – not just a change of direction, but an apparently complete change of character. I'm surprised it hasn't attracted more attention.'

Layla frowned, tapping her pen on her pad.

'So what happened in 1938? What prompted this sudden change of interest?'

Dupont shrugged. 'No-one seems to know. One minute Hoth and his team are excavating in Egypt, at a site just outside Alexandria; the next he's rushing back to Berlin for some top-secret meeting with Himmler – a meeting, incidentally, that is deemed so important Himmler actually puts off a dinner date with the Führer in order to attend it. And then a couple of days after that Hoth turns up in Jerusalem taking measurements in the Church of the Holy Sepulchre and asking questions about some eight-hundred-year-old legend of buried gold.'

'William de Relincourt,' Layla said.

The Frenchman nodded.

'That's just the start of it, however. For the next five years Hoth zig-zags back and forth across Europe and the Levant investigating what seems like every madcap treasure story known to man. He visits libraries, goes through private manuscript collections, digs holes everywhere from Turkey to the Canary Islands before eventually turning up at Castelombres in September 1943, which somehow seems to be the culmination of the whole bizarre episode.'

'And there's no indication of why he was doing

any of this?' she pressed. 'What he was looking for?'

Dupont shook his head. 'Of course it's possible he was simply acting under orders. Fulfilling some quixotic fantasy of Himmler's. He was a devoted Nazi after all. Would have done whatever his superior told him. Or maybe he simply lost the plot. He wouldn't have been the first academic to be driven mad by his work.'

'But you don't think so.'

'No,' replied Dupont, 'I don't. I think he was genuinely on to something. Something so important, of such immense significance to the whole Nazi history machine, that he was prepared to turn his entire life upside down in order to pursue it.'

He contemplated the end of his cigarillo, then looked up at her.

'And whatever he was looking for, I think he found it at Castelombres.'

He held her eyes for a moment, then, with a wry smile, slipped off his stool and went over to the kettle, switching it on again.

'I can't prove it, sadly. From the outset the Castelombres excavation was shrouded in a degree of secrecy that was intense even by Nazi standards. All we know is that Hoth arrived there in mid-September 1943, bringing with him heavy digging equipment and a crack unit of the Sonderkommando Jankuhn, an SS division specializing in excavation and looting. And he left three weeks later taking with him some sort of mysterious box or crate.'

Layla leant forward, her chest tight with excitement.

'Do we know what was in it?'

Dupont shook his head. 'Unfortunately not. We do know where it was taken, though, because three days after they left Castelombres, Hoth and the crate turned up at Wewelsburg Castle in north-west Germany where they were met by no less a welcoming party than Heinrich Himmler and the Führer himself.'

'No!'

'It was certainly most unusual,' concurred Dupont, puffing on his cigarillo. 'We have a diary entry from one of Himmler's adjutants recording how the moment he arrived Hoth was presented with the Knight's Cross you saw earlier, after which Hitler made a speech in which he declared that the contents of the crate were a clear sign that what Titus had started he, the Führer, was destined to finish.'

Layla's eyes narrowed.

'Meaning?'

'Well, the diary entry is somewhat short on detail, but I'd say it's almost certainly a reference to the Holocaust. Titus was the man who in AD 70 conquered Jerusalem and expelled the Jews from the Holy Land, and in a sense the concentration camps and gas chambers were the logical extension of that act. How precisely Hoth's discovery was relevant to the Final Solution . . .' He threw up his hands as if to say 'I have absolutely no idea'. 'One of the many fascinating elements of Hoth's five-year excursion into the world of medieval arcana, however, is the sudden interest he starts to show in Judaism and Jewish history. He even taught himself to read Hebrew. This from a man renowned for his virulent anti-semitism.'

There was a click behind him as the kettle came to the boil.

'More coffee?'

Layla shook her head, leaving him to spoon Nescafé into a cup for himself while she stared down at her pad, spooling everything she'd just heard through her mind, trying to fit it into the framework of what she had already discovered over the last few days. Hitler's Wewelsburg speech struck her as particularly significant. If the object at the centre of this whole mystery was in some albeit obscure way tied up with the expulsion of the Jews from the Holy Land and their subsequent perse-cution by the Nazis, then that would explain some-thing that had been perplexing her from the very outset – why it should be of any interest to someone such as al-Mulatham. She was still no closer to discovering what the damn thing was, however.

'So what happened then?' she asked. 'After Hoth arrived at Wewelsburg?'

Dupont was pouring water into his mug, ciga-rillo clamped between his teeth.

'So far as we can tell, nothing. The mysterious crate disappears into the depths of the castle; Hoth returns to Berlin where he takes up a desk job with the Ahnenerbe; the whole strange affair seems to come to a rather abrupt end.'

He stirred the cup, removed the cigarillo, took a sip.

'Although there is one rather curious coda, which may or may not be linked. It occurred just over a year after Hoth arrived at Wewelsburg, at the end of 1944. By this point the tide of war had turned well and truly against the Nazis. The Americans and British were pushing into Germany from the west, the Russians from the east, and although the Führer was still insisting they could recover the situation, deep down the Nazi high command knew the Third Reich's days were numbered. They started moving gold and looted art treasures out of the path of the advancing Allied armies and either spiriting them abroad or else hiding them in secret locations within Germany, usually inside abandoned mines.'

He took another slurp of his coffee and returned to his swivel stool, cup in one hand, cigarillo in the other.

'In the middle of all this, in December 1944, Dieter Hoth suddenly appears at Dachau concentration camp in southern Germany, bringing with him, according to a deposition given by the deputy camp commandant Heinz Detmers, two trucks, one containing some sort of large wooden crate.'

Layla's eyes widened. 'The—'

'Maybe, maybe not,' said Dupont, anticipating the question. 'It must have been something pretty important for Hoth to have come all that way in person, but whether it was the same crate he brought back from Castelombres . . .' He shrugged. 'All we know is that he commandeered a work party of six prisoners and left again. It's possible he was taking the crate to hide it somewhere nearby, or maybe to have it shipped abroad. Then again, he might have had some wholly different purpose. We simply don't know. The following day he was back at his desk in Berlin. The crate is never heard of again.'

'And he was killed at the end of the war? Is that right?'

Dupont nodded. 'He and a group of other SS officials were trying to get out of Berlin before it fell to the Russians. Got hit by a *katusha* rocket as they tried to sneak across the Weidendammer Bridge. Wasn't much left of him, by all accounts – head blown off, both legs. They only managed to identify him because he was wearing his Knight's Cross and was carrying a number of artefacts from a site he was known to have looted in Egypt.'

He took a final puff on the cigarillo and ground it out in the ashtray.

'No more than he deserved, I imagine. Fascinating man, brilliant scholar, but a deeply flawed human being. Tragic, when you think about it – such a great mind harnessed to such terrible ends.'

He sighed and, clasping his hands behind his neck, gazed up at the skylight overhead. Layla sat back in her chair and rubbed her eyes, suddenly overcome with weariness. Whatever William de Relincourt had found in Jerusalem, whatever he had sent to his sister at Castelombres, whatever had been taken to Montségur for safekeeping, whatever Dieter Hoth had subsequently dug up and carried back to Germany, it now seemed to be lost again. So near and yet so far.

'If you've got time you really should visit the St Sernin,' Dupont was saying. 'Parts of it date all the way back to the time of the First Crusade, you know.'

Layla mumbled a distant 'yes' but wasn't really listening. All she could think of was where the hell she should go from here.

CAIRO

After leaving the Gratzes' apartment block Khalifa wandered around El-Maadi for a while, gazing at the plush houses, stopping to peruse a street vendor's stall where, on a whim, he bought a carved wooden statue of the hawk-god Horus, thinking it would make a nice present for his wife Zenab. Then, still with the best part of four hours to kill, he turned his feet back to the Metro station and took a train towards the centre of town.

Whenever he found himself in Cairo with time to spare he invariably gravitated towards the Museum of Egyptian Antiquities on Midan Tahrir, and it was where he thought he'd go now, hoping to lose himself, if only for a while, in its wondrous collection of ancient artefacts. His old friend and mentor Professor Mohammed al-Habibi, the museum's chief curator, was away lecturing in Europe, which was a shame, because there were few things in the world he enjoyed more than wandering around the museum's galleries in the professor's company. Even without him, though, it was still a magical place, and as his train rattled its way northwards through the dusty suburbs he felt an excited tingle of expectation at the prospect of the distractions ahead.

It was eight stops from El-Maadi to Sadat, the station closest to the museum. Precisely why he got out four stops short of his intended destination he had no idea. One minute he was swaying back and forth in the packed carriage, staring at the higgledy-piggledy tenements juddering past outside the window, the next, without any conscious awareness of having actually left the train, he was on a deserted street outside Mar Girgus Metro station, clutching his wooden Horus statue and gazing across at a neatly dressed stone wall behind which were corralled an asymmetrical jumble of houses, monasteries and churches – Masr al-Qadimah, the Old City of Cairo.

Although he knew most of the capital like the back of his hand, this was one quarter he had never visited before – a curious gap in his geography given his fascination with history, since, as its name implied, it was the most antiquated section of the metropolis, with buildings, or parts of buildings, dating right the way back to the Roman era (there had been no town here in ancient Egyptian times, when the capital had been further south, at Memphis).

For almost a minute Khalifa stood where he was, blinking, disorientated, as if he had woken from a heavy slumber to find himself in a wholly different location from that in which he had originally gone to sleep. Then, propelled by an imperative he could neither explain nor resist, he crossed the street and descended a set of worn stone steps that led him beneath the enclosure's perimeter wall and into the tight honeycomb of buildings within.

It was silent in here, unnaturally so, and very still, the air dense and musty, timeless, as if the physical laws that held sway throughout the rest of the city had in this particular corner of it somehow fallen into abeyance, leaving everything suspended in a sort of hushed, immutable vacuum. He stopped, uncertain what on earth he was doing there, yet at the same time struck by a sudden curious sense that his presence was perhaps after all not entirely random, that rather it had some underlying purpose to it. Then he started forward again, following a narrow paved street that ran away in front of him like a deep scalpel-stroke cut through the quarter's tangled entrails. Crumbling brick and stone buildings rose in walls on either side of him, punctuated here and there with thick wooden doors, like leathery mouths, most of them closed tight but a few slightly ajar, affording fleeting glimpses into secret worlds beyond – a neatly tended courtyard garden; a room piled high with lumber; a shadowy Coptic chapel, its fluted pillars wound round with soft skeins of candlelight.

Every now and then other streets opened up to his left or right, silent, deserted, inviting him to divert to some other part of the quarter. He held his course, following the paved avenue as it dog-legged back and forth until eventually, like a stream issuing into a large pool, it emerged into a dusty open space at the centre of which stood a square, two-storey building in yellow stone, with arched windows and a band of carved cornicing around the edge of its flat roof. A sign outside read BEN EZRA SYNAGOGUE – PROPERTY OF THE JEWISH COMMUNITY OF CAIRO.

He had never seen a synagogue before, let alone been inside one, and for a moment he hesitated, part of him wanting to turn right round and go back the way he had come. The feeling that he was somehow meant to be there, however, that he had, in some inexplicable manner, been *called*, was by now so strong that it overcame whatever doubts he had. Clasping his wooden statuette, he walked up to the building and passed through its arched entrance.

The interior was cool and softly lit, silent, with a grey-white marble floor, a row of brass lamps suspended from the ceiling and, to either side, a procession of pillars supporting a low wooden gallery. The walls were painted with geometric patterns in green, gold, red and white, while at the far end of the room, beyond an octagonal marble pulpit, a set of five steps led up to an exquisitely decorated wooden shrine, its surface inlaid with ivory and mother-of-pearl, its doors inscribed with lines of Hebrew lettering.

Again he hesitated, a curious sense of expectation

swelling in the pit of his stomach; then, slowly, he started forward, walking the length of the synagogue until he was standing at the foot of the steps leading up to the shrine. A pair of curiously shaped brass lamps, almost as tall as he was, stood to either side, each with a long vertical stem from which six branches curved gracefully outwards and upwards, three on one side, three on the other, each crowned, as was the stem, with a flame-shaped light-bulb. Despite the magnificence of the building's other ornaments it was for some reason these lamps that most compelled his attention, that were somehow the focus of his sense of expectation. Stepping up to one of them, he reached out a hand and clasped it around the smooth stem.

'And you shall make a lampstand of pure gold, and there shall be six branches going out of its sides, and its cups, its capitals and its flowers shall be one piece with it.'

Khalifa wheeled round, startled. He had thought he was alone, had been certain he was alone. Now, however, he saw that away to his right, half-hidden in the gloom beneath the gallery, a man was sitting on one of the wooden benches that ran along the synagogue's walls. He was wearing a dark blue robe and skullcap that seemed to blend with the shadows – the reason, probably, why he hadn't noticed him before. As well as a long white beard that came down almost to the level of his chest, he had the most extraordinarily bright blue eyes, which seemed to glow in the darkness like stars against a night sky.

'It's called a menorah,' said the stranger, his voice soft, faintly musical.

'Sorry?'

'The lamp you are holding. It is called a menorah.'

Khalifa realized that his hand was still clasped around the light's spiralling stem. He withdrew it, embarrassed, as if he had been caught touching something he wasn't supposed to.

'I'm sorry,' he repeated. 'I shouldn't have . . .'

The stranger waved a hand, smiling.

'It is good that you are interested. Most people, they walk past without noticing. If you want to touch, please, be my guest.'

He remained where he was for a moment, staring at Khalifa – the detective had never seen such bright blue eyes – then got to his feet and walked over to him, his movements curiously fluid and effortless, almost as if he was floating. Although his hair and beard were white as ice, now that he was in the light Khalifa could see that his skin was smooth and taut, unlined, his body erect, so that it was impossible to guess his age. There was something faintly disconcerting about him. Not threatening, just . . . strange. Unworldly, as if he was not actually there in real time, but rather part of a dream.

'You are the . . . imam here?' asked the detective, his voice sounding strangely thick and unfamiliar, as though he was talking underwater.

'The rabbi?' Again the man smiled, his eyes lingering momentarily on the Horus-statue clasped in Khalifa's left fist. 'No, no. There has been no fulltime rabbi here for over thirty years. I am simply a . . . caretaker. Just as my father was before me, and his father before him, and his before him. We . . . look after things.'

His tone was matter of fact, conversational. There was something about his choice of words, however, the way his gaze held and enveloped Khalifa, flooded right into him, that seemed to hint at some deeper meaning, some level of mutual understanding beyond what was being openly expressed. Although he had always been disdainful of those who believed in the paranormal – 'hunkum-funkum' as Professor al-Habibi called it – the detective could not escape a sudden, unsettling conviction that not only did the man know exactly who he was, but that he was in some indeterminable manner responsible for his presence here today. He shook his head, flummoxed, and moved backwards half a step. There was a long silence.

'It means something, the word "menorah"?' he asked eventually, trying to make conversation, to ease the air of intensity that seemed to have wrapped itself around them.

The stranger stared down at him – he was almost a head taller – then, with a faint, knowing smile, as if he had been expecting the question, turned towards the lamp, his sapphire eyes sparkling in the glare of its flame-shaped bulbs.

'It is the Hebrew for candelabrum,' he said quietly. 'The lamp of God. A symbol of very great power for my people. *The* symbol. The sign of signs.'

Far from easing the atmosphere, Khalifa sensed that his question had only served to thicken it. Despite that, despite himself, he couldn't help but be drawn in by the man's words, as if he was listening to some sort of incantation.

'It's . . . beautiful,' he mumbled, his gaze climbing up the lamp's stem and along the smooth, curving arc of its branches.

'In its own way,' said the man. 'Although like all reproductions it is but a shadow compared to the original – the first lamp, the true lamp, the lamp that the great goldsmith Bezalel made, way back in the mists of time, in the days of Moses and the Exodus from Egypt.' He touched his fingertips to the outermost of the lamp's curving arms. '*That* was very beautiful,' he said, eyes flickering as though a pair of bright-blue butterflies had settled to either side of the bridge of his nose. 'Seven branches, capitals shaped like flowers, cups like almonds, the whole of it beaten from a single block of solid gold – the most beautiful thing that ever was. It stood in the desert tabernacle, and in the First Temple that Solomon built, and in the Second Temple too, until the Romans came and it was lost to the world. Almost two thousand years ago, that was. Whether it shall ever be seen again . . .' He shrugged. 'Who knows. Maybe one day.'

He was silent for a moment, gazing at the lamp, a strange, distant look in his eyes as if he was recalling times long past. Then he dropped his hand and turned back towards Khalifa.

'In Babylon,' he said, 'that is what the prophecy tells us. In Babylon the true Menorah will be found, in the house of Abner. When the time is right.'

Again, for no reason he could explain, the detective was struck by an unsettling sense of subtext to the man's words, a feeling that, although he didn't fully understand what was being said, it was nonetheless in some way significant. He held the man's gaze for a moment, then looked away, eyes roving around the interior of the synagogue until they came to rest on a clock hanging above the entrance.

'Dammit!'

He was certain he had only been there for fifteen minutes, twenty at the outside. Yet according to the clock it was nearly five, which meant he had been in the synagogue for well over three hours. He checked his own watch, which confirmed the time, and with a bewildered shake of his head, said that he had to be going.

'I completely lost track of time.'

The man smiled. 'The menorah can have that effect. It is a very mysterious force.'

The two of them stared at each other – Khalifa experiencing a momentary, giddy sensation of falling, as if he was plummeting from a great height into a clear blue pool – then, with a nod, the detective stepped past the lamp and started back across the synagogue.

'Might I ask your name?' the man called after him when he was almost at the entrance.

Khalifa turned. 'Yusuf,' he replied. There was a beat, then, more out of politeness than genuine interest, he asked, 'Yours?'

The man smiled. 'I am Shomer Ha-Or. Just as my father was before me, and his father before him. I hope I will see you again, Yusuf. In fact, I know I will.'

Before the detective could ask what he meant by this the man waved and, again with that curious floating motion, walked back into the shadows at the side of the synagogue, disappearing from view as if he had stepped right out of this world.

JERUSALEM

The Kfar Shaul Mental Health Centre, a nondescript cluster of yellow and white stone buildings shaded by trees and hemmed in by a low perimeter fence, sits on a steep rise at the north-western fringe of Jerusalem, at the point where the city's outskirts start to stutter and fragment, segueing into the bulging, pine-clad slopes of the Judean Hills. Ben-Roi arrived late in the afternoon and, after parking up outside the main gate, walked across to the security cabin and informed the guard inside that he had an appointment to see one of the patients. A call was put through to another part of the compound, and three minutes later a plump, middle-aged woman in a white doctor's coat arrived, introducing herself as Dr Gilda Nissim and escorting him out of the cabin and up into the hospital grounds.

Coming here was, if not exactly an act of desperation for Ben-Roi, at least the last obvious line of enquiry left open to him at this juncture. Despite working right through the previous night and all that day he had singularly failed to establish any link whatsoever between Piet Jansen and Hannah Schlegel. Sure, he'd unearthed a few extra details about Schlegel's past: the precise dates of her internment in Auschwitz; the fact that she and her brother had been transported to the camp from Recebedou, a transit centre in southern France. But the information was way too fragmentary to formulate anything approaching a clear picture of the victim's life, let alone explain why Piet Jansen, or anyone else for that matter, should have wanted to murder her.

There had been just one faint glimmer of light and that had come from a visit to the Holocaust Memorial at Yad Vashem, where Schlegel had been employed part-time as an archivist. According to one of her former colleagues her work there had involved basic filing, indexing and assistance with simple research queries – general stuff, nothing out of the ordinary. At the same time – and it was this that had given Ben-Roi pause – she had also, apparently, been engaged in some sort of private research of her own. Exactly what this research entailed the former colleague hadn't been able to say. He did think, however, that it was in some way connected with Dachau, since on a number of occasions he had come across Schlegel poring over records and survivor testimonies from that particular concentration camp. Mrs Weinberg, Schlegel's former neighbour, had also mentioned seeing her with files on Dachau, while Majdi, the guy who had burnt out her home, had described how the flat was full of papers and documents 'like some sort of archive'. There was, the detective felt certain, some significance to all of this, some way in which Schlegel's 'private research' tied in with her murder and with Piet Jansen. He had been unable to clarify the connection, however, and in the end had been forced to concede that, while it was clearly an important line of enquiry, it also seemed to be a hopeless one.

Which left him with Isaac Schlegel, the dead woman's twin brother. And from everything Ben-Roi had heard, he was a complete fruitcake.

'I've been told Mr Schlegel's pretty screwed up,' he said as he and Dr Nissim climbed through the hospital grounds, following a steep tarmaced road past scattered stone buildings interspersed with terraces of flowers and pine and cypress trees.

She shot him a faintly disapproving look.

'He's extremely disturbed, if that's what you mean,' she replied. 'He was already suffering from acute post-traumatic stress disorder as a result of his wartime experiences, and then when his sister died . . . well, it pretty much pushed him over the edge. They were very close. I shouldn't expect too much from him. This way.'

They angled left around a fenced enclosure in which two overweight men in pyjamas were playing table-tennis before coming to a modern, single-storey, white-stone block with a sign outside announcing NORTH WING PSYCHOGERIATRIC

CENTRE. She ushered him through the glass entrance and along a deserted, softly lit corridor, a vague smell of cleaning fluid and boiled vegetables in the air, everything silent aside from the hum of the air-conditioning and, from a room somewhere ahead of them, the muffled sound of a man's voice wailing, shouting something about Saul and Zedekiah and the Day of Judgement. Ben-Roi shot the doctor a glance.

'That's not . . . ?'

'Mr Schlegel?' She gave a humourless grunt. 'Don't worry. Isaac has many problems, but fantasizing that he's some Old Testament prophet isn't one of them. Besides, he's barely spoken a single word these last fifteen years.'

They stopped in front of a door near the far end of the corridor. Nissim gave a gentle knock, then opened it, putting her head through into the room beyond.

'Hello, Isaac,' she said, her tone soft, soothing. 'I've brought you a visitor. There's no need to be afraid. He's just going to ask you some questions. Is that OK?'

If there was any answer, Ben-Roi didn't hear it.

'You can have twenty minutes,' she said, withdrawing into the corridor. 'I'll come and fetch you when the time's up. And remember, this isn't a police station, so go easy on him. Yes?'

She held the detective's eye for a moment, then, with a curt nod, set off back the way they had come, her plimsolled feet squeaking on the smooth marble floor. Ben-Roi hesitated, uncertain what to expect, uncomfortable – he had always hated these sort of places, their blank, characterless sterility, the soporific atmosphere, as though the air itself was drugged – then stepped through the door and pushed it to behind him.

He was in a bright, sun-filled room, very sparse, with a bed, a table and, taped all over the walls, covering them from ceiling to floor like badly pasted wallpaper, dozens upon dozens of crayon drawings, very simple, like something you might find in a children's nursery. Schlegel was sitting opposite, in an armchair beside the window, a frail, haggard-looking man wearing pale green pyjamas and carpet slippers. He was staring fixedly at the rockery outside, a book clutched in his bony hands, its green cover creased and dog-eared.

'Mr Schlegel?'

The old man didn't respond. Ben-Roi hovered for a moment, then, picking up a wooden stool, crossed the room and sat down in front of him.

'Mr Schlegel,' he repeated, trying to keep his voice soft, unthreatening. 'My name is Arieh Ben-Roi. I'm with the Jerusalem Police. I wanted to ask you some questions. About your sister, Hannah.'

The man didn't even seem to register his presence, just continued staring out of the window, his eyes sunken and blank.

'I know this is difficult for you,' pressed the detective, 'but I need your help. I'm trying to catch the man who killed your sister, you see. Will you help me, Mr Schlegel? Will you answer some questions? Please?'

Nothing. No acknowledgement, no reaction, no answer, just that blank, catatonic stare, glazed and expressionless, like a fish gazing up from a monger's slab.

'Please, Mr Schlegel?'

Still nothing.

'Can you hear me, Mr Schlegel?'

Silence.

'Mr Schlegel?'

Silence.

'For fuck's sake.'

Ben-Roi brought his hands up and cracked the knuckles behind his head, at a loss. If he'd been interrogating a criminal suspect he would have pushed and harried, threatened, demanded information; but, like the doctor said, this wasn't a police station, and he couldn't employ police-station methods.

Several minutes passed, the two of them just sitting there in silence like a pair of chess players; then, accepting that conversation seemed to be futile, Ben-Roi stood up and wandered across the room, running his eyes back and forth over the crayon drawings taped to the walls. There must have been close on a hundred of the things, and initially he didn't take much notice what each one was specifically depicting, just glanced this way and that, not particularly interested, assuming them to be no more than the random outpourings of a damaged mind. Only gradually did it dawn on him that, childish as they were, clumsy-handed scrawls that any five-year-old could have produced, the pictures were perhaps not quite as disconnected as he had at first thought. On the contrary, taken together they actually seemed to form some sort of meandering, mural-like narrative.

He slowed his eyes, focusing on a drawing beside the door. There was a boat with a funnel, undulating blue lines denoting waves, and, standing on the boat's prow, two stick-like figures with joined hands. The next two pictures depicted almost exactly the same scene, but then came one in which the two figures, still hand in hand, seemed to be suspended in mid-air in front of the prow, as if jumping into the sea. He recalled the story Mrs Weinberg had told about how Schlegel and her brother had been forced to swim ashore after the boat in which they had travelled to Palestine had been turned back at Haifa by the British, and with a sudden electric jolt he realized it was exactly this scene that the picture was showing.

'It's his life,' he whispered to himself.

He wheeled round.

'It's your life, isn't it? It's the story of your life.'

He spun round again and picked up the narrative, following it first forward through time, then back, slowly revolving as his eyes hopped from picture to picture, up and down and around the walls, piecing together the story.

Many of the images corresponded with things he had already found out about Hannah Schlegel's life. On the wall above the bed, for instance, among the last pictures in the collection, were three depicting a small stick figure being beaten on the head by another, much larger figure, against a yellow, desert-like background – presumably a reference to her murder in Egypt. Likewise, a whole block of pictures around the door, more than twenty of them in total, all in black or grey, were unambiguous portrayals of the horrors of Auschwitz – a smoking chimney, loops of barbed wire, six bodies hanging from a gibbet and, horrific in its simplicity, two stick figures strapped onto beds, zig-zags of red-crayoned blood issuing from their groins, slashes of black bursting from their mouths in what Ben-Roi took to be a depiction of agonized wailing.

Other pictures were less easy to interpret. The very first image in the narrative, for instance, was of a large pink house with a bright sun rising behind it and four faces peering out of separate windows, all with wide, curving smiles. Was this a recollection of Schlegel's early life, he wondered? The brother and sister at home with their parents, before their world fell apart? Or did it have some other, wholly different meaning?

Similarly, interspersed at regular intervals throughout the collection, like a recurring motif, a refrain within a song or poem, were a series of images of a seven-branched menorah in bright yellow crayon. An allusion to the artist's faith and heritage, perhaps? Or was it simply a shape that for whatever reason the old man found soothing? It just wasn't clear.

One group of pictures in particular held Ben-Roi's attention, mainly because they seemed to chart some sort of transition between the childish optimism of the first few pictures, which were drawn in bright, cheerful colours, and the darker, more melancholy shades of the rest of the collection. There were four of them in total, all featuring the same arched door or gateway, very tall and narrow, its sides wound round with coiling tentacles of green ivy. The first in the group showed two stick figures, presumably Schlegel and his sister, standing in the centre of the gateway, holding hands and smiling. The next depicted almost exactly the same scene, save that the figures were now hidden behind some sort of bush, watching as another group of figures hacked at the ground in front of the gateway with pickaxes. The sequence was then broken by the first of the menorahs that were to recur throughout the collection before resuming with an image of Schlegel and his sister apparently running away from the gateway, pursued by the figures with pickaxes. The final picture in the sequence showed a malevolent, giant-like creature with fierce red eyes clutching the two smaller figures, one in each hand. Their smiles had gone, replaced by the arcing black parabolas of terror and distress.

The more Ben-Roi looked at them the more something inside him – a gut instinct, a bellyache – told him that of all the drawings in the collection they were somehow the most significant, the moment when everything started to go wrong for Isaac and Hannah Schlegel, and thus, in some unspecified way, the key to Hannah's subsequent life and death. He stared at them for a long while eyes taking in every nuance and crayon stroke; then turning, he went back to his stool and sat down again.

'Mr Schlegel,' he said, 'can you tell me about the pictures over there by the table? The pictures with the arch.'

He asked the question more for the sake of it than in any hope that he'd actually get an answer. To his surprise, Schlegel slowly revolved his eyes away from the window, turning his gaze first on Ben-Roi then down to the book in his lap, then up at Ben-Roi again. The detective scraped his stool forward a couple of inches so that his knees were almost touching those of the old man.

'They're important, aren't they?' he pushed, trying to keep his voice calm and slow, like someone tip-toeing towards an injured bird, doing their utmost not to startle or distress it. 'They're when bad things started to happen to you and your sister. They're the reason your sister was murdered.'

It was a guess, this last statement, a long-shot, but it obviously struck a chord, for the old man blinked and, as if in slow motion, a single crystalline tear welled in his left eye, teetering like a tightrope walker on the cusp of his lower lid before dropping down onto the cheek below.

'What happened at the arch?' asked Ben-Roi softly. 'Who are the people with the pickaxes?'

Again Schlegel dropped his gaze to the book, then lifted it, his pupils moist and grey, a misty, faraway look in his eyes as though he was gazing not at something within the room but rather at a place far removed in both space and time.

'Please, Isaac. What happened at the arch? Who's the giant with the red eyes?'

The old man did not respond, just stared into the distance, humming softly to himself, one hand caressing the book in his lap. Ben-Roi tried to hold him, to keep him in the present, but it was no good; after that brief fragile spark of connection the old man had once again disappeared into his own world, drifting away like a pebble slowly sinking out of sight into the depths of a deep, dark lake. The detective questioned him a while longer, then, acknowledging it was a waste of time, that the moment had passed, he sighed, sat back and looked at his watch. His twenty minutes were almost up. As if on cue there was a distant squeak of approaching feet in the corridor outside.

'Bloody fuck it,' he mumbled.

He drummed his fingers on his knees, defeated, then reached into his pocket and pulled out his hip-flask, bringing with it, accidentally, a crumpled sheet of paper – a copy of the picture of Piet Jansen Khalifa had faxed over to him the previous afternoon. He had brought it in the hope that Schlegel might be able to tell him something about it, but he now accepted that that was wishful thinking. Leaning forward, he dropped it into the bin beside the old man's chair before sitting back again, unscrewing the cap of his flask and taking a long gulp.

So intent was Ben-Roi on getting as much of the liquid down his throat as he could before Dr Nissim arrived that he didn't notice Schlegel slowly craning forward, picking the paper out of the bin and staring down at the grainy black and white image. Only when he had drained off the flask's entire contents and was starting to rescrew the cap did he register what the old man was doing.

'Ring any bells?' he grunted, slipping the flask back into his pocket, talking more to himself than to Schlegel. 'But then I guess you haven't any bells left to ring, have you?'

If he caught the sarcasm, the old man didn't show it. What he did do, suddenly, shockingly, was to hold out the picture towards Ben-Roi and, levering open his mouth, unleash the most ferocious, ear-piercing scream the detective had ever heard.

He might not have got all the answers he'd wanted, but one thing at least was clear: Isaac Schlegel knew exactly who Piet Jansen was. And he was terrified of him.

CAIRO

The moment he left the tangled labyrinth of the Old City, passing beneath its walls and back into the outside world, the encounter in the synagogue seemed to recede in Khalifa's mind like a dawn mist evaporating in the heat of the rising sun. By the time he got into the Metro station he was already struggling to recall the interior details of the synagogue and the precise appearance of the man he had met there; and by the time he was back in El-Maadi, walking swiftly along its tree-lined avenues towards the Gratzes' apartment block, he had genuinely started to wonder whether the whole thing hadn't simply been some sort of elaborate day-dream. Only those piercing, sapphire-blue eyes and the curious seven-branched lamp lingered with any residual clarity, and even those were catapulted away into the furthest recesses of his consciousness when, rounding a corner, he saw a cluster of police cars and ambulances gathered in front of the Gratzes' apartment building. There must have been dozens of other residents in that particular block, but he knew immediately, instinctively, that it was Piet

Jansen's friends who were somehow the focus of all this commotion. He broke into a trot.

'What's going on?' he asked, coming up to the police cordon and flashing his force ID at one of the uniforms on guard there.

'Shooting of some sort,' replied the man. 'Two dead.'

'Oh God! When?'

'A couple of hours ago, maybe more. I'm not sure. I only just got here.'

Cursing himself for not anticipating something like this, Khalifa ducked beneath the tape and, his wooden Horus-statue still clutched incongruously in his hand, hurried into the building and up to the third floor.

The Gratzes' flat was full of people – plain-clothes officers, photographers, forensics guys in white suits and rubber gloves – the air echoing with the hushed, staccato chatter that always seemed to accompany these sort of scenes, part excitement, part nervousness. He asked who was in charge and was pointed towards a door about halfway along the hall from which blared the strobe-like pulse of flashing cameras. He pushed his way down to it, and after a second's hesitation – 'This is my fault,' he was thinking, 'I caused this' – turned inside.

He was in a bedroom, a large double bed in its far corner, the wall behind it spattered with a heavy fan of congealed blood. The bed itself was covered with what Khalifa at first took to be some sort of sheet or throw, but after a moment realized was actually a large red flag with a swastika emblazoned at its centre. This too was drenched in blood and what looked like flecks of meat and skin, its surface depressed and crumpled, as though someone had been lying on it. There was still a faint whiff of cordite in the air – sour, corrosive – and another smell that he couldn't quite place, like burnt almonds. A single black body-bag lay on the floor beside the bed, smooth, shiny, like a giant pupa.

'Who are you?'

A fat bearded man, the detective in charge to judge by his manner, was looking at him from across the room. Khalifa came over and, again flashing his ID, explained why he was there.

'What happened?'

The man grunted, removing a Mars bar from his pocket and tearing away the wrapper.

'Some sort of suicide pact, by the looks of it. Guy blew his brains out' – he nudged the body-bag with the toe of his shoe – 'woman drunk half a bottle of prussic acid. Neighbours heard the gunshot, called us. No third party involved, so far as we can tell.'

He took a hefty bite out of the bar, apparently unperturbed by the blood-spattered walls and sheets.

'Never seen anything like it,' he garbled, mouth full of chocolate. 'The two of them lying there on the bed, hand in hand, place like an abattoir, him in some sort of military uniform, her in a wedding dress, for God's sake. Weird.'

He crammed the rest of the bar in his mouth, and, turning away, gesticulated at a photographer, indicating that he wanted more pictures of the blood-stained flag. Khalifa pulled out his cigarettes, received a disapproving look from one of the forensics guys who were crawling around the floor, and pocketed them again.

'It's cursed,' he thought to himself. 'This whole case. Everything I do, everywhere I turn, nothing but dead ends and death and horror. I hate it. Hate the whole thing.'

'Where's the woman's body?' he asked after a moment.

'Hmm?' The detective turned back to him. 'Oh, they've taken her up to As-Salam International. Pumped her stomach, or whatever the hell it is they do in these situations.'

It was a second before the significance of these words struck Khalifa.

'I thought . . .' A sharp jolt speared up his spine. 'I was told they were both dead.'

'What? No, no, the old woman survived, although only just. Another twenty minutes and she'd have ended up like her husband.' He gave the body-bag another nudge with his foot. 'Lucky. Or unlucky, depending on which way you look at it. Wearing a fucking wedding dress, she was. Weirdest thing I ever—'

He didn't get the chance to finish the sentence, because Khalifa had already swung round and hurried from the room.

LANGUEDOC, FRANCE

Layla pulled the hire-car, a bruise-coloured Renault Clio, over into the lay-by and, leaving its engine running, leant forward and looked up through the windscreen at the ramparts of Montségur Castle high above. She remained like this for a moment, taking in the blank grey walls, the rearing, skull-shaped dome of rock on which the castle perched like a ship riding the crest of a tidal wave; then, sitting back again and throwing a glance at the map on the passenger seat beside her, she swung back out onto the road and continued on her way.

It took her another twenty minutes to reach Castelombres. She had bought a couple of guide books back in Toulouse, which was fortunate because without them she would have struggled to find Castelombres village – no more than a scattered string of houses and farm buildings that didn't even show up on the map – and would have had no hope whatsoever of locating its ruined castle, which was three kilometres outside the hamlet and well off the beaten trail. Even with the books the ruins were still by no means easy to find, involving a bumpy ride along a steep track that hairpinned its way high into the hills, and then a walk across two boggy fields and up through a thick coppice of hawthorn and giant boxwood, following a sharply climbing path that must once have been reasonably well kept but was now so overgrown as to be virtually indistinguishable from the surrounding vegetation. So remote was the castle's location, so completely hidden away, that she was actually on the point of retracing her steps, thinking she must have taken a wrong turning somewhere, when the coppice suddenly dropped away to either side of her and she found herself standing on abroad, grassy terrace cut deep into the hillside with spectacular views over the surrounding hills and down into the river valley below. A broken wooden sign to her left announced ÂTEAU DE CASTELOMBRES.

Whoever had razed the castle had done a thorough job, because there was almost nothing of it left, just a few scattered blocks of stone, a couple of collapsed walls – the tallest of them no more than knee height – and a single pock-marked pillar lying on its side in a clump of grass like a rotten log. Only one thing hinted at what must once have been a substantial building, and that was a magnificent arch at the far end of the terrace, very tall, very narrow, its stonework clasped by winding tendrils of black ivy, its apex rising to a sharp point that seemed to scratch at the sky like a pen-nib scrawling across a sheet of grey parchment.

Layla walked over to it, assuming it must be some sort of door or gateway, only realizing as she got up close that it was actually the remains of a window, beautifully constructed, with a delicate tracery of loops and spirals incised into its face, and here and there, just visible beneath the heavy jacket of ivy, tiny flowers carved out of the stone. There was something unbearably melancholy about it, standing there all on its own, a solitary eye gazing out over the hills, and after staring at it for a moment she turned away again, pulled her jacket around her against the chill wind that had suddenly blown up from the south, and wandered off around the remainder of the ruins.

Whatever the Germans had been doing here they seemed to have left no trace of their presence, and after twenty minutes she grew bored of the place and started back towards the path that had led up through the coppice. As she did so there was a swoosh and rustle of branches from below, accompanied by the slow pad of feet, the sounds growing steadily louder until eventually an elderly, red-faced woman emerged through the foliage onto the terrace. She was wearing Wellington boots and a heavy brown coat, and had a large wicker-work basket three-quarters full of mushrooms clutched in her hand.

'*Bonjour*,' she said when she saw Layla, her thick Languedoc accent elongating and twisting the word so it came out more as 'bangjooor'.

Layla reciprocated the greeting, adding, for the

sake of politeness, a couple of complimentary remarks about the size of the woman's mushroom harvest.

'Oh, it's not a bad haul,' she said, smiling. 'It's not really the season, but you can still find them if you know where to look. You're Spanish?'

'Palestinian.'

The woman raised her eyebrows, a mildly surprised look on her face.

'You are on holiday?'

'I'm a journalist.'

'Ah.'

She crossed to the nearest stone block, set the basket down on top of it and began working her way through its contents, sifting the mushrooms, examining them.

'I suppose you're here to do an article on the Germans,' she said after a brief silence.

Layla shrugged, driving her hands into the pockets of her jacket.

'You remember them?' she asked.

The woman shook her head. 'Not really. I was only five at the time. I remember them all staying in a house at the end of the village, and my father telling us that we weren't to talk to them, weren't to go anywhere near the castle, but apart from that . . .'

She shrugged, held up a large yellow mushroom and sniffed its crumpled cap, giving a satisfied nod and holding it out towards Layla.

'Girolle,' she explained.

Layla leant forward and breathed in the mush-room's scent, her nostrils filling with a rich, earthy odour.

'Beautiful,' she said. And then, just for the hell of it, 'What do you think they found up here?'

The woman grunted, dropping the mushroom back into the basket.

'I don't think they found anything. It makes a good story, but the truth is people have been digging holes up here for centuries looking for buried treasure. If there was anything to find it would have been discovered long before the Germans arrived. Or at least that's what I think. There are others who would disagree.'

From somewhere far off there was a distant rumble of thunder.

'You didn't hear about the crate they took away with them?' asked Layla.

The woman waved a hand dismissively. 'Oh I heard about it. But I never saw it. And even if they did take a crate away, that doesn't mean there was anything in it. It could have been full of rocks for all we know. Or empty. No, I think the whole thing's an old wives' tale. Complete rubbish.'

She held up another mushroom, examined it, then, with a tut, threw it aside into the undergrowth.

'If you want to do a story about Castelombres, you should write about the children.'

Layla frowned. 'The children?'

'The Jewish children. The twins. I sometimes

think it's the reason everyone in the village spends so much time going on about treasure and crates and what-not. To try and forget what happened to them. Divert attention.'

Again Layla frowned, not understanding. 'What twins?'

The woman paused for a moment, then, laying aside the basket, sat herself down on the stone. There was another faint rumble of thunder, the trees whispering and hissing as their branches shuddered in the wind.

'Their parents sent them down here from Paris,' she said, gazing out over the wooded hills. 'After the Germans invaded. Paid a local farmer to take them in. Thought they'd be safer here, in the south, out of the occupied zone, being Jews and all that. Like I said, I was only five at the time, but I remember them very clearly, especially the girl. We used to play together, although she was older. Ten or eleven. Hannah, that was her name. And her brother Isaac.' She sighed and shook her head. 'A terrible thing, it was. A terrible thing.' She looked up at Layla. 'The Germans found them, you see. Up here, at the castle. Playing. They didn't mean any harm, they were only children, but it didn't make any difference. No-one was supposed to go near the ruins. The man in charge – horrible man, wicked – he brought them down to the village and stood them in the street: I'll never forget it, as long as I live, the two of them standing there side by side, terrified, so small, and the man screaming that if anyone disobeyed his orders again he would do to them what he was going to do to these Jew vermin. That's what he called them. Jew vermin. And then he beat them, right there in front of us, with his own hands. Little children. Beat them unconscious. And no-one in the village, not a single person, did anything to help them. Not a single voice was raised, not even when they threw them in a truck and drove them away.'

She shook her head sadly.

'Isaac and Hannah, that's what they were called. I sometimes wonder what happened to them. Died in the gas chambers, I expect. It's them you should be writing about, the real secret of Castelombres, not all this rubbish about buried treasure. But then, being a Palestinian, maybe that sort of thing doesn't interest you.'

She swung her eyes out over the hills again, then, with a sigh, got to her feet, picked up her basket and, with a glance up at the sky, which had turned a forbidding slate grey, said that she ought to be on her way.

'It was nice meeting you,' she said. 'I hope you enjoy the rest of your stay.'

She smiled, raised a hand in farewell and, turning, set off across the terrace, disappearing into a clump of fir trees on the slope above, her basket of mushrooms swinging in her hand. There was a third groan of thunder, nearer this time, and it started to rain, heavy drops spilling down from above as though the sky was weeping.

CAIRO

'Oh, my poor Anton. My poor darling Anton. Why couldn't you let us die together? Like we were supposed to. Why are you torturing me like this?'

Inga Gratz's hand crept its way across the bedsheet and clasped Khalifa's wrist, her grip cold, clammy, surprisingly firm. The detective winced, repelled by her touch, as if some large venomous spider had curled its legs around his arm. He made no move to pull his hand away, however. He sensed that the entire investigation had somehow narrowed itself to this meeting, and if allowing her to hold on to him encouraged the old woman to be more forthcoming, tell him what he needed to know, then he was prepared to put up with it, even if it did make him feel faintly nauseous.

It was past eleven at night. For five hours he had paced up and down the corridor outside Inga Gratz's hospital room, chain smoking, going over and over the scene back at the apartment block, waiting for her to regain consciousness. When she finally did the doctors had been reluctant to allow him into the room, saying that she was still too weak to speak, that he should wait until the following morning. With uncharacteristic bluntness, he had insisted on being let in to see her, had threatened to take the matter to the highest level, and in the end they had relented, allowing him fifteen minutes with her, on the proviso that a nurse was in attendance.

'Vermin,' she was mumbling, fingers clenching and unclenching around his wrist, her voice dull and vague, presumably a result of the drugs she had been administered. 'You must see that. Vermin. Every one of them. Bloodsuckers. We were doing the world a favour. You should be thanking us.'

She stared up at Khalifa, face deathly pale in the soft glow of her bedside lamp, a pair of plastic tubes descending from her nostrils like thin worms slithering out of the burrow of her skull. Then she turned away and began to weep. There was another intravenous tube plugged into her arm, and with her spare hand she started to claw at it, prompting the nurse, who was hovering beside the door, to come forward and lift the hand away, gently tucking it back beneath the sheets. There was a long silence, the only sounds the halting, uneven flutter of the old woman's breathing and, from outside the window, the rhythmic fut-fut of a water sprinkler in the hospital grounds.

'Dieter,' she said eventually, her face still turned away from Khalifa, her voice barely audible, just a low whisper.

'I'm sorry?'

'That was Piet's real name. Dieter. Dieter Hoth.'

It took a moment for the detective to make the connection. When he did, he dropped his head and sighed, a faint smile pulling at the corner of his mouth, although there was no humour in the expression, just a sort of weary self-reproach. For God's sake! *Hoth* – that's what Hannah Schlegel had whispered to Gemal fifteen years ago, as she lay dying on the temple floor at Karnak. Hoth, not Thoth. All this time he'd been chasing the wrong name. How many other things had he got wrong, he wondered; how many other blind alleys had he run down?

'He was . . . a Nazi?' he asked.

She gave a weak nod. 'We all were. Were proud to be. To serve our country, our Führer. No-one understands now, but he was a good man. A great man. He would have made the world a better place.'

She turned her head back to him, that helpless, imploring look still in her eyes, although he now saw something else there as well, deeper down, something he hadn't noticed before: a cruelty, a hardness, as if her feeble body was no more than an outer casing within which was contained a wholly separate, altogether more malevolent being. He clenched his teeth, more repelled than ever by the clammy clasp of her hand.

'And Hannah Schlegel?' he asked. 'He killed her? Piet Jansen – Dieter Hoth.'

She gave another weak nod, no more than a

fractional inclination of the head. 'She knew who he was, you see. Came to find him. Vermin. They never stop looking.'

She puckered her mouth and rolled her eyes up towards the ceiling, little shudders rippling through her body as though she was receiving tiny electric shocks. There was another extended pause, the ticking of a clock on the wall sounding unnaturally harsh in the enveloping silence; then slowly, falteringly, she began to talk again, spilling out bit by bit, fragment by fragment, the story of her own life – Elsa Fauch was her real name, wife of Wolfgang Fauch, both of them former guards at Ravensbruck concentration camp – and that of their friend Dieter Hoth: who he was, where he came from, his work with the SS. Khalifa allowed her to tell it at her own speed, in her own way, occasionally interjecting the odd question or comment when it seemed as if she was losing the thread of her narrative, but otherwise listening in silence, all the different elements of the case, all the things that had so confused him these past two weeks, gradually resolving themselves in his mind into a clear, coherent whole.

'We all got out together,' she mumbled, staring up at the ceiling, eyes half closed. 'At the end of the war. April 1945. Me, Wolfgang, Dieter, another man named Julius Schechtmann. Julius went to South America, we went to Egypt. Dieter had contacts, you see, people who could help us.'

In Khalifa's mind another fragment of the jigsaw slotted into place.

'Farouk al-Hakim,' he said.

She nodded. 'Dieter knew his family. He was just a young man then, a clerk. Clever, though, ambitious. We'd brought money with us, bullion, whatever we could lay our hands on. We paid Farouk, he helped us disappear. Later, others came out; Farouk organized things for them as well. We used to pay him an annual retainer; he made sure no questions were asked. It was a good business for him.'

The meeting with Chief Mahfouz reared in Khalifa's mind. *I told al-Hakim about Jansen, but he said he was off limits. Said dragging him into it would only make matters worse. Piss the Jews off even more.* No wonder, he thought. Investigating Jansen would have brought the whole Nazi thing out into the open; exposed Egypt as a haven for murderers and war criminals; and deprived al-Hakim of what was clearly a lucrative sideline. Far better to leave Jansen alone and have someone else convicted for Schlegel's murder. Even if that someone else was entirely innocent.

'We had a good life,' the old woman was saying. 'Started a business, made new friends. There was quite a little group of us at one time. All gone now. Me, Wolfgang, Dieter – we were the last. Just me now.'

She sighed, and shifted her frail body slightly

beneath the sheets, her hand still clasped around Khalifa's arm.

'We had to be on our guard, of course. Especially after what happened to Julius. They hanged him, you know, the dirty animals. In general, though, we just got on with things, minded our own business. Thought we'd live out the rest of our days in peace and quiet.'

'Until Hannah Schlegel arrived,' said Khalifa quietly.

She grimaced at the name, her thin, pale lips pulling back off her teeth so that the detective had the momentary, unnerving impression that he was looking not at a human being but rather at some fierce snarling animal, a dog or a wolf.

'God knows how she found Dieter,' she muttered. 'He'd been so careful, done everything he could to cover his tracks. Faked his own death before we left Berlin, left some of his personal possessions on a dead body so that it looked like he'd been killed during the Russian bombardment. But then, that's the Jews for you, isn't it? Vampires. Always hunting, always looking for blood. Always, always, always.'

She was becoming agitated, turning this way and that in the bed, her breath coming in short, sharp gasps. Stepping forward again, the nurse laid a hand on her putty-grey forehead, trying to settle her. Khalifa took the opportunity to free his arm, no longer able to bear the touch of her skin, as though the contact would somehow infect him, leak poison into his bloodstream. He shifted his chair backwards, out of her reach, crossed his legs and waited for her to recover herself.

'He never told us the full story,' she resumed eventually, the nurse having calmed her down sufficiently. 'Something about France, an excavation . . . it was never entirely clear. All he said was that he'd sent her to the camps back in 1943, and then, forty-five years later, she suddenly calls out of the blue from a hotel in Luxor and demands to meet him.' She shook her head. 'At first he thought she wanted to blackmail him. Typical greedy Jew. But then, when they met up, the stupid bitch started shouting about justice and revenge, said she had a knife, was going to kill him. He was in his seventies at the time, but he was still strong, fit. Gave her a good beating, then finished her off with his walking cane. Or at least he thought he'd finished her off. We later heard from Farouk that she was still alive when he left her.' She grunted. 'Like cockroaches, they are. So hard to kill cleanly.'

Khalifa shook his head, barely able to believe what he was hearing, that such things could be said so coldly, so matter-of-factly, and by a little old lady too. 'I can't comprehend this,' he thought to himself. 'Everything about this case, everywhere it takes me – it's like I'm in an alien world. Fumbling my way around a pitch-black room where all my instincts and senses, everything I know and value, count for nothing. I just don't understand it. I don't understand any of it.'

'Hannah Schlegel's flat?' he managed to ask. 'It was Jansen who asked you to burn it?'

The old woman nodded. 'He called us, explained what had happened, warned she might have left notes, details of how she'd tracked him down. He'd taken her wallet, and that had her address in it. Wolfgang contacted some business associates in Jerusalem. They took care of everything.'

She closed her eyes, her ugly, withered fingers tweaking the edge of her bedspread.

'Poor Dieter. He was never the same after that. None of us were, but he took it worst of all. Terrified, he was. Convinced more of them were going to come, that they were going to take him back to Israel, put him on trial. He stopped seeing anyone, had locks put on all his windows, slept with a pistol beside his bed. And then, when Farouk died last year, he was even more frightened because with him gone there was no-one to protect us any more. It gave him cancer. I genuinely believe that. The worry, the constantly looking over his shoulder. He might have killed her at Karnak, but the old Jew bitch got him in the end. Got all of us in the end. They always do. Scum, they are. Vermin.'

She was reaching the end of what little strength she had left, and the nurse, who was still standing beside the bed, coughed and tapped her watch, indicating it was time to bring the interview to an end. Khalifa nodded, got to his feet and turned towards the door, only to turn back again.

'Before he died, it seems Mr Jansen was trying to contact the Palestinian terrorist al-Mulatham. Said he was in possession of some weapon he could use against the Jews. Do you know anything about this?'

To his surprise, the old woman chuckled, a nasty, viscous sound, like bubbling mud.

'Dieter's riddle,' she said, a little strength seeming to return to her voice. 'That's what we used to call it, me and Wolfgang. He was always going on about it, especially after he'd had a drink or two. How he'd found something that would help destroy the Jews. "I can still hurt them, Inga." That's what he used to say, "I can still hurt the bastards."'

She chuckled again and, lowering her hands, sank back into the pillow as though into a drift of snow, eyes fluttering open and shut.

'Did he tell you what it was, this thing?' asked Khalifa.

'No,' she replied, 'he never said.'

'Where?'

She gave a frail shrug. 'I think he mentioned a safe deposit box once. But then another time he said he'd left the details with an old friend, so who knows? He could be very secretive, Dieter.'

She sighed, staring up at the ceiling.

'A new generation, that's what he was hoping for. Someone he could pass it on to, who would help Germany become strong again. But the years went by and no-one took up the mantle, and then he found out he had cancer so he decided to hand it over to the Palestinians instead. "Give it to the people who need it," that's what he said. We sent a letter for him.'

'A letter?' Khalifa's eyes narrowed.

'To a Palestinian woman. In Jerusalem. Dieter thought she could help him. Al-Madani, that was her name. Layla al-Madani. No idea if she ever got back to him. I hope she did. We have to keep fighting. Show the Jews they can't have it all their own way. Vermin, they are. A plague. We were doing the world a favour. You must see that. Surely you must see that? We're your friends after all. We've always been your friends.'

Her eyes were gradually slumping shut, her voice growing weaker and more distant. Khalifa stared down at her, trying, and failing, to dredge up even a shred of pity, then walked to the door. As he reached it she somehow managed to heave herself up in the bed and called after him.

'I'll be all right, won't I? You won't tell the Israelis? You'll look after me? They're your enemies too, after all.'

He paused for a fraction of a second, then, without answering, stepped out into the corridor and closed the door behind him.

KALANDIA REFUGEE CAMP, BETWEEN JERUSALEM AND RAMALLAH

Yunis Abu Jish rose before first light, after just a couple of hours' uneasy sleep, and, having washed himself at the tap outside their makeshift cinderblock house, returned to his bedroom and began his dawn prayers, trying to keep his voice low so as not to wake the four younger brothers with whom he shared the room.

It was three days since he had received the call from al-Mulatham, during which time those closest to him had noticed a dramatic change in the young man. His face, already gaunt and sunken, seemed to have receded even further into the bony catacomb of his skull, as though sucked inwards from behind, while his heavy-lidded eyes had expanded and darkened, assuming an unfathomable, opalescent blackness, like peat-stained water. His manner, too, had altered beyond recognition. Formerly talkative and outgoing, he had withdrawn into himself, shunning the company of others, spending all his time alone, lost in prayer and solitary contemplation.

'What is wrong, Yunis?' his mother had pleaded with him on more than one occasion, alarmed at this sudden change in her son's appearance and manner. 'Are you ill? Should we call the doctor?'

He would have liked to explain, share a little of the burden. He had been expressly forbidden from discussing the matter, however, and had therefore simply assured his mother, and anyone else who asked, that he was fine, that he just had things on his mind, that they weren't to worry. That in time they would understand.

He finished his prayers, reciting the final *rek'ah* and the *shahada,* and stood for a moment gazing down at the youngest of his brothers, six-year-old Mohammed, fast asleep on his mattress on the floor, his breathing soft and helpless, a skinny arm splayed at his side as though he was reaching out towards something. Not for the first time these last couple of days he was speared by a sharp pang of horror at what he was being asked to do, at the fact that it would remove him forever from those he so loved and cherished. It lasted only a few seconds, giving way almost immediately to a conviction that it was *because* he loved and cherished these people so much that he had taken the course on which he was now embarked.

He bent forward and stroked the boy's hair,

whispering to him, telling him how much he cared, how he was sorry for any pain he might cause him, then straightened and, taking his Koran from the shelf beside his bed, went outside into the cool grey dawn to continue his solitary preparation.

JERUSALEM

It was past eleven a.m. when Layla eventually got back to her flat in East Jerusalem, an oppressively hot morning – unnaturally so for the time of year – with a low, cloudy sky and heavy, soporific atmosphere that wrapped itself around the city like a sticky gauze. She threw her mobile and overnight bag onto the sofa, listened to the messages on her answerphone – the usual slew of insults, death threats and queries about late copy – then took off her clothes and went through into the bathroom for a shower.

What do I do now, she thought to herself, water cascading across her head and face? Where do I go from here?

Whatever Hoth had found at Castelombres – and despite the scepticism of the old Frenchwoman with her basket of mushrooms, Layla felt certain Hoth *had* found something – it seemed to have disappeared again during the mayhem at the end of the Second World War. If any records had been left as to its whereabouts they hadn't been made public; and although there were still, according to Jean-Michel Dupont, thousands of pages of Nazi files and documents that had yet to be properly examined – tens of thousands of them – it could take months, years even, to dig out the information for which she was looking. If, indeed, the information existed at all, which was by no means certain.

What else? There was the Palestinian kid, the one who had delivered the mysterious letter to her in the first place. She could, she supposed, make more enquiries as to his identity, try to track him down, pick up the trail back to the letter's originator. Or else return to the Church of the Holy Sepulchre and talk to Father Sergius again, see if there was something she'd failed to pick up on during their first meeting, some tiny clue as to what it was William de Relincourt had dug up beneath the church's flagstoned floor.

Again, both options seemed futile. Father Sergius had been adamant there was no extant evidence of what de Relincourt had found, while trying to find the Palestinian kid would be like looking for a needle in a haystack. In a field of haystacks. A country full of the damn things. Whichever way she looked at it she seemed to have come to a dead end.

With a despondent sigh she wound the hot tap off and turned the cold one up to full jet, allowing the icy water to lash down across her head and torso. As she did so, something flashed momentarily across the margin of her mind, a half-thought, a memory, something that was in some way relevant to the problem in hand. It was gone almost straight away, like a shooting star that fades as soon as it appears, leaving her with the frustrating sense that she had somehow missed something important, some minute chink of light. She turned off the tap and closed her eyes, trying to follow her train of thought backwards: Palestinian kid, Father Sergius, church, flagstoned floor. The floor, that's what it was. The church's flagstoned floor. Why was that important? What was she trying to recall?

'*Yalla*,' she mumbled to herself. 'Come on. What am I thinking of? What is it? What?'

For a moment her mind remained a blank, then, very faint, she heard a sound. A clack. A strange echoing clack, as of something tapping on stone. Clack, clack, clack. What the hell was it? A hammer? A chisel? She couldn't pin it down. She opened her eyes, closed them again, forced herself to think of something else, then veered her mind back, as if trying to sneak up on the sound from behind, catch it unawares before it could escape. It worked. Of course! It was the sound of a walking stick, the one belonging to the old Jewish man Father Sergius had pointed out. *Every day he comes in, regular as clockwork. Convinced de Relincourt found the Ten Commandments, or the Ark of the Covenant, or King David's sword – I forget which. Some ancient Jewish thing.*

At the time she had simply dismissed the man as yet another of the deluded crackpots that seemed to hover around the de Relincourt story like moths round a candle flame. The likelihood was still that this was what he was. After what she had discovered about the Secret of Castelombres, however, and particularly the way it seemed somehow to be bound up with Judaism and Jewish history, a part of her couldn't help wondering whether perhaps the old man might know something that could help her. It was clutching at straws. Given that every other line of enquiry seemed to have petered out, however, straws were just about all she had left. At the very least it was worth following up, even if it did turn out to be nothing, which it almost certainly would.

Stepping from the shower, she grabbed a towel, dried herself and went through into the bedroom, pulling on pants, bra and a shirt before she was interrupted by a sudden loud hammering on the front door.

'Hang on,' she called.

Whoever was outside either didn't hear or else wasn't prepared to wait because the hammering continued, growing heavier and more insistent with each thud, the whole flat seeming to reverberate with the sound of the blows. Annoyed, and suddenly suspicious – the hammering was way too forceful for Fathi the caretaker, or anyone else she knew for that matter – she heaved on a pair of jeans and trainers, grabbed a hand towel with which to dry her still-damp hair and, going to the door, came up on tiptoe and peered through the spyhole drilled into its wooden face.

A huge, broad-shouldered man was standing outside in the gloom of the landing, Israeli, with a craggy, big-nosed face and a Jericho pistol wedged threateningly into the belt of his jeans. For some reason she had an immediate bad feeling about him, a premonition of danger.

'Yes?'

The man froze, one hand raised in the act of knocking, then leant right forward so that his eye swamped the spyhole.

'Jerusalem Police,' he growled. 'Open up.'

Ben-Roi had driven over as soon as he'd got off the phone to Khalifa, covering the distance from the police station to the Nablus Road in fewer than three minutes, in the process shooting two red lights and narrowly avoiding a collision with an elderly Haredi man who had stepped off the pavement without bothering to look for oncoming traffic.

Hoth, Gratz, Schlegel, the fugitive Nazi community – it had been an extraordinary story, fascinating. Disappointing too, in a way, that in the end the Egyptian seemed to have solved the thing alone; that his own input, while filling in a few details, had not in the end proved fundamental to the case's resolution.

Neither fascination nor disappointment were what was firing him now, however, not after what

565

Khalifa had told him right at the end of the conversation, almost as a parting shot: about Layla al-Madani and the letter Hoth had sent her requesting her help in contacting al-Mulatham. Now he was running on adrenalin, the pure, ferocious adrenalin of the fighter who after months of build-up is finally on the point of stepping into the ring to confront a long-awaited opponent.

He'd always known he'd confront her eventually. Or at least he had for the last year, ever since reading that article she'd written. He could offer no clear reason for his obsession with her, no rational explanation as to why she should give him such a bellyache. Sure, if you looked closely, really closely – and he'd been doing little else for the last twelve months – you *could* pick up hints, vague glitches in the fabric of her life and work, like the interviews she'd done (almost every bomber, for God's sake, almost every fucking bomber!). Nothing overt, however. Nothing conclusive. Nothing, certainly, to warrant the degree of suspicion and hatred she had aroused in him. All he knew was that with that article she'd somehow fixed herself in his mind as the one tangible, human link with the man who had butchered his beloved Galia, and as such he had never doubted for one moment that at some point their paths must eventually cross. That it had happened as a result of this case was unexpected. Or, then again, maybe it wasn't. Maybe it was the reason he had been drawn to the investigation in the first place – a subconscious awareness that it would some-how be the trigger, the thing that finally brought them together. He couldn't say, nor did he really care. All that mattered was that after a year of watching and waiting, of researching, following, fixating and bellyaching, now, finally, the moment had come to meet her face to face, to look into her eyes and see what he could see there.

'Come on,' he repeated, giving the door another heavy crash with his fist. 'Open up.'

'Badge first,' came her voice from the other side.

Muttering, Ben-Roi reached into his pocket and produced his police ID, thrusting it at the spyhole. There was a long pause, a lot longer than was necessary for her to take in the card's details, as though she was deliberately making him wait, emphasizing the fact that she wasn't intimidated by him, before eventually there was the click of a catch and the door swung open.

'Always a pleasure to welcome the Israel National Police,' Layla said, rubbing at her hair with a towel.

She was shorter than he'd expected, slighter, something almost adolescent about the small, tight swell of her breasts, her narrow hips, details you didn't get in the photographs from sitting opposite her apartment night after night looking up at her windows, watching her go in and out. There was a toughness there too, though, a hardness, especially in her emerald-green eyes; the way she stared at him without blinking, unfazed by his size, by the fact that he could have picked her up and swung her round with a single hand.

'Well?' she asked.

He was so absorbed in the minutiae of her appearance that the question didn't immediately register and she had to repeat it.

'Well?'

He shook his head. 'I've got some questions,' he replied, coming forward a step, as if to enter the flat.

She reached a hand across to the door-jamb, blocking his way.

'Not without a warrant you don't. You got a warrant?'

He didn't.

'I can go and get one,' he snarled. 'And when I come back I won't be nearly as friendly.'

She gave a derisive snort. 'I'm fucking trembling. Now, either you show me a warrant, or you ask whatever you've got to ask from right there. And you're going to have to do it quickly. I'm late for an appointment.'

Her manner was calm, assured, contemptuous, and for a brief instant he found himself thinking of his first meeting with Galia, when he had arrested her at the anti-settlement demonstration and been treated with a similar haughty disdain. He grimaced, as if shocked by the analogy, and came forward another half-step so that his body filled the entire door-frame.

'You were sent a letter recently. A letter asking for your help in contacting al-Mulatham.'

She said nothing.

'You know what I'm talking about?'

There was a fractional pause, as though she was weighing up how to answer; then, throwing her towel over her shoulder, she acknowledged that, yes, she had indeed received such a letter.

'And?'

Another pause, another weighing up of the options.

'And nothing. I read it, I tore it up, I binned it. Like I do with all my junk mail.'

Ben-Roi scanned her features, seeking out those small tell-tale clues that she was lying – a tightening of the mouth, a dilation of the pupils, a tremor of sweat. Nothing. Either she was telling the truth or she was better, way better, than anyone he'd ever encountered before.

'I don't believe you,' he said, testing her.

Layla laughed, her eyes never leaving his. 'I don't give a fuck what you believe. I got the letter, I read it, I threw it away. And before you ask, no, it's not still in my bin. Athough I'm sure if you go down to the municipal dump it should only take you a couple of weeks to find it.'

He clenched his fists, trying to resist the urge to lash out at her.

'What did it say, this letter?'

'It seems you already know,' she replied.

'What did it say *exactly*?'

She crossed her arms and sighed, like a teacher dealing with a backward pupil.

'*Exactly* I couldn't tell you, given that I didn't bother memorizing it. "I'm trying to get in touch with al-Mulatham, I think you can help me, I'll pay you whatever you want" – something along those lines. Bullshit, basically. I only skimmed it. If you want the full version you'll have to get in touch with your mates in Shin Bet. I presume it was them who sent it in the first place.'

Again, even though his eyes were boring into her, his ears straining, he failed to pick up the least hint that he was being lied to, the faintest shimmer of dissemblance in either her features or her voice. Which was unsettling, because every instinct in his body told him that he *was* being lied to, she *was* dissembling, so that either his instincts were all wrong, his radar irredeemably scrambled, or else she was possessed of a level of self-control that was almost superhuman in its impermeability. Only in her eyes, way down, was there a rumour of something other than what she was openly expressing, a sort of faint cloudiness, like silt disturbed deep underwater. Whether it reflected mendacity or some wholly different aspect of her psyche, however, he couldn't say. Maybe it was just a trick of the light.

'Did it mention a weapon, this letter?' he pushed. 'Something that could be used to damage the state of Israel?'

Not that she remembered, she replied. If it had, maybe she would have taken more notice of it.

'Does the name Dieter Hoth mean anything to you?'

Nope.

'Piet Jansen?'

Same response.

'I have heard of David Beckham, if that's any help.'

And so it went on, Ben-Roi firing questions at her, Layla batting them back with sneering, scornful disdain, until eventually he ran out of things to ask and fell silent.

'Is that it?' she asked, placing her hands on her hips and staring up at him. 'Because, much as I'm enjoying myself, I have got things to do.'

Behind her, the phone started ringing.

'Is that it?' she repeated.

He glared down at her, fists clenched, aware that whatever he had been expecting to get from the meeting, whatever revelation he had been hoping to prise from her, it hadn't happened. She'd won. This round, at least.

'For the moment,' he replied.

'Well, you know where I am. Like I said, it's always a pleasure to welcome the Israel National Police.'

She nodded at him, indicating that he should step backwards out of the doorway, and started to close the door. When it was half-shut she leant round and looked up at him through the gap, the phone still ringing behind her.

'Just for the record, I have absolutely no fucking idea who al-Mulatham is, where he is, or how to find him. I'm sure it won't stop you coming round and hassling me, but I thought I'd mention it anyway, just on the off chance it finally sinks in.'

In the study, the answerphone clicked on, her tinny, recorded voice echoing through the flat: 'I can't come to the phone right now. Leave a message and I'll get back to you.'

'And on a personal note,' she added, 'I've no idea what that aftershave you're wearing is, but it stinks. You should try another brand.'

Ben-Roi's eyes narrowed. Behind her, there was a loud beep and another voice drifted out into the hall-way, deep, gravelly.

'Layla! Magnus Topping. Just thought I'd give a quick call to see if you got back all right, tell you . . . um . . . well, what a pleasure it was to meet you. Also, something I forgot to mention while you were here, an interesting fact for that article you're doing. Apparently that German archaeologist, the one who was digging at Castelombres, Dieter Hoth – he had webbed feet. Thought you might like that, little bit of colour. Anyway, give me a call if you like. All the best.'

Another beep, then silence.

Layla stared up at Ben-Roi, Ben-Roi stared down at Layla. There was a fractional pause, then, with a growl, the Israeli flung out a hand to push his way into the flat. She was too quick for him. The door slammed shut in his face; there was a click of locks and the muffled patter of running feet.

'You lying bitch!' he cried.

He snatched his Jericho from his belt and, taking a step back, charged. The door held firm. He tried again, giving himself a longer run-up. There was a cracking sound, but still the door held.

'You lying Arab bitch!'

He tried a third time, snorting like a wounded bull. This time the door gave. He stumbled forward, regained his footing, looked wildly around. Her bag and mobile phone were lying on the sofa. No sign of her. He ran into the study, the bedroom – empty. In the bathroom he saw the concrete stairs leading upwards, the open door at the top. He took them three at a time, barrelling out onto the roof terrace, the sky vast and white above him, the city spreading out all around. Nothing. He turned to double back on himself, thinking perhaps he'd somehow missed her down in the flat; then, hearing a car horn from the street below, he veered away to the edge of the roof, grasped the rusty iron rail running along its parapet and stared down at the Nablus Road beneath. He spotted her immediately, weaving through the traffic, too far away for him to stand any chance of catching up with her.

'You fucking bitch!' he yelled impotently. 'You fucking lying bitch!'

If she heard him she gave no sign of the fact, just hurried onwards, crossing Sultan Suleiman

Street and disappearing into the throng of people jostling around the entrance to the Damascus Gate. He gazed after her, cursing, then, heaving his mobile phone from his pocket, jabbed a number into the keypad and held the unit to his ear.

'Duty desk? Ben-Roi. I need an immediate alert on Layla al-Madani. That's Layla al-Madani. Yes, the journalist. Top priority. She's somewhere in the Old City. I repeat – top priority.'

LUXOR

'**S**even-thirty, eight at the latest. As soon as I get everything finished here. I love you too. More than anything in the world.'
Khalifa touched his lips to the phone and popped a flutter of kisses down the line, eyes half closed, as if it was Zenab's mouth he could feel rather than the cold impersonal plastic of the receiver. He lingered thus for a moment, then, with a final 'I love you', hung up and sat back in his chair, staring at the wooden Horus statue he had bought in Cairo, eyes red and puffy with exhaustion.

It was almost over, thank God. He'd already filled Ben-Roi in on everything. Now all he had to do was type up a report for Chief Hassani, set a few bureaucratic wheels in motion – getting the artefacts in Jansen's basement transferred to Luxor museum; filing an application for a posthumous pardon for Mohammed Gemal – and then he could wash his hands of the whole damned case and return to some semblance of normal life.

A holiday, that's what he wanted. Time alone with his family, away from thoughts of death and murder and hatred. Maybe they could all travel down to Aswan, visit his friend Shaaban, who worked there at the Old Cataract Hotel; or else go over to Hurghada for a few days, something they'd been talking of doing for years now but had never got around to. Yes, that's what he'd do: take the family to the seaside. They couldn't afford it, but what the hell. He'd scrape the cash together somehow. He smiled at the thought of Ali and Batah's faces as he told them about the planned trip; then, with a sigh, he lit a Cleopatra and leant forward over his desk.

Because before he could start thinking about holidays, close the case down once and for all and consign it to the gloomy netherworld of the station archives, there remained one final strand of the investigation to be resolved: the identity of the mysterious 'weapon' Piet Jansen had been trying to hand over to the Palestinian terrorist al-Mulatham.

It was a peripheral strand, and one to which, in all honesty, he could simply have turned a blind eye. He had, after all, done what he'd set out to do: he'd proved it was Jansen who murdered Hannah Schlegel, why he'd done it, and why al-Hakim had been so intent on protecting him. The weapon thing was a side issue, of importance to the Israelis perhaps, but with no obvious relevance to his own investigative remit. Despite that, and despite the uneasy throb in the pit of his stomach warning him that to continue delving could only bring more trouble and confusion and heartache, there remained a part of him – the 'pernickety, pig-headed, tight-arsed old biddy' part, as Chief Hassani styled it – that simply couldn't let the matter drop.

He dragged on his cigarette and picked up the sheaf of notes he'd scribbled after his interview with Inga Gratz. In a safe deposit box. That's what the old woman had said when he'd asked her about the weapon. *I think he mentioned a safe deposit box once. But then another time he said he'd left all the details with an old friend, so who knows?*

As far as deposit boxes were concerned, he already knew from legwork he'd put in earlier in the investigation that none of the major Egyptian banks had any safe deposit account under the name Piet Jansen. A quick ring-round after he had finished speaking with Ben-Roi had been enough to confirm they had no Dieter Hoth on their records either. There were other enquiries he could make, with smaller banks, private banks, international banks, and that was before he even started looking into banks abroad. But even if he called every single bank in Egypt, in the entire world, he sensed it wasn't going to do him any good. Everything he knew about Piet Jansen, everything he had found out these last two weeks, told him that he had been too cautious an operator, too canny and sly not to make sure he covered his tracks thoroughly, especially when it involved something as evidently important as this. If he did have a box somewhere it would be well hidden. Too well hidden, certainly, for him to track it down without a long and complicated search.

Which left the old woman's other comment, about leaving the details with an old friend. What friend?

All the way back from Cairo he had dwelt on this, turning the old woman's words over and over in his mind, visiting and revisiting every aspect of the case, trying to work out who Jansen might have been referring to, who he would have trusted sufficiently with that sort of information. The Gratzes clearly didn't know. Al-Hakim was a possibility, but he was dead, as were all the other members of the fugitive circle to which Jansen had belonged. Maybe it was someone he hadn't yet come across in his investigations. Someone from Jansen's days with the SS, perhaps, or his work as an archaeologist. Or maybe from even further back. Someone buried deep beneath the sands of time. Someone it would be even harder to track down than it would Jansen's safe deposit box. It seemed hopeless, absolutely hopeless.

He went through his notes once, twice, three times, then, with an exhausted sigh, pushed himself away from the desk, stood up and wandered over to the office window.

'Let it go,' he muttered to himself. 'For once in your bloody life stop being a pernickety, tight-arsed old biddy and just let it go.'

He finished his cigarette and, leaning his elbows

on the windowsill, gazed down at the scene below: a tourist haggling with a shop-owner; two old men sitting on the pavement edge playing *siga* in the dust; a young boy petting a scrawny Alsatian dog, the animal kicking its legs and waggling its tail, evidently enjoying the attention. This last tableau momentarily reminded him of something, some scene he'd witnessed before, although he couldn't recall what. After thinking about it for a while he shrugged it away, pulled his head back into the room and, returning to the desk, started to tidy up his notes.

Under one pile of paper he found a plastic evidence bag containing Jansen's pistol, under another the dead man's house keys and wallet. He lifted the latter, stared at it, put it down, continued with his tidying. After a couple of moments, however, he stopped and again picked up the wallet, a frown suddenly crumpling his forehead. He turned it over in his hand, glanced at the window, then, opening it, sunk his fingers into one of the inside pockets and slipped out the crumpled black and white photograph of Jansen as a young boy, squatting beside his Alsatian dog. As he did so, the words of Carla Shaw echoed at the back of his mind, from the night they'd interviewed her at the Menna-Ra.

Arminius. A childhood pet. Piet was always going on about him. Used to say he was the only real friend he'd ever had. The only person he'd ever really trusted. Talked about him like he was a human.

579

Safe deposit box, old friend.

'Dammit,' he whispered, a curious, confused expression spreading across his face, part excitement, part reluctance.

He hesitated. Then, leaning forward, he picked up the phone.

It took just two calls. Bank of Alexandria, Luxor branch, safe deposit account in the name Mr Arminius.

'Bloody dammit.'

JERUSALEM

'*Yalla, yalla*. Come on, come on. Where the fuck are you?'

Layla glanced down at her watch, aware that every minute would be bringing the Israelis closer, then stepped back into the fog of shadows gathered around the margins of the Church of the Holy Sepulchre, the pounding of her heart seeming to vibrate through the entire building as if someone was banging at its foundations with a heavy iron sledgehammer.

She had no idea how the detective had found out about the letter she'd been sent, the request to help contact al-Mulatham, Dieter Hoth, any of it. At this juncture it wasn't relevant. What she did know – had known from the moment she'd first clapped eyes on him – was that he was dangerous, more dangerous than any Israeli she'd ever encountered, except possibly Har-Zion. That's why she'd lied to him. That's why she'd done a runner (in the process clocking the battered white BMW parked outside, the same BMW she had seen so many times before keeping tabs on her apartment late at night). And that's why she'd come here to find the old Jewish man, take this one, last, desperate opportunity to shed some light on what it was William de Relincourt had found beneath the floor of the church. It was a long-shot. The old man was almost certainly mad, or senile. Probably both. It was the only shot she had left, however. She had to find out what she was dealing with here. Give herself at least one small bargaining chip . . .

'Come on,' she hissed, banging her fist against the dark, sweaty pillar beside her. 'Please! Where the fuck are you?'

Another twenty minutes passed – slow, agonizing minutes, a water-torture of nervous expectation – and she had all but given up, convinced the old man wasn't going to come, when finally, from the far side of the church, she at last heard the sound for which she had been so desperately waiting – the distant, rhythmic clack of a walking stick.

The old man hobbled into the Rotunda and, as he had done when she'd seen him before, made his way across to the covered cube of the Aedicule. He removed a *yarmulke* and a small Torah from his jacket and began to pray, his body creaking back and forth, the soft, staccato rasp of his voice floating upwards into the dome above like the sound of leaves whispering in a breeze. She remained where she was until he had finished, watching, waiting; then, as he returned the skullcap and prayer-book to his pocket, she stepped from the shadows and, casting a nervous glance towards the church entrance, went across to him and gently touched him on the elbow.

'Excuse me.'

He turned, unsteadily, like a clockwork toy whose mechanism has all but wound itself down.

'I was wondering if I could talk to you about a man called William de Relincourt. One of the priests here told me you might know something about him.'

Up close, he seemed even more geriatric than he had done from a distance, his body twisted and bent, his face so deeply lined it looked as if the least jolt would cause it to shatter and disintegrate. An unpleasant, faintly sickly smell hung about him, unwashed clothes mixed with something deeper, more elemental – an odour of poverty, failure, decay. Only his eyes seemed to tell a different story, for although they were jaundiced and bloodshot, they were also alert, suggesting that if his body was all but clapped-out, his mind certainly wasn't.

'It won't take long,' she added, flicking another anxious look towards the entrance. 'Just a couple of minutes. Five at the most.'

He said nothing, just stared up at her, his mouth hanging half-open like a gash sliced in a piece of worn leather. There was an uneasy silence, the only sound the whoosh and flutter of wings as high above them a pigeon flew round and round inside the Rotunda's white and gold dome; then, with a grunt and a shake of the head, the old man turned and began to shuffle away. She assumed he wasn't going to talk to her and her heart sank. To her surprise, and relief, rather than heading towards the church entrance he hobbled over to the bench on which four days earlier she'd sat with Father Sergius and lowered himself down onto it, indicating that she should join him. She threw yet another look towards the doorway, then went over and sat down.

'You're that Arab woman, aren't you?' he said once she was settled, leaning forward on his stick, his voice broken and faltering, as if heard over a bad telephone connection. 'The journalist.'

She admitted that, yes, she was a journalist.

He nodded. 'I know your work.' A beat, then, 'Sewage. Lies, bigotry, anti-semitism. It disgusts me. You disgust me.'

He swivelled his head towards her, then away again, dropping his eyes to the floor.

'Although to be fair, not as much as I disgust myself. My *onesh olam*, my eternal punishment: to live in a world where the only people who wish to listen to what I have to say are the ones to whom I least wish to say it.'

He smiled faintly, the expression somehow conveying the exact opposite of amusement, and, hunching forward, prodded with his stick at a line of ants processing along the edge of a crack between paving stones.

'Sixty years I've been trying to tell them. Written letters, made appointments. But they won't listen. Why should they, after what I did? Maybe if I had something I could show them . . . but I don't. It's just my word. And they won't listen to that. Not after what I did. So maybe I should be grateful for your interest. Although I doubt even you'll believe it. Not without the proof. And there is no proof. No photographs, no tracings, nothing. It's hopeless. Hoth kept the lot.'

She had been on the point of interrupting this rambling monologue, desperate to bring the conversation back to William de Relincourt, terrified that at any moment a squad of Israeli police were going to come bursting into the church to arrest her. This last comment stopped her in her tracks. She swivelled on the seat, her fears receding as her attention homed in, laser-like, on what the old man had just said.

'You knew Dieter Hoth?'

'Hmm?' The old man was still poking at the line of ants. 'Oh, yes. I worked for him. In Egypt. Alexandria. I was his epigrapher.'

One minute Hoth and his team are excavating in Egypt, at a site just outside Alexandria; the next he's rushing back to Berlin for some top-secret meeting with Himmler. Layla's stomach tightened as she recalled the words of Jean-Michel Dupont. He *does* know something, she thought. My God, he does know something. Except . . .

'I thought Hoth was an anti-semite. Why would he—'

'Employ someone like me?' Again the old man's mouth twisted into that bitter, grimacing smile, his fingers clasping and unclasping around the handle of his stick. 'Because he didn't know I was a Jew, of course. None of them did – Jankuhn, von Sievers, Reinerth. None of them. Never suspected. Why should they when I was the biggest Jew-hater of the lot?'

He sighed, a thin, despairing sound that blew from deep within him like air escaping from a punctured balloon, and, sat back against the pillar behind the bench, gazing up into the dome above.

'Fooled them all, I did. Every one of them. So clever. Went to the rallies, sang the songs, joined in the book burnings. The perfect little Nazi. And you know for what?' He winced. 'Because I loved history. Wanted to be an archaeologist. Can you believe that? Cut out my own heart because I wanted to dig holes in the ground. And as a Jew I couldn't get the necessary qualifications, not the way things were in those days. So I stopped being a Jew and became one of them instead. Changed my name, got false papers, joined the Nazi Party. Betrayed everything. Because I wanted to dig holes in the ground. Is it any wonder they won't listen to me? A Jew who turned his back on his own people. A *moser*. Is it any wonder?'

He looked across at her, eyes moistening, then away again. She could see that he was upset, knew that she ought to tread carefully. There wasn't time, however; there just wasn't time.

'What happened in Alexandria?' she said, trying, and failing, to hide the urgency in her voice. 'What did you mean when you said you don't have any photographs or tracings?'

He didn't reply, just stared up at a heavy beam of sunlight slanting downwards from the skylight in the apex of the dome high above, like a thick golden rope.

Layla paused a second, then, more from instinct than any clear notion that it might help the situation, added: 'I know what it's like. To lie. The loneliness. I understand. We're the same. Please help me. Please.'

From somewhere behind them there was a shout and the sound of hurrying feet, which caused her to start and turn. It was only a couple of Syrian Jacobite priests hurrying to prayer, their black robes billowing around them like wings, and she turned back almost immediately. The old man was staring directly at her. He held her gaze, his eyes seeming to push right into hers, his lower lip quivering slightly. There was another unbearable pause.

'November the fourth.' It was barely audible.

'Sorry?'

'That's when we found it. November the fourth. The inscription.'

His voice was so low that Layla had to lean right forward to catch what he was saying.

587

'Sixteen years to the day after Carter found Tutankhamun. Ironic, when you think about it: the two greatest finds in the history of archaeology made on exactly the same date. Although ours was the more important of the two. By far the more important. Almost made all the lies and betrayal worth it, just to be there.'

There was another commotion behind them – voices, the slap of feet on stone – and a group of tourists processed into the Rotunda, all dressed in identical yellow T-shirts. She barely registered them.

'Yes,' the old man mumbled, 'almost made the lies worth it. Almost. Not quite.'

He grunted and, raising a trembling hand, wiped at the corner of his mouth where a bulb of spittle had gathered in the angle between upper and lower lip.

'It was on a sandstone block. Oblong, about so big.' He raised his other hand to indicate the dimensions. 'Early Byzantine, about AD 336, reign of Constantine I. Tripartite text in Greek, Latin and Coptic. An imperial proclamation, to the citizens of Alexandria. It had been reused in the foundations of a later Islamic building which was why it had survived in such good condition.'

Layla could feel her heart thudding, lungs twisting, like the times as a child when she'd tried to see how long she could hold her breath. Tell me, she willed him. Come on, tell me.

'It announced the completion and dedication of the Church of the Holy Sepulchre,' he continued.

'This church. Described Constantine's conversion to Christianity, his devotion to the one true God, his rejection of all other faiths. Standard stuff. Nothing extraordinary. Except for the last part. It was the last part that was important.'

The tourists in yellow T-shirts had gathered themselves in front of the Aedicule where their guide was explaining the history of the church. One of their number, a young man with greasy, shoulder-length hair, was taking digital pictures with his mobile phone, the apparatus making a pinging sound each time he took a shot.

'At first we couldn't believe it,' the old man whispered, his head shaking from side to side. 'The *lukhnos megas*, the *candelabrum iudaeorum*. We thought we must have got it wrong, that it was referring to something else. It was just too incredible. Everyone thought it had stayed in Rome, you see. That Gaiseric and the Vandals had carried it away in 455 when they sacked the city.'

Layla bit her lip, confused. 'I don't understand. Carried what? What do you mean?'

He didn't seem to hear her.

'Two hundred and fifty years it had been there, in the Templum Pacis, the Temple of Peace. Ever since Titus brought it back from the ruins of Jerusalem. Titus took it from Jerusalem, and two and a half centuries later Constantine returned it. That's what the inscription said. That's why it was so extraordinary. It recorded how it was brought back from Rome and buried in a secret chamber beneath the floor of Constantine's new church, an offering to the one true god, a symbol of Christ's eternal light.'

He held out a shaking hand.

'Right there, it was. Right there in front of us. For eight hundred years. Hidden. Forgotten. Until William de Relincourt found it. I've tried to tell them. Told them when I turned myself in at the end of the war, told them during the inter-rogations, have been telling them ever since. But they won't believe me, not after what I did, not without the evidence. And there is no evidence. Hoth kept everything. Right there in front of us it was.'

Layla could barely control her desperation. He was talking in riddles!

'What was?' she hissed. 'What was right there in front of us? What did Constantine bury under-neath the church?'

He opened his eyes and looked towards her. There was a ping as the lank-haired tourist snapped another shot with his mobile phone.

'I told you. The *candelabrum iudaeorum*. The *lukhnos megas*. The *lukhnos iudieown*.'

'But I don't understand!' Her voice seemed to fill the Rotunda, causing several of the tourists to look round at her. 'What is that? I don't understand!'

The old man seemed startled by her vehemence. There was a pause, then, slowly, he explained.

'Oh God,' she whispered when he had finished. 'Oh sweet God Almighty.'

She was still for a moment, too shocked to move. Then, eyes fixing on the man with the mobile phone, she got to her feet and moved quickly towards him.

LUXOR

The safe deposit box was ready for Khalifa when he arrived at the Bank of Alexandria, sitting on a table in a room in the bank's basement. He was shown in by the assistant manager, a middle-aged woman with rouged lips and a silk headscarf, who took him through some paperwork, unlocked the box's lid and left again, telling him that if he needed anything she'd be outside.

He waited until the door had clicked shut, fingers drumming on the table, the windowless room seeming to press in all around him. Then, with a deep breath, as if he was about to leap into a pool of icy water, he leant forward, opened the box and looked in.

A purse, that was the first thing he saw. A cheap plastic lady's purse sitting on top of a thick cardboard folder. He lifted out the purse and opened it, knowing instinctively, before he'd even examined its contents, that it was Hannah Schlegel's. There were some Egyptian pound notes and Israeli shekels; a laminated, green ID card; and, tucked away in a side-pocket, two small, passport-sized photographs, black and white, their borders frayed with age. He slipped them out and laid them side by side on the table. One was of a family group, a man, a woman and two small children – Hannah and Isaac Schlegel with their parents, he guessed – the four of them standing in the doorway of a large house, smiling and waving at the camera. The other showed the same children, older now, sitting on the back of a wooden cart, laughing, their legs dangling from the tailboard, their arms round each other's shoulders.

Khalifa had only ever related to Schlegel as an old woman, a battered, blood-covered corpse lying splayed on the floor at Karnak. Somehow these images of her as a child – so beautiful, so innocent, wholly unaware of the horrors awaiting her – upset him more than anything else he had yet encountered in this investigation. He stared at them for a long moment, struck by how like his own daughter she looked with her long black hair and scrawny legs; then, with a sigh, he slid the pictures and the purse to one side and turned his attention to the cardboard folder.

Whatever he had been expecting – and over the last few days all manner of madcap ideas had been going through his head as to what Hoth's mysterious weapon might actually be – the folder's contents proved an anti-climax. Interesting, certainly, intriguing even. Not, however, the sort of dramatic revelation for which he'd been bracing himself. Photographs and documents, that's what he found when he undid the ribbon with which the folder was bound and opened it up – a bulging, miscellaneous wodge of material that on closer inspection turned out to be less concerned with weapons and terrorism than archaeology and history. There were tracings, maps, photocopies of pages from books he'd never heard of (*Historia Rerum in Partibus Transmarinis Gestarum; Massaoth Schel Rabbi Benjamin*), photographs of everything from excavation sites and the interiors of churches to a large triumphal arch with a frieze in raised relief depicting a crowd of toga-clad men carrying a giant seven-branched lamp (the Arch of Titus in Rome, according to a note on the back of the picture). Nothing, however, not a single thing that was in any way suggestive of any sort of armament, something that could be used, as the Gratz woman had said, to 'help destroy the Jews'.

He worked his way through the collection, bemused, skimming some things, spending longer on others: a tracing of an ancient inscription in Greek, Latin and Coptic; a blown-up photograph of a handwritten Latin sentence ('Credo id Castelombrium unde venerit relatum esse et ibi sepultum esse ne quis invenire posset'); a protective plastic sleeve containing an aged sheet of yellowed parchment with six lines of script made up of an apparently random selection of letters and signed at the bottom with the initials GR.

What it all meant he had absolutely no idea, although the more he looked at the material the more he got the feeling its constituent elements were perhaps not quite as random as he had at first assumed, that on the contrary they were in fact linked in some way, part of a single research project. What that project was he couldn't even begin to guess; nor, despite his fascination with all things historical, did he intend to start trying. What was important was that the further he got through the folder's contents the more convinced he became that Hoth's boast about possessing some sort of secret weapon, some terrible force that could be unleashed against the Jews, was in fact precisely that – a boast. The hollow, last-ditch bragging of a lonely, frightened, paranoid old man desperate to persuade those around him, and perhaps himself as well, that he was still someone to be reckoned with.

'You were bluffing, weren't you?' Khalifa murmured as he approached the bottom of the pile. 'There never was any weapon. You were bluffing, you murdering old fool.'

He smiled, relieved that all his fears seemed to have come to nothing, and, lighting a cigarette, picked up the final item in the collection – a brown manila envelope on the front of which was scrawled the word 'Castelombres'. Inside were a series of photos, black and white, the first few general shots of the grass-covered remains of some long-ruined building – a tall arched window was just about the only identifiable architectural feature – the remainder charting the digging of an excavation trench right in the centre of those remains, the work carried out by a group of overall-clad men using pickaxes and mechanical diggers.

He started to flick through them, quickly at first, as if he was shuffling a deck of cards, then more slowly as, despite himself, he began to be drawn into the progress of the dig. In each shot the trench was shown a little wider and a little deeper. At about three metres some sort of box started to reveal itself – gold to judge by the metallic glint of its surface – with nearby what looked like part of a curving branch or arm. A similar arm emerged beside it, then another, and then more of the box, which seemed to have a second, smaller box sitting on top of it, only it now appeared that they weren't boxes at all but rather the tiers of some elaborate pedestal from the centre of which a thick stem projected off in the direction of the curving arms. Inch by inch the curious object was coaxed from the ground, each stage of its painstaking emergence faithfully captured on film until eventually, in the very last of the photographs, it had been completely prised from the earth's grip, lifted from the trench and set on a tarpaulin in front of the stone window, the latter's arching outline seeming to surround and enclose it like the frame of a picture.

Khalifa stared at this last image for almost a minute, his cigarette burning away unnoticed between his fingers, his eyes narrowed. Then, leaning forward, he rifled through the papers he'd already looked at, pulling out the photograph of the triumphal arch with its frieze depicting a seven-branched lamp. He held the two photographs together, comparing their subjects, the lamp in the frieze and the lamp from the excavation. They were identical.

The curious meeting in the Cairo synagogue filtered back into his mind. *It is called a menorah . . . The lamp of God. A symbol of very great power for my people. The symbol. The sign of signs.*

He gazed at the two pictures, eyes flicking back and forth between them; then, slowly, he stood up and crossed to the door. The assistant manager was waiting for him outside.

'Is everything OK?' she asked.

'Fine,' he said. 'Fine. I was just wondering . . . is it possible to send a fax to Jerusalem from here?'

JERUSALEM

Layla leant her head back against the wall of the holding cell and gazed up at the ceiling, bringing her knees up to her chest and wrapping her arms around her ankles. She needed to pee, and flicked a glance down at the seatless aluminium lavatory bowl plumbed into the corner of the room. She resisted the temptation to use it. She knew she was being watched, and didn't want to give them the satisfaction of seeing her exposed in that way. She'd have to go eventually, but for the moment she could hold out. She sighed and pressed her thighs together, trying to ignore the insidious blind rectangle of one-way glass set into the steel door opposite.

They'd picked her up the moment she'd stepped out of the Church of the Holy Sepulchre, four hours ago now, a whole squad of them, including the detective who'd questioned her at her flat – gun to head, spreadeagled on the ground, handcuffed. She hadn't bothered to resist, knowing it would only make things worse for her. Back at the station she'd been left to stew for a bit, then interrogated – two hours, just her and the detective.

This time she'd played along, told him everything: William de Relincourt, Castelombres, Dieter Hoth, the Menorah – everything she'd uncovered these last few days. Not because she'd been scared – although she certainly hadn't felt comfortable, the way he'd sat there staring at her, eyes seeming to bore right the way through her skull and deep into the brain behind, clawing at her deepest thoughts. No, she'd co-operated because there was simply no longer any reason to go on lying. He already seemed to know about the Lamp; all the other details he could piece together by going through her notebooks, contacting the people she'd spoken to. Evasion would have been a waste of time. Her one, slim hope now, her only hope, was that he would realize the significance of the Menorah's discovery, the appalling impact it might have if it fell into the wrong hands, and would accept the offer she had made him right at the end of the interview.

'You need me,' she had said, holding his gaze, wrestling with it. 'I don't give a shit about the Menorah. But I do give a shit about what would happen if someone like al-Mulatham got hold of it. You have to let me help you. Because if al-Mulatham gets there first . . .'

She doubted she'd convinced him, but it was the best she could have done in the circumstances. The wheels had been set in motion. Whether she'd play any further part in the whole thing, however – that, as her father used to say, was something only God and deep blue sea could tell. All she could do now was sit and wait.

She squeezed her thighs tighter together and, leaning her forehead on her knees, closed her eyes, the screen of her mind filling with a disturbing and unsolicited image of a gold menorah from whose lamps, for some reason, sprang not rays of light but viscous gloops of sticky red blood.

On the opposite side of the door Ben-Roi gazed at her through the observation window, a hazy blizzard of thoughts swirling round inside his head. The Menorah, al-Mulatham, the newspaper article, Galia, aftershave – all jostled and collided within the crucible of his skull, appearing, disappearing, merging, disintegrating. Only one thought remained fixed and clear, standing firm at the centre of the maelstrom like a lone redwood in the eye of a hurricane, and it was this: the Menorah can help me.

How, he wasn't sure. Not yet. He had no clear plan in mind. All he knew was that this was somehow the opportunity for which he had so long been waiting; the means, if not of recovering his beloved Galia, at least of avenging her. The Lamp would be his weapon. And, also, his bait. Yes, that's how he would use it. As bait. A lure to draw out his lover's murderer. To bring him to al-Mulatham. Or to bring al-Mulatham to him.

He took a swig from his hip-flask and, turning away down the corridor, went back to his office, closing and locking the door behind him, crossing to his desk and pulling out the images the Egyptian had faxed over to him earlier.

'Dear God,' he mumbled, just as he had done when he'd first seen them. 'Dear God Almighty.'

He stared at the pictures, hands trembling with the magnitude of the whole thing; then, putting them away again, he picked up the phone and dialled. Five rings, then a voice echoed at the other line.

'Shalom,' he said, keeping his voice low, fingers tweaking at the miniature silver pendant around his neck. 'Can you talk? It's just that something's come up and I think you ought to know about it.'

JERUSALEM

At the heart of the Old City's Jewish Quarter, at the southern end of the Cardo, on public display inside a thick plexiglass cabinet, there stands a gold menorah – six sinuous arms curving outwards from a central stem, three to one side and three to the other, the whole rising, tree-like, from a tiered hexagonal base. The accompanying inscription explains that it is a precise replica of the original Menorah, the true Menorah, the Menorah that the great goldsmith Bezalel made, the first such replica to have been cast since the fall of the Temple two thousand years earlier.

As the day faded and evening slowly drew in around him, Baruch Har-Zion stood in front of this reproduction and, throwing back his head, laughed – a deep, long, vibrant laugh of joy and gladness, such as he had thought he would never let out again. Only last night he had been praying for a sign, some assurance that what he was doing was right, that all the blood and horror were necessary. And now it had come. Clear, sharp, unambiguous. The true Menorah. After all these centuries. And to him it had been revealed. To him, of all people. He couldn't stop laughing. Behind him, Avi his bodyguard came forward a step.

'What do we do?'

Har-Zion raised a gloved hand and touched a finger to the plexiglass screen, his laughter gradually subsiding.

'Nothing,' he replied. 'Not yet. We wait, we watch. They mustn't know that we know. Not yet.'

Avi shook his head. 'I can't believe it. I still can't believe it.'

'That's what they all say, Avi – all those who are called by God. Abraham, Moses, Elijah, Jonah – all of them doubted at first. But it is His voice. He *has* revealed this great thing. And He would not have revealed it had He not intended it to come to us. It is the sign. It is the time. Blessed are we, for in our day we shall see the Temple rise again.'

He rolled his shoulders, the skin tight beneath his shirt, and came up even closer to the screen. Who would have thought it? Who would have imagined? Yet somehow he had always known. He was the chosen one. The saviour of his people. And now all he had to do was wait and watch. Let Ben-Roi track it down. And then, when it was found . . .

'Thank you, Lord,' he whispered. 'I will not fail you. *Ani mavtiach*. I promise. I will not fail you.'

LUXOR

'That's fifteen pounds you owe me. You want another one?'

In response, Khalifa drained off the remainder of his tea and, getting to his feet, slammed the leaves of the backgammon box together, signalling that no, he didn't want another game.

'Coward,' said Ginger with a grin, puffing on his *shisha* pipe.

'Always have been, always will be,' replied Khalifa, opening his wallet and counting out his losses. 'Although right now it's not losing to you I'm afraid of but being late for Zenab. She's cooking, and I promised her I'd be home by eight.'

His friend exhaled a cloud of apple-scented tobacco smoke and, extending his thumb, drilled it into the table-top, the gesture indicating that he thought Khalifa was 'under the thumb'. There were loud chuckles from the other tea-drinkers sitting around them. The detective's devotion to his wife was a source of common knowledge, and general amusement.

'Time for Inspector Hen-Pecked to get off home!' one of them called.

'Pussy-whipped Khalifa!' yelled another.

'By day the police rottweiler,' chanted a third, 'by night . . .'

'Zenab's mouse!' everyone chorused, the refrain accompanied by a barrage of squeaking sounds.

Khalifa laughed. It had never bothered him, this sort of good-natured teasing, and this evening he actually rather enjoyed it, signalling as it did a return to normal life after all the upheavals of the last two weeks. He handed Ginger his winnings – he couldn't remember the last time he'd played backgammon with his friend and actually come out on top – and, telling everyone to go drown themselves in the Nile, picked up the two plastic bags he had leant against the leg of his chair and left the café, the squeaking sounds pursuing him for twenty metres down the street before dissolving into the more generalized babble of the evening souk.

He felt good. Great. Better than he had done for ages, as if a weight had been lifted from his shoulders. He'd handed in his final report to Chief Hassani, sent all the stuff about the Menorah over to the Israelis, who could do with it whatever the hell they wanted, and now he was heading home to Zenab and the kids with a bag full of brochures for the Red Sea resort of Hurghada. There was just one discordant note: when he'd asked Hassani to pass a copy of the case report on to Chief Mahfouz, his boss had informed him that the old man had passed away late the previous night. The news had saddened Khalifa, although not overly so. As Mahfouz himself had said, at least he'd died knowing he'd done the right thing in the end.

He stopped to say hello to Mandour the T-shirt seller, a plump, partially sighted man whose habit of chasing punters up and down the road extolling the virtues of his wares had almost become a tourist attraction in itself, then continued on his way, swinging his bags beside him, thinking of beaches, and waves, and, best of all, Zenab in a swim suit – God, what an image! Before he knew it he was standing outside the drab grey apartment block in which he lived, one of a row of identical blocks lined up on the northern fringe of town like a line of pock-marked stone monoliths.

He paused a moment to finish the cigarette he was smoking, then climbed the bare concrete staircase to the fourth floor and, as quietly as he could, inserted his key into the door of his flat. He didn't open it immediately. Instead, leaving the key in the lock, he kicked off his shoes, squatted down and, rooting inside one of the two plastic carriers, produced first a pair of cheap rubber flippers, which he pulled onto his socked feet, then a diving mask and snorkel, slipping the former over his face and the latter into his mouth. Then he let himself into the apartment, barely able to control his amusement at the joke he was about to play.

'Tsonly ee,' he called, his words distorted by the rubber mouthpiece wedged between his lips. 'I hoh!'

No response. He slapped forward into the hallway, wondering where everyone was.

'I hoh!' he repeated, louder. 'The deef sea diver has surhaced!'

Still no response. He put his head into the kitchen – empty – then edged his way around the fountain in the middle of the floor and padded, duck-like, towards the living room at the far end of the flat, struck by the sudden thought that maybe *they* were playing a joke on *him*. What a laugh! The door to the living room was ajar and, pausing for a moment to clear his mask, which had become fogged, he pushed it open and stepped through, making what he hoped looked like an underwater swimming motion with his arms.

'Wow, it's a-azing down here with all the hish and the—'

His words trailed off. Zenab, Ali and Batah were all sitting on the sofa, their faces pale, frightened. Opposite, one sitting, one standing, were two men in grey suits, the standing one's jacket hanging open slightly to reveal the unmistakable outline of a Heckler and Koch machine pistol. Jihaz Amn al Daoula. No doubt about it. State security service.

'Daddy!' Ali leapt from the sofa and ran to his side, eyes bright with tears. 'They want to take you away, Daddy! They say someone wants to talk to you. They're going to send you to prison.'

Khalifa removed the mask and snorkel, flicking a glance down at Zenab, who looked terrified.

'What's all this about?' he asked, trying to keep his voice calm, be strong for his family.

The sitting man – the elder and thus, presumably, the more senior of the two – got to his feet.

'It's like the boy says: someone's got some questions for you. You're to come with us. Now. No arguments.'

He looked across at his companion and the two of them smiled.

'Although you might want to change out of your flippers. I don't think you'll be needing them where you're going.'

There was a limousine-style car waiting in a lay-by across the street – sleek, black, smoked-out windows; he couldn't imagine how he'd missed it earlier – and, escorted by the two men, he was ushered into the rear seat, the younger of the agents slipping in beside him, the older one taking the passenger seat in front. A third man, in the same uniform of tailored grey suit and crew-cut hair, was already waiting behind the wheel. Even before the doors were properly closed he had started the engine and moved off, the car gliding out onto the uneven tarmac with the smooth, predatory grace of a prowling panther.

Khalifa tried to ask what was going on, where he was being taken, if all this was to do with Piet

Jansen and Farouk al-Hakim, as he knew it must be. The men said nothing, just stared fixedly ahead with the blank, menacing impassivity of professional executioners. After a couple of minutes he gave up trying to communicate, lighting a cigarette and gazing out of the window, cursing himself for his naivety, for imagining he could expose someone as powerful as al-Hakim and not be made to pay for it. The Jihaz always looked after their own. And always punished those who crossed their own. God, how could he have been so naive? Beside him in the darkness the tip of his Cleopatra scratched orange patterns against the window from the trembling of his hand.

Initially they headed back towards the middle of Luxor, making, he presumed, for one of the many government offices clustered in the centre of town. As they passed Luxor General, however – and this only served to increase his anxiety – they swung off onto a trunk road and headed out again, eastwards this time, towards the airport. Again he tried to ask the men where they were going, again they refused to answer, the silence seeming to push in on his chest and lungs as though his torso was being slowly constricted within a thick loop of rope, making it hard for him to draw breath.

At the airport, the front barrier was thrown open for them without question and, skirting the car park, they were waved through a side gate out onto the runway area, the dial of the car's speedometer veering round to 150 km/h as the driver put his foot to the floor, rushing them across the expanse of smooth, empty tarmac towards the very furthest corner of the airport enclosure where they pulled up alongside a Learjet, its twin engines already running. As he was ushered out of the car he asked for a third time, his voice desperate now, what this was all about, where they were going, what was going to happen to him. Still the two agents said nothing, just marched him up the steps into the jet's cabin and pointed him into a leather seat, indicating that he should fasten his safety belt.

The door was closed, instructions shouted towards the cockpit, and the plane taxied out onto the runway, slowing for a brief moment as if to gather its strength before accelerating again and lifting gracefully into the air. Khalifa stared down at the floodlit bulk of the terminal building as it slowly receded beneath him, then leant back and stared at the cabin ceiling. Behind him he could hear one of the agents mumbling into a mobile phone.

Amazingly, given the circumstances, he must have dozed off, because the next thing he knew his shoulder was being shaken and he was being told to get up. Groggily, he undid his seat-belt and got to his feet. They were on the ground again. For a muddled moment he thought perhaps he'd only dreamt the take-off and they were actually still in Luxor. As he was prodded through the cabin door and down the steps onto the tarmac, however, he realized it couldn't have been a dream because this was a new airport, smaller than Luxor, differently configured, an unfamiliar smell in the air that at first he couldn't place but then realized was the brackish tang of salt water. The sea. Where the hell . . . ? He glanced down at his watch. Not Hurghada, certainly, they'd been in the air too long, almost fifty minutes. Alexandria? Port Said? Hadn't been in the air long enough for those. So where? Sharm el-Sheikh? Yes, it could be Sharm el-Sheikh. Or Taba, maybe. Yes, Sharm el-Sheikh or Taba, although what the hell they were doing on the Sinai Peninsula he couldn't begin to imagine. Wherever they were it clearly wasn't their final destination because at the bottom of the steps he was led round to the far side of the Learjet where a Chinook CH-47 helicopter was waiting for them, crouched on the runway like a giant praying mantis. They barely had time to clamber into its long, narrow belly and strap themselves into their seats before its rotors whined into life and they were airborne again, wheeling away across the airport and off into the night.

'God help me,' Khalifa whispered, remembering all the stories he'd heard about the Jihaz throwing people out of helicopters way out in the middle of nowhere, their bodies left to rot amid the rocks and the sand. 'Please, God, help me.'

They flew north, to judge by the position of the

moon outside the window, the cabin vibrating with the rhythmic wub-wub of the engines, a barren, mercury-coloured desertscape rushing past beneath, its surface torn by sharp ridges and criss-crossed with a meandering tracery of wadis, like snake-trails slithering across the landscape. Twenty minutes went by, then they came down again, the helicopter's bulbous wheels settling themselves onto the desert's back, its rotor blades slowing to a standstill, swamping the interior with a dense, eerie silence. One of the agents leant forward and tapped Khalifa on the arm.

'Up.'

He undid his seat-belt, hands shaking, and followed the men to the front of the cabin where they heaved open the door, revealing a dim rectangle of night within which he could just make out a jumbled landscape of slopes and ridges beneath a star-filled sky.

'Out.'

Khalifa hesitated. Why had they brought him here? What were they going to do to him? Then he jumped, shoes crunching on the gravelly desert floor, a rash of goosebumps rising like bubblewrap across his forearms from the cold. The two agents remained behind him in the doorway of the Chinook.

'Over there,' said one of them. 'Go.'

The man raised the muzzle of his gun, pointing to the right, towards a low stone building about a hundred metres off at the foot of a rocky incline, its outline murky and indistinct, its windows lit by a faint yellowy glow like monstrous eyes peering out of the gloom. A Bedouin shelter? An old army border post? Either way Khalifa didn't like it. He turned back towards the men, but they simply patted their guns and waved him forward, so he started walking.

After fifty metres he stopped and looked back, noticing for the first time two other helicopters sitting side by side beyond the one he had come in, then continued, the conviction growing with every step that this was it, he was going to be executed, there could be no other possible explanation for his presence out here in the middle of the night in the middle of nowhere. Maybe he should make a run for it, he thought, scuttle off into the desert, hide among the rocks. At least he'd have some chance, albeit a remote one. But he couldn't bring himself to do it, couldn't force the necessary adrenalin down into his legs, so he just plodded forward until he came to the building and was standing on the step in front of its rusted iron door.

He threw a final glance back towards the Chinook, then, mumbling a prayer, by now certain that his life was about to end, reached out a shaking hand, pushed the door open and stepped inside, wondering in a detached sort of way whether he'd actually hear the shot that killed him or whether everything would simply go blank and he'd suddenly find himself transported to a completely different world.

'*Mesa el-khir*, Inspector. My apologies for bringing you here like this, but given the urgency of the situation we had little other choice. Please, help yourself to tea.'

THE SINAI DESERT, NEAR THE BORDER WITH ISRAEL

Khalifa blinked. He was standing in a low, spartan room – stone walls, bare concrete floor, corrugated tin roof – with a collapsible camp table at each end and, on the tables, a pair of oil lamps, the latter illuminating the room with a heavy orange light, viscous and shimmering. In front of him three men were sitting in worn armchairs. A fourth man was standing in the far corner of the room, leaning against the wall, his face half-lost in the shadows. The air was dense with the odour of kerosene and cigar smoke.

Relief – that was his immediate reaction. A surging, bowel-shuddering wash of euphoria that whatever else he'd been brought here for, it clearly wasn't to be killed. Almost instantaneously it gave way to shock, for the person who had addressed him, one of the men in the armchairs, unmistakable with his thick square glasses and silver-grey hair, was none other than Ahmed Gulami, his country's foreign minister. Khalifa opened his mouth to say something, ask what the hell was going on, but such was his surprise, and awe, that no words would come out, and after a moment he shut it again. There was an extended silence, the four men all staring at him, the only sounds the soft hiss of the lamps and, outside, the rusty creak of the iron window-shutters. Then Gulami waved a hand towards a thermos flask sitting on the table nearest to him.

'Please, inspector, do have some tea,' he repeated. 'I expect you need it after your journey. And if you could close the door . . . It's a cold night.'

In a daze, Khalifa pushed the door to and walked across to the table where he filled a Styrofoam cup from the flask. Once he had done so Gulami beckoned him onto a low canvas stool beside him. The standing man remained where he was; the other two shuffled their chairs round so as to face Khalifa directly.

The younger of them – a handsome man in his late thirties, with a mop of black hair and a red and white checked *keffiyeh* slung over his shoulder – the detective had already recognized: Sa'eb Marsoudi, the Palestinian activist-turned-politician, a hero not merely to his own people but, after his leadership of the First Intifada back in the late 1980s, most of the Arab world as well (Khalifa still remembered those iconic television images of Marsoudi, wrapped in the Palestinian flag, kneeling down and praying in front of a line of advancing Israeli tanks). The other, older man – medium height, stick-thin, with a white skull-cap on his head, a cigar clamped between his teeth and, on his right cheek, a ragged, sickle-shaped scar arcing from his eye down to the level of his chin – this man too Khalifa had seen before, although at first he was unable to pinpoint precisely where. Only after a few seconds did he remember that it was in Piet Jansen's villa, that first night he had visited it, in the picture on the front of *Time* magazine. Masan, Maban? Something like that. A politician. Or was it a soldier? Israeli, anyway. The fourth figure, the one standing, he couldn't place, although there was something about him – the lumbering, bear-like frame, craggy face, the way he kept swigging from the silver hip-flask he held in his hand – that Khalifa didn't like. Thuggish, that was his immediate impression. And drunk too, by the look of it. Disgusting. He stared at him for a moment, then dropped his eyes and took a sip of his tea.

'So,' said Gulami, pulling a set of amber worry beads from the pocket of his jacket and beginning to tell them off between the finger and thumb of his left hand. 'Now we are all here, let's get down to it.'

He turned to Khalifa.

'To begin, inspector, I must emphasize the absolute confidentiality of what you are going to hear tonight. The *absolute confidentiality*. You were not brought to this place. You did not see these people. This meeting is not happening. Do I make myself clear?'

617

The detective had a head full of questions he wanted to ask, and a few choice comments to make to boot about the way he had been treated. He wasn't about to make them in front of someone as powerful as his country's foreign minister, however, and just mumbled a simple 'Yes, sir'. Gulami held him in his eyes, the worry beads processing through his fingers with a soft clicking sound, then, with a nod, sat back and crossed his legs.

'Sa'eb Marsoudi, I believe, needs no introduction.'

He indicated the man with the *keffiyeh* slung over his shoulder, who tipped his head at Khalifa. His hands, the detective noticed, were clasped so tightly together the knuckles looked like they would burst through the skin.

'Major-General Yehuda Milan.' Gulami went on, nodding towards the cigar smoker, 'was one of his country's foremost soldiers, now one of its most respected politicians. One of its most enlightened and courageous politicians as well, I might add.'

Milan also tipped his head towards Khalifa, taking a slow puff on his cigar.

'Detective-Inspector Arieh Ben-Roi' – Gulami gave a flick of his worry beads towards the figure standing in the corner – 'I believe you already know.'

Out of politeness, Khalifa half-raised a hand in greeting, annoyed with himself for not having guessed the man's identity sooner. Ben-Roi made no effort to reciprocate the gesture, just stared at him out of the shadows, his expression distinctly hostile.

'Let me repeat, inspector,' Gulami continued, 'what you hear tonight is to go no further than these four walls and the inside of your head. There is a very great deal at stake, more than you can possibly realize, and I will not have it jeopardized with loose talk. Is this understood?'

Khalifa mumbled another 'Yes, sir', desperate to know what all this was about but sensing that it was not his place to ask, that whatever the reason for his presence out here it would be revealed to Gulami's timetable, not his own. The foreign minister peered at him through his heavy, black-framed glasses, then turned to Milan and Marsoudi, both of whom gave the faintest inclination of the head, as if to say, 'OK, tell him.'

'Very well.' Gulami sat back in his chair and stared down at his beads. When he spoke again the level of his voice had dropped, as if even out here in the middle of nowhere he was still worried about being overheard. 'For the past fourteen months the government of the Arab Republic of Egypt has made this building available to *sais* Marsoudi and Major-General Milan as a secure and neutral environment in which they can meet and talk, away from the media spotlight and the pressures of their domestic political situations. Both have spent their lives fighting for their respective peoples, both have suffered great personal losses in the name of those peoples' – Milan shifted in his seat, throwing a half-glance back towards Ben-Roi – 'and both have, independently, reached the conclusion that those same peoples are doomed to catastrophe unless they can find some wholly new way of engaging with each other, some different path to tread. Their purpose out here: to try to forge that different path; to develop proposals for a viable and, *insha-allah*, lasting settlement to the conflict that has blighted their land for so long.'

Whatever Khalifa had been expecting, it wasn't this. He bit his lip, eyes sliding from Gulami to Marsoudi to Milan and back to Gulami, a vague sense of dread marshalling itself behind his ribs, like a swimmer who, already aware that he is too far from shore, starts to realize he is even further out of his depth than he had previously imagined.

There was a pause, Gulami's words seeming to hover in the air like an echo lingering at the furthest extremity of a deep cavern, then the foreign minister opened a hand towards Marsoudi, inviting him to speak. The Palestinian shuffled forward on his stool.

'I won't waste your time with details, inspector,' he began, his brown eyes glinting in the glow of the kerosene lamps. 'All you need to know for current purposes is that in our meetings here over the last fourteen months we have, and not without some bitter words I can assure you' – he threw a glance at Milan – 'hammered out a set of proposals that go further in the name of peace, take greater risks, give up more than has ever been contemplated before, by either of our two sides.'

There was a cup of water on the floor beside him and, lifting it, he took a short sip.

'Understand, we are just private individuals. We do not represent our governments, we have no official backing for these talks, we possess no legislative authority to implement the proposals we have developed. What we do have, precisely because, as *sais* Gulami has explained, we have spent so long fighting for our respective causes' – again he flicked his eyes towards the Israeli – 'is the faith and trust of the majority of our people. Enough faith and trust, I believe, for them to listen to and, please God, support ideas that coming from any other of our countrymen would be dismissed out of hand as at best hopeless idealism, at worst outright treachery.'

Beside him, Milan exhaled a cloud of cigar smoke, the scar on his cheek seeming to glisten in the half-light like a thin vein of crystal.

'We harbour no illusions,' said the Israeli, picking up the discourse, his voice deep, husky and slow, like a series of notes played on the very lowest keys of an oboe. 'The proposals we have formulated are hugely controversial, will require immense sacrifices, on both our parts. Their implementation will be fraught with pain and conflict and suspicion. A generation, two, maybe even three, that's how long it will take for the wounds to start healing. Even then there will be many on both sides who refuse to come with us.'

'Yet despite that,' Marsoudi put in, taking over again, 'it remains our belief that, if we can persuade a majority of our people to accept them, these proposals offer the best, perhaps only chance for a realistic and durable solution to the problems in our land. And it is also our belief that when they see the two of us standing side by side together, bitter enemies for so long, now united in the cause of peace, a majority of our people *will* be persuaded. Have to be persuaded, frankly. Because as things stand now . . .'

He shrugged and fell silent. Milan puffed on his cigar; Gulami worked his worry beads; in the corner, Ben-Roi fiddled with his hip-flask, a deep frown concertinaing his forehead, whether from disapproval at what he'd just heard or because of some other thought festering inside his giant head, Khalifa couldn't tell. He took another sip of his tea, which was already starting to go cold, pulled out his cigarettes and lit one. Fifteen seconds ticked past, twenty.

'I don't understand,' he said. His voice sounded weak, overawed, the voice of a child sitting in a room full of adults. 'What's this got to do with al-Hakim?'

For a moment Gulami seemed confused by this comment, then he gave an amused grunt, realizing what was on Khalifa's mind.

'You thought . . . ?' He tutted and shook his

head. 'Farouk al-Hakim was a piece of shit. A disgrace to his profession and his country. You have done us all a favour by exposing him for what he was. Rest assured we have not brought you here as punishment for uncovering his sordid little secrets.'

Khalifa took another nervous pull on his cigarette, exhaling the smoke almost before it had had time to penetrate his lungs.

'So why? Why are you telling me all this?'

Gulami held him in his eyes for a moment, then looked across at Milan. The Israeli sat back in his chair, staring at Khalifa. There was an interminable pause.

'What do you know about the Menorah, inspector?' he asked eventually.

Again, this took the detective by surprise. He hesitated, confused, Milan's gaze seeming to burn into him.

'I don't see what that has—'

Gulami's hand came down onto his arm, gentle yet firm, the pressure indicating that he should answer the question. Khalifa shrugged helplessly.

'I don't know. It's . . . it stood in the Temple of Jerusalem; it was lost when the city fell to the Romans . . .'

He mumbled his way through everything he'd found out over the last couple of days, which wasn't very much. Milan listened in silence, eyes never leaving him. When he'd finished, the Israeli got slowly to his feet and, crossing to the thermos flask, poured himself a cup of tea, gazing down at the flickering flame of the kerosene lamp, its light tingeing his cigar smoke orange so that it looked as if he was enveloped in a shimmering blanket of fire. There was another long pause, then Milan started speaking, his voice, already a low baritone, seeming to become even deeper and more gravelly, barely audible.

'Every faith, inspector, has something – some object, some symbol – that is sacred to it above all others, that more than any other serves to encapsulate the essence of that faith. For Christians it is the True Cross, for Muslims the Ka'ba in Mecca. For the Jewish people, my people, it is the Holy Lamp. "And the Lord shall be unto thee an everlasting light" – this is what the prophet Isaiah told us, and this, for us, is what the Lamp has always represented: the light of creation, of belief, of being. That is why, of all the objects in the ancient Temple, it was the most venerated and the most beloved; that is why, in our own day, it was chosen as the emblem of the state of Israel. Because there is nothing more precious to us, nothing more holy, no purer symbol of what we are and strive to be as a people. Because, quite simply, in the light of the Holy Menorah is revealed nothing less than the face of the Lord God himself. I absolutely cannot overstate its power and significance.'

He took a long, slow pull on his cigar, allowing this last sentence to linger a moment, his face disappearing behind a heavy curtain of smoke.

'And now, inspector' – he turned to Khalifa, slowly, his shadow looming and shifting on the wall behind him – 'thanks to you, the original Menorah, the first Menorah, the Menorah of Menorahs that Bezalel made way back in the mists of time and that was thought to be lost for ever – now, suddenly, after all these many centuries, it has returned. Again, I cannot overstress the significance of this. Nor, more importantly, the danger.'

His voice rose slightly on this last word, its syllables seeming to swell and resonate, filling the room. The sense of dread that had been gnawing at Khalifa for the last ten minutes, the feeling that, against his will, he was becoming ever more entangled in something that was way beyond his understanding, grew suddenly more intense.

'This isn't my—'

Again Gulami's hand squeezed Khalifa's arm, signalling him to be quiet, to listen. Milan pulled on his cigar, eyes never leaving Khalifa's face.

'It is a curious quirk of the region in which we live, inspector, that symbols have always counted for a lot more than human lives. The death of an individual might be tragic, but in time the sadness fades. The desecration of something sacred, on the other hand, that is never forgotten, nor forgiven. Imagine the reaction of your people if, say, the Holy Ka'ba was to be razed by Israeli jets. It is the same for us with the Menorah. If an object as iconic as that were to fall into the wrong hands, the hands of someone such as al-Mulatham, to be despoiled by him, destroyed – take it from me, the collective wound such a sacrilege would inflict would be deeper than that of a thousand suicide bombings. Ten thousand. Human loss can be redeemed. The loss of something holy, however – the pain would never abate. Not in one generation, two, three. Never. And nor would the fury.'

He tapped the ash off the end of his cigar and, raising a hand, rubbed at his eyes, his face suddenly looking haggard, his shoulders slumping as if something was pressing down on them from above.

'Our two peoples are teetering on the edge of the abyss, inspector. Sa'eb and I, we believe we can pull them back, even now, even after so much blood has been spilled. But if the true Menorah were to be found by al-Mulatham, or, conversely, by any of the fundamentalist lunatics on our side – of whom there are plenty, I can assure you, all of them just waiting for a banner such as this behind which to rally the forces of fanaticism' – in the corner of the room Ben-Roi shifted uncomfortably, fingers playing with the pendant around his neck – 'if that were to happen, believe me, we would plunge headlong into the void, and no peace process on earth could ever pull us back out again.'

Khalifa's cigarette had burnt itself out in his hand, leaving a tenuous claw of ash dangling from the butt. There was something coming, he could feel it. Something he didn't want to hear.

'Al-Mulatham doesn't know about the Menorah,' he mumbled weakly. 'Hoth died before he could tell him.'

Marsoudi shook his head. 'We can't be certain of that. We know Hoth was doing everything he could to contact al-Mulatham. Maybe he failed; but then again, maybe he didn't. Maybe al-Mulatham is searching for the Menorah even as we speak. Maybe others are searching for it. We just can't take that risk.'

Khalifa's throat was dry, his stomach tight. He was being manoeuvred, he could feel it; cornered, like the time when he was a kid and a gang of older boys used to chase him through the Giza backstreets, always running him down in the end, boxing him in.

'Why are you telling me this?' he repeated.

There was a snort from the far side of the room.

'Why the fuck do you think they're telling you?'

It was the first time Ben-Roi had spoken.

'It was you who started this thing. Now help finish it.'

Khalifa looked around, his forehead throbbing, as though there was something alive inside it, thrashing against the inside of his temples.

'What does he mean, "help finish it"? Why have you brought me here?'

He sounded desperate. Gulami removed his glasses, examined them, put them back on again. Like Milan, his face too suddenly looked weary and pinched.

'The Menorah has to be found, inspector,' he said quietly. 'It has to be found quickly. And it has to be found without any other parties being made aware of its continued existence.'

There was a pause as his words sank in, then Khalifa got to his feet.

'No.'

He practically shouted it, startled by his vehemence yet unable to stop himself, even in front of someone as powerful as Gulami. He didn't want to be part of this. Didn't want to know about Israel, Judaism, menorahs – any of it. Had never wanted to know, not from the very beginning, whatever Zenab might have said about seeking out what you don't understand, growing and becoming a better person. All he wanted, all he had ever wanted, was to lead a small, normal, regular life, to be with his family, to get on with his job, to move on up the ladder. But this – it was too big. It was all just too big for him.

'No,' he repeated, shaking his head.

'What the fuck do you mean, no?'

Ben-Roi had come forward a step, eyes blazing. Khalifa ignored him, addressing himself to Gulami.

'I'm a policeman. This is . . . it's nothing to do with me!'

'It's everything to-fucking-do with you,' hissed Ben-Roi. 'Haven't you been listening?'

Still Khalifa ignored him. 'This isn't my

responsibility. I don't want to be a part of it. I don't want to be involved.'

'Who gives a fuck what you want?' snapped Ben-Roi, face reddening. 'There are more important things here.'

'Please, Arieh.' Milan tried to lay a hand on Ben-Roi's shoulder, but it was shrugged away.

'Who the fuck does he think he is!'

'Arieh!'

'"I don't want to be involved." Who does he think he is, the cheeky Muslim cunt!'

Khalifa wheeled, fists clenching. Two, maybe three times in his entire life he had completely lost his temper, uncontrollably lost it, and this was one of them.

'How dare you!' he hissed, no longer caring where he was, who he was with. 'How dare you, you arrogant Jew bastard!'

'Khalifa!'

Both Gulami and Marsoudi were now on their feet as well.

'*Ben-Zohna!*' bellowed Ben-Roi, surging forward, arms swinging. 'Son of a bitch! I'll fucking kill him!'

Somehow Milan managed to grab his jacket, pulling him back. Marsoudi stepped in front of Khalifa, who was also advancing, seizing his shoulders, holding him.

'*Lech tiezdayen, zayin!*' spat Ben-Roi, jabbing a finger at the Egyptian. 'Fuck you, prick!'

'*Enta ghebee, koos!*' retorted Khalifa, also jabbing a finger. 'Fuck you, vagina!'

There were more insults and expletives, both men straining towards each other, before eventually Gulami shouted, '*Halas!* Enough!' and they both fell silent, breathing heavily. Gulami, Marsoudi and Milan looked at one another tight-lipped, then the foreign minister ordered Khalifa to leave the room, to calm himself down. Throwing a withering glare at Ben-Roi, the detective crossed to the door, yanked it open and stepped out into the night, slamming it shut behind him. He took a couple of deep breaths of air – clean, cool, refreshing – then stomped off towards a row of jagged black rocks looming thirty metres away where he sat down and lit a cigarette.

Several minutes passed, the world silent aside from the faint whisper of the breeze, the sky overhead spattered with an impossible number of stars, like sprays of blue-white paint. Then there was a creak as the door opened again, and the crunch of feet on gravel. Someone came up behind him. Marsoudi.

'*Ezayek?*' asked the Palestinian, laying a hand on Khalifa's shoulder. 'You OK?'

The detective nodded. '*Ana asif,*' he mumbled. 'I'm sorry. I shouldn't have . . .'

Marsoudi's hand squeezed reassuringly. 'Believe me, that was tame compared to some of the things this place has heard these last fourteen months. This is a difficult time. It is inevitable there will be harsh words.'

He squeezed again and sat down beside Khalifa.

There was a long pause, the world around them completely still – that perfect, pristine stillness you only ever encounter in deserts and on high mountaintops – then, raising his arm, Marsoudi pointed up at the sky.

'You see there?' he asked. 'That constellation with the four bright stars? No, there. Yes, that's it. This we call the tank. That line of stars at the bottom, those are the caterpillar tracks, then the turret, and there, the gun.'

Khalifa followed the movement of the Palestinian's finger, watching as he slowly traced out the shape, which, now he looked, did indeed resemble the crude outline of a tank.

'And there' – Marsoudi swung his hand towards another constellation – 'the Kalashnikov. See, its butt, its muzzle. And over there' – he took Khalifa's elbow and turned him – 'the grenade: body, arm, pin. Everywhere else in the world people gaze up into the heavens and see beauty. Only in Palestine do we look up and see the objects of war.'

Somewhere out across the desert a jackal started to wail, the sound tailing off almost as soon as it had begun. Khalifa dragged on his cigarette and pulled his jacket around him against the cold.

'I can't do this,' he whispered. 'I'm sorry, but I just can't work with them.'

Marsoudi smiled sadly, and, dropping his head back, gazed up into the night.

'You think I didn't feel the same? My father, he died in an Israeli prison. When I was nine I watched my own brother blown up by a tank shell, right in front of me. You think after that I wanted to talk with them, come out here and negotiate? Take it from me, I have more reason to hate them than you ever could.'

He continued to stare upwards, his face deathly pale in the light of the moon.

'But I did come out here,' he said quietly. 'And I did talk to them. And you know what? These last fourteen months, Yehuda and I, we have become friends. We, who've spent our whole lives fighting each other. Good friends.'

Khalifa finished his cigarette and flicked it away into the shadows, its butt continuing to glint for a moment like the tail of a glow-worm before gradually fading into darkness.

'It's Ben-Roi,' he mumbled. 'If it was someone else . . . but Ben-Roi . . . he's dangerous. I can see it in his eyes. Everything about him. I just can't work with him.'

Marsoudi drove his hands into the pockets of his trousers.

'You have a wife, inspector?'

Khalifa nodded an affirmative.

'Apparently Ben-Roi was going to get married.'

'So?'

'A month before the wedding his fiancée was killed. In a suicide bombing. Al-Mulatham.'

'*Allah-u-akhbar.*' Khalifa hung his head. 'I didn't know.'

Marsoudi shrugged and, pulling his hands out

of his pockets again, raised his first and middle finger and tapped them against his lips, asking Khalifa for a cigarette. The Egyptian pulled one out of the pack and lit it for him, the Palestinian's thin, handsome face momentarily illuminated by the flare of the lighter before sinking back into the shadows again.

'In six days' time there will be a rally in central Jerusalem,' he said quietly. 'Yehuda and I have chosen that rally as the place to make public what we have been doing here this last year. We will outline our proposals, and we will announce the formation of a new political party, a joint Israeli-Palestinian party of co-operation and peace, one that will work to have our proposals implemented. As Yehuda said, it's going to take years, generations, to turn things round, but I think we can do it, I genuinely think we can. Not if the Menorah falls into the wrong hands, though. If that happens everything we've worked towards, everything we've hoped for, everything we've dreamt of . . .'

He took another long drag, and stared at the ground.

'Help us, inspector. From one Muslim to another, one man to another, one human to another – please, help us.'

What could Khalifa say? Nothing. He let out a deep sigh, scraped at the ground with his foot, nodded his assent. Marsoudi reached out a hand and touched his shoulder again, then looped an arm through his and led him back towards the building.

The meeting continued for another hour, Khalifa and Ben-Roi doing most of the talking now, coldly formal, avoiding each other's eyes, going over all the information they had about Hoth and the Menorah, trying to narrow down the search and develop possible lines of attack, the other men occasionally interjecting the odd comment but otherwise listening in silence as the two detectives hammered things out between themselves. It was past midnight when they eventually fell silent.

'One final thing we should discuss,' said Milan, grinding out his cigar butt. 'The al-Madani woman. What's to be done about her?'

Gulami drained off the contents of the cup he was holding in his hand.

'She can't be kept in custody till this is resolved?' he asked.

Marsoudi shook his head. 'She is well known to my people. And well loved by them. To keep her under arrest would attract much attention. Something we don't need in the current situation.'

'So?' Gulami said as he crunched the cup into a ball and launched it across the room.

No-one answered, all of them staring off into space, sunk in their own thoughts, the room now thick with velvety wedges of shadow as the kerosene lamps slowly burnt themselves down. A full minute went by.

'She can work with me.'

It was Ben-Roi. Everyone looked up.

'She knows as much as we do,' he said, 'about Hoth and the finding of the Menorah, probably more. And she understands what would happen if al-Mulatham got his hands on it. We should use her.'

It seemed a reasonable suggestion, and Gulami, Marsoudi and Milan all nodded. Only Khalifa seemed uncertain, his brow furrowed, his eyes scanning Ben-Roi's face – the way his tongue kept flicking out to moisten his lips, a mannerism he had often seen during police interviews when the interviewee was nervous, trying to conceal something. There's more here, he thought to himself. Something you're not telling us. Not a lie, just . . . some other agenda. Or was it simply that he disliked the man so much he could take nothing he said at face value? Before he could decide, Gulami came to his feet and declared the meeting closed.

Outside, as they trooped back towards the helicopters, Khalifa found himself walking just behind Ben-Roi, who towered over him, higher by a head and almost twice as broad. After all that had happened that night he felt no great inclination to address him, to have any contact with him at all save what was absolutely necessary to get the job in hand completed. His sense of decency got the better of him, however, and, coming up alongside the Israeli, he told him that despite what had been said earlier he was sorry for what had happened to his fiancée, that he had a wife and children himself, could not imagine what it must be like to lose a loved one in that way. Ben-Roi looked down at him, then, with a muttered 'Fuck you', strode away again.

'It is a strange coincidence, no?' Gulami's voice drifted back to them from up ahead. 'An Egyptian, an Israeli and a Palestinian began this whole process. And now it is upon an Egyptian, an Israeli and a Palestinian that its survival depends. I like to think that maybe this is a good sign.'

'Please God it is,' said Milan.

'Please God,' echoed Marsoudi.

KALANDIA REFUGEE CAMP, BETWEEN JERUSALEM AND RAMALLAH

The envelope was waiting for Yunis Abu Jish when he woke at dawn, slipped beneath the door of his house, although who had delivered it, how and when, he had no idea. Inside was a simple type-written note informing him that his martyrdom was to take place in six days' time. At exactly five p.m. on the afternoon of that day he was to be outside the payphone on the corner of Abu Taleb and Ibn Khaldoun streets in East Jerusalem, where he would receive his final orders.

He read the note three times, then, as instructed, took it outside into the narrow dirt alley that ran along the back of the house and burnt it. As its paper curled, blackened and crumbled into ash he felt a sudden rush rising from his stomach. Collapsing onto all fours, he began to vomit uncontrollably.

PART III

THREE DAYS LATER

LUXOR

'What is it? What have you found?'

Khalifa leant forward over the veranda rail, his voice urgent, excited.

'A bicycle frame, ya inspector.'

'Dammit! You're sure?'

'I think my men know a bicycle when they see one.'

'Bloody dammit!'

The detective spat out his half-smoked cigarette and stomped it beneath his foot, muttering in frustration at this latest false alarm. In front of him, leaning on their *tourias* amid the remains of Dieter Hoth's garden, its neatly tended rose beds and immaculately clipped lawn now scarred with an unsightly assault course of pits and trenches and heaps of sand and mud, stood four dozen workers in earth-stained djellabas. Three days and nights they'd been digging, *Gurnawis fellaheen*, peasant labourers from the villages on the west bank of the River Nile, the best excavators in Egypt. If there was anything buried in the garden, they would be the ones to unearth it. Yet they'd found nothing, just a couple of concrete utility pipes, the rotted remains of an old wooden *shaduf* and, now, part of a bicycle. Wherever Dieter Hoth had hidden the Menorah, it certainly wasn't here. As, deep down, Khalifa had always known would be the case.

He gazed out at the mess in front of him, weary, despondent; then, lighting another cigarette and signalling to the gang's *rais* that his men should call it a day and pack up their tools, he turned and wandered back inside the villa. Here too the scene was one of utter devastation: half the floor-boards were up, drifts of books and papers lay scattered everywhere, ragged holes gaped in the white plaster walls and ceilings – the detritus of three days' increasingly frantic searching. Three days' vain searching, because here too he'd drawn a complete blank: no Menorah, no clue to the Menorah's whereabouts, not even a mention of the damned thing.

Standing in the hallway now, cigarette dangling limply from between his lips, mayhem all around, Khalifa acknowledged that he'd reached the end of the line. Jansen's office at the Hotel Menna-Ra – a play on the word menorah, he now realized – his former house in Alexandria, even his blue Mercedes: all had been thoroughly gone over and all had yielded precisely *mafeesh haga* – nothing. The only other possibility, that Hoth's friend Inga Gratz had kept something back when he'd inter-viewed her the other night, was for the moment unverifiable, the old woman having fallen into a

642

coma a few hours after he'd left her bedside, a state from which, according to her doctors, she was unlikely to emerge for some while, if at all. There was no-one else to talk to, nowhere else to look, no stone still to be turned. Whatever Hoth had done with the Lamp, the answers weren't, it seemed, going to be found in Egypt.

He remained in the villa for another twenty minutes, trudging aimlessly from room to room, uncertain whether he ought to feel relieved that he'd done all he could and could now abandon the hunt with his honour intact, or disappointed that he hadn't got more of a result. Then, locking up the house, he set off back to the station to call Ben-Roi, to tell him his search had failed. The Israeli wasn't going to be happy. From the conversations they'd been having over the last few days – curt, stiff, monosyllabic – it was clear that his end of the investigation had been going no better than Khalifa's. Time and options were both running out, and still the Lamp remained resolutely hidden.

JERUSALEM

As the two of them walked up through the grounds of the Kfar Shaul Mental Health Centre, past its pretty terraces of flowering plants and collage of neatly spaced stone buildings, Layla was tempted to make some reference to the place's history, to ask Ben-Roi if he was aware that the older buildings had once formed part of the Palestinian village of Deir Yassin, scene, in 1948, of an infamous massacre by Jewish paramilitaries: two dozen men, women and children shot dead in cold blood. One look at her companion – his eyes bloodshot from lack of sleep, his mouth set into a seemingly permanent rictus of stress and displeasure – was enough to tell her the information wouldn't be appreciated, and she said nothing, just carried on up the hill in silence.

A joint Israeli-Palestinian investigation – that's what he'd proposed when he'd marched into her cell out of the blue three mornings ago. The two of them working together as a team to try and track down the Menorah, plus some other guy called Khalifa following up leads in Egypt, all

644

officially sanctioned, all top secret, all for the greater good. Was she up for it? Would she help?

Of course, she'd been surprised. Suspicious too, even though it was she who had mooted the joint-investigation idea in the first place (never for one minute believing he'd take her up on it). That manic glitter in his eyes, the not entirely successful attempt to sound calm and reasonable; everything about him had screamed out that there was more to his proposal than he was letting on, some concealed agenda. There was too much at stake for her to refuse to co-operate, however, and she had agreed immediately and without question to do whatever was required.

Equally unexpected had been his insistence that for the duration of the search she should move into his apartment in West Jerusalem. Again, every warning system in her body had rung out, told her the arrangement had less to do with them having somewhere they could work together without arousing suspicion, as he claimed, than his wanting to keep tabs on her, follow her every movement. Again, she had kept her concerns to herself, said that, yes, in the circumstances that would be a very good idea, accepting that if she wanted to remain in the hunt for the Menorah she was going to have to play by his rules. And anyway, with the stakes this high she was just as anxious to keep an eye on him.

So he'd signed her release forms, driven her over to her apartment to pick up her laptop and a change of clothes – she saw immediately that the place had been thoroughly gone over in her absence – and then back to his flat in Romema, whose living room had been turned into a makeshift office. And that's where they'd been ever since – three solid days, tense, uncomfortable, claustrophobic. Each morning they would start work first thing, calling, emailing, surfing the net, chasing up every lead they could possibly think of, continuing thus all day and deep into the night, living off coffee, sandwiches and, in Ben-Roi's case, endless swigs of vodka. In the early hours she would collapse onto the sofa for a few hours' uneasy sleep and he would disappear into his bedroom, although he didn't seem to do much sleeping there because on several occasions she'd jolted awake in the dead of night to hear him pacing up and down, whispering into his mobile phone, and once to find him standing in the corridor staring in at her, his face deathly pale, his lips trembling. A couple of times, near the beginning, she'd tried to break the ice, get some sort of dialogue going, asking him about his background, the photograph of the young woman on his bookshelf, anything; but he'd simply snarled and told her she was there to help find the Menorah, not write his fucking biography. So she'd just got on with it, phoning, emailing, researching, trying to stay focused. And all the while that insidious, choking atmosphere of mutual antipathy and suspicion.

Hoth's visit to Dachau – from the beginning that

646

had formed the main thrust of their investigations. There seemed little doubt that the crate he'd brought with him had contained the Menorah. But where had he taken it afterwards? Why had he commandeered the six prisoners? These were the questions they needed to answer. And these were the questions they had singularly failed to crack. Dachau experts, Third Reich experts, Ahnenerbe experts, experts in tracking down looted Nazi treasure, even experts in World War Two German transport infrastructure – they'd contacted them all, questioned and delved, but to no avail. Most hadn't even heard of Hoth; those that had could offer no clue whatsoever as to why he'd visited the camp or where he'd gone subsequently. She'd contacted Magnus Topping again – yes, she'd love to have dinner with him when she was next in England – Jean-Michel Dupont again, half a dozen friends and associates of Dupont, all in vain. No-one knew anything, no-one could help them.

In three long, hard days of researching only two new pieces of information had come to light: the type of trucks Hoth had had with him – Opel Blitzes, three-ton, standard German Army transport – and, from the archive at Yad Vashem, the names of the six Dachau inmates Hoth had commandeered: Janek Liebermann, Avram Brichter, Yitzhak Edelstein, Yitzhak Weiss, Eric Blum, Marc Wesser, the first four Jews, the last two, respectively, a communist and a homosexual.

None of them had been returned to the camp; every attempt to try and track them down, to discover if any of them had survived the war, had failed. In short, they had come to a dead end.

Which is why, after three days, they had finally left Ben-Roi's apartment and made their way to Kfar Shaul. Because the only other possibility was that during her long quest to locate Hoth, Hannah Schlegel had somehow tracked down the Menorah as well. And that she in turn had communicated that information to her brother Isaac.

'Waste of bloody time,' Ben-Roi had grumbled during the drive over. 'The guy hasn't spoken for fifteen years. He's a cabbage.'

But it was the only possibility left.

As arranged over the phone, they made their own way up to the North Wing Psychogeriatric Centre, where they were met by Dr Gilda Nissim, the woman who had escorted Ben-Roi on his previous visit. She greeted them both with a perfunctory nod and, throwing a suspicious glance at Layla, led them through the wing's glass doors and down the softly lit corridor, their shoes squeaking on the polished marble floor, the overhead air-conditioning filling the building with a ghostly whispering sound. When they reached Schlegel's room she delivered a brief lecture, informing them that her patient had been extremely disturbed by Ben-Roi's previous visit, that she would not tolerate him being upset again in that manner, and that they could have fifteen minutes only, no more. Then she opened the door and stepped aside. Ben-Roi strode through; Layla hesitated, then followed, the doctor half-opening her mouth as if about to issue further instructions before Ben-Roi turned round and, with a curt 'Thanks', closed the door in her face.

'Fucking busybody,' he muttered.

The room was unchanged from his last visit: bed, table, crayon drawings all over the walls and, in an armchair by the window, pyjama-clad and thin as a scarecrow, Isaac Schlegel, his gaze locked onto the same dog-eared book in his lap. Ben-Roi grabbed a stool and sat down in front of him. Layla remained where she was, eyes flicking around the walls, taking in the numerous drawings of seven-branched menorahs.

'I'm sorry to have to trouble you again, Mr Schlegel,' began the detective, launching straight in, 'but I need to ask you some more questions. About your sister Hannah?'

He tried to keep his tone calm and reassuring, so as not to frighten the old man. It didn't work, because the moment he heard the detective's voice Schlegel's eyes widened in distress and he began to rock back and forth in his chair, hands clasping and unclasping around the spine of the book, a faint whimpering sound emitting from his mouth. Ben-Roi bit his lip, clearly not in the mood for this sort of thing.

'There's no need to be afraid,' he said, forcing

a not entirely sympathetic smile across his face. 'We're not going to hurt you. We just need to talk to you. It won't take long, I promise.'

Again, his attempts at reassurance had the opposite of the desired effect. The whimpering grew louder, the rocking more pronounced.

'I know this is difficult, Mr Schlegel, and I'm sorry if I upset you before, but it's extremely—'

Schlegel's hands bunched into fists and came up to either side of his head, like a boxer trying to ward off a barrage of blows, his whimpers expanding into a high-pitched wail, filling the room. Ben-Roi's mouth crumpled into an irate grimace, his own fists clenching in frustration.

'Look, Schlegel, I know you—'

'For God's sake!' Layla stepped forward, throwing the detective a cutting look as if to say 'What the hell's wrong with you?' before squatting down beside the old man and cupping one of his fists between her palms. 'Ssssh,' she said gently, stroking the pale, translucent skin. 'It's OK, it's OK. Calm down.'

Almost immediately the fit began to abate, the old man's rocking gradually slowing, his wailing subsiding into a low-pitched purr, like the background murmur of a fridge or a computer.

'That's it,' she said softly, continuing to caress the old man's hand. 'There's no need to be afraid. Everything's going to be OK. There's nothing to be scared of.'

Ben-Roi watched her, a momentary flicker of

uncertainty registering in his eyes, as though he was discomforted by this show of tenderness, confused by it; then, removing his hip-flask, he sat back and took a swift gulp. Layla carried on talking to the old man, soothing him, relaxing him, humming the odd bar of a lullaby her father used to sing to her when she was a child, until eventually he was completely calm, his opaque grey eyes staring downwards into his lap, his hand clasped around hers. She gave it another half a minute, then, judging that she had gained as much of his confidence as she was going to, shuffled round so that she was kneeling directly in front of him, her back to Ben-Roi.

'Isaac,' she said gently, her voice little more than a whisper, 'we need your help. Will you help us?'

Behind her, Ben-Roi gave a dismissive snort. She ignored him, focusing all her attention on the scarecrow figure in front of her.

'Will you tell us about the Menorah, Isaac? You saw it, didn't you? You and Hannah. At the ruined castle. Like in your drawings. Do you remember? At Castelombres. When you were children.'

Schlegel just stared down at his book, a beam of early-morning sunlight slanting through the window onto his skeletal face, the faint humming sound continuing to drift from his nostrils.

'Please, Isaac.' She squeezed his hand, silently willing him to speak to her. 'We're trying to find the Menorah. To protect it. Do you know where it is? Do you know what happened to it?'

651

Nothing.

She asked again, and again, and again, all the while trying to rein in her frustration, keep her voice level. Then, when there was still no response, not even a flicker of understanding or connection, she sighed, slipped her hand out of his and dropped her head, acknowledging that Ben-Roi was right, it was a waste of time.

'Yellow.'

It wasn't even a whisper; more a faint disturbance of the air around Schlegel's lips that might or might not have actually constituted a word. Layla looked up, thinking she must have imagined it. The old man was still staring down at his book.

'Yellow.'

The word was stronger this time, although still so low as to be barely audible. Behind her she could feel Ben-Roi tensing, leaning forward.

She reached out, took Schlegel's hand again.

'What's yellow, Isaac? What do you mean?'

Slowly, the old man looked up. He held Layla's eyes a moment, his own now seeming to glow faintly, like bright light seen through frosted glass. Then, slipping his hand from hers, he raised it and pointed a trembling finger up and to his right, to the four drawings depicting the arch at Castelombres, with in their midst a fifth drawing of a seven-branched Menorah.

'Yellow,' he whispered for a third time, his entire body shaking as though with the effort of forcing the words up from within him.

'What do you mean, yellow?' Ben-Roi had come so far forwards his knees were pushing into Layla's back. 'That the Menorah's yellow?'

The old man continued to point for a long moment, then dropped his arm again, clasping his hands tightly around his book.

'Look at the yellow one.'

Layla half-turned, throwing a bewildered glance at Ben-Roi, then dipped her head and looked up into the old man's face, laying her hands on his again.

'Is that what Hannah told you, Isaac? Did Hannah say that?'

Schlegel was squeezing the book, twisting it, bending the spine.

'Look at the yellow one,' he repeated.

'But what does it mean?' Ben-Roi's voice was harsh, loud. 'What yellow one?'

Schlegel said nothing, just continued to twist the book.

'The yellow picture?' pushed the detective. 'Is that what she meant? Look at the yellow picture? The picture of the Menorah?'

There was a pause, then a scrape of wood on linoleum as Ben-Roi pushed back his stool and got to his feet, striding over to the Menorah drawing and gazing at it, searching for some hidden meaning in the simple, yellow-crayon image. Nothing. He ripped the sheet from the wall and looked on the back. Blank. He threw a glance at Layla, then started round the room examining the other Menorah drawings, tearing them down, his movements increasingly agitated. Still nothing. Schlegel just gazed down into his lap.

'Please, Isaac!' whispered Layla, clasping her hands around his. 'What did Hannah mean? What did she want you to tell us? Please help us, Isaac. Please!'

He was receding, she could feel it, sliding back into himself. She continued to press him, squeezing his hands, gently kneading the bony palms as if by so doing she could somehow force one final piece of information out of him. The moment had passed, however, and with an exasperated groan she sank back on her haunches and stared up at the ceiling, shaking her head.

Ben-Roi slammed his hand against the wall.

'Fuck it,' he muttered.

Afterwards, as the two of them trudged in despondent silence back down through the hospital grounds, the only sounds the atonal twittering of the birds in the pine and cypress trees and, from somewhere away to their right, the faint pop and clack of a ping-pong ball being knocked back and forth, Ben-Roi fought to focus his mind, work out what his next move should be, how the hell he could still make this whole thing work.

Aside from a few snatched minutes here and there he hadn't slept for seventy-two hours, and he was shattered, more shattered than he'd ever thought it possible to be, everything inside his head all fogged up and confused so that he was no longer entirely sure what the fuck he was doing any more, or why he was doing it. Three days ago it had all seemed so clear: the article, the interviews, the aftershave – it had all fitted, all tied in. Keep her close, keep watch, wait for the cracks to appear. But the cracks hadn't appeared – she was too clever, too controlled – so that despite himself he was starting to have doubts, to wonder if maybe he'd got the whole thing wrong (the way she'd been with Schlegel just now . . . could someone like that . . . ?). Sure, he still had the belly-ache – God, did he have the bellyache! – but could he trust it? Could he trust himself? He didn't know, he just didn't fucking know any more. And he never would unless they could find the Menorah. That's when she'd—

'What do we do now?'

'Hmm?' He was still half-sunk in his reverie.

'What do we do now?' Layla repeated.

He shook his head, trying to drag himself back into the present. 'Pray that schmuck Khalifa's found something.'

'And if he hasn't?'

'Then we get back on the phones. And we stay on them till we find what we're looking for.'

He slowed and looked across at her, pupils swelling with suspicion and antipathy, before turning away again and striding on down the hill, Layla trailing in his wake. At the bottom they got into his BMW and drove out through the hospital's white metal gates, turning onto the main highway back towards central Jerusalem. As they did so, just for an instant, Layla caught sight of a blue Saab parked on the forecourt of a derelict garage on the corner opposite the hospital entrance, the driver leaning forward over his wheel apparently staring directly at them. It only lasted a split-second and then they were past and speeding off back into the city.

Behind them, Avi Steiner started the Saab's engine.

'OK, they're moving again,' he murmured into his walkie-talkie. 'Kanfei Nesharim, eastbound. I'm with them.'

He engaged first and slipped out into the traffic, weaving his way through the cars until he was hovering directly on their tail.

LUXOR

Back in his office, Khalifa crunched a pickled turnip from the bag of *torshi* he'd bought on the way back from Hoth's villa and, with a reluctant sigh, lifted the telephone and dialled Ben-Roi's mobile number. The line rang four times, then clicked into life. As usual, the Israeli didn't bother with formalities.

'So?'

'Nothing,' replied the Egyptian.

'Fuck it!'

'You?'

'What does it fucking sound like?'

Khalifa shook his head, wondering if the man was capable of forming a sentence that didn't hinge on an expletive. Never in his life . . .

'You've seen the brother again?' he asked, trying to keep his voice civil, not to dwell on how utterly objectionable he found the Israeli.

'Just finished with him.'

'And?'

'Fuck all. The man's a zombie. Just sits there fiddling with his book making weirdo humming noises.'

There was the echo of a female voice – Layla al-Madani, presumably – asking Ben-Roi what was being said, the Israeli responding with an aggressive 'Wait, will you!'

'And there was definitely nothing in Hoth's house?' Ben-Roi's voice stormed down the line again. 'You're certain?'

'Certain,' replied Khalifa. 'I've gone over every inch of it.'

'The garden?'

'That too.'

'What about—'

'And his car. And his hotel. And the Alexandria Police have gone over his former residence. There's nowhere left to look, Ben-Roi. Not here. Not in Egypt. There's nothing.'

'Well, you must have missed something.'

'I have not missed anything.' Khalifa clenched his fist. 'There's nothing here, I tell you.'

'Well, just keep looking.'

'You're not listening to me. There's nowhere left. What do you want me to do? Dig up the whole of Luxor?'

'If that's what it takes, yes! We have to find it. I have to—'

The Israeli broke off, abruptly, as if reining himself back from some comment he hadn't wanted to make. There was a fractional pause, then he resumed, struggling to keep his voice level.

'You know what's at stake here. Just keep looking.'

The Egyptian threw up a hand helplessly. Like talking to a bloody brick wall! He mumbled a tight-lipped 'OK, OK, I'll see what I can do' and leant forward, ready to put down the phone.

'What's the book, by the way?' he asked.

'What?'

'You said Schlegel's brother had a book.'

There was another fractional pause, the Israeli clearly floored by the question, then a brief muttered exchange as he asked Layla. The next thing, so loud it made Khalifa jerk the receiver away from his ear, there was a high-pitched squeal of tyres on tarmac as of a car abruptly changing direction, accompanied by a chorus of outraged beeping.

'Ben-Roi?'

'I'll get back to you!' shouted the Israeli. Then, to Layla, 'Why the fuck didn't you—'

The line went dead.

JERUSALEM

The young man picked his way carefully across the building site, a heavy holdall clutched in his right hand, stopping frequently to check he wasn't being watched or followed, an unnecessary precaution since the site had been abandoned for the last five months, and anyway, it was way out on the fringes of the city, well beyond any populated areas. He passed a pile of breeze-blocks, skirted a network of crumbling foundation trenches from which lines of rusted iron rods stuck up like wind-blasted saplings, before eventually coming to a large metal shipping container at the very centre of the site, its door secured with a chunky padlock. After taking another cautious look around he produced a bolt-cutter from the holdall, snapped the lock and, easing open the door, went inside, the air hot and musty, thick with the smell of dust and tar. At the far end lay a crumpled heap of tarpaulin – the interior's only contents – and, crossing to this, he carefully concealed the holdall beneath it, smoothing the material back to its original shape before going outside again and re-securing the door with a new padlock. He threw a final lingering glance around, then removed a single key from his pocket, stooped and buried it in the sand at the container's front left-hand corner before straightening and hurrying back across the site, the tassles of his *tallit katan* flicking from beneath his shirt like anenome tentacles swirling in a strong current.

JERUSALEM

'Why the fuck didn't you tell us this before?'

'Because you didn't ask,' snapped Dr Gilda Nissim, striding ahead of them down the corridor towards Isaac Schlegel's room. 'I might be a psychiatrist, but that doesn't mean I can read people's minds! And kindly control your language!'

Ben-Roi opened his mouth, apparently about to yell at her. Somehow he managed to control himself and instead just let out an exasperated growl. Layla quickened her pace, coming up level with the doctor.

'And you say his sister gave it to him just before she left for Egypt?'

Nissim gave a curt nod, clearly struggling to master her own temper. 'Mrs Schlegel stopped off on her way to the airport. Spent fifteen minutes with him, gave him the book, then left again. It was the last time he ever saw her. He hasn't let it out of his sight since.'

'For fuck's sake!' muttered Ben-Roi underneath his breath, glowering at the back of the doctor's head.

They reached Schlegel's room, but instead of stopping Nissim led them on down the hallway and out through a set of glass doors at the far end of the unit, explaining that at this time of the morning her patient liked to sit outside in the sunshine. They climbed a set of steps up through a rockery planted with flowering geraniums and purple-headed lavender bushes, then followed a narrow, white-stone path up to the very top of the hospital compound, where there was a grassy knoll surrounded by pine trees, very still, very peaceful, the air redolent with the bitter-sweet tang of pine needles, the hazy forest sea of the Judean Hills spreading out all around. Nissim nodded towards a solitary figure sitting alone on a concrete bench at the far side of the knoll, and, throwing Ben-Roi a severe look over the tops of her glasses, withdrew. The two of them continued walking until they reached the bench, Ben-Roi taking up position behind it, Layla sitting down beside the old man. The book, as ever, was clasped tightly in his lap. She laid a hand gently on his arm.

'Hello again, Isaac,' she said. There was a brief silence, then, 'Will you let us see your book? The one Hannah gave you. Can we look at it? Is that OK?'

She had been worried he might not wish to show it to them, would be panicked by her request. Far from it. With a faint sigh, as if he was relieved finally to be asked the question, Schlegel slowly lifted his hands away, allowing her to take the book from his lap. Ben-Roi leant forward, craning his head to get a look.

It was a slim volume, paperback, very creased, with a green cover on which was printed a simple black line-drawing of a pine tree. Underneath, in English, was the title *Summer Walks in the Berchtesgaden National Park*. Layla glanced up at Ben-Roi, raising her eyebrows, then flicked the book open to the contents page.

There were ten walks listed, each with a name – the Konigsee Trail, the Watzmann Trail, the Weiss-Tanne Trail – and also a colour code, the latter apparently corresponding to coloured markers on the ground. The last in the book, the Hoher Goll Trail, was designated yellow.

'Look at the yellow one,' Layla whispered, her heart starting to pound.

Ben-Roi said nothing, just came round and sat down beside her. She began leafing through the book, rapidly, searching for the relevant section.

'Hoher Goll Trail,' she announced after a moment, flattening the book out on her lap.

Like the other nine chapters, this one started with a simple black-ink line drawing, in this case of a mountain, its summit flat and craggy, a long hogs-back ridge sloping away from it towards the right before ending in a sheer cliff on the edge of which was perched what looked like a small house. There followed some basic facts about the walk – Length 19 km; Time 5–6 hours; Difficulty Level 3 (out of 5) – a scale map on which its course was marked out by a zig-zagging dotted line, and then six pages of text describing the walk in detail, with inserted boxes providing extra information on local flora and fauna, points of historical interest, etc. Two-thirds of the way through the text a paragraph at the end of a page had been highlighted in red felt-tip pen:

Cross the road and take the track directly opposite, behind the derelict pumping station. After a thirty-minute climb – steep in places – you will come out into an open space in front of the entrance to the abandoned Berg-Ulmewerk salt mine (for more on the region's salt-mining tradition see introduction, p. 4). High above you, weather permitting, you will see the summit of the mighty Hoher Goll (2522m), to the right the roof and radio mast of the Kelsteinhaus, or 'Eagle's Nest', formerly Hitler's tea-house (see box). Below there are wonderful views down to Obersalzburg, Berchtesgaden and the Berchtesgadener Ache river. The trail continues to the left, beside the small stone cairn (see box overleaf).

Layla and Ben-Roi exchanged a look, confused, uncertain what any of this had to do with Dieter Hoth or the Menorah. She flipped the page. The box mentioned had also been highlighted. It was titled 'The Hoher Goll Skeletons'. They glanced at each other again, then started reading.

> In May 1961, at the spot marked by this cairn, six skeletons were discovered by passing hikers after a night of unusually heavy rainfall had washed away the topsoil from the shallow grave in which they were buried. All were male, all had died from gunshot wounds. Fabric remains suggested they were concentration camp victims although their identities have never been established, nor the reason for their presence up here in the foothills of the Hoher Goll. They are now buried in the cemetery at Berchtesgaden. When passing, it is customary to add a small stone to the pile as a mark of respect.

There was a momentary silence as they processed this information, then, both speaking at the same time, 'The Dachau prisoners.'

Their voices were charged, excited. Layla shoved the book at Ben-Roi and began rooting through her bag, pulling out her notepad and flicking through its pages, the paper making an urgent rasping sound beneath her fingertips.

'Jean-Michel Dupont,' she muttered. 'He said something, about the Nazis, the way they . . .'

She found the page she wanted, ran a finger down it, started reading.

'At the end of the war the Nazis either sent looted treasure abroad or hid it at secret locations within Germany, *usually inside abandoned mines.*'

She looked up again. For an instant their eyes held, then they both started scrambling. Layla snatched the book back and began scribbling down details of the mine and its location, her writing so juddery with excitement that after a few frantic scrawls she was forced to rip the page out, screw it up and start again. Ben-Roi was on his feet, speaking rapidly into his mobile phone, his voice fading in and out as he paced back and forth across the knoll, left hand scooping at the air as if to try and speed everything up.

Five minutes later it was all arranged: two seats on the 11.15 flight from Ben-Gurion to Vienna, then a connection on to Salzburg, the nearest airport to Berchtesgaden, where a hire car would be waiting. Barring any unforeseen delays they'd be in Germany by late afternoon.

'Let's get a shift on,' said Ben-Roi, striding off down the side of the knoll. 'If we miss this flight there's not another one till tomorrow.'

'Khalifa?'

'Fuck him. We know where it is now. He's irrelevant.'

He disappeared beneath the brow of the knoll. Layla turned to Schlegel, who through all of this had sat silent and motionless, gazing out across the forested hills. Taking his hands in hers, she pressed the book back into them.

'Thank you, Isaac,' she whispered. 'We won't let Hannah down. I promise.'

She hesitated, then leant forward and kissed the old man on the cheek. He gave the faintest of nods and seemed to mumble something, although it was too low for Layla to make it out – 'my sister', possibly, she couldn't be sure. She squeezed his arm, then stood and went after Ben-Roi, the two of them jogging down to the bottom of the hospital compound and out onto the street. She was still clutching the crumpled-up ball of paper she had ripped from her notepad earlier, and as they came up to the car she launched it into a bin at the roadside before slipping into the passenger seat and slamming the door.

From his position opposite, Avi Steiner watched as they pulled off and disappeared into the traffic. Then, murmuring something into his walkie-talkie, he started the engine of his Saab, idled off the garage forecourt and, turning the corner, pulled up at the bin and got out.

JERUSALEM

Har-Zion was beside the phone when it started ringing, gazing out of his apartment window while he massaged balm into his bare arms and torso. He bent and lifted the receiver, wincing slightly as he did so – even with the cream his skin seemed to have been getting ever tighter these last few months – answering with a brief '*Ken*' and then listening in silence to the voice at the other end. Gradually the pained expression that had twisted his mouth when he first bent down rearranged itself, first into a pucker of concentration, then a smile.

'Get the Cessna ready,' he said eventually. 'And speak to whoever we've got at the airport – we'll need to plant a tracker, just to be certain. Meet me downstairs in twenty. Oh yes, Avi, I'm coming. I'm definitely coming.'

He replaced the phone and, squeezing more balm into his hand, slowly circled it over his stomach, staring out at the Old City beneath, with its domes and towers and, just visible, the long patchwork rectangle of the Western Wall. For a moment, just a brief moment, he allowed himself to daydream: an army, a great army, all God's children, Israel united as one, marching past the Wall with the Menorah at their head before passing up onto the Temple Mount and tearing down the Arab shrines. Then, screwing the cap back on the ointment bottle, he went through into the bedroom to start getting ready.

LUXOR

'Well, ask him to call me, will you? Khalifa. Khalifa! Kal-ee-far. Yes, of course he knows . . . What? Yes, it is urgent! Very urgent. Sorry? OK, OK, thank you, thank you!'

Khalifa slammed down the phone. For a moment he sat where he was, rubbing his temples; then he got to his feet and stormed out of the office and down the corridor into another room where he snatched an atlas from a bookshelf on the wall. Back at his desk he flipped rapidly through the index, then yanked open the relevant page and began tracing the lines of latitude and longitude with his fingers until he had located the place-name he wanted: Salzburg. He lit a cigarette and stared down at it.

It was an hour since he'd last spoken to Ben-Roi. As agreed, he'd waited for the Israeli to call him back; then, having heard nothing from him and impatient to know what, if anything, they'd found out from Schlegel's brother, he'd rung his mobile. Engaged. He'd given it another five minutes, then called again. Still engaged. He'd called a third time, ten minutes after that, but now the mobile was switched off. For no reason he could explain he had started to get an uneasy feeling in the pit of his stomach, a vague premonition of trouble that grew stronger as the minutes ticked by and still the mobile stayed dead, until eventually, convinced there must be something wrong, he'd contacted the David police station.

As with his first encounter with Israeli police bureaucracy he'd had to put up with a deal of stonewalling and obstructiveness before finally getting through to a secretary who, in faltering English, had informed him that Detective Inspector Ben-Roi and a colleague were currently on their way to Austria. To Salzburg. Why, and when they were due back, she had no idea, nor would she be at liberty to reveal that information even if she did. He'd wanted to push her, demand to speak to someone higher up, but that would have meant explaining why it was he was so anxious to get in touch with the detective; and since this whole damned Menorah thing was supposed to be confidential, he'd had no choice but to back off, asking her to get Ben-Roi to call him if he happened to make contact and leaving it at that.

'What the hell's he doing?' he muttered to himself, staring down at the open atlas. 'What the bloody . . . ?'

The office door flew open and Mohammed Sariya put his head into the room.

'Not now, Mohammed.'

'I've got—'

'I said not now! I'm busy!'

His tone was sharper than he'd intended, but the news about Ben-Roi had rattled him and he wasn't in the mood for trading jokey banter. Sariya looked faintly put out by his abrupt manner, but said nothing, just shrugged, held up his hands as if to say sorry and withdrew again, pulling the door shut behind him. Khalifa thought of going after him – he was never short with his deputy, never – but he was just too wound up and instead sucked away what was left of his cigarette, threw the butt out of the window and buried his head in his hands.

They'd found something, that much at least seemed clear. Something important. Something that necessitated going all the way to Austria to follow up. For a brief moment he wondered if he was simply over-reacting, if there was some perfectly innocent explanation for Ben-Roi's silence, like he'd just forgotten to call in the excitement of unearthing this new lead, or else couldn't get a signal on his mobile and was in such a rush for his plane that he didn't have time to stop and use a payphone.

But no. The more he thought about it, went through everything that had happened over the last few days, everything he'd seen and heard of

Ben-Roi, the more certain he became that this wasn't simply a case of an innocent oversight on the Israeli's part, but a deliberate move to cut him, Khalifa, out of the picture at the crucial moment. Why? A personal thing? Because Ben-Roi didn't like him? Wanted to claim all the credit for the Menorah's discovery himself? Or was there some bigger, more insidious game being played out here, some wider agenda? He had no idea. All he did know was that the Israeli was absolutely not to be trusted.

He lit another cigarette, drummed his fingers on the desk, then, coming to a decision, picked up the phone and dialled the private mobile number Gulami had given him the other night, in case of emergencies. Five rings, then a voice-mail message. He rang off and dialled again. Same result. He called Gulami's office. The minister was in a meeting with President Mubarak, wouldn't be free till the end of the day, not to be disturbed, under any circumstances. Dammit.

He stood, crossed to the window, rapped his knuckles impatiently on the frame, then went back to his desk and called a contact of his on *al-Ahram*, asked how he could get in touch with Sa'eb Marsoudi. The contact gave him a contact in Ramallah, who gave him a contact in Jerusalem, who gave him a contact back in Ramallah who gave him the number of an office down in Gaza, which told him they had no idea where Marsoudi was. Bloody dammit!

He phoned around a while longer, then, having got nowhere, he went down the corridor to splash some water on his face, try and clear his head. As he passed the last office before the washroom he noticed Mohammed Sariya sitting alone at a desk inside, eating his lunch. Feeling a pang of guilt for his earlier behaviour he slowed and put his head through the door.

'Mohammed?'

Sariya looked up.

'I'm sorry. I didn't mean to snap at you like that. I've been a bit . . .'

His deputy waved a spring onion at him, dismissing the apology. 'Forgotten.'

'Nothing important, was it?'

Sariya bit into the onion.

'It was just about that doorway.'

Khalifa shook his head, not understanding.

'You know, the picture you gave me, the slide. The one you found in Jansen's villa.'

With so many other things on his mind Khalifa had completely forgotten about it.

'Listen, can we do this another time, Mohammed? Right at the moment tombs aren't high on my list of priorities.'

'Sure,' said Sariya. 'Although that's kind of why I thought you might be interested.'

Again Khalifa shook his head. 'How do you mean?'

'Well, it wasn't a tomb.'

'Not a . . . so what was it?'

'A mine,' said Sariya. 'In Germany. Salt mine to be precise.'

For a moment Khalifa hovered by the door; then, intrigued despite himself, he came into the room.

'Go on.'

His deputy crammed the remainder of the onion into his mouth and, bending down, retrieved a large cardboard folder from beneath the desk, removing first a sheet of A4 paper with notes scribbled all over it, then three large photographs, then the slide Khalifa had found in Hoth's villa.

'I got a regular six-by-four print done,' he began, indicating the slide, 'but it didn't show anything you couldn't already see. It was only when I got the guys down in photographic to do a proper blow-up that I found something interesting.'

He held up the first of the large pictures. It was the same doorway Khalifa remembered: dark, forbidding, opening up at the base of a high wall of flat grey rock. Now, however, just above the doorway's lintel, he could make out crude lettering scratched into the bare stone, so faint as to have been invisible on the original slide. He bent forward, squinting at the words.

'*Glück Auf*,' he read, struggling with the pronunciation.

'Means good luck,' explained Sariya. 'German. I spoke to their embassy.'

'And they could identify the tomb just from that?'

'Mine,' corrected Sariya. 'And no, they couldn't.

It's a traditional miner's greeting, apparently. Used all over Germany.'

'So how?'

'Well, just for the hell of it I got the photographic guys to zoom in on the upper part of the door and blow the picture up again, really enlarge it, and . . .' He held up the next print. 'Notice anything?'

Khalifa ran his eyes over the picture. It seemed exactly the same as the last image, save for what looked like a tiny white blob at the top right-hand corner of the doorway, just below the 'f' of GLÜCK AUF.

'What's that?'

'Very good!' said Sariya with a grin. 'We'll make a detective of you yet.'

He held up the third and final photograph, very grainy, just a small segment of lintel, the word AUF and, beneath it, blurred but legible, painted onto the rock in an area no bigger than the size of a coin, the legend SW16.

'At first I thought it was graffiti,' he said. 'I sent it over to the embassy anyway, just on the off-chance it might ring a bell. They got in touch with some mining expert back in Germany, and he finally came back to me this morning. It turns out it's actually—'

'Part of a numbering system?'

'Exactly. Used around a town called' – he consulted the note-covered sheet of A4 – 'Berchtesgaden. To identify old salt mines. This particular one's a mine called' – again he consulted his sheet – 'the Berg-Ulmewerk. Abandoned since the end of the nineteenth century. They even faxed me a map and some stuff about its history. Bloody efficient, the Germans.'

He delved into the cardboard folder again and pulled out a sheaf of fax-paper which he handed to Khalifa, who sat down on the edge of the desk. There were a couple of pages of writing in German – useless, since he couldn't speak the language – a map, and also a picture of a mountain. He couldn't be sure, but with its flat, craggy summit it looked distinctly like the oil painting hanging in Hoth's front room. He felt a slight tightening of his chest, a tickle of adrenalin.

'This town, Berder-whatever-it's-called. Where is it exactly?'

'Berchtesgaden,' corrected his deputy. 'Southern Germany. Near the border with Austria.'

There was a fractional pause, then Khalifa was on his feet sprinting back to his own office. The atlas was still open on his desk and, grabbing it, he began running his eyes back and forth over the page. It took him precisely five seconds to find what he wanted. Berchtesgaden. Fewer than twenty kilometres from Salzburg, which was the nearest airport. He snatched up the phone and punched a number into the keypad. Three rings, then Chief Hassani's voice echoed down the line.

'Sir? Khalifa. I need to request some travel expenses.'

A tinny, jabbering sound.

'A bit further than that, I'm afraid, sir.' He bit his lip. 'Austria.'

The jabbering suddenly became much louder.

BEN-GURION AIRPORT

By the time they'd picked up their passports, driven the sixty kilometres to the airport and made their way into the terminal building, their flight to Vienna was already boarding. Ben-Roi flashed his police ID to get them through the initial round of security checks in the departures hall – the first and only time Layla had managed to negotiate the latter without being subjected to minute and interminable questioning – and straight to the check-in desk. The second security control, at the entrance to the departures lounge, proved more difficult, one of the duty guards insisting on taking Layla aside into a private cubicle to search her, despite Ben-Roi's insistence that she was in his custody and posed no threat. By the time she'd been given the all-clear their flight was being called for the last time.

'*Ghabee!*' Layla hissed impatiently as her knapsack was handed back to her, its contents thoroughly rifled. 'Idiot!'

She hefted the bag over her shoulder and turned to go after Ben-Roi, who was already moving towards their departure gate. As she did so, back beyond the passport control booths, half-hidden behind a pillar, she caught sight of a tall, muscular figure who seemed to be staring directly at her. Their eyes met for the briefest of instants, then he stepped backwards and disappeared from view.

Outside, Avi Steiner crossed the car park and slipped into the back of a Volvo.

'They're boarding.'

Har-Zion nodded and, leaning forward, patted the driver on the shoulder. The car started up and they moved off, passing through a security gate at the far end of the terminal and out across the tarmac, driving past a row of cargo bays before pulling up beside a hangar in whose open doorway sat a black Cessna Citation Jet. Four other men – tall, honed, expressionless – were waiting for them beside the boarding stairs, each wearing a black *yarmulke*, each clutching a canvas holdall. Har-Zion and Steiner got out and, with a silent acknowledgement of each other's presence, the six of them disappeared into the jet, its door thunking closed behind them, its engines starting to whine and purr.

EGYPT

Khalifa had already missed the one daily direct flight from Egypt to Austria, so had to scramble round trying to put together an alternative itinerary to Salzburg via some other European capital. After almost an hour of phoning the best he'd managed to come up with was a tortuous route via Rome and Innsbruck which wouldn't get him to his destination till past midnight. By that point Ben-Roi would almost certainly have reached the mine, done whatever he was going to do there and left again, and he was just starting to think he was wasting his time, that there was no way he was going to catch the Israeli, when, with his very last call, he finally found what he needed: a tourist charter from Luxor direct to Munich, departing at 1.15 p.m. Munich was only 130 kilometres by road from Berchtesgaden, and although it wasn't the ideal solution it was the best he could do in the circumstances.

He just had time to call Zenab, tell her he was going on a short business trip – 'Nothing to worry about, I'll be back by this time tomorrow' – before charging off to the airport. So rushed was the whole thing that it was only when he was actually on board the plane and roaring down the runway that it occurred to him this would be the first time in his entire life he had ever been out of his native Egypt.

SALZBURG

They landed in Vienna at 3.30, and Salzburg an hour later, picking up their hire car and speeding south along the autobahn. Ben-Roi drove and Layla map-read, the Bavarian Alps closing in around them like a ring of shattered battlements, steep, tree-covered slopes leaping upwards to either side. Although their lower parts were free from snow, further up, at the level where the forests of birch, elm, ash and juniper gave way to tightly serried ranks of spruce and mountain pine, everything suddenly became swathed in misty white, and though nothing was actually said, they both gazed upwards in growing concern, fearful they had come all this way only for their intended destination to be inaccessible. There was nothing they could do about it at this stage, however, and they sped on in silence, turning off the autobahn after ten kilometres and picking up a looping A-road that ran direct to Berchtesgaden, a frothing river pacing them to their right, the damp tarmac rushing past beneath like a spooling tape.

684

Ben-Roi, Layla noticed, kept flicking glances into the rear-view mirror, even though the road behind was completely free of traffic.

MUNICH

lthough his flight landed twenty minutes ahead of schedule, Khalifa lost all that time and more at passport control, where even with his Egyptian Police ID he struggled to persuade the official on duty – a large, sour-faced woman with bobbed hair and the most enormous breasts he'd ever seen – that he wasn't an illegal immigrant trying to sneak into the country to sponge off its social security system (the fact that he had an open-ended ticket and spoke no German didn't help things). By the time he *had* persuaded her, and then bought a map, picked up his Volkswagen Polo hire car and negotiated his way out of the airport and onto the eastbound autobahn, it was already early evening, the last breaths of daylight swiftly dissolving into the thick, uncertain haze of dusk.

Under other circumstances he would have taken things more gently, given himself time to absorb his new surroundings. The lush pastures; the rolling, wood-covered hills; the pretty villages with their onion-domed churches and neat, red-tiled houses – it was all so utterly alien to him, so completely different from the sun-baked desert vistas that constituted his own world. With Ben-Roi already well ahead of him, however, there was no time for such indulgences, nor was he in the mood for them. Rather, with barely a glance at his surroundings, he swung the car into the outermost and fastest of the autobahn's three lanes, pushed down the accelerator as far as it would go and roared on into the deepening twilight, oblivious to the flashing overhead signs declaring a speed restriction of 130km/h.

Only once during the ensuing journey did he allow this steely focus briefly to waver. He had swerved into a Dea service station to top up with petrol and buy some cigarettes and was about to climb back into the car when, on a grassy bank on the far side of the pumps, he noticed a small patch of snow, no larger than a child's blanket, a lingering remnant of what must originally have been a far more extensive covering. He had never seen snow before, not real snow, let alone touched it. Although he could hear the seconds ticking away inside his head, he couldn't resist trotting over and laying his hand on the patch's crusted icy surface, holding it there for a moment as if petting some unfamiliar animal before hurrying back to the car and screeching on his way again.

'Wait till I tell Zenab,' he thought to himself, palm still tingling. 'She'll never believe me. Snow! *Allah-u-akhbar!*'

BERCHTESGADEN

They stopped off at a small roadside hardware store about five kilometres short of Berchtesgaden to buy torches and winter clothes, then turned left off the main highway and started up into the hills. Although it was now dark, the sky above was clear, pricked here and there by the first evening stars and with a full, ice-coloured moon that bathed everything around them in a dull silvery luminescence, as though the landscape had been cast out of pewter. Here and there huddles of glinting lights marked isolated villages and farmsteads, while in the low-lands behind, pairs of headlamps inched their way through the darkness along the main Berchtesgaden-Salzburg highway. They encountered no other cars on the road they were on, however, and once they had passed through the village of Oberau, with its patchwork of red-and-green-roofed alpine houses, the dwelling lights dropped away as well, leaving the world silent and empty and still, devoid of all traces of humanity save for the road itself and, every kilometre or so, a large sign announcing they were following something called the Rossfeld-Hohen-Ringstrasse.

'You're sure this is the right way?' asked Ben-Roi, flicking the headlamps on to full beam.

Layla nodded, holding a finger to the map. 'It loops round underneath the Hoher Goll and then goes down again towards Berchtesgaden. According to Schlegel's book the path to the mine starts just past its highest point. We need to look out for some sort of ruined building.'

The Israeli grunted and, throwing yet another glance in the rear-view mirror, he dabbed the brakes, swerved the car through a tight bend and accelerated again, grit clattering off the wheels and bodywork, the headlamps punching deep holes in the enveloping gloom.

They were by this point well above the snow line, everything around them sunk beneath a pristine blanket of glinting white: snow on the ground, snow on the trees, snow banked up in sugary, metre-high walls to either side of them. The route itself remained clear, however, and they were able to continue upwards unimpeded, winding back and forth through a succession of ever tighter hairpins, higher and higher, the rearing, cliff-like face of the Hoher Goll looming ever more threateningly in front, until eventually they started to level out, the road running flat for a kilometre or so through thick pine forests before starting to drop down again. As it did so, ahead of them, at the apex of a long sweeping bend, the car's headlamps picked out a small ruined building sitting in a clearing to the left of the road, its crumbling stone walls clasped in a thick muffler of drifted snow. As they came up to it and slowed, Layla pointed to a small wooden sign at the roadside with a yellow arrow aiming upwards into the trees above.

'The Hoher Goll Trail,' she said.

They pulled over and got out. For a brief moment they stood there, taking in their surroundings, the silence enveloping them, ribbons of icy steam billowing from their mouths; then, without further ado, they pulled on their boots, coats and gloves, turned on the torches and started up into the forest, following what was in warmer weather presumably some sort of path or track, but was now just a glistening avenue of virgin snow curving gently upwards through the tightly massed ranks of pine trees.

For the first couple of hundred metres the going wasn't too difficult, the track rising gently, their feet sinking into the snow no deeper than the level of their ankles. Gradually, however, the gradient started to become harsher and the snow deeper, coming up first to their calves, then their knees, then, in places, their thighs, making progress slow, and cumbersome and exhausting. It was bitterly cold, and with tree-trunks crowding in all around they became increasingly disorientated, stopping ever more frequently to make sure they were still actually on the track, which refused to hold a straight line but rather twisted sharply back and forth as though deliberately trying to shake them off. Had it not been for the yellow arrow signs nailed at regular intervals to tree trunks along the route, and the fact that they knew that whatever else they did they needed to keep moving upwards, they would long since have lost all sense of where they were going.

Isaac Schlegel's book had reckoned it was a thirty-minute climb to the mine. With conditions as they were it was almost an hour and a half before they finally felt the ground starting to flatten out beneath them and, as if emerging from a tunnel, staggered forward into a wide clearing at the foot of a rearing wall of black rock, their bodies from the waist down caked in a powdery crust of snow.

'Thank God,' panted Layla, gasping for air.

Beside her, Ben-Roi pulled his hip-flask from his pocket and, between coughs, took a series of long, deep swigs.

They gave themselves half a minute, then, both still fighting to catch their breath, they moved forward a couple of steps and raised their torches, playing the beams back and forth across the rock face in front of them until they had picked out the mine entrance – a dark rectangle across whose mouth thin slats of wood had been nailed to prevent anyone getting in. They exchanged a brief look, neither able to make out much of the other's features behind the veils of steam issuing from their mouths, then started forward across the clearing, weaving their way through mounds of snow-covered rock and slag until they had reached the mine.

Three not particularly hard kicks and a bit of tugging was enough to dismantle the flimsy barricade across its doorway, revealing a dank, forbidding corridor running backwards into the hillside, its ceiling supported at regular intervals by wooden props, its narrow confines choked with a blackness so thick Layla felt she could reach out and scoop up a great chunk of it into her hand. For a brief, distressing moment she found herself pitched into her recurring nightmare – the underground cell, the lurking animal, the same hideous, all-enveloping darkness – before she was snatched back to the present by the sound of Ben-Roi moving forward into the shaft. She went after him, the walls seeming to press in on her, her heart hammering, continuing for about ten metres before the Israeli suddenly stopped, his bulky frame blocking the entire corridor.

'Fuck!'

'What?'

'Fuck!'

She came up beside him, the beam of her torch combining with his to punch a bulging tube of light into the blackness ahead. Forty metres further on the shaft came to an abrupt end, blocked by a wall of massive tumbled rocks where the mine's roof had caved in.

'Fuck!' repeated Ben-Roi.

BERCHTESGADEN

Khalifa came into Berchtesgaden from the north, on the road from Bad Reichenhall, the Polo's interior by that point thick with cigarette smoke, its dashboard ashtray overflowing with a mass of crumpled butts. He pulled over in front of the town's train station to consult his map, then set off again, casting a brief, quizzical glance at a group of men walking down the opposite side of the street dressed in leather shorts – my God, in this weather! – before swinging right over the Berchtesgadener Ache river and heading upwards out of town into the mountains.

According to the map the Germans had faxed to Sariya, the Berg-Ulmewerk mine was accessed by some sort of path or track that led upwards from the Rossfeld-Hohen-Ringstrasse, the road he was now following. Precisely where that path started, however, or if it was marked in any way, wasn't made clear, either on the faxed map or the one he had bought at the airport, and the higher Khalifa climbed and the deeper the snow got and the thicker the pine forests, the more worried he became that unless he happened upon some large sign saying MINE THIS WAY, he was never going to be able to locate the damned thing.

He was actually starting to wonder if maybe he shouldn't turn round and head back to the nearest village, try to get more detailed directions, when, coming out of a bend at what seemed to be almost the road's highest point, his headlamps swung across the face of a ruined stone building huddled in a clearing to the right. Beyond it a car was pulled up at the roadside, with a trail of footprints churning an untidy wake up into the forest above. Ben-Roi. It had to be. He stopped, cut the engine and got out.

If he thought it had been cold down in the lowlands it was nothing to the bitter, icy atmosphere that now enveloped him, the raw mountain air seeming to shred away his clothes so that he felt as if he was standing stark naked inside a giant refrigerator. For a moment it quite literally knocked the breath out of him, as though he had been punched in the stomach, and even when he'd recovered himself sufficiently to get a cigarette in his mouth and light it, his teeth were chattering so much he struggled actually to draw any smoke.

He stomped up and down for a bit, forcing whatever warmth he could into his body, then, leaning back into the Polo and stuffing every bit of loose paper he could find into the pockets of his jacket – maps, car-hire paperwork, even the Volkswagen's log book – he slammed the door, locked it and set off up into the forest, his shoes crunching and squeaking in the snow, the pine trees closing around him like the bars of an enormous cage.

They managed to shift a couple of smaller rocks off the top of the ceiling fall, hoping against hope that it might just be a limited collapse and they would somehow be able to wriggle through into the shaft beyond. No chance. Behind the smaller rocks were bigger rocks, much bigger rocks, great jagged slabs of rock. It would have been a struggle to move them with ten people and proper lifting equipment. With just the two of them, and nothing to use but their bare hands, it was a lost cause. They worked at it for thirty minutes, their flashlights balanced precariously on an old tin bucket on the floor, then gave up.

'Wasting our time,' panted Layla, her face bubbled with sweat despite the cold. 'No way we're going to get through. No way.'

Ben-Roi said nothing, just leant against the wall breathing heavily. Then, with a muttered 'Fuck it,' he snatched up one of the torches and started back along the shaft towards the dim, grey rectangle of the mine entrance. Layla lingered a moment, then moved forward and picked up the second torch. As she did so its beam wheeled momentarily across the floor, picking out what looked like a faint groove in the rock at her feet, no more than a few centimetres across and barely visible beneath the dust and dirt with which the floor was caked. She pointed the beam downwards, frowning, then dropped and, holding the torch with one hand, brushed at the ground with the other. More of the groove became visible, and other grooves as well. She brushed harder. They seemed to run in parallel lines, one set following the direction of the corridor from the entrance to the rock fall, the other curving off at the point where she was squatting and running directly into the wall between two of the wooden ceiling props.

'Look at this,' she called, still rubbing at the ground.

Ben-Roi had by now almost reached the mine entrance. He stopped and turned.

'There were rails in here,' she shouted. 'On the floor. They ran back into the mine. But then, just here, another set branched away.'

The Israeli hesitated, then came back down the shaft to where she was squatting, the light of his torch beam combining with hers to illuminate the parallel grooves arcing off from the main axis of the tunnel. He stared at them, then moved back and ran his torch over the area of wall into which the grooves disappeared. Layla did the same. Although it was grimy and uneven, now that they looked closely they could see that that particular section of rock was of a lighter hue than that of the rest of the shaft, and of a vaguely different texture as well. Ben-Roi went up to it, ran his hand over its surface, thudded a fist against it.

'It's concrete!' he hissed. 'There was an opening

here. Someone's blocked it up, tried to make it look like the rest of the tunnel.'

'You think . . . ?'

He didn't reply, just thumped again, harder. Layla couldn't be sure, but she thought she caught a faint hollow sound. There was an old pick-axe head lying on the floor nearby and, picking it up, she slammed it against the wall. Again that hollow sound, louder now. They glanced at each other, then Ben-Roi grabbed the pick-head, handed her his torch and started hacking. One blow, two, three and a small crack opened up. He adjusted his position, gave himself more room to swing, resumed the attack. The crack widened and spread, ancillary cracks radiating outwards from it like the spokes of a wheel, the hollow sound growing louder with every blow until eventually a heavy flap of concrete sheared away and dropped to the floor, revealing a crude breeze block wall behind. On it, in white paint, were daubed the words MEIN EHRE . . .

'Heisst Treue,' whispered Layla, completing the legend, the last section of which was still lost beneath the concrete rendering. She looked across at Ben-Roi. 'The motto of the SS.'

'You sneaky bastard, Hoth,' he murmured. 'You sneaky Nazi bastard!'

He slapped a hand against the blocks to gauge how solid they were, then, using the point of the pick, started scraping around one of them, loosening the chunky globs of cement that held it in place. They came out easily, crumbling almost as soon as the pick-point scored into them, and within a minute he'd all but freed the block from its neighbours. He dropped the pick and kicked at the wall. The block trembled, but stayed in place. He kicked again, putting all his strength into the blow, and this time it dislodged, flying backwards and disappearing with a loud thud like a cork bursting from a bottle, leaving a dark, rectangular cavity. He took his torch back from Layla and, leaning forward, shone it into the hole.

'*Oy vey!*'

'What can you see?'

'*Oy vey!*'

'What?'

Ben-Roi stepped back, allowing Layla to take his place. She raised her own torch and, pressing her face to the cavity, peered through into the darkness beyond, the steam of her breath swirling and twisting in the light of the beam. Another tunnel ran away in front of her, narrower than the main shaft and at right angles to it. Lined up along its walls, looming briefly in the torchlight before receding into blackness again as she swayed the beam from side to side, were dozens upon dozens of boxes and crates, some wood, some metal, some big, some small, most, so far as she could make out, stamped with a swastika and the twin lightning-bolt insignia of the SS.

'God Almighty,' she whispered.

She took in the scene for thirty seconds, transfixed, then, uneasy suddenly at having her back to Ben-Roi, turned again. The Israeli was standing directly behind her, hand clasped around a rusty iron chisel that he must have picked up while she was peering through the cavity. For an instant she tensed, thinking he was about to attack her. But he simply handed her the chisel and, stooping, lifted the pickhead from the floor where he had dropped it.

'Let's get it down,' he said.

It took them fewer than five minutes to expand the cavity into a fully fledged opening. As soon as they'd punched a big enough hole they threw aside the tools and, Ben-Roi going first, clambered through into the tunnel beyond, the uneven rasp of their breathing seeming to fill the entire shaft as if they were standing inside some vast stone lung.

They played the torch beams back and forth, trying in vain to see how far the corridor extended, then stepped up to the nearest of the boxes and squatted in front of it. It was square, metal, with a hinged lid on which a skull-and-crossbones had been sprayed in black. Ben-Roi flicked the catches and opened it.

'*Chara!*' he growled. 'Shit!'

Inside, wrapped in a waxed paper like lumps of cheese, were two dozen blocks of plastic explosive. They gazed at them nervously, then moved to the next box along, this one wooden, oblong. There was a crowbar lying on top and, grabbing it, Ben-Roi sprung open the lid, brushing aside a layer of straw to reveal a nest of gleaming, wooden-stocked Mauser rifles. A compartment at the end of the crate was crammed with ammunition clips.

'It's an arsenal,' murmured Layla. 'It's a fucking arsenal.'

They lifted one of the rifles out and examined it – it seemed in perfect working order, unaffected after sixty years of being bricked up in the darkness of the mine – then laid it down again and started moving deeper into the tunnel, stopping every few metres to open up other crates and chests. Most contained weapons and demolition equipment. There were other things as well, however. One box was crammed with hundreds of Iron Crosses, another with bundles of neatly wrapped banknotes, another with dusty bottles of wine. A small flat crate leaning against the wall about twenty metres into the tunnel had a tag attached to it on which was scrawled '1 Vermeer, 1 Breughel (Altere), 2 Rembrandt'.

'God Almighty,' Layla kept murmuring to herself. 'God Almighty.'

For all that the collection was spectacular, they found no sign of the Menorah, so they just kept moving along the shaft, deeper and deeper into the mountain until eventually, after about fifty metres, they saw that ahead of them the tunnel seemed to widen out, its mouth filling with a blackness even more impenetrable than that which they had so far encountered. They slashed their torch beams back and forth trying to see what was going on, then continued, covering another twenty metres before the tunnel walls suddenly disappeared and they found themselves standing on a broad, flat ledge gazing out into emptiness.

'It's a cavern,' said Layla, whispering for some reason.

They moved forward to the front of the ledge where there was what appeared to be some sort of rudimentary elevator system giving access to the cavern floor below – just a rectangular wooden platform with a handrail at each end, running on two vertical tracks bolted into the rock face. They tested it with their feet, gingerly, making sure the wood wasn't rotten, then stepped onto it and shone their Maglites out into the void.

With everything swamped in darkness it was impossible to get a proper sense of the cavern's dimensions. Given that their torch beams were already weakening by he time they hit the ceiling, however, and had been completely smothered before they were able to pick out the far wall, they could tell it was big. Very big. Below – ten, fifteen metres – they could make out more crates. A lot more crates.

'How much of this fucking stuff is there?' muttered Ben-Roi.

They wheeled the Maglites around for almost a minute, trying to piece together a picture of their surroundings, then started looking for a way to get the elevator working. There was a control box clamped to one of the handrails with a long loop of electrical cable dangling from its underside and a lever on its face. Ben-Roi pulled the lever. Nothing.

'No power,' he said.

He put down the crowbar he was still holding and leant over the rail, shining his torch down into the blackness, trying to locate the lift's electricity source. There were more cables coiled on the cavern floor, some snaking away among the crates, one – the thickest – running up the rock face beside the elevator. He traced it with his beam, following it up over the lip of the ledge, across the stone balcony and through a low doorway a few metres to the left of the tunnel opening. They went over to it and ducked into a small, rock-cut room where the cable fed into a large generator, a rusted crank mechanism dangling from its side like a withered arm.

'You think it still works?' asked Layla. 'After all this time?'

'Only one way to find out,' said Ben-Roi, handing her his Maglite.

He grasped the crank with both hands and yanked, turning it half a revolution. Nothing. He tried again. Still nothing. He cricked his shoulders, squatted to give himself more leverage, and heaved. The generator let out a weak cough, its body shuddering slightly.

'Come on,' hissed Laya.

Ben-Roi jerked the handle again, and again, and

again, each revolution producing a louder and more protracted splutter until eventually, on the ninth attempt, the machine suddenly roared into life, a brilliant, shocking explosion of light flooding the cavern behind them. They hurried back out onto the ledge.

'Oh fuck,' gasped Layla.

As they had already worked out, they were standing on a natural balcony at one end of a vast, hangar-like cave, thirty metres high, forty across, seventy long, its walls and ceiling striped with undulating bands of orange and grey rock. It was not the cavern itself which left them standing with mouths agape, however, but its contents, for if in the tunnel there had been dozens of crates and boxes, here – illuminated in the frosty glare of eight giant arc lamps – there were hundreds of them, line upon line, row upon row, stack upon stack, divided into neat blocks by a grid of narrow avenues that were themselves choked with a jumbled traffic of miscellaneous objects and clutter – statues, machine guns, paintings, oil drums, even a pair of old motorbikes. Suspended from the ceiling at the back of the cavern, covering almost its entire rear wall, was a huge flag – red, white and black with, at its centre, a crooked-armed swastika.

'Oh fuck,' repeated Layla.

They moved forward onto the elevator platform again, the generator thudding and growling behind them, their Maglites clasped redundantly in their hands.

'We're never going to find it,' she murmured. 'It's impossible. It'll take days, weeks.'

Ben-Roi said nothing, just ran his eyes back and forth around the cavern. Ten seconds passed, then he held out his torch, pointing.

'No it won't.'

Beneath them, running the length of the cavern from the elevator to the rear wall, was a broad central aisle, the only part of the floor that was reasonably clear of clutter. At its far end, standing alone directly beneath the Nazi flag as though it had deliberately been set apart, was a single large crate, square, about the height of a man.

'That's the one,' he said.

'Yes,' whispered Layla. 'Yes.'

They stared at it, then, picking up the crowbar again, Ben-Roi eased forward the elevator's control lever. There was a loud click, and with a tremble and a judder the wooden platform slowly began to descend, rumbling downwards with a rattle of machinery before jerking to a halt a few centimetres above the cavern floor. They stepped off and started walking, their feet falling sound-lessly onto the flat stone, the stacks of crates rising like walls to either side of them, the cavern somehow feeling even more vast and imposing now that they were viewing it from ground level. About halfway along the growl of the generator momentarily faltered, plunging them into dark-ness for a few seconds before the motor recov-ered itself and the cavern once more flooded with icy light. They paused, waiting to see if it would happen again, then continued walking, the Nazi flag looming ever larger in front of them, the crate coming ever closer, until eventually they came to a halt a couple of metres in front of it, their breathing fast and uneven, their foreheads glistening with sweat. Ben-Roi held the crowbar out to Layla.

'Lady's privilege.'

She hesitated, noting how dilated his pupils had suddenly become, sensing that whatever he'd been plotting these last few days it was fast approaching its denouement. Then, taking the bar and laying aside her torch, she stepped up to the crate.

'The moment of truth,' she said, forcing a nervous smile across her face.

'Oh yes,' whispered Ben-Roi.

The crate's back left-hand corner was damaged, the wood cracked and splintered, and, going round to it, she worked the bar's head into the gap and began to prise off the lid. It was securely fixed and she had to fight to get it moving. Ben-Roi stood watching her.

'Galia,' he said after a moment.

'Sorry?'

'Her name was Galia.'

She pulled the bar out and moved it a little further along, yanking it down with all her weight.

'Whose name?'

'In my living room. The photograph. Of the woman. You asked who it was. Her name was Galia.'

She looked up at him. What the hell was he talking about?

'Right,' she said.

'My fiancée.'

'Right,' she repeated.

The lid was starting to come now, the nails whining and squeaking as one after the other they were torn from their housings. She moved round to the side of the crate and then the front so that her back was to Ben-Roi, yanking and heaving. Behind her the Israeli had begun flipping his torch from one hand to the other, eyes fixed on the back of her head.

'We were going to get married.'

There were only a couple of nails left now. Beneath the lid she could see a mass of yellow straw.

'Beside the Sea of Galilee,' he said. 'At sunrise. It's beautiful at that time of day.'

Layla threw a glance over her shoulder – why the fuck was he telling her this? – then turned back to the crate.

'What happened?' she asked. 'She ditch you?'

The torch came to rest in Ben-Roi's right hand.

'She got blown up.'

Layla's shoulders tensed.

'A week before the wedding. In Jerusalem. Hagar Square. Al-Mulatham.'

There was a loud shearing sound and the last of the nails gave, the lid levering backwards and dropping to the floor with a clatter. She barely noticed. Oh God, she thought, that's what this is all about. They killed his fucking fiancée. And now . . .

Behind her she could feel Ben-Roi stepping forward, raising a hand. With a furious, desperate burst of energy she swung, lashing out at him with the crowbar, trying to drive him away, protect herself. He was ready for her, ducking the blow and smashing her across the side of the face with the Maglite barrel, sending her sprawling to the floor.

'You have to believe me,' she choked, groggy, confused, feeling his knees pushing into the small of her back as he came down on top of her. 'I'm not . . .'

She felt her knapsack unzipping, his hand swirling around inside it, then his palm slapping beneath her chin and yanking her head back. He was snarling like an animal.

'I wear Manio, you murdering Arab bitch!' he spat. 'You understand? I wear Manio! Now, where the fuck is he? Tell me! Tell me or I'll break your fucking neck!'

In the end the climb up to the mine wasn't quite as bad as Khalifa had expected, although it was bad enough, particularly the last section when the cold really started to bite into his hands and feet. The fact that Ben-Roi and Layla had already forced a path through the drifted snow made the going easier than it would otherwise have been, however, and by stopping every hundred metres or so to light some of the paper he'd brought with him and frantically rubbing his hands over the transient conflagration of maps, fax sheets and log-book pages, he was able, if not exactly to stay warm at least to prevent himself freezing to death.

At the top, at the forest edge, he paused for a moment to get his bearings, the world silent apart from the lurch of his breath and the soft crack-ling of icy twigs, then moved towards the mine. As he did so, picking his way across the clearing, he became aware of another sound, a sort of vague throbbing grumble, so faint as to be barely audible, but growing stronger the further he went. By the time he reached the mine entrance it had resolved itself into the distant but unmistakable growl of a generator motor.

He stepped into the shaft and stopped, listening. The noise was definitely coming from within, although where exactly he couldn't tell. He craned his head forward, squinting into the murk, but aside from a small section of wall and floor directly in front of him that was dimly visible in the glow from the moon outside, he could see nothing, just velvety, impenetrable blackness. He clicked on his cigarette lighter and, holding it aloft, started shuf-fling his way along the corridor, the rumble of the generator growing more distinct with every step, the beating of his heart more violent.

He went twenty metres, then halted. There was something ahead, barely discernible, a sort of dim, ghostly haze hovering in the air hard against the tunnel's right-hand wall, like a will-o'-the-wisp. He rubbed his eyes, thinking perhaps he was imagining it, then moved on again, the haze seeming to expand and thicken the closer he came to it until he realized that what he was seeing was not some paranormal apparition but a faint corona of light issuing from an opening in the shaft's right-hand wall. He came up to it and, bending, looked through into the tunnel beyond.

'*Allah-u-akhbar!*' he mumbled, taking in the shadowy rows of boxes and crates, the brightly lit cavern at the tunnel's far end.

He clambered through. As he did so he heard what sounded distinctly like a woman's scream. He straightened, listening – yes, there it was again, definitely a scream – then continued to walk. Two metres in he found an open crate packed with rifles. Mauser, the same as he'd used at police training school. He pulled one out, examined it, then banged in an ammunition clip, slipped a spare clip into his pocket and continued on his way, the glow at the end of the tunnel getting ever brighter, the putter of the generator ever louder until eventually, blinking, he emerged onto the broad stone platform on which Layla and Ben-Roi had been standing fifteen minutes earlier.

At the same moment the generator stalled for a second time, the cavern lights blinking and failing so that barely had his eyes had time to take in the high arched ceiling, the mass of boxes and crates, and the giant Nazi flag hanging from the rear wall before everything was suddenly swamped in a giddy tide of blackness. He froze, disorientated, remaining that way for what seemed like an age but was in reality only a few seconds before the motor somehow coughed itself back into life again. As swiftly as it had invaded the cavern, the darkness was driven off by a brilliant burst of light. He crossed to the front of the ledge, dropped to one knee and, raising the rifle, played its muzzle back and forth over the sea of crates beneath.

'Ben-Roi!'

No response.

'Ben-Roi! Are you there?'

Still no response, and he was about to shout a third time when, like a snarling wolf bursting from a thicket, the Israeli's voice suddenly raged upwards from below.

'Khalifa, you stupid cunt! What the fuck are you doing here?'

There was movement about a third of the way down the gallery, and Ben-Roi emerged from between two crates, a Schmeisser sub-machine gun held in one hand, the other clasped around the collar of Layla's jacket. He dragged her out into the middle of the central aisle and yanked her to her knees. There was blood caked around her nose, and a fan of bruising on her upper left cheek, purple, like a birthmark.

'You animal,' Khalifa thought. 'You dirty Jew animal.'

He clicked back the bolt of the rifle and sighted down the barrel.

'Drop the gun, Ben-Roi!'

The Israeli's mouth was twisting this way and that, his eyes wide, bulging and bloodshot. He looked crazy, deranged.

'Listen to me, Khalifa!'

'I was top marksman in my class and I'm aiming right between your eyes,' shouted the Egyptian, finger tightening around the trigger. 'Now, drop the gun.'

'Listen, you fucking idiot!'

'Drop the gun!'

'He's coming! You understand? Al-Mulatham. He's coming here. For the Menorah! She works for him. She fucking works for him.'

In front of him Layla was staring up at Khalifa, her eyes frantic, imploring. She gave a faint shake of the head and mouthed the word *la* – no. Khalifa shifted his weight slightly, trying to keep the rifle steady despite the trembling of his hands.

'I'm not going to tell you again, Ben-Roi. Drop the gun and move away!'

'For fuck's sake. Khalifa,' bellowed the Israeli. 'She admitted it. She works for him. He's coming! He killed Galia and now he's coming here!'

His voice had risen to the point where it was now almost a scream. He's cracked, thought Khalifa. Having some sort of breakdown.

'Just drop the gun and we can talk,' he cried.

'There's no time, you fucking fool! He's coming! Al-Mulatham's coming.'

He seized a handful of Layla's hair, stabbing the gun against the back of her head.

'Tell him!' he cried. 'Tell him what you told me!'

'Leave her, Ben-Roi!'

'Tell him, you bitch!'

'Ben-Roi!'

'How you recruit the bombers! How that whole article was a lie! Tell him, you murdering Arab whore!'

He was shaking her like a rag doll, jerking her head back and forth.

'Please!' she screamed.

Khalifa increased the pressure on the trigger, taking it almost as far back as it would go. He yelled another warning, then, when the Israeli showed no sign of backing off, fired, aiming at the floor just to his left. The bullet pinged off the stone, pinged off the back wall, ricocheted away into the crate stacks. Ben-Roi froze, his breath coming in short, desperate gasps, his eyes blazing insanely. For a brief moment he just stood like that; then, with a snarl of impotent fury, he released Layla's hair and took a step backwards, the machine gun still clutched in his hand. Khalifa jerked back the bolt to engage another bullet. Layla slumped to the floor.

'Thank God,' she coughed, clasping her head, wincing. She took a couple of breaths, then looked up at Khalifa. 'He's working for Har-Zion,' she croaked. 'The Warriors of David. They know about the Menorah. They're following us.'

The Israeli let out an incredulous bark of laughter, eyes flicking wildly from Khalifa to Layla and back to Khalifa again.

'That's bullshit!' he spat. 'She's bluffing you!'

'It's the truth! I've seen them. In Jerusalem, at the airport. He's been feeding them information all along.'

'She's lying, Khalifa! She's fucking lying!'

'He's been playing us all,' she said, stumbling up onto her feet, backing away against a crate. 'You, me, everybody. He's Chayalei David. They're coming for the Lamp. They're going to start a fucking war.'

'Don't believe her!'

'We have to get it out. Before it's too late.'

'You lying Arab . . .'

He took a step towards her, raising the Schmeisser. Khalifa fired off another shot, the bullet again ricocheting around the cavern before disappearing among the box stacks.

'That's the last warning, Ben-Roi!' he shouted, working the bolt. 'Now drop it!'

'You don't know what you're doing!' screamed the Israeli, flecks of spittle bursting from between his lips. 'Please, Khalifa, you have to believe me. I've been watching her, following her. She works for al-Mulatham!'

He was starting to jabber. With a superhuman effort he reined himself in, slowed his delivery.

'Listen,' he said, drawing in great gulps of breath, his voice straining with the effort of holding itself steady, 'she wrote an article. A year ago. Just after Galia died. An interview, with al-Mulatham. She said he was wearing aftershave – Manio. Said she recognized it. But I wear Manio, Khalifa, and she didn't recognize it. I wear Manio and she had to ask me what aftershave I was wearing. She didn't know. She didn't fucking know!'

Khalifa flicked a bemused glance down at Layla, who raised her eyebrows as if to say 'I don't understand either.' Ben-Roi caught the exchange, jerked his head in frustration.

'For God's sake, you must see!' he cried. 'It was fiction. She made it up. The aftershave, the meeting, the whole fucking article. She invented it. To put people off the trail. To protect the real al-Mulatham. To protect her master.'

His voice was speeding up again. He fought to control himself, raising a hand and clasping it around the menorah at his neck.

'I've investigated her. Ever since that article. A whole year. Every bomber, Khalifa. Every fucking al-Mulatham bomber – she's interviewed them all. Every single one. That's how he recruits them. Through her. She interviews them, makes sure they're suitable, then passes their names along. That's how the whole thing works. That's the system. She's in it up to her neck!'

'He's crazy!'

'Explain it, then!' he yelled, glaring at Layla, his

eyes so wide and wild it looked as if they were going to burst right out of his head. 'Explain how it is that every al-Mulatham bomber happens to be someone you've interviewed!'

'I can't explain it!' she cried, shaking her head helplessly, her own voice now beginning to rise. 'Coincidence, I'm being set up . . . I don't know! I went through all this with Shin Bet after I wrote the article.'

'She had a tracker on her, for fuck's sake!' Ben-Roi fumbled in his pocket, withdrew a small metal object about the size of a cigarette packet, brandished it triumphantly in the air. 'It was in her bag, Khalifa! He's following us. Al-Mulatham. He's fucking following us!'

'They went through my bag at the airport,' she cried. 'There's no way I could have got something like that through.'

'Then how? How?'

'I don't know!' she yelled, raising a hand to her forehead, confused suddenly, disorientated. 'Someone must have planted it on me. I don't know!'

'You filthy lying bitch!' bellowed the Israeli, no longer making any attempt to sound calm or rational. 'Don't believe a word she says, Khalifa. She's play-acting. She works for al-Mulatham. She's always worked for al-Mulatham. She's a murderer! She murdered my Galia!'

'We're all murderers as far as he's concerned!' she screamed. 'Every Palestinian, every Arab.

715

Al-Mulatham killed his fiancée and we're all to blame. That's why he sold out to Har-Zion.'

'Bullshit, you fucking bitch!'

'They're following us!'

'Don't believe her, Khalifa! She's a filthy fucking—'

A third shot rang out, silencing them, the bullet disappearing harmlessly into a heap of tarpaulins, the cavern echoing to the sharp retort of the rifle. Layla sank back against a crate, Ben-Roi stood with his arms at his side, both staring upwards at the stone platform, motionless, like defendants awaiting a verdict in a courtroom. Khalifa bit his lip, blinked away a pearl of sweat that had dropped onto his eye-lid, tried to get his thoughts clear. That Layla was right about Ben-Roi he had no doubt. Yet there was something in the Israeli's eyes, the way he had pleaded his case . . .

Mohammed Gemal, that's who it reminded him of, during the Schlegel interrogation all those years ago – the same desperate fury, the same frantic, wide-eyed protestations of innocence. Gemal had turned out to be telling the truth. But Ben-Roi . . . The words of his father echoed at the back of his mind: *Be careful of them, Yusuf. Always be careful of the Jews.*

He blinked away another sweat droplet, gazed from Layla to Ben-Roi and back to Layla again, then snapped back the rifle bolt.

'Drop the gun, Ben-Roi.'

'No!'

'Drop it and get on your knees!'

'You don't know what you're doing! You don't know what you're doing, you stupid Arab—'

A fourth shot rang out, the bullet grazing the floor less than an inch from Ben-Roi's right foot. The Israeli looked down, up, to the side, eyes flaring like sparks of molten steel, his mouth so contorted with fury it looked as if the whole lower part of his face was going to shear away; then, with a high animal howl of despair and impotence, he cast the Schmeisser aside and sank to his knees. Layla hurried across, snatched up the weapon and, backing away, motioned him down onto his belly.

'These Warriors of David people,' called Khalifa. 'How long before they—'

He broke off, silenced by the cold nudge of a gun barrel in the nape of his neck.

'I think that answers your question. Now, put the rifle on the floor and raise your hands.'

For a fraction of a second Khalifa thought about trying to shout a warning to Layla. It was a suicidal notion, and he dismissed it before it had even fully formed, laying the Mauser on the ground and locking his fingers on top of his head. The gun barrel was withdrawn and a rough hand yanked his arm up behind his back, hoisting him to his feet and turning him.

There were six of them, including the one holding his arm – tough, stern, expressionless, all wearing ski-jackets and, somewhat incongruously, black skullcaps. Five were armed with Uzis. The sixth, the eldest and, it seemed, the one who had just spoken – a squat, thickset man with gloved hands and a pale, heavily bearded face – was clutching a Heckler and Koch pistol. With the pristine clarity of thought that fear confers, Khalifa instantly recognized him from the picture on the front of the *Time* magazine in Piet Jansen's living room: Baruch Har-Zion.

'You bastard, Ben-Roi,' he thought. 'You lying Jew bastard.'

Words were exchanged in a language he didn't understand, Hebrew presumably, and as one the group moved to the front of the ledge, the man holding Khalifa's arm yanking him around so that he was again looking out over the sea of boxes. By this point Layla had clocked there was something going on above and had shrunk back against one of the crates, her face white, her Schmeisser still covering Ben-Roi, who was lying face down on the floor. For a moment Khalifa was worried the Israelis were going to start shooting, but they merely stood staring down at her, stony-faced, their Uzis held ready at their sides, while one of their number – a tall, crew-cut man who seemed to be Har-Zion's second-in-command – stepped right up to the edge of the stone balcony and leant out, gazing at the elevator below.

There was another muttered exchange, then, slinging his Uzi over his shoulder, the crew-cut man turned, dropped to his knees and, shuffling backwards, eased himself over the ledge's lip and started to climb down, using one of the vertical elevator tracks as a ladder. Thirty seconds passed, and then there was a whirr of machinery as the elevator started to ascend, the man slowly rising before them as though levitating. When he was level with the ledge he cut the power and, at a nod from Har-Zion, they all moved onto the platform, Khalifa's arm still jammed up behind his back, the barrel of an Uzi pressed into his ear. Another nod and they began to descend, the stage sliding downwards with a rattle and a judder before jerking to a halt at the bottom.

On the floor, Ben-Roi was trying to crane his head around to see what was going on; Layla had moved out into the centre of the aisle and half-raised her Schmeisser as if to block their path. As they came up to her Khalifa tried to catch her attention, convey that she should stay calm, not do anything stupid, but her focus was locked on Har-Zion. For a moment the two of them just stood staring at each other, eyes glued, his grey and hard as granite, hers emerald green and fierce, a faintly defiant twist to her mouth. Then, with a nod, she handed her gun to one of Har-Zion's men, swiped a cuff across her bloodied nose and stepped aside.

'You took your bloody time.'

It was so unexpected it was a moment before Khalifa actually realized what she'd said. When he did, his mouth fell open in shock. On the floor, head twisted round at an unnatural angle as he struggled to peer at them over his shoulder, Ben-Roi likewise didn't seem immediately to register what was going on, his eyes jinking this way and that, his features spooling through a whole slew of expressions before finally settling themselves into a grimace of horrified disbelief.

'Oh God,' he whispered, turning away and pressing his forehead into the cold stone floor. 'Oh please God no.'

For a moment everyone remained motionless, the scene freeze-framed; then, slowly, Ben-Roi heaved himself up onto his knees and then his feet, dazed, like a boxer rising drunkenly from the canvas. Layla backed away so that she was standing with the Israelis, her eyes flicking momentarily towards Khalifa, a faint rash of red staining her cheeks – whether from shame or some wholly different emotion the Egyptian couldn't tell. Ben-Roi no longer seemed to notice her, his gaze now focused exclusively on Har-Zion.

'The Palestinians simply aren't that good,' he murmured, voice tight with suppressed fury. 'The way the brotherhood operates is way too sophisticated for a renegade Palestinian cell. The impetus has to be external.'

Khalifa was still trying to marshall his thoughts, work out what was going on.

'I don't understand,' he mumbled, looking from Ben-Roi to Layla to Har-Zion and back to

Ben-Roi again. The latter's face had completely drained of colour, the skin a dirty translucent white, like stained alabaster.

'It's like I told you, Khalifa. She works for al-Mulatham. Recruits his bombers, writes bullshit articles about him, just like I said. Only one thing I missed.' Ben-Roi's fists clenched, eyes never leaving Har-Zion. 'It turns out al-Mulatham's been murdering his own people.'

Again it took the Egyptian a moment to process this, to get his thoughts arranged.

'You mean . . . ?'

Ben-Roi's entire body had started trembling.

'He's al-Mulatham,' he snarled. 'He's the one who's controlling it. Arab bombers, Israeli master. Butchering his own people. His own fucking people!'

Khalifa stared aghast, the entire cavern seeming to contract around them. There was a momentary silence, then, with a shocking animal howl of loathing and fury, Ben-Roi launched himself forward. He was a powerful man, but he was also overweight, exhausted and up against professionals. Before he had even got close to his target two of Har-Zion's men stepped up and, with cool, choreographed precision, halted him in his tracks, one smashing an Uzi butt into his stomach, doubling him over, the other coming round behind him and taking him in an arm-lock, yanking him upright again. Khalifa tensed, fists clenching, but with a gun pressed into the side of his head there was nothing he could do. Layla stared down at the floor, the red on her cheeks deepening and spreading.

'Why?' choked Ben-Roi, gasping for air, struggling against the arm-lock. 'In God's name, why?'

Har-Zion rolled his shoulders, trying to ease the constricting clasp of his burnt skin, which was becoming increasingly tight and itchy beneath his jacket.

'To save our people,' he replied, his voice, in contrast to Ben-Roi's, cold, measured and toneless.

'By butchering them?'

'By proving to them once and for all that there can never be peace with the Arabs. That their purpose is and always has been to destroy us, and that to survive we have no choice but to do the same to them.'

Ben-Roi bucked, struggled, spat.

'You killed her!' he choked. 'You killed her, you filthy animal!'

Again Har-Zion rolled his shoulders. His face was empty.

'If there was any other road I would gladly take it. But there is no other road. Our people have to see the Arabs for what they truly are.'

'Hamas aren't doing a good enough job of it?' screamed Ben-Roi. 'Islamic Jihad?'

'Unfortunately not.'

'Unfortunately?'

'Yes, unfortunately,' said Har-Zion, his tone hardening slightly, his eyes betraying the first vague flicker of emotion. 'Unfortunately because however many of us they kill, still we try to convince ourselves that if only we negotiate, concede a little, then everything will be all right, everything will be OK, they will leave us alone to bring up our children in peace and security.'

'You're fucking mad!'

'No,' snapped Har-Zion, the annoyance in his eyes now unmistakable, 'it is those who speak of compromise and retreat who are mad! It was compromise that fired the ovens of Auschwitz, retreat that dug the death pits at Babi Yar. And now we're intent on making the same mistake again, the mistake we have always made, year after year, century after century, the cardinal error of the Jewish people: to believe for a single moment that the *goyim* can ever be trusted, can ever be our friends, desire anything other than to herd us into the gas chambers and wipe us from the face of the earth!'

His voice was starting to rise, the words barking from his mouth like bullets from the muzzle of a gun.

'We don't need peace processes,' he spat. 'Treaties, accords, road maps, conferences – none of it. If we wish to survive we need one thing and one thing alone, and that is fury. The same fury that has been directed at us through all the long, dark night of our history. It is this alone that will protect us, give us the strength to survive. And it is this that al-Mulatham has provided. This is why we have made him. That is why he exists.'

He broke off, his high, pale forehead beaded with sweat, little shivers running through his body from the itching of his skin, which was starting to become unbearable, as it always did when he failed to apply his balm at the appointed time. Ben-Roi stared at him, no longer bothering to struggle against the arm-lock, his eyes dull and glazed, his mouth opening and shutting as though unable to find any words appropriate to convey the depth of his loathing.

'*Moser*,' he whispered eventually. '*Rodef.*'

Har-Zion's lips tightened. He held the detective's gaze, then raised a gloved hand and motioned to the man with crew-cut hair, who stepped forward and, without actually seeming to draw back his arm, slammed his fist into the base of Ben-Roi's pelvis, just a few centimetres above his groin.

'*Allah-u-akhbar*,' mumbled Khalifa, wincing, fists clenched impotently at his side.

Ben-Roi let out a deep, choking gargle and slumped, his legs giving way beneath him. He was hauled up again, punched again, this time at the very top of his chest, just beneath his throat, then left to sink down onto his knees, and then his elbows, a narrow string of vomit dribbling from his mouth onto the stone floor.

'There is only one traitor here and that is you,' said Har-Zion, standing over him, his voice back to its former cold, measured monotone. 'You and, from what I have heard of her, your fiancée too. There are deaths I regret, but hers is not one of them.'

Ben-Roi mumbled something and tried to flail out an arm, but he was still winded from the punches and there was no power in the movement. Har-Zion signalled again and the crew-cut man slammed his heel into the side of Ben-Roi's head, splitting the top of his ear, sending him crashing into a crate.

'Stop it!' shouted Khalifa, no longer able to contain himself, the Uzi pressing into the back of his neck forgotten in the shock of revulsion he felt at what he was witnessing. 'In God's name, stop it!'

Har-Zion turned, slowly, stiffly. He stared at the Egyptian, a hard, unpleasant look, then said something in Hebrew. The Uzi was lowered and Khalifa suddenly found himself clasped in a suffocating neck-lock. On the floor, Ben-Roi had struggled up into a sitting position, his torn ear streaming blood.

'Let him go, Har-Zion,' he rasped. 'He's not part of this.'

Har-Zion let out a derisive snort. 'You hear that? Us he condemns for defending our own people while he pleads for his friend the Arab. Whatever else he is, believe me, this piece of shit most certainly isn't a Jew.'

He nodded to the crew-cut man, who raised his

boot again and crunched it down into Ben-Roi's crotch, the detective convulsing in agony. Then he crossed to Khalifa and without pausing drove his fist straight into the Egyptian's solar plexus, the blow delivered with the controlled, businesslike precision of a surgeon dissecting a cadaver. Khalifa had been hit before, numerous times – half his youth seemed to have been spent getting into fist-fights in the Giza backstreets where he'd grown up – but never anything like this. The fist seemed to sink halfway into his stomach cavity, splaying his vital organs, driving the air out of his lungs. A tangled kaleidoscope of thoughts and images swirled through his mind – Zenab, the patch of snow at the motorway service station, that strange blue-eyed man in the synagogue in Cairo – before suddenly, unexpectedly, just for a moment, the mist of pain evaporated and he found himself looking up into the eyes of Layla al-Madani.

'*Ley?*' he whispered. 'Why?'

If she responded he didn't hear, because almost as soon as it had come the moment of clarity disappeared again. His mind clouded, his head dropped back, and then everything went dark.

How long he remained unconscious he couldn't be certain, but it must have been a while because when he came to he was being dragged down the central aisle by two of the Israelis, feet trailing uselessly on the floor ('They're scuffing my nice shoes!' was his first, incoherent thought). Ben-Roi was ahead of him, limping along with an Uzi pressed into the back of his head, his neck and jacket stained with a congealed crust of blood from his torn ear; Har-Zion and Layla were now at the far end of the cavern, watching as the crew-cut man worked at the front panel of the Menorah crate with a jemmy. As they came up to it, the panel sheared off with a squeal of rending wood, revealing a dense block of straw from within which peeped tantalizing glints of gold.

Realizing that their prisoner had regained consciousness, the Israelis hoisted Khalifa upright and pushed him roughly against one of the box stacks, a wave of nausea causing everything to bulge and swim around him before gradually settling down again. Ben-Roi was beside him, and for a moment their eyes met and held, each giving the faintest of nods to acknowledge the other's presence, to indicate they were OK, before turning away again and focusing their attention on the scene in front of them.

There was a pause, the atmosphere charged suddenly, expectant; then, stepping forward, Har-Zion and his second-in-command started stripping away the protective straw. Their bodies blocked Khalifa's view so that he was only able to catch vague glimpses of the object they were revealing – a curving arm, the corner of a pedestal, fleeting flashes of gold – and it was not until the thing had been revealed in its entirety and the two men had stepped back and to the side that he was able to view it properly.

He had seen it before, of course, in the photograph in Dieter Hoth's safe deposit box. That had been in black and white, however, and had wholly failed to convey the full, breathtaking magnificence of the artwork at which he now found himself staring. It was about the height of a man, its base made up of two hexagonal tiers from the centre of which, as though from some ornate pot, a vertical stem shot upwards, six branches curving outwards from its sides, three to the left, three to the right, one above the other, each crowned, as was the stem, by a lamp-cup cast in the shape of a small cymbal. Such was the Menorah's basic form. There was more to it than that, however, so much more. Its branches were decorated in the most exquisite manner with knops and bulbs and calices shaped like almond-blossoms; around its base were wonderfully worked images in raised relief of fruits and leaves and vines and flowers, so lifelike you almost felt you could smell their fragrance. Its gold was so deep it was almost red; its symmetry possessed of such perfect balance, such sinuous, effortless poise, that it seemed not to be cast of metal at all but rather to be something alive, something that grew, breathed and coursed with sap. Groggy, in pain and probably with not long left to live, Khalifa could still not help but be awed by it, his head shaking from side to side at the sheer glittering splendour of the thing. The Israelis' reaction was even more intense, Ben-Roi muttering 'Oy vey' over and over again; Har-Zion's granite face had softened into an almost childlike expression of rapture.

'And God said let there be light,' he whispered, 'and there was light. And God saw that the light was good.'

Only one person seemed unmoved by the whole thing, and that was Layla. She stood slightly apart from everyone else, barricaded inside her head, betraying no emotion whatsoever unless it was in the faint red stain that still marked her upper cheeks, and in the way her hands seemed involuntarily to clench and unclench. For the briefest of moments her eyes snagged on Khalifa's before immediately swerving away again, unable to hold his stare.

Several minutes passed, everyone just gazing at the Lamp, its beauty, far from diminishing with familiarity, actually increasing as the full richness and subtlety of its decoration became apparent, until eventually the spell was broken by the crew-cut man.

'We should get it out,' he said, his voice sounding harsh and crude, like a rock thrown into a pool of still water.

For a moment Har-Zion didn't respond, just continued staring, eyes moist with emotion. Then, with a nod, he motioned to three of his men. They stepped forward, draping their Uzis round their necks, and grasped the Lamp, counting *echat, shtayim, shalosh* – one, two, three – before starting to lift. Fit and muscle-bound as they were, its weight was too much for them, and it was only when they were joined by a fourth man that they were able to manhandle it up onto their shoulders, faces contorting with the strain, legs buckling.

Steiner levelled his gun at Khalifa and Ben-Roi, and, as one, the group started to move back down the aisle, stopping every twenty metres so that the Lamp-carriers could catch their breath. Eventually they reached the far end of the cavern and the Lamp was lowered onto the elevator platform, its wooden planks creaking beneath the weight. The Israelis climbed up beside it, Layla going with them, and the control lever was eased back, the detectives remaining on the cavern floor as the platform slowly ascended in front of them. Three metres up it came to a halt again, a line of Uzi muzzles pointing down.

'This is where we part company, gentlemen,' Har-Zion called, his mouth curved into a triumphant smile. 'Us, by God's providence, to begin the rebuilding of the Temple and the inauguration of a new golden age for our people. You . . .'

He gazed down at them for a moment, again rotating his shoulders to try to loosen the suffocating glove of burnt skin in which his body was clamped. Then he indicated that his men should fire.

'No!'

Layla's voice echoed shrilly around the cavern. 'No!' she repeated. And then again: 'No!'

Har-Zion's men looked at their leader, but he gave no signal, either to shoot or to lower the guns, so they remained as they were, fingers tight around the Uzis' triggers. Below, on the cavern floor, Ben-Roi and Khalifa exchanged a glance.

'No!' Layla yelled for a fourth time, her tone desperate, hysterical almost, hands clenching and unclenching. She had wanted to speak out before, when they had beaten the two men, but she hadn't been able to do it, choked as she was with shame and self-loathing. Now, however, she couldn't stop herself, barely even conscious of what she was saying, just sensing that her entire existence had somehow narrowed itself to the focus of this moment, and that despite it all, despite the years of lies and betrayal, she could not just stand mute while two people were shot dead in cold blood in front of her. Pointless, of course, given how many people had been butchered over the years because of her actions, how indelibly steeped in blood she was. There could never be any redemption from what she had done. Nor was she looking for it. All she knew was that as she had stood there gazing down at the two detectives – their faces pale, resigned – her father's voice had suddenly rung out inside her head like a clear bell, stronger than it had ever rung out before. The words he had spoken on the night of his death:

I can't leave someone to die in the dust like a dog, Layla. Whoever they might be.

And as soon as she had heard those words she had experienced a fierce, uncontrollable yearning to know that there was still something of her father left deep inside, some last tiny lingering vestige of his beautiful light. That she was still his daughter, however dark the world she had made for herself.

She pushed to the front of the elevator, eyes catching Khalifa's for a fraction of a second before she turned to face the Israelis, her slim body blocking their line of fire.

'You've won,' she cried at Har-Zion. 'Don't you see that? You've won, for God's sake. Just leave them. For once, just stop the killing and leave them.'

There was a pause, the cavern throbbing with the roar of the generator, the Menorah glinting in the glare of the arc lamps. Then, slowly, Har-Zion nodded.

'She is right. It is time for the killing to stop.'

Layla's body seemed to relax slightly. Almost immediately she tensed again as she noted the cold smile spreading across Har-Zion's face.

'Or at least some of the killing. These' – he waved stiffly towards Khalifa and Ben-Roi – 'their lives mean nothing. Al-Mulatham, however – he, I believe, has served his purpose. As Miss al-Madani says, we have won. With the Menorah on our side our cause is unstoppable. One final reckoning, and then we can dispense with the Palestinian

Brotherhood altogether. And all the apparatus that goes with it. *All* the apparatus.'

As he said this last phrase he glanced across at his crew-cut sidekick, at the same time tipping his head towards Layla. The man nodded in understanding and, with shocking calmness, stepped forward and slammed his palm hard into Layla's right breast, launching her backwards off the elevator platform and out into space, arms and legs flailing. For a brief moment she just seemed to hang there, hovering in mid-air as if suspended from the ceiling of the cavern by an invisible wire; then she cart-wheeled silently downwards and slammed to the floor with a sickening thud.

'Thank you, Miss al-Madani,' called Har-Zion. 'The state of Israel will be eternally grateful for your efforts. Arab or not, you have indeed earned yourself the title *Eshet Hayil*. A woman of valour.'

She knew immediately that her back was broken, probably a load of other things as well, although since she seemed to have no feeling from the neck down she couldn't be sure. It didn't much matter. She'd be dead in a few short moments anyway. Which was fine by her.

Strangely, as if to compensate for the fact that she could no longer feel anything, her other senses seemed suddenly to grow much sharper. Her nostrils quivered with the rich, resinous tang of the pine planks from which the crates were made; her ears seemed almost unnaturally attuned to sounds that in normal circumstances she would never have noticed. Most curious of all, she seemed to have developed the uncanny ability to see four or five different things all at once, without even moving her head. There was Har-Zion, standing up above on the lift, laughing with his followers; Ben-Roi a little to her left, looking unexpectedly shocked given how much he must have wanted something like this to happen to her; and, kneeling right beside her holding her hand – how on earth had he got there so quickly? – Khalifa. She could even see her own face, as if she was standing above herself looking down, the very faintest of smiles twisting the corners of her mouth, although there was no humour or satisfaction in it, more a sort of infinite, despairing loneliness that could find no other expression with which to manifest itself.

She'd always known it would end like this. Ever since she'd come back from England all those years ago and started working as an informer for Har-Zion and Israeli Military Intelligence. The precise circumstances were a surprise – in a giant cave full of looted Nazi treasure, for God's sake! – but not the violence. That had always been a given. Frankly, she was surprised she'd lasted this long.

Beside her, Khalifa was saying something, although she couldn't seem to hear his voice, which was strange given how many other less tangible noises she was picking up. She didn't need to hear, though, because she could make out what he was saying from the movement of his lips. It was just one word, repeated over and over again, a question, the same question he'd asked her earlier.

Ley? Why?

What could she say? Nothing, really. She would have liked to explain. Really she would. Let at least one person know. Deathbed confession and all that. But then, how could she? How could she ever make him understand? Make anyone understand? That she had done what she had done not for any of the usual reasons people collaborated – money, coercion, ideology. No, she had done it because on the night of her fifteenth birthday, on a dirty patch of waste-ground on the edge of Jabaliya refugee camp, beneath a star-filled sky and with wild dogs howling in the distance, she had watched the person she loved more than any other in the world, her beautiful, brave, gentle father, the greatest man there had ever been, being beaten to death with a baseball bat. By his own people. Watched over by his own people. That's why she'd contacted Har-Zion and offered to work for him. That's why she'd gone along with the whole al-Mulatham thing; that's why, the moment she had found out about the Menorah, she had called Har-Zion from the Church of the Holy Sepulchre, done everything she could to secure the Lamp for him. Because they'd killed the only person she had ever really loved, and because from that moment forth she had hated them, all of them, vowed that whatever else she did with her life she would make them pay for that, suffer for it, every last Palestinian. That was the reason. That was the answer. But how could she explain it? Make him understand? Communicate even a fraction of the misery and pain and hatred and torment that had consumed her all these years? She couldn't. It was impossible. Beyond her powers to illuminate. Always had been, always would be. She was just so desperately alone.

She looked up into Khalifa's face – a kind face, brave, handsome; like her father in many ways – and tried to squeeze his hand. At the same moment, with that curious gift of multiple sight that she seemed to have acquired as a result of her fall, she could see above her that Har-Zion had extended an arm and was aiming his pistol directly at her head. Go on, she thought, just do it. It's time. At least I tried to do one good thing before the end. One thing my daddy might have been proud of.

She closed her eyes and there she was again, lying at the bottom of the hollow, clutching her father's hand, her dark hair soaking up his blood.

'Oh God, my daddy. Oh God, my poor daddy.'

And then the shot rang out.

Her head jerked and snapped, and a neat black hole opened up just above her left eyebrow, a ribbon of blood spooling out across her cheek and chin and down onto the floor where it formed itself into a viscous, plate-sized puddle. For a moment Khalifa was too shocked to move, her hand hanging limp in his, the echo of the gunshot rebounding angrily around the cavern; then, shaking his head, he laid the hand gently down, came to his feet and backed away so that he was standing beside Ben-Roi, the two of them gazing up at the line of Uzi muzzles above.

He should have felt scared. More scared than he did, given what was about to happen to him. Whether it was because he was still drained from the beating he had taken, or simply because his death was now so inevitable his body just couldn't see any point in getting worked up about it, he felt a curious sense of calm. Zenab and the kids, they were his only real concern. That and the fact that he probably wouldn't get a proper Muslim burial. But then he was sure Allah would understand. Allah understood everything. That's why he was . . . well, Allah.

He glanced across at Ben-Roi and their eyes met. There were people he would have preferred to die with. But then again, maybe he'd been a bit harsh on the guy. Rude, yes. Arrogant, belligerent. Not the sort of person he'd choose as a friend. He was a good cop though, seemed to have worked things out pretty well. And who knows, if his own wife had been killed like that, butchered needlessly, maybe he, Khalifa, would have ended up exactly the same. You never could tell. He tried to mumble something, to apologize, to admit that his earlier decision to trust Layla's word over Ben-Roi's had been informed not by an objective assessment of the situation, but rather by blind prejudice, by the fact that he simply couldn't bring himself to believe a Jew over one of his fellow Arabs. He couldn't seem to find the words, however, and fell silent again. They held each other's gaze a moment longer, then, with a nod, turned away and looked up at the elevator, fists clenching, waiting for the bullets.

Everything went black.

For a brief, confused instant, Khalifa thought he was dead. Almost immediately, from the shouts of Har-Zion's men, he realized the generator must have cut out again, killing the lights. So unexpected was it, and so disorientating, that he didn't react, just stood rooted to the spot. Ben-Roi's instincts kicked in quicker, the Israeli seizing Khalifa roughly by the collar and propelling them both forward out of the line of fire. A split-second later the Uzis opened up, the darkness torn by crackling bursts of red and white, bullets pinging off the floor and thudding away into the crate stacks with a rat-at-at of punctured wood. The detectives tripped, crashed down, somehow managed to find their feet again and stumbled on, eventually banging into the rock wall directly beneath the elevator platform. There were more shouts and, as abruptly as it had started, the shooting ceased. They froze, eyes straining against the blackness.

When it had cut out earlier the generator had restarted itself almost immediately; this time it remained silent. They could hear whispering, a torch came on, then another, and then there was a faint creak and slap as someone started climbing the vertical elevator track towards the ledge above, presumably to try to get the generator working again. One of the torch beams was shone upwards to light the climber's way; the other started arcing back and forth over the crate stacks in front of them, vainly trying to pick them out in the blackness. The possibility that they might be directly beneath seemed not to have occurred to Har-Zion's men. Not yet, at least.

'Must move,' whispered Ben-Roi, cupping a hand around Khalifa's ears, his voice so low as to be barely audible. 'Need to get among crates.'

Khalifa squeezed his arm to show he understood. A shout from above indicated that the climber had got himself up onto the balcony and was now moving towards the generator room.

'Must move,' hissed Ben-Roi again. 'No time.'

Twenty seconds ticked by, both of them frantically trying to come up with a suitable course of action, aware that the moment they emerged from beneath the platform they would almost certainly either be heard or picked up by the torch beam. Finally, in desperation, Khalifa drove a hand into his jacket pocket and yanked out the five-bullet ammunition clip he had put there earlier, pressing it against Ben-Roi's arm. The Israeli guessed immediately what he was thinking.

'Throw left,' he whispered. 'We go straight. Hold hands.'

'What?'

'So we don't lose each other, idiot!'

From above there was a loud mechanical sputter as Har-Zion's man started cranking the arm of the generator. At the same moment the torch beam suddenly slipped away from the crates and started circling the floor at the foot of the elevator. For a moment it lingered on Layla's body, then started moving backwards towards their hiding place. It was now only a matter of seconds before they were spotted. Grasping Ben-Roi's hand and drawing back his free arm, Khalifa lobbed the bullet clip as hard as he could towards the far side of the cavern. It seemed to remain airborne for an impossible length of time and the torch beam was swishing in front of the tips of their shoes when, with a loud clatter, it came down again.

The effect was instantaneous. The beam swept away and there was a stamp of feet as the Israelis moved towards the left side of the elevator, followed by a deafening rage of gunfire. The moment it began Khalifa and Ben-Roi started running, sprinting hand in hand straight ahead into the blackness, following what they guessed – hoped – was the line of the central aisle, wincing with every step lest they should slam face-first into a crate or some other impediment. Somehow they held their course, fear and adrenalin driving them on, covering about half the length of the cavern before they slowed, unlocked hands and felt their way into one of the narrow passages between the crate stacks, stumbling over the miscellaneous clutter of objects with which the passage was clogged. Behind them the gunfire gradually dropped off, and then stopped altogether.

They stood where they were, trying to catch their breath, the darkness smothering them like a swathe of black velvet, the cavern silent save for the repetitive thunk of the generator crank and the chatter of Israeli voices, low at first, but gradually becoming more urgent. Ben-Roi craned his neck, listening.

'Shit,' he whispered.

'What?'

'Fire.'

'What?'

'The shooting. It's set the crates alight.'

Even as he spoke their nostrils caught the first faint tang of burning wood.

'This place is a fucking powder-keg,' snarled Ben-Roi. 'It's going to fucking erupt!'

Khalifa didn't need to be told. He'd seen the cavern with his own eyes: oil drums, ammunition crates, explosives, stacks of tinder-dry wood.

'Dammit!' he hissed. 'Dammit!'

He flicked on his lighter and, cupping a hand over the flame to mask its light, began frantically casting around, searching for something, anything, they could use to fight their way out of the cavern. Har-Zion's men were shouting now, their voices increasingly panic-stricken as the fire apparently strengthened and spread. The coughing of the generator crank grew more urgent.

'Come on!' growled Ben-Roi. 'We need guns!'

'There aren't any!'

Khalifa pushed further into the crate passage, no longer caring about the noise he was making, weaving his lighter back and forth. He found paintings, sculptures, what looked like part of a large chandelier. No weapons, however, and he was beginning to get desperate when finally, hefting away a sack full of bank notes, he uncovered a long metal case which, when opened, turned out to contain a dozen brand-new Schmeisser submachine guns. An identical case beside it was stacked with ammunition clips.

'*Hamdu-lillah*,' he murmured.

He grabbed one of the guns and handed it with a couple of clips to Ben-Roi. He took another one for himself, and was just checking it over, getting to grips with the unfamiliar mechanism, when there was a sudden protracted crack of gunfire. They dropped, assuming it was being directed at them, only to realize from the alarmed yells of Har-Zion's men that it was actually an ammunition box exploding.

'It's going to go up like a fucking volcano,' hissed Ben-Roi.

They stood and forced their way back along the passage, a thickening orange corona filling the cavern away to their right. As they reached the gangway mouth there was a whumping explosion – an oil drum, Khalifa guessed, or maybe several oil drums – followed almost immediately by the roar of the generator as it finally burst back into life, a wash of icy-white light sweeping through the cavern, throwing everything into sharp and brilliant focus. Har-Zion's men let out a cry of delight, and with a whine and a clatter, the elevator resumed its slow ascent. Ben-Roi peeked out into the aisle, then withdrew his head.

'They're halfway,' he whispered. 'One on the ledge above. I'll take him. Count of three, OK?'

They cocked their guns.

'One . . . two . . .'

Another loud explosion, the entire cavern seeming to shiver and tremble.

'Three!'

They charged out into the aisle.

The conflagration was worse than Khalifa had anticipated. Already, in just a matter of minutes, it seemed to have got hold of a whole raft of boxes away to their right, a yawning maw of fire that lurched and snapped at everything in sight, eating its way ever deeper into the crate stacks. Plumes of flame snatched at the cavern walls; fragments of blazing debris drifted through the air like fireflies.

Overhead, a dirty froth of grey smoke rolled slowly across the ceiling.

All of this he took in in a split second before dropping to one knee and opening fire, the Schmeisser jolting and juddering in his hands. Beside him Ben-Roi was doing the same, strafing the far end of the cavern with an unbroken salvo of bullets.

The attack seemed to take Har-Zion and his followers by surprise. Ben-Roi was able to pick off the one up on the ledge, Khalifa took out two more on the elevator, the second of them slumping forward over the elevator's control lever, throwing the mechanism into reverse. The platform clunked to a halt, then, with an outraged squeal of machinery, starting to descend again, the Menorah standing impassive at its centre, its gold branches glinting in the strengthening firelight.

Their advantage was short-lived, however. After an initial moment of confusion the three remaining Israelis – Har-Zion, Steiner, one other – dropped flat onto the elevator floor and launched their own return volley of gunfire, viciously accurate. Khalifa was driven back into the passage between the crate stacks; Ben-Roi held his ground a moment, then dived into another gangway on the opposite side of the aisle.

'Don't let them get to the controls!' he yelled.

One of the Israelis was already trying to do just that, Har-Zion and Steiner covering him while he rolled across the platform and tugged at the body slumped over the up-down lever. Khalifa bobbed out and unleashed a barrage of shots at him, but was forced back almost immediately. Ben-Roi had more success, swinging out and despatching a volley of bullets down the cavern that thudded straight into the Israeli's flank, hoisting him into the air before slamming him down again at the base of the Menorah.

The elevator was now almost back on the cavern floor. In a last desperate effort to get it moving upwards again Steiner emptied his Uzi down the aisle, yelled something at Har-Zion and, while the latter covered him with his Heckler and Koch pistol, scrambled across the platform, seized the slumped corpse and, neck muscles bulging, tore it away, smacking his hand against the control lever to reverse its direction. The elevator stopped, paused a moment as if to catch its breath, then, grudgingly, started to rise.

Har-Zion let out a cry of triumph, only for the sound to die on his lips as his pistol ran out of ammunition. A man with normal freedom of movement would have taken only a matter of seconds to whip out a new clip and snap it into the magazine. Because of the constricting tightness of his burnt skin, however, he was unable to reload anything like that quickly. He shouted something, Steiner shouted back, indicating that he too was out of ammunition, and in that brief moment of confusion Ben-Roi saw his chance.

Yelling at Khalifa to follow, he leapt from his

hiding place and started sprinting towards the elevator, stumbling momentarily as a massive explosion somewhere behind him rocked the entire cavern before regaining his footing and charging on, finger yanking at the trigger of his gun. His first shots went wildly astray, disappearing into the inferno away to the right. So did his next ones, which pinged harmlessly off the rock wall well above the elevator. His third burst found its target, punching into Steiner's neck and torso, slamming him backwards into one of the vertical tracks up which the elevator ran. For a moment he just stood there, blood bubbling from his mouth, a faintly surprised look on his face; then, slowly, as the platform rose beneath him, his body slid down the track and caught beneath the chunky metal wheels that ran along it, snarling them. There was a squealing as the lift's motor tried to fight the blockage, the wheels chewing and grinding at the corpse, before eventually, unable to take the strain any longer, the engine exploded in a shower of sparks and the elevator came to a dead halt, a metre and a half off the floor.

Har-Zion was still clawing desperately for a new ammunition clip, screaming in agony as the strain of his movements caused his desiccated flesh to split and tear beneath his clothes. Seeing that he was helpless, Ben-Roi slowed to a trot and then a walk. He approached him, lifted the Schmeisser and pressed its muzzle hard against Har-Zion's head, seemingly oblivious to the plumes of flame now leaping all around.

'This is for Galia,' he whispered.

He took the trigger to within a hair's breadth of firing, then stopped. He had dreamt of this moment for so long, every day for the last year – to hold a gun against the head of the man who had murdered his fiancée, butcher him, just as Galia herself had been butchered. Yet now it came to it, now that the gun was in place and he need do no more than twitch his finger, he somehow couldn't bring himself do it. Not like this, not in cold blood. He bit his lip, willing himself to shoot, to give in to his hatred, but still it didn't happen; still a lone, small voice deep inside him – her voice – told him that it wouldn't be good, wouldn't be right, would somehow hurt him more than it would heal him. Har-Zion seemed to sense his reluctance.

'Help me,' he croaked, craning his head up to stare at Ben-Roi. 'Do whatever you want to me outside, but for God's sake help me save the Menorah.'

Ben-Roi stared down at him, hand trembling, face sheened with sweat from the ever-increasing heat of the fire. Then, with a hopeless growl, he pulled the gun away. Har-Zion immediately started to pull himself to his feet, choking in pain.

'We'll have to hoist it up,' he coughed. 'We need cable or rope. Where's the Arab?'

Ben-Roi looked around. He had assumed Khalifa was right behind him, had followed when he had first charged the elevator. The Egyptian had indeed tried to do just that. As he had emerged from his hiding place, however, a thunderous explosion – the same one that had almost knocked Ben-Roi off his feet – had sent half a dozen crates tumbling down on top of him, knocking him unconscious. He was lying now in the middle of the aisle, face down, a large crate pinning his legs. Ben-Roi sprinted up to him and heaved the crate away, dropping to his knees.

At first he thought he was dead. He managed to find a pulse, however, and with no time to worry about broken bones he hoisted the Egyptian roughly onto his shoulder and hurried back to the elevator, coughing with the smoke. Har-Zion had found a length of rope and was wrapping it around the stem of the Menorah.

'We'll get the Lamp out and come back for him,' he said. 'Help me.'

Ben-Roi shook his head. 'I'll take him up first.'

'No! We have to save the Menorah!'

'I'll take him up first,' repeated Ben-Roi, heaving Khalifa onto the platform, climbing onto it himself and hoisting the Egyptian back onto his shoulder. As he did so the muzzle of a pistol was jammed hard into the back of his neck.

'It's reloaded,' growled Har-Zion. 'Now, put him down.'

There was a fractional pause, another oil drum

exploding at the far end of the cavern, a geyser of flame shooting upwards almost to the level of the ceiling, engulfing and vaporizing the giant Nazi flag; then, shrugging the gun away, Ben-Roi stepped up to the nearest of the elevator tracks. Har-Zion raised the pistol and fired off a shot into the air.

'Drop him!' he yelled. 'You understand? We have to save the Lamp. Drop him and help me!'

'If you kill me you'll never get it out,' shouted Ben-Roi, eyes scanning up and down the track. 'I'll take him up and come back.'

'No!' screamed Har-Zion, firing off another warning shot. 'We have to save it now! Now! Do you understand?'

The detective ignored him, stepped over Steiner's bloodied corpse, grasped one of the horizontal metal bars that ran upwards between the tracks like the rungs of a ladder and started to climb, Khalifa's body dangling from his shoulder like a giant rag doll. Behind him Har-Zion was screaming, waving his gun.

'We have to save it! Don't you understand? It's your faith! Your faith!'

Ben-Roi just kept going, all his attention focused on the task in hand, ascending one rung at a time, eyes bulging with the effort, wafts of blazing embers swirling around him, burning his arms and cheeks. The first quarter of the climb went just about OK, but by halfway he was flagging badly, vicious shafts of pain spearing through the muscles of his legs and arms, his progress getting slower and slower as his burden sapped more and more of his strength. He tried to think of Galia, his family, Al Pacino – anything to take his mind off the agony in his limbs, to trick his body into thinking it wasn't quite as drained as it was. He managed to drag himself up to the three-quarter-distance mark, three metres below the ledge, but there he came to a halt and knew he wasn't going any further, that there was no more gas in the tank, not even enough to get him down again.

'I'm going to have to drop him,' he thought, hands trembling with the effort of holding onto the track, legs buckling. 'I'm going to have to drop him or I'm going to fall.'

Why, in that moment of drained desperation, he suddenly started reciting the *shema*, he had no idea. He wasn't even aware he was doing it until he'd got a few lines in. It just seemed to well up from somewhere deep inside him, like water from a parched spring. Before Galia's death he used to recite it every day. This last year it hadn't even passed his lips. Yet now he was mumbling it to himself again, the great prayer of the Jewish people, his people, the proclamation of their faith in God.

Hear, O Israel, the Lord is our God, the Lord is one . . .

His voice grew louder, the mumble swelling into a chant, and the chant into a song, just as old

750

Rabbi Gishman had taught him in Hebrew classes all those years ago.

And you shall love the Lord your God,
With all your heart, with all your soul, and with
  all your might.
And these words which I command you this day
  shall be upon your heart.

And as he sang, he felt the strength returning to his limbs, slow at first, but then more forcefully, power swelling and coursing through his body, so that without even realizing he was doing it he had moved up another rung, and another, and another, and then suddenly he was on the ledge and running – literally running – down the first of the tunnels back towards the outside world. He reached the gap in the wall, clambered through, started along the main shaft, Khalifa bumping and slapping on his shoulder, the distant echo of explosions rumbling behind him, on and on until eventually he stumbled through the mine doorway and out into the night, his feet crunching on the pristine snow, the sky overhead ablaze with stars.

He stood there gulping down air – deliciously cold and clean after the smoke-filled interior of the cavern – then he carried Khalifa across to the small stone cairn at the side of the clearing and laid him on the ground beside it. He groaned and mumbled something, but Ben-Roi didn't have time to linger, just rubbed a handful of snow on the Egyptian's face to try and revive him and, turning, sprinted back into the mine.

By the time he came out onto the stone ledge again the entire cavern seemed to be ablaze, great twisters of flame rearing and swirling everywhere he looked, devouring the crate stacks, clawing at the walls and ceiling. In his absence, Har-Zion seemed somehow to have climbed all the way up onto the ledge and left the free end of the rope there before for some reason descending again. He was now standing below on the elevator platform as though on a tiny island in a sea of fire, looking wildly around at the fast approaching wall of flame. Ben-Roi called down to him.

'I tried to get it up myself but it was too heavy!' screamed Har-Zion as soon as he heard the detective's voice. 'Start pulling! I'll have to support it from underneath.'

Shielding his face against the heat, which was now nigh on unbearable, Ben-Roi grabbed the rope and, moving back a few metres, started heaving, slowly inching the Menorah off the platform and up while Har-Zion grasped its base and lifted. When it was high enough he got himself underneath it and, supporting it with his shoulders, started climbing the elevator track, rung by rung, wailing in agony as beneath his jacket his skin split and tore like a tissue-paper shirt, rivulets of blood streaming down his arms and legs and into his gloves and shoes.

'Oh God,' he screamed, 'oh please God!'

They got the Lamp about three metres off the cavern floor before a huge explosion sent a billow of heat pulsing into Ben-Roi's face, knocking him backwards and over, the rope sliding uselessly through his hands as the Menorah crashed down onto the platform again. He lay where he was for a moment, dazed, then stumbled to his feet and staggered back to the edge.

'*Oy vey*,' he whispered.

Beneath him, Har-Zion was lying prone underneath the Lamp's stem, gazing up through its branches as though through the bars of a cage, a trickle of blood oozing from the corner of his mouth, although he was clearly still alive because his lips were moving, his gloved hands clenching and unclenching around the outermost of the Menorah's curving arms. Flames were now lapping right up against the platform, and as Ben-Roi watched in horror, they slowly rolled forward and engulfed it, the Menorah buckling and twisting in the heat, its arms bending this way and that, its gold seeming to shrivel away from it like flaking skin to reveal something dull and black beneath until eventually the whole thing melted, slumped and liquefied over Har-Zion's jerking body.

He watched until it was gone, then, unable to bear the heat any longer, he turned and moved back into the tunnel. As he did so another huge explosion rocked the cavern behind, and another, and another, the blasts gradually seguing into a single deafening roar, a thick fist of flame punching down the corridor at his back. He broke into a sprint, diving through the hole in the wall, barrelling along the mine's main shaft and out into the night again. He just had time to get over to Khalifa and drag him round to the far side of the cairn before there was an almighty boom and, like an express train hurtling from a tunnel, a surge of flame burst from the mine entrance and fired all the way across the clearing, smashing into the trees on the edge of the pine forest and setting them ablaze. It seemed to go on for ever, the ground beneath them quivering and trembling, debris dropping all around, before eventually it subsided again, the flame slowly retracting itself until it was no more than a hesitant flicker around the shattered mine entrance.

Behind the cairn, Khalifa, conscious again, fumbled out a hand and grasped Ben-Roi's arm.

'Thank you,' he croaked. 'Thank you.'

The Israeli was shaking his head, arms flung out to either side of him as if he was floating in a pool.

'It was lead,' he whispered. 'It was made of lead. Gold covering, lead underneath.'

He snorted and, scooping a handful of snow, held it against his cut ear.

'Typical bloody Jews, eh? Never miss a chance to save money.'

They thought the best thing would be to get out of Germany as quickly as possible. Ben-Roi made a few calls on his mobile, couldn't get a flight to Israel, but did manage to find one to Cairo – a charter from Salzburg, direct, leaving at six a.m. He booked tickets.

'I'll get a connection to Ben-Gurion from there,' he said. 'Better than waiting around here.'

They drove in convoy to the airport, dropped off the cars, got a wash and a few hours' sleep, departed on schedule. Once they were airborne, Ben-Roi dropped off again immediately. Khalifa tried to do the same, but exhausted as he was he couldn't manage it, so he just sat there sipping his coffee and staring out of the window, watching as away to the east a faint rim of red slowly seeped its way into the sky, gradually strengthening and spreading until the whole horizon was ablaze with light.

Something was bugging him. It shouldn't have been. The events of the previous night had brought the whole Schlegel case to about as definitive a conclusion as it was possible for an investigation to have. Despite that, he couldn't shrug off a niggling feeling – not even a feeling, really, more a sort of vague flicker right at the very back of his head – that there was still some loose end to be tied up, some final tiny detail to fill in before the picture could finally be declared complete.

He finished his coffee, fought the urge to sneak into the toilet for a cigarette, and gazed out at the expanding dawn, his mind drifting in a disjointed way over everything that had happened these last few weeks, flitting to and fro through the confusion of people and places and events before eventually ending up back in the Valley of the Kings where the whole business had started. Ginger, Amenhotep II, little Ali chattering away about pharaohs and treasure and booby-traps. What was that name he'd come up with? Horrible Inkyman. He smiled. Horrible Inkyman indeed! Priceless.

'Coffee?'

The air hostess was leaning over him with a flask. He held out his cup, sat back, picked up his chain of thought.

Horrible Inkyman. Hor-ankh-amun. Vizier to the pharaoh Tuthmosis II. His tomb had been discovered only a few months ago, at Saqqara, its burial chamber still intact, crammed to the rafters with a fabulous array of grave goods, including a magnificent sandstone sarcophagus. That alone made it one of the most important finds of recent years. What was unique about it was that beneath the main chamber the excavating team had stumbled on a carefully concealed subsidiary chamber containing an even more extraordinary array of artefacts, and an even more spectacular sarcophagus, the latter containing the tomb owner's actual body. The upper room, it turned out, had just been a blind, a perfect facsimile to fool robbers into thinking they'd found the main prize when in fact that prize was directly beneath their feet. Extraordinary.

He blew on his coffee and stared out of the window

– the entire sky was now a glittering sheet of red and gold – his thoughts zig-zagging around again before eventually homing in on that curious meeting in Old Cairo, in the Ben Ezra Synagogue. What was that guy's name? Shobu Ha-Or. Shobu? No, Shomu. Shomer. That was it. Shomer Ha-Or. Odd man, weird. The way he'd seemed to be expecting him, had told him all about the synagogue menorah.

Like all reproductions it is but a shadow compared to the original . . . That was very beautiful. Seven branches, capitals shaped like flowers, cups like almonds, the whole of it beaten from a single block of solid gold – the most beautiful thing that ever was.

He could certainly attest to that. It had been beautiful. A fabulous piece of work, even if it was lead underneath.

In Babylon, that is what the prophecy tells us. In Babylon the true Menorah will be found, in the house of Abner:

Behind him they were starting to serve breakfast, the hostess's voice drifting down the aisle as she asked passengers whether they wanted cooked or continental.

Babylon. Single block of solid gold.

Something was bugging him.

Hor-ankh-amun. Fake chamber: Fooling robbers.

Really bugging him.

The food trolley came level with their row and the woman started serving. Ben-Roi grumped himself awake, asked for the cooked breakfast. Khalifa went for the continental.

'Shomer Ha-Or.'

'What?'

'The name Shomer Ha-Or?' asked Khalifa. 'Does it mean something? In Hebrew.'

Ben-Roi was picking the foil off his plastic plate, ripping his cutlery from its cellophane wrapper.

'Guardian of the light,' he replied. 'Guardian, protector, something like that. Why?'

The Egyptian didn't reply, just stared down at his tray. A few moments ago he'd been starving. Now, suddenly, his appetite seemed to have fallen away.

CAIRO

They landed just after eleven, a warm, clear morning with a blue sky and a fat yellow sun floating in the centre of it, like a lump of tallow.

Ben-Roi wanted to get a connecting flight immediately. There was nothing till that evening, however, so he agreed to share a cab into town where he could go to the Israeli Embassy and get a shower and a change of clothes, have his ear looked at by a doctor. Khalifa gave the driver instructions in Arabic, and they set off.

They didn't talk during the journey, just sat staring out of the windows as the metropolis swiftly enveloped them. When they hit the Nile they turned south along the Corniche, following it for a couple of kilometres before veering inland again, back into the thick of the town, weaving through the chaotic surges of traffic before eventually rounding a corner into a broad, empty street with a Metro station on one side and, opposite, some sort of walled enclosure full of trees and churches. They pulled over.

Ben-Roi had never been to Cairo before, but he

was pretty certain this wasn't the Israeli Embassy. Annoyed, he asked Khalifa what was going on.

'I just need to check something,' replied the Egyptian, getting out. 'It'll only take a few minutes. I think you should come as well.'

Ben-Roi grouched and grumbled, but Khalifa was insistent and eventually the Israeli got out too, muttering to himself. They paid the driver, crossed the road and, descending a set of stone steps, passed into the interior of the enclosure, emerging onto a narrow paved street between high walls of red and yellow brick. It was very still in here, and very quiet, the atmosphere dense and musty.

'What the hell is this place?' asked Ben-Roi, gazing around.

'It's called Masr al-Qadima,' replied Khalifa, removing his cigarettes and lighting one. 'Old Cairo. The most ancient part of the city. Parts of it date right the way back to Roman times.' He took a drag. 'Although I seem to remember it had a different name then.' He flicked a glance at Ben-Roi. 'It was called Babylon. Babylon-in-Egypt.'

The Israeli raised his eyebrows, as if to say 'Is that supposed to mean something to me?' Khalifa didn't respond, just wedged the Cleopatra in his mouth and, with a wave of the hand, led the way down the street. Every now and then they passed a doorway or a shuttered window, but they saw no other people, nor heard any sound save for the slap of their feet and, once, a faint waft of song, soft and ethereal. The street doglegged right, then left, then right again before issuing into the open, tree-fringed space in front of the Ben Ezra Synagogue.

Again the Israeli asked what was going on, again Khalifa didn't reply, just flicked away his cigarette and beckoned Ben-Roi into the building. They paused a moment in the entrance, taking in the marble pulpit, the wooden galleries, the intricately decorated walls and ceiling, then walked forward until they were standing in front of the high wooden shrine at the synagogue's far end, flanked to either side by the brass menorahs.

'Welcome, Yusuf. I knew you would return.'

As on his previous visit, Khalifa had been certain the synagogue was empty. Yet there was the tall, white-haired man again, sitting as before in the shadows beneath the gallery. He raised a hand in greeting, staring at them both for a moment before standing and coming over to them. Khalifa introduced his companion.

'Arieh Ben-Roi,' he said. 'Of the Israel Police Force.'

The man nodded, as if he had been expecting some such answer, eyes lingering on the menorah pendant hanging around Ben-Roi's neck. Khalifa shuffled uneasily from foot to foot. Now that it came to it he wasn't entirely certain how to vocalize what was on his mind. Wasn't even entirely certain what it was that was on his mind. The man seemed to understand his dilemma

761

because he came forward a step and laid a hand on his shoulder.

'It was brought here a very long time ago,' he said gently. 'Seventy generations now. Matthias the High Priest ordered it. When he knew the holy city would fall to the Romans.'

Khalifa blinked at him.

'The . . .'

'Other one?' Again the man seemed to understand what he was thinking even before Khalifa himself did. 'Eleazar the Goldsmith cast that. To mislead our enemies. The original was sent to Egypt with my fore-father, here to wait until better times should come. Our family has guarded it ever since.'

Ben-Roi opened his mouth, then shut it again, bemused. There was a long silence.

'You've never told anyone?' asked Khalifa eventually.

The old man shrugged. 'The time was not right.'

'It is now?'

'Oh yes. Now the time is right. The signs have been fulfilled.'

His eyes, to Khalifa's surprise, seemed to well with tears – of gladness, not sorrow. He gazed down at the detective, then, slowly, turned away towards the nearest of the menorahs, reaching out a hand and touching his fingertips to one of its branches.

'Three signs to guide you,' he recited softly, his voice distant suddenly, as though echoing across a wide expanse of space and time. 'First, the youngest of the twelve shall come and in his hand a hawk; second, a son of Ishmael and a son of Isaac shall stand together as friends in the House of God; third, the lion and the shepherd shall be as one, and about their neck a lamp. When these things come to pass, then it will be time.'

There was another silence, the man's words seeming to linger in the still, cool air of the synagogue's interior, then he turned again, sapphire eyes sparkling.

'Your coming fulfilled the first sign,' he said, smiling at Khalifa. 'For the youngest of the twelve sons of Jacob was Joseph, Yusuf in the Arab tongue. And you brought with you a hawk. The second sign' – he spread his hands to encompass both detectives – 'this you both fulfilled. For it is to Ishmael that the Muslim people trace their ancestry, and from his brother Isaac that the Jewish race is descended. A Muslim and a Jew side by side in the House of God. As for the third sign . . .'

He tilted his head, indicating Ben-Roi's pendant.

'Lion?' asked Khalifa, his voice sounding strangely thick and foreign to him. 'Shepherd?'

The man said nothing, just looked over at Ben-Roi.

'My name,' mumbled the Israeli. 'Arieh is the Hebrew for lion. Roi is shepherd. Listen, what the fuck's all this about?'

The man's smile broadened and he let out a soft

chuckle. 'Let me show you, my friend. Let me show both of you. Seventy generations, and now, finally, the time has come for it to be revealed.'

He took them both by the arm and led them to the rear corner of the synagogue where he produced a key and opened a low door set into the wooden panels lining the walls.

'Our synagogue was built in the late ninth century, on the ruins of an old Coptic Church,' he explained, ushering them down a staircase into a large flag-stoned basement, empty aside from a stack of folding wooden chairs and, in the middle of the floor, a large rush mat. 'That in turn, however, stood on the ruins of an even older building, one dating right the way back to Roman times. When my ancestors first came here that building was the home of the leader of the Jewish community in Babylon, a very wise and holy man. Abner was his name.'

He crossed to the mat and, leaning down, grasped its corner.

'Nothing now remains of that original house save one small part – a vault, very deep, once used for storing wine. That has survived untouched while above it the centuries have slowly passed and the buildings come and gone.'

He drew the mat aside, revealing a stone slab with a socket at its centre, larger than the surrounding flags, smoother, older somehow, much older. With the detectives' help he lifted it aside, opening a hole within which a set of worn steps led downwards. Khalifa couldn't be certain, but he thought he caught a faint hint of light down below.

'Come,' said the man. 'It is waiting.'

He led them down the steps and into a narrow arched passage with a corbelled ceiling and dusty brick walls. The light was now unmistakable, a rich warm glow emanating from round a corner at the passage's far end. They moved towards it, the glow growing stronger with each stride, deeper and more intense, their nostrils picking up a vague suggestion of perfume on the air, barely noticeable and yet at the same time strangely intoxicating so that they began to feel light-headed. They came to the end of the passage, turned the corner and halted.

'Oh God,' choked Ben-Roi.

In front of them was a vault hewn out of bare rock, its walls and ceiling rough and uneven, its interior suffused with the warmest, sweetest, most exquisite light Khalifa had ever known. Standing at its far end, the source of the light, was a seven-branched Menorah, seven flickering flames rising from its lamps, identical to the one they had found in the mine yet at the same time wholly different, its gold infinitely richer and more alluring, its form infinitely lighter and more graceful, its decoration so subtle and lifelike that beside it real flowers and leaves and fruits would have seemed no more than tawdry imitations.

The detectives looked across at each other, eyes

meeting and holding for a moment before they turned away again. Following the white-haired man, they walked forward until they were standing directly in front of the candelabrum, its light washing over them like a wave of gold, streaming into their eyes, flooding the remotest recesses of their bodies, filling them.

'You keep the lamps lit?' asked Ben-Roi, his voice barely audible.

'The lamps have not been touched since the Menorah was brought here,' replied the man. 'They were lit then, and have remained so ever since. Their wicks have never burnt down, their oil has never run out.'

They shook their heads in wonder and shuffled forward a few more inches, gazing into the flames. They were unlike any Khalifa had ever seen before, made up of all the colours of the rainbow and more, colours Khalifa didn't even know existed, colours so pure, so perfect, so hypnotic that thereafter every colour he saw would look unbearably drab and monochrome by contrast. They seemed to draw him inwards, swirling and spiralling around him, caressing his face as though he was passing through some diaphanous veil before it suddenly parted to reveal vast open spaces, spaces that somehow – and he never was able to explain it properly – contained every person he had ever known, every place he had ever been, everything he had ever done: his entire life spread out in front of him, all perfectly clear, perfectly real. There were his father and mother, his brother Ali, his police graduation, the day as a five-year-old when he had run away from home and climbed all the way to the top of the Great Pyramid of Cheops. And right in the midst of it all, clearest and brightest by far, laughing and waving at him as if he was looking at them through a window, Zenab and the children.

'I can see Galia.'

Khalifa turned. To his horror he saw that Ben-Roi had reached out his hand and was holding it right in the middle of one of the flames. He raised his own hand, intending to pull the Israeli's back, but the white-haired man restrained him.

'The light of God cannot harm those who at heart are truly righteous,' he said quietly. 'Let him be.'

Ben-Roi was smiling, the flame seeming to expand and swell so that it encased his entire hand, wrapping it in a brilliant glove of golden light.

'I can feel her hair,' he whispered, 'her face. She's here. Galia's here.'

He began to laugh, fingers moving back and forth through the flame as though he was stroking a loved one's skin, continuing thus for several moments before suddenly his face crumpled in on itself and he let out a deep choking sob. Another one came, and another, and another, each more violent than the last, his entire body seeming to convulse with the force of his grief. He withdrew his hand, bent forward, clutched his sides, but the convulsions grew stronger and eventually he was driven down onto his knees, sobbing uncontrollably, the tears pouring out of him like water from a broken dam, on and on, emptying him.

'I loved her so much,' he kept saying. 'Oh God, I loved her so much.'

Khalifa tried to mumble some words of comfort, but they seemed wholly inadequate and, stepping forward, he laid a hand on Ben-Roi's shoulder. Still the sobbing continued, tears coursing down the Israeli's craggy face, his breath coming in short, agonized howls. Eventually, hardly even aware he was doing it, Khalifa came forward another step, sank to his haunches and wrapped his arms around the big man.

'I loved her so much,' choked Ben-Roi. 'I miss her. Oh God, I miss her.'

The Egyptian said nothing, just held him close, the light of the Menorah enveloping them both like a glittering cloak, drawing them together, binding them. The old man smiled, turned and walked from the vault.

When they finally climbed back up into the synagogue the man was nowhere to be found. They called his name, but there was no response, and after wandering around for a few minutes they went outside again.

It had been midday when they arrived. Yet now, inexplicably, it was dawn again, as if the conveyor belt of Time had somehow slipped and surged, breaking the normal rhythm of the day's cycle. They gazed east at the swirls of pink and green staining the sky above the ragged heads of the Muqattam Hills, then walked forward and sat down on a bench beneath the bole of a giant India laurel tree. As they did so a little boy in a white djellaba came up carrying a tray with two glasses of tea on it, his eyes blue and bright as sapphires.

'Grandfather said to give you these when you came out,' he said, extending the tray. 'He'll be waiting for you in the synagogue when you're ready.'

They took the glasses and he scuttled off again. Khalifa lit a cigarette and gazed up at the last faint stars still twinkling in the sky above. There was a long silence.

'So, what do we do with it?' he asked eventually.

Beside him, Ben-Roi had hunched forward, blowing on his tea.

'Do good things,' he murmured. 'Try to make a difference.'

'Hmm?'

'The last thing Galia said to me. Before she died. Do good things. Try to make a difference. It was this phrase we had.' He glanced up at Khalifa, then down again. 'I've never told anyone that.'

The Egyptian smiled and sipped his tea. It was very sweet and very strong, the liquid clear and reddish brown, almost ruby-coloured – just how he liked it.

'It's going to cause trouble,' said Ben-Roi after

769

another brief silence, sipping his own drink. 'If people know it's been found. The way things are at the moment. There are other Har-Zions out there. Other al-Mulathams, too.'

Khalifa took a puff on his cigarette. The head of the sun was just peeping up above the hills, a thin sickle of brilliant red.

'It's just too . . . powerful,' continued Ben-Roi. 'Too . . . special. If it was to go back . . . I just don't think we're ready for it. Things are complicated enough as they are.'

He laid his glass aside and folded his arms. A pair of bee-eaters fluttered down from the branches above, pecking at the ground with their long, quill-like beaks, hopping back and forth. The two men looked at each other, then nodded, knowing they were both thinking the same thing.

'Agreed?' asked Ben-Roi.

'Agreed,' said Khalifa, finishing his cigarette and grinding the butt out beneath his shoe.

'I'll call Milan. Tell him it's safe. He won't want to know any more.'

'He can be trusted?'

'Yehuda?' Ben-Roi smiled. 'Yes, he can be trusted. That's why I called him about the Menorah in the first place. He's a good person. Like his daughter.'

'His daughter?'

'I thought I told you,' said Ben-Roi. 'I'm sure I did.'

'Told me what?'

The Israeli ran a hand through his hair. 'Yehuda Milan was Galia's father.'

They were concerned their decision would upset the old man. When they found him and told him, however, he merely nodded and smiled that enigmatic smile of his.

'Our task was to guard the Lamp, and when the time was right reveal its whereabouts,' he said quietly. 'This we have done. No more was expected, either from us or by us.'

There was a patter of feet and the little boy came running into the synagogue, taking up position at his grandfather's side. The man put an arm around his shoulders.

'What will you do now?' asked Khalifa.

'Now?' The man shrugged. 'We are the caretakers here, this is our home. That will not change. Nothing will change.'

'The Lamp?'

'The Lamp will remain where it is. Until it is God's will it should be moved. While its cups burn there will always be light in the world, however dark things may seem.'

The little boy tugged his robe and, coming up on tiptoes, whispered in his ear. The man chuckled and kissed the boy on the forehead.

'He says to tell you that when I am dead and gone and it is he who is caretaker, you will both be welcome to come and see the Lamp whenever you wish.'

The detectives smiled.

'May God be with you, my friends. The light of the Menorah is in you now. Do not let it fade.'

He held them in his eyes for a moment, both men experiencing a sudden strange feeling of weightlessness, as if they were floating on the air. Then, with a nod, he took the little boy's hand in his own, turned and walked into the shadows beneath the synagogue's wooden gallery, the two of them disappearing from sight as if they had never existed.

As they left the synagogue, Ben-Roi suddenly raised a hand to the side of his head.

'My ear's healed up,' he said.

CAIRO

'Last call for Egyptair Flight 431 to Aswan via Luxor.'

It was six p.m. and, finally, Khalifa was on his way home. He would have got an earlier flight, but when he'd spoken to Zenab she had insisted that since he was in Cairo he might as well take the time to make some social calls. So he'd had breakfast with their old friends Tawfik and Narwal at Groppi's on Midan Talaat Harb, then spent the day in the Antiquities Museum with his mentor, dear old Professor al-Habibi – recently returned from his lecture tour in Europe – before finishing up back at Groppi's with his childhood mate Fat Abdul Wassami, who, true to his name, had managed to work his way through six eclairs, three pieces of *basbousa* and a massive slice of honey-soaked *katif* ('I'll call it a day there,' he had announced virtuously. 'We're out for dinner tonight and I don't want to spoil my appetite.').

Now, however, Khalifa was ready for home.

'Last call for Egyptair Flight 431.'

On the other side of the security barriers he

could see the last few passengers filing through the glass doors and into the bus that would carry them out to their plane. He turned, scanning the departures hall, looking for Ben-Roi, who was booked on to an eight p.m. flight out of the International Terminal and had agreed to meet here to say a final goodbye. The place was crowded with tourists, including a large group of English women all of whom were for some reason wearing matching sombreros. No sign of the Israeli, however. He gave it another minute, then, with his flight again being called, started towards the security point.

'Khalifa!'

The Israeli was pushing his way through the herd of English women, two enormous carrier bags clasped in his hands. The Egyptian went forward to meet him.

'I thought you weren't going to make it.'

'Couldn't find the fucking terminal.'

Ben-Roi dropped his bags, wiped a hand across his sweat-stained forehead and, pulling out his silver hip-flask, unscrewed the lid and took a long gulp. As he lowered it again he noticed the faintly disapproving look in Khalifa's eyes.

'Keep your bloody hair on,' he grunted. 'It's just that hibiscus stuff. What do you call it?'

'*Karkaday?*'

'That's the one. Very refreshing. Thought it was time to, you know . . . flush the old system out a bit.'

Although he was unfamiliar with the phrase, Khalifa got the gist of what the Israeli meant and smiled. They looked at each other, then away again. Now that it came to it neither of them was entirely certain what to say. Khalifa glanced down at the plastic bags, noting their contents.

'Colouring books?' he asked, surprised.

'What? Oh, yes. I was having a wander round town, saw them in a sale. There's this teacher I met, works in a school where they teach Palestinian and Israeli kids together, and they can't afford . . .' The Israeli broke off, embarrassed suddenly. 'Anyway, I thought she could use them,' he mumbled.

Khalifa nodded. 'She's beautiful, I think, this teacher.'

'She is actually. She's got this long hair that . . .' Again Ben-Roi broke off, scowling, as if he'd somehow been tricked into saying something he didn't want to say. 'Fuck you, Khalifa.'

There was no maliciousness in his tone, and behind the scowl there was a flicker of amusement. The tannoy rang out again.

'Last call for Egyptair Flight 431. Would all remaining passengers please report to the departure gate immediately.'

'That's me,' said Khalifa.

There was a pause, both of them still struggling for the right words, shuffling nervously from foot to foot, then Ben-Roi extended a hand.

'*Ma-salaam, saheb.* Goodbye, friend.'

Khalifa laughed. 'I thought you told me you didn't speak any Arabic.'

'Asked someone at the embassy,' said Ben-Roi with a shrug. 'Thought it would, you know, be polite or whatever.'

Khalifa nodded and, reaching out his own hand, grasped the Israeli's.

'*Shalom, chaver*. Goodbye, friend.'

This time it was Ben-Roi who chuckled.

'I thought you told me *you* didn't speak any Hebrew.'

'Looked it up in a phrase book,' said Khalifa. 'Thought it would be . . . polite, or whatever.'

They held each other's hands for a moment, eyes locked, then, releasing their grip and repeating their farewells, turned and started moving away. Khalifa had just passed through the security barrier, the last passenger to do so, when he heard a shout behind him.

'Hang on! Hang on!'

He stepped back through the barrier.

'I'll forget my own bloody head one of these days,' muttered Ben-Roi, fiddling in one of the bags and producing a small package, which he handed to Khalifa.

'For your wife and kids. *Halva*. Our national sweet. I picked it up at the embassy.'

The Egyptian protested, but Ben-Roi waved a hand and, delving into his pocket, produced another packet, smaller, only the size of a matchbox, done up in brown paper.

'And this is for you. Just a small thing.'

Again Khalifa protested, again the Israeli dismissed it, reaching out and slipping the packet into the Egyptian's pocket. They stood looking at each other, a sort of enforced hesitancy to their stance as if they were both holding themselves back from doing something they wanted to do but weren't at all sure was appropriate. Then, as one, they threw caution to the wind, stepped forward and embraced, Ben-Roi's arms completely enveloping the smaller man.

'I'll be seeing you, you cheeky Muslim cunt.'

Khalifa smiled, face pressed into the Israeli's massive barrel chest.

'You too, you arrogant Jew bastard.'

They remained like that for a moment, connected, then broke and went their separate ways. Neither of them looked back.

Later, once his plane was in the air and carrying him south back towards his home and his family, the only place he had ever wanted to be, Khalifa reached into his pocket and pulled out the packet Ben-Roi had given him. He gazed down at it, thinking he knew what it might contain, then, carefully, tore away the wrapping to reveal a small plastic box. Inside, on a bed of tissue, was the silver menorah Ben-Roi used to wear around his neck. He tipped it into his palm, smiling, and, closing his hand around it, leant his head against the window and stared down at the tiny thread of the Nile below, a miniature blue vein that against all the odds brought life and hope to the otherwise barren desert.

JERUSALEM

It was a big crowd, several thousand strong, packed fifteen deep along the edge of Sultan Suleiman Street, crammed shoulder to shoulder on the semicircle of stone steps leading down to the Damascus Gate – men and women, old and young, Israeli and Palestinian, some holding aloft flaming tapers, others banners and placards, others framed photographs of loved ones who had died in the violence between their two peoples. All of them were looking down at the makeshift stage in front of the gate, where two figures – one wearing a white *yarmulke*, the other a checked *keffiyeh* – were standing side by side in front of a single microphone. Every now and then there was a ripple of applause, but in general the crowd was quiet, taking in what was being said.

It was through the centre of this multitude that Yunis Abu Jish now slowly eased his way, the explosives-packed vest tight around his midriff, his face grey and drenched with sweat. As instructed he had gone to the payphone on the corner of Abu Taleb and Ibn Khaldoun, where al-Mulatham's people had given him his final orders: collect the vest from the abandoned building site, make his way down to the Damascus Gate, get as close to the stage as possible then pull the detonator cord.

'*Allah-u-akhbar*,' he mumbled, inching his way forwards, carefully, so as not to jolt the explosives. '*Allah-u-akhbar; Allah-u-akhbar; Allah-u-akhbar.*'

In front of him the men were taking it in turns to speak, leaning into the microphone and then away again.

'. . . end to violence . . . sacrifices in the name of peace . . . hatred or hope . . . our last chance . . .'

He was only dimly aware of their voices, lost as he was in the maelstrom of his own mind. He came to the bottom of the steps, edged across the esplanade in front of the gate, reached the stage and took up position right in the middle of it, directly below the speakers.

'. . . unequivocal withdrawal from the West Bank and Gaza Strip . . . acknowledgement of Israel's right to exist . . . abandonment of the Right to Return . . . compensation for refugees . . . Jerusalem as our shared capital . . . respect and understanding.'

'*Allah-u-akhbar; Allah-u-akhbar, Allah-u-akhbar.*'

Sick, nauseous, terrified, he forced his hand up into his jacket, yanked the first of the cords to arm the explosives, dragged it down and clasped the second cord.

'. . . a new world . . . together as friends . . . hope out of despair . . . light instead of darkness . . .'

'*Allah-u-akhbar, Allah-u-akhbar, Allah-u-akhbar.*'

He pulled a little. Stopped. Pulled again. Froze. And there he remained, gripping the detonator, while above him the two men embraced and all around the crowd started to sing . . .

GLOSSARY

Abba Father (Hebrew).

Abbas, Mahmoud Successor to Yasser Arafat as President of the Palestinian Authority. Born 1935. Also known as Abu Mazen.

Abraham Jewish patriarch, considered the father of the Jewish people.

Abu Simbel Archaeological site in southern Egypt. Location of one of Egypt's greatest monuments, the Sun Temple of Ramesses II.

Abu Za'abal Egyptian prison near Cairo.

Abydos Cult centre of the god Osiris and burial ground of some of Egypt's earliest pharaohs. Located 90km north of Luxor.

Ahl el-Kitab Literally, 'People of the Book'. Muslim term for Jews and Christians, whose scriptures were incorporated into Islam.

Aish baladi Pitta-type bread made from wholemeal flour.

Akhenaten Eighteenth Dynasty pharaoh. Ruled c.1353–1335 BC. Father of Tutankhamun.

Al-Abram Literally, 'The Pyramids'. Best-selling Egyptian newspaper.

Al-Akhbar Egyptian newspaper.

Al-Quds   Arabic name for Jerusalem.

Alim al-Simsim   Egyptian version of US children's show *Sesame Street*.

Aliyah   Literally, 'Going up'. Emigration to the land of Israel.

Al-Wadi al-Gadid   Egyptian prison in Kharga oasis.

Amarna Modern name for Akhetaten, a city built by the pharaoh Akhenaten on the east bank of the Nile midway between Cairo and Luxor.

Amenhotep I Eighteenth Dynasty pharaoh. Ruled *c.* 1525–1504 BC. His tomb has never been conclusively identified.

Amenhotep II Eighteenth Dynasty pharaoh. Ruled *c.* 1427–1401 BC.

Amenhotep III Eighteenth Dynasty pharaoh. Ruled *c.*1391–1353 BC. Father of Akhenaten, grandfather of Tutankhamun.

Amir, Yigal Jewish extremist. Assassinated Israeli Prime Minister Yitzhak Rabin in 1995.

Ankh Cruciform symbol. The ancient Egyptian sign of life.

Antonia Fortress Fortress adjacent to the Temple complex in ancient Jerusalem. Built by Herod the Great.

Arafat, Yasser Figurehead and de facto leader of the Palestinian people from the late 1960s until his death in November 2004. President of the Palestinian Authority from 1996. Born 1929. Also known as Abu Ammar.

Arminius Ancient German warrior hero.

Lived *c.*18 BC–AD 21. Famed for defeating the Roman army at the Battle of the Teutoberger Wald (AD 9).

Ashkelon An Israeli prison.

Aya A verse of the Koran.

Ayalon, Ami Former head of Shin Bet (1996–2000).

Babaghanoush Egyptian dish made from tahina and mashed aubergine.

Babi Yar A ravine near Kiev, site of an infamous World War Two massacre in which a hundred thousand people, mainly Jews, were shot dead by Nazi firing squads.

Banana Island A Luxor beauty spot. Renowned as a haunt for homosexuals.

Bar mitzvah Jewish ceremony marking a boy's coming of age.

Barak, Ehud Former Israeli Prime Minister (1999–2001).

Barghouti, Marwan Popular Palestinian activist and politician. Born 1958. Imprisoned by the Israelis in 2002.

Basbousa Egyptian sweet pastry made with semolina, nuts and honey.

Batya Gur Popular Israeli author.

Beir Zeit University Palestinian university, in Ramallah.

Beni Hassan Important Middle Kingdom necropolis on the east bank of the Nile, midway between al-Minya and Mallawi.

Bezalel Revered Jewish craftsman from the time

of the Exodus. Created the Ark of the Covenant and the first Menorah.

Borscht Beetroot soup.

Buchenwald Nazi concentration camp, in Germany.

Butneya An area of Cairo renowned for its thieves and drug dealers.

Cabbala Mystical teaching of Judaism.

Caleche A horse-drawn carriage.

Camp David The US President's country retreat in Maryland. Scene of abortive peace talks in July 2000 between the then Israeli Prime Minister Ehud Barak and Yasser Arafat.

Cardo Covered street in the Jewish quarter of Old Jerusalem. Formerly the main thoroughfare of Roman Jerusalem.

Carter, Howard English archaeologist, discoverer in 1922 of the tomb of Tutankhamun. Lived 1874–1939.

Champollion, Jean François French scholar who deciphered hieroglyphs. Lived 1790–1832.

Chicago House The home of the University of Chicago Archaeological Mission in Luxor.

Chicken *kneidlach* Chicken soup with dumplings. Popular Jewish dish.

Constantine I Known as 'The Great'. First Roman emperor to convert to Christianity. Lived c.AD 274–337.

Dahlan, Mohammed Palestinian politician and activist. Born 1961.

David Jewish hero and king. Lived *c.* eleventh to tenth centuries BC. Father of Solomon.

***Debir* (Holy of Holies)** The most sacred part of the ancient Temple.

Deir el-Bahri Site of the mortuary temple of Queen Hatshepsut (ruled *c.*1473–1458 BC). On the west bank of the Nile at Luxor.

Deir el-Bersha Middle Kingdom necropolis on the east bank of the Nile, opposite the modern town of Mallawi.

Deir Yassin Former Palestinian village on the outskirts of Jerusalem. Scene of an infamous massacre by Jewish paramilitaries in 1948.

Deutsche Orient-Gesellschaft The German Oriental Society. An institution devoted to studying the history and archaeology of the Near East.

Djellaba Traditional robe worn by Egyptian men and women.

Djellaba suda Black robe worn by Egyptian peasant women.

Djoser Third Dynasty pharaoh. Ruled *c.*2630–2611 BC. His step pyramid at Saqqara was the world's first monumental stone building.

Dunum Measurement of land, equivalent to a quarter of an acre.

Ecole Biblique Institute founded in 1890 for the study of the Bible and the archaeology of the Holy Land.

Eid el-Adha The Feast of Sacrifice, one of the most important festivals in the Muslim calendar.

Eighteenth Dynasty   Ancient Egyptian history is divided into Kingdoms (Old, Middle and New) which are in turn subdivided into dynasties. The Eighteenth Dynasty comprised fourteen rulers and covered the period *c.*1550–1307 BC. It was the first of the three dynasties of the New Kingdom (*c.*1550–1070 BC).

Elijah   Hebrew prophet.

El-Kab   Archaeological site on the east bank of the Nile, 70km south of Luxor. Has a spectacular town enclosure dating from the Early Dynastic Period (2920–2975 BC).

Erekat, Saeb   Palestinian politician and academic. Born 1955.

Eretz Israel Ha-Shlema   Literally, 'the Whole of Greater Israel' – i.e. the entire land that in the Bible God granted to Abraham.

Erez Checkpoint   Main crossing point from Israel into the Gaza Strip.

Even Shetiyah   Literally, 'Foundation Stone'. The exposed rock of Mount Moria on which the ancient Temple was built.

Ezra   Ancient Jewish lawgiver.

Faience   A material made of fired quartz, with a glazed outer layer. Used extensively in ancient Egypt for jewellery, small vessels etc.

Farid   A make of Middle Eastern cigarette.

Fatah   Palestinian faction founded by Yasser Arafat in the late 1950s. The word is both the Arabic for 'victory' and an acronym for 'The Movement for the National Liberation of Palestine'.

***Fellaha* (pl. *fellaheen*)**   Peasant.

Frumm   Yiddish word meaning 'strict in religious observance'.

Gaddis, Attaia   Famous Egyptian photographer. Lived 1887–1972.

Gaiseric   King of the Vandals AD 428–477. Sacked Rome in AD 455.

Garden Tomb   Site considered by some to be the burial place of Christ.

Gebel Dosha   Archaeological site in northern Sudan.

Gefilte fish   Traditional Jewish dish of boiled fish balls.

Goldstar   A make of Israeli beer.

Goldstein, Baruch   Jewish extremist. Shot dead twenty-nine Muslim worshippers in Hebron in 1994 before he himself was beaten to death. Regarded as a hero by right-wing Jewish settlers.

***Goy* (pl. *goyim*)**   Derogatory Yiddish term for a non-Jew.

Groppi's   Famous chain of Cairo coffee houses.

Gross-Rosen   Nazi concentration camp in Poland.

Gush Shalom   Literally, 'The Peace Bloc'. Israeli peace group.

Ha'aretz   Israeli daily newspaper.

Halakhah   The entire body of Jewish law, both written and oral.

Hallah   A plaited loaf eaten by Jews on the Sabbath.

Hamas   Militant Palestinian nationalist Islamic movement, founded in 1987. Hamas is both the

Arabic for 'zeal' and a reverse acronym for 'The Islamic Resistance Movement'. Its figurehead, Sheikh Ahmed Yassin, was assassinated by the Israelis in 2004.

Hanukkah Jewish festival commemorating the victory of Judah Maccabee over the Seleucid Greeks and the cleansing of the Temple.

Haram al-Sharif Literally, 'the Noble Sanctuary'. The enclosure in Old Jerusalem containing the al-Aqsa Mosque and the Dome of the Rock, the third holiest site in the Islamic world. Overlies the remains of the ancient Jewish Temple.

Haredi Ultra-orthodox Jew.

Hasidic A branch of ultra-orthodox Judaism.

Hawagaya Egyptian term for a foreigner.

Hazzan A cantor. One who leads the singing in synagogue.

Hizbollah Literally, 'Party of God'. Militant Shi'ite Islamic group based in Lebanon.

Horemheb Last pharaoh of the Eighteenth Dynasty. Ruled *c.*1319–1307 BC.

Horns of Hattin Battle in 1187 in which Saladin defeated the crusaders.

Horus Ancient Egyptian god, son of Isis and Osiris. Portrayed with a human body and the head of a hawk.

Houris **(pl.)** Virgins who minister to the needs of Muslims in the afterlife.

Humvee Acronym for High Mobility Multi-Purpose Wheeled Vehicle.

Hypostyle hall   A hall with a roof supported by columns.

IDF   Israel Defence Force. The Israeli army.

Imam   Leader of congregational prayer in the mosque.

Imma **(pl.** *immam***)**   Headscarf or turban. Worn by men throughout Egypt.

Insha-allah   Literally, 'if Allah is willing'. Common Egyptian term.

Intifada   Literally, 'shaking off'. A popular uprising by the Palestinians of the West Bank and Gaza Strip. The First Intifada lasted 1987–1993. The Second, or al-Aqsa Intifada, erupted in 2000 and is ongoing.

Isaac   Jewish patriarch. Son of Abraham and half-brother of Ishmael. It is from Isaac that the Jewish people are said to be descended.

Ishmael   Eldest son of Abraham, by the concubine Hagar. It is from Ishmael that the Arab people are said to be descended.

Isis   Ancient Egyptian goddess. Wife of Osiris and mother of Horus. Protector of the dead.

Islamic Jihad   Militant Palestinian Islamic group, founded in late 1970s.

Jacob   Jewish patriarch. Son of Isaac and grandson of Abraham.

Jeremiah   Jewish prophet of the sixth century BC. Foretold the destruction of the Temple of Solomon by the Babylonians. Said to have died in Egypt.

John of Gischala   One of the leaders of the

Jewish revolt against Rome of AD 66–70. Sentenced to life imprisonment after the fall of Jerusalem in AD 70.

Jonah A Hebrew prophet.

Joshua Brother of Moses. Leader of the Israelites after Moses' death.

Judah Maccabee Jewish military leader of the second century BC. Reconquered Jerusalem from the Seleucid Greeks.

Ka'ba Cube-shaped building within the precincts of the Great Mosque at Mecca. Holiest shrine in Islam.

Kahane, Meir Brooklyn-born Jewish extremist. Advocated forcible removal of all Arabs from the Biblical land of Israel. Born 1932. Assassinated 1990.

Karkaday An infusion of hibiscus petals, popular throughout Egypt.

Katif Shredded wheat soaked in honey. Popular Egyptian dessert.

Keffiyeh A headdress worn by Arab men.

Ken Yes (Hebrew).

Kerovah A Jewish prayer that can either be chanted or sung.

Ketziot Notoriously harsh Israeli prison in the Negev Desert.

Khaghoghi derev Traditional Armenian dish of stuffed vine leaves.

Kiddush Jewish prayer recited on the Sabbath and at festivals.

Klog iz mir Yiddish for 'Woe is me!'

Kneidl   Dumpling.

Knesset   Literally, 'Assembly'. The Israeli Parliament.

Kohenim (pl.)   Hereditary priests of the Temple.

Kor   Archaeological site in northern Sudan.

Kufr   Name given to those who do not follow Islam. Unbelievers.

Mangonel   A war engine used for hurling giant stones.

Maniak   Hebrew for arsehole.

Mashrabiya   Traditional Egyptian woodwork.

Matmidim (pl.)   Jewish scholars devoted to the study of the Talmud.

Matzah   Unleavened bread eaten by Jews during the Passover festival.

Mauristan   An area in the Christian Quarter of Jerusalem's Old City.

Mea Sharim   A suburb of Jerusalem, just north of the Old City.

Mendil   Headscarf worn by Palestinian women.

Mengele, Josef   Nazi doctor at Auschwitz. Nicknamed the Angel of Death. Escaped to South America after the war. Died in Brazil in 1979.

Menorah   A seven-branched candelabrum, one of the oldest symbols of Judaism and the emblem of the state of Israel.

Merenptah   Nineteenth Dynasty pharaoh, ruled *c.*1224–1214 BC.

Meshugina   Yiddish for 'crazy person'.

Mezuzah   A small box containing verses from the book of Deuteronomy attached to the doorpost of orthodox Jewish homes.

Midan Tahrir   Literally, 'Liberation Square'. The hub of modern Cairo.

Mishnah   The corpus of Jewish oral law, compiled in the second century AD.

Molochia   Green leafy plant similar to spinach.

Moser   Yiddish for betrayer or traitor.

Mount Moria   Site of the ancient Temple in Jerusalem, where Abraham was supposed to have almost sacrificed his son Isaac.

Mubarak, Hosni   President of Egypt since 1981.

Muezzin   Mosque official who summons the faithful to prayer five times daily.

Nebbish   Yiddish for someone who is weak-willed or timid.

Nemes **headdress**   A type of headdress worn by ancient Egyptian pharaohs.

NGO   Non-government organization.

Occitane language   A French dialect, now largely defunct, used in the Languedoc region of southern France. The lingua franca of medieval troubadour poets.

Osiris   Ancient Egyptian god of the underworld.

Oslo Peace Accords   Set of peace proposals between Israelis and Palestinians, negotiated in secret in Oslo and signed in Washington in 1993.

Ostracon (pl. ostraca)   Piece of pottery or limestone bearing an image or text. Effectively the ancient equivalent of the modern-day doodling pad.

Palestinian Authority (PA)   Semi-autonomous Palestinian governing body with authority over the West Bank and Gaza Strip. Created by the Oslo Peace Accords (1993).

Pe'ot **(pl.)**   Sidelocks worn by ultra-orthodox Jews.

Peace Now   Main Israeli peace movement. Founded 1978.

Pesah   Passover. Jewish festival commemorating the Exodus from Egypt.

Pilum   Spear or javelin used by Roman soldiers.

Protocols of Zion   Bogus document published in Russia in 1905 purporting to be a Jewish masterplan for world domination. Although it was subsequently proved to be a forgery, it has fuelled anti-semitism ever since.

Pylon   Massive entrance or gateway standing in front of a temple.

Qasr Dush   Site of an ancient Roman temple, near the oasis of Kharga.

Qubbat al-Sakhra   Arab term for the Dome of the Rock, the principal Islamic shrine in Jerusalem.

Quftan   Caftan. A long-sleeved cloak.

Qurei, Ahmed   Palestinian Prime Minister since 2003. Also known as Abu Ala. Born 1937.

Rafah   Palestinian town in the Gaza strip, near the Egyptian border. Scene in 2004 of a heavy-handed Israeli military operation that left many Palestinian civilians dead.

Rais Foreman.

Rajoub, Jibril Palestinian activist and politician. Born 1953.

Ramadan War Arab name for the Yom Kippur war of 1973.

Ramesses II Third pharaoh of the Nineteenth Dynasty. Ruled c.1290–1224 BC. One of ancient Egypt's greatest pharaohs.

Ramesses III Twentieth Dynasty pharaoh. Ruled c.1194–1163 BC. His mortuary temple at Medinet Habu is one of the most beautiful monuments in Egypt.

Ramesses VI Twentieth Dynasty pharaoh. Ruled c.1151–1143 BC.

Ramesses IX Twentieth Dynasty pharaoh. Ruled c.1112–1100 BC.

Ramesseum Mortuary temple of Ramesses II, on the west bank of the Nile, at Luxor.

Rashi Jewish scholar and commentator, lived AD 1040–1105. Real name Solomon ben Isaac.

Rek'ah Prayer cycle.

Rodef Hebrew for traitor.

Romema A suburb of Jerusalem, in the northwest of the city.

Rosicrucians An esoteric religious society. Its emblems are the rose and the cross.

Sabra Nickname for a native Israeli. The *sabra* is a cactus plant and, like the cactus, Israelis are supposed to be prickly on the outside with a soft centre.

Sabra and Chatila Palestinian refugee camps

in West Beirut, scene of an infamous massacre in 1982. Although the atrocity was carried out by Lebanese Christian militiamen, Israel was considered complicit since its army controlled West Beirut at the time.

Saladin Anglicized form of the name Salah al-Din. Great Muslim military leader. Lived AD 1138–1193.

Saqqara Necropolis of the ancient Egyptian capital at Memphis. A vast desert burial ground covering almost seven square kilometres, including the famous Step Pyramid of Djoser, 20km south of Cairo.

Schal Cloth shawl or wrap worn by Egyptian men.

Schlomo Artzi Israeli musician.

Sephardee A Jew of Spanish origin.

Seti I Nineteenth Dynasty pharaoh, father of Ramesses II. Ruled *c.*1306–1290 BC.

Shaaban Abdel-Rehim Egyptian musician.

Shabbat Hebrew word for the Jewish Sabbath.

Shabti Small mummiform figure, usually of wood or faience, placed in a tomb in order to perform tasks for the deceased in the afterlife.

Shaduf A wooden hoist used to lift water from the Nile.

Shahada Muslim profession of faith.

Shaheed An Islamic martyr.

Sharon, Ariel Controversial Israeli soldier and politician. Prime Minister of Israel since February 2001. Born 1928.

Shebab   Literally, 'youth'. Young Palestinians.

Shema   The central prayer of the Jewish faith, made up of three Biblical passages: Deuteronomy 6: 4–9, Deuteronomy 11: 13–21, and Numbers 15: 37–41.

Shin Bet   Israel's internal security service. The equivalent of MI5 or the FBI.

Shisha **pipe**   A water pipe. Smoked throughout the Middle East.

Shtetl   Yiddish for 'small town'. Term used for settlements in Eastern Europe with a mainly Jewish population.

Shtreimel   Large fur hat worn by ultra-orthodox Jews.

Shul   Yiddish word for a synagogue.

Shuma   A staff or walking stick.

Siga   An Egyptian board game, also known as *tab-es-siga*. Similar to draughts.

Simon Bar-Giora   One of the leaders of the Jewish revolt against Rome of AD 66–70. Executed after the fall of Jerusalem in AD 70.

Solomon   King of Israel in the tenth century BC. Son of David.

Soujuk   Traditional Armenian dish of spicy sausages.

Star of David   A six-pointed star, one of the primary symbols of Judaism. Known in Hebrew as the Magen David – The Shield of David.

Sura   A chapter of the Koran, the holy book of Islam. Each of the 114 *suras* is divided into a number of *ayat*, or sections.

Table of the Shewbread   One of the holy objects in the ancient Temple of Jerusalem. It held the sacred bread used in temple services.

Tallit   A prayer shawl worn by Jews for worship.

Tallit katan   A shirt-like garment with fringes at each of its corners, worn by ultra-orthodox Jews beneath their everyday clothes.

Talmid Hakhamim **(pl.)**   Literally, 'Disciples of the Wise'. Those devoted to the study of Jewish law.

Talmud   Collection of scholarly opinons and debates on Jewish law.

Tamar bindi   Refreshing drink made from dates.

Tarboosh   Fez.

Tarha   Cloth worn over the head by traditional Egyptian women.

Taybeh   A Palestinian beer.

Teffilah **(pl. *teffilin*)**   Small box containing Biblical passages. Orthodox Jews bind these to their forehead and arm during certain types of prayer.

Tel el-Fara'in   Literally, 'Mound of the Pharaohs'. Archaeological site in northern Egypt.

Termous   Type of bean.

Theban massif   Range of hills on the west bank of the river Nile at Luxor.

Theban Triad   Amun, Mut and Khonsu. The three ancient Egyptian gods to whom Karnak was sacred.

Thobe   Embroidered dress or caftan worn by Palestinian women.

Tish B'Av   Literally, 'The ninth of Av', the date in the Jewish calendar when both the First and Second Temples were destroyed (by the Babylonians and Romans respectively). A time of great mourning for Jews.

Titus   Son of the Emperor Vespasian. Commander of the Roman army that conquered Jerusalem in AD 70. Ruled as emperor AD 79–81.

Torah   The central text of the Jewish faith, comprising the first five books of the Bible. Also referred to as the Pentateuch.

Torly   A traditional Egyptian casserole or stew.

Torshi   A mixture of pickled vegetables. Popular Egyptian snack.

Touria   Hoe.

Tuna el-Gebel   Archaeological site on the west bank of the Nile, near the town of Mallawi.

Tuthmosis II   Eighteenth Dynasty pharaoh. Ruled *c.* 1492–1479 BC.

Umm ali   Cake soaked in milk, sugar, raisins and cinnamon. Popular Egyptian dessert.

Umm Kulthoum   Iconic female Egyptian singer. Lived *c.* 1904–1975.

Ummah   The Muslim community.

'umra   A pilgrimage to Mecca. Unlike the more important Hajj pilgrimage, it can be made at any time of the year.

Vandals   Germanic tribe who sacked Rome in AD 455.

Vespasian   Roman Emperor AD 69–79.

Via Dolorosa   Literally, the 'Way of Sorrow'.

The route through old Jerusalem that Christ supposedly followed on his way to the cross.

Wadi Biban el-Muluk Literally, 'Valley of the Gates of the Kings'. Arab name for the Valley of the Kings.

Wadi Halfa Town in northern Sudan. Site of many important archaeological remains from pharaonic times.

Ward-i-Nil Literally, 'Nile flower'. Common Egyptian water plant.

Western Wall The remains of the retaining wall of the ancient Temple in Jerusalem, the only part of the building left after the Romans destroyed it in AD 70. Also known as the Wailing Wall and, in Hebrew, the Kotel. The most holy site in the Jewish world.

Yad Vashem Holocaust memorial and museum in Jerusalem.

Yahrzeit The anniversary of the death of a relative or loved one.

Yansoon Popular Egyptian aniseed drink.

Yarmulke Skullcap worn by Jews during prayer. Orthodox Jews wear one all the time.

Yathrib Original name of the Arab city of Medina.

Yediot Ahronot Highest circulation Israeli daily newspaper.

Yehudi **(pl.** *Yehudi-een***)** Jew.

Yeshiva A Jewish religious school devoted to study of the Talmud.

Yutzim **(pl.)** Yiddish for fools, simpletons.

Yuya and Tjuyu A noble couple, lived in the

fourteenth century BC. Great-grandparents of Tutankhamun.

Za'atar Aromatic Middle Eastern plant. From the mint family.

Zedakah box Charity box. A fixture in many Jewish homes.

Zemirot (pl.) Literally, 'Songs'. Psalms and hymns sung by Jews during worship.

Zonah Whore (Hebrew).

ACKNOWLEDGEMENTS

I owe a debt of gratitude to a great many people for helping in the research and writing of this book, and what follows is, of necessity, but paltry recognition for the support and assistance they have given.

Huge thanks to my agent, Laura Susijn, for always being there in times of difficulty, and to Simon Taylor of Transworld, whose skills as an editor are matched only by his Herculean levels of patience in waiting for a manuscript to actually edit.

Rudi Eliott Lockhart, Emma Woolerton and Tessa Webber provided invaluable help with the medieval Latin translations; James Freeman did the same with ancient Latin and Greek.

For advice on the nuances of Palestinian Arabic a massive thank-you to Ghassan Kharian and Henrietta McMicking; likewise to my dear friend Mohsen Kamel for correcting my (woeful) Egyptian Arabic. For Hebrew transliterations I am beholden to Rabbi Warren Elf, a teacher in the finest traditions of Judaism.

In no particular order, but with equal gratitude to all, my thanks to Professor Dieter Lindenlaub,

Rolf Herget, Gilad Atzmon, Dr Nick Reeves, Bromley Roberts, Nigel Topping, Xan Brooks, Andrew Rogerson, John Bannon, Charlie Smith, Marie-Louise Weighall and Sue and Stanley Sussman.

Finally, three special thank-yous. First, to the staff and officers of the David Police Station in Jerusalem, who were unfailingly kind, helpful and informative during the time I spent researching in Israel.

Secondly, to the many Palestinians who took the time to meet and talk with me, and give me an insight into their world. Because of the current political situation there was understandable nervousness about allowing their names to appear in print. They know who they are, and I will always be grateful.

Last, and most important of all, to my beautiful wife, without whose love, support and strength this book would never have been finished.